ISLAND IN THE SKY

From behind the dirigible, the sun cast an almost shadowless radiance. Crystalline, blue-black, the stratosphere made a chalice for the pearl which was Skyholm. Then as the craft drew nigh, that pearl became a moon indeed, a world.

Two full kilometers in diameter, it nonetheless kept an airiness, a grace to rival anything man had ever created. Transparent, the outer skin had a shimmer across it, a ghost of rainbows. Beneath were the interlocking hexagons of slender hollow girders and thin cables, as if the god of the spiders had been everywhere weaving. A hundred meters behind this was a vast ball of night, over which the web went agleam.

Its pattern disappeared at the equator. There homes, meeting places, workshops, laboratories, control centers, all the manifold spaces that humans used were nested among the ribs of Skyholm. Positioned around it were four observation domes, four laser complexes, two missile launchers, two flanges on which—dragonflies at this distance—jetplanes rested, and eight engines belonging to the aerostat itself. Small inspection platforms and banks of solar collectors studded the rest of the sphere.

And this was Skyholm, which men before the Judgment had dreamed of, and built in modules and lifted on wings of helium to assemble in the uppermost air. . . .

POUL ANDERSON

ORION SHALL RISE

This is a work of fiction. All the characters and events portrayed in this book are fictional, and any resemblance to real people or incidents is purely coincidental.

A Baen Book

Baen Publishing Enterprises
P.O. Box 1403
Riverdale, NY 10471

ISBN: 0-671-72090-2

Cover art by Paul Alexander

First Baen Printing, November 1991

Printed in the United States of America

Distributed by Simon & Schuster
1230 Avenue of the Americas
New York, NY 10020

AUTHOR'S NOTE

Those who remember other tales from the world of the Maurai will perhaps notice what appear to be inconsistencies with them in this book. However, consistency is not an either-or matter. New data and insights often cause us to revise our ideas about the past and even the present. Surely the future is not exempt.

Variations from present-day languages, including orthography, grammar, names, geographical identifications, etc., are due to changes wrought by intervening centuries—not necessarily to ignorance on my part.

Dr. Ernest Okress of the Franklin Institute very kindly sent me a wealth of material about the Solar Thermal Aerostat Research Station on whose design he and others have worked. (The tensegrity concept is Buckminster Fuller's.) From a class in wilderness survival given by Tom Brown, Jr., I learned a great deal, a little of which I have attempted to describe here. For good counsel and friendly encouragement I am indebted to Karen Anderson (above all), Mildred Downey Broxon, Víctor Fernández-Dávila, Larry J. Friesen, David G. Hartwell, Terry Hayes, Jerry Pournelle, and "Vladimir iz Livonii" of the Society for Creative Anachronism.

No person named in these acknowledgments is in any way responsible for whatever errors and infelicities I may have perpetrated.

POUL ANDERSON

TO KAREN—
again, and always

When you stand on the peak of time
it is time to begin to perish.

—Robinson Jeffers,
"The Broken Balance"

PROLOGUE

There was a man called Mael the Red who dwelt in Ar-Mor. That was the far western end of Brezh, which was itself the far western end of the Domain. Seen from those parts, Skyholm gleamed low in the east, often hidden by trees or hills or clouds, and showed little more than half the width of a full moon. Yet folk looked upon it with an awe that was sometimes lacking in those who saw it high and huge.

Yonder they had, after all, lived for many generations under its rule. The Clans were daily among them. The Breizheg peninsula had joined the Domain, through treaties rather than conquest, less than a century before Mael's birth. Outside its few towns of any size, a man of the Aerogens was still a rare sight, a woman well-nigh unknown. Common speech named such a person a saint, and common belief gave him the power to work miracles.

The home of the pysan Mael stood by itself on an upland where heather and gorse bloomed purple and gold in their season. Farther down was a forest, and in the valley which the house overlooked were meadows, grainfields, and cottages. Whatever of this earth that he could see from his gate was Mael's, worked by him, his sons, his tenants, and their sons, with its horses, cattle, sheep, timber, crops, fish, game.

He was frequently gone from it, because as a man of substance he had public duties. The Mestromor, who reigned over Ar-Mor, had made him his bailli, to keep the peace and judge quarrels throughout this district. On visits to the city Kemper, Mael had then come to know the Coordinator, Talence Donal Ferlay, whom Skyholm kept there to advise the state government and make certain that the advice was followed.

They got along well, those two. Mael was bluff, Donal reserved; but Mael knew better than to suppose a member of the Thirty Clans, the Aerogens, was a being more mysterious than any other mortal, while

Donal knew better than to suppose a family whose roots were ancient in the land when Skyholm went aloft must needs be ignorant of the outside world. They could thus enjoy each other's company. Besides, each felt himself under a duty to learn as much as might be. So they would talk at length when chance allowed, and now and then get a little drunk together.

After a few such years, one day a man came a horseback to the pysan's dwelling, and it was Donal.

In early spring, snow patched the brown ground, water gurgled and glimmered, an orchard nearby had just begun to bud, cloud shadows scythed from horizon to horizon. Those clouds raced across a pale sky, before a wind that whooped and smelled of the dampness and streamed chillingly across face and hands. Rooks wheeled and cawed through it.

Such men as were present gathered outside the main gate to meet the visitor. Mael carried a spear. Not too long ago, everyone would have been ready for trouble, grasping their few precious firearms as well as edged metal. Nowadays Skyholm would send its lightnings against any pirates or invaders; thus it had freed the Mestromor, his baillis, and their deputies to put down what banditry remained. Besides, this newcomer rode alone. Mael simply intended to dip his spear in a traditional gesture of welcome. When he saw who reined in, he reversed it instead, and bowed, while his followers crossed themselves.

They had never met Donal before, but a Clansman was unmistakable. Even his clothes—loose-fitting shirt beneath a cowled jacket, tight-fitting trousers, low boots—were of different cut from their linen and woolen garb, and of finer material. At his ornate belt, next to a knife, hung a pistol; a rifle was sheathed at his saddlebow; and these were modern rapid-fire weapons. His coat bore silver insignia of rank on the shoulders, an emblem of a gold star in a blue field on the left sleeve. Before all else, his body proclaimed what he was. He sat tall and slender, with narrow head and countenance, long straight nose, large gray eyes, thin lips, fair complexion but dark hair that hung barely past his ears and was streaked with white. Though he went clean-shaven in the manner of his people, one could see that his beard would be sparse. He carried himself with pride rather than haughtiness, and smiled as he lifted an arm in greeting.

"A saint," muttered the pysans in wonder, "a saint from Ileduciel—from *there.*" Some pointed toward Skyholm. It showed only a faint crescent, for the sun was in the east and daylight always paled it in men's vision. Nonetheless, many dwellers hereabouts, who had never been far from their birthplaces, still believed that Deu Himself had placed it in heaven, as an unmoving moon, to watch lest humans bring a new Judgment on the world.

"Yonder is Talence Donal Ferlay," Mael explained. His words heightened respect, or outright reverence, for everybody knew that Clan Talence was the one from which the Seniors of the other twenty-nine always chose the Captain of Ileduciel.

Mael turned back to the rider. "Sir," he asked, "will you honor my home? I hope so, and for more than a single day." He was a sturdy man, though age was grizzling away the ruddiness of his mane and beard.

Donal nodded. "Many thanks," he said. "You have invited me enough times, and promised excellent hunting." They spoke in Francey, since the Clansman knew little Brezhoneg and the native less Angley. "A week, if that will not burden you overmuch. No longer. You see, I am on my way to Tournev." Mael recognized the name of that city in the Loi Valley which lay straight beneath Skyholm: with its hinterland, the sole part of the Domain that the Aerogens ruled directly. "My term of service here has ended, and I shall be taking on new duties elsewhere." He smiled. "However, first I think I have earned some rest and sport."

"Indeed you have, sir," Mael replied. He was no flatterer. Donal had in fact done considerable to bring outside commerce, and thus prosperity, to Ar-Mor, as well as to strengthen the lately founded Consvatoire in Kemper, where knowledge both ancient and new was preserved and where promising youngsters could study.

To his men, in their own language, Mael gave orders about Donal's mount, pack mule, and baggage. The Clansman descended and accompanied his host on foot through the gate.

Buildings of stone and tile formed a tight, defensible square, with guardian towers at the corners, around a well-flagged courtyard where much of the life of the farm went on. In these peaceful days, livestock sheltered elsewhere; barns had been changed into workshops, storerooms, expanded living quarters. Women and children stood more or less ranked under the walls to offer salutation. They kept an awkward silence, not knowing quite what to do, for manners in this countryside were boisterous but here was a saint come to them.

"At ease, at ease," Mael boomed. "Get busy, break out our best stuff, make a feast ready for evening." That brought a relieved fluttering of curtsies, happy expressions, a few giggles. Dogs barked, cats scampered clear of suddenly fast-moving feet.

A handsome woman whose braids hung gray over her gown remained in place. Beside her stood a boy of ten and a girl of seventeen. "Talence Donal Ferlay," Mael said, "here is my wife Josse." Politely, the newcomer gave her a soft salute. "Our older sons and daughters have homes of their own—we'll send for them—but these are my youngest son, Tadeg, and daughter, Catan."

Donal's glance reached the maiden and stayed. A slow flush spread across her cheeks and down her bosom. She lowered her lashes above dark-blue eyes. Her form was willowy, her features cleanly sculptured; that countenance might have passed for a Clanswoman's. When her turn came to voice a welcome, the rest could barely hear. She spoke good Francey, though; most children of well-to-do Breizheg families learned it in chapel school, now that their land was part of theDomain.

Donal smiled in his austere fashion and took her hand. "Be not afraid of me," he murmured. "You must know I am simply a man, a friend of your father's, your guest for what will be all too short a while."

Her youth surged up in her and she blurted: "Is that true, sir? I mean, of course you wouldn't lie, but, but aren't the saints reborn, again and again, in . . . your race—?"

Josse drew a sharp, scandalized breath. Donal calmed her by answering, "Well, the anims of ancestors do live in us, but this is true of everybody. Or so many people believe. Your father has told me that he—and you—carry blood of Ileduciel. And I, all my kind, we have countless forebears who were not of the first Thirty. Let us be friends, Catan."

Between the parents passed a look, knowing and eager.

After a few days, Donal got a small radio transceiver from his gear and sent word that he would arrive late. Skyholm relayed it line-of-sight back to Kemper, where he had ordered an airplane for a certain date, and down to the Ministry of Coordination in Tournev. There nobody questioned his decision. They knew him for an able and conscientious man, who gave more of himself to the Domain than he did to Clan and family affairs. Shortly afterward, Skyholm passed another communication on, in a private cipher, to his wife. She had left Kemper ahead of him, to oversee their estate in Dordoyn.

A month went by. The last snow melted, warmth and sunlight

breathed a mist of green across the country, blossoming exploded, verdancy strengthened, the migratory birds began returning, plowman and plowhorse labored, rains blew gentle out of the west, larks jubilated while lambs and calves and winter-born infants lurched forth into amazement.

It was a time of hard work on the farms, but Mael could always arrange companionship for his highborn guest, hunting or fishing or sightseeing. Sometimes there were festivals in a village not too far off, otherwise there were the evenings at home, by lamplight in front of a tile stove.

Generation by generation, as the need for defense grew less urgent while the soil regained its fertility and trade reached ever farther, landholders here had made their houses more spacious and gracious. Between heavy-beamed ceiling and heavy-carpeted floor, the plaster of the main-room walls was well-nigh hidden by draperies, pictures, bookshelves, finely carved chests and seats, olden relics. Folk sat together drinking wine or beer—on special occasions, the coffee, tea, and chocolate that were lately coming from abroad. Some smoked tobacco. Mostly they talked or played games, but one among them might well read aloud or they might join in song while bagpipe and drum and a wooden flute or two rollicked around their voices.

Shyness before Donal Ferlay soon vanished. Aloof by nature, he therefore got more deference than any law required. Yet he was amiable in his way, willing both to listen and to tell about the outside world, the territories elsewhere in the Domain that strangeness made magical for the pysans.

Mael himself found it hard to grasp the vastness of that realm which Skyholm viewed and therefore commanded. The circle swept out the whole of Franceterr, Flandre, the Rhin, the Pryny range, the mountains of Jura, most of Angleylann, a corner of Eria (though the Aerogens had no wish to gain suzerainty over the patchwork countries on those islands), and westward across the entire Gulf of Gascoyn, to the Ocean. It held a score of states, each with its own geography, industries, government, history, laws, customs, dialect or even language. Men muttered earthy words of surprise, women gasped, children shrilled when Donal described what he had seen. And Ileduciel itself—but that was beyond any comprehension, and folk were obscurely afraid to talk very much about it.

Just the same, they grew to like the Clansman. Whatever the powers that laired within him, whatever knowledge he bore that was forbidden to ordinary folk, what he showed them was his human side;

and as a human being he was good, if perhaps a little too earnest. Before everything else, he was giving Mael and Josse great honor, an honor that should bring luck to everybody in the neighborhood.

For he sought out Catan daily, and soon they two were walking hand in hand amidst the young blossoms, and soon after that she spent her nights in his room.

Such joinings were common in regions where usage allowed. It certainly did in Brezh. No family would take a wife for a son until she had proved she was not barren, and many weddings waited until the child was born and seen to be healthy. A union with a saint could never lead to that, for the Clans married only among themselves, but it might endure for long years. Whether it did or not, it conferred glory on the woman's kin, and often valuable connections to the Aerogens. If it ended, it had made her a supremely desirable bride for any unwed man of her own community, and he would welcome into his house the offspring of her earlier mate.

Mael owed much of his well-being to the fact that a grandfather of his had been Vosmaer Pir Quellwind—and the latter had simply chanced by while looking over this newly acquired land, and had never returned. The daughter who came of it married the heir of the upland farm, though the daughters of far wealthier households would gladly have done so. Liaisons like that were still rare in Brezh.

And . . . it seemed as though Talence Donal Ferlay was not merely amusing himself, nor was Catan merely hero-struck or scheming. Women who saw those two together would sigh, chuckle, shake their heads a bit, and gossip about it.

—Yet the twilight came when he and she stood alone beneath an apple tree whose flowers glimmered wan in cool blue dimness, with an odor of oncoming summer, and he laid his hands about her waist, looked into the reflections of the first stars in her eyes, and said: "Tomorrow, at last, I go."

Her head drooped. "I know," she whispered. "But why did you set just that date?"

"Because I must set a date, and abide by it, or I would never leave."

Her palm shivered upward and across his cheek. "Why must you, ever?"

He stiffened his back. "I have my duty." After a moment: "Too few of the younger among us understand that. They think the Domain has become almighty, and nothing is left for them but pleasure. It isn't true. Espayn, Italya, the barbarians beyond the Rhin—the Gaeans, the Maurai, and who knows what else, dissolving every old certainty that was ours— No, I cannot stay idle. My honor would rust away."

"Then why can't I go with you?" she pleaded.

"I have explained that. My duty is also to my wife. And to you. You would be lost, bewildered, sick with longing for this your home." Again he paused, until he could wrench the words forth. "Besides, I am not a young man. I should not stand in the way of the life you have before you."

"Oh, beloved! You *are* my life." She cast herself against him and wept.

He held her close and said into the fragrance of her hair, "Well, I'll come back. As often as may be. As long as may be."

2

At midwinter, Catan brought forth a son. She gave him the name his father had chosen, Iern.

Many were the suitors for her hand, but she refused them and Mael would not force her. Instead she remained on the estate, taking her share of work, raising her child as best she could, and living for the times when Donal returned.

To Iern as he began growing, his father was a figure of might and enigma, who brought him gifts and asked how he did but who really arrived in order to claim his mother's heed. He did not resent this, for her joy spilled over onto him. Besides, his grandfather and his uncles were men enough to steer his world.

They taught him what a boy should learn and then, because of his heritage, did more. They took him on journeys through all Ar-Mor, its stern sea-cliffs and nestling villages and port of Kemper where ships came from halfway around the globe. This was a land haunted by ancientness. Strongholds from the bad old days scowled on guard, but some of them incorporated remnants of works built before the Judgment—sometimes long before, a medieval city wall, a Stone Age tomb. The menhirs, cromlechs, dolmens, and passage graves of peoples who had died even earlier stood gaunt in sight of hovering Skyholm. Upon a few of them, blurred by weather and lichen, remained signs chiseled by those who lived afterward: a Celtic face, a Roman figure, a cross for believers in Zhesu-Crett. Iern was too small for real understanding, but he got into him a sense of time as an endless storm-wind, on which men and nations and gods were blown like autumn leaves, forever.

Otherwise he was a bright, merry, and well-liked lad.

Grateful for this and much else, Donal saw to it that Mael's household got every chance to prosper further, as the Domain knitted Brezh more closely into itself—

—until after seven years he came back to claim his son.

3

Darkness keened. Rain dashed against walls and shutters. The single lamp in a private chamber left its corners full of shadows, and its air was chill. Donal stood gazing into Catan's tears. She was still fresh and fair, but his skin was furrowed and his hair mostly white. "I'm sorrier than I have words to say," he told her.

"But you'll take him anyhow!" she cried.

He nodded. "I must. Didn't you hear me? No doubt is left. Rosenn —my wife will never bear a child that lives. She cannot."

"Then why did you marry her?"

"We didn't know." Half a smile twisted his mouth. "Besides, our ways are not yours, my dear. It was a good arrangement for the Talence Ferlays and the Kroneberg Laniers to make. Not that we aren't fond of each other, Rosenn and I—one reason why I can't deny her a child to call ours."

He laid fingers along Catan's jaw and made her look at him. "You can have more children, beloved," he said. "That's no longer as ill-advised for you as we thought it might be. She—well, it's always been so, that certain Clanswomen have trouble with childbirth. Too fine-boned . . . too inbred, in spite of adopting groundlings . . . too high a mutation rate, from stays in the stratosphere . . . but I don't suppose you know what that last means." The breath gusted out of him. "Never mind. What you surely will see, and not begrudge me, is my need for an heir."

"You have the right in law to take him away," she said forlornly. "Could you take me with him?"

He shook his head. "No. It would uproot you, and you would wither. It could destroy Rosenn. She isn't jealous, but only imagine having you there. . . . Be at ease, Catan. She will be as kind to him as I myself. He'll grow up to be a man of the Aerogens, with everything that that means. And he'll come see you when he can. His first call won't be soon. He's already past the usual age for enrolling as a Cadet, and the training is rigorous. But later—" He started to draw her close. "Meanwhile, I'll bring you news of him."

She stiffened and pulled free. His clasp fell from her. "No," she said. Pride rang through the grief in her voice. "Not ever again."

He clenched fists, though his face showed scant surprise. "I was afraid you would hate me."

"Not that." She stamped despair beneath her heel. "I love you yet, Donal. I suppose I always shall. But it's time I became my own woman."

 4

The Clansman had arrived in a light aircraft, landing on a pasture. Next morning he flew off with the boy, east toward Skyholm. He never came back.

He did send letters and opportunities and, when possible, Iern on a holiday.

Catan married Riwal the Stout, a widowed proprietor of several ships and fishing boats in Carnac. They lived calmly, and received Iern well on his visits.

Folk recalled a night shortly after his birth, when a wander-woman who claimed second sight had stopped for a while under Mael's roof. Staring at the infant by the light of a candle she had made in the form of a dagger, she mumbled, "Watch him well. He will bring their doom upon the gods." But this may be only a tale of the sort that arises long after the thing has happened.

I

Somewhere in the western Ocean, a storm came into being. No man ever knew the place. Once moonlets on sentry-go around the planet would have seen and warned, but most of them had come down as shooting stars, centuries past, and the rest gone silent. The Domain could not keep a global watch; metals for aircraft were too scarce, fuel too costly in the manufacture. Unseen by any, save maybe a few sailors, whom it would have drowned, the storm gathered strength as it lumbered eastward. By the time that vessels off the Uropan coasts were radioing news of it, observers in Skyholm had seen the earliest sinister changes in cloud patterns far below them, and called for the Weather Corps.

Iern got word only upon his return to Beynac. He had been riding circuit through the Ferlay lands in Dordoyn, as was his seasonal task—hearing tenants, freeholders, villagers, herders, timbercutters, their complaints, ideas, hopes, prides, dreads, gossip; easing grievances, arbitrating disputes, negotiating arrangements as best he was able; presiding over various festivals and ceremonies as tradition demanded; rewarding good deeds or faithful service; letting himself be entertained, and in return being a pleasant, accessible guest, from whom there flowed tales of scenes beyond these horizons; in general, reweaving the bonds between his family and the people it led.

Now he and his attendants rode home along the river road. Autumn flamed in hillside forests, but air was mild and sweet. Sunlight slanted from the west, cliffs shone, the stream glistened down the steep length of its valley. From afar, a woodsman's horn sounded lonesome, and found answer in echoes. The cloaks of the men lent vividness, while dust thumped upward by hooves caught light and swirled against shadows like firelit smoke.

Ans Debyron, secretary to Iern, made his horse trot until he rode alongside the master. "A very successful trip, I'd say, sir," he ventured. A native of these parts, lately graduated from the Consvatoire of Sarlat, he was inclined to be pompous, though otherwise he was a competent and agreeable fellow. The soft Occitan enunciation of his Francey redeemed his choice of words.

"Well, things seemed to go fairly smoothly," Iern replied. "I'm too new at this to be sure."

"Sir," Ans declared, "they *like* you. You're fair-minded, and you don't need much explanation before you understand a matter—oh, they appreciate your taking the trouble to learn this dialect and its nuances—but you're also . . . you're genial. That's not been too common among castlekeepers here."

"Like my father, when he served his hitch?" The groundling's dismay brought a grin from Iern. "No disrespect intended, Ans, or at least no more than comes naturally from a son. He's a great man, in his own right as well as in the Domain, but he and I are quite different." He paused, then plunged; a mission completed gave a special sense of comradeship. "To tell the truth, when he wanted me to take over this post, I came near to rebellion."

"Really? May I ask why?"

Iern shrugged. "Consider. I was newly commissioned, in line for advanced training in aircraft and meteorology, the things I'd been aiming at through most of my Cadetship. Besides, I had a large backlog of pleasures in mind for my free time. And I insisted I had no talent for administration. If he absolutely must put me in charge of a family holding, then couldn't it be in some territory where the girls were ready to hop into bed with me? Certainly I knew nothing about Dordoyn. You remember my ties are to Brezh, where the very language is different."

He paused before he went on: " 'Take your share of the load,' my father said, and ended the matter. He's that sort of man. I'm not sorry now. It's lovely country here, grand people. And, of course, I only have to be on hand for two or three months, scattered through the year. Otherwise I fly."

Enough reserve remained in him that he was glad to break off his confession abruptly, when they rounded a bluff and saw Castle Beynac ahead. "Hoy, there she is!" he exclaimed and spurred his mount forward and then up the side road.

Ans gaped after him before also setting into gallop. Talence Iern Ferlay was not altogether of Ileduciel; he continued to surprise those who remembered lords more grave.

His stature was only average for a man of the Aerogens, though this made him tall among the stocky Dordoynais. Thanks to the pysan side of his ancestry, he was more muscular than his father; and in him the sharp face was somewhat broadened and blunted, with cheekbones wide and high, eyes bright blue, hair brown and unruly, voice a light baritone. His taste in clothes ran to the flamboyant.

The castle welcomed him with a bravery of banners and sungleams off tower windows. Its handsomeness was another thing which reconciled him to his station here. Throughout Franceterr, too many such medieval buildings, reoccupied after the Judgment when there was again a need for fortresses, had been remodeled over the centuries until they were jumbles of styles and functions. The Ferlays had usually had better taste, and when it faltered, later generations demolished the mistakes. Beynac reared mighty on its height above the river, and modern additions—even the radio mast or the airy residential wing—seemed to be treasures that it was natural for the old warrior walls to protect.

As always in these peaceful times, the gates stood open; the few small cannon, armored cars, catapults, and dartthrowers were relics; the sentry who winded his bugle was ornamental. Courtyard stones clattered beneath horseshoes; Clan Talence could afford the iron thus to equip its leading men and their immediate attendants. Dwellers spilled from the buildings and ran to greet the keeper, shouting and windmilling their arms in the Southern manner. Almost as exuberant was the concubine Iern had brought along from Tournev. Eagerness leaped in him. Three weeks or so, out among the chaste Dordoynais, had grown confoundedly long.

Then Talence Hald Tireur, his first officer, pushed through the crowd to his stirrup. The man's face was grim. "It's well you're back, sir," he said without preamble. "A message came today for you from Weather Corps headquarters. You're to call in at once."

Iern swore at himself for not having taken a transceiver in his kit. Inexperience. It wouldn't happen again. He swung from the saddle and raced to the donjon.

Lamplight relieved its gloom, furnishings and artwork its starkness. Iern hardly noticed. He believed he knew why they in Skyholm wanted him, and his nerves thrummed.

A circular staircase led to the tower room where the radio equipment was. He took it three hollowed-out steps at a bound, and flung himself into the operator's chair. His fingers sped across the keyboard. Through the clicking he heard a buzz, and he smelled a pungency as the set warmed up. It was big, for the vacuum tubes in its wooden console filled much space, and crude compared to the transistorized portables—those were trade goods from the Maurai Federation—but, powered by the castle's coal-fired generator, it could fling a signal as far as Skyholm, and that sufficed.

From this elevation he spied the aerostat, low above a ridge to the north. Closer here than it was to the country where he had been born, it showed correspondingly larger, almost the size of a full moon, pale and faintly webbed in the window. A hawk sailed by, briefly hiding the sight behind wings which the declining sun turned fiery gold. A slight shiver passed through Iern. All his training in science and logic had never quite erased what Breizhad pysans muttered by their firesides in his childhood, of omens and fates.

He shoved superstition aside. The set was ready. He transmitted his identification code. After a moment that hummed, a female voice came from the speaker: "Communications Center. Lieutenant Dykenskyt Gwenna Warden on duty." Her Angley bore a Rhinland accent; she must spend most of her groundside time there. "You are . . . are you Talence Yern Ferlay? I'll switch you directly to Weather Command."

"Iern," the man corrected, pronouncing the unaccented first syllable as *ee.* A part of him snickered at himself. Why did he care how his name was spoken? Why, because the odds were that what lay ahead would bring him glory, if he survived, and in his youthfulness he wanted no confusions about who the hero was.

"Apologies," Gwenna replied indifferently. Was she brusque because the business was urgent, or because she was young too and, like so many of today's young, chafed at formality and restraint? He wondered fleetingly what she looked like. When the Thirty Clans numbered some sixty thousand individuals, the officers among them ten thousand, you couldn't meet everybody in your lifetime. And how did she feel, off in her aerie thirty kilometers above earth and sea and oncoming storm? That must be a terrifying piece of weather on the march. Why else summon all the Stormriders in the Corps? It had to be the whole of their small elite, for otherwise Iern would have been left to finish his tour of obligation among his groundlings.

Buzz, click-click, mutter, and another female voice, but now of a person he knew, his superior, Colonel Vosmaer Tess Rayman: "Lieutenant Iern!"

"Madame," he said into his microphone. "I salute."

"You've doubtless guessed. A hurricane is in the Gulf, aimed at the Zhironn coast. Force Twelve. It'll flatten the Etang area, drown a score of fishing villages, and probably wreck Port Bordeu, with everything that that implies for shipping. Local authorities say they can't evacuate more than a third of the inhabitants. The loss of life will be enormous."

"But you think we can break it?" Trumpets resounded in Iern's head. The hair stood up on his arms. "Ready for service, madame!"

Anxiety softened her tone. "Are you certain? You've had a day's journey, you must be tired, and this mission is an order of magnitude beyond any previous entries you've made. The least error— We need every data point we can get, but we *don't* need a wrecked plane and a dead pilot."

"You won't get either one from me, madame."

Tess sighed; he could almost see her head shake. "No boy realizes he can die, does he?" Crisply: "Very well, Lieutenant. Proceed to Port Bordeu. They'll have a briefing ready for you, though I'm afraid it will be brief indeed. Too little information as yet. You're the closest Stormrider; you'll reach the objective first, in spite of this late call-in. What you discover will be critical." She paused. "On your way, then. Blessings fly with you."

"Thank you, madame." Iern snapped up the main switch, left his chair, and ran.

2

From his aircraft as he neared, the hurricane made a black mountain range under which the sun had already set. Clouds flying before it hid the Gulf below their rags, though now and again he glimpsed water lashed into white violence—once a ship, sails furled, sea anchor out, crew waiting to learn if they would live or die. Elsewhere the sky was clear, violet in the east where stars blinked forth, blue overhead, greenish in the west. As yet, Skyholm caught sunlight and cast it from the north, sheen and shadow chased each other across the clouds beneath, but soon it would darken.

Well, Iern thought, he'd be blind anyway, after he invaded the tumult ahead.

Ever more strong through the murmur of the jet engine he heard the air, and he felt how his craft shivered and bucked. As hands and feet danced through the rhythms of control, he laughed for delight.

This was not the little propeller-driven sparrow, half wood and canvas, which had taken him from Beynac to Bordeu; this was a falcon, as good as anything the Maurai themselves possessed. The alloys in it were worth a Captain's ransom, and it burned fuel in torrents, hence few of its kind existed on Earth—but it could outpace sound or ascend to Skyholm. It traveled unarmed, for what could attack it? Not that it would see use in war; it was too valuable. If Iern went into combat, he would fly a machine scarcely better than the one which belonged to the estate.

Across his mind flickered a question about how that would feel. The Espaynian conflict had occurred before his birth, and he had been an adolescent Cadet during the Italyan campaign. Would there be more affrays? The Domain had failed to keep Lonzo de Zamora from bringing most of Iberya under his Zheneralship, but later it did check his son's ambition to get control of the western Mediterr Sea. . . . Iern hoped the peace would endure. He didn't relish the idea of killing men. He didn't even hunt—

A voice in his earphones recalled him. "What was that, Lieutenant? You sounded amused."

"Oh. Oh, nothing," he answered. A blush went warm over his cheeks. It wasn't professional to admit enjoyment of a dangerous mission. Hastily: "I hear a bit of static. How are you receiving from my instruments?"

"Satisfactory. We now have three more units on the fringes and are receiving from them too, so we're beginning to get a picture. Take heed." Aloft in the aerostat, with the Domain's single powerful computer, the analysis officer rapped forth a series of technicalities and figures.

Iern scowled. "Not enough, not enough information by a dozen bowshots."

"Of course. Your assignment—"

"Listen," Iern interrupted. "I expected this. By the time we've learned what we need to know, being cautious, the brute will've reached land. No, I'll make for its middle instead. I recommend my fellow pilots dive at least halfway into the cyclone pattern, at appropriate altitudes, from where they are."

"Lieutenant!"

"You will transmit my recommendation, Major." Iern knew his teammates would follow it; pride of self as well as the honor of the Corps commanded them. "I am about to accelerate. Prepare for a high rate of input."

Did he hear a gulp? "Very good, Lieutenant."

A glow as from wine mounted within Iern. In the present kind of situation, a Stormrider awing outranked everybody but the Captain of Skyholm. This was his first exercise of that authority. It felt almost like having his first woman.

And here was his first proper foe, too! He had plunged into wild weather often before, but simply for practice and to collect data for the forecasters and scientists. A storm so great that men fought against it came but twice or thrice in a career.

From beneath his fingers on the controls, power surged. The jetplane shot upward on a slant that pressed Iern into the leather of his seat. Ten kilometers high, he throttled back, tilted over, and peered downward while he circled. His enemy filled most of his vision with roiling, lightning-shot murk, though eastward across the curve of the world he glimpsed open water and the shores he hoped to help save. The sight had a wild magnificence, but to dawdle over it would be treason to his cause.

Radar beams probed from the craft. Infrared sensors converted radiation into measurements. A television camera relayed an optical image to flesh out what Iern saw through his calibrated magnifiers and described in semimathematical language. (A recent addition to the arsenal, that television, a scarce and expensive import from the Maurai—but he blessed the commerce which had brought it to Uropa.)

Though he had located the eye of the storm, he had yet to map it. "I am ready to descend," he announced.

"Zhesu ward you," said the major shakily.

Iern shrugged. He attended services because that was what a proper Clansman did, but made no bones about being an agnostic. "Thank you, sir," he replied. "I'll spiral in loops of three kilometers' radius, two kilometers apart. That looks to me like the best flight plan." He couldn't resist bravado: "Ask my comrades to wish me good hunting, as I wish them it!"

His falcon stooped.

Night closed in. Wind raved and tore, lightning flared, thunder crashed, rain and sleet smote metal and hammered the pilot's canopy. Flung back and forth, up and down and around, half deafened by skirl and roar, he lost himself in the fight to keep his antagonist from ripping his craft asunder or casting it into the sea. Sometimes he lurched out into the calm at the center, but instantly speared back into the wall. And always as he whirled, his instruments gauged, while a hard-driven ultrahigh-frequency beam sent their messages outward —pressures, velocities, ionizations, potentials, gradients—the numbers of the beast.

Afar in Skyholm, computer technicians fed their engine what he and his fellows gave. To the meteorologists it returned an understanding that grew. Its program was the product of hundreds of years of study, thought, trial, and ofttimes fatal error. Even during the Isolation Era that the Enric Restoration ended, that work had gone forward. For was not the Aerogens king and queen of heaven?

Iern's radarscope glowed a warning at him. He was close to hill-high waves; he had done what he could, and his next duty was to escape. He reeled out of turbulence, into the central quietness, stood his vessel on its tail, and climbed. Above him the sky was a disc of purple wherein a star trembled.

He broke free, arched above the monster, and streaked eastward. "Iern Ferlay reporting," he sang into the microphone at his throat. "Finished and safe. Did you copy my transmission?"

"Yes. Well done, Lieutenant."

"What about the rest?"

"They're safe too. We'll be ready for action in minutes. Get clear. Set course for Tournev."

Iern nodded and obeyed. His plane, like the others, required inspection, and perhaps repairs, of the sort that only the facilities at the headquarters city could perform. As for the pilots, they would get the traditional conqueror's welcome, followed by at least a week of ease and celebration.

Whether or not they were conquerors— Not every attempt succeeded.

Slowly Iern realized that he had spoken and acted automatically. His awareness had been elsewhere, in some unknown place, and was just now returning to him. He could not quite recollect how he rode the storm; the experience had been transcendental, he had been one with his adversary. . . . His body throbbed and ached. Padded jacket or no, the safety harness had probably striped him with bruises. But peace and joy welled up within him . . . yes, it *had* been a kind of lovemaking. . . .

The excitement wasn't over! The real show was about to start.

He had won fame, promotion, honor for his family and Clan. He had not won the right to waste a single liter of fuel by hanging around to watch the spectacle. He could, though, fly high and slowly, unbuckle, kneel on his seat and look backward. Barely soon enough, he remembered to don dark goggles.

The laser beams struck.

Throughout each day, never hindered by cloud or mist or rain, sunlight played across the aerostat. On a sphere two kilometers in diameter, that was an input measured in gigawatts. A fraction of it, shining through the double skin, kept hot the air at the center, and thus held Skyholm aloft. More went into solar collectors or thermal converters and became electricity. Of this, a portion ran the jets which maintained station against stratospheric winds, and supplied other needs on board. A portion, sent earthward, powered synthetic fuel plants and similarly essential industries. However, those were few, and except for them and local generators here and there, the Domain had no electricity; metal for conductors was too costly. Most of the sun cells waited idle, against a day of war or of tempest.

Now circuits closed, shutters opened, a tide of current flowed into the great accumulators and thence to the outsize lasers. Fiercer than lightning, the beams leaped off to battle.

They were not random thrusts of wrath. Cool minds aimed them, guided by those data the Stormriders had snatched out of destruction's self. Their energy was small compared to that which drove their target. Its intensity, focused on well-chosen spots, was something else.

What Iern saw was firespears out of heaven. Air blazed and thundered around them. Where they struck the darkness, brilliance fountained. Without his goggles, he would have been blinded for at least a while, maybe for always. As was, his vision quickly filled with dazzle and he dared watch no longer.

Again and again accumulators discharged and collectors refilled them. Some beams held steady, drilling, eroding; others flashed briefly, upsetting the balance at single places, turning the hurricane's own force upon it. Pitiless, Skyholm stabbed, slashed, ripped, while Iern and his comrades fled.

The struggle fell behind him, and he flew above a Franceterr darkling beneath stars. The aerostat still shone bright, catching rays of a sun he could no longer see, but would soon fade. He wondered if that would happen before the task was done.

Incandescence winked out. Triumph bawled in his earphones: "That's it! The pattern's broken!"

"Prediction?" asked tones that remained dry. Iern recognized Colonel Tess'.

"Ah-h-h . . . a preliminary evaluation, madame. We've dissipated the fringes. The core continues active, but much reduced in force and veering northwest. Strong winds and heavy rains along the coast, trending north, for the next two or three days. But nothing disastrous, and further energy input would too likely drive the core against Eria."

"Which would be inhumane, as well as angering little countries that bid fair to become good trading partners of ours. Aye, we'll let well enough alone. . . . Weather Command to all Stormriders, congratulations, thanks, and welcome back!"

Iern flew on. At his altitude, on his left he glimpsed a piece of Brezh —Ar-Goat, not Ar-Mor, yet Brezh. A sudden wish to see his mother tugged at him.

Skyholm rose and waxed in his view. With only starlight upon it, it was a moon vast but ashen, save where electric lamps sparkled. And now, also before him, the Loi River hove in sight, a silver thread looped across rich lowlands. He began his descent.

3

Originally Tournev was an outgrowth of Old Tours, some of its material quarried from abandoned parts of the latter. Folk settled thereabouts to get not simply protection, but the comforting nearness of Ileduciel. They rebuilt because most former structures were either fallen into ruin or had been taken over for the special uses of the Aerogens. They made it a distinct town because those early Clanspeople-to-be, few in numbers and badly overworked, did not want the day-to-day responsibility of governing it. Time passed, industrial plants wore out or grew obsolete; the easy and sensible thing was to start new ones in the thriving new city. By degrees, Tournev became the lower capital of the Domain, as Ileduciel was the higher. Old Tours was an enclave, a cluster of piously restored buildings where none but caretakers and shopkeepers lived and none but the curious visited.

Nevertheless it was a romantic setting. Iern stood on a tower at twilight, a young woman by his side, and felt himself falling in love.

The air held a chill, breath smoked, but hooded cloaks kept them warm and likewise did hand linked with hand. Beneath them lay roofs and darkened streets. Beyond, windows throughout Tournev were coming aglow, and gas lamps along the boulevards. Elsewhere lanterns bobbed like fireflies as workers sought homeward. Farther on shimmered the river, around darknesses that were moored barges and boats. From its right bank the ground swelled northward, flecked by farmhouses and hamlets, to the hill of the Consvatoire. Those ivied walls were not wholly nighted; here and there, across kilometers, another light burned where a scholar sat late. In immemorial belief, which endured among many pysans, that site was hallowed. It was the highest ground along an arc where at certain times of year you saw sun or moon pass behind Skyholm.

Seven and a half times the size of either in heaven, the aerostat hung directly overhead. Still touched by the sun, as it was for about twenty minutes after nightfall and before daybreak, it cast muted radiance across the land. In that light, Ashcroft Faylis Mayn seemed to Iern almost a being of Breizheg legend, a haunter of woods and dolmens, too beautiful to be real.

"How often have I lingered here and dreamed," she said low. "But I never dreamed I would do it with . . . a saint."

Her musical Bourgoynais accent redeemed a thin voice. And apart from that— Iern's pulse thuttered. She was small, delicately featured, with large gray eyes and long, lustrous golden hair. She was intense and intelligent, a student of history at the Consvatoire yonder. She was no girl to tumble straight into bed, but a well-born maiden. His kinsman Talence Jovain Aurillac had introduced them a few days back, and Iern quickly lost interest in tumbling the harbor girls.

"Oh, come," he said, with an awkwardness that seldom burdened him, "you're no back-country shepherdess, you're a Clanswoman and know we're all human. I, well, I did my job, nothing more."

Her gaze sought his. "But we carry our ancestral anims, don't we? I think yours may come from the First Captain himself."

"What? No, surely our present Captain— Anyway, not only do you flatter me, but frankly, I'm skeptical about that belief."

She smiled. "And I . . . frankly. Yes, I'd rather suppose you're a—" She hesitated. "An organelle that is truly evolving."

Taken aback, he swallowed. "Are you a Gaean?"

"Oh, no. I think the Gaeans have certain insights, but—but I'm simply a little delver in dusty old books. A dreamer—" She looked upward and sighed. "I do believe there is a purpose behind existence. Else nothing would make sense, would it, Iern? Just consider history.

How could we, you and I, stand here this evening, safe and happy, if a fate, a force, had not possessed our ancestors?"

"Well—" He searched for words but gave up. Why argue and risk spoiling the hour? His own view of the past was prosaic.

Immediately after the War of Judgment, when chaos and radioactivity rolled to and fro across Uropa, the original crew members moved Skyholm from its station above Paris to one above Tours. The latter city had escaped obliteration. It did not escape famine and pestilence in the years that followed, but the aerostat held off desperate outsiders. Thus a measure of recovery became possible relatively fast.

While they tried, in a rough-and-ready fashion, to be benign rulers, the Thirty—twenty-two men, eight women, from half a dozen nations which no longer existed as anything but terrains and memories—had their own survival in mind. Aloft, they were safe. But they must eat and drink; aircraft perched on landing flanges must have fuel and spare parts; the skin of their home demanded replacement about once a decade, panel by panel, as the ultraviolet and ozone of the stratosphere gnawed at its material; their needs were countless, and nothing could supply them but an advanced technology whose industrial base was gone.

Around the world, sister aerostats fell for these reasons. The Thirty were fortunate. Guarded and reorganized, the people of the area could divert their scant excess energies to restarting or rebuilding the essential facilities. They were willing. If Ileduciel went, most likely what little they possessed would soon go from them too. Poor in equipment, resources, trained personnel, the plants were inefficient at first, their output barely sufficing to maintain Skyholm and its machines. Yet it did suffice, and meanwhile farms were becoming more productive again, and a little trade revived, and some persons found leisure to rescue books from decay and study them.

Meanwhile, also, the power of Skyholm spread. This began almost willy-nilly, a matter of suppressing raiders or marshaled, covetous enemies. Later, generation by generation, it became a matter of policy—of duty and destiny. Sometimes the Aerogens used groundling troops, with flyers to help and the lasers in reserve. Oftener an area was glad to be annexed, by way of shrewd diplomacy, dynastic marriages, or the like. After all, entry into the Domain conferred many benefits. Peaceful borders and free trade were the most obvious. Surveillance from above increased public safety, spotted incipient crop diseases or rich fishing grounds, provided up-to-date maps. Weather forecasts and occasional weather modification were of incalculable value. The Consvatoires which Clansfolk founded were schools, libraries, laboratories, museums, repositories and wellsprings of knowledge; from them came physicians, agronomists, learned men and women of every kind. Nor did Skyholm require much in return: modest tribute, enactment of a few laws which chiefly concerned human rights, cooperation in business of importance to the whole Domain. Otherwise, except for the region around Tournev, states remained autonomous.

Or so the theory went, and for centuries theory counted for a great deal—or myth did, awe, a sense of fate, a hope that this race, divinely chosen, would restore the whole world.

That could not be, of course. The limit of achievement came at last, in debatable lands where Skyholm was on the horizon. To move it closer to them would have been to remove its protection from others whose fealty was ancient. The Aerogens could not master the planet; despite all, its members were only mortal.

The globe overhead grew dim. Stars blinked forth. "I must go back," Faylis said. "I wish I didn't have to, but my reputation and—" She broke off. He could barely see her lashes flutter.

"And mine?" he ventured. His heart leaped. "You're safe with me." A chuckle. "Curse it. But you are."

"I know. And I wish— But we met such a short while ago!"

"What difference does that make?" She did not resist when he drew her to him. In a minute she was learning how to kiss a man.

It stopped with that. He dared not push his luck further, yet. Aided by his flashlight—emblem and perquisite of an elect few—they made an unsteady way down the stairs, out the door, and along the streets. Several times they laughed together, or skipped over the paving stones.

When they entered Tournev, they had better be more decorous. They were not in the riverside district, but a section for Clansfolk and wealthy groundlings. Ordinarily she lived in a dormitory at the Consvatoire, but this chanced to be a holiday week, Harvest. For that period she had moved over to the comfort of a mansion belonging to the Aurillac family, together with several fellow students. It had ample space, and such courtesies to their kind were usual.

The ranking occupant at present was Talence Jovain Aurillac, here on business of the estate he governed in the Pryny Mountains. As the butler admitted Iern and Faylis, he came out of a writing room. Lamplight cast shadows over his face, making it a lair for his eyes. "Great Charles, girl!" he exclaimed. Where he came from, the name of the First Captain was seldom used as an oath. "What have you been doing? Do you know what the time is?"

She bridled. "Do *you* know what right you have to ask me, sir?" she responded. "None!"

Jovain stiffened. After a second, his stare swung to his kinsman, and Iern thought he saw a birth of hatred.

It mattered nothing to the Stormrider, then.

II

"Orion shall rise."

Terai Lohannaso first heard those words from a small girl, bereaved and embittered, in the home she was about to leave, under a snowpeak in a land where he was an unwelcome alien. He was never sure afterward why they haunted him. It was not in his nature to brood, and while he always hated to bring sorrow upon others, he recognized that often there was a blunt necessity for action.

Maybe it was because he had known her father, seen him die, and been the one who came to tell her mother what had happened. Maybe it was because the sad little scene triggered within him an awareness of which he was not quite aware, memories of things done and seen and heard about, which at their times had seemed mere flashes, but taken together pointed toward something that might prove terrible. In any event, during the years that followed he often harked back to that moment, and beyond it to Launy Birken.

The two men had been acquainted before the Power War. This was not strange. Terai was skippering a tramp freighter based at Awaii; Launy was part owner of a factory, modest-sized but innovative, producing electronic gear that found a market also in the Maurai Federation.

Like many of her kind, Terai's ship would sail through the narrows past Vittohrya, a town more cultural and political than mercantile, to Seattle. (Folk in the Northwest Union had had no qualms about rebuilding on former sites, even before the radioactivity had become unmeasurably slight. In such cases, the community was apt to preserve its name better than did those which had not been hit.) Upon docking, his supercargo sent messages to whatever people were appropriate. When Launy received an order, he would bring the consignment himself from his hinterland village, and stay to make sure it got properly stowed. Then he and Terai went out for dinner and an evening's drinking. He spoke no Maurai, but his companion was fluent in Unglish. Eventually Terai met Launy's wife as well.

The fact that the men had served on opposite sides in the recent conflict put no constraint on their friendliness. The Whale War had been undeclared and short, the aims of either party strictly limited, and a chivalric code prevailed.

Terai, eighteen years of age and newly enlisted in the Federation Navy, won a medal when he took charge of his dismasted, burning frigate after all officers perished at the Battle of the Farallones, and kept her afloat under a jury rig the whole way back to Hilo Bay. He always remembered how the nearest of the victorious Union vessels hove to and sent men to help put out the fire, who expressed regrets that they could do no more than that because they must pursue fleeing Maurai units.

As for Launy, he, somewhat older, had captained one of the privateers that brought commerce to a standstill throughout the eastern Pacific Ocean. With her diesel auxiliary and lavish armament, his craft captured nine merchantmen, plundered them, and sent them to the bottom; but first he transferred their crews, not forgetting ship's cats. Fascinated by Maurai culture, he treated his "guests" with good cheer equal to any they would have offered in their homes.

Thus the two could respect and like each other.

Once or twice they did argue the rights and wrongs of their causes. The last such discussion before the next war occurred in quiet, wainscotted surroundings, a dining room in the Seattle chapter house of Launy's Wolf Lodge.

He had invited Terai there for a gourmet meal and a look at something of what his civilization had accomplished, besides manufacture, trade, and exploration. The chamber was large, high-ceilinged, the tables spaced well apart and bearing snowy linen, fine china, ivory utensils. Flames danced in a stone fireplace but were only decorative; electric heating staved off the cold while wind hooted and rain dashed against glass. Likewise electric were the lights, though kept soft. Waterpower was abundant in these parts. In addition, the use of coal throughout the Union increased year by year at a rate that Maurai found horrifying.

"I don't understand you, Launy," Terai said. A bottle of wine and a fair amount of local whiskey had lubricated his tongue. Sober, he was chary of words. "A decent fellow like you, fighting to keep a bunch of whalers in business. It's not as if you had to. There's no conscription here, and the war was not called a war anyway. Yes, you've told me you did well off your raiding, and it was a great adventure. But you're doing better off your company, and if a man feels restless—Lesu Haristi, he's got a whole planet to roam, and half of it still mostly unknown!"

"And more than half of it full of nothing but backward starvelings," Launy retorted.

"Oh, now, I've traveled rather widely, and it isn't that bad. Not everywhere."

"Bad enough, and in enough places." Launy's speech quickened. "I haven't just read books, I've seen."

"M-m, how?"

"My father was an Iron Man till he grew arthritic. He took me, a kid, along with him on his final trip. We went clear to the Lantic coast, prospecting. Plenty of stuff yet in the dead cities. We didn't run into any danger. But I almost wish we had, because the main reason was that the natives were too miserable to be a menace. Instead, they begged. A lot of women tried to rent themselves out, with their families' consent—for a needle, a plastic cup, anything useful we could spare. I was too young to pay much heed, but I don't think those poor, scrawny, rickety-boned creatures got many takers."

I like him more than ever, Terai thought. *He's straying from my question, maybe on purpose, but he's not using the change of subject to glamorize himself.*

That would have been easy, his mind went on. The Iron Men were picturesque, and their early exploits had been heroic in a raw fashion as they fought, sneaked, or bargained their way across the Mong-occupied plains in search of metal. Today, however, treaties regulated their passage; Lodge-owned plants near the sources processed materials before those were loaded onto trains that then chugged uneventfully over the prairies and up the mountains; sometimes the freight came from lodes that had been rediscovered, rather than from salvage; coal enormously exceeded it in tonnage. But, true, expeditions did still range through the wilds and barrens of the far East, hunting for the means to give Union industry more muscle. *If it could only be given more brain and heart. . . .*

"No, I'll take a civilized country," Launy continued. "I've been south as far as Corado, and the countries there are all right: political puppets of yours, but living all right. The Mong, too. I've visited the Mong, and they're as different from us as ever in spite of modernizing, but even their serfs eat well and are better educated than you might expect. I'd certainly love to travel through your Federation someday—I mean as a private person—oh, yes. And could be I'll make it to Yurrup one of these years. Trade's really begun growing in that direction, hasn't it? Skyholm must be a wonderful sight. And you can name other lucky areas. But most of 'em—" He shook his head vehemently. "No, thanks. I know about countries where the rich have it good, but I know about their poor, too, and I know about those where everybody is poor, and I tell you, I've seen enough."

Terai returned to the attack. "If you're so tender-hearted," he asked, "how can you support the slaughter of whales?"

"You Maurai hunted them in the past. And you tried ranching them, like cattle."

"That was before our scientists learned—what scientists were finding out shortly before the Downfall—how intelligent the cetaceans are." Terai gripped his glass, snuffed the smoky odor, tossed ardency down his throat. "Oh, you've heard all this. Bit by bit, we decided the world isn't so impoverished that men need to kill beings like that for meat and oil."

He regarded the other across their table. What he saw was a big man, though not as big as himself, heavy-featured, ruddy, with yellow hair combed down to the shoulders and a close-trimmed red-yellow beard. The Norrman was rather typically clad for an evening out: scarf of imported silk tucked into the open collar of a plaid wool shirt, buckskin trousers, solid half-boots. An ivory ring on his left hand declared him married.

In this climate Terai dressed similarly, but his clothes were plain and their cut, as well as his appearance, foreign to the diners around. Those, mostly husband-and-wife couples, kept trying not to stare.

"You could decide it on your own account," Launy said. "Not on behalf of the whole human race. When you started seizing Northwest whaling ships—"

"As we'd long been seizing slave ships. You never objected to that."

"No. We don't care for slavery here." Launy raised a palm. "Wait. We care for freedom. But that means the freedom of people, not horses or chickens. Sure, whales are smart animals, and I'd rather we left them alone. But you've never proved they're more than animals. Be honest; all you have is a theory."

He drank and spoke fast: "You took it on yourselves, in what you thought was your almightiness, to tell free captains what they could and could not do on the high seas. Maybe you realized whaling's carried on almost exclusively by members of the Fish Hawk and Polaris Lodges, and you didn't think the rest of this loose-jointed country would help them with its blood. But of course no Lodge forsakes another; the Mong wars taught us loyalty. Of course we told you busybodies to go to Rusha. And when you got violent, why, the Lodges raised men and money, they armed and convoyed, they got violent right back at you."

And in pitched battles, as well as raids, you persuaded us we had better not insist, Terai admitted. He recalled vessels that were the core of the Union fleet at Farallones, steam-powered, steel-plated, devoid of catapults but dragon-headed with cannon that fired explosive shells and tubes that launched rockets. *We didn't understand you. We never guessed—in our, oh, yes, our "almightiness"—that anyone would squander resources on that scale, for no larger reason than yours.*

Launy's voice dropped. He leaned forward. "Look, Terai," he proceeded earnestly, "let's not squabble. Let me just add one thing, and afterward we can get drunk and sing songs and whatever else we feel like. But look. We need sperm oil for fine lubrication. Sure, I know jojoba oil will do. But we can't import enough from areas where the jojoba plant grows, because there isn't enough being raised, nor enough trade with them to stimulate it. As for whale meat and lamp fuel and baleen and such, mainly we sell them to the Mong, and buy stuff they have that we want, like coal or the tolls on our railroads through their nations. After we've got our industry really well developed, why, we won't *need* to go whaling. It won't *pay* anymore. Instead of bitching about our development and ob—uh—obstructing it every way you can short of provoking a full-dress war . . . why don't you encourage us? We'd stop our whaling that much the sooner. Could it be that you—no, not you, Terai, but your politicians, your merchants—could it be that they don't want anybody, anywhere in the world, to get as important as the Maurai Federation?"

"No!" Terai denied, and wished for an instant that he were completely sincere. *Well, I am as far as I myself go, I suppose.* "How often have we said it? We don't want any single civilization lording it over the rest, nor any industry that damages the planet—"

Launy threw back his head and interrupted his guest with a shout of laughter. "Sorry," he apologized. "It suddenly struck me . . . how we're parroting our newspapers and professors and orators . . . when you're sailing on tomorrow's tide. Talk about waste!"

Terai relaxed and boomed forth a chuckle. "You're right about that, at least. Good drinking time is a nonrenewable resource. And didn't you mention a girl show?"

"I did that."

Neither man felt need of the sleazy resorts in Docktown. Launy's wife had accompanied him to Seattle, though agreeing not to interfere with his stag night; Terai's crew included wahines as well as kanakas. However, Seattle strip dances were quite a contrast to the demure Awaiian hulas. It became a memorable evening.

They had few more. Five years after the Whale War ended, the Power War began; and it was declared—by the Federation upon the Union—and went on for three grisly years, because this time each agonist was determined to break the other.

That Launy and Terai had become friends was nothing extraordinary. The curious chance was that they met again, early in the second year of the second strife between their peoples.

A naval engagement took place off the Aurgon coast. The Maurai forces won, as the Maurai were winning everywhere at sea. They had learned their lesson earlier, had closely studied a society which they no longer underestimated, and had made ready for a conflict that the realists among them knew was ineluctable. The strength, skill, wealth, manpower had been theirs all along, needing only to be mobilized—though at that, the Norrmen gave them a hard fight.

The ship that bore Terai sank an enemy vessel and set about rescuing survivors. Those who were hauled from the water included a radionics officer named Launy Birken.

2

Waves ran blue, green, white-laced, foam-swirled, from a shadowiness to starboard that was the continent, westward to the world's edge. They brawled, they whooshed, they hissed and chuckled; the surge of them pulsed upward through timbers and into human bones. The sun stood past noon where a few clouds and many gulls flew like spatters of milk. Air blew spindrift and chill into men's faces, tossed their hair, filled their ears with skirling.

Despite her size and the fact that she was beating upwind, *Barracuda* bounded on her way at twenty knots. She could have gone faster if her lift motors had raised more sail, but would have outpaced most of her flotilla. A science of hydrodynamics that, in the course of centuries, had become almost as precise as ballistics underlay her design. The trimaran structure was intended for speed and maneuverability rather than volume. Her rigging was more conventional—not that Maurai shipbuilders followed a uniform convention—but equally subtle and efficient. Five masts down the length of the main hull each bore five courses of squaresails (translucent synthetic fabric, strong and rot-proof) that were actually airfoils. Computer-controlled, their aileron edge panels created vectors that rotated the masts to whatever the optimum angle of the moment might be; no stays were needed, nor many running lines. Nor were more than four sailors—

—if she had been a merchantman carrying express cargo. In the event, dozens of crewfolk were on deck. They had ample room. Save for a streamlined bridge, cabins were below; machinery, weapon turrets, lifeboats, and other apparatus occupied little space; the solar collectors were deployed, to charge accumulators and refresh bacterial fuel cells as well as to furnish power, but they were elevated on hydraulic shafts and so formed pergolas in whose shade people might gather. Hardly any did, for Maurai found these waters and this atmosphere cold.

On a civilian craft, the setting would have been less austere. Probably the main prow would have borne a figurehead: very likely religious, the carven Triad, Tanaroa the Creator, Lesu Haristi the Saviour on His right, shark-toothed Nan the Destroyer on His left. Surely planters would have been bright with flowers. As it was, apart from the hues of indurated wood in strakes, planks, and spars, all the color was aft, where the Cross and Stars of the Federation streamed at the flagstaff.

Yet the crewfolk provided ample gaiety, as they took their pleasure between battles. Some defied the weather and wore nothing but a sarong, plus beads, bracelets, garlands, or leis they had woven from blossoms grown in pots in their quarters. Young, lithe, skin tones ranging from amber through umber to black, they were doubly beautiful amidst their more fully clad mates. Here and there, intricate tattoos rippled to the play of flesh. The majority were male, but, as nearly always on Maurai vessels, adventurous women, not yet married, were enrolled as well.

In little spontaneous groups, they celebrated their aliveness. Japes flew. Feet bounded, hips swayed, hands undulated. Through the wind came sounds of flute, drum, fiddle, accordion, koto, song. Dice rattled; stones moved over a chalk-marked go board. Two persons told stories from their homes to listeners from distant islands; neither printed pages nor radio waves could transmit the entire diversity of a realm that sprawled across half the Pacific Ocean. A couple embraced; another couple went down an open hatch to make love. Three or four individuals sat apart and contemplated the waves, or their souls.

Amidships at the port rail, Launy hunched his shoulders and dug hands deep into the pockets of the pea jacket lent him. "Who's on watch, anyway?" he wondered.

Terai shrugged. "The usual," he replied. "First, second, or third officer. First, second, or third engineer. Quartermaster at the wheel. Radio officer; except in emergencies, she's in charge of the radar too. And, yes, the cook and bull cook must be starting to prepare tea about this time. And I daresay a few more—the carpenter or the gun chief, for instance—have found things that need doing. But Navy or no, we Maurai aren't much for strict schedules or busywork." He grinned. "I've heard us called sloppy, and not just by Norries like you, but by the Mericans south of you—our own clients, that we converted from freebooters to civilized ranchers and whatnot! However, somehow we manage."

"You do," said the captive bleakly, and stared for a while at the man beside him.

There was considerable to stare at. Terai Lohannaso loomed a sheer two meters in height. Iron-hard, contoured like a hillscape, his body was broad and thick out of proportion to that. His features were largely Polynesian, wide-nosed, full-mouthed, with a scant beard that he kept shaved off; but the square jaw, gray eyes, and complexion ivory where seagoing years had not turned it leather-brown, those were a heritage from Ingliss forebears. His voice was pitched like thunder. Reddish-black, his locks were bobbed under the ears and banged across the bow in the style of N'Zealanner men. A short-sleeved shirt revealed hairless chest and forearms, the latter tattooed —on the left, a standard fouled anchor, but on the right, a hammer and tongs. (He had mentioned once that blacksmithing was a hobby of his.)

"Oh, yes, you manage," Launy said. "You call yourselves easygoing and happy-go-lucky, but your outposts are along every coast of Asia and Africa . . . and the western side of Normerica and Soumerica, from our border on down . . . and native rulers do whatever your local 'representatives' 'suggest' if they know what's good for them. Meanwhile your explorers and traders—your vanguards—are pushing into Yurrup. . . . Oh, yes."

His glance went across the rest of the flotilla. Most of the craft in it were monohull, less fast though more capacious than *Barracuda.* (Stabilities were identical, given extensible spoilers to forestall capsizing.) Their rigs varied, as did their sizes: everything from an archeological-looking schooner to a windmiller whose vanes drove a screw propeller. All were wooden, with scant metal fittings; all appeared frail and innocuous at a distance, even the carrier on whose deck rested a score of airplanes. None bit ferociously through the waves, belching smoke, a-bristle with cannon, like a Northwestern ironclad.

But none, either, were like the big-bellied merchantmen he had taken during the Whale War. He had seen these dancers on the waters pluck apart the squadron in which he served. Now they were bound north to rendezvous with the rest of their kind. Thereafter the combined force would seek the main Union fleet, whose whereabouts were incessantly tracked by Federation scouts. (It was seldom worthwhile to fire shells or rockets at those high-hovering blimps and hydroplaning boats. They were astonishingly evasive; if hit, they were astonishingly durable; if destroyed, they bore life rafts, and the Maurai had astonishingly effective rescue teams.) And later . . . he supposed Federation marines would land on Union shores.

Terai shuffled his feet. "No, hold on," he said uncomfortably. "I, uh, I sympathize with you—you've lost shipmates—but we *don't* want to rule the world. What'd that get us except a bellyful of trouble? Anyhow, the whole idea is to let the world stay, uh, diverse, so different cultures can learn from each other—" He flushed and clicked his tongue. "Sorry, old chap. I didn't mean to repeat propaganda at you. But it's true."

"Right. You like quaint customs and ethnic music," Launy lashed out. "But never something really different. Never something that might upset the Maurai predominance."

"That might wreck every civilization again, or life itself," Terai said back. His lips tightened off his teeth. "Sometimes I wonder if the Downfall didn't come barely in time, to save the whole biosphere from what the old industry was doing to it."

"You talk like a Gaean."

"Lesu forbid!" Terai attempted a laugh. "The Mong dislike us worse than you do, and I doubt a single Maurai ever gave Gaeanity a second thought."

"Then why do you make 'ecology' and 'diversity' your catchwords for a holy war?"

Long-smoldering anger spat forth a small blue flame. "We share this planet," Terai growled. "Your reckless coal-burning and chemical effluents were bad enough. When you collected fissionables and set out to build a *nuclear powerplant*, that was too buggering much. When you turned down our ultimatum, what could we do but declare war? Now we're going to curb you, for everybody's sake!"

His temper abated as fast as it had flared. He was not a choleric man. "Don't fear, Launy," he said, and fumbled in his pockets. "We're not after your kind, just after the exploiters and crazies who've grabbed the rudder from you. The few who don't know, or don't care, that Earth's cupboard is flinking close to empty." He drew out briar pipe and tobacco pouch.

"Oh, I know it is," the Norrie answered. "Remember, my father was an Iron Man—a scavenger—and I've read the books and heard the lectures."

His mind repeated them in synopsis:

The Doom War and its aftermath didn't wipe out knowledge. Too many records of every sort were left, and in certain lucky areas, certain lucky people sooner or later got a chance to study them. They could have rebuilt—except that the earlier technological civilizations had consumed the abundant, easily accessible materials which had made it possible to build in the first place. No Mesabis were left, no Prudhoe Bays, no vast virgin timberlands, no tonnes of fertile topsoil on each arable square meter. More and more, the ancestors had been making do with substitutes and rearrangements. The successor societies, cursed with low energy and lean resources, could not afford to restore the industrial plant necessary for that.

So, mostly, those who survived kept going by creating new versions of savagery or barbarism. Few of them have yet climbed any further back. Few, if any, ever will, unless—

The Maurai hold a key, and beyond the door they guard is a stairway to the future. Their own ancestors were lucky. N'Zealann wasn't hit. Yes, it got its dose of ultraviolet when the bomb explosions thinned the ozone layer—diebacks and mutations in the microbial foundations of life, famines and pestilences and chaos. But it wasn't hit. The structures remained, usually. Factories, laboratories, hydroelectric facilities, not to speak of unexhausted iron and coal mines. City people died, but country dwellers tended to live, and on their reservations the aborigines had a tribal fellowship with institutions that were adaptable to the new conditions. As nature began to recover, the N'Zealanners wanted to reconstruct, and found themselves facing a terrible labor shortage. They invested coal and iron in ships that went out recruiting immigrants, who were mainly from the Polynesian islands. It was natural for them to evolve a scientific but parsimonious technology. . . .

We're different, we in the Northwest. We started with a richer base. And we didn't change from what we had been. Throughout the hard centuries, we never stopped looking forward, we never stopped hoping and dreaming.

His pipe charged and between his jaws, Terai produced a lighter. It was a small hardwood cylinder with a close-fitting piston. He removed the latter and shook some tinder from a compartment of his tobacco pouch down the bore. After he had tucked the pouch away, he rammed the piston home, withdrew it again, and emptied the tinder onto his tobacco. Air compression had heated it to the combustion point. With careful inward puffs, a hand screening off the wind, he nursed the fire into complete life.

"You know," Launy murmured, "that clumsy thing comes near to being a world-symbol for your civilization."

Terai smiled; crow's-feet meshed around his eyes. "Oh, it isn't clumsy when you've gotten the knack. Don't tell me you'd prefer sulfur matches! Why, a smoke would cost you a day's wages."

"What people carry at home is a torch about the size of your thumb. Plastic case, flint-and-steel igniter. The fuel, generally butane, we derive from coal or by destructive distillation of sawdust."

"I know. I've seen. A drunken sailor is less extravagant."

"Now wait a minute, Terai. Your people make use of forests as well as farms. Why, you farm and mine the seas themselves."

"We replant. We maintain a balance."

"We do too, as far as we're able. We'd be better able if we had more energy to spend. That's the solution to everything, energy."

Terai pointed around the ocean, into the wind, and upward.

"Oh, sure, your chosen sources," Launy said. "Sun, wind, water, biomass—but it all goes back in the end to the sun, and the sun's good for hardly more than a kilowatt per square meter, at high noon on a clear day; a hell of a lot less in practice."

"We do use some coal, you know," Terai answered, "but we treat it for clean burning. You could do likewise."

"Not if we're to live the way we think human beings are entitled to. That calls for high-production industries. Petroleum's too precious a feedstock to burn, of course, and wood's too valuable as lumber or just as forest. What's left but coal? I admit it's dirty, and it won't last forever."

Excitement mounted in Launy. "Why won't you Maurai allow nuclear development?" he challenged. "The plants we designed would've been harmless and safe. We'd've disposed of the wastes perfectly safely, too, glassified and stored in geologically stable desert areas—innocent compared to coal mines, acids, ash, gases. We were willing to cooperate in precautions against any weapon-making. We'd also have cooperated in research on thermonuclear power, unlimited energy for as long as Earth lasts. Energy to start us back toward the stars."

He shook his head and sighed. "But no. You'd have none of it, nor let us. Why?"

"That was explained a million times over," Terai said, a little wearily. "The dangers, in case present systems break down, outweigh any possible gain. Even if the systems worked perfectly, forever, the planet itself would suffer too much from industry on the scale you want."

"So you say," Launy retorted. "But what about power politics, greed, maintaining your, uh, your hegemony? Those have been a mighty big part of your motivation, Maurai. I don't mean you personally. You've always struck me as an honorable man. It puzzles me how you could serve as a spy between the wars. You could have refused the assignment."

"I wasn't a spy," Terai said mildly. "Yes, my role as a merchant skipper was a disguise, I was a naval intelligence officer the whole time, but I didn't steal any secrets. I only got to know your country better."

"Against the day when you'd fight us!" Launy struggled to keep hold of his feelings. "No doubt you think of yourself as a simple patriot, a loyal subject of your Queen and member of your tribe. And no doubt that's true, as far as it goes. Underneath, though—in your quiet, relaxed-looking way, you Maurai are fanatics."

He paused before he added: "My history professor in college had a saying, 'Nothing fails like success.' He was right, and your civilization is the prime example. Your achievements were great in their time, but you've gotten fixated on them. You worship them more devoutly than you do your Triad. If anything might change the status quo in any real way, you'll stamp it down . . . and congratulate yourselves on your stewardship of Earth."

He snapped after air, gripped the rail, and turned his gaze back over the sea, away from his beleaguered land.

Terai stood mute, exhaling blue fragrance. Finally he laid a hand on the Norrman's shoulder and rumbled, "I'm not offended. Say what you like. You need to. I'm still your friend. I'll take every chance that comes by to prove it."

3

The armadas clashed off the mouth of the mighty Columma River, on a day when half a gale drove icy rain mingled with sleet out of the west. Currents lent trickiness to the enormous waves; eastward, reefs and shoals lurked beneath. It was as if nature herself fought in defense of this her country.

If so, she fought in vain.

There were skilled sailors among the Union crews, but virtually every Maurai was a child of the great waters, with a dolphinlike sense for them and for the winds that caressed or stirred or lashed them. The Union ships were well built, but most of them on lines that were antique before the old civilization destroyed itself, and they were driven by clumsy rigs or clumsier coal-fired engines, with a very few synfuel diesels. The Maurai ships were aerodynamic as much as they were hydrodynamic, as maneuverable as shark or albatross; those with auxiliary power ran electric motors smoothly off fuel cells. Neither side had many aircraft, but the primitive Union machines were weatherbound, while the Maurai pilots could fly. Rain did not blind radar, sonar, heat detectors, and other such instruments; those of the Maurai were incomparably superior.

As for weapons, the Union guns used explosive powder of mineral origin. Scarcity restricted the supply. The Maurai had been accumulating ammunition from sources more diffuse but unlimited. Their violent combustibles were of largely biological origin, from pelagic farms or bacterial cultures. What metals they used had principally come, by patient electrochemistry, from the sea. Oxygen and hydrogen were similarly borrowed; solar cells had maintained their cryogenic state on the long voyage hither.

Rockets blazed, torpedoes churned, bombs whistled downward, and each of them pursued a precise target. Manmade lightning racked the storm. Union ironclads wallowed amidst their dying companions and shot wildly back. Then the biggest invader missiles arrived, bearing cargoes of liquid gases that reacted upon impact. Volcanoes awoke. The armored ships broke apart. Water fountained upward, fell back, rushed about in its torment to fling hulls, wreckage, survivors crashingly together.

The battle was done in less than two hours. Afterward the wind died away, as if awed into silence, and the rain fell softly, as if weeping for men dead and treasure lost, hope lost. The Maurai did not exult, they went about searching for whom they might rescue, and horror dwelt behind no few of their faces.

They had taken some damage themselves, of course. For example, a shellburst put *Barracuda* out of action until she could be repaired and killed a number of persons aboard her. They included Launy Birken.

The war writhed on for two more years, because it had become a land war. And the land was gigantic. From the Klamath Mountains of Calforni it reached up the seaboard to embrace all of Laska. In its northern parts, its eastward parapets were the Rockies; farther south they were the Cascades, the country narrowing thus because Norrmen cared little for treeless dry plains. Theirs was a realm of uplands, deep valleys, rushing streams, intricate straits and fjords—of woods and swamps, never distant from the richest farm or the lustiest coastal city—of rain, fog, snow, shy sunshine, but sometimes unutterably clear winter nights where stars glittered and auroras flared—of strongholds, hiding places, secret trails, ambushes.

And its folk, men, women, children, were warriors. Terai came to believe that natural selection had worked upon them. Their ancestors had suffered immensely more in the Downfall than his, and meanwhile the Mong poured across from Sberya, over a channel that for years lay frozen for months on end because nuclear detonations had filled the upper air with dust. Through the Yukon plateau the newcomers punched, over the heights beyond and down the tundras and prairies, irresistible—save by the forebears of the Norrmen. Those rolled the tide back in blood from their mountains; they regained Laska, cutting off the influx out of Asia; during centuries of warfare they held off the aliens, wore them down, built their own strength, wrested back what eastern tracts they desired, until at last quietness fell and peace rather than strife became the norm along their borders.

Their descendants were not surrenderers either. They were not insane; when beaten beyond doubt, they yielded, sullenly. The Maurai captured their cities and production centers without inordinate killing. However, that did not end the contest. It did no good to take Seattle, Portanjels, Vittohrya, and send a detachment of marines to occupy the fisher hamlet on Sanwan Island where the Grand Council of the Union met ("off by themselves to keep 'em from doing too much mischief," Launy had once explained). The powers of the central government were so limited that it scarcely qualified as one. More authority resided in the Territorial capitals, but was nonetheless scant. The bone and brain of this society were its Lodges, and they were everywhere. A local Lodgemaster could field a regiment overnight, and disperse it to anonymity when its mission was completed.

With hellish slowness, the Maurai found how to make their enemies lay down arms. They had neither the manpower nor the will to overrun the country, and the thought of devastating it—*Earth*—never occurred to them, except perhaps in nightmares. But they could choke off supplies of war matériel at the source. Meanwhile they could offer relief, medicine, unstinted help in reconstruction, technological improvements, trade, scholarships at their universities for the gifted young.

In this endeavor, High Commissioner Ruori Haakonu became a hero more useful than any combatant. His intelligence, charm, unfeigned warmth, and kindliness gave a glow to his quite real achievements. His masculine beauty did no harm. At the same time, he tolerated no nonsense and was uncannily well informed. (His father, Aruturu, was chief of the intelligence division, Terai Lohannaso's ultimate commander.)

Thus, piecemeal, the Lodges were persuaded to give up and make the best of things. The situation remained acridly bad for them. By treaty, the Northwest Union forswore future attempts to get energy from the nucleus. Its navy was limited to a coast guard and its industry to whatever the Maurai Ecological Service should decide was not too dangerous. For enforcement, the Federation would keep bases at strategic spots and exercise unlimited rights of inspection. Such inducements as favorable terms of commerce scarcely healed the bleeding pride or lessened the weight of the shackles.

But at least there was peace. Terai could soon go home.

4

Walking down the village street, he had seldom felt so alone. The place was lovely. Frame houses with flowering sod roofs stood well back from the pavement, surrounded by lawns and gardens, jauntily painted, many displaying carved designs on doors, gables, or beam ends. Behind them reared a fir forest; its odor brought the springtime coolness alive. To south, the snowpeak of Mount Rainier filled heaven with purity.

Yet isolation radiated from Terai, the outlander. Fair-skinned Norries and occasional squat brown Injuns stiffened when they saw him; children ceased their games; dogs snuffed wrongness, bristled, and snarled. None ignored him but a cat sunning itself on a porch and a raven that flapped hoarse overhead.

Well, he thought tiredly, *what else did I expect? Maybe I shouldn't have come. But I told you, Launy, I'd show you my friendship whenever I could.*

He found the house he wanted, mounted the steps, swung the wooden knocker. Anneth Birken opened the door. She was a tall woman, well formed, brown braids hanging down over the mid-calf dress that was customary in this part of the Union. "Good day," she said, and recognized him and stepped back. Her eyes widened till white ringed blue. "Oh—!"

Terai honored local custom by tipping his cap. He had been careful to don dress uniform, white tunic and trousers, but to leave off his decorations. "Good day, Mizza Birken," he said. When previously they met, almost four years ago, it had been on first-name terms. "I hope I'm not intruding. If you want, I'll leave immediately."

She made no response.

"I wrote ahead, but I suppose you didn't get my letter," he plowed on. "The mails are still in poor shape. I learned your community radiophone is out of order too. This was my last chance to visit you, though. Next week I return to N'Zealann."

Resolution congealed in her. "What do you want?" she demanded.

He stood humbly, as if the upper hand were hers, and answered, "Only to call on you, for old times' sake and to see whether I can help with anything. And, uh, and . . . if you wish . . . I can tell you about Launy's last days, and his death. I was there, you see."

She stood for a number of raven-croaks before she said, "Come in," and led the way.

The house was pleasant, in its somewhat dark and cluttered Northwestern fashion; it was full of mementos. She took him to the living room and gestured him to a chair as heavily built as the rest of her furniture. Above the fireplace he saw an oak panel carved with the emblem of the Lodge that had been Launy's, and was hers too, as it happened: a wolf at full speed, a broken chain around its neck, and underneath it the motto *Run Free.*

"Please be seated, Commander Lohannaso," Anneth said. "I read your insignia correctly, don't I? You have commander's rank now? Can I offer you refreshment? I'm afraid we've no coffee or proper tea at the moment, but there's herb tea, or milk or beer or cider if you prefer."

"Not unless you want it, thank you," he replied, thinking what an effort hospitality would be for her and what explaining to her neighbors she might have to do afterward. He longed for a smoke but remembered that she didn't indulge, common though the vice had become in the Union as trade with the Southeast revived, and decided against hauling out his pipe.

She poised above him. Her mouth was drawn tense, her nostrils were flared and white. "You can tell me how Launy met his end," she said, flat-voiced. "I'm sure it was gallantly. But I've received nothing except the bare news, a year late."

Terai nodded. "He was a prisoner aboard my ship. A random shell from his side killed him instantly. I never saw him flinch. In fact, he was standing by prepared to help give first aid if needed."

"I see. Then I'd like our daughter to hear this. Our sons, too, but they're older and in school." She stepped into the hall and called upstairs: "Ronica! Come down here!"

A girl of perhaps five obeyed. If that was her age, she was big for it, within a tomboy's smudgy sweater and jeans—but had she been cuddling a teddy bear in her room? When her mother made introductions, she grew mute and motionless, but not stiffly; Terai thought of a lynx kitten.

"Sit down, Ronica," Anneth said, saw to it that the child did, and followed suit. "You are kind, Commander Lohannaso, and we're fortunate. Also in your timing. In a month, we move to—" She broke off. "No matter. Please tell what you have to tell."

Terai had rehearsed the account in his mind, over and over. Despite that, he stumbled through it.

And Ronica's green eyes got larger, narrower, larger, narrower. Tears coursed out, but silently, apart from the gulped breath. Her blond head never bowed. Did she remember her father at all? Very likely not—but from her kinfolk, chapter members of his Wolf Lodge, whatever memorial service they had been able to hold for him in wartime—yes, surely she did.

And at the end, although Terai gentled his narrative, she sprang to her feet, fists clenched, and cried in a tempest of rageful sobbing:

"You killed 'im! You old Maurai killed 'im! But we'll kill you! Orion shall rise!"

"Ronica!" Anneth swept from her chair to grab the girl to her. "Be still."

"Orion shall rise!"

The look that Anneth gave Terai was stark. "Excuse us, Commander," she said. "I made a mistake. If you don't mind waiting, I'd better carry her upstairs and soothe her."

"I quite understand, Mizza Birken," he answered, lifting himself. "Take your time. I have a room at the inn, and don't plan to catch the Seattle train till tomorrow. We'll talk about Launy, or anything, as much as you want meanwhile." Awkwardly: "If you'd rather not, I can explore your woods, maybe get in a spot of birdwatching."

"Thank you, Commander," she said—the least bit less frozenly than before?—and hurried her daughter out.

He sank back into his chair. *What odd words for a youngster to scream,* passed through him. *Something she overheard from adults, I imagine, but something meaningful. . . . What meaning? Only a slogan, I suppose. Orion is the Hunter or, in some parts of the world, the Giant in Chains. It's a winter constellation here, and the Northwest Union extends past the Arctic Circle. Nevertheless . . . this may bear watching.*

For the next twenty years, off and on, as far as he was able, he watched.

III

"The Otter stream took me and drowned me and carried me—
Quietly, quietly—
Throughout that summer day
From reeds as they rustled at Fallen Bridge fishing hole,
On into Idris Wood,
Where sun and shadows play.

"The shaw opened up on the meadows of Arwy farm.
There was the apple tree
Where first I kissed my girl.
(Oh, afterward, hand in hand, stood we on Honey Hill,
Wild with surprise at how
The world was all awhirl.)

"Past Alfenton village and dreams in its thoroughfares,
Toyed with and broken by
A boy who once was me,
The river sent rolling whatever was left of him
South toward Budley Bay,
Where first he saw the sea.

"At Ottery Simmery, high gleamed the weathervane
Crowning a steeple through
These thousand years and more,
For here is our market, that traffics in memories.
Inns full of fellowship
Were beckoning from shore.

"But on flowed the river, to Tipton where formerly,
Underneath ivy leaves,
I tried to learn a trade.
The signboard was there still, and greeted the ne'er-do-well
Faring unseen beyond
The friends that he had made.

"At Harpford they knew me right well as a drinking man,
Singing man, gambling man,
A worker when I chose,
Adorer of womankind, rambler of countryside—
None saw me pass it but
The minnows and the crows.

"A little way south of the place I called Otterton
Ended my pilgrimage,
Where willows roof a shoal.
My bones lie there nameless, but everywhere whispering,
Wind-borne and stream-borne, go
The names that were my soul."

Plik ended with a shiver of fingers across the strings of his lute, laid the instrument down on the table at which he sat benched, seized a goblet of wine and drained half of it in a gulp.

"What was that?" asked Sesi.

Plik shrugged. "I suppose I'll call it 'Names.' "

Standing before him, the barmaid raised a finger in reproach. The motion made her hips undulate. They were nicely rounded, like the rest of her. A low-cut, knee-length gown set that shape off to advantage. Her face was rather pretty too, with dark ringlets to frame brown eyes, snub nose, heavy lips, clear complexion.

"I mean what's it about, silly," she said. "You know I don't know much Angley."

Plik drank more slowly. "Well, it isn't quite autobiographical—thus far, anyhow—though it does describe the area I come from."

She gave a slight, seductive shudder. "Now don't you tell me more. I caught barely enough to make me nervous. Honestly, Plik, when you get into one of your weird moods, it scares me."

"No harm intended to you, ever, dearest Vineleaf." A smile twisted his mouth. "I'll make amends. My next will be in Francey, and in praise of you. Incidentally, I'm near the end of learning Brezhoneg —not everyday Brezhoneg, but the literary language. Soon I'll do a ballad in it, all for you and all about you."

She bent over and bestowed a swift kiss on him. He reached for her, but she swayed backward with an ease that bespoke practice. "You are an old dear." She giggled. "But, please, not *all* about me."

"Oh, no." Plik uttered a rusty chuckle. "I've too much competition as matters stand." He emptied his goblet, reached into his belt pouch, and slapped down an iron coin. "Another, if you will."

She took money and vessel while she looked archly across the table. "You, sir?"

Iern shook his head. "Not yet, thanks."

Both men's gazes followed her as she walked to the barrel near the bar. This early in the afternoon, they three were alone in the Pey-d'Or. It was a tavern mostly for laborers and sailors. Smoke-blackened beams upheld a low ceiling above a clay floor. Benches flanked four tables. A basement room with a dusty-windowed clerestory, it was already dim.

"What a pleasant sight," the pilot murmured in Angley. "To tell the truth, I could have tossed mine off, but I'll wait till you get your refill so she'll make another trip. She wags her tail in such a cheerful fashion."

Plik started. "What?" he said in his dialect of the same tongue. "Your usage—are you of the Aerogens?"

Iern nodded. "We needn't make a fuss about it. I admire your song. It's eerie, yes, but I liked it, and you fitted the words very well to that old folk tune." He offered his hand. "I'm Talence Iern Ferlay."

"The same—?—the Stormrider who— An honor, sir." The poet accepted the clasp. "I'm Peyt Rensoon, from Devon across the Channel. Everybody here calls me Plik, though."

They regarded each other. The Angleyman was tall and lanky and ungainly in his movements. A narrow skull bore a face thin and deeply lined, jutting nose, long chin, pale-blue eyes. Alcohol and tobacco had hoarsened what was once a melodious voice. Like Iern, he was clean-shaven, and he kept his receding sandy hair cut more short. However, his blouse, trousers, and shoes were in worse shape than the Clansman's rough but sturdy outfit.

"May I ask what brings you to us?" he inquired.

"Oh, I was visiting my mother and stepfather in Carnac. His oldest son has lately become skipper of a small freight schooner, among several that the father owns. He set off on a trip down the Gulf to Port Bordeu, stopping first at Kemper to get his cargo. I thought I'd ride that far. I used to carouse in Kemper, on furloughs while a Cadet, often in this very den, but I hadn't seen the town for years. It hasn't changed much, has it? Except for our charming servitrice, of course."

Plik grimaced. "No, places like this don't change easily. They're too haunted."

Surprised, Iern considered the remark for a few seconds. Haunted? Why, Kemper was the largest community in Brezh, its chief seaport, capital of Ar-Mor. . . . Wait. More than history and prehistory brooded above its narrow streets. A cathedral raised in the Middle Ages to honor St. Corentin, who was among the Bretons when they arrived from the province of Britannia, which Rome had let go; today its crumbling majesty knew the rites of three separate faiths. . . . A museum, rebuilt after centuries had gnawed away the former episcopal palace that had been its predecessor, housing relics more ancient than Breton or Roman or Gaul, megaliths like those which stood in arrays outside Carnac. . . .

Iern guessed Plik meant ghosts more newly made, though amply old by now. Kemper became consequential because it was spared the destruction that fell on the great cities of Brezh during the Judgment, and because engineers afterward did not find it impossible to broaden and deepen the upper Odet River enough, and dig out a harbor basin big enough, for such ships as their world was able to launch. If he had a sense of history, as he appeared to do, then wherever he looked as he wandered about, Plik perforce remembered billionfold deaths and high hopes crushed.

"Why did you come, then?" Iern blurted. "Why do you stay?" He checked himself and prepared to apologize. Most groundlings were flattered, overjoyed, when a Clansperson asked about them, and ready to confide at embarrassing length. This man wasn't typical, not of anything Iern had met.

Sesi cut him off. She had returned with the wine and Plik's change, and poised watchful. "Must you talk Angley?" she complained. "I mean, it's sort of dull for me at this time of day. Later it's more fun, but then they keep me busy, the fellows do."

Iern suspected some of them kept her busy with more than fetching and carrying.

"Vineleaf," said Plik in Francey, "you should know that we have with us—"

"Iern," the pilot interrupted. "Plain 'Iern' will do." He didn't want her overexcited.

"Ah, well." Plik waved expansively. "Why don't you join us, Vineleaf? Tap yourself a glass, on me."

"Oh, I really shouldn't— Well, thanks. A girl does get tired and thirsty. Iern, are you ready for another?"

The Clansman drained his own goblet. "I suppose. But please let me treat. You too, Plik. Aren't poets traditionally paid in wine?"

"Ah, you know more than I realized." The other man's large Adam's apple bobbed as he gulped what he had. "Yes, it's been said down the ages that the Spirit shuns wealth. I suspect this may have been promulgated by lords who wanted to get their entertainment cheap, but no matter. I at least am in no peril of riches." He spoke with an exaggerated precision that suggested he was drunk.

He confirmed that in Iern's mind when he leaned back, elbow on table, shank over knee, and stared after Sesi while words tumbled out of him:

"You wondered what I'm doing in exile. Well, I've always been an exile, and more in my birthland than here. Do you care to listen? I'm never loath to talk about myself, but my friends in the Pey-d'Or have heard my story too often. Therefore I retell it in bits and pieces, in the songs I make for their amusement and for the drinks they stand me, and they never recognize it. Vineleaf, darling," he called across the room, "don't pout. I promise I'll keep it short this time.

"I mentioned being a national of Devon in southern Angleylann. Do you know it at all?"

"Yes, I was there once with my stepfather, when he had merchandise to trade," Iern said. "A beautiful country."

"Peaceful, pastoral, and dull," Plik answered, "aside from those strangenesses you find in any rural area. They're different from the strangenesses of cities, you know. My father was a village shopkeeper but my mother had Welsh blood in her—still does, I hope. I left in disgrace eighteen years ago, when I was twenty.

"You see, I was always a moody, solitary boy, the first of three who lived but not much help at home, always with my nose in any book I could find when I wasn't drifting around the landscape. In my teens I made a halfhearted attempt to become respectable—but you heard my song. A clergyman of the Free Church that governs Devon liked a few of my early efforts, and on his recommendation I received a scholarship at the college in Glasstobry. It was a wonderful chance, those thousands and thousands of books. . . . I tried to be a good student. I truly did, for more than a year. But the opportunities were so numerous to drink and gamble and chase women and—and at last I played an elaborate practical joke which got me expelled."

"Why did you do that?" Iern inquired. He'd pulled his share of pranks while a Cadet, but kept them within reason. He would never have risked not becoming a flyer.

Sesi brought the three filled cups on a tray and set them down—and herself, beside the Clansman.

At that, pain crossed Plik's countenance and he replied harshly:

"The Bishop couldn't understand that I had to do it. Had to. Glasstobry is so old, so haunted, oh, far more haunted than Kemper."

His tone leveled off, though now a trifle slurred: "Well, I couldn't stomach the idea of slinking back home. I oddjobbed my way abroad. The captain of the ship that happened to bring me here enjoyed my songs, and introduced me to the owner, who engaged me to perform at a banquet he gave in honor of the Mestromor. His Benevolence, Arnec IV, was actually impressed, and wanted to keep me on hand. He gave me a position in his library—oh, books, books, books! The Book and the Bottle—do you know, you don't really require a group of fellow drinkers. You can find a book such a companion that it's quite possible to drink with it and none else. . . . His Benevolence summoned me to many court functions, where I was well rewarded for my talents."

Iern studied the down-at-heels figure. "Something went wrong," he deduced.

Sesi tossed her head. "What'd you expect?" she said impatiently. "He went back to lushing, not drinking but lushing. He'd arrive soused at court and make a fool of himself." She leaned close to Iern. He felt her breath on his cheek. "Let's hear about you," she insinuated.

"My demon was in me," Plik declared stiffly. "I leave it to your judgment whether the word 'demon' is to be taken in its Classical or medieval sense. *I* think the trouble was that gradually I lost interest in composing nice little ditties for nice little people. What I offered instead disturbed them."

"Foof!" Sesi bounced to her feet. "Pardon me, Iern. I have to go behind the house. I'll be back in a minute." She swayed over the floor. Mute, Plik watched until she had climbed the rear staircase out of this basement and closed the door.

Then he shook himself and finished: "At last the Mestromor told me to keep away. He's a kind man; he let me stay on at the library. But all I care to do with the books is read them. My duties are deadly simple. Hence I pay a succession of poor students half my salary to handle them for me. What's left, I eke out by occasionally performing in a better class of taverns than this, where the tips are good, and by occasionally sitting in a marketplace booth as a public scribe. A grubby life, but mostly a merry one."

He took a deep draft. Silence fell. Iern sipped his own wine. It was cheap stuff, thin and sour. Plik had known far better.

"I don't wish to pry," the Clansman said at length, cautiously, "but it seems odd to me that, well, that you stick in Kemper. You could make a fresh start in, well, even Tournev."

"Why don't I?" the poet rasped. "Why do you think?" His glance sought the door above the rear stairs.

"Oh. She's attractive, in her way, but—" Iern decided to say no more.

"In me is my demon," Plik mumbled. "In her is the very Goddess. And me a Christian who deplores the heresies into which my Breizhad friends have fallen. Sometimes she lets me sleep with her."

He rattled forth a laugh and turned his look upon the pilot. "She's right about my making an ass of myself," he said. "I've done it afresh. Could we talk about you for a while?"

"You seem to have heard of me," Iern said, a shade self-consciously. "There isn't much I can add."

"There's everything." Plik made a wobbly gesture. "Not the showy things—your exploit against the whirlwind, year before last; your father, whom the Clan Seniors will probably choose for Skyholm's next Captain when old Toma Sark dies; your slightly legendary status among the pysans of Ar-Mor and, I understand, your unusual popularity among many pysans elsewhere; your leadership of the Weather Corps aerobatic glider team; your coruscant social life—no, not even your championship of such peculiar causes as kindness to animals, or your outspoken opinion that Gaeanity is a menace to the Domain— Let those be. I'd rather know what it feels like to be you. To stand in Skyholm, looking thirty kilometers down to Earth while infinity surrounds you. To believe that the anim, the basic identity of Charles Talence himself, may someday pass into you, coalescing with the uniquenesses of ancestors who already indwell. To know that your Aerogens and its lofty citadel are more than the governors and guardian of an entire civilization, they are its central myth. For every society must have a myth to live by, else it's a walking corpse that will soon fall to the ground—"

"O-o-oh!"

The squeal passed through his grandiloquence and nailed it to the spot. He and Iern yanked attention to Sesi. Unnoticed by either, she had come back from the outhouse and stood on the landing with ears open wide as her eyes.

"Oh, you're a saint! You're *Talence Iern Ferlay!*" She scampered down the stairs and across the floor to cast herself on her knees before him. "Oh, sir, oh, sir!"

Oh, damn, he thought.

Although—well, Plik seemed a person worth talking with, but perhaps not when this drunk and fulsome. And Sesi had arranged her posture of adoration to give Iern a good look down her cleavage.

"Now never mind that," he said. Rising, he bent over, grasped her beneath the arms, and helped her to her feet. She stumbled against him. The sensation was delightful. "Let's be friends together," he urged.

"But this is so marvelous," she breathed. "I'm actually in, in your embrace."

"Sesi, the Aerogens doesn't really encourage superstitions about itself. We're men and women like any others."

She dipped her lashes. "A most handsome man, sir." She raised them and plucked his sleeve. "Could we go off in a corner for just a second? Please? You don't mind, do you, Plik?"

The poet sent her a wry smile and returned to his wine.

Sesi led Iern aside, stood on tiptoe very close, laid her hands over his, and whispered rapidly: "Please don't think I'm bold or wanton or anything. If you tell me no, well, I know my station in life, and only being in the same room with you this afternoon is something I'll always remember. But I've adored you ever since— Anyway, on week nights the landlord, he'll tend bar later, the landlord generally closes up about twenty hundred, because the kind of customers we get have to go to work early. I'm sure you're staying somewhere too fine for the likes of me. But if you felt like it, I do sleep in a room upstairs, and I'd be so honored—"

Iern consulted his conscience. Faylis? No. After nearly two years of marriage she remained indifferent in bed; she loved the glamour and luxury of being his wife, but when they were alone she was apt to rail at him; she was reading Gaean texts, and he knew she corresponded with Talence Jovain Aurillac, who was a Gaean convert. This wouldn't be his first romp away from her. Besides, few Clansfolk took such things seriously anymore.

But Plik. He would like to see Plik again, get to know that curious man better, hear more songs.

He cast a glance yonder. The poet met it, grinned on the left side of his face, hoisted his goblet in toast, and said: "No fears. I'm used to this. Doubtless I'll pass out before long, and awaken with a headache and stagger off to my lodgings. Besides, my Vineleaf can do no wrong."

IV

"Orion shall rise."

Those were the first words that Ronica Birken remembered uttering. Earlier recollections out of childhood stood apart from each other, vaguely perceived, like islands in a fog—her mother singing her to sleep each night; her father (home on leave from the war, he must have been) flinging her in the air and catching her while she laughed for joy; a stately wapiti that hung around the village as a sort of public pet and took lettuce leaves from her fingers; hours of practice at throwing a ball, for she was determined to do it as well as the boys; rain on the windows of a darkened house wherein her mother wept—

But she remembered how she came home, saw Uncle Emon and another man in the living room with Anneth, was so struck by the grimness on all three that she stopped in the doorway and stood unobserved while the other man (Rikko Torsun? He was the local Lodgemaster of the Wolves then; but his face was unclear in her mind) spoke of winning back freedom, and from her uncle rolled forth the words she did not understand (for the starry Hunter *would* gleam again above snowfields—wouldn't he?) but that held a deep and shivery magic.

The very next day, or almost, the stranger came. She did not recall what name he gave himself, but his size and alien features remained always with her, vivid as a scar; and though he talked gently, it was of Daddy's death he talked, and he was one of the troll Maurai, the first she had ever seen. At last she hurled the magic words at him for a lightning bolt. Nothing happened except that Mother took her away. However, from that hour onward, Ronica's memories were more and more linked, as if this marked the beginning of her real life.

In a way it did. Soon after, the family moved to Portanjels on the Strait of Wandy Fuca, where Anneth took a job about which she told her children merely that it was for her Lodge. (A minor harbor, therefore scarcely noticed by the Maurai Inspectorate, the town was an excellent terminal for the seaborne part of the secret traffic with Kenai; and recordkeepers were no less indispensable to the growth of that traffic than were sailors, engineers, or armed guards.) Presently she married Tom Jamis, also of the Wolf Lodge (and also in the secret, as a computerman concerned with procuring hardware). In the course of a few years, the undertaking reached a point where their services were in demand at the volcanoes. The family moved to Kenai, and there—later in the forests behind it, on into the vastness that was Laska—Ronica grew up. By her mid-teens, through alertness and thinking, she had gained a shrewd idea of what the thunders really were that sometimes rolled from behind the mountains across the inlet.

She kept silence. At that time, she was aiming to become a Survivor; and she did learn, pass her tests, start to act as a guide and provider, occasionally a tracker and rescuer of lost persons, for those who would reclaim the wilderness for man. She also became a postulant of the Wolf Lodge. That was nearly inevitable, for not only was it her family's, it had by far the largest membership in the area. (Here as elsewhere, Injuns and Eskimos generally preferred their own traditional groupings, though some belonged to it.) At the age of eighteen, she completed her studies, performed her First Duty—in her case, backpacking medicines to a snowbound settlement that had radioed news of its need—and stood her Vigil.

When she had been ceremoniously initiated, Lodgemaster Benyo Smith called her to his office. With him were her stepfather Tom Jamis and that Eygar Dreng who was rarely seen in Kenai. The men wore blue robes, and Benyo kept a hat on his head and gripped his emblematic staff. It was clearly a solemn moment. Above the Lodgemaster's desk, carved into the wainscot, the wolf that had broken its chain ran free.

"Ronica," Benyo said, "your elders have watched you for a long while, and by and large, what we've seen has pleased us. You're intelligent, brave and adventurous but not reckless, loyal, and . . . discreet." He paused. "How much do you know of what's going on amongst us?"

Her throat felt thick. "Orion shall rise," she got out past the thutter of blood.

Benyo nodded. "Let's not say anything more just yet. A work this big, this meaningful—aimed at the upheaval of the whole world—is hard enough to hide. It would have been impossible to hide, year after year, before the Doom War made places like Kenai lonely again. It gets harder to hide as it goes."

He gusted a sigh. "We've got to recruit new people, and not simply because many of us have grown old or died in the service of Orion. We've come so far along that we require some special new combinations of abilities. You seem promising. But let me first warn you, it won't be a lot of thrills—scarcely ever. Mostly it'll be labor and sacrifice, for a cause of liberation that you can hardly have noticed in this backwater where the Maurai never come. If you aren't prepared to give up a great deal of what you enjoy, what you love, well, tell us right now, straight out. There'll be no hard feelings, I promise you. You can continue your life as you've been leading it. After all, a Survivor is socially useful."

"But I'll have to stay in Laska," she foretold.

"Until Orion rises," Benyo answered.

"If ever it does," Eygar Dreng said. "We don't yet have what we must have. Maybe we never will."

Tom Jamis gave his stepdaughter a crooked smile. "Yes, the Lodge will expect you to avoid civilization," he told her. "I myself haven't left these parts for ten years, you recall. It's not that anyone's afraid I'll betray them, it's that I can do my work right here; and why take an added risk? But I like it well enough, and you're entirely at home, aren't you?"

Ronica wet her lips. "What . . . would you want me . . . to do?"

Eygar Dreng regarded her for a span that felt long before he replied slowly: "I've examined your school records and talked with your teachers. You could be an engineer. You could work on Orion—not as a leader; frankly, you aren't brilliant in that area—but as a valuable junior . . . . when you aren't using your Survivor skills in a search that is vital to us. We'd like to send you south, to study at the University of Vittohrya. It'd be on a scholarship of the kind that Lodges regularly give deserving kids."

"The first thing you must think about, and think hard," Benyo Smith added, "is whether, in that atmosphere, at your age, you can keep the greatest secret on the planet. If you have any least doubt, say no, and we'll thank you."

"Couldn't you teach me, you people?" Ronica wondered. Though this interview was not altogether unexpected, she was half stunned by the implications. "My brother Bill—he's already vanished across the water, into the mountains."

"And your brother Zakki is reasonably content to be a lumberman," Tom said. "Yes, we do have in-house facilities for education, and that's where Bill is, but— You're different, Ronica. If you join, you'll need to know more about the world outside."

Of course she accepted.

Four years passed before she returned, and then she was soon off again, this time northward and into wilderness.

2

She came afoot and alone over the Chugach Mountains and down to the peninsula. Her entire journey she had made thus, for it was through country where none but a few hunting tribes dwelt. Except when she happened on one of these and took hospitality, she herself traveled as a hunter and gatherer.

That did not slow her much. Her rabbit stick knocked down small game along the way; her eye was quick to find berries, roots, every edible that the land yielded so abundantly; water was never a problem; in the evenings, after she had spent maybe half an hour putting together a brushwood shelter, collecting fuel, starting a fire, she might construct a deadfall while her dinner cooked, with a good prospect of finding a squirrel or the like in it next morning. When perchance she went hungry for a day or two, it was the sort of minor discomfort that she ignored. Occasionally she stopped to wash and dry her clothes, or to inquire among natives in what pidgin she and they could improvise. Otherwise she strode.

Nevertheless, hers became a three months' faring. The subarctic fall was well along when she reentered the tamed country. Here forests had dwindled to woodlots while meadows grew into pastures. Down the shore road she went, Cook Inlet aglitter on her right and snowpeaks rising sheer behind, aspen and birch still yellow amidst the darkling spruce on her left, more mountains beyond them, smoke blowing ragged from the chimneys of stoutly timbered houses, sometimes an eagle at hover with its wings golden against sky and clouds, and past this the ramparts of the peninsula itself, staving off the bleakness of the sea—this and more she saw, when rain was not falling. Rain fell most of the time, but she ignored it too; else she would never have gotten far.

Now she could spend her nights beneath roofs, among friends.

Dwellers were not so many but that everybody knew almost everybody else. Folk were eager to have company. In Ronica's case, the older sons of a household were especially happy.

At twenty-two years of age, she was tall, long-limbed, broad in shoulders and hips, full-bosomed; her face was wide, with green eyes under level dark brows, blunt nose, strong mouth and chin, fair and slightly freckled complexion; wavy amber-colored hair, contained by a beaded headband, fell to the base of her neck. Not that she was anything exotic. Her woolen shirt, trousers, and hat were battered and travel-stained, and scarcely more was in her backpack than a change of clothes and boots, a couple of utensils, and her prospecting gear. In these parts she had discarded her rabbit stick and fire drill, which she could make anytime.

Regardless, she was handsome, and lately come back from her studies in Vittohrya, *the* city. Young men speculated about her morals, were disappointed, and settled down with their kin to hear whatever she chose to tell of her experiences outside these horizons. She gave them gossip, generally amusing, from the South, and they were content. Of her present expedition, begun shortly after she returned home, she said nothing specific, and nobody inquired. For nearly two decades, Wolf had been doing something hereabouts, aided by individuals from other Lodges, but it did not especially touch inhabitants in their lives and they had an ethic of minding their own business. Also, the majority belonged to Wolf themselves; they heeded the Lodgemaster's hints and discouraged any neighbors who grew unduly curious.

Besides, Ronica Birken was a Survivor, who had been four years away from her wilds. It was understandable that she would wish to refresh her knowledge of them, and perhaps meanwhile do a little surveying or investigating—or whatever—on behalf of her Lodge and people.

Therefore she walked undisturbed to Kenai.

One by one, landmarks hove in view and fell behind. Long abandoned, a fortress from the early Mong Wars period crumbled toward the same oblivion as that Ancrage from which most of its materials had been quarried. Ammonia Hill was a grave mound above what was left of an ancient petrochemical plant after it too had been stripped of its useful substances, hundreds of years ago. A fairly modern industrial building also lay deserted, since the last trickle of the natural gas that it processed gave out, and roots and weather were reclaiming what parts of it man had not removed.

Not far onward, though, stood a newer and hopeful workplace, turning waste and by-products such as sawdust into fuel for today; and this was on the edge of Kenai, which lived as intensely as ever.

Five thousand inhabitants made the town the principal community in an enormous area. Houses clustered along irregular streets, many of which were paved with asphalt rather than wood blocks. Most were gaudily carved and painted, like those in the hinterland. Some belonged to traders, merchants, brokers, doctors, veterinarians, and other professionals, who conducted their business on the ground floors. There were a few warehouses, factories, smokehouses, a lumberyard . . . an inn, a bar and grill, a school, two churches and a pagan shrine-park . . . looming over the rest, triple-tiered, with shingle roofs, totem colonnade, and watchtower, the Wolf Lodge Hall, which included such things as municipal auditorium and library . . . emblems on private homes telling that various other Lodges met in them. . . . Fishing boats were out, but three freighters lay at the docks, their spars rakish athwart the mists that hid the farther heights; and a ferry threshed with ox-driven paddlewheels on its way across the channel from Tyonek.

Traffic was sparse, half of it seeming to consist of children at play, white, Eskimo, Aleut, Injun, mixed-breed, among excited mongrels and dignified malemute dogs. Now and then a rider clopped by or a horsecart trundled past. Adult pedestrians usually gave Ronica a hail. Men and women were clad much alike, in her style though often affecting ornaments; men tended to beards and long hair, women to braids halfway down their backs. A town smell filled the air, blent of salt water, tar, fish, smoke, humanity. The sun was clouded over in the west; lamplight glimmered from windows.

Ronica proceeded to the Wolf building, climbed its steps, crossed its porch, went through its main door. The lobby was spacious and gracious, floored and paneled in swirl-grained hardwoods, with ancestral portraits and trophies on the walls, a stone fireplace where logs blazed to pick rafters out of shadow. Of the several exits, most were open to anybody. Ronica identified herself at the reception counter and got admission up a particular staircase, to a particular office.

Its door was closed. Through the dimness of the corridor, she saw that the emblem of a Lodgemaster had been newly repainted—rifle and plowshare crossed above an open book, reminder that the Lodges had originated out of the need to fight as well as to cooperate and conserve knowledge. She scowled at that. The Mong Wars had long since died away, but the Maurai—

The clerk below had not said Benyo Smith demanded to be left undisturbed. Ronica wanted to discharge her immediate obligation by reporting to him, then seek her mother and stepfather. She rapped. "Come in," said his voice over the transom.

Obeying, she saw weariness on his aquiline countenance; but he sat erect behind the desk, white hair and goatee like banners of defiance. A visitor rose to give her a courtly bow. *Maurai influence,* she thought in distaste. The gesture was doubly out of place because he wore the blue tunic and trousers of a Union naval officer, insignia of captain's rank embroidered on the sleeves.

"Ronica!" Benyo exclaimed softly. "Welcome . . . welcome home, my dear."

"Will the lady permit me to introduce myself?" the stranger said. "Mikli Karst."

"Ronica Birken." She shook hands. He made the clasp linger a trifle while they observed each other by lampglow and fading daylight.

He seemed to be in his late forties, short and scrawny but agile in his movements. His head was large, bearing a long sharp nose, small ice-blue eyes, close-cropped gray hair and beard. Between thin lips, his teeth showed snaggly. His voice was rather high and hurried. Yet when he smiled, a transformation went over that face; he knew well how to charm.

She turned to Benyo. "Sir, the expedition was successful," she declared. "Shall I give you the details tomorrow?"

"No, please, at once." Joy shone from the old man. "Sit down. This calls for a celebration." He went to take bottle and glasses from a cabinet.

"Which my arrival did not." Mikli Karst chuckled in Ronica's direction. "Quite all right. You're far better-looking than me."

"You can speak freely," Benyo assured her. "Captain Karst is in the Intelligence Corps. He knows about Orion, probably more than I do, and he's served us well. In fact, he was just relating his most recent exploit against the enemy."

"Not to brag," the newcomer said. "Mind you, I'm as great a braggart as the next man. But in this case, experience convinced me we need improved security, fast. I came here to discuss that with your leaders on the spot."

Ronica shed her pack and accepted a drink. It was fine whiskey, which smoked across her tongue and down her gullet. Relaxation felt equally warm throughout her muscles.

Mikli Karst took forth a pack of cigarettes, offered her one, was refused, and lit it for himself. His fingertips were stained yellow. She was glad that half-open windows let out the stench. "I take it," he said, "you've been questing for fissionables."

"How do you know?" the Lodgemaster asked.

The officer shrugged. "Obviously Missy Birken has been in the outback." ("*Missy,*" "*outback,*" she thought—*Mauraiisms.* But they gave no reason to doubt his loyalty. She had seen foreign influence aplenty in the cities of the South, and heard ever more people of her generation questioning the values of the Northwest Union, the entire civilization that it embodied.) "Her accouterments, her suntan." He grinned. "It takes considerable exposure to get a suntan in this climate. What would have required that, and been so important that immediately upon her return she comes to none less than you, sir? What but a search for nuclear explosives?"

He blew a smoke ring. "We know how the material salvaged for the power project was confiscated by our esteemed opponents after the war," he continued lazily. "However, I've always taken it for a certainty that there were military stocks, tactical weapons, in Laska before the Doom, and it seems unlikely to me that every last missile got ejaculated in that spectacular orgasm. The problem would be to find the remnants, centuries later, in a tremendous and sparsely settled territory." He glanced at Ronica. "I daresay you had clues."

"Not I, at first," she said. "Men who went through the Rangle Mountains—traders and trappers, mostly—heard rumors from the native tribes that might indicate something. They had no idea what. But we always question their kind about everything that's happened to them, whenever they show up. That's no giveaway, you realize. Why should the Lodge *not* want to keep tabs on the wilderness? It's bloodyfart little—uh, pardon me, Master Smith—damn little we do know. Anyhow, the accumulated stories seemed to call for investigation, and I volunteered."

"Ronica is a special person," Benyo said with pride. "She's a professional Survivor who now has a degree in electronic engineering. She'll work across the channel, in between checking out possibilities like this."

"An admirable idea," Mikli Karst said. "My compliments to the chef."

Benyo leaned over the desk. His gaunt frame quivered. "How much did you find, Ronica?"

"Three intact warheads," she told them. "And evidently more that've disintegrated; but the stuff should be recoverable from the soil. Uranium, to judge by the radiation pattern, so no serious toxicity problem." Excitement came to life again. It was as if once more she stood on that rocky slope, in that thin cold rain, and heard her counter cry out. Her husky voice dropped lower. "Half-life, millions of years, you know. I estimate we can go fetch us a dozen kilotonnes' worth. The site's above timberline, so hardly anybody ever comes by, but it's got enough remnants of construction, deep rust stains in the rock, and so forth, that stray hunters shortcutting between valleys noticed. Don't worry about them blabbing. They're savages pure and simple, deathly afraid of the Old Ghosts."

She leaned back, crossed her legs, and tossed off a gulp of liquor that made Mikli raise his brows, most respectfully.

He contracted them after that, turned to Benyo, and said: "Sir, we'd better plan the recovery operation as carefully as porcupines make love. As I was warning you, the Maurai Inspectorate has become suspicious. Inevitable, no doubt. Secrets are notoriously fragile, even when they're tucked away in the back of beyond. We've managed to misdirect the opposition thus far."

He chuckled. "If I may claim credit, and just try to stop me, it was my idea, years ago, to start the notion that mutterings about 'Orion' were nothing but the standard legend that a subjugated nation commonly develops, of a sleeping hero or god who will someday awake to set it free and reign over it in peace and justice and every such implausibility. I persuaded various anthropologists to publish papers—" He sobered, stubbed his cigarette, took a fresh one, and added, "But we can't dine out on that forever. The latest Maurai mission got far closer to goal than I liked."

"You were about to tell me," Benyo said. Ronica decided she was in no hurry to get home; this should be interesting.

"Well," the other began, "it started with an intelligence officer of theirs coming to the liaison headquarters in Vittohrya and demanding a tour north. Information pointed toward something under way in Laska, something forbidden by the peace treaty, and he had orders to go check up. I'd guess the recent demise of the High Commissioner had exacerbated matters."

Ronica frowned. She had been saddened by that news. While a student at the university, she heard nothing but good of Ruori Haakonu. Yes, he was in charge of curbing the sovereignty of the Union, lest it massively revive that high-energy technology the Maurai abhorred; but he did his task with tact, humanity, helpfulness. She would fight what he stood for, but she could well understand why many of her contemporaries were doubting that their parents had been right after all. A number of her female classmates had confessed to being in love with him.

"He had to go," Mikli Karst said, "but we were bound to get a reaction among his friends."

Benyo and Ronica started in their chairs. "What?" the Lodgemaster whispered. "It was an accidental death, wasn't it? A fete, an archery contest, a blind man who wanted to try under guidance but misheard the instructions—"

"As you will," the officer replied. "In any event, he was too effective. When Orion rises, we don't want our people full of self-doubt, do we? They'll be stunned as is. Better they first spend a few years under a less likable Maurai High Commissioner."

He seemed to feel the shock in his listeners, for he went on deftly: "This agent of theirs, then, insisted on going north to poke around. As per doctrine, his principal guide, allegedly civilian, was from my corps, and happened to be me. I must say that Terai Lohannaso is an impressive fellow. Middle-aged but bull-strong, bull-sized; possessed of an adequate if perhaps not exactly scintillating mind; withal, a disarmingly soft-spoken and friendly sort."

Ronica's own mind stirred. That name— No, she couldn't lay hand on whatever the memory was.

"Like the rest of us, most of whom were entirely sincere, I told him I knew of nothing illicit, but he was welcome to look wherever he chose, and I'd make the trip as easy as possible for him and his staff," Mikli continued. "Oh, that became quite a trip!

"I took him to a Tlingit settlement, hoping their well-known festiveness would distract him. Instead, he ate and drank *them* to the ground, and was champing to be off next morning. Not far from Kenai, he noticed faint signs, broke out his instruments, dug down, and found a buried power cable—a monstrously thick thing, but he lifted it in his bare hands, seeing the current was off. I did my best to convince him it was ancient—who'd be that lavish with copper nowadays?—but well preserved by its insulation, and used by a hydroelectric station serving the locality. I took him to the station, but plainly he was skeptical, and I decided best he and his party suffer a regrettable accident. He was climbing a mountain, carrying an infrared detector, to make sure a heat source he'd spotted was not artificial. My assistant triggered an avalanche in the snowfield above. Nobody else with him escaped alive, but he did. Incredible! It was as if he *swam* in that roaring mass. . . . He was injured, though, besides having lost most of his group, and must needs give up and go back to recuperate."

Mikli scowled. "He'll return, or colleagues of his will," he finished. "Communications may be thin and transportation slow, compared to the past before the Doom; likewise, intelligence corps are naive; but brains are as functional as ever. We shall have to improve our cover, to the point where we can safely receive Maurai inspectors right in Kenai."

"Can we?" Benyo asked, a small tremor of age in his voice.

The visitor gestured expansively. "Oh, yes. I and my colleagues have given the matter a heap of thought. Our organization is ready to move; I'm only here to survey the area in detail and make specific recommendations. For example, in this vicinity—not hard by, but in this general vicinity—we can start work on what appears to be a clandestine nuclear powerplant that a syndicate supposedly is building to produce synthetic fuels. We can let the Maurai discover it, with enough difficulty to make them believe they've cracked the secret. Less elaborate arrangements might suffice, to be sure. We'll see. Don't worry, Master Smith. Orion shall rise. The safeguards will be directed by a highly competent troublemaker, namely me."

Benyo did not look altogether happy.

Mikli switched his jaybird glance to Ronica. "You've made a magnificent contribution, my lady," he said. "I'm not sure but what you're being wasted in Laska. How would you like to see the rest of the world? I go to and fro in it."

Taken aback, she could merely reply, "You're moving a little fast, aren't you, Captain?"

He laughed. "The offer is honest, or presumably will be after I've had a chance to learn more about you. We might make a first-chop team. If you also choose to explore how we might do recreationally, I'll be enchanted; but if not, don't worry, I can behave myself. Your physique suggests I'd better."

He made social talk for a while longer and took his leave, arranging to meet Benyo again in the morning.

When the door had closed behind him, Ronica shifted her weight. The windows were now full of dusk, the room full of its chill. "I should be on my way too, sir," she said. "I'll write up my notes and give them to you as soon's may be. If you want, I can guide the recovery team, but that isn't necessary, and, uh, to be frank, I'm kind of anxious to try my hand at the work undermountain."

Benyo nodded. "Quite." He hesitated. "You'll probably have more dealings with Captain Karst."

"M-m-m. . . . I dunno. What can you tell me about him?"

"Nothing in depth, but we have had encounters in the past, he and I. And one hears things." Benyo searched for words. "Be careful, dear. He's a strange and not very savory character. Grew up as a guttersnipe in the slums of Seattle; some say his mother was a prostitute. Got into trouble, was sent to sea. Served on a privateer in the Whale War, later joined the regular Navy and distinguished himself as an intelligence officer in the Power War. Meanwhile he'd been accepted into the Salmon Lodge, and afterward expelled. The reason was never made public, as usual, but the story goes it was because of misconduct with a boy. Possibly that's untrue. He did marry, into a wealthy house, his father-in-law a Wolf, and his wife seems devoted to him in spite of everything. And as you heard today, he is invaluable to Orion. He may well be our next head of security here; Ab Munso is about ready for retirement. But have a care."

"Thanks." Impulsively, Ronica leaned across the Lodgemaster's desk and patted his hand. "You are a sweetheart, did you know? Don't worry. I'm not a simple backwoods maiden. I'll cope."

Not a maiden at all. Pain flashed. She'd had her love affairs in oh-so-sophisticated Vittohrya (if young Maurai are free to indulge, why not young us?), but the last had not been fun or romance or anything, it had been with a professor of hers who was a family man, and in the end they'd agreed they should not destroy his home. That was shortly before she graduated and took ship for Kenai. *The forest and the mountains, in them there is healing.*

She rose. "Well, goodnight," she said. "I'm certainly willing to talk further with Captain Karst, if he is, but have no fears for my virtue. The prospect of visiting some foreign countries is mighty interesting."

A thrill went through her. *God damn and hell rejoice, but it is!* Karst had been much too casual about the deaths he described. Orion was supposed to liberate without killing. But done was done, and had apparently been necessary under the circumstances, and she had her own life to attend, clamorous within her.

V

With a whirr of propellers the dirigible left its mooring at Tournev airfield and ascended. It was among those which regularly carried goods and people to Skyholm.

Passengers were few this trip. Iern and Faylis could stand at the forward observation window during approach and see wonder grow huge before them.

"O-o-oh," she whispered, and clasped his hand. Tears started forth. "Oh, darling."

He smiled, brought an arm around to tilt the exquisite face up toward him, leaned down, and kissed her. The lips beneath his were cool but trembled in response. Ever since he had told her about his assignment, she had been more affectionate than at any time after their honeymoon.

Happiness brought that about, he supposed. It would be her first visit aloft, and for three whole months! She went about their town-house singing. She commissioned a new wardrobe, with furs and silks and embroideries and jewels, extravagance which he could not find the heart to scold her for. *She's so young,* he told himself repeatedly —not much younger in years than he, but in experience, in spirit, like a child. *She loves the elegance she never knew before, luxury, gaiety, familiarity with important persons—prestige of her own, and few things carry more prestige than a station in Skyholm. I shouldn't worry about expenses. Beynac gives me a pretty good income. Maybe I can cut back on my private spending. And, yes, not let her coldness or her tantrums drive me away, but also give her more of my company than my habit has gotten to be.*

Here was certainly a chance for that. He wouldn't travel for thirteen weeks, except when he took his Cadets on short practice flights. Otherwise he would be lecturing, grading papers, doubtless giving occasional counsel. He had not drawn this duty before, since it rotated among pilots, but felt he could probably handle it well. He might actually enjoy it. In any event, in his leisure time he could find ample diversion . . . *with Faylis, of course,* he reminded himself.

"No picture shows this, really," she breathed. "None." She reached out and touched the glass. He thought of a baby reaching for the moon.

From behind the dirigible, the sun cast an almost shadowless radiance. Crystalline blue-black, the stratosphere made a chalice for the pearl which was Skyholm. Then as the craft drew nigh, that pearl became a moon indeed, a world.

Two full kilometers in diameter, it nonetheless kept an airiness, a grace to rival anything man had ever created. Transparent, the outer skin had a shimmer across it, a ghost of rainbows. Beneath were the interlocking hexagons of the tensegrity structure: slender, hollow girders and thin cables, as if the god of the spiders had been everywhere weaving. A hundred meters behind this was a vast ball of night, over which the web went agleam.

Its pattern disappeared at the equator. There homes, meeting places, workshops, laboratories, control centers, all the manifold spaces that humans used were nested among the ribs of Skyholm. They seemed a broad, intricately ornamented belt, mostly dark but with flashes of color and metal. Positioned around it were four observation domes, four laser complexes, two missile launchers, two flanges on which—dragonflies at this distance—jetplanes rested, and eight engines belonging to the aerostat itself. Small inspection platforms and banks of solar collectors studded the rest of the sphere.

Approach from ground revealed an opening at the lower pole, where the ribs gave way to a frame in the form of pentagram. It supported a great pipe leading to the interior. As a plane took off on some mission and dropped below the globe, on the far side, its image briefly quivered, troubled by the heat that poured forth.

And this was Skyholm, Ileduciel, Hemelhuis (the names were many), which men before the Judgment had dreamed of, and built in modules, and lifted on wings of helium to assemble in the uppermost air.

Faylis was long silent. When at last she spoke, her voice was small and timid: "Suddenly I realize how little I know about it. I mean, it's always been there, like Earth. I don't—well, nobody quite knows why and how it was made. Do they?"

"What?" asked Iern, startled. "And you set out to be a historian?"

"You know my main interest has been Iberyan history."

"Well," he said, "a lot of records were lost in the War of Judgment and its aftermath, but considerable was preserved, and the Thirty found time to chronicle certain matters themselves. A consortium of nations in West Uropa decided to have an Okress aerostat, as a few elsewhere already did. The crew made Angley—its ancestral version —their common language because it was, then, the standard language of aeronautics—"

She flushed. Indignation sharpened her tone. "I'm not a complete ignoramus, whatever you think. I learned that much in chapel school."

"I'm sorry," he answered fast. "I misunderstood you. What did you mean?"

She relented. "The technical reasons for the undertaking. I'm such an idiot where it comes to science. I remember my teachers explaining, but I don't remember exactly what they said."

"Oh, there were plenty of uses for a base in the stratosphere," Iern told her. "Most of them were the same ones you're familiar with, that we still have. Surveillance for both civilian and military purposes. Monitoring of weather and oceans. Communications relay. Nighttime illumination by searchlights, when necessary. A place for aircraft, missiles, astronomy and other research. Collecting solar energy — But you know that. In addition, there were plans to launch spacecraft from it." Sudden wistfulness locked his tongue. Once human beings had reached outward to the moon and beyond.

She didn't notice. "Yes, dear. I'm afraid it remains arcana to me." She giggled. Her awe had been short-lived. Now, he guessed, she was again anticipating the life of a Skyholm officer's lady. *Well, that's better than dwelling on that Jovain wretch and his vicious Gaean foolishness,* Iern decided. "Why," she said, "I can't even understand what holds the balloon up."

He welcomed the chance to forget Luna and talk about yonder globe. Perhaps it was a minor triumph, when set against the briefest cosmic voyage, but it was among the few triumphs that had endured.

"Not a balloon," he corrected. "A rigid configuration like this airship we're on. Different principle, however. That framework saves weight by relying on tensile much more than compression strength. And the sphere isn't full of hydrogen, with an anticatalyst against fire. It's essentially two skins of polymer, the inner one equipped with light absorbers. Sunlight gets trapped and heats the air at the middle; greenhouse effect, we say. The pressure stays the same because of that vent at the bottom, but the air inside is less dense because of its high temperature, so buoyancy equals thousands of tonnes. The sun supplies energy for everything else too, by way of solar cells and thermal converters. Energy to run all apparatus, maintain a comfortable environment, replenish nighttime radiation losses, power factories and synthetic fuel plants on the ground by microwave transmission—and those motors. Skyholm's engines don't burn anything; they're electrically driven fan jets."

He stopped for breath. "Thank you for the lecture," she said. "But it's more information than I can absorb in five minutes."

He swallowed, then saw wryly that he had been delivering a short version of a talk he intended to give the youngest of his students. They needed solid facts as well as whatever inspiration Skyholm itself, and he as a popular hero, could provide. The years between enrollment at six and graduation at twenty were arduous. They seemed interminable to a little boy or girl; those whom he would instruct in high-altitude flight were sixteen and over.

"I'm sorry," he said as before, and wondered if he truly was. Other women did not require endless apologies and reconciliations. Sesi in Kemper danced across memory. Yes, he must go back—though mainly for companionship with Plik of the songs. . . .

Faylis left him, to seek the prismatic downviewer around which several fellow passengers were clustered. "Gaea!" she cried softly.

He joined her. The sight was old to him, but not the less imperial for that. Seen from thirty kilometers of altitude, their planet curved away across the length and breadth of the Domain, green, brown, white-swirled with clouds. Rivers, lakes, Gulf lay burnished, Angleylann and Eria like emeralds on the silver band of their channels. Along the edge of the world, a narrow blue-white ribbon deepened upward to azure and thence to the abyssal clarity which surrounded him.

With an effort, he dismissed from his mind the name she had uttered. It was not unnatural for her to use "Gaea" for the living Earth. Quite a few people did these days who were anything but Gaeans. He laid an arm about her marvelously slim waist.

A steward entered the cabin from the control section of the gondola. "Sirs, ladies, we are preparing to rendezvous," he announced. "Please take your seats and secure your harnesses."

"Why?" Faylis asked Iern. "It's calm outside, isn't it?"

He found relief in explaining. "The vent that I mentioned causes turbulence. Also, often Skyholm's engines have to be on, to maintain position against winds. Yes, the stratosphere has winds; they're thin but fast. A lighter-than-air ship is a clumsy thing, except for fuel efficiency. A jet operating nearby can bounce it around."

"I see." She swayed against him, and they settled down, and everything was glorious—

—until the dirigible moored, and a pressure tube extended through which they debarked, and waiting in the reception area was Talence Jovain Aurillac.

His greeting was courteous, though, and he was entitled to be here. True, he must have exchanged his term with somebody else; and he must have gotten the dates from Faylis. Yet Iern could not forbid anyone to make such bargains, nor forbid her to correspond with a friend who had met her before he did. Skyholm belonged to all the Clansfolk.

The Thirty took unto themselves wives and husbands from among the people over whom they had assumed authority, were fruitful and multiplied. Later generations built new living quarters for their larger numbers, until they reached a limit. More dwellers meant either sacrificing space devoted to scientific and military capabilities, which was unthinkable, or crowding unpleasantly close together. By then the original families had become the Clans, marrying only among each other save when they adopted worthy groundlings into their ranks; their properties in the Domain were widespread and prosperous; converting apartments into barracks would be absurd. Instead, they changed their law.

None but the Captain and his or her immediate kin might stay permanently aloft, and through the following centuries, few Captains chose to do so. If nothing else, background radiation in the stratosphere was stronger than it now was anyplace where nuclear weapons had wrought their havoc during the Judgment. From time to time an individual, generally a dedicated scientist, petitioned for an extended leave of residence, which was granted if the reason was valid, and of course that person's spouse and children got the same privilege; but those cases were exceptional.

Gradually the population of Skyholm stabilized around two thousand, with slight fluctuations. About half were adults. Approximately a hundred were officers and technicians, serving tours of duty, together with marriage partners of these. (Professional staff alternated three years here, with frequent visits groundside, and three years at support facilities throughout the Domain.) More than half the subadult group were Cadets, in training for eventual commissions; it demanded several sessions in the aerostat.

The remaining persons were there for the month which was the right of every grown Clan member, every seven years. At certain times, others arrived—the Seniors, to decide matters of great moment, perform the rituals of summer and winter solstice, or give the most honored of the dead a funeral. It was fitting and proper that all should thus have their parts in the life of Skyholm. They shared no single creed; in the eyes of many, the services that the chaplains conducted were merely another of the traditions which it would be ill-bred to flout; but to each of them, in some deep and inexpressible sense, Skyholm was holy.

Or so the case had been through cycle after cycle of birth, begetting, and death. In the end, time wears everything away, even sacredness.

VI

After the house in Tournev, not to speak of ancestral estates in different regions, an apartment in Skyholm felt still more meager than it was. Of its three chambers, the bedroom had just enough floor space that Faylis and Iern could reach the bed. The one that combined kitchen and dining area was scarcely bigger, equipped with only a sink and a minuscule electric stove. Refrigeration lockers, like the bathroom, were at the end of a corridor onto which opened the doors of those half-dozen couples who shared them. For the first time in her life, she must do her own cooking, housecleaning, and laundry. She hated the chores and did them badly, with bursts of rage or tears. Before long she and Iern were eating their suppers in the aerostat's single restaurant; other meals consisted chiefly of sandwiches.

The living room was somewhat larger and much more gracious. However, it was windowless, the habitations being inboard of the working sections. Fluorescent panels and landscape paintings could not open a way out of her feeling of imprisonment. Anyhow, they weren't *her* pictures, they had been hung there by people generations in the grave, nor were the draperies and carpet and lightweight furniture hers. Thank foresight that she'd brought along a number of books. But she hadn't expected that her stay in heaven would give her an opportunity to catch up on her reading.

A knock at the door brought her from it. She hurried across the floor with her heart aflutter. Who—? Iern was at work, and as for Jovain, she was to meet him this afternoon.

Opening, she saw an auburn-haired young woman in an elegant, if slightly immodest, calf-length gown. "Blessing be upon you," the stranger greeted formally, but with a wide smile. "If this is an intrusion, I depart in good will."

"Oh, no," Faylis said. "Please come in."

The other did. They exchanged respects, hands crossed on bosoms, heads bowed. "I'm Ricasoli Anjelan Scout," the newcomer explained. "We haven't met because my friend and I are three halls away. We're taking our month . . . and to think it's half gone already, and not till yesterday did we learn that Talence Iern Ferlay has been here all along! You can imagine how thrilled we were. I came to ask if you'd care to visit us."

"Why, why, yes, of course. Thank you. Won't you sit down? I'll make coffee."

"No, please don't." Anjelan laughed. "That would be a poor way to start an acquaintance, putting you to such an expense."

"A glass of wine, then?" On getting agreement, Faylis set forth a decanter and goblets. They were beautiful antique crystal, but they belonged to Skyholm, not her.

Anjelan quickly made herself welcome. Her chatter was vivacious and amicable and it broke the solitude. By birth she was of Clan Bergdorff, from Toulou in the South. Lately she had divorced—something which no few of her age group had decided was not a betrayal of kinship, as their forebears had supposed—and was now sharing quarters with one of her lovers. The settlement had given her an independent income, and she saw no reason to work. "Not that I'm selfish," she added. "At home I belong to a little theater society. We go on tour for three weeks every year—bring some culture to the pysans, you know, or at least a bit of fun. Maybe it makes them less restless." She cocked her head. "I hope I haven't shocked you."

"No," Faylis replied, unsure whether or not she quite spoke truth. "I know there are many nowadays who think like you, and who am I to call it wrong? Foreigners and their ideas have been arriving ever since the Isolation Era ended, and it's becoming a flood. Inevitably, that forces us to question our own assumptions."

Anjelan regarded her. "You're different, aren't you, dear?"

"Well, I was a student when I met Iern, and since we got married, most of the people we see have been, are, they're inclined to be old-fashioned and make a big thing out of duty." *Most of the people we see,* passed through her. *Not those he goes off to make merry with.*

"And you're a very serious person, too; that's clear." Anjelan's glance dropped to an open book on the table between them. "A reader. My, that does look learned, as thick as it is. What's it about?" She leaned closer, to see the title at the head of a page. "*Principles of Gaean Thought.* Oh!" She straightened in her chair and registered some shock of her own. "Is that your religion? I'd never have guessed."

"Gaeanity is not a religion," Faylis answered. "It's a set of insights and practices."

"Really? I don't want to be rude, but frankly, I always took for granted—a cult that began among barbarian nomads away off in Merique—"

"The Mong are not barbarians," Faylis declared with a touch of irritation. "They're not exactly nomads, either. They've been civilized for centuries, even though it's a civilization unlike ours."

"But—do forgive me; I'm fascinated—we hear about the danger from Espayn—yes, I distinctly remember an article in a newspaper, quoting your husband as calling Gaeanity a menace."

"I am not required to share his every opinion. Being in the Air Force, he's naturally concerned about military threats. But I think he exaggerates our problems with Espayn. Yes, the Domain tried to keep Lonzo from conquering the larger part of Iberya, but failed, and the Zhenerals have held that against us ever since—especially when we did later force them out of Italya. And yes, Gaean missionaries have made many converts there, who're anxious to convince everybody else. But they aren't plotting to invade us. I have a close friend whose estate is in the Pryny Mountains, in Eskual-Herria Nord, on the very border. He fought in the Italyan campaign, by the way. And he says the Espaynian leaders aren't insane. They may nibble away here and there on the fringes, where Skyholm is below the horizon, but that's normal. Think about the tribes beyond the Rhin."

"You *are* an interesting person, Faylis," Anjelan said. "So quiet, until the fire lights in you." She paused. "Could you explain to me, then, what Gaeanity is? I never paid attention before, I only heard what you'd call the clichés."

Faylis relaxed, touched in spite of herself, and smiled. "That's what Iern would describe as a three-bottle mission," she replied. "I couldn't possibly in an hour—and mind you, I'm not a Gaean. Not yet. Maybe I never will actually embrace the philosophy. But I'm learning whatever I can, because I do think there's a basic, really basic truth in it."

"Could you give me just a few words?"

"Well, let me read them to you." Faylis picked up the book and turned back to its preface. As she pronounced the sentences, her voice grew low and it was as if something glowed within her.

" 'Life upon Earth is One. This is no metaphor. It is a statement of fact, simple and tremendous.

" 'Nor is this knowledge altogether new. Some faiths, most notably in Hinja, have maintained from time immemorial that existence has a fundamental unity. Ancient records, lately discovered by archeologists and studied by historians, show that toward the end of the Age of Plenty, a few thinkers were expressing the idea in secular terms.

" 'The War of Judgment cast their work into oblivion. Karakan Afremovek never heard of it. But that Yuanese philosopher-ecologist, inspired by the Buddhism and Christianity of his nation but drawing on scientific principles, reached the same conclusion, and proceeded thence to understand the nature of Gaea.

" 'The core teaching is this: that Gaea, our living planet, is a single organism. From the first chemical stirrings in primordial oceans, onward to human awareness, a force within life has made it bring about its own evolution toward ever greater majesty and meaning. That evolution has not ended with us. It will go on as long as Gaea Herself endures.

" 'We are organs, or rather organelles, that She has developed in order that She may think. We no more exist separately from Her than the cells of our bodies exist, in any viable fashion, separately from us. We live because we belong; we serve the immense Oneness, as does every animal, plant, or lowliest microbe.

" 'The teaching of Karakan is true. Therefore it is not sentimental. Evolution has thus far been the working of a blind force, often going wrong though always in the end correcting itself. The brain that humanity has provided life with is primitive. Intelligence went horribly astray in the Age of Plenty, when a recklessly exploitative industrial civilization degraded the biosphere and could have destroyed it, like a cancer destroying a man. The War of Judgment was not a plain human mistake, an unleashing of powers more vast and lethal than anyone had truly comprehended. It was a fever whereby Gaea freed Herself of a disease.

" 'Let us never forget. Else the Life Force may well cast us off entirely, as it cast off the dinosaurs, and spend the next few millions of years evolving a creature that is both sentient and sane. Our part is to serve the supreme organism of which we are a part. Ours is to revere life, while developing ourselves as human beings because that is to develop an aspect of Gaea.' "

Anjelan threw up her hands. "Stop!" she laughed. "It's far too heavy for me."

Faylis took the volume off her lap and reached for her wine. "But I hope you'll agree it isn't a jumble of pagan superstitions," she said.

"Yes, indeed. I'm impressed. Though I'm afraid it's scarcely my cup of tea."

"Hm-m, all kinds of people have accepted it. I admit, no doubt most of them have quite a superficial understanding, and get much of it wrong. Really studying it is hard work."

"And you're such a studious type. I suppose you think I'm shallow."

"Oh, no—"

"I don't pretend to be deep. I only like to enjoy myself. What else is there in life?" Quickly: "Yes, dear, you've tried to explain what there is . . . for you. But don't you like a good time now and then?"

Faylis bit her lip. "When it happens."

Anjelan grew sympathetic. "Not so often, am I right? Your man's work keeps him away from home a great deal, and you haven't anybody else, and your associates aren't too sprightly, are they?" Her smile turned sour. "And be honest, Skyholm has been a disappointment, hasn't it? It has to me. I don't care for the sports in the gymnasium. Plays, concerts, lectures get boring. The dances and other social activities are unimaginative. Meditation on the centuries of history around us—ha!"

Faylis smiled faintly. "I admire your frankness."

Anjelan leaned across the table and patted her hostess' hand. "Well, my Zhoen and I can help you to some pleasure while we're here. And you can help us. Everything I've read or heard about Iern says he's a jolly sort when he chooses to be. When can you come?"

"I'll have to ask him, but surely soon."

"Good. I'm an excellent cook, even with this miserable equipment, so bring an appetite. Afterward—well, I own a record player and took it along. I have unusual discs for it, too. Have you heard the Balearic Ensemble? Super-erotic. Especially when you're smoking— Now don't look that disapproving. We won't press it on you, if you don't want any, but really, marijuana isn't for brutish back-country yokels. Most young Clansfolk use it, at least in my circle, and take no harm."

"Um, would you care for some more wine?"

—Both women were mellowed when Anjelan left. At the door she said, "One last thing, darling. Your husband has been my hero ever since he rode into that hurricane. Would you mind if I borrow him? A girl I know has told me he's fabulous in bed."

Faylis could only stare. In a peripheral, half-denying fashion she had recognized that Iern did not always sleep by himself when away from home. Perhaps he seldom did. But if this was common gossip—

Anjelan tittered and stroked Faylis' cheek. "Thank you," she said. "Never fear, I'll return him in mint condition. Goodbye, now."

The door closed behind her. Faylis kept staring at it, until she recalled that the hour was near for her to meet Jovain.

2

Fitted in between the ribs of Skyholm, corridors were short, companionways were steep, both were narrow and heavily trafficked. Faylis must continually squeeze by people: stern-faced officer, brisk technician, pondering scientist, solemn chaplain, sophisticated city woman, rural squire full of marvel, young couple on their first visit but intent only on each other, aged couple on their last visit and also hand in hand, Clansfolk who affected the costumes of whatever states they lived in, once a dark alien—Maurai, surely—who had some professional reason to come aloft. . . . Usage had stylized such encounters, made them into a dance of movements and expressions whereby you avoided jostling and, simultaneously, the appearance of indifference. In the beginning Faylis had been enchanted. Later she found it monotonous, meaningless, maddening.

She wondered how anybody could endure repeated assignments here. Well, they had their work to keep them interested. Doubtless they grew accustomed to the crowdedness, and accepted the—the decorum, the reverence for Skyholm as the heart of civilization, that was expected. She could try to empathize. After all, though raised in the spaciousness of a Bourgoynais estate, she had accepted dormitory quarters when she entered the Consvatoire, that she might dwell in the brilliance of books and intellects.

She had imagined Skyholm as an intensified version of that, until she arrived and found that Iern had taken more than one virginity from her. Never again could she look heavenward and see a kind of divinity in this hollow globe. It was merely a thing humans had made, which kept some of them in power over others. The mystery and grandeur of life inhered in life itself.

Fragrance welled up a companionway. She hastened into the Garden.

The bottom tier of the inhabited belt did more than help freshen the air. Mostly aeroponic, to save the weight of soil, it nevertheless seemed totally natural. It restored the spirit with leaves, blossoms, playful waters, singing and winging birds, intricacy, intimacy. Children could rollick along the walks and steps without troubling lovers in an arbor, oldsters in talk or reverie on a bench, a meditator before a shrine, a wanderer in search of peace and beauty. The art of centuries had learned how to create lushness out of very little, where it was desired, and elsewhere make sparseness delightful.

Where Faylis entered from above, a catwalk began. Its rails were elaborately trained grapevines, its carpeting was moss, it went on into moist green dusk through a tunnel of foliage wherein orchids glowed. Following this, she came to a bridge over a tiny stream that ran through a channel of indurated wood whose irregularities made it swirl, jump, and chuckle. Presently she took a stairway, whose own wood had been selected for its grain, that curved downward and around, into a stand of bamboo rustling and clicking in warm ventilator breezes. Leaving that, she saw the brooklet ring as a waterfall across a sculptured panel, into a basin where goldfish flickered.

Her way then grew austere for a while. The walk was bare metal, a structural member undisguised though inlaid with geometrical patterns. Fluorescents shone upon struts and cables. They were positioned so that light and shadow brought the endless interplay of hexagons forth into chiaroscuro. Ivy, morning glory, occasional shrubs softened chosen lines. Woven among them, a huge cage of monofilaments gave room for songbirds to fly; their notes reechoed through these spaces. Hummingbirds and butterflies—tiger swallowtails—darted free, living jewels.

A filigree arch marked the boundary of a court where grass and flowerbeds were. Having taken a hidden course from the fish basin, here the stream leaped as a fountain and chimed sparkling back over bowls of aluminum anodized in rich hues. Several tracks radiated hence. Faylis picked one that went between rows of bonsai and by a statue of the Winter Lord—a Juran legend—whose lucite was icily illuminated from within. Beyond was a passageway also made of low-weight synthetic, dim and damp but clustered with showy fungi. It gave on beds of amaryllis, whose colors the ribs of Skyholm pierced; harmless but brightly patterned small snakes basked under heat lamps.

A ramp, whose surface changed from rough wood to parquet, slanted farther downward between two actual trees. Fruit hung lanternlike amidst the leaves of the orange, while a house in the branches of the dwarf oak tempted children to enter. At the bottom, a path where bubbles of pseudo-gravel scrunched underfoot went between formal hedges, past a bower over whose lattice roses rioted, red, white, yellow, purple, night-blue.

There Talence Jovain Aurillac waited.

He stepped forth and took Faylis' hands in his, without ritual greeting. For a space they regarded one another.

Approaching forty, he was not exceptionally tall in the Clans but slender, lithe, graceful in his movements. On him, the typical long skull and narrow face bore a curved nose, golden-brown eyes, olive complexion, black and slightly gray-shot hair. Strong in his veins, blood of the Midi let him do what few of his kinsmen could with success: cultivate a mustache and pointed beard in the style of the Pryny groundlings whom his estate dominated. His clothes were somber but tasteful, fur-trimmed velvet tunic, tight hose, opal pendant, amber-studded belt and half-boots. When he spoke, his voice was musical, the Angley bearing a marked accent from Eskual-Herria:

"I began to fear you were detained, my dear."

"Why, I am just on time." She pointed to the wristwatch that was among her most expensive pieces of jewelry: not much iron in it, nor even much precious alloying metal such as manganese, but many hours of highly skilled handicraft.

"Really?" He bent to look, holding her arm, and lingered unnecessarily. His military service, if nothing else, must have made him familiar with miniature clocks. Her enjoyment of his touch made her feel a little guilty, until she recalled how Iern flirted with every attractive woman in sight. And frequently did more than flirt.

"Right you are." Jovain straightened. "The time simply appeared long." He smiled. It was a rather nervous smile, and the words jerked out of him as if rehearsed but badly rehearsed. Very likely they were. He lacked Iern's glibness. In his gaze was only honesty.

She wondered if *he* stayed true to his wife. They had been wedded fifteen years, with three children who survived—something of an accomplishment for a Clanswoman, though of course the father's descent included hardy mountaineers. Yet, while he had never complained directly, Faylis gathered that a chill had fallen on the marriage since Irmali refused to join her husband in his conversion to Gaeanity.

Despite that, she thought, *the ancient honor of his family abides in him. His ancestors stood guard for generations against Iberyan raiders. He still does, no matter that most of Iberya has become a single nation with which the Domain trades. He himself is a pilot who saw combat over the Italyan peninsula, won decorations and the devotion of his men, and later, as castlekeeper, earned the affection of his pysans.*

She knew little more than that, and most of her information was from others. He and she had not met except when he had occasion to be in some region where she was, and then their conversation had not dwelt on themselves. Nor did the letters which they exchanged at an ever-increasing rate. *It's his mind, his wonderful mind that draws me to him; and, yes, his soul, coming aflame when he speaks to me of Gaea.*

His tone, gone matter-of-fact, made her realize with a start that she had been trying to think of him in the stately phrases of an Alainian Era chronicler. "Ah, well. I hope you had no trouble finding this place?"

"No, no," she said. "The Garden is certainly complicated, but even if the way-markers are inconspicuous, they're easy to follow." She drew a perfumed breath. "Why did you want me to come?"

His voice dropped. "This high above Earth," he answered slowly, "you can experience an incomparable aspect of Gaea."

Taking her arm again, he led her into the bower. Roses filled it with dusk and sweetness. Through ventilation murmur she caught a hypnotic buzzing of Skyholm's stingless bees. The flowers made a frame, a crown of thorns and petals like that upon the brow of Zhesu, around a prismatic window which revealed the world below.

Her moodiness departed from Faylis. This would always remain a miracle, the ever-changing sight of clouds, waters agleam, rich plains and manifold uplands dappled with field, heath, forest, meadow, rock, snow, shadow, sunlight or moonlight or starlight, save when the planet roofed itself with weather. Today was clear, scraps of blue-tinged whiteness adrift above a summerscape that the afternoon turned golden. Gaea dreamed.

After a long while, standing behind her, Jovain asked low (she felt his words in her hair): "Isn't this an especially fine setting?"

"Yes," she replied as softly.

He clasped her shoulders. "I wanted you to see, Faylis, and for more than the view alone. I hoped to share this experience of the All . . . with you."

On the instant, overwhelmingly, memory rose and filled her.

They were at the Aurillac house in Tournev. She had left the Consvatoire after her betrothal but stayed in the city, rather than go back to Bourgoyn until the wedding, so that she could be near Iern. His duties often took him away, though. Meanwhile Jovain prolonged his business and exerted himself to break a coolness that had come between him and her. He succeeded; she was allured by the world-view he sought eloquently to explain.

A late hour, one stormy night, found them in the common room, seated across from each other before its great stone fireplace. Only embers were left there, piecemeal dying, and only a candelabrum on the mantel raised flames. Everybody else had gone to bed. In spite of the air being warm, slightly smoke-pungent, a noise of rain against windowpanes made the darkness throughout most of the chamber feel somehow thickened.

"How cold we'd be if these walls weren't heated," she ventured.

"Why, no," he said. "We could dress for it. And at that, people usually overdress. They make an ample thermostatic system atrophy, that they had at birth from Gaea."

"Would you rip the wiring out of here if the family let you?"

He shrugged. "That would depend on whether I knew of a better use for the metal. After all, it isn't for lack of power that electricity is scarce. Skyholm could pour energy down to us, if metal for conductors were less costly."

"But I thought—" she said. "I've heard about plans to import aluminum and things from the Northwest Union, where they have the coal to produce it—"

"Oh, yes." Earnestness took him over. He leaned forward. "Faylis, my young friend, do you share the vulgar misconception? That Gaeanity is hostile to any technology, that it would bring down Skyholm if it could? Not true!"

"But," she said weakly, "I've heard, Iern's told me, and, and I've read for myself—"

He sighed. "I grant you, there are fools and fanatics among us. But they aren't many, and on the whole we've been misrepresented, by fools and fanatics among our enemies. They take sentences out of context and try to prove we'd abolish every advance that's been made since the Stone Age. That we'd return civilized countries to the same ignorance and wretchedness that rule everywhere outside them—" his utterance harshened—"famines for lack of pest controls, plagues for lack of medicine and sanitation—as if we believed defense against natural rivals is not a driving force of evolution!" His eyes caught candlelight and glimmered through the gloom like drawn steel. "Do you think *I* would destroy the work of my forefathers?"

"No, not you, not you," she said in haste. "But I'm confused sometimes. Everything will seem clear, and then—oh, for instance, you told me the book I'm reading is important, but I've just finished a chapter called 'The Myth of Progress'—"

"Surely you agree with the author that we can't let the Northwest Union and its kind bring back an industry that flays and sears and poisons the planet. The Maurai are absolutely right in forbidding it." He frowned, pursed his lips, shook his head. "Unfortunately, they're letting the Norrmen keep, or actually rebuild, far too much. And now the Domain is admitting traders from the Union, to enrich those filthy technocrats. It must be stopped."

"Yes, that part's easy," she said, "but he writes as if he believes the Maurai are still more dangerous."

Jovain nodded. "They fancy themselves the wardens of living Earth. And they have done some good. But their entire spirit is wrong. Cold, rationalistic, no matter how warm-hearted they claim to be. They want to conserve the biosphere in order to use it, not be in and of it but use it. Their genetic engineering is an obvious example—imposing their will on Gaea, as if men had the wisdom to steer evolution. Yes, in certain matters they may have been our allies, but I suspect they are the ultimate enemy and the final war will be against them."

"And afterward?" she prompted.

He shook his head anew, though calm was descending upon him, a hint of that peace and joy beyond measure which (Karakan foretold) would come when all humanity was fully One with Gaea. "I can't say. Nobody can. Except that we won't forget what we've learned. Including our mistakes; mistakes are a way of learning, for life as well as our little part of life. We'll preserve what is good. We may build several more Skyholms, for instance. If we do, we'll keep them for benign purposes. The price of civilization will no longer be the pain of not knowing Gaea. No more loneliness, no more ugliness, no more poverty, oppression, war— Instead, our race will be Her eyes, hands, mind, turned outward on the universe."

She had heard that before, or read it in the writings he urged on her. Tonight she inquired about future aerostats. She knew, from Iern and printed sources, that the Maurai were negotiating to get plans and information that would help them float their own. They could do it by themselves, and would if they must, but technical data from the Domain would expedite matters. She also knew that they wanted them for tasks similar to those of the original. What would a Gaean world do with such devices?

'A few of the same things," Jovain told her. "Pure science. Gentle helpfulness; storm warnings, for instance." He disapproved of breaking up hurricanes, which might have a biological role that was not yet understood. Likewise, he would only agree to a very limited amount of message relay, lest people get enthralled by words at the expense of direct perception. "And that we may adore Gaea from above, too."

And at this hour she and Jovain *were* above, together. No, not above, she thought, if that meant detachment. They were still within the Whole, and of it; they had simply reached a level where they could more fully look upon its majesty.

The floor of the arbor was a sponge-soft material on which you could recline or kneel. "Come," he said, "let us seek Oneness."

For an instant she was alarmed and hung back. He sensed it. His smile was sympathetic. "Have no fears," he assured her. "I have nothing planned besides the perfectly chaste practices you know, contemplation, meditation, yoga, exercises you've already tried. I hoped that here, in this special place, they might give you special help."

Suddenly happy, she laid palms together over her bosom and lowered herself beside him.

3

Later, somehow—she was never sure what had happened—they kissed, shyly at first, then ardently.

She drew back at last and sat huddled, dizzy and shuddering. "No," she gasped, "no, please, I mustn't."

He kept his hands quiescent but stayed close. "Why not?" His speech was likewise unsteady, and a vein throbbed in his left temple.

She stared through tears at her feet. "It would, would be, it's wrong."

"Iern doesn't agree. Or do you cling to the double standard? You're too free-souled for that, Faylis."

With an effort, she lifted her face. On his she thought she saw less passion than pleading. *In the Gaean future there is to be marriage, but as a deepening of mystic unity with the All, purified of suspicion, possessiveness, jealousy.* Nevertheless— "I'm sorry, Jovain." She swallowed, and tasted the salt on her lips. "You're my dearest friend, but I can't. My father—it would break him if he knew."

The man slumped for a moment before he straightened and said, "I must respect your wishes, madame. If I have given offense, in humility I crave pardon."

The conventional formula was soothing. "You have not, sir," she replied, equally by rote. "Let it continue between us as it has to my pleasure been."

Their glances met afresh and lingered, until they both laughed just a little. "Thank you," he said. "You ease the loneliness for me, more than you know."

"And you ease mine—" She veered away from that. "I felt you must be lonely, but too proud to admit it. Why do you stay in that drafty old castle, off among half-barbarian shepherds who don't even speak Francey?"

He settled into a more relaxed position, as did she. His gaze went to the land and sea beneath them. The territory of his overlordship lay wrinkled at the edge of vision.

"I mean," she persisted with growing boldness, "they don't need you for more than a few weeks total out of the year. The rest of the time, your first officer can handle matters, and send for you in emergency. You could have a place in Tournev, as we do, and occupy yourself with something you enjoy, like Iern and his flying."

And be nearby when Iern is gone. . . .

He scowled. "My sons are uncertain about their Gaeanity, in the teeth of their mother's opposition. I'm not afraid that exposure to Clan ways would make them lose faith. But modern skeptics—or, worse, the foreigners who're swarming in, Maurai, Northwesterners, Mericans, Beneghalis—No, let them grow up in the clean mountains."

Almost, she heard Iern gibe: "*I notice that among those subversive foreigners you don't list Mong.*" To her and in public he had said: "One of the scariest things about the Gaeans is that if they got in charge, they'd censor everything they don't agree with. Read their books, or consider Espayn and the Zheneral's 'information commissioners.' It'd be like the Isolation Era, but worse. At least then the government was trying to protect the Domain's native traditions." *And by the way, Jovain,* Faylis added, *what you said isn't entirely convincing. It seems an excuse rather than a reason. What are you really doing in your borderland?*

She dismissed that as unworthy. "Your belief means everything to you, doesn't it?" she murmured.

" 'Belief' is a misleading word," he responded. "Gaea is not Deu. Gaea is the life on Earth. There must be other living worlds, and there may well be an ultimate cosmic Oneness, but the universe is too big and strange for us. We'll never know anything beyond what we can see from this planet, and never understand most of that. Perhaps the next organelles that Gaea develops, in thousands or millions of years, perhaps they will."

She stopped his monotone by reaching forward and stroking his arm. "I know. But you haven't answered me. I asked if your . . . philosophy . . . isn't what you live for, you, Talence Jovain Aurillac."

He nodded, while peering outward, downward. "It has come to be."

"You've never told me why."

"Why does anybody do, or accept, anything? We can't be sure. Our conscious minds are mere prototypes. The chief part of us, in the brain, too, is the old mammal, the ancient reptile." He turned to her and formed a lopsided smile. "I preach too much, don't I?"

"No," she said. "Not for me. But I do suspect something happened to you."

He grimaced. "Yes. The Italyan campaign. No large affair, as wars go. Nothing but our 'assistance' to a 'friendly nation' against 'Espaynian aggression and its local cat's-paws.' It succeeded. We kept the Zheneral's client warlord from subjugating our client warlord." His mouth tightened. "I was a military flyer. I didn't see the worst of it by any means. But what I did see—death, maiming, agony, grief, destruction, waste—and for what? How were we threatened, when Skyholm hangs ready to blast any invaders of the Domain into smoke? But, yes, our commerce might be inconvenienced, and another land might turn Gaean and therefore stop heeding us.

"I went home and accepted—requested—the castlekeeper's post for my Clan in the Prynys. It would give me the freedom from distraction I needed, to think, to try making sense out of what I had witnessed.

"And presently Ucheny Mattas came up from Espayn, traveling afoot, explaining and converting as he went. I've mentioned him to you, haven't I? He isn't Mong, he's Douroais, though he did study under Tsiang Sartov. I was interested, and invited him to stay for a time." Once more Jovain smiled. "He's there yet. Dismiss any image of a gaunt, monomaniac ascetic. Mattas revels in life. I wish I could, the way he does. But the upshot was, he proved to me that life is neither empty happenstance nor at the whim of some inhuman supernatural Thing. No, it creates and it is its own meaning, its own purpose and destiny."

His tone softened: "From this I got peace within myself. Do you wonder that I want to share it with my countrymen?"

"Oh, Jovain!" She moved to hug him.

She was half angered, half relieved when, at that instant, another couple appeared in the entrance. The man had the ruddy blondness of Flandre upon Aerogens features, and wore the coarse garments of that state: unmistakably a Maartens of Clan Dykenskyt. The woman, small and dark, was just as clearly a Silber, though her family wasn't self-evident.

"Greeting, sir and lady," the man said. He had the accent, too. Probably he seldom left his ancestral holding. "We would not intrude."

"This is everybody's place." Jovain made amends for brusqueness by rising and bowing. "Let us bid you welcome. You will find that the view today is extraordinary. We were about to depart, and we do in good will."

Faylis followed his lead. After appropriate courtesies, she found herself on the path beside Jovain.

They walked off. When out of earshot, he said, "Well, we were lucky to have privacy as long as we did."

"But we've so much more to talk about," she protested. "Your time ends in a week. When afterward can we meet?" On an impulse, she seized his hand. "Let's go to my apartment." Having come alone, he must share his with a man who had also arrived solitary.

He hesitated. "Iern doesn't like me."

"Iern won't be back for hours. He's taking his advanced squadron to look at a storm out in the Gulf." Quickly: "I'm not being forward. We'll have a little wine, and talk."

And—? she wondered. Her pulse accelerated.

"I accept with joy," he replied.

They wheeled and went back fast, along the lane, up the ramp, through the amaryllis and fungus tunnel. "You always give me joy," he said. "I'm glum by nature. You're lovely, and Gaea laughs with your mouth."

I shouldn't let him say such things. But it warms me. I tingle. Faylis tried to make the conversation light. "Thank you, kind sir. I agree you are of sparing habits. I've heard you called a man who has no redeeming vices. But that must be unjust, I'm sure."

"Oh, I have my recreations. I enjoy keeping fit—mountaineering, skiing, playing a hard game of pelota. I play the flute fairly well too, did you know? And appreciate the arts in general. And am an amateur astronomer. On a clear highland night, the stars call my spirit skyward, and when it returns to Gaea—"

Avidly discoursing, they went by the Winter Lord and the fountain, fared among the hexagons, saw the minikin cataract, penetrated the bamboo cluster, climbed the staircase, entered the tunnel of leaves, crossed the whimsical bridge, and proceeded along the mossy catwalk. Thence an ordinary companionway brought them back to ordinary Skyholm, but that didn't matter. They passed people correctly but automatically, bound for their special destination.

Faylis opened the apartment door. Her left hand remained in Jovain's right.

"Oh!"

Iern surged from his chair. "What the blaze?" he exclaimed.

"But you, you said, you told me—" Faylis stammered.

"The storm was disappointing, not worth the fuel as an example." Iern's eyes narrowed, his tone sharpened, he stood fists on hips. "You didn't expect me this early, eh?"

"Sir," Jovain said, and it was as if metal clashed against metal, "your wife invited me here for an hour or two of *polite* conversation."

"About what?" Iern jerked his head in the direction of the book. "You'd've had it squirreled away when I got home, wouldn't you, darling? And any other evidence."

She stiffened. She felt her cheeks kindle. "Don't speak to me like that!" she cried.

Jovain had released his grasp but not left her side. "Lieutenant Colonel Iern," he said, "I shall not forget my manners and make untoward remarks, but honor seems to demand that I remind you your wife is born a Mayn of Clan Ashcroft."

Faylis stamped her foot. Letting fury loose was incredibly exhilarating. "Not a harem slave in Khorasan! A Clanswoman, free and civilized!"

Iern whitened. His nostrils flared. Sudden fear struck her. He had never badly hurt anybody she knew of, but he was as touchy as a Gascon. (Through her flashed memory of his stepmother confiding a belief that that was because of his divided heritage. Enrolled in the Academy a year late, a stranger to city ways, the accent of Brezh thick on his tongue, he had had to fight, over and over, before he won respect from his compeers.) Once Faylis had seen him explode. They were traveling through Normaney, where neither the Ferlays nor the Mayns had any property, any prerogatives; they came on a pysan flogging a tied-up dog bloody for some offense; Iern sprang off his horse and gave the man a drubbing, and afterward in Clan court was callously cheerful about paying for the teeth he had knocked out.

He mastered himself and said through taut lips: "Major Jovain, I imply no breach of propriety. No technical breach. I do declare that my wife is young and innocent—naive, if you wish—and you have been exposing her to vicious nonsense against which she has no defense. I have no legal means of stopping that, but I shall know what your honor is worth when I see whether or not you stop meddling in our family life. Meanwhile you are unwelcome in my home. You will depart."

Rage flared from the older man. "It's her home too!"

Appalled—*This is worse than a fight*—Faylis stared from one to the next. Dismay went over her like an Arctic tide. She sank to the floor and wept.

Contrite as fast as he had been infuriated, Iern fell to his knees and took her in his arms. Jovain hovered in a corner, trapped. Etiquette demanded he go, but if he did, it would be a surrender from which he might never win back.

Resolution congealed his countenance. He stayed.

After a while Faylis was merely, quietly sobbing. "Please," she brought forth, "I'm so fond of you both. . . ." Iern raised her, assisted her to the couch, got her to stretch out on it and laid a cushion beneath her head. He stroked her hair. "Be calm, sweetheart," he said. "Everything's going to be all right."

He sought the cabinet and set forth cognac and three glasses. At Jovain he threw a sour grin. "A big emotional scene would be uncivilized," he admitted. "We should talk this out in a reasonable way. I offer you drink, Clansman."

"I thank you," said Jovain as properly.

Iern poured. He handed the potions out, but touched rims only with Faylis. She ventured a shaky smile.

Palms cupped around vessels evoked a comforting aroma. Jovain cleared his throat. "Sir," he began, "may I make a suggestion?"

Iern inclined his neck. "If you wish, sir."

"We have too much accumulated tension between us," Jovain stated. "We've each resented what we saw as the other's interference in what should be your lady wife's personal development, but we have scarcely met, and then under public circumstances. We do need to discuss matters honestly and privately, but first, I believe, we need to discharge that tension."

Iern grew wary. "What do you propose?"

Jovain shaped a chuckle. "Oh, nothing barbaric. No Italyan duello, no Angley fistfight, no Erian drinkdown—but a good, rousing sunwing contest."

Surprised, Iern gave him a close look.

"It won't be important which of us wins," Jovain said. "The point is that we will have fought our symbolic fight and be free to go on from there."

"Um-m-m . . . fairness—"

"I know. You are a Stormrider. Well, a sport of mine is gliding. You must be aware of how tricky the Pryny airs are."

"I am. And you've flown against Espaynian fighters—" Excitement gathered. "By Charles! It would be interesting, wouldn't it?"

They worked out details while they finished their brandies and Faylis regained her equilibrium. Thereafter, tactfully, Jovain left.

VII

Normally a sunwing contest was an event watched by thousands, and several took place in succession. That would happen as part of a festival, at which the games, competitions, and performances were many, everything from handball, footraces, and acrobatics to live chess, dressage, and ballet. Flags of Clans and states would fly above a stadium that holiday clothes made gaudy, music and cheers resound, the Chosen Lady strain forward in her youthful eagerness to know who the winners were to be whom she would garland, while up amidst blue the craft swooped and glittered wherein the lords of the air matched skills.

Maybe that was why Faylis had, from the first, a sense of dreadful wrongness about the encounter between Iern and Jovain, a feeling —which she kept futilely telling herself was absurd—that naught but evil could come of it. Here was no crowd, no noise, no ceremony and celebration, no revelry ahead that would roil the streets until dawn. She stood in a pasture, beyond sight of any habitation. Ankle-high grass reached as far in every direction as she could see, from this flat part on toward a wooded ridge in the north. Before a changeable breeze, ripples went silvery over its greenness. Cattle grazed in the distance, and to the south lay a weed-grown rubbleheap that might have been a building before the Judgment. (Passing by, she had noticed pieces of crumbled concrete scattered in a line—an ancient highway, less durable than the stones at Carnac. Nobody since had had reason to clear the stuff away and make a new dirt or gravel road.) In spite of moving, the air was hot; pungencies of soil, dung, bruised plants rolled upward through it. The sky was cloudless, paled by a sun which slowly climbed toward the great wan crescent of Skyholm. Against that brightness, she could not make out the shadowed part of the aerostat. It was as if shade had vanished from Earth.

Tethered nearby were the horses that had borne people from Tournev, and those that had drawn the flatbed wagons on which the sunwings rested. By either vehicle waited a few retainers. While all were groundlings, with shoulder patches of Clan Talence on their various liveries or workaday garb, they seemed to share Faylis' forebodings, or at least to understand that this was no play of friends; their two groups did not mingle, and their words were scant.

Beyond, on spidery wheels and struts, the aircraft poised. No matter the twenty-five-meter wingspans or the bright brave emblems on control surfaces, to Faylis they looked hideously fragile. The bodies were films of clear plastic, stretched over exiguous frames between propeller at the nose and empennage at the end of a boom thin enough to tremble in this light wind. After they had been offloaded, each had been borne away by a single man, the axle on his shoulders; companions had nothing to do but keep wings from hitting the ground and crumpling. These were toys—Iern's owned by himself, Jovain's borrowed from the local Academy on his authority as a flight officer—but toys such as had sometimes killed men.

Her husband came to her. He had exchanged his riding outfit for loincloth, sandals, and parachute; every gram he could save would work for him. Sweat sheened on muscular torso and broad visage, his eyes sparkled sapphire, the draft ruffled brown locks, teeth flashed arrogantly white. When he kissed her, the odors of male flesh were nearly overwhelming. "Wish me luck, macushla," he said. (That was a word he had brought back from Eria. On how many lasses there had he used it? But of course he wasn't married then.)

"Be careful," she pleaded.

"I promise. Not so careful that it would be stupid, but within reason, I promise." He grabbed her close and growled into her ear: "After all, I've got plans for this evening, oh, yes. Tomorrow it's going to be you that's careful, about walking and sitting down." He whooped forth laughter and bounded off.

Farther away, Jovain stood alone . . . how very alone. He had chosen to wear white shirt and trousers under his parachute harness. That kept for him a dignity which Iern had shed. Likewise did the soft salute he gave her, before he turned and strode to his machine.

You be careful, Jovain! her heart cried. She clutched to her the fact that he had insisted on taking the craft lent him to a vacant workshop, that he might spend some hours by himself inspecting and servicing it.

The pilots scrambled into their cockpits, strapped their bodies into skeletal chairs, sent fingers across rudimentary controls. On the upper wing surfaces, solar cells drank energy from heaven. Electric motors wakened. Propellers whirred. Slowly, on parallel tracks into the breeze, the sunwings rolled off. They gathered speed.

If only one of them would hit a rock, Faylis prayed. *That wouldn't harm anything except the plane. It would stop this affair.* But obviously it could not happen. The men had checked every centimeter of their takeoff routes.

The sunwings lifted.

Why am I afraid? she asked the chill within her. *It's just a sport, with strict sporting rules. The winner forces the loser back to earth. Iern claims it's less dangerous than polo.*

His in bravura spirals, Jovain's in a steady climb, the damselflies sought altitude. Light shimmered on propeller circles and off the lower wing surfaces. Already she could not see through the skin to the reed-slender ribs, but she knew, she knew.

Jovain got well above his opponent. Abruptly his craft slanted about and dived. His aim was to shade his opponent's solar cells, but it appeared almost that he meant to ram. Faylis crammed a knuckle between her teeth.

Jovain executed a bank, a turn—she didn't know the language, she could scarcely follow the action, but all at once Iern's wings were in shadow. Jovain had the sun gauge of him. If he could hold it for a minute, denying his rival sufficient power, Iern must either glide down or crash.

Or break free! The lower airboat went into a wild roll. Its wingtips came near brushing the other. If they did, both machines would be wrecked. Jovain fell away from that risk, and from stirred-up currents which tossed his gossamer vehicle about. Iern leveled off and swooped around. He must be taking help from an updraft—a thermal, was that the word? He must have planned this.

Now it was he overhead and eastward. He kept well back, so that he blocked light from only about half Jovain's cells—Faylis guessed. But the Southerner, thus underpowered, disadvantaged by geometry, could not yaw clear of him.

Yet Jovain could ride the wind too, and maybe with greater skill. Between that and his remaining engine capability, he could keep aloft. For how long? Faylis had heard of engagements that went on for hours, until sheer exhaustion brought a contestant to such slowness and clumsiness that it became easy to hold him under complete eclipse and make him descend.

It isn't fair! Iern's thirteen years younger!

As if in a mating dance, the sunwings swung around the sky. She could not hear them, she could hear nothing but the hiss of air through grass, the drumbeat of blood in her ears.

And, yes, a retainer who addressed the man beside him. "Plumb loony, them, heh?"

"It's their way, Hannas," replied the second. They spoke what must be their mother tongue, Alleman in the Elsass version, believing that nobody else understood it. Faylis had studied the entire linguistic family, as a case history of divergence after the Judgment.

"Yah," the fellow went on, "Clansfolk can afford expensive fun, Gott knows. They've hooked onto the best land, everywhere in the Domain, and got the biggest factories and what all else. And on top of that, they tax us."

"Ah, now, Friedri, they don't. You know that. Our lords in the states tax us, then pay Himmelburg its due."

"What difference? Out of our pockets, however you reckon it."

"It's not much, really. No, not much, next to what I hear the pysans get squeezed for in places like Espayn. And we get a lot for it, too. Safety, first and foremost. My uncle once thought he'd make him a bit of money as a mercenary beyond the Rhin. What he's told me about war— No, you be glad, Friedri, glad for that big old moon up there."

" 'Twas you called those two flyers loony, Hannas."

"Yah, that I did. I see a lot of funny doings and high living—wasteful, shameless—amongst the Clansfolk, 'specially the youngsters. Not like it used to be."

"And on the backs of us groundlings. Mind you, I don't want to rebel or anything, but it's damn well past time we got more say in the Domain."

Such grumbling was on the increase. As yet, few people seemed to feel grossly oppressed, but many were restless. Change blew in on the winds from the sea, the winds in the sails of foreign ships.

Faylis dismissed the thought and the guttural mutters. She sent her whole mind back aloft. Jovain tried a stallout in hopes his rival would overshoot, but the sunwings were not built to drop straight down and Iern quickly recovered position. The dance wheeled on.

Which of them do I want to win? And why? What difference will it make? Iern is my man, my brash, heedless, faithless man. Jovain is—is what? Strong but tender, thoughtful, and underneath his armor, oh, how woundable. He loves me. Does Iern, any longer? Jovain is closer in spirit to Iern's father, Donal, than to Iern. Much closer, no matter how antagonistic their world-views are. To them, power spells duty. (Yes, Iern is conscientious enough, after a fashion, but he just carries out his Clan obligations, he never looks for extra burdens he might assume. The nearest Jovain ever came to losing restraint and saying ill of him to me was that day as we left the Garden, when he called Iern "the golden boy" and bitterness corroded his tone.) Jovain has been guiding me into the understanding, the reality, I have always sought, always since I was a girl and first began to doubt Zhesu. Later I, like those two poor workmen, began wondering if the Clans are perfect rulers by absolute right. Jovain has told me we can regain our legitimacy if we, like the ancestors, bestow something new on the people. They gave peace and prosperity. We can give Insight. . . .

The Aurillac aircraft came around and made north toward the high, forested ridge. Relentless, the Ferlay aircraft dogged it. Faylis must needs admire Iern's mastery, the way in which he steadily denied his opponent light.

What if they go out of view? What if something terrible happens, and nobody is there to see?

The contenders dwindled in sight. She struggled for breath. The servitors mumbled.

On the edge of visibility over the treetops, tiny at its remove, Iern's flitter suddenly reeled. Jovain's slipped free of it, banked, circled, and rose like a shark toward it.

Both disappeared from Faylis.

She stood locked for a moment that went on. Shouts roused her. She raised a yell of her own, "Come, come! Bring the medical kit!" and stumbled toward her saddle horse.

Wreckage lay intertwined and scattered on the far slope. The sun stood at noonday and all breezes had died. From here you glimpsed houses, barns, sheds, windmills, in clusters along the northern horizon. Closer were rail-fenced wheatfields. Ghostly overhead passed the daily dirigible from Tournev to Marsei, and vanished.

Parachuting from too low a height, Jovain had broken his right leg. He rested stoic on the grass and let a man trained in first aid tend it. The remainder of those who had accompanied Faylis stood aside in a nearly mute group.

Iern had sustained no worse than bruises. He stalked like a panther to take stance before them and say bleakly: "We collided. That happens once in a while, you know. Collect the pieces and bring them back to my hangar at the airport for salvage. Make Clansman Jovain as comfortable as you can and transport him to the hospital. My lady and I will go home by ourselves." He offered no explanation of the long object, wrapped in a piece of cloth, that he held. Turning to Faylis: "If you please, madame, we have something to discuss."

She followed him for a hundred meters. He stopped, confronted her, and rapped forth: "Jovain tried to kill me. It was his idea from the beginning."

No— She stood more dumb than the servitors.

Taking care to hide it from them, Iern unrolled the cloth for her.

She saw a high-powered rifle. He reswathed it.

"He must have had this ready in his cockpit, to use when he'd drawn me well away from everybody else," Iern related. "A crack, a whine, two holes in my fuselage and me a few centimeters off the line of them—I looked, and there he was, aiming his weapon. He was shooting through the skin of his plane. What could I do? These bugs are too slow for me to escape every shot he could fire. Instead, I crashed us and jumped."

She could not answer, she could not, nor could she tell if she could believe.

Iern rattled a laugh. "We had a short session together on the ground before you arrived. I'll yield him this, he swallowed his pain and listened. I said that for the honor of our Clan I wouldn't denounce him. Officially, we had an accident. But I'll keep the firearm, with whatever fingerprints of his are on it. I'll also keep sherds of plastic with bullet holes in them. Who'd have thought to search for bullet holes in me? And he could've climbed, gone into a dive, and bailed out. He'd hide the rifle, and nobody would notice the punchouts in what was left of either vessel. He'd tell the woeful story of how we got too close and collided.

"What do you think of your Gaean mentor now, Faylis?"

Darkness crossed her in waves. "What more will you do?" came out of her.

"Nothing, if he keeps his nose clean. Which means pulling back into his castle, minding his proper business there, having no more contact—ever—with us, you and me."

Iern swept her to him. Battle had turned the smell of him acrid. His breath bore the muskiness of rut. She had never liked that. At this moment she must fight not to gag. "By Charles!" he exulted. Stubble scraped her cheek. (Jovain's beard felt silky.) "It's been well worth the loss, disposing once for all of that son of a camel, hasn't it, darling? Let the servants take care of things here. Let's us start back right away, on the gallop. Are you going to get laid!"

I suppose I can pretend.

2

Rain fell softly, like tears, through a gathering twilight. Beneath street lamps and lighted windows, pavement glistened wet. In this newer part of Tournev, houses built in the affluence that first blessed the Domain five centuries ago were mostly brick, tile-roofed, rearing three and four stories high; but steep façades, massive doors and shutters harked back to the unrest which had prevailed earlier. Faylis, who had grown used to her sunny modern town dwelling, felt as if their weight were on her breast. The going was lonesome at this hour, none but a few pedestrians like herself, a bicyclist, a carriage whose horse's hooves struck with a measured dullness that reminded her of funeral drums. When she reached her goal and wielded the knocker, unseen fingers took her by the throat.

The door opened. Observing the Talence crest on her cowl, the butler laid palms together and bowed low. "Madame honors this house by her presence," he said ritually but as if he meant it. "In what way shall we serve you?"

She was barely able to reply. "I . . . must see . . . Major Jovain."

"I believe he is resting, madame. Does he await you?"

"No . . . but . . . I must. He will want it."

"Please enter, madame. May I take your cloak? . . . If you will please follow me, we will inquire the master's wishes."

The house was family property, but Aurillacs seldom visited these parts. Nobody was present tonight but Jovain, the entourage he had brought from Eskual-Herria Nord, and the permanent staff. Carpets whispered beneath Faylis' feet as she passed between age-blackened wainscots from which portraits of the dead regarded her, up a staircase, and down another hallway to one of the suites. The butler took a speaking tube in his hand and glanced at her. "Whom shall I announce, madame?"

"Not my name. Tell him—tell him I'm from Skyholm."

The butler looked surprised, but obeyed. Jovain understood. Gladness shook through his voice: "Yes, let her in!"

She crossed to a room full of heavy antique furniture and deep-red drapery. The door closed behind her. Jovain had climbed out of his armchair and leaned on a crutch. He wore a robe whose black velvet made him appear sallow beneath the gaslight, and she saw that the lines had deepened in his eagle face. Then he moved to meet her, and swung along nimbly. *He can't be too much hurt,* she thought, and some of the load dropped off her.

They stopped and stood before each other, gaze upon gaze. "I dared not hope for this," he whispered.

"I would have come before, but couldn't get away," she told him as quietly. "I was terrified that you'd have gone home."

"I was planning to leave tomorrow. But—" He wet his lips. She was profoundly moved, that such a man should be afraid of what she might say. "I could remain awhile if— Why aren't you back in Skyholm?"

"I told Iern I wanted a rest in more comfortable surroundings, after the shock of . . . of everything. He agreed to a week, and went aloft on the shuttle this afternoon." *Why not? Anjelan will keep his bed warm, and somebody else after she's gone.* The idea angered her enough to burn timorousness off. She spoke louder, with no more hesitation. "I couldn't come here before, and he mustn't find out, because he's forbidden me to have anything further to do with you."

Grimness responded. "What has he told you about the incident?"

"Something I can't really believe. That you had a gun and started shooting at him. That he had no choice but to crash you and bail out. He showed me the gun, but—" Anguish smote. She gripped his free hand; her nails dug in. "It can't be! Can it?"

Jovain shook his head. "An absolute lie," he declared flatly. "He did cause a collision, on purpose. It sheared a wing off my plane so I couldn't glide but fluttered down fast and couldn't get free in time to have adequate parachuting space. Surely he meant for me to be killed. His propeller was broken, but he managed to keep altitude before he jumped. Afterward, while we were still alone, he showed me that rifle and threatened to accuse me of having brought it and used it, if I didn't break off relations with you and stop taking an active role in Domain politics."

Sickened, she leaned against him. He positioned his crutch in a manner that let both his arms embrace her. His lips played across her hair. Through the soft cloth, her ear and cheek felt his heartbeat.

"The rifle was his," Jovain said. "I imagine he had it in reserve. In case I wasn't killed, I could be blackmailed."

"No. Fight back. Demand a Clan court."

He chuckled sadly. "My word against his. In fact, I can't prove to you that I am not the liar, the frustrated murderer."

"He talked about fingerprints. Make him show them. And bullet holes in the fabric."

"They'll be there, if they aren't already. As for fingerprints, yes, I did handle the weapon, in my pain and amazement, when he thrust it at me. He snatched it back at once. His must be on it too. Not that any prints won't likeliest be smudged beyond identification." Jovain sighed. His clasp upon her tightened. "No, what purpose could I serve by pulling the whole sordid mess forth? Nothing could be proved. There would only be scandal, and you, Faylis, would suffer the worst, though you are innocent of any wrongdoing. I can't have that. Retirement to my beloved mountains is not a terrible fate."

She broke free, stepped back, clenched her fists, and cried into his face: "But why *would* he? He's selfish and vainglorious and—and—but I never imagined he was a monster!"

"Oh, he probably isn't." Jovain shrugged. "Call it a base impulse that we can hope he will live to regret. He saw me as dangerous—a high-ranking advocate of the Gaeanity he hates, who has connections in the Espayn he distrusts. Mainly, though, I think the driving force in him was jealousy. He fears losing you, and knows you and I have been close friends in spirit, however rarely we meet in person. He saw a chance to get rid of me, and he tumbled." Pause. "Yes, let us give him his due. He could have finished me off as I lay helpless—smashed my skull with the rifle butt, then hidden the rifle. Nobody would have suspected. He contented himself with blackmail. It's possible he never intended my death at all."

She shuddered. "Tell me that again," she begged. "Tell me, over and over. I have to believe it. That Iern simply went a little crazy for a while."

"Because you must live with him?" Jovain murmured. "Must you? For that matter, he has no right to choose your associates."

"But—but he could make such trouble for you—" Faylis gulped. "As for why I don't leave him, I've told you. My family is rural, old-fashioned. If I did go, it would hurt my father twice over, because my father-in-law will likely be the next Captain, and Dad always says there's too much self-doubt in the Domain already; the Captain's household must stay pure."

She paced to a table where she let her fingers explore a cut-crystal bowl, something old, beautiful, enduring. "Besides," she said, "Iern hasn't mistreated me. By his lights, he's reasonably kind and generous. We got married because of an infatuation, yes, and it hasn't worked well, but he does keep trying—not just the material things he gives me, but when he's home he tries to be affectionate and patient—and even when his temper snaps and he storms out of the house, he's soon back with a bouquet or an offer of a first-class restaurant dinner or whatever else he can think of. I admit I may have been doing less than my share in the effort."

She swung around to confront Jovain. "But he's shallow!" broke from her. "And now this. I thought he was at least honest, but after what he's done to you—"

The man crutched across the floor to her. At the hemline of his robe, she saw that his injured leg was not in a cast but splinted and swaddled. The fracture must be slight; it ought to heal without complications and meanwhile not handicap him too badly.

"Darling," he said, "don't go in fear of your life or anything like that. I've explained how this seems to have been an aberration. I can't actually blame him very much. You are so lovely."

You are so noble, she wanted to say.

He reached her. Again they stood close. Decision came. "Listen," she said. "I am going to stay in touch with you regardless. If you want me to."

"What else could I want?"

"I need your, your guidance. . . . Let me write to you as I've done before. When you write back—I'll give you an address where I can pick up your letters, your dear letters."

"I hate to think of you being clandestine," he said slowly. "You are too good for that."

"But I have to. For a while, till we've found how to change things around."

"Which we will!" He took her to him and kissed her. She kissed him. "We will, beloved."

—"We have a week. . . . You aren't completely crippled?"

"Oh, no, Faylis, oh, no."

"I've never before— Be gentle, darling."

He was.

VIII

Having attained a measure of Insight, Vanna Uangovna Kim possessed a serenity about her life which was more than contentment or even happiness. Those all sprang from the certainty that she was One with Gaea.

It was not that she was invulnerable. Pain and sorrow could strike her yet. They sometimes did, when she must witness the trouble of others. Reading history, she rejoiced that Krasnaya had long been at peace, in well-being, and knew that she did so on her own account as well as on her country's, because she was spared having anguish around her.

Just the same, Gaea being what She was, there were rewards in misfortune, if only those inner rewards that come from helping somebody else. Vanna strove never to be smug, but honesty—the fundamental honesty required by her vocation—forced her to confront such a sense of worth and growth. *Well,* she told herself, *a muscle feels good when it is used, does it not?*

This was as she turned from the deathbed of an old man. She left him asleep and knew he would not awaken. Her words, her guidance through the mantras to the meditation, her final blessing had brought him ease; his body now believed what his mind already understood, that the time had come to let go. After his eyes closed, she impulsively brushed her lips across his, and saw him smile. He was still smiling a little when she departed.

His family waited outside. As she closed the bedroom door, they rose and bowed low. "He is at rest," she told them. "I think it will last until the end, which will surely come soon."

They bowed again. "Reverend lady," said his gray-haired eldest son, "we have no words fit for thanks to you. None other could have done what you did."

Vanna raised a hand. "Oh, you are overwrought," she protested.

"I only talked with him. Be sure to have your physician come and see if any further care is needed."

The son tugged his wispy beard, as if he must have something to clutch. Tears shimmered at the edges of his eyefolds. "No, I beg to remind you, it was you he asked for, not a doctor or a priest but you. Else we would never have dared rouse a proróchina in the night."

"I would have been grieved if you had not. Your father served the Library faithfully for many years before his retirement. That the Library, in my small person, could requite him a little, that is an honor for which I thank you and your house, Tsai Ilyich."

Silence fell. Dawnlight slipped through a windowpane to glow on porcelain displayed in a cabinet. A bookcase stood heavy with volumes and shadows. Otherwise the room was humble. These folk were Soldati, but not of high rank or especial wealth; there were slugai who lived better. Straw mats covered a clay floor. A bench and a couple of chairs stood about a table where the dwellers ate. Warmth and odors of cooking wafted from behind a screen in front of a kitchen alcove.

The eldest wife spoke shyly. "Would the Librarian care to breakfast with us?"

Vanna considered. She wasn't hungry. At most, she wanted her usual porridge and tea, followed by a bath and fresh clothes, at home. They would feed her too much here, while making awkward conversation just when she desired solitude.

But it would mean a great deal to them. "You are kind," she said.

—Afterward she did not go straight to her own place. She left the cottage as if she meant to, lest she raise a distressing question in the hearts there, then doubled behind a windbreak row of poplars. This location being on the outskirts of Dulua, the maneuver put her on a road pointed west through meadowland, away from town and lake. She would walk for an hour or two before returning to make herself presentable. No matter that she would be late for work. Nobody would ask why, nor doubt that she had a good reason. *And I am not quite indispensable anyway,* she thought dryly. She would, though, be a bad influence, however subtle, if she had not first come to terms with that which had happened.

The sun caressed her, turned grass and leaves wonderfully green, grazing cattle wonderfully red, struck brilliances from dewdrops, called forth scents of earth and blossoms. Quietness lay under heaven, making her doubly aware of her footfalls and thence of her flesh in motion, alive, apulse, One with the entire living planet.

And dear old Ilya Danivich Li was too—still was, always would be. The Life Force was taking back his worn-out self, but his existence had given its minute urge to the onward streaming; thus he would forever be a part of reality, also after those who loved him had likewise surrendered their separateness. It was enough, overwhelmingly enough.

Vanna Uangovna took a while to realize this, not as words but as something more direct than the breath she drew. When she had won to knowledge, a task in which previous victories over loss aided her, grief departed like the morning's dew and chill. Peace welled up, and an ineffable joy. She went eagerly back to her duties.

The irony seemed acute that it was later in the same day that the foreign soldiers arrived.

Events did not release her until evening. Home alone, she could not at once shake herself free of them. Instead, she forgot about making supper while she sounded her books and memories, in search of an understanding that might bring calm, if not acceptance.

Dusk deepened to night. She lit no lamp but sat motionless among the glooms that were her few furnishings. Light from sky and street trickled through windows she had left open to the breeze. She kept her eyes focused on the ghost-vision of a flower arrangement beneath a calligraphic scroll; it was her chosen mandala.

She had taken the news composedly, and proceeded composedly to organize the search which the bearer of evil tidings demanded. Underneath, a voice screamed that it was futile. But then what might be helpful? Before she could think, she must overcome horror. The end of a long life was natural, yes, right; this other thing that was going on was neither.

Gaea, Gaea All-Mother. . . . We cannot appeal, out of our agony that we bring upon You. . . . Time is both entropy and illusion. That which we name the past is real and unreal equally with that which we name the present or the future. Let me marshal the chronicled centuries as well as the hours of this afternoon. Thereby I may perhaps once again overcome the feeling, which destroys courage, that my troubles and I are in any way unique.

Dulua was a bare forty kilometers north of the nearest cairn marking the border. Thus, in the course of history, the Krasnayan town had often been penetrated by Yuanese troops, when war broke out. Wars had been common between the two nations, almost as common as those which Yuan, Chukri, Bolshareka, and Ulun fought in the West against the Norrmen and the Free Mericans.

Here there were no such aliens. All Mericans had long since been domesticated (if you didn't count hillmen well to the east, and the people beyond them as far as the Sunrise Ocean, wretches whose territories had never been worth conquering). It might seem that the Soldati had no reason to contend with each other. Indeed, it might seem curious how they remained divided among five sovereignties. In the view and the languages of the aborigines, were they not "Mong" together?

Vanna knew matters were not so simple. It was her business to know things, as well as to help folk into the communion of Gaea. The society of the Soldati was founded on war, or at any rate on the warrior in his regiment. It had been from the beginning, of necessity, when the ancestors fought their way out of desolated Asian lands and across this continent. Moreover, the society was not really one. A Chukrian dweller in the cold forests or on the colder tundras of the North was not, could not be very like an Ulunian rider on the prairies and sagebrush deserts of the South. On the plains in between, Bolsharekans and Krasnayans kept a distinct Rosiyan element in their cultures and bloodlines, whereas the Yuanese were closer kin to the Khalkan, Manchu, Korean, and Sinese parts of the original immigrations.

Still, their mutual clashes had usually been less ferocious than their strife with the natives. The Lodges of the Northwest Union, the city-states and tribes of the Mericans southward, the Dons of Meyco beyond the Rio Gran, were utterly foreign. When Soldati took land from them, or they took land that Soldati had possessed, it meant more than occupation; it meant the rapid transformation of the defeated, their way of life demolished, their grandchildren growing up strange to them.

On the other hand, whatever their differences, all Soldati had a common heritage. Their causes of dispute were limited, territory, dynasty, trade, pride. Their masters had no reason to ravage, when the wealth of a region they had invaded might well become theirs. Pillage was generally the work of a beaten army on its retreat—and even then, by ancient law and military discipline, a woman of the Soldati was almost always safe; only female slugai of the enemy's were to be raped. If a province changed hands, the lives of its inhabitants changed little. It seldom mattered much to the average soldier-herdsman that his regiment now—for example—owed service and tax to the Tien Dziang of Yuan rather than to the Supreme Gospodin of Krasnaya, or that its colonel took its affairs to the Imperial Court in Chai Ka-Go rather than to an encampment of the Sovyet. Many of its sedentary Merican slugai, among the farmers if not the town-dwelling workers, might never know that anything whatsoever had been altered.

Thus the streets of Dulua remembered how hostile hoofbeats and trumpets had racketed, hostile lances swayed and glittered, again and again; but only once had they seen a bloodbath, only twice a sack, and they had seen nothing but commerce for the past two hundred years or more. Peace had descended on the plains like a twilight; a generation ago its blueness spread up the mountains of the West, and mothers no longer told unruly children, "If you do not behave, the Norrmen will come get you."

Vanna Uangovna had encountered war nowhere but in history books, reminiscences, and fragmentary news out of distant realms. Rather, she had when young gone into Yuan herself, on a regimental scholarship, to complete her study of physics at the Grandfather University in Chai Ka-Go; in that same country, in the House of Revelation, she had had an experience of Gaea that decided the whole meaning of her life, and later spent years as a disciple of a Yuanese ucheny. Back in her homeland, gaining the name of a proróchina, a seeress, she had no few seekers of enlightenment come to her in their turn across the border. Merchant caravans—wagons in summer, sleighs in winter—from the neighbor were an ordinary sight here, as were freighters and fishing boats from those southeasterly shores of Ozero Visshi that Yuan held. Friction occurred occasionally, but never—by radio, journal, letter, or word of mouth—had she received any hint of serious trouble between the two nations.

Hence it was a double-pronged stab through her when a Yuanese troop rode unheralded into Dulua, armed for battle.

She heard the noise and came forth to see what was happening. This was a summer day of a brightness rare in these parts. Her eyes needed a moment to regain full sight, her mind the same time to understand. At first she was mainly aware of warmth that streamed from overhead, drawing resiny odors out of a nearby lumberyard. The second-floor balcony on which she stood overlooked a paved street kept clean by the slugai; the two regiments that shared ownership of this community made a habit of neatness. Likewise well-scrubbed were the cottages of those workers, from steep red tile roofs to painted frame walls. Here and there reared the townhouse of an officer family, dragon-raftered, or the bulk of a mercantile establishment, or the heaven-blue onion dome of a temple. Beyond were the docks, and then the lake reached past the horizon, its glitter of hot silver broken by idle sails or by cargo barges striding along on their oars. Inland, at Vanna's back, close settlement gave way abruptly to pasture, vegetable fields, and timberlots, with pine woods in the distance, but the Library building hid that.

Fleetingly she grasped familiarity to her, before she focused on the intruders. They numbered about a hundred horsemen, trailed by pack animals and remounts in charge of boys—a full company. Tunics and trousers were gray-green, helmets crested, which was not true of any Krasnayan unit. Bodies tended more to stockiness, faces to flatness, eyes to obliqueness than was the case in her country. The gonfalon borne in the van did not display a white star on black, but a golden sun on crimson. Otherwise the gear was the same as what she was used to, everyone carrying a sword, principal weapons divided equally among lances, bows, and costly rifles, a radio transceiver on the back of a mule. . . . Well ahead, Vanna spied a squad of local troopers, quietly reined in. Alarm began to drain from her.

And yet—why have they come?

Hard by the standard, a man who had seen her emerge brought his horse around for a closer look. He was as roughly clad as the rest, but insignia on his shoulders flashed beneath the sun, actual metal. His voice boomed at her: "Ho-oh, greeting! I want the Librarian."

Somehow that sent the last fright out of Vanna. Indignation came in its place: deplorable, no doubt, but she was not just a Gaean, she was a daughter of the Soldati and charged with duties that had been sacred long before Karakan Afremovek had his first Insight. She stiffened where she stood, kept her own voice low but projected it in the way she had learned as part of her Gaean body-consecration: "This is the Library at Dulua, open like all Libraries to any who come in desire of knowledge, and the honor has befallen me that *I* am its Librarian."

The man sat for several heartbeats, erect and motionless in the saddle. Was he ashamed, or did he resent being reproached—by a formula, and on the lips of a woman—before his soldiers? When he spoke again, his tone was level: "No disrespect meant, reverend lady. I've got urgent business here, and it's important to Krasnaya too. We aren't invaders, we've come by invitation."

A wryness brought the corners of Vanna's mouth slightly upward. *Invitation by demand,* she thought. *The last peace treaty may have recognized our right to independence, but it deprived us of our richest holdings. Ever since, we have been a country of meager grazing and niggardly farmlands. Our sole real wealth is in the forests, but timber and furs will not support a large population. Whenever mighty Yuan whistles, Krasnaya wags her tail. . . . Mostly they've left us alone. They wouldn't arrive like this without strong cause.*

"You shall be received, then," she called. It would have been more impressive to go inside at once than to linger, but she could not resist watching for a while. The officer gave orders to a subordinate, who passed them on to his sergeants. Bugles sounded, gongs clanged. The company formed ranks and trotted on up Minyasota Street, preceded by the Krasnayans. Probably they were off to a field close by town where they could pitch camp. The commander spoke to a couple of men who had stayed behind, and dismounted. Timidly, Mericans began to emerge from the cottages and mingle with the Soldati who already stood and stared.

For a moment the Yuanese leader himself paused to gaze. Well he might. The Library at Dulua was old, famous, and well endowed. Including the garden and shrine, its grounds spread over a hectare. They were dominated by the main building, huge, gracefully colonnaded, its whitewashed brick inlaid with the words of sages, the Eye of Wisdom above its portal as a mosaic of marble, jade, lapis lazuli, onyx, and gold.

But this was mere housing. What counted was within. Of the estimated million books, some were physical relics of civilization before Death Time and the Migrations—whether Old Merican or imported later from abroad. More were reprints, meticulously done from originals in other collections. Most represented the art and scholarship of later generations, especially of the past two or three centuries. And there were maps, periodicals, indices, drawings, photographs, charts, research facilities—even, nowadays, a computer shipped the whole way from N'Zealann. . . .

Vanna left the balcony. In the cool dimness behind, she summoned her assistants and acolytes. The first group she reassured; they were mainly slugai, albeit of professional status, and therefore bone-terrified of anything warlike. "Go about your tasks," she said. "You have nothing to fear." (Inwardly, she wondered the least bit.) The acolytes were Soldat-born, serving in the Library and learning its skills incidentally to their search into the Gaean mysteries under her direction. They numbered a dozen or so, young men with a few young women among them. In Krasnaya, oftener than elsewhere on the plains, girls who showed aptitude were sometimes encouraged to become something other than wives.

"Assume the Excellent Formation and follow me," she ordered. A robed and slowly gliding party at her back would help put the foreign officer in his place.

He waited in the foyer. Sunlight through stained-glass windows splashed the stone floor with color. As she and her followers swept down the grand staircase, he saluted. She decided he was not a bad man. His manners were coarse, but that wasn't his fault. Already her linguist's ear had identified him by his accent as hailing from Yo-Ming Province. Quite likely he had been in the final border skirmishes with the Northwest Union when he was a youth; very likely he had led hunts for bandits in the foothills.

"Greeting, reverend lady," he said. "My name is Orluk Zhanovich Boktan, and I'm noyon of the Bison Polk." The brass hawks on his tunic repeated it; he ranked just below the colonel of the entire regiment. While he had brought no more than a company with him, his presence bespoke the seriousness of his mission.

"I hight Vanna Uangovna Kim, Librarian of Dulua, who bid you welcome and offer assistance," she replied. They both bowed.

Thereafter they considered each other. She saw a middle-aged man, compact and leathery, shaven-headed and fork-bearded. He saw a woman in her late thirties, small, almost childlike in her slenderness, but with a large head bearing a sharply delicate face. Her gown of office was gray, unadorned save for an embroidered Sinese "Knowledge" character in gold; but at her throat hung a disc of jade, a cross carved into it, the emblem of a Gaean adept.

He smiled rather stiffly. "Don't be afraid," he told her. "I'm not going to paw through your books. Your Major Kharsov said that if anybody here can help us, it's you. Could we go off by ourselves and talk?"

"Certainly." Dismissing her attendants, Vanna led the way to her sanctum. He seemed a bit surprised by its austerity, amidst an ornateness of murals, but settled down, in cross-legged Western fashion, on the bench in front of her desk. She took the tall, uncushioned stool behind it, raised her brows inquiringly, and waited.

"This is secret," he warned. "If word got out to the wrong people that we know what we do, and if matters are as buggered up as they maybe are, why, such demons might be loosed that Oktai himself couldn't chase them back to hell."

Momentarily, irrelevantly, she wondered if he was a pagan, or simply used the name of the Stormbringer to give force to his words. In either case, his sincerity was unmistakable; beneath his toughness gnawed a rat of dread. Her skin prickled with cold. "Say on," she murmured.

He scowled and tugged his beard. Doubtless he wished he could light one of the cigars she saw in a breast pocket. After half a minute, he got it out: "Has anyone come by looking for . . . uranium, plutonium . . . nuclear explosives?"

It was like a detonation in her brain. Appalled, she could only stare while he slogged relentlessly on:

"We've got reason to think someone's been collecting them, and for a lot of years. Unexpended missiles from Death Time, their sites forgotten and overgrown—because Maurai agents, you know, tracked down every gram of fissionable they could, around the world, long ago, and I believe their claim is true, that they encased it and sank it in the deepest part of the sea.

"Nevertheless, lately—and I've not been told, but I'd guess it's because the Maurai warned the Imperial Court—lately we in Yuan have had expeditions out, hunting for overlooked missiles, whether big ones in launch holes or mobile units left behind by the Old Merican army when it scattered and died. We've found a number; and the warheads were missing. Stripped—*not* by Maurai hundreds of years back, but by somebody else within the past decade or two. You can tell by signs like scratches on the metal, how oxidized. . . . Well. Somebody seems to have plans, like maybe for putting his saddle on the world. And Yuan occupies just one of the territories where the ancients kept their weapons.

"No offense, reverend lady, but Krasnaya doesn't have the manpower or the organization to go into this as thoroughly as must be. We've got to ransack your wildernesses, find the lost hellmakers or at least, we hope, get an idea of who those graverobbers are. The Tien Dziang wrote personally to your Supreme Gospodin. They agreed Yuanese search parties should come. I'm leading the first."

He stopped, hoarsened, and now Vanna suspected he most wanted a drink from the canteen at his hip, which surely did not hold water.

But am I mad? she wailed to herself. *Japing about a thing as terrible as this!* She willed ease into her muscles, drew several long breaths, silently voiced a mantra while calling up, before her mind's eye, a mandala. After a few seconds she could reply steadily:

"I understand, Noyon, and with my whole being wish I could help. If that cancer on Gaea recurs, the Life Force may be driven to a more radical cure than another Death Time. But I fear I have no information."

"You may. Somewhere, buried in that mass of material you keep, somewhere may be a lead to some of those sites."

"I doubt that. Naturally, I'll start my staff investigating on a priority basis, but after all the centuries that it's been maintained, the ancient collection is well catalogued and indexed. And newer acquisitions will be of no use, will they?"

"They might. Who knows? Mention, maybe, of something curious that a trapper noticed, far off in the woods. And you, reverend lady. You get a good many people here, wanting to find out about this or that. You must supervise them, especially if they borrow old books."

"True." Vanna frowned, harking back, until she sighed and spread her hands. "No. I'm sorry, but I'm sure no one has done research that might have been aimed in that direction. If you think about the matter, Noyon, you may agree it's implausible anyone would. Why leave precisely the sort of clue for you that you've mentioned?"

Instead, she thought, *the searchers will have traveled inconspicuously through the forests and along the lakes, always alert, ready to ask certain innocent-seeming questions of every local person they met. You might try to find such persons, Noyon, but to me it looks hopeless. Among isolated, naive backwoods folk, the searchers can have passed themselves off as practically anything, anybody, they chose.*

Twenty years of purpose, did you estimate, Noyon? We may well already be too late. She could not repress a shudder.

2

Abruptly, while visiting a holding of his Clan in the Vosges, Talence Donal Ferlay gasped, caught at his chest, and fell dead.

It was totally unexpected. Though he had entered his seventy-first year, he continued hale, without need of other artifice than reading glasses, and Ferlay men often survived thus into their nineties. Unspoken but unquestioned had been the assumption that the Clan Seniors would soon elect him Captain, when aged Toma Sark passed away.

Many looked forward to that, not wishing their head of state any ill but feeling the need of a stronger hand on the Domain. These were years of menace as well as of hope. Outland visitors and goods, outland ideas above all, were breaking old certitudes apart. More and more, groundlings chafed at the suzerainty of Skyholm, while the young in the Aerogens wondered if they were not right to do so. Gaeanity found ever more converts, and the implications of its doctrine were revolutionary—which implied a split with those who kept by traditional beliefs, even a chance of eventual civil war and breakup of the Domain. Behind the Prynys, the Zheneral of Espayn licked his wounds after Italya, built his strength, and waited for opportunities. Some of the tribes beyond the Rhin, emerging from backwardness, were forming a confederation that would be powerful, and buying arms from abroad. A new Isolation Era was improbable; the economy had become too dependent on outside trade, and therefore on the whims of events around the planet. And of late, intelligence officers had received a sinister word from their Maurai counterparts. . . .

And suddenly Talence Donal Ferlay was dead.

The Clans honored him in every way they were able. With military escort, shrouded in the Tricolor of his remote ancestors, his body was brought aloft to Skyholm. Each Senior who could possibly come was on hand to receive it; but pride of place went to his immediate household. Rosenn, his wife, and Catan, the mother of his son, stood side by side and offered prayers, the first in Francey, the second in Brezhoneg, and both in Angley. Iern led the pallbearers down the corridors, bearing horizontally the staff of a furled flag; after them marched the guard, plumed helmets bent low, drums slowly athutter. In the Funeral Chamber there was music more soft, a few brief eulogies were given, and Captain Toma read the Farewell. Then the coffin slid past a steel door whereon stood engraved the Twenty-third Psalm; laser energy poured white; a hatch, bearing words to recall the anim, flew open; and the ashes of Talence Donal Ferlay drifted forth upon the winds of upper heaven.

—When the memorial feast was over, the Seniors held a meeting. Despite his being a mere twenty-six years of age, they elected Iern to their ranks. It was not a gesture of respect for his father. The power —to vote on Domain matters, to serve as a mediator and court of appeal—was never bestowed that lightly: for no Clan could have more than one Senior per hundred adults. The thought was that Talence Iern Ferlay was a strong young man, intelligent if not profound, perhaps a little frivolous but basically responsible, a dramatic figure well liked not only by the Aerogens but by pysans from Brezh to Dordoyn and onward. He should be an asset in Council. He might prove the best choice for Captain.

3

The castle at Valdor had always been isolated. Near the southern frontier of the Domain, it had been raised on its crag as a base for militia who were to keep raiders from descending out of the Prynys onto the farms and towns below. Gradually such barbarians were pacified and civilized, until Eskual-Herria Nord was organized as a state. However, the highlands could support little but a shepherd folk, thinly spread, more in touch with their fellows across the border in Iberya than with the Gascons north of them. As the Espaynians recovered likewise, commerce did, but it generally preferred the sea lanes to the mountain passes. Save in time of war, Valdor seldom got visitors, and most castlekeepers of this Talence possession spent the bare annual minimum of weeks there. Few troubled to learn the native tongue—admittedly difficult, unrelated to any other in Uropa. Rather, they employed interpreters whenever they dealt with a person who commanded no Angley or Francey.

Jovain Aurillac was exceptional in both respects. Moreover, he took a genuine interest in the welfare not only of his estate's servants and tenants, but of the nearby villagers and surrounding rancher families. They liked him for that, and looked to him for leadership. Such ties strengthened when he spent an entire year in residence, which it seemed he might continue indefinitely. People were vaguely aware that this was because of some unspecified trouble he had gotten into, but any resentment was on his behalf. And if he no longer went to Ileduciel and Tournev to speak for them, who would? Government of their land was parceled out among local magnates, all of them fiercely parochial; the king was ornamental.

Ileduciel itself seemed nearly as unreal, for it stood beneath these horizons unless you climbed onto a peak. What had it done for the Eskualdunak—muttered many a pysan—but get them into wars against their brethren in Iberya? The spread of Gaean belief among them whetted their suspicion of the Aerogens; so did tales of outlanders bringing outlandish ways into Franceterr. The Clans in their haughtiness would do well to remember that every male Eskualdun above the age of twelve kept weapons and knew how to use them!

Before he went to his meeting with the officer from Espayn, Talence Jovain Aurillac stood for a while in a tower room by an open window. It was a frightening thing that he had finally brought himself to do—or had Faylis?—and he hoped Gaea would first give him of Her infinite inner peace.

The summer of the High Prynys was waning. A breeze that blew in had crossed snow on the crown of a mountain opposite him and sipped of its chill. Grass farther down had gone tawny, and leaves on scattered oaks were turning bronze. The valley beneath remained half green, in paddocks and orchards, but grain rustled pale, ready for harvest, and the river had taken on a sheen like steel. From here he could see a couple of houses, hunched low under their sod roofs;

smoke whipped in tatters from the chimneys. Closer, on the slope below the castle, a flock of sheep grazed, startlingly white in bleak sunlight. The girl in charge was playing a wooden flute; he caught her minor-key notes. Otherwise he sensed only a whisper of wind and the tension that he must will out of his body.

I do what is right, because it is what best serves the Life Force, he declared. *Yes, it serves my desires as well, but they are honorable, they are evolutionary. To rescue the woman I love from her misery, be again with her, get children upon her. To rescue the Domain from its present insanity, guide it into paths of wisdom and the knowledge of Gaea, make Skyholm a beacon of truth for all mankind.*

His fingers twisted together. *Do I absolutely believe that? I have never had a real Insight. My conversion was intellectual, when I strove to make sense out of the horrors I had partaken of. Bibulous, gluttonous, lecherous old Ucheny Mattas, he has direct experience of the Oneness of Life, over and over. In him it is an ecstasy; in others whom I have known it appears to be a total serenity; but always the seer transcends self. Meanwhile, those like Faylis and me stand wistfully inside the prison of ego. Sometimes my telescope almost releases me (the Orion Nebula, where new suns and worlds are coming to birth even as I watch!) but never quite.*

Well, if I can prepare the way for my children—

A footfall dropped into his consciousness and made him turn around. His wife had entered. She halted at the middle of the floor. They exchanged stares.

She seemed phantomlike to him, white-gowned, her hair hidden by a scarf that was also white, the fair skin of her family—Ayson in Clan Lundgard—turned bloodless, eyes enormous in the pinched countenance. "I was looking for you," she said at last, so low that he had trouble following. "Can you spare me a few minutes?"

"Well, I have an appointment very soon," he answered. "Can't the matter wait?"

"No." Irmali sighed. "Most matters between us can wait, because they must, but this concerns that same appointment."

Unease touched him. "What do you mean?"

"I watch people closely," she said. "I've had to. That man who's come to confer with you—about a trade agreement with his company, you've announced—he isn't a plain Espaynian merchant. No, he walks like a career soldier."

"Um-m . . . I've heard he, um, he used to be. What of it?"

She started to draw nearer but stopped, as if afraid to touch her husband. Perhaps she was. Plainly, she had had to nerve herself up to this talk. Her fists clenched at her sides. "Jovain," she said, "the fact that I can't swallow your Gaeanity doesn't mean I'm a fool. I watch, and think, and fit things together. For the past year or more, you've been involved in correspondences you don't speak about; but I've paid heed to where the letters come from. Messengers have gone back and forth, and I've known—by accent, dress, a thousand clues —where they were from. Radio's easier and cheaper, but you've used the radio for nothing but routine communications. You must have something else to discuss that you don't want overheard. Besides, Jovain, I know you. However far apart we've strayed, I know you."

"What do you imagine I'm doing?" he snapped.

"I can't tell for certain, of course," said her dogged diffidence, "but I'm afraid it's a political plot—and you've called in a foreign agent — Oh, Jovain, don't!"

The wind blew in more stiffly, stirring his hair, seeking under his robe, the living wind of Gaea. He drank the strength he needed, and challenged her: "Yes, I do have confidential negotiations underway, but I swear to you they are not to the harm of the Domain. I am not a traitor. If you think I am, your duty is to denounce me to Skyholm."

She shrank back. "I couldn't do that," she breathed. "I love you. But I fear—for you, our children—"

Now he could stride to her, take both her hands in his (how cold they were), smile down into her face (she was wearing the rose perfume that he had especially liked when they were first married), and assure her: "Irmali, dear, this is a large business indeed, and I won't deny that it involves righting a terrible wrong done us. I can't say more than that, not yet. But stand true, Irmali, and you'll have your reward." He bestowed a brief kiss and tasted salt. "I'm sorry, I must go. Stand true."

He left her there, knowing that she would stay until she had gotten her weeping done in private. *Zhesu-Crett!* growled within him. *If only she didn't* cling *so!* The winding way downstairs seemed to weave his mood back together. *No, I'm being unfair. She has her courage, as witness the way she's stood up for her faith against mine, year after year. I wish I could be honest with her.*

A smile passed over him. "*Hypocrisy is the axle grease of society,*" *Mattas remarked once, and accompanied this bit of advice with a thunderous belch. I wonder if an ucheny more solemn, less earthy, yes, less rascally could have won me to the Gaean philosophy. For I am a man of action as well as an idealist. . . . Ha, had I but succeeded in killing Iern Ferlay, when we dueled in our sunwings! My failure has cost Faylis another year with him. It will cost her more, poor beautiful darling. But I have her liberation in train. This day we should move a long way toward our reunion, Faylis, Faylis.*

I wonder if I will ever be able to tell you that he spoke truth about the affair. Probably not. I love you too much to give you an unnecessary shock like that.

And love belongs to the Life Force.

The stairway gave on a corridor lined with tapestries and trophies. Household staff whom Jovain met bent the knee to him; he remembered to give back a nod and a smile. At the intersection of a second passage he encountered Mattas Olvera.

They nearly collided, in fact. The older man was well into his regular afternoon drunkenness. His swag-bellied form wrapped in a robe stained with food and rancid with sweat, he waved a wine bottle while he lurched and hiccoughed and muttered snatches of bawdy song. The fat face glistened, the broken-veined nose was a lamp. Tumbling halfway down his chest, an unkempt grizzled beard hid the jade Earth-sign that proclaimed him a seer—prorók—as well as ucheny—teacher of truth. But then he had always insisted, since the day when he came stumping dustily up the road from Iberya as a mendicant preacher, that Gaea required no formality. She was not a god; She *was,* and her Oneness was for humans to find by whatever means were individually best for them.

"Oh, ho, ho!" he roared, and flung an arm around the castlekeeper's neck. "Well met, my friend, eh, what? You on your way to your little conspiracy and I on my way to my little maidservant. Enjoy yourself!" After all the years he had lived here, his Francey remained atrocious.

Jovain stiffened and drew back. "I beg your pardon, sabio," he said, choosing the honorific with care. "I have a conference, yes. A conference, on certain questions of trade."

It was a reminder about discretion. Mattas had been involved from the start, as Jovain's lead to the network of adepts in Iberya (and across the Ocean to Merique, bypassing and overleaping governments, nations, races, in the service of Gaea). The apostle cheerfully admitted that otherwise he was useless; his calling was not practical politics, but explaining that Life was One and helping those who heeded him to enter into the ineffable communion. Aside from that, he said, life was there to be lived. Jovain envied him.

For a moment, the ucheny's small eyes were aimed rifle-straight, his grin fell away, his voice sank, and Jovain wondered how drunk he really was. "Castlekeeper," he said, "geology and history both show that moments occur when evolution takes a new turn, for better or worse. It may be that this is such an hour. If so, may it be for the Onwardness."

Thereafter he laughed, ripped out a fart, swigged from his bottle, wished the Clansman well, and rolled off toward his newest doxy.

Jovain proceeded.

Yago Dyas Garsaya waited in the agreed-on room. He was a short man, spade-bearded, clad in the linen blouse and striped trousers of a well-to-do burgher from central Espayn; but as Irmali had observed, he bore himself like the soldier that he actually was. He rose when Jovain appeared, and stood as if at attention. After all, he might well be confronting the next Captain of the Domain.

"Good day, sir," he greeted. His Francey was impeccable, with a Gascoynais intonation.

"Greeting. Please be seated. May I offer you—?" Jovain fussed about with cognac and cigarettes, though he himself did not smoke. It was more than the courtesy due from a host to a guest. He was a member of Clan Talence, but Dyas Garsaya was a spokesman for the Zheneral of Espayn.

He was also disconcertingly direct. Within minutes he was asking: "How serious are you about this proposed coup?"

Jovain mustered courage to reply with equal bluntness: "One hundred percent. I've done my best to explain the issues, but let me recast them briefly for you. Then, if you find my position reasonable, we can go on to practicalities."

He let a sip of brandy burn its comforting way down his gullet before he itemized:

"I belong to the Domain of Skyholm. That's where my loyalties lie, please understand. I've fought for it, taken wounds, risked my life—all the while unsure why it was *your* country whose men I traded shots with. Afterward—well, your people are largely Gaean by now, and I began to imagine a whole new cycle of world civilization— But we needn't repeat slogans.

"The fact is"—anger grabbed him; his fist slammed down on the arm of his chair—"Talence Donal Ferlay has died. He was the obvious heir to the Captaincy when Toma dodders off, and would have been bad enough. But the Clans immediately raised his son Iern to Senior status, and talk is that that jackanapes, that technolater, may well be chosen—" He gulped. "Precisely because I'm his personal enemy, I feel I'm in a position to make a move for Gaea. Hatred can be an energy of the Life Force, can't it?"

Dyas Garsaya nodded. "I suppose so," he replied. "I'm no adept, you realize. I'm an officer in the service of my Zheneral. We'd naturally like to see the next government of the Domain friendlier to legitimate Espaynian goals than past ones have been. If, in addition, it should be a Gaean government . . . why, there is indeed the nucleus of the next civilization!"

He drew hard on his cigarette. "Very well," he said, "let's discuss contingencies. Nobody knows what will happen. For instance, a candidate less controversial than Ferlay might be impossible to push aside. But just in case—

"You want weapons. Espayn can't supply them directly. If nothing else, Skyholm intelligence would learn we were producing more than we were using, and set out to trace where they were being sent. However, we have connections to Yuan, in Merique . . . and can be the intermediary and arrange the conduit, do you see? And these mountains are a good place to train men discreetly. . . . Yes, let us by all means talk, sir."

In Jovain's breast, glory mounted.

4

"Vineleaf, O my Vineleaf, now pour the hoarded sunshine out
From bottles where it lay in a dream of summers lost
To the sunsets wrought by frost
All throughout the vineyards where grapes had swollen purple
And well-nigh sweet as kisses that from boy to girl were tossed
When their lightfoot pathways crossed—
Nor count the cost!
Aldebaran is not so red within the Hyades
As is the hearthside claret heartward flowing;
No gold or whiteness quivers across the winter seas
Like that which gleams where chardonnay is glowing.
Drink, before our time shall come for going.

"Once again the vintners have wrought their humble miracle—"

Plik broke off. "Bah!" he snorted, swept a crashing discord out of his lute, and banged the instrument down. "Plenty. Indeed, too bloody much. Fill my glass, will you, dear?"

Seated opposite, Sesi gave him a surprised look through the candlelit dimness. Likewise did the four—a sailor, a couple of laborers, a pysan come to market—benched at the adjoining table. They and the singer were the only customers in the Pey-d'Or. Not expecting heavy trade until later, when most men would have finished their evening meals at home, the landlord was upstairs enjoying his.

"Why'd you stop?" the barmaid asked. "That's a nice song."

"Puerile," the Angleyman sneered. "So conventional it creaks. Nothing of the Goddess there. Suddenly I couldn't go on quacking banalities about drink and love, when I might instead be drinking" —his mood shifted to impudence—"and maybe, later, get in a spot of lovemaking?"

Sesi tossed her head. "Wasn't that song for me? And you stopped right in the middle."

Plik sighed. "Yes, I intended a tribute, but this wasn't worthy of my Vineleaf." He shook his head, clicked his tongue, twisted his mouth upward on the left side. "Or perhaps it was, which would be rather worse. I'll compose you something better, I promise." He paused. "Ah . . . you could provide a bit more inspiration, you know, sweet-pants. Starting with a recharge of burgundy."

"I'll buy, Plik," a workman offered. He spoke Brezhoneg.

"Why, thank you, Roparzh," the poet replied in the same language. "Do that twice and I'll probably feel like committing a different song —a real one, with blood in its veins."

"And in our lingo, hey? I wasn't following the Angley too well. How about that 'Bandit Ballad' of yours?" Roparzh turned to his companions. "You like it too, don't you, Koneg? And you out-of-town fellows will, I know. It's a rouser."

Plik considered. "It's subversive, is what it is." In many stanzas, it celebrated the exploits, combative as well as gustatory and amorous, of the half-legendary outlaw Jakez, who five centuries ago spear-headed pysan resistance to an oppressive Mestromor. "It wouldn't be popular among your sort—I've heard it bellowed from end to end of Kemper, and in the countryside as well—it wouldn't be, if it didn't vent a real grudge or two."

Roparzh scratched in his mane and thought about that. Koneg grunted, "Yah-uh. You know what the cost of food's gone up to? And rent and everything else. Except wages. Can our Ligue get the Trademaster to allow us a raise? No!"

"The city Ligues have given in—" began the farmer.

Koneg nodded vehemently. "They won't so much as go over the Mestromor's head and appeal to the saints on our account."

"Don't your precious saints know about your plight, or care?" scoffed the sailor.

His was not the first voice between these walls to speak thus of the Aerogens, but Sesi stuck out her tongue at him, which made Plik say: "It's not their fault. By their own law, the annexation treaty, they can't interfere in the domestic affairs of this state. If ever they did, you Breizhads would howl as furiously as any people in the Domain."

"Don't blame us food-growers either," said the pysan. "We'd be as squeezed as you are, except that our association still has, oh, one ball left to it. And even so, it can't keep cheap grain from the South out of Ar-Mor. We'll be ruined if we don't get some modern ten-horse combines, and do you know the price on those things?"

"Argh, forget your Ligue," the seaman growled. "Scrap it. Scrap 'em all. They may've been useful once, in old times when people needed to band together for everything, but now they're a meddlesome yoke on you."

"The thought of a yoke running about meddling in business has a certain elfin charm," Plik remarked. Sesi flounced off after his wine.

"What would you put in place of them?" Roparzh asked.

"Nothing," the sailor said. "Abolish them. Abolish the Trademaster's office too—every damned official we've inherited from the past. Let people earn their keep however they personally please, and sink or swim by themselves. If they want to cooperate, fine, but let them do it by free choice, and have a right to opt out anytime."

The pysan regarded him in astonishment. The townsmen, who had had more exposure to strange notions, grew thoughtful. Sesi brought Plik his filled glass. He took a long draft.

"You wouldn't know what or who you could depend on," said Koneg at length.

"That's how they do it in Merique—the Northwest Union, anyhow," replied the sailor. "And it works, it works. Not that I've been there myself or ever expect to, but I've talked with crewmen of theirs who've come this far—"

The door at the head of the stairs opened. A cold breath of air pierced the tavern smokiness. Snow was falling through an early dusk. Colored lanterns shone across the street, as they did everywhere in the city, for Solstice was only three days in the future.

Two persons closed the door behind them and descended into the taproom. Snow dusted their cloaks and caps. Their shadows followed them, huge and restless as the glooms around the hearthfire. Plik peered, and suddenly exclaimed:

"Why, talk of an ace and draw a royal flush! Here comes authority's own self, if you wish to continue debating about the Northwest Union." He raised his lanky frame and sketched a bow. "Welcome, sir and lady," he said in Angley. "Come drink with us. That's obviously your intent, but let us invite you nevertheless."

The pair approached. "Many thanks," the man responded in accented but fluent Francey. "Ah, isn't this language preferable for the rest of the group? It behooves foreigners to be polite."

He reached the table and stopped, a small and rather ugly individual with a blade of a nose, glacial eyes, beard short and gray around bad teeth. His garments were nondescript, like his companion's. It was on her that the men's attention dwelt, and not simply because a woman in trousers was a rare sight here. She was big, blond, young, handsome, and there was a feral quality about her though she stood quietly.

Himself still on his feet, gesturing with his goblet, Plik performed grandiose introductions. "—And this is adorable Sesi, whose true name I have decreed to be Vineleaf, prepared to serve you. What shall it be? My treat, unless these gentlemen care to contribute. We don't get ranking officers of the Northwest Union in our down-at-heels favorite inn very often. In fact, have we ever? No. Therefore, on behalf of the management, welcome."

The man formed a curiously charming smile and waved at the company. "My name is Mikli Karst," he said.

"Ronica Birken," the woman informed them. "Sir, are you the poet we have heard about?" Her Francey was barely serviceable.

"From time to time I perpetrate various doggerel," Plik answered. They settled themselves at his table and Sesi took orders—"including whatever you desire, my loveliness, within the limits of this lean purse."

Mikli Karst brought forth a cigarette case, proffered it around, was refused—instead, Plik asked Sesi to bring him his clay pipe—and lit up with a fuel device that drew much comment. Presently, though, the foreigner could take a sip and ask: "How did you instantly know where we're from? Norries aren't exactly common in Uropa, yet."

"Ah, but a ship from your country arrived two days past," explained Plik. "A most impressive ship," he added for the benefit of Sesi and the pysan. "You ought to go see her while you have the chance. A giant catamaran, four-masted, actually carrying an aircraft." He flicked his glance back at the newcomers, especially Ronica. "Several of her crewmen wandered in yesterday. I was singing and they seemed to enjoy it. I daresay you heard from them, and came when your duties permitted."

Ronica nodded. "Right," she said. "I like a good song. And maybe you'd like to hear a sample of ours."

"Absolutely, whether or not I can decipher the words." Plik drew out a tobacco pouch and began stuffing his pipe. "Your men—two of them could mangle their way through a little Angley—they said you'd come directly to northern Espayn, and laid to in Bylba harbor for three weeks before proceeding here. They didn't know exactly why. Can you tell us?"

Mikli spread his palms. "We're on what amounts to a diplomatic mission," he said. "My associates and I had business in the Espaynian interior. Sightseers in Kemper needn't hurry, because our ship will probably be docked for months, while our team conducts further business with your people. Some of it relates to trade—tariffs, for example—and some to other matters of mutual concern. I regret not being free to say more."

Nobody minded much. Aristocrats of the Domain, both Aerogens and groundling, did not make their own proceedings public. "Well, then," Plik replied, "I hope that whenever your tasks bring you back to Kemper, you'll visit the Pey-d'Or. Meanwhile let's buckle down to the really serious thing in life, namely getting drunk."

It became a memorable evening, though not one that anybody remembered clearly. A few did recall afterward that toward the end, Ronica Birken leaped onto a table, beaker aloft, and shouted something about Orion rising. Mikli Karst was quick to hush her. Nobody knew what it signified. Foreigners had peculiar ways.

IX

As his yacht entered the bay, Terai Lohannaso swarmed up the rigging. For a minute he crouched on the spreader beneath the masthead and let the world flood him.

Wind whooped fresh and salt from the port quarter, through a brilliance that laved his flesh and skipped across whitecaps. The waves were like diamond-dusted sapphire, swirled with emerald where sunlight met crests, but moving, molten, alive. This far aloft, he still heard how they rushed and chuckled. Their vigor throbbed upward, into him. Gulls wheeled and piped overhead. Forward, mountains encircled the shore where his town nestled. They were mostly forested, summer-green in a thousand hues, save where a river cataracted down toward the sea or where an occasional hayfield ripened toward harvest. Above them in the west, cloud banks loomed, their whiteness deeply blue-shadowed and faintly gold-tinged by a declining sun.

Terai bawled in delight, sprang to his feet, and dived. The sloop was heeled far over. He struck the water cleanly and knifed down through cool depths that darkened from amber to amethyst as they caressed his whole body. Rising, he saw a long shape approach. Hiti, the family dolphin, had accompanied the party all day, playing tag with the hull but also, more and more, begging in every leap and fluke-flicker for somebody to come join him.

They broke surface together. The helmsman, Terai's older son Ranu, brought the boat around in a rattle of jib, main, and boom. The girl he had invited along kept an arm around his waist. Likewise engaged were Terai's second son, Ara, and, by her boyfriend, his older daughter, Mari. Slender, lithe, tawny skins aglow, dark hair tossing, scantily dressed or nude, they all made a pleasing sight along the rail. (Parapara had elected to spend this first of the school holidays at a party for children. Unspokenly, she seemed clear about the fact that at ten she was old enough to be perturbed by an erotic atmosphere which she was not yet old enough to share.)

"Ahoy!" Terai shouted. "Drop the hook and let's have a swim!"

The group exchanged glances. "Well, Dad," Ranu called back, a touch embarrassedly, "I think we'd better get on in. We, uh, were planning— Anyway, I think we'd better."

Terai grinned. *What should I have expected? At their age, eight hours is a long time to be out sailing with a chap they can't help thinking of as ancient. Fun while it lasted, but now they want privacy to make love.*

"As you like," he replied, waving to show he was not offended. "I'll stay for a bit, but you go ahead."

"Are you sure that's wise, Father?" Mari asked.

Terai swam closer. "My dear," he said, "I can still wrestle either of your brothers to the ground, three falls out of three; and here's Hiti to carry me along if I should get tired."

I can also still show your mother a hell of a good time; but I want a swim first. I've been too much away.

That was as the member of the Electoral College for his Uriwera tribe. The Queen was old and in failing health; the times were stormy; it was wise to debate in advance what person should next be honored by elevation to the throne, for the powers of the monarch were theoretically quite limited but in practice could be considerable if he or she fully used the moral force—the mana—of the office. Terai had repeatedly declined the request of the elders that he, as a magnate, represent Uriwera in Parliament. Not only would that have entailed his resignation from the Navy, but he had no taste for politicking, even the formalistic politics-by-consensus of a civilization as conservative as the Maurai. However, he felt he owed his tribe some service, over and above what he gave to the country as a whole.

Ranu laughed. "We might try that wrestling again tomorrow," he said. "Very well, Dad, I'll take the boat in. Uh, we may none of us be home for dinner."

"I'd be disappointed in you if you were," Terai said, and the craft left him amidst general merriment.

They're good kids, he thought. *I don't suppose it'll happen, unless maybe between Ranu and Alisabeta—youngsters want to explore before they settle down —but I'd be glad to see any of ours marry today's sweetheart.* He wrinkled his nose. *Not like those I've watched too bloody often in the cities.*

Why? he wondered for perhaps the thousandth time. *Breakaway from old decencies, aping of foreign styles, belly-rumble about "moral corruption, when we keep the world locked up in a cage of outworn institutions," while recruitment for the Navy has dropped alarmingly low. . . . Oh, yes, the Power War was a shock; it showed me too that we aren't angels. But it had to be fought —didn't it?—if we were to pass a clean and safe planet on to those same children who now complain about what we did—and Lesu Haristi, it ended twenty years ago!*

Hiti's beak nudged him out of his thoughts. He felt thankful for that. Brooding wasn't his nature, wherefore it hurt whenever he fell into it.

He and the dolphin romped on into the bay. Numerous boats were out. Those crews that spied him swung close to give a cheery hail. Reaching a reef, he went below, aided by his companion, to admire the formations and brightly colored fish. He could only stay underwater about three minutes at a time, but then, he was merely revisiting scenes familiar to him from many scuba dives.

What a beautiful, mysterious, protean Earth this was—and how heartbreakingly vulnerable!

A little weary after he finished, Terai got on Hiti's back and rode the last kilometer to the wharfs. There he climbed aboard his deserted yacht, found a treat of sliced ham for his steed, toweled himself dry, and donned shirt, trousers, sandals. The sun had gone behind the western clouds and he felt the need of more than bare skin or a sarong. Maybe, he thought, he was starting to show his years a mite, in other ways than gray hair and furrowed countenance.

The town was not large, primarily a marketplace plus a few minor industries. More like inhabitants of a remote island than the average modern N'Zealanner, Uriwera tribespeople generally preferred to live on separate family grounds scattered over a wide territory, holdings which gave them a substantial part of their support directly, as well as cash products. Those who had moved here from the hinterland left hard work and long hours to a handful of entrepreneurs.

Airy houses, their wood fancifully carved and painted, lined brick-paved streets that wound steeply uphill. Children played among pets, musical instruments and voices resounded from verandahs, laughter filled the tavern and dancing feet the plaza. Trees arched above, palm, kauri, matai, elm, where birds flitted and sang; flowers and vines surrounded nearly every dwelling; the evening was warmed by their perfumes and by savory kitchen odors.

Everywhere, kanakas and wahines greeted Terai. Several wished him to stop and gossip, or come inside for a drink, but he declined in polite, circuitous fashion. He wanted home, a rum toddy, his wife in bed, little Parapara to welcome when she returned, dinner before a log fire. Nevertheless the invitations pleased him. Some old-established families had gradually become half strangers to common folk, and surely the Lohannasos were as prominent as any. He, though, had succeeded in managing his property, his partnership in the Red Ox freight line, and his missions as an officer of naval intelligence, without losing the friends of his boyhood.

His house scarcely differed from theirs, either. It did command a magnificent view from a showplace garden, but except for its size was typical; and the cottages where the staff—mostly kinfolk—lived had their exact counterparts on many a farm or ranch. While the buildings included stables and kennels, as well as the workshop where Terai enjoyed making things, none were ostentatious. Beneath his roof he kept a jackdaw collection of objects from around the world, but that was nothing unusual either, in the globe-navigating Maurai Federation.

He bounded through the open front door. Beyond, straw mats, ash paneling, and broad windows kept the entryroom full of light. "Hal-lo-o!" he bellowed.

His wife appeared. He moved to embrace her. In her mid-forties, Elena continued thoroughly embraceable. Herself built on a generous scale, hair streaked with white like a sea phosphorescent in the dark, she was born a Bowenu of the Te Karaka tribe; they had met when the Navy sent him for advanced education to the engineering school where she was a student, had become lovers almost immediately, written back and forth while he was off to the Power War, and married as soon afterward as their parents could sign the customary agreement and arrange the customary festivities.

"M-m-*m*," he purred into her ear. "You smell of woman, you do." Then he sensed how tensely she stood, stepped back, kept his hands on her hips but looked down into a faceful of trouble. "I say, what's wrong?"

"I don't know," she answered. "A radio call today from Aruturu Haakonu in person. He said you were to come at once if convenient —if inconvenient, come all the same."

Terai scowled and gnawed his lip.

"He told me he knows you've been away as an Elector, and is sorry to haul you off to duty in such haste," Elena went on. "Otherwise he explained nothing. But I don't believe he ever jokes unless there's a sticky situation."

"No, he doesn't," Terai agreed. "Hasn't, since his son was killed. . . . So be it. I'll get the morning train from Napiri. Do you want to ride along to the station and take my horse back?"

"Of course. Who else should?" Achieving a smile, she stroked his cheek. "We needn't leave before sunrise to catch the train, and you can sleep on it. How tired are you now?"

"Not half as tired as we both shall be," he laughed. They were a Navy couple of the old-fashioned sort.

2

Most buildings in Wellantoa were substantial, brick, stone, tile, often whitewashed or brightly plastered, a solar collector on every roof. Here too people disliked crowded housing. The hills above the bay gave more area to family gardens and public parks than to homes. This frequently meant going a distance of kilometers from place to place. Few in the city minded, despite their reputation as a hustling and bustling lot. After all, they could take bicycles, horses (properly diapered while in town), carriages, trams in the flatlands, their own feet anywhere; the mild climate usually made transit a pleasure; for the rare emergency, motor vehicles existed, taxicabs, ambulances, fire engines, police cars. The waterfront was busy and noisy, as were the railway station and various factories, but on the whole, this was a gracious community.

Silhouetted on its height against the Tararua Mountains, the Admiralty overlooked much of it, from Parliament and the Palace at either end of the same ridge, down past the loveliness of the University campus and stateliness of the Royal Science Museum, and across the strait toward South Island. On this day, however, wind brawled out of the Tasman Sea, rain slashed, sight lost itself in silver-gray: weather to disquiet a believer in omens.

Terai was not, but he couldn't help thinking how it fitted the lair wherein he sat and the purpose that had called him here.

Just under the ceiling, the emblem of the Intelligence Corps was the most colorful thing in the big room; but its image, a falcon stooping upon a kea, reminded visitors of that evil which the sheep-killing parrot symbolized. The only personal items were photographs of Aruturu Haakonu's dead son Ruori and his surviving household, on the desk; a tabletop model of the ship aboard which he had served as a young man in the Okkaidan War, placed next to an outsize terrestrial globe; and a crossed pair of spears, acquired in Africa during his years as a field agent, on the wall behind him. Everywhere else were bookshelves and filing cabinets, of well-chosen hardwood but strictly devoted to reference material. The customary Triad images were lacking. The chief of the Corps was not a devotee of Tanaroa, Lesu, and Nan—not of anything, he had remarked to Terai in a rare unguarded moment, except human steadfastness in a universe that was also mortal.

"Thank you for such a prompt response, Captain Lohannaso," he said when the other entered. Thereupon he rang for his secretary to bring tea, inquired after Terai's family, and spent a few minutes discussing the prospects of the local soccer team. He well understood the value of good manners toward a subordinate. Underneath them, he remained an aristocrat of the Aorangi tribe, into whom something of the starkness and splendor of their mountain had entered.

Presently he sat straight at the glassy sweep of the desk, and his single eye came to such intent focus that the artificiality of the left one was unmistakable. The eye was gray, his hair and a beard that fell to his breast were white, his features craggy and pallid. In him the Ingliss side of the ancestry was dominant—spirit as well as body, Terai imagined.

Nevertheless, he was not discourteous, he did not go too hastily at matters. His concession to the Maurai temperament took the form of didactic discursiveness.

"I've recalled you partly because you're among our ablest field operatives, Captain, in a period when we're damnably short even of run-of-the-mill personnel," he said. "And you understand the present danger better than Her Majesty's average subject does. We've had it too easy for centuries. *You* don't take our hegemony for granted."

"The admiral is kind," Terai muttered, and reached for his pipe.

Aruturu made a harsh sound that might have been meant for a chuckle. "It's not precisely kind of me to bring you here when you've earned a long leave, and for the mission I have in mind. A mission which should never have been required in the first instance."

"Really, sir?"

The monocular gaze went afar. "Our colleagues before the Downfall would not have been caught by surprise as we've been. Compared to them, we—everyone like us on Earth—we're naive, ignorant, understaffed, underequipped, undersupported. We've never had any enemies who required us to become efficient. But you've heard me on this topic before." Aruturu returned his look, sharpened, to Terai.

"Now we seem at last to be up against somebody who has given the business a great deal of thought and done a great deal of groundwork. Somebody with whom you may be uniquely well qualified to cope."

Terai raised his brows and waited.

"In view of your trip to Laska five years ago," Aruturu explained.

Terai winced. "That was hardly a success of mine, sir. I suspect I was rather cleverly hoodwinked, and lucky to get out alive, but I found no proof of anything."

"*I* suspect you came closer to making a discovery than all the agents we've had in those parts before or since. The sheer size and wildness of that country—a society too loosely organized, in its damned Lodges, for us to infiltrate in any useful degree— Well." Aruturu's tone grew metallic. "What brought your name to my mind was another name in a report lately received from Europai. Mikli Karst."

Terai nearly dropped his smoking gear, recovered, and got busy with it. "I'm surprised the admiral remembers me in that connection."

"I've an excellent memory, Captain Lohannaso, and a better data retrieval system. Your own recollection may have gotten a trifle dim, after the range of later assignments you had." Aruturu formed the smile of a carnivore. "Yes, of course you made yourself too conspicuous among the Norrmen to be very useful there, again. But how would you like to meet your old opponent on ground that is new to you both?"

Wind shrieked, rain dashed against panes, the noise of a typewriter in the outer office suggested skeletons holding carnival on Ghost Night. Terai started his pipe. The smoke scratched his palate in friendly, reassuring wise. "Please say on, sir."

"This will take time," Aruturu warned. "I shall have to ramble through the background of it all.

"Our operatives in the Domain of Skyholm are miserably few, in spite of the increasing Maurai presence in the country. The well-developed domestic communication and air transportation systems do enhance their capabilities somewhat, and they send regular dispatches via GRC." Terai recognized the abbreviation for coded radio, relayed by the sea stations which the Federation maintained worldwide.

"They report that a large Union ship, complete with an aircraft, has reached a port on the western peninsula and settled down for an indefinite stay," the chief continued. "Earlier she was in Espayn. They've sent us as many names and ratings as they could learn, and Mikli Karst's is at the head of the list, seemingly the leader of the expedition. Its purpose is undisclosed, aside from vague talk of 'commercial and diplomatic negotiations.' It arrived about two months ago, following similarly secretive scurryings about in Espayn. Karst is seldom at the harbor, but has been seen in places such as Tournev, the principal city. Several members of his party have not been seen at all since shortly after the landing. Certain rumors recently heard, and passed on to me, are what have perturbed me enough to decide we had better get properly cracking on this. They tell of strangers in the eastern marches of the Domain, who crossed the Rhin River and vanished among the Allemans. They sound as if that party may well be from the ship."

"How so, and how did they reach our men?" Terai inquired.

"They scarcely would have, and in any event they would not have included any worthwhile description—save that the leader of the band is a rather spectacular woman. *That* raised gossip along many a trade route." Aruturu repeated his grin. "The Norrmen make mistakes too. Though perhaps they had no choice; perhaps she was the best they could get for the task, whatever it is."

"What do you think they're up to, sir?"

"It is a capital mistake to theorize before one has data. Yet consider." Aruturu ticked points off on his bony fingers.

"First," he said, "none of this would be possible without the connivance of aristocrats high in the Domain. Its states have extensive autonomy, but Skyholm keeps basic control. Of recent years, that control has been faltering. Regardless, no gang of foreigners could establish a base, travel about as they please, and never offer a real explanation—unless they had some intrigue afoot with powerful men.

"Second, the Domain is riddled with intrigue. Its Captain is nearing the end, like Her Majesty here; but the Captaincy of Skyholm carries authority several orders of magnitude above what our monarchy does. Contending for it are traditionalists, Gaeans, a dozen different cabals of malcontents. If the Northwest Union can help engineer the succession of a government favorable to it vis-à-vis us, we'll not only be eased out of a growing market, our Europaian operations —our intelligence—will be slowly strangled.

"And the Norrmen will fare as they choose. . . . What are that woman and her followers doing beyond the Rhin? Could they be after fissionables? Could that be the basic reason why Norrmen are plotting with members of the Aerogens?"

Terai, who was no coward, shivered. The gale outside was less terrible than that which Aruturu bespoke. "Sir, I've, well, I've heard what you might call whispers about this, but it's hard to, to accept. Didn't the Federation scour the world for that stuff, long ago, and throw it into a subduction zone?"

"Yes, but the search was cursory in wilderness or in devastated areas, and afterward the supposition was that the remainder could be confiscated as it was discovered. That didn't work so well, did it? The Norrmen before the war found fuel for several reactors, without undue difficulty. There must be rather more lying about in forgotten nooks and crannies. And lately— We're keeping it secret for the time being, if only to avoid public panic, but we have gotten definite evidence that somebody is foraging again. You'll be briefed."

The calm statement came to Terai like a kick in the belly. He felt sick, half stunned. "But it doesn't make sense!" he protested.

"Why not?" his superior replied.

"Because—teeth of Nan, because it doesn't!"

Aruturu leaned back in his chair. "Give me your reasons, Captain. I've obviously been through the argument before, but you need to clarify your own thinking."

"Well—" Terai puffed hard, raising a small guardian cloud for himself. Dismay drained from him and horror receded to the bottom of his mind. Monstrosities could be slain; but first they must be understood. His thoughts grew methodical.

"Well, the logic of it," he said. "Suppose somebody—call him X —suppose somebody did get together a few hundred kilos of uranium-235, plutonium, or whatever else. Let X make bombs of it, too. What then? I presume the bombs would be for use on us," *since we dominate Earth.* "How shall they be delivered? A fleet of bombers or rockets is ridiculous. Quite aside from the metal, where's the fuel to come from? Oil wells are treasures in the firm grip of the chemical industry. Synfuels depend in the last analysis on solar energy, and that's too diffuse. X couldn't build an adequate plant, or divert the amount he'd need from the civilian economy, without us noticing.

"Therefore X can only mount a sneak operation, bombs in the holds of merchant ships and so on. Supposing he could coordinate the thing, against our bases and outposts around the world—and I don't see how he could—it wouldn't destroy us. We're too widespread; too much of our strength comes from village and family enterprises; what was left of our Navy would still be stronger than anything he could muster. Besides, surely most of the human race would join us, to stamp on anybody who'd risk a second Downfall.

"No, sir, if X is crazy enough to try that, then X is too crazy to be any real menace."

He stopped, short of breath after such an unwontedly long speech. For a while, the storm keened.

"To tell the truth," Aruturu said, "I agree with your reasoning. A nuclear attack on us would be a grisly absurdity. However, we cannot reason the data away."

"What *could* the motive be?" Terai implored.

Aruturu sighed. "I've spent more sleepless nights than I care to number, trying to answer that. Your X might build a powerplant, as the Norrmen wanted to do before the war. But given our policy of prohibition, that doesn't make sense either. It would have to be tucked off at the back of beyond, where it could play no worthwhile industrial role.

"What else? An attempt at extortion? Or, controverting both sanity and morality, an actual attempt at bringing the Federation down? Whatever the aim, it's necessarily hostile to us, because the ban is ours."

Terai made no comment. None was needed. You could argue against the right of the Maurai to be the custodians of Earth, but you could not dispute the fact that nuclear energy, in whatever form and for whatever purpose, meant the possibility of nuclear weapons.

"Who is X?" Aruturu pursued. "Probably the Northwest Union. Oh, not officially. An entire nation can't hide so hellish a secret, especially when it's so weakly governed. But a close-knit consortium of their Lodges might."

"We shouldn't dismiss others," Terai counseled. "The admiral remembers how Beneghal made an undercover effort of that sort."

"Indeed. And you know what a close watch we've kept on Beneghal ever since. Who else? X has to have the technological capability, which excludes the vast majority of mankind today. Besides, most societies are sympathetic or, at worst, resigned to us. In the case of the Northwest Union, we stand foursquare between them and their dearest dreams."

"The Gaeans don't like us either," Terai reminded.

Aruturu nodded. "True. However, can you imagine them splitting the atom? They'd hang any of their own people who tried. Aye, aye, the Corps is investigating them. It's investigating every candidate, the whole way from Okkaido to the Domain itself. But let us not play games, you and I. We have just a single prime suspect. Or, rather, and much more difficult for us, a number of prime suspects; but the guilty group, with ninety percent certainty, is Northwestern. Our task is to find them, prove their guilt, and break them, before it is too late."

He fell silent for a space. The gale ramped. When he spoke further, it was most quietly:

"Terai Lohannaso, I do not order you on this mission. Think first. Refusal won't be held against you. It's lonely and weird and may lead you nowhere but into death. You have earned better."

The big man braced muscles and will. "If nothing else, Admiral," he said, "I've my kids to think about, and whatever kids they'll be having. I accept."

Aruturu's smile this time held a touch of warmth. "Well, then, I promise you'll find it fascinating, as great a challenge as you can ever meet. Our men presently in the Domain are routine information collectors, not spies; their identities and duties are known to Skyholm. I ask you to go there on a roving commission.

"The Norries may not be after fissionables at all . . . in Europai. In any event, that can scarcely be their primary goal. Ferret out what is happening, Captain, and take whatever measures may be indicated. In effect, you'll have plenipotentiary authority."

"Just what does that mean, sir?" Terai asked cautiously.

"Well, you should send your findings here, for the Cabinet and the Navy. But if you can't, then, whatever you decide to do, Her Majesty's government will back you down the line. It has that much faith in me; I have that much faith in you."

Aruturu waited a little before finishing, with a visible measure of pain: "Besides the regular sort of staff, you'll have an associate who, I believe, is quite extraordinary. And I ought to know. He's my grandson—in part; in a way, a strange way."

3

Had the ancient canal through either Panama or Suez been restored—projects thus far rejected as demanding too many machines and too much fuel—or had *Hivao* traveled, spendthrift, under power, she could have reached the antipodes in less than the two months it actually took. Heavy weather and foul winds did not impede her particularly; but around Cape Horn they combined with icebergs drifting up from Antarctica to make her creep along. Later, as she headed north, most currents were unfavorable until, near the end of her journey, she entered the Gulf Stream.

The planners had foreseen the slowness. Indeed, the ship was a monohull chosen for sturdiness and capacity, not speed. The Corpsmen aboard required the time for study, and at that, they must be intense about it.

They were bound for a country, an entire and alien civilization, which none but the two who instructed them knew at first hand. Language was only the most obvious hurdle to overleap. Angley was not like the dialects of Ingliss flourishing in such places as Stralia and Awaii, nor was Francey like the Faranasai heard in the Taiiti region. It was also essential to grasp the elementary facts of geography, ethnology, history, laws, customs, traditions, faiths, contentions . . . the list continued.

Modern psychopedagogics made the learning possible, but just barely. The voyage was no pleasure cruise for either the intelligence team or the sailors. Women were absent from both groups, their abilities as well as their company sorely missed; be he right or wrong, the admiral had decided that frustration at sea would distract his agents less than would possible emotional involvements.

Terai noticed early on that Wairoa Haakonu attended few lectures and joined nobody in memorization exercises or speech practice. Instead, he shut himself up in his cabin with books, or spent hours on deck saying never a word to anybody. Terai determined to find out why. The fellow was supposed to be his partner, the other ten mainly support personnel for those two, but they had only met twice, brief and formal encounters, before they embarked.

Terai's opportunity came on the evening when *Hivao,* bearing south of east, crossed the sixtieth parallel. He emerged from his classroom below in search of cold air to blow the haze of concentration out of him before dinner. In that bleakness the deck appeared abandoned by all but the two crewmen on lookout. Twilight made their heavily clad, hooded forms goblinlike. Aft, a last streak of crimson smoldered on the horizon. Thence an overcast darkened toward the night rolling in from ahead. The sea glimmered dull gray as its waves marched to meet yonder gloom. A pair of albatross soared on high, only visible trace of life beyond the hull. Running before the wind, *Hivao* bore little sense of its sound or force, but its chill struck deep and spindrift laid salt on Terai's mouth.

He strode off on what he planned as several laps around. It would be a respectable distance. *Hivao* was a five-masted squarerigger, a hundred and fifty meters in length, twenty meters in beam. A low deckhouse, whose glassed-in front was the bridge, and a shelter for the aircraft she carried were the principal interruptions in the sweep of her topside; nearly everything else, even the lifeboat bays, was below for the sake of streamlining. On a vessel this size, that did not limit cargo space too severely.

Those sails that were set made a spectral firmament but doubled the murkiness beneath. On his way to the rail, Terai almost stumbled over a rigging engine crouched at the foot of the mast it served. Lanterns burned far apart. He walked on across a ventilator grille, hearing the faint whirr of the fan, catching the odorous warmth of expelled air. When he got to the side, he thought he could hear an intake under the gunwale.

He went forward. Although no sculpture adorned the prow, reflections off the radar as it turned at the foremast head suggested Lesu's watchfulness against shark-toothed Nan, and Terai offered a soft salute. Religion was no large part of his life, but the Triad seemed to him as sensible a way as any of symbolizing an ultimate mystery; on the whole, its church served the nation fairly well, and the rites ranged from pleasant to awesome.

He started aft along the port rail. Beyond the deckhouse, he made out the aircraft pod near the stern. A frown crossed his brow. He wished they didn't have to bring that beast. Its presence was not quite easy to reconcile with their cover story: that they represented a private company sending assorted wares to the Domain on a venture, in hopes of creating a steady trade; that finding the right markets for the different items would require time and travel.

Well, the fact that the Norrmen had a plane left the Maurai no choice. Probably both were simply a reserve against emergencies—bad emergencies, inasmuch as security officers of the Domain denied foreigners permission to make overflights. If Mikli found reason to violate that edict, Terai would too, and his craft was superior to anything owned by anyone in the Union. The peace treaty after the Power War had set limits which the High Commission and its Inspectorate enforced.

A man stood at the rail near the pod, hands in pockets, staring outward. As he neared, Terai saw it was Wairoa.

Ah-ha!

He drew alongside and halted. "Good evening," he said.

"Good evening to you, Captain," answered a rather high tenor voice. The accent belonged to no island; it was a composite, like the man himself.

"A bit raw to hang around motionless, isn't it?"

"Most of our folk find it so." A slight note of scorn: "Altogether unnecessarily. Individual Polynesians have managed well in every climate, once they let their bodies adjust. The Maurai have gone soft."

Terai made his gambit. "But it is naturally easier for you to adapt, isn't it?"

No response. Wairoa continued gazing out to sea. Dusk thickened, minute by minute. Already Terai had lost sight of all but the closest waves that boomed and hissed around him.

"Nothing to see now," he persisted. "Why not join me in some turns around the deck, and then in my cabin for a tot of rum before mess?"

"I see amply well. And hear, smell, taste, feel with every sense. But I can't explain."

The rudeness stung Terai into aggression. "Look here," he said from the depths of his throat, "we're supposed to work together in Europai. How the deuce can we, when we're scarcely acquainted? Like it or no, we'd better do something about that. I'm trying, and I want cooperation."

Surprised, Wairoa turned to confront him. For a moment they regarded each other. Terai could make out little, and that was clothed, albeit more lightly than he or the sailors were. He had, though, seen Wairoa sunbathing among men off duty on the first day, before work commenced in earnest. At the time he had wondered if the display of that unnatural body was an act of defiance or an attempt at forestalling curiosity.

Taken on its own terms, it was not a body deformed in any way. Wairoa Haakonu stood tall, chiefly because of his cranelike legs; his torso was squat, with a thick chest but ropy arms. His skull was very long, his face very broad, bearing wide nose and narrow lips, high forehead, heavy brow ridges, pointed chin. His right eye was blue, his left black. His hair was straight and striped black and brown, back from forehead to nape. His skin was golden except for numerous ebon blotches, one of which covered the upper half of his visage like a mask. An observer from a different planet might well have deemed him handsome.

"My apologies, Captain," he said low. "I often make mistakes when dealing with people. Especially my own people."

If the Maurai are yours, thought Terai in sudden compassion. *If you can ever have any people, anywhere in the world.* "That's all right, Lieutenant Commander. Just so we do come to an understanding. I'm especially anxious to know why you've been skipping class."

"Don't you?" Again the astonishment seemed genuine. "Most of that involves subjects I've already mastered or that I can learn better by myself. I only need occasional data input from the instructors."

"What? Do you mean you, uh, you learned those languages beforehand?"

"No. But I am learning them fast. The instructors have made the pronunciations clear; grammar and vocabulary are in the texts, idioms in the literary material I took along. Listen." Wairoa rattled off sentences first in Angley, then in Francey. As far as Terai, who had a good ear, could tell, he spoke flawlessly.

"The same for the sociology," Wairoa continued. "Once I've caught the drift of a topic, why hear a lecturer drone on and on? You may have noticed me borrowing notes from classmates, speed-reading them, and asking specific questions. Logic and the unconscious logic called intuition fill in the gaps well enough for me." He shrugged. "After all, no one expects a freak to follow the nuances of social intercourse. I shall do better to acquire more hard facts. I hope you'll be able to help me there, Captain. I'm woefully ignorant about the Northwest Union. My work has been in countries remote from it."

He stopped as if switched off and waited for response.

His use of the word "freak" had been so casual that it would haunt Terai for days. The big man stood long mute, hunting for a way to be kind. Through the back of his awareness streamed:

Superman or monster? Does either mean anything, here? Suddenly I'm confused. I thought I knew something about his origins, but whether I do or not, I realize now that I don't fathom them. I had better start by putting the information in order.

The Royal Genetic Institute had an honorable mandate, not just to carry on pure science but to go after practical ends such as control of mutations and improvement of breeding stock. Its vanguard laboratories were isolated on Rangatira for safety's sake. But that may have brought on too strong a feeling of mana. Certainly the career personnel became a kind of society or tribe in their own right.

There was nothing immoral about experiments on human material. The goal was knowledge, and everything that that spelled for human well-being. Failures were terminated painlessly, or if they weren't too bad, they were decently taken care of on the island. Wairoa came from an early attempt at combining desirable traits that never naturally occur all in an individual. The hope was that this would throw new light on the molecular biology involved and its functioning throughout the life of the organism.

Genetic mosaic: Take two fertilized ova in vitro. Let them divide about three times, then nudge them together. If they fuse successfully, implant them in a uterus to grow. The result is a single fetus, but with four parents. It was an old technique, invented before the Downfall, in limited use by modern agriculture and mariculture. Human cells were only the next stage to try.

The donor-parents were chosen for chromosomes that the researchers thought could be selected from to make an interesting, viable hybrid in which the interplay of heredities would be reasonably clear. They were a Sinese, a black Stralian, a white Merican, and a Maurai. Although he was then in his teens, the Maurai was Ruori Haakonu, Aruturu's son, who grew up to become High Commissioner in the Northwest Union and die there. . . . The woman who carried the child to term was also Maurai, a scientist on the island. Thus Wairoa had two fathers and three mothers.

Or nine mothers, he remarked to me when we talked about it for a couple of minutes in Wellantoa—because they raised the children communally, but his fosterer and six other women took the most care of him. I imagine the first half-dozen years of his life were not unhappy.

Then the laboratory was closed and its staff scattered.

Their work had never been illegal or secret, but more and more, they had found it best to stay discreet. Controversy continued to the present day over whether they were in fact pushing things closer to the limit than was wise and right, or whether a multitude had begun taking an old motto, "The Federation is the steward of living Earth," too seriously. After the Whale War the sentiment against "violating nature" came nigh to hysteria. Journalists discovered what was happening on Rangatira, and the furore that resulted led to the shutdown of the laboratory.

Wairoa's fosterer took him to N'Zealann, where she soon married. He didn't get on with his stepfather. He became a tribeless misfit, a pariah in his age group, lonely, moody, brilliant.

Aruturu learned of it and adopted this grandson of his.

I've been in that house on Mount Aorangi. It's odd in many ways, but it was *a home for the boy. With no social life, he went into his own brain for companionship; he entered the University at fourteen, took honors in logic and linguis-*

tics, transferred to the Academy, and graduated from it into the Naval Intelligence Corps. There he's been ever since, and he's now—thirty, is that it? Of course, nobody with his appearance can be a conventional spy, but I've heard rumors of exploits. . . .

And that's pretty much the extent of my knowledge of Wairoa Haakonu.

"I can tell you more if you wish, Captain. Your background information is essentially correct. Thank you for your sympathy, but the fact is that I don't feel sorry for myself."

"Aii?" After a second, Terai pulled his jaw back up. "Can you read minds?"

"Not directly. I have hyperacute hearing, and can lower the threshold of perception at will. It enables me to catch subvocalization at close range. Meanwhile hyperacute vision supplies body language, and as for odors— In short, I obtain clues from which logic can often reconstruct an interior monologue."

"While the damn thing is going on," Terai marveled.

"Actually, it is seldom translatable into grammatical sentences," Wairoa admitted. "Yours wasn't, though I daresay you had the concurrent impression that it was—except at moments when your conscious mind was fully engaged and you started literally talking to yourself. Given the general context, I knew what that talk referred to." Teeth flashed white in the dusk as he barked a laugh. "The temptation to shock you was irresistible."

"Hu!" The older man shook his head. "I begin to see why the admiral sent you along. You compensate for your conspicuousness in quite a few ways, don't you? What are the rest?"

"We should not discuss them where we might be overheard, Captain. And, of course, you won't tell anyone about the demonstration I have given, will you?"

"Oh, no, oh, no." Terai rubbed his chin. "I'll need a day or so to realize exactly how glad I am to have you. This changes the whole strategy I was laying out. I begin to think those stories I've unofficially heard, about what you did in southern Africa, aren't overblown but underplayed."

"What stories, please?"

"How you, bloody near singlehanded, restructured a society that was coming apart, and left it stable and friendly to us."

Wairoa turned his face back seaward. Terai suspected his night vision was not greatly inferior to a cat's. "That's a long and complicated tale, Captain," he said low. "To oversimplify, they had tried to modernize, failed, and lapsed into worse misery than before. Chaos ensued. The Beneghalis have never forgiven us for sabotaging their clandestine thermonuclear research, and they had traders and political agitators in the area. For them, it was a potential entry to the African interior, and we—we are the Sea People; we can't occupy the inner continents.

"I was instrumental in helping the distressed nation establish a social order compatible both with its own ethos and with a degree of scientific technology: a hierarchy of classes, as it happened, from king to serf."

I've heard it muttered that in the course of that, you played a queer part, Terai thought. *You took a woman for each class to be, and begot a prototype child on her. . . . Was that necessary, given the culture and the objective, or was it your choice? I should imagine you have trouble getting bedmates, except in primitive areas where your appearance lends you mana, or in civilizations that have prostitutes.*

He remembered what he was doing, and swallowed.

Wairoa laughed anew. It sounded like the coyotes Terai had heard in eastern lands of the Northwest Union. "No, I wasn't listening in on you, Captain," he said. "I was hearing a whale broach out there —a magnificent sound— You couldn't?" He drew breath. "Mind you, I wasn't alone in Africa. I took the initiative in certain respects, but my associates did the essential grubbywork. We were moderately well pleased with the results—things looked promising when we left—but to publicize them would have been to destroy them. We Maurai talk endlessly about encouraging different folk to go their different ways and learn from each other. However, if word got around about an encouragement of serfdom—"

"Right-o," Terai said. "I've dodged the idealists too. Especially in the aftermath of the Power War."

"Yes, it's been the great one of this century." Still Wairoa's attention went northward, darknessward. "And it isn't finished yet. That's why we're bound where we are, you and I." The wind took the sigh that he heaved and strewed it over the ocean. "Destiny is a pernicious illusion, isn't it, Captain? We Maurai thought we had the world under control, that we'd built a firm foundation for a humane and ecologically sound world order. But we built on sand, because sand is all that's available to men, and it's begun sliding out from underneath our house."

"Hoy, wait." Terai forced a chuckle. "Pessimism is more dramatic than optimism, but I always say that the one sure way to lose hope is to give up hope. If you're convinced we're doomed, why are you aboard?"

"Oh, we may still have a chance," Wairoa replied. "In any case, it's exhilarating to be a sort of watchman; and come worst to worst, it will be exciting to blow the last trumpet."

The ship plunged on into night.

X

Talence Toma Sark's final illness began in spring of his twenty-ninth year as Captain of Skyholm. He received the best medical care. Not only were his doctors skilled and well read, they used the Maurai seaborne relays to send television pictures to the specialists in Wellantoa whom they consulted. Given such help, his tough old body endured until a month past solstice.

Then he said: "Enough. I can't carry out my duties any longer with any competence; I'm a burden on my Domain, my Clan, my family, and myself; let my anim seek a new home." The doctors respected his wishes, and soon after setting affairs in order as well as he could, he departed his pain.

Word flew from end to end of the realm he had governed. Because it was no surprise, the Seniors had already been in conference, at first piecemeal, later more widely. It seemed best to terminate the interim leadership of the Administrative Board as fast as possible, by choosing the new Captain immediately after the funeral.

Often in the past the electors had not assembled for months, and their deliberations had paraded onward for weeks, but these times looked too sinister; stateliness had better go by the board. This meant that a voting majority must reach a consensus in advance. They did so unofficially and quietly. Nevertheless, they must consult the wishes of prominent Clansfolk and groundlings. The wiser among them also sounded out pysans and ordinary towndwellers. There was no way to keep truly secret the trend of the proceedings, nor any thought that that might be advisable.

Again and again the dirigibles from Tournev came to harbor at Skyholm, and from them trod the Seniors, spouses, and entourages. Some were missing for various reasons, but they were a minuscule minority. More than a thousand men and women gathered in solemnity to pay Talence Toma Sark his last honors. The weight was such that all visitors and Cadets had perforce been dismissed from the aerostat, with the promise that they could come back later and the assurance that this was their part in the work, for them to carry out with pride.

Words and music rolled forth; the sun-fire blazed; the ashes blew out and mingled with the dust of shooting stars. Afterward came a memorial feast in Charles Hall, and performances—orchestral, lyrical, athletic, dramatic, military—representing the different states. Everything was very reverential, but it ran very late.

The following day was free, that Seniors might rest and, if they chose, converse among themselves. The day after that, their Council would assemble.

2

"Come with me, Faylis," Iern said. "We've got to talk, and this apartment feels like a cage. Let's go to the Garden."

Silent and stiff-backed, she accompanied him. The passageways were crowded, but not bustling or noisy. Rather, gravity, slow movement, low voices suggested the quietness that can fall before a thunderstorm explodes. Farther down, comparatively few had sought the country of the leaves. It was as if most people dared not risk yielding to its peace.

Iern took a route he had always liked. It led him and his wife past the Winter Lord statue, through the fungus corridor and amaryllis beds, down a ramp between two trees, and along a path to a rose bower. "Nobody here," he said. "Let's go inside. It has a viewer—Hai, what's the matter, dear?"

Faylis had flinched and doubled her fists. They unclenched but she remained pale. "Nothing," she mumbled.

He studied her. "Are you well? You've been as tense as a fiddlestring these past several days, more all the time till I expect something will snap and recoil. Why?"

She wet her lips. Perfume did not entirely blanket a rankness from the sweat that misted her brow and darkened her sleeves below the arms. "I'm . . . nervous. Aren't you?"

"In a way, of course." He took her by the elbow and guided her into the fragrant dusk that trellis and flowers made. In the prism Earth curved enormous, green and brown and silvery where clouds did not interpose their snowbank forms. Turning toward her, he laid his other hand on her other arm as well. For a time he stood looking into her eyes. They flickered about; he thought of trapped birds.

"Faylis," he asked finally, "do you want to be the Captain's lady?"

"I—What do *you* want?" Her voice had gone scratchy.

His lips pinched together before he answered. "When it first started looking possible I'd be chosen, I took for granted you'd think it was the most wonderful thing that could happen. But this past couple of years, if not longer— Well, you never said much, but you acted less than elated when I was raised to Clan Senior, and now, when I can almost certainly be the next Captain, you've turned downright grim."

She gave him a whiff of defiance: "If I never said much, that was because you never listened much."

"Zhesu! Must we go over that ground again?" He mastered his temper. "Let's not argue rights and wrongs," *your sullenness, your body flaccid in bed, your shutting yourself away hour after hour, your open study of Gaean books and even attendance at Gaean communions—* "Can't you understand? This is the most important decision of my life so far. If I decide no, it'll be the most important ever. I want to consult your wishes because, chaos take it, our marriage does matter to me." *Really? Well, a fair amount, I suppose. I hate to see you aching, if only because you're a living creature; and, to be sure, once we were happy together.* He recognized the calculation that followed for what it was: *Besides, a Captain who got divorced would lose a certain respect among the conservatives of the Aerogens, and I'll need their wholehearted support. My bedmates and I will have to be very discreet. What a nuisance. Is that a reason why I shilly-shally about this?*

"Are you looking for an excuse to say no?" she flung at him.

Taken aback, he stood staring down at the world, hearing a hum of bees, feeling a pulse in his throat. Finally he shaped a grin. "Maybe I am, Faylis. Maybe I am."

"Why might you not want the post?"

Again he was astonished, for he thought he sensed eagerness and, yes, hopefulness in her tone, such as he had almost forgotten could be hers. He returned his gaze to her and saw how she strained forward, wide-eyed, lips parted, the small bosom rapidly rising and falling.

"The responsibility," he confessed. "Oh, I think I could pick sound advisers, and I know I can delegate authority, but at the end, I couldn't let myself be a figurehead."

"Why not? Many Captains have been."

"Mostly in the Isolation Era, and the Enric Restoration put paid to the account of the Great Houses, didn't it?" Iern shook his head. "No, if I don't take the lead, I'll simply have all the drawbacks of the office with none of the satisfactions. And the drawbacks are countless. Starting with being tied to the Domain, except possibly for dull official visits abroad. You know how I've dreamed of traveling over the whole planet. And then, it'd be cheating the Seniors who elected me, the people who trusted me. I understand how they expect me, a young man, to collect sage counsel and heed it. But they also expect a head of state who'll give of himself, make the hard choices and see them through." A second passed by. "My father used to say that no man or woman who actually wants to be Captain is fit to be. By that standard, I qualify."

"Why do you think nobody else does?"

"I didn't say that." *Charles! She is different today. Why?* "Although . . . what other realistic prospects does Clan Talence have to offer? Aidwar Turain is a reactionary who frankly wishes the nasty, upsetting foreigners would go away, and will certainly be no good at making deals with them. Hald Simonay has Gaean leanings. Emma Zhiraudou doesn't, but she believes we can safely reduce the military forces and devote the money saved to social betterment. The list goes on."

He saw her nostrils flare and wished he had been less blunt about the pro-Gaean candidate. "What would you do as Captain?" she demanded.

"What seems indicated," he answered. "Who can read the future? But I do feel—in a marrowbone way that most Domain folk can't yet—I feel the future will be different from the past, whether we like it or not, and we'd better get busy trying to hammer it into a shape that we'll have a chance of liking. For instance, this argument over whether we should give the Maurai the benefit of our data and experience on their own project to construct Okress aerostats. Why not? They'll do it regardless. If we don't help, it'll merely slow them down; and I suspect they'll develop an improved model. Why not cooperate, earn their goodwill, make this an opening for really close relationships? Yes, the reactionaries are afraid that'll bring on huge changes at home. The Gaeans are afraid it'll be a victory for us technophiles and leave them forever in the shadow. Doubtless both are correct. Good, say I!"

"You'll permanently alienate many of our own people," she sought to warn, "not to mention Espayn and the Northwest Union."

Now why's she suddenly concerned about the Northwest Union? I thought she was hardly aware it exists. . . . One of her correspondents may have wakened her interest. Iern could not help knowing that she wrote and received many letters, but after some rebuffs—in the form of "A classmate of mine; the topics we discuss would bore you"—he had given up inquiring about them. Honor forbade that he snoop, and he didn't particularly care in any event.

"It wouldn't be an either-or proposition, nor would revolutions come overnight," he told her. "Tradeoffs, a balancing act—it would be a challenge." He sought to gentle the conversation. "And there are so many other things I'd like to see done, that won't stand big in the history books but that I could hug to me on my deathbed. Laws against cruelty to animals, for instance." He nodded. "Yes, that's the real bait, the idea that I, myself, might change the world a little bit for the better."

She appeared stricken. "Then you will agree to election."

"I more than halfway have already, you know," he reminded her. "But I did want to ask you. Leave public benefit aside. What is your own wish?"

He saw her summon up resolve, a convulsion that forced tears from the big gray eyes. "Don't!" she cried. "Refuse it—openly, for everybody to hear—*now!*"

He could only gape at her. She reached toward him like a blind woman. "Oh, please, please, Iern. I don't want you hurt, in danger—"

Alarm shrilled through him. "What the devil do you mean?" *Simple hysterics? But she's educated. She must know that no Captain has died violently for something like five hundred years.*

She brought knuckles to mouth and shrank from him. Her left hand made fending motions. "Nothing," she gasped, "nothing, really, except—oh, please—"

He tried to thrust anger down. He was too often angry with her. A flash on the edge of vision seemed a lucky chance, a possible diversion while they calmed down a trifle.

He bent over the prism. "Hul-lo-ah," he murmured. "Look, darling. An airship bound this way from below." He peered. "And a jet for escort, seems like." The shapes were still tiny in chasm-dark heaven, the sunlight fierce off metal, but he knew well every type of flying machine in Uropa and had seen pictures of most sorts elsewhere. "Not a regular shuttle; that's a Clan transport. And . . . the plane's a Stormrider model. Who's spending that much fuel?"

"Already?" Faylis wailed. "I thought—" She whirled about and fled. Her skirt flapped back to brush him, the yellow hair stirred likewise at her haste, and she was gone. For a minute he heard her running from him.

He started to follow, but halted after one stride. *No. She's overwrought, for whatever reason. Give her time to recover.* He forced his attention back outward.

As the dirigible neared, the emblem on its flank became identifiable, the gold rosettes on black of Clan Bergdorff. *So . . . Senior Pir Verine, who called in sick, feels enough better that he's coming for tomorrow's Council. A vote against me; he's favorable to Gaeanity, if not an outright convert. . . . But why has he brought that hulking vessel all the way from the South, instead of taking the liner to Tournev and a shuttle up to here like practically everybody else?*

Spiraling about to maintain lift in the tenuous air, the jet passed close. Iern squinted after it. He had glimpsed protrusions sleek along the wings, but the sight went by too fast for him to be certain what they were. Cowls over machine guns? Talk had gone around for years of arming a few meteorological superplanes. They'd be invincible against anything this side of the Maurai Federation. The obstacle was their fuel consumption. Besides the starving of equipment that was needed worse, such as scout cars and field ambulances, on a distant battlefront it would pose a nearly insoluble problem of supply.

But the officers in charge of one could quietly have gone ahead and had it modified, as an experiment. They'd have the authority, I imagine. My corps is always tinkering with its gear, including vehicles. . . . But why bring it here, unannounced? Is Bergdorff Pir Verine planning a splashy demonstration of achievement that he hopes will swing votes to Hald Simonay?

Iern rubbed his chin. Bristles scratted slightly against his finger. *Hm. Why don't I go meet the party and find out? I've nothing better to do just now.* It wrenched in him. *Nothing better.* He left.

3

Skyholm loomed immense amidst endlessness. Talence Jovain Aurillac's heart shivered in its bone cage. He wanted to strain against the window before which he stood, like a child long confined by illness who sees Father riding homeward with an armful of birthday presents. Birthday in truth. This day he was reborn, to the kingdom and the power and the glory—kingdom over the land that had nurtured him, power to guide it on the way of life, glory that was Faylis.

But no. He must not compromise his dignity. Threescore men waited at his back, hushed and tense before the shattering thing they were about to try. If he could plan and work in secret for more than two years, at risk of everything he had and loved, he could wait these few remaining minutes in the calm that his followers needed from him.

He turned to face them. Seated, in the green uniforms he had designed—green for Gaea, though he would not provoke added resistance by proclaiming that—they filled the shadowy length of the gondola. About half, including all officers, were Clansmen, mostly young idealists but with a healthy fraction of hardheaded, ambitious opportunists. The rest were Eskualdunak from the Valdor region, tough, aggrieved, not precisely sworn enemies of the Aerogens but not friends either. He could have had Espaynian soldiers as well; however, their presence would have made him a traitor, rather than a reformer, in too many eyes throughout the Domain. For the same reason, he kept clandestine the help he got from Northwestern adventurers.

"The hour of decision," he said with rehearsed softness, through the rumble of engines, and added in Eskuara, "The moment of truth," before returning to the Francey that everyone here understood. "You know our purpose—to avert the next Uropan war, that reckless militarism could easily cause; to bring under control the alien influences that are poisoning our civilization; to right long-standing wrongs and establish a new justice; on that foundation, to build a gateway to the future, when everywhere upon Earth life shall be truly One.

"Let me give you a final word before we launch our enterprise. We have practiced over and over what each squad is to do, which key point it is to seize and hold, how we will maintain communication among ourselves, what actions are appropriate to meet which contingencies. Your leaders are familiar with Ileduciel; never fear that you are getting lost in a maze. There are no firearms, or virtually none, anywhere in the aerostat—scarcely a single weapon more dangerous than a kitchen knife. Your entry will be a total surprise."

At this moment, I trust, passed across Jovain's mind, *the pilot is on the radio, "explaining" why Bergdorff Pir Verine sees fit to arrive in such style—to demonstrate that airships serving as tankers, protected by certain new devices, make a limited number of high-powered warplanes feasible—a development that is bound to affect policy, and therefore should be taken into account when electing the new Captain. . . .* In point of fact, Bergdorff Pir Verine lay low in an Alpine hunting lodge. He had proved willing to conspire, but had been frank to Jovain about his intention—if the coup failed—of declaring shock and grief that his trusted colleague could so misuse vehicles lent him for what had been alleged to be patriotic research and development.

"On that very account, men, it is crucial that you restrain yourselves. We dare not inflict serious damage on Ileduciel, and our goal must be to inflict none whatsoever. Almost as urgently, we dare harm no person except in case of direst necessity. We shall need the skills of some from the beginning; we shall need the acquiescence of the rest shortly after, and eventually the support of most. Remember, besides vital technical personnel, these are the *Clan Seniors,* their spouses, their immediate assistants. They are more than human beings who have a right not to be wantonly hurt or insulted. They are leaders, symbols, embodiments. Ileduciel is mighty, but not almighty. At best, our troops on the ground will have taken only a few areas. They cannot hold those, let alone spread control over the countryside, if our behavior here has outraged the entire Domain."

Small and thinly spread would the garrisons be indeed. You couldn't introduce many newcomers into a town, the neighborhood of an airfield or important factory, a defensible hill, without attracting undue notice, even over a period of months and under many different ingenious pretexts. Still more difficult were the smuggling and concealment of their weapons. The operation would probably have been impossible in most parts of the world; but guarded by Skyholm, the Domain had rested in peace for so long that it took its own security for effortlessly granted, like air and sunshine.

They are ready, though. Or else I shall soon be dead. That knowledge was not daunting to Jovain; in him, it tingled and trumpeted.

When the signal flashed from on high, that Skyholm was his, the men on the ground would don their uniforms, take up their arms, and occupy their ordained places. If all went well, there would be little fighting, or none. People would be too stunned, too disorganized; and they would be under bombardment of messages from the aerostat, that the soldiers were on hand by right, strictly as protectors during a period of emergency. Castlekeepers, commanders of military bases, skippers in the navy, might not believe it, and did possess forces. But they would hesitate to risk destroying town halls, Consvatoires, depots, transportation and communication centers, whatever facilities the Jovainists held—not to mention hazarding the annihilation that Skyholm itself could thunder down on them.

And while everybody mills about and temporizes, the Council of Seniors meets aloft to choose the new Captain.

For this, the Seniors must be alive.

"Never be frightened. Always remember that the strength is yours. Fire no shot except in extreme danger, and then only on orders from your ranking officer. Use lesser degrees of force if you must, but only if you must and only to the degree absolutely necessary for you to carry out your assignment. We are not invaders, we are liberators."

Jovain raised a hand, palm toward them. "You know this, brave friends. I spoke to remind myself as much as to remind you. Now let us go forward to victory!"

A muffled cheer lifted. Teeth, eyeballs, and drawn steel gleamed. He sat down and secured his safety harness. The dirigible had begun to pitch and yaw a little in the currents around the great globe. It moved carefully in toward the dock.

Contact shivered through its mass. Grapnels went out to engage mooring rings. Engines whirred to silence. Men in altitude suits, breathing from tanks on their backs, moved across the flange to secure the vessel properly, with spring cables. Thereafter they unfolded the entry tube, as they dragged it from its bay to the gondola door it was to osculate. When the seal was firm, pumps brought air pressure within the tube to sea-level value. Their noise died away. The chief of the docking crew examined a gauge, closed a valve, and signaled that doors might be opened.

Ashcroft Lorens Mayn took the lead. Jovain had wanted to, but his chief associates persuaded him that would be lunacy. The whole undertaking turned on him, when no other Talence whatsoever had joined it. Amply bad was having him participate in the assault at all; but that concession must needs be made to archaic emotions. Faylis' handsome blond brother, recruited by her, had the presence, prestige, and military experience to be the spearhead.

A dozen picked men filed after him. They bore no guns on their shoulders, and would not take out their pistols and knives until they had deployed in the reception room and reached every egress. Surprise was essential to the capture of that bridgehead.

Sudden shouts and clattering footfalls told how swiftly they worked. In a minute or two, the whistle shrilled that hung from Lorens' neck: *Success—thus far!*

Jovain heard a yell burst from his own throat. He could enter his kingdom. He sprang forward and sped through the tube. Its colorless lining, lit from the doorways at either end, enclosed him in white dusk and seemed to stretch on and on forever. Boots thudded and breath sounded rough at his back, but he scarcely heard amidst his heartbeat. Sweat prickled across his skin, twice chill against the fire beneath.

He reached the chamber beyond, ran on to its center where Lorens stood, and stopped to stare around. Excitement sank to an inner thrumming. Never had his mind and senses been more keen.

The space was large and echoful in the light of fluorescent tubes. Ancient heroes looked out of time-faded murals, down upon benches, counters, baggage-inspection area, and people. More than the usual functionaries stood aghast, in huddled little groups, around the floor, under the gaze of armed and uniformed men who sealed off the corridors radiating hence. Fifty or sixty others had noticed the airship arriving and come to see what it brought. Jovain recognized a couple of gray heads, Seniors.

"Reassure them, Colonel," he directed. The rest of his troop were debarking, on the double and a bayoneted rifle in the grasp of every fourth man. As many among them bore cocked crossbows, the rest long knives, and at each belt hung a truncheon.

"Aye, sir. The megaphone, Sergeant." Lorens took the instrument, put it to his lips, and boomed: "Attention, attention! Please be calm, sirs and ladies. You have nothing to fear. We are not pirates, nor are we foreigners; we are of the Domain just like you. We have come in response to an emergency, for the protection of Skyholm and of all persons within. Stay calm, do not interfere with us as we carry out our essential tasks, and all will be well, everybody will be safe."

A gaudily clad young man stepped from a knot of bystanders. They had screened him from view, for although muscular, he was shorter than many males of the Aerogens. Pysan blood showed, too, in broad countenance and tousled brown hair. "Lorens!" he cried. "I couldn't understand— Have *you* brought that snake Jovain here?"

Faylis' brother let the megaphone sink. Dismay blurred the resolution on his own features. "Iern, be careful," he called back.

Fear and triumph flared together in Jovain. He had not expected to meet his enemy this fast. Nor this publicly. The potential for riot, for resistance blazing up everywhere in the labyrinth that was the aerostat— He turned to the officer on his left and pointed. "Lieutenant, take your squad and arrest that man," he rapped.

"Sir!" The group trotted across the room.

"Is that wise, sir?" Lorens asked unevenly.

"It is my command," Jovain answered.

"Yes, sir. But he's impulsive. Allow me." Lorens raised the megaphone anew. "Iern, don't make trouble. Go along quietly. You'll be all right, I promise. I'll explain this business as soon as I possibly can."

Iern had been sidling back from the men who advanced upon him. "Jovain's business?" he howled.

In a blur of motion, he spun about and bounded toward the nearest exit. "Stop him!" Jovain screamed and himself dashed in pursuit. The guards in the doorway tightened their line, pistoleer between two Eskual steel-wielders. Shrieks resounded through the chamber, folk scrambled to get clear, some flung themselves prone.

Full tilt, Iern left the deck and soared. A foot scythed before him, into the pistoleer's belly right under the breastbone. That soldier went down like a sack of meal. His mates sought to close in. Iern swept the blade of a hand at one, against the throat. The knifeman lurched back, fell, and lay choking and writhing. Iern dodged the third and pelted on through the corridor.

"After him!" Jovain drew his sidearm. "Shoot him!" He fired. The crack was astoundingly loud. The bullet whistled through emptiness and clanged off a corner which Iern had just rounded.

Lorens overtook his chieftain and grappled. "Sir, sir," he pleaded, "this isn't doctrine, it could wreck our whole operation, let him go, he can't escape, we'll get him later—"

Jovain yielded. For a moment he shuddered, breathed deep, fought back a dizziness that had taken hold of him. "You're right," he said. His voice came hoarse out of a tightened gullet. "Carry on."

By evening, Skyholm was his.

Occupation of its heart and its nerve centers had taken scarcely more than an hour, with nothing except minor scuffles before unarmed crewfolk gave up. A pilot tried to flee in a small jet, but heeded a warning that the warcraft would shoot him down if he did not return. No flyer ventured upward from the ground, and presently the fighter stood parked on a dock, ready for instant battle but probably not to be needed.

Afterward, though, time stumbled very slowly along. Jovain's men must organize, set watches, come to agreements with those technicians who were indispensable, arrange quarters and mess. Patrols must make certain that order prevailed. Spokesmen must reassure whomever they could that nobody was in peril of life or property, that a full and satisfactory explanation of events would be forthcoming, that meanwhile everyone should cooperate. It took long before the Seniors were assembled where Jovain could address them, fend off a gale of questions and protests, promise them that their conclave would take place tomorrow as planned and that he would open it with revelations that ought to prove the rightness of his actions. Before and after that meeting, he was closeted not only with his officers but with those of Skyholm—including a number of the Seniors—who had known he was coming and had done what they were able to prepare the way for him. . . .

Vaguely aware that he was ravenous, he swallowed a sandwich and coffee that an orderly fetched and went back to studying the information that his investigators brought, to arguing, persuading, threatening, issuing directives, deciding, deciding, deciding. . . .

The sun sank, the moon rose, a measure of calm seeped in from the night. Lights began to go out, men and women to sleep, however uneasily. Jovain shoved his work aside, told the sentries where he would be should a crisis arise, and left the office he had appropriated. At last he could seek his love.

The corridors were dim. They resounded hollowly to his footsteps. A few times he encountered a man of his, who saluted but did not speak—a feeling more lonely than he had expected. After a while this tenanted section came to an end. Passageways to the next were simple catwalks among tensegrity members, whose spiderwebs lost themselves in distance and dimness. The outer skin glimmered milky with moonlight, the inner was full of murk; Jovain walked as if between a blank sky and a barren earth. The aerostat was keeping station against a strong night wind, and the sound of the jets surrounded him here, low but like the noise of a waterfall pouring into an abyss without bottom.

Somewhere skulked Iern. Over and over, Jovain's hand sought comfort from a knurled pistol grip. *Two serious casualties in all; and he put both those men in sickbay. The one with the damaged larynx may not live. I didn't know our Golden Boy was that savage. What shall we do when we've tracked him down?*

Jovain realized drearily that he had never quite faced this problem. He had thought in terms of an accomplished fact, against which his rival would be no more than a moth fluttering at a pane. If Iern bade fair to make a real nuisance of himself—why, then, detention for him as a threat to the commonweal, and afterward, presumably, release under surveillance. *I don't know if that will serve.*

His behavior today justifies arresting him, and the order is out. If he should happen to be killed, resisting arrest with the homicidal violence he has already demonstrated—it might forestall a good many difficulties. Or he could die later, in an attempt at escape.

Jovain drew a quick breath. *What am I thinking of? I am no murderer!*

That day in our skywings— And Faylis need never know. I'm sure she would never inquire too closely.

Stop that. Think about her. You are going to her. Jovain hastened his gait.

The next filled section was residential: hers. Two years' exile or no, the route to the Ferlay apartment was burned into him. He smote the door. It opened. She was there. A blue robe clung to her slenderness. He took a step forward. She nearly fell against his breast. They stood hugged together and kissing for minutes before they remembered to shut the door.

"Oh, darling, darling," she gasped through tears, "I've been so afraid for you, alone hour after hour—"

"I'd have been more afraid for you, if you hadn't stayed in safety." He stroked her hair. How soft it was. "Thank you for keeping that promise. Thank you for everything you've done."

"It was, was wretchedly little."

"No, it was much."

He wasn't sure how truly he spoke. He had almost had to browbeat her into taking an active role. At first her letters (schoolgirl hand, convoluted phrases with bursts of passion) insisted that she need only leave Iern and he leave Irmali, and he had been tempted, but Ucheny Mattas brought him to acceptance of his destiny and he wrote sternly to her. Yet he had neither trusted her gifts for conspiracy nor wished her to attempt anything dangerous. Her part had been to supply information, mainly to sound out individuals she met and identify those to him whom she deemed were potential supporters of his cause. *But that was important,* he thought. *There I was, isolated in the mountains . . . oh, yes, I had my agents, but who else could have done precisely what you did for us? And exceeding your instructions, you recruited your brother Lorens directly, as valuable a man as I have. Yes, you have earned well of the Life Force, beloved.*

"Hold me close again," she begged.

He did, and inhaled the fragrance of her. "Poor dear," he murmured, "I can imagine the strain you've been under."

She gulped and nodded her head against his breast. "Not afraid, really, most of the time, but, but, oh, torn. I always had faith in you, never doubt I had faith in you, Jovain, but—poor Iern. He does have good intentions, mostly." She pulled free. The eyes that stared upward were white-rimmed. "How is he? Is he all right?"

Jovain scowled. "I'm sorry to tell you he—well, he was reckless today, a madman. But he's not been hurt. If he'll come to his senses — You do know, don't you, I wish him no ill, in spite of everything?" *I just wish him dead in some convenient fashion. Afterward I'd be glad to deliver a carefully phrased eulogy and sponsor a modest monument.* He related briefly what had happened.

She shuddered. "But then he's hiding, by himself, I suppose, hungry, desperate. I never wanted that!"

Jovain strengthened his embrace. "Nor I," he said, *though if ever anybody deserved it, Talence Iern Ferlay does.* "Have no fears. He'll surely do the intelligent thing and surrender tomorrow. I'll do what I can to save him from the consequences of his folly. Now, though—Faylis, now is ours. After two years, ours."

He drew her to him. She was slow about growing lively and warm in his arms. Finally they sought the bed. He found he was too worn and worried for the achieving of her desire.

4

Iern rose and pressed for a time display. The data screen came aglow with numerals: 2051. "I'd better start off," he said.

Vosmaer Tess Rayman, Senior in her Clan and colonel in the Weather Corps, gave him a troubled look from her chair. "This early?" she asked. "The guards should be drowsy later on."

"Not if they're well disciplined, madame, which they've certainly been acting like. And the longer a period of night I have ahead of me, the better my chances of making myself untrailable."

"I thought you might rest some more. You never did succeed in falling asleep."

"Too high-keyed. It'd be strange if I weren't."

"Your scheme is dicey at best, you know."

Iern shrugged. "What will happen if I stay aloft, playing mouse to Jovain's cat? I reckoned they'd be too busy at first to search for me, and I could safely hole up with somebody I knew I could trust. But I'll give you any odds you want, madame, tomorrow they'll check every apartment, and ransack the rest of Skyholm meter by meter, nor stop till they have me." He grinned. "Or till they're convinced I escaped. Let them wonder how."

The lean, white-haired woman did not share his eagerness. "I think they'll guess right, but I hope they won't be able to trace it back to Dany." That was her son, come along as her aide, whom she had summoned to her lodging after Iern appeared and had sent after the gear that Iern wanted.

"I hardly think so, madame. Things were confused, while technical services must go on. Most of the interlopers seem to be groundlings, completely unacquainted with the routines here. Who'd pay any special attention to a fellow that calmly opened a locker and walked off carrying an altitude suit? They'd take for granted he had a job to do outside."

"If he left with you—you'd have a companion, a comrade in arms, and Zhesu knows you'll need one."

"No. Thank you, but we've covered this before. He's inconspicuously back in his bachelor dormitory. If he turned up missing tomorrow, though, that'd point straight to you."

Tess lifted her head. "You're right. In fact, Iern, you're proving smarter than I, frankly, expected. It gives me double reason to stay and do whatever I can on your behalf at the Council."

"You're a valiant lady, madame. Which *I* frankly expected, or I wouldn't have come to you."

Her sharp profile turned toward a photograph of her late husband. "I try to do what Aric would have wanted."

Iern went into the bedroom, where the equipment lay. He started to draw the curtain. "Nonsense," the colonel said. "Leave that open and we'll talk while you change." It muffled sound. "I won't peek, if the idea makes you blush."

"Well—" He laughed. "Madame, I confess that when I first joined your command, I regretted the age difference between us. Is it a court-martial offense to daydream about a superior officer?"

"Oh, I knew you did," she answered calmly, "and enjoyed knowing, but was rather glad of the age and rank gap. It would never have done, my becoming one more trophy." Her tone sobered. "In that respect, Iern, you have yet to grow up. I wonder what it may have had to do with bringing on the disaster today."

Grimness took him. *I likewise. If my brother-in-law has joined the enemy, what of my wife? I think of so many things she's said and done, or left unsaid — No. Can't be.* He shed his clothes and busied himself with the altitude suit. In this cramped room, he must do it on top of the bed.

Tess' voice went on: "We won't really know how to act, we loyalists, until we understand the whole situation. I don't look for a full accounting tomorrow, either. But Jovain will be persuasive, oh, yes; less than candid, but persuasive. And he has avowed allies on the Council, and doubtless others who haven't avowed it; and still others are less than satisfied with you, and will listen if Jovain brings charges — Don't let the news you hear shake you, Iern. It's sure to be bad, whatever it is. And don't take foolish chances. I believe we'll have to bide our time and see what develops, before we can even decide what countermeasures to take. Perhaps we'll have to decide against taking any."

He worked the inner layer onto his feet and up his body, centimeter by centimeter, smoothing the slick black fabric to make its engineered molecules adjust their configurations and cling to him like an extra skin.

"Yes, I'll lie low," he promised.

"Can you tell me where?"

"No. Depends on the winds tonight. Dordoyn is ideal guerrilla country, but Brezh has its own advantages for me—to name the two most obvious."

He could almost hear how she frowned. "Don't think of resorting to arms, Iern. Not yet."

"Oh, no. I meant that I can hide in the Dordoyn hills, and the pysans will help me. But maybe I should go abroad."

"That might be your best hope." Tess was quiet for a space. "May I live to see our hope flower."

Having sheathed himself to the neck and secured the slide fastener, Iern donned a heavy coverall. Its chief function was to protect the material beneath, lest that suffer a rip and expose him to stratospheric near-vacuum, but it gave him pockets and loops as well, to carry various necessities which he stowed in them.

He returned to the living room and Tess helped him with the rest. Socks and boots protected his feet. The helmet shell went over a padded coif and, at its base, sealed itself to the inner skin. He left the faceplate open. After he had passed arms through straps and buckled the harness, an oxygen tank was riding between his shoulderblades. Tess connected it for him and adjusted the valves. Those were critical. He must breathe, and he must sweat. The elastic that would keep his blood from boiling also blocked perspiration, but the air unit would vent sufficient water vapor given off from his head that heat prostration would not strike him.

The parachute rig that followed was not the standard type required for workers when outside. A fall off the aerostat being rare, they got verbal instructions, not a practical training that might claim lives. Hence the equipment must needs be simple. Dany had brought a pack of the kind favored by experienced skydivers, some of whom jumped from the aerostat itself.

Iern had done that once, years ago. Tess heard of it, called him on the carpet, and forbade him explicitly and profanely to repeat the stunt ever again. "We spent a fortune qualifying you for your wings," she snapped, "and yesterday you risked spattering yourself over half the Domain, for a thrill!"

Tonight is different, he thought. He drew on his airtight gloves. She snugged them to his wrists.

They stood before each other while silence grew. "Well," he said at last, "I, um, I'd better be on my way. Thank you for everything."

Her grin wavered. "See to it that you make me a proper return, you rascal. I'm angling for grandchildren, and I want them to enjoy all we've had."

She rose on tiptoe and kissed him, fleetingly as swallowflight. "Farewell, Talence Iern Ferlay. Fare always well."

More awkward than he was wont, he departed. She waved as he went out the door.

Thereafter he strode purposefully. The faceplate, halfway lowered, should veil him, unless somebody saw him loitering along and wondered why. He met no one. Skyholm had drawn back into itself to await the morning.

A green-clad guard did stand at the airlock to C–3. He lifted a rifle. "Halt!" he called. Echoes shivered in the locker-lined space. He spoke nervously, with a thick Eskuara accent. "Where do you go?"

"Outside, on regular duty," Iern said. "Let me by."

"Have you a pass?"

Iern was prepared to edge close, whip out a knife, and kill. He would rather not take the chance of failure in the attack; and abruptly he discovered that he would rather not succeed, either. "Why should I need a pass for a piece of routine?"

"What do you want?"

Iern sighed elaborately. "Look here, compadre. That isn't a parking dock out there, or a laser emplacement, or anything else you can imagine I might sabotage. It's nothing but a small observation platform. I'm supposed to inspect as much of the skin as I can see from there. Afterward I go on to the next platform, and the next. Ultraviolet light and ozone make the material deteriorate. We want to replace every panel before it blows out. Your interference today kept us from checking. Pressure changes at sunset generate stresses. My chief told me to make certain nothing is about to pop. Now may I do my job?"

The sentry was quick to stand aside. "Yes, go, go," he said.

Iern leered inwardly. Except for pretending to be at work, he had uttered no lie. He had merely put urgency in his voice, and omitted to mention that, the average lifetime of a panel being ten years, inspections were performed annually, using precision instruments, and never at night. He had implied that a blowout would bring Skyholm crashing down, when this was not even true of the buoyant inner sphere; outward movement of air would automatically unroll an adhesive patch, good for hours of service, before pressure had dropped noticeably. The ancestors had built some big safety factors into their creation.

But they never imagined it would be betrayed.

Iern closed his faceplate and cycled through. Having done so, he must needs spend minutes looking, for this might be his last sight from on high.

Eastward the full moon glowed dazzling bright in a hyaline blackness. Elsewhere stars crowded heaven, unwinking ice-glints of a hundred different hues, and the galactic bridge swept sword-sharp from horizon to horizon. The night was cloudless below him, he saw Gulf and Channel and outlines of land, here and there a river or lake or snow-crown glimmered, but otherwise Earth lay blurred, all grays and silvers and moon-haze, more distant and less real than ever he had known it before.

Stranger still, somehow, was the vast opalescent curve of the captive stronghold. Its lattice showed faint; he thought of veins blue in a woman's milk-swollen breast and then, so keenly that he gasped, of his mother. Sun energy stored during the day kept the sleeping giant aloft, in place, alive. When he gripped the platform rail, he felt a slight quiver as air surged from two of the jet engines, and imagined he could hear its *br-r-roo-oo-oo-m-m* that had challenged the upper winds for eight hundred years.

He shook himself, as if he had just come out of a wintry river. "Time to start, lad," he muttered.

Awe faded, excitement crackled. What a leap he was about to make!

He swung his legs over the rail, poised for a second, and jumped.

At first it was dreamlike. Weightless, disembodied, he passed through silence and moonlight. He tumbled, but slowly and gently; Earth revolved through his vision, followed by the white globe from which he, thistledown, drifted. Did he hear the air sing, or was it too thin? Surely it was cold enough to freeze his eyeballs, but in his suit he floated womb-warm, encompassed by stars. The part of him that gauged and calculated made no call upon his awareness, any more than heart or lungs did. His true self had dissolved into the distances around.

Must delay chute release till the right atmospheric density, else the rig will most likely foul and become a winding sheet for my meteorite corpse. When, though? I could overheat and be cooked, streaking unchecked into those lower levels. About fifteen kilometers' altitude, but when I did this last time, I had instruments — Make an estimate, bird-boy, and act on it.

He pulled a ripcord. The drogue and then the primary parachute came free, trailed, expanded, stiffened. Harness slammed brutally against his flesh. He hung for a while before he regained the strength to dismiss the pain. *I overdid the waiting. I'll be bruised and sore tomorrow.* Exultation: *But I'll be free!*

That brought him entirely back to consciousness. Never mind eldritch beauty, he was an aviator with a landing to make. He lacked precise data, but he could observe. Warily, he began manipulating the shrouds. Winds generally blew east in the stratosphere, his last choice of directions, but he could counter them to some degree by judicious spilling, and after he entered the troposphere, they should be going different ways at different heights. He could partly collapse the canopy and drop fast when the set was wrong, open it wide and fall slowly through desirable flows.

Skyholm dwindled above him. Presently a heaviness and a whistling told him he had indeed crossed into the nether kingdom of air. Stars faded from view until those that were left formed the familiar constellations. He swung a bit, clapper underneath a broad pale bell, and navigated as best he was able. Channel and sea were not shrinking much on the horizon, were they? . . . Ah-ha! He had a wind from east of south. It made the lines quiver.

He nerved himself and pulled another cord. The parachute let go of him and fluttered off, shrouds twisting about in the moonlight like tendrils on a jellyfish. He started falling swiftly—not free-floating, in this denser gas, but falling, buffeting through it—until his second chute deployed and put on a brake.

He was gambling, he knew. The primary one would have brought him down safely, though he would not have had a great deal to say about where he touched ground. The second was a modern device, Maurai-inspired, an intricate and comparatively fragile thing of vanes, battens, ailerons, venturis, well-nigh as steerable as a hang glider. You weren't supposed to open it more than a few kilometers above turf.

His conscience twinged. People counted on him—Tess, Dany—his friends, his pysans—Faylis?— Well, if he smashed, he smashed. The point was that he could use this chute to reach Brezh, the country of his mother.

His whoop made the helmet ring.

—He came down almost softly, on a road he had chosen. Dust puffed from his bootsoles, gray-white. On either side, trees stood hoar under the moon and dew glittered on grass in ditches. When he stripped, he felt a breeze slide cool around him, he drank its moist earthy odors and heard an owl hoot afar.

First he should dispose of the telltale half of his gear. He went a small distance into the woods and used a knife to dig it a shallow grave. Footwear and coverall he resumed; insignia removed, they could pass for garb of an itinerant laborer.

Then he started walking on the road. He had a fair idea of where he was. Not far ahead there ought to be a trail leading to the ruins of a castle, abandoned centuries before the Judgment. The hermit who dwelt in it would give him shelter, and keep quiet after he was gone.

The moon rose higher. Its lambency outshone by far a Skyholm on which the sun's rays no longer fell.

XI

The news came to Ronica Birken soon after she had crossed the River Seyn on her way back from lands beyond the Rhin. A sweep-driven ferry let her group of half a dozen and their wagon and horses off at its left-bank wharf. They mounted to seat and saddles and started on the last three or four kilometers to Fonteynblo.

Alek Zaksun urged his steed forward until he rode in front, beside the woman. "A fine evening, hm?" he remarked.

She looked around her. Trees, mostly alder and beech, formed a vaulted corridor full of shadows, wherein leaves that caught the last level sunbeams gleamed green-gold. It was no longer quite warm, but summer odors lingered. The road was graveled, crunchy beneath hoofs and wheels. Birds twittered. For a moment, homesickness tugged at her—but Laska lay beyond the Pole, and its wildernesses weren't really akin to this domesticated forest in the middle of the Domain. "Yes, beautiful," she said.

"Why not spend tomorrow resting?" Alek proposed. "You've pushed us like a muleskinner."

"We'd've been fools to dawdle," she snapped. "You know that."

Recollection: *Maybe not so much among the barbarians of the eastern parts. They seemed in awe of us, and had no firearms in any case. There, what we had to sweat at was the Doom-near impossible traveling conditions. But half-civilized western Allemans, yeh, I didn't want to give them time to brew up ideas about robbing us. The fact that their plunder would kill them shortly after they pried it open would've been a mousefuck-small consolation.*

"We're safe now," he pointed out. "Have been for the past week, at least. And still you crack the whip over us. What's the rush, Ronica?"

"We may be needed at the ship."

"If we were, you'd have heard from Captain Karst, wouldn't you?"

She must nod. In the outlands they had been cut off from communication, but here the situation was different. The tiniest hamlet, anywhere in the Domain, kept a public radio receiver. For an hour out of each twenty-four, Skyholm devoted its relay capability to messages, for a price, which were transcribed at the designated post offices and held until called for. Mikli had had her memorize a list of code phrases. To date she had gotten nothing, and she had no reason to expect anything before she reached Kemper—perhaps nothing there, either, if he was away at the time, busy with his machinations.

"The Domain is a clutch of states, though, each running by its own rules," she reminded Alek. "So far our papers have gotten us past every checkpoint, but we are a conspicuous gang of foreigners, and if we loaf on our course, some official may notice us enough to grow too poxy curious."

"What if he does? He'll read our documents, won't he, and not meddle with archeological salvage for a, uh, a Consvatoire."

Salvage—four intact plutonium warheads, from that ancient battleground in the Czechy Range, shunned and dreaded by the natives—but they have nothing to tell them that the lethal contents of other missiles, broken or corroded, have leached away into Earth's entire biosphere—

"It'll scarcely happen anyhow," Alek persisted. "None of the jurisdictions we're passing through is given to fussiness. They've been at peace for centuries, and we're a breath of fresh air to them. Take my word for it, Ronica. I do know this country."

Again honesty forced her to nod. "M-hm. How you do." Without him, her expedition would have been hopeless. She could make a way through forest and swamp, over roadless heights and rivers in spate, all the while keeping her party well fed off the land and well sheltered at night. When trouble arose, as it had done a couple of times, she could order them into such a formidable array that the troublemakers slunk off. At the end, she could direct a search for the objects they sought. But she had no acquaintance with Franceterr, let alone the tribal patchwork eastward; and her knowledge of Yurrupan languages amounted to little more than limited Angley and less Francey, studied while the ship fared from Seattle. Alek Zaksun had spent a total of years on this continent, as an anthropologist. He was fluent not only in Francey and several Alleman dialects, but in a few Shlavic ones. His had been the talk that eased their path among the barbarians, the tactful inquiries that yielded clues for them to follow in their quest.

"Well, then, why not take a day or two off in Fonteynblo?" he asked. "It's a delightful place, it and its hinterland. If nothing else, think of our poor beasts."

Ronica looked downward. She saw how her horse's head drooped, she felt how its hooves plodded. Guilt pricked her. *He's right. I have been setting a tough pace, and it's not necessary anymore. At home I don't kill an animal or cut down a tree without whispering, "I'm sorry, my brother (my sister); I have need." Should I abuse these creatures, only because I'm in a hurry to—to what? I'm not even sure of what. Although—*

"Okay," she decided. "If we don't find a message calling for us to make tracks."

"Wonderful! You won't be sorry." He edged his mount close, until his knee touched hers and he could pat her hand, unseen in the dimness by their followers. "I'll show you around. The local wines are superb, the food is excellent, the sights interesting, the countryside ideal for a picnic, and—m-m-m. . . ." He let his voice trail off, but not his hand over hers.

It seemed to burn, yet she did not withdraw from it. Her pulse quickened. Something of a cramp passed through her, but not like a period or a sickness. Well-nigh furtively, she glanced aside at him. He was no counterpart of the tough, burly men at the rear, soldiers and mechanics. Whipcord-slender, clean-featured, neatly clad and jauntily bearded under the harshest conditions, and a sparkling conversationalist, Alek minded his manners with her as properly as the others did. But somehow he never let her forget that her chastity was merely for the sake of maintaining discipline.

Damn, but it feels like forever since— She remembered temptations on trek, especially after she'd picked up a smidgen of lingo. It would have been easy to sneak off with a handsome young tribesman, and nobody else ever the wiser. The trouble was, she had no immunity to numerous nasty diseases endemic in those populations, and not all of them yielded to antibiotics. (On this suddenly dizzying evening, she rejected memories of stenchful shacks, niggard fields, people gnarled and toothless and nearing the grave at forty, infant after infant in primitive cribs, obviously dying, while flies buzzed around. According to what she had read, East Yurrupans were better off than most of the human race.) For the same reason, she hoped, her men had confined themselves to anticipations of Franceterr. She felt sure Alek had.

I'm no floozy. I can go without as long as I must, and often have for months. There's plenty else in life. However— All at once she grinned. *Admit it, Ronica. You want to get yourself discreetly but thoroughly laid. Why not here?* She patted her horse's mane. It was coarse and warm beneath her palm. *Courage, my friend,* she thought at it. *You'll have a holiday now. Lord knows you've earned one.*

Alek released her, for they were leaving the woods and the town stood before them.

Outbound, they had taken a northerly route, in order that they not be seen coming and going—when Maurai agents scuttled ratlike around the Domain. This sight was new to Ronica. "Hoy-ah!" she exclaimed, and clapped her hands together for joy.

The forest swung off to the right in a darkling arc. Elsewhere land rolled away as vineyards, here and there a meadow or orchard, poplars along the roads, farmhouses snug in the hollows and lamplight mellow in their windows. The town clustered neatly around a time-blurred gracefulness of remnant palace walls. The sky was clear, shading from violet in the east, through gray-blue overhead, to greenish in the west above a newly sunken sun. Southwestward stood Skyholm, the size in vision of the full moon that would shortly rise. Swallows darted and flicked. An angelus bell pealed, coolness given a voice.

"Oh, yes," Ronica murmured. "Oh, yes." She clicked tongue at her horse and put heels in its ribs to urge it onward, but gently. Alek kept beside her. The followers clattered and the wagon rattled behind, on into town.

Streets were paved, noisy under hooves. Walls, made of the sandstone that was a local product, gave back a hint of the day's ardor. Most folk were indoors, having dinner, but some gaped and squinted at these foreigners bound for the inn. That house fronted on a marketplace whose booths were shuttered for the night. In the middle of the square rose a post, the lamp on top not yet kindled. Lower down was a loudspeaker. Ronica clattered across.

The loudspeaker came to life. She reined her steed in so harshly that, no matter its weariness, it reared. The Francey roaring forth meant nothing to her; the tone, and the people who spilled from their doors and swarmed onto the plaza, meant everything bad.

She brought her animal under control, drew close to Alek, and seized him by the arm. "What is it?" she demanded. "What's gone wrong?"

His features were unclear in the gloaming, but she thought she made out a starkness upon them. " 'Attention, attention, burghers,' " he translated in a slurred, hurried tone. " 'Special announcement from Ileduciel to the Domain—' " Abandoning the effort, he turned to her and said in Unglish, amidst ongoing oratory from above and jabber of those who seethed everywhere around: "Some kind of political coup. Talk of a crisis, an emergency. Word is, everybody should stay calm, but— Nothing's definite, except that hell's boiling over."

Immediately she was in command of herself. "Then we proceed on to Kemper as fast as may be," she said. "Better not stay in town; Yasu alone knows what'll happen. We'll camp somewhere beyond, and eat what rations we've got left. Tomorrow dawn, we hit the trail again."

Calculation clicked, as if she were back among the volcanoes. *We can't hope for much speed. The best road in the Domain is a cowpath, compared to any main highway in the Union. Our wagon's light, scarcely more than a cart, but it's a drag on animals close to exhaustion. Maybe we can make a swap, ours for stock inferior but fresh. A week or so to Kemper—can we shave a day off that?*

We'll goddamn well try. She drew her sword, not to cut at the frightened dwellers but as a wand of authority to open a lane through them. "Let's go, boys!" she cried. "On the bounce!"

2

Two years ago, a detachment of Maurai from the Inspectorate had landed at Kenai, established themselves, and used the town as a base for a month's searching around the area. They claimed they had reason to think a treaty violation was afoot, nature unspecified because—their chief eventually admitted to Lodgemaster Benyo Smith—uncertain. Although careful to behave correctly, the strangers met with scant friendliness and no helpfulness worth mentioning. Laskans were apt to be independent even by standards of the Northwest Union, and to resent the High Commission still more than did Southerners, for whom it was a fact of everyday life. This was especially true since Ruori Haakonu's death; his successor meant well but lacked charm.

In the course of their mission, the inspectors demanded to visit those mountains across Cook Inlet where none but a chosen few had gone for close to twenty years.

"Why is it restricted?" Commander Okuma Samuelo asked.

"Not exactly restricted," Benyo replied, in Maurai better than his visitor's Unglish. "People are strongly requested to stay away, and most hereabouts belong to the Wolf Lodge, whether from the start or by later marriage and reallegiance. Voluntary cooperation is the basis of our whole society, you know." His tone grew a trifle sardonic.

"Social pressure too, of course. It gets mighty powerful in a frontier area like this, where mutual goodwill is important to survival. Non-members respect the reservation also, for that reason. Why not? We have no shortage of real estate."

"Please don't play games with me, sir," Okuma said. "What are you doing there?"

"Why, you know that after the industrial project failed, we took over and established a wildlife refuge. Partly it's insurance—in view of population growth throughout the North—but mainly it's for scientific purposes, ecological studies, genetic, everything that I'm sure you can well appreciate. The Wolf Lodge is doing it, with help from individuals who belong to others, because ours has always had an intellectual tradition. For centuries we've supplied more than our share of scientists, scholars, teachers, and military officers."

"Yes, military," Okuma muttered. "You're paramilitary at least, to this day, aren't you? . . . Why has your team published so little?"

A smile creased the old man's face. "We may be competitive businessmen, we Norries, but we aren't competitive academics. A Lodge looks after its own, gives them time to develop their undertakings—generations, if need be—and doesn't hanker for immediate glory. Besides, there are never many persons involved yonder. A large group would spoil the very things they hope to observe."

"I have reason to believe substantial shipments have frequently been made to the site, not only in the past but every year since."

"Some," Benyo agreed. "Laying down sensors throughout a territory that big and rugged is no kiddie game. Also, for experimental purposes, occasionally some landscape has gotten modified, and this has involved heavy equipment. Aside from that, I think you must have an exaggerated notion of the activity. You've probably heard about cargoes that were actually meant for someplace else. An easy mistake to make, at your remove and in a country this different from yours."

He wagged the stem of his churchwarden pipe. "Look here, Commander," he said. "I know you want to go see for yourself. Okay. Let's arrange it. Give me a few days to recruit guides." Anticipating the objection: "No, no. You can go wherever you want, and we could scarcely remove something big overnight, now could we? The guides will just be on hand to assist, advise, and keep you out of trouble. It can get a tad dangerous—snowfields, talus slopes, that kind of thing. Also, frankly, we'd like to prevent your disrupting the environment too much. I'm sure you'll go along with that. Your Federation is a science-oriented society, like the Union."

Okuma and his technicians found nothing suspicious across the firth. Granted, what they did find was wilderness, vast, tilted, cragged, totally alien to them. They realized how easily they could miss traces of—of what?—and under better conditions might have done a better job. However, the short subarctic summer was drawing to a close in rain, sleet, fog, lashing winds, waning daylight. And now a team farther east radioed the exciting news that it had found what seemed to be evidence of clandestine activity in the recent past, near Yakutat—possibly an attempt to develop an aircraft of more speed and range than the Union was allowed under the treaty—a project that, outgrowing its facilities, could well have moved on into the sparsely mapped Yukon region or, conceivably, by secret agreement, into the Mong nation Chukri. . . .

The inspectors left Kenai and did not return. Said Okuma to Benyo, bitterly, at their farewell: "I've no choice but to assume you're honest. If any Lodge besides yours—Salmon, Beaver, Polaris, Avengers, Juniper, Chinook, any of scores—is carrying on something illicit, you wouldn't know, nor would its average member. I can only beg you, if by chance information should come your way, put parochialism aside, think of the good of mankind, yes, of life on Earth, and call us."

The reply was not unkindly: "I don't envy you your job, Commander, trying to make the world stay put."

In the next two years, rumbles and shocks had gone through the land more often than aforetime. The volcanoes grew restless, folk said. Nobody among them was a geologist. A Wolf expert addressed a town meeting on the subject. They had little to fear, he told them, provided they were sensible. If they saw a bright flash and heard no immediate noise from the peaks across the straits, best would be that they take cover and avert their eyes.

The outburst came on a windless morning in summer. Fog had settled in overnight, so thick that people groped their way after dawn through its dripping dank grayness, themselves wraithlike in vision. Houses were shadows, wanly and blurrily puddled where lamplight shone through glass, invisible two doors off. Mournful, muffled, from out on the water came the lowing of a buoy horn.

Then brilliance flared in the murk, lurid blue-white. It strengthened and spread, a fire, a lightning ball, a sun. Those who did not heed the warning and immediately look away would have suffered retinal burns were it not for the cloud that lay over land and sea and heaven; as was, they clapped hands to faces and afterimages danced before them for a long while. Those whose backs were turned saw an enormous ring of rainbow in the mist, like a suddenly opened portal.

A second blaze smote, but weaker because it was far higher up. Afterward the sound arrived. Even over a great distance, it crashed through ground as well as air, sent waves up into human bones to shake the heart and call forth dread that had no name.

It faded out. Vapor swirled toward quiescence. Men and women exchanged stares of astonishment—they were alive, unhurt—and hastened to soothe terrified children. An Eskimo who had coolly counted his pulse went around declaring that the volcano was about a hundred kilometers off. He opined that its brief rage had cast a gout or two of molten lava aloft, which would make an all-time splash and steam-puff when it hit the water, or a devil of a mess if it struck on land.

In a chamber across the strait, deep underground, director Eygar Dreng and his immediate staff looked wildly at a bank of instruments. "She's going," he said. His fists knotted, his breast heaved, tears ran down his cheeks. "By the Seven Thunders, *how* she is going!"

On radio wings, a coded message sought three ships, hove to at far-spaced stations. Captains announced the news to their men, who cheered, capered, embraced, flung caps in air, before they buckled down to work. Before long, they ardently hoped, one of their crews would be very busy indeed.

3

Tables cleared away and chairs placed in rows, Charles Hall became the auditorium of Skyholm—or the assembly room where the Clan Seniors met. Displayed on the walls at the appointed places, their banners transformed it, reduced the murals of historic scenes to background for a kaleidoscope of colors and devices, were arrogant with diversity and solemn with centuried memories. Waiting on the stage, knowing how dwarfed he was by the gold-embroidered curtain of blue silk at his back, Jovain had seldom felt more solitary.

The trumpets rang, the sergeant at arms called to order, the chaplain gave an invocation, the president of the Administrative Board rendered formalities. From down on the floor, the Seniors looked at Jovain.

No matter his troopers, that audience was daunting, six hundred-odd men and women elected to represent their Clans. They sat in blocs, separated by a couple of meters. Acoustics were adequate; he made out slight rustlings and murmurs, that only emphasized silence. They were variously clad, in military uniform, in regional costume, in somberly rich town garb, but on every shoulder, a Clan patch mirrored a banner. Most were middle-aged, some old, some young *(like Iern, damn him, damn that slippery bastard, where is he?)*, all alert and chary. Nearest to him were the Talences, who could speak but not vote in the choice of a Captain. He read such hostility upon several of their countenances that his glance went around among the twenty-nine groups franchised today, seeking for persons he knew would uphold him. Air gusting from a ventilator felt gelid on his skin.

Stop that! he scolded himself. *You have a destiny to fulfill.* And when the president announced him and he advanced to the lectern, courage returned, will, confidence. True, this wasn't what he had imagined. He had not anticipated nervousness, doubts, nagging thoughts about details he must not forget to attend to, an itch between his shoulderblades, the smell and coldness of his own sweat, a dismal memory from the night before and grit in his head because he hadn't slept well afterward. But was anything ever quite what you had expected?

He required no written text. The lectern was for a public-address microphone, and for him to rest a hand on in an effective manner as he began:

"Sir President, honored Seniors, Clansfolk and people of the Domain, let me first thank you sincerely and humbly for your patience. This occasion is unprecedented and therefore twice difficult—"

Not altogether meaningless noise. Monkeys groom each other with fingers, humans with words. Also, the preliminaries let him find his rhythm, gather his momentum, feel the beginnings of exaltation. *I don't think Faylis will be disappointed again tonight!*

For hours to come, he must ride out a storm and quell it. Who had faced a greater challenge, since that day after Judgment when radioactive smoke blew across the world and Charles Talence rallied his crew to carry on? *Do I really feel his anim uniting with mine? No, that's vainglorious; I never would, whatever the truth. Besides, the Gaean philosophy doesn't encourage any such belief . . . though it doesn't forbid, either.*

"—I will proceed straight to the hard, practical facts of our situation. Skyholm is in danger. Our entire civilization is. By swift, decisive action we have, I trust, avoided a peril I am about to describe. But larger, more enduring perils lie ahead . . . as do unlimited opportunities, if we can organize ourselves to seize them." A number of listeners were producing notebooks and pencils. He would hear some pointed questions later on.

"—my profound apologies for yesterday's intrusion. Never before has the peace, the sanctity of Skyholm been troubled. I can merely plead that a far worse, an infinitely tragic disruption might have occurred—in my considered opinion, would have occurred—had my loyal friends and I not acted. We dared not consult you beforehand. It seemed essential to bring an armed force, but that was unheard-of. A Captain could have ordered it; we had no Captain. This distinguished assembly would have felt impelled to ask for evidence, debate the matter, search for the wisest decision; and meanwhile the enemy could strike.

"You ask who this enemy is. Let me summarize briefly what I have learned, deduced, and conjectured. Later I will go into more detail. The actual evidence will be made available in due course to such trustworthy persons as this Council may select."

Now the billow crests and surges to shore! "We are accustomed to thinking of Espayn as a unified nation under a monolithic government. However, those of you who are versed in the subject know well that that is not the case. It is a nation recently and forcibly hammered together. . . .

"—my position on the border, my connections across it . . .

"—factions . . .

"—a cabal . . .

"—information brought me by peace-loving individuals and organizations . . .

"—It may have been exaggerated, yes. It may just have been the dream of a few, heedless and ambitious, who lack the forces to seize Skyholm under any circumstances. I do not know for certain. I did not know. But I dared not take the risk.

"For tens of generations we have been complacent in our stratospheric aerie. We forgot that bold men will always find unexpected new instrumentalities. Today we are safe again—for the time being. I wish to assure that safety for the time to come.

"Dismiss me and my men if you choose: but not, I pray you, before our new Captain has replaced us with an adequate, permanent guard for Skyholm, our heart.

"Perhaps I should step down at this point, that you may go about your deliberations." *No, I mean to overwhelm you.* "Command me to do so if that is your will." *First remember who commands the guns here.*

Pause.

"Well, then, I beg your indulgence for a while. I have said that the danger we barely avoided was—is—hardly more than a wave breaking on reefs through which we have yet to sail. I trust you will decide that the welfare of the Domain requires you hear me out."

Courtesies; questions; arguments from the floor. Jovain's supporters were well briefed; his sympathizers rallied around in predictable fashion.

"Thank you, thank you. What I have to say is as manifold as the world itself, the complex, changeable, dangerous, but hopeful world from which we cannot hide away in a new Isolation Era. Our brush with disaster"—*we make axiomatic, without further discussion, that that's what it was*—"has shown that we too can go down to extinction, as whole societies have done throughout history, as every society did in the War of Judgment. But it is not inevitable. We have the alternative of seizing the future. . . .

"—dangers arise from our own ranks also. The case of . . . esteemed . . . Talence Iern Ferlay is appalling. I had hoped to prove, before this gathering and to his face, that his militarism, his technolatry would close off any possibility of cooperation with those elements in Espayn who would like to be our friends. Rather than a civilized debate, he chose murderous assault on innocent persons, and flight from justice. Sirs and ladies, I am not a psychiatrist. It is not for me to pass judgment, to diagnose. But I ask you whether the balance of peace or war should rest in such hands. . . .

"—and his favoring of the Maurai Federation, that colossus which has for too long bestridden the world . . .

"—cultivate relationships with the Northwest Union, as it resurges from the bonds that the Maurai laid upon it." *Give them a laugh.* "I am supposed to be a devout Gaean. Well, I admit Gaeanity has an important message for us. Many of you agree. But if it's Gaean devoutness to encourage the machine-heavy Northwest Union, not as an ally or anything like that but as a counterweight to the biologically minded Maurai Federation, why, what can I say except that they aren't putting the kind of stuff into Gaean devoutness that they used to?"

Nothing, ever, about Northwestern emissaries who've sought me out and worked with me. That peculiar little man Mikli Karst—He was busy in Uropa before the Espaynians approached me. Rumors about somebody collecting nuclear explosives . . . Rumors only, as far as I'm concerned. There may be reports in the secret files of the Captaincy. I'll find out.

"—For its own survival, for the sake of everything it can contribute to mankind, the Domain must cease looking inward and begin looking outward. We must become a world power, not for empire but for peace. . . .

"—Seniors can always meet and vote a bad Captain out of office. It has happened twice in our history. . . ." *No soldiers occupied Skyholm then.*

"—In all humility, in reverence for the past and hope for the future, I offer the Domain my services."

4

Ironically, Terai and Wairoa were bound for the Prynys when they heard the news. A month of travel, talk, and watchfulness, in their guise of merchant adventurers, had given clues to something brewing in those mountains. Likewise had indications picked up by other agents covering other parts of the Domain.

Terai and Wairoa had garnered the most data themselves. Bluff, genial, the former could usually steer conversation with a local man —whether groundling or of the Aerogens, somebody whose affairs had him in touch with widespread regions—toward the matters that really interested him, once they had finished with his ostensible business and were relaxing over a drink. "—Yes, of course we Maurai have no monopoly on visiting your country. I hear that these days you're meeting scouts like me, or even tourists, from as far as Merique. —Mong missionaries, yes. —That many Northwesterners? Really? I'm surprised. —Do you happen to know if they tend to concentrate on particular areas? It would give me a hint as to what sort of competition to expect. —Thank you, sir, you're very kind. I won't forget, after we've gotten our enterprise established here. And if ever you happen to visit N'Zealann—"

Meanwhile Wairoa sat quietly observing, with his special senses and his special mind. He did the same when wandering about in the apparent aimlessness of any curious newcomer to town. His physique made some persons shun talk, some eager for it, but always it put them off balance, vulnerable to his talents. He was a copious reader of newspapers and magazines, a listener to radio broadcasts, who paid special attention to such matters as markets and shipping.

Pieces of the puzzle fell together. Mikli Karst had ranged extensively about, mostly contacting aristocrats, but the focus for him and his associates was in the Prynys, and perhaps beyond. "They're too few to be engineering trouble by themselves," Terai said. "Or are they?"

"It doesn't take much catalyst to make a reaction go," answered Wairoa. "There is a magnate in the South by the name of Talence Jovain Aurillac. We should investigate him."

"Eh? Why?"

"You may recall that mention of him has occurred occasionally. Body language at those times suggested he might be more important than he seems to be. Why has he kept himself in virtual exile these past two years? What did happen between him and that Iern Ferlay we hear of as a good prospect for the next Captain? I have nothing but hints, and an intuition that we need more than this."

Intuition, Terai thought. *Subconscious logic? I don't know; but Wairoa's hunches are worth more than most fellows' demonstrations.* "All right. We'll drift in that direction."

To travel straight and fast could raise too many questions. Terai zigzagged at a leisurely pace, by air, rail, and the generally execrable roads of a country where mechanized ground vehicles were rare. He sought men prominent in commerce. He was affable and gossipy as he inquired about possible demand for copra, coral, maricultural products, synthetic fibers, bacterial fuel cells, and the like. Their friends, including Clansfolk, heard about it and often wanted to meet him too. He was invited to homes, shown the local sights, sometimes given a romp in bed. He did not consider that an infidelity when Elena was half a world away, nor would she. His "assistant" Wairoa stayed in the background, observing and thinking.

The news of Jovain's takeover reached them in Toulou. "Oh-oh," Terai muttered; and as soon as he and Wairoa were alone: "We'd better get back to the ship. Every one of us. Nan the Destroyer knows what's about to happen—I don't."

"Won't that look suspicious, when we have just arrived?" Now and then Wairoa showed a curious ignorance about standard-issue human beings.

"Not if we don't mind looking rather timid. Strangers in a strange land and so forth; it's natural for us to feel nervous. I'll bluster out a feeble excuse. That should be in character for me. You contact the rest."

Wairoa nodded and slipped off. A suitcase in their baggage contained a radio set capable of activating a sensitive recorder anywhere within five hundred kilometers. The signal was scrambled; outsiders who chanced to tune in would suppose they heard a burst of static. Agents who got the message also got instructions to relay. *Back to Kemper, as fast as compatible with not blowing your cover!*

Next morning the two Maurai boarded a dirigible for Renn, capital of Ar-Goat. There they would change for their destination in Ar-Mor. Passengers sat in tense quietness, waiting for newscasts. The music that a cabin loudspeaker brought them in between times did not ease them, nor did food and wine.

Renn felt close to explosion, during a night's layover there. Wairoa went prowling through the dark, overhearing or eavesdropping. He sought Terai again at dawn. "The place reeks of fear and anger," he reported.

"Well, nothing like this has ever happened before," Terai said. "It's a terrible shock."

"Many people believe Jovain did frustrate a conspiracy. At any rate, they want to believe it. But then who are those shadowy figures behind the conspiracy, and what further evil have they in train? Many others think it's a hoax, and are afraid Jovain means to stuff Gaeanity down their throats. And many others—The Domain is not the tranquilly unified realm that it has seemed for so long to be, from the outside. It's shot through with rivalries and antagonisms, ethnic, religious, social, economic. When nobody knows what to expect, everybody dreads that somebody else will become able to take a sudden advantage."

Terai scowled. "A civil war here is bloody near the last thing the Federation wants. The Domain's our natural partner, or should be, as interested as us in keeping the world stable. . . . Well, let's hope this doesn't come to blows. And let's go get us some breakfast. If a miserable Fransey roll and cup of herb tea count as breakfast."

They heard on their flight to Kemper: the Council of Seniors had chosen Talence Jovain Aurillac the new Captain. "I can imagine the scene," Terai grunted to Wairoa in their language. "His supporters will have been ready to argue and put on pressure in organized style, though I don't suppose many of them knew in advance what he planned to do. Those who like part of what he stands for—Gaeanity, for instance, or opposition to foreign influences—they were easy to persuade. The cautious and the cowardly would mostly fall in line. I daresay an armed hillman looks persuasive, no matter what assurances his boss has given, and in any event, it'd appear safest to vote yes and scuttle home."

"At that," Wairoa pointed out, "he received a bare plurality. He probably could not have won if the opposition weren't split among several candidates."

"And surely not if Iern Ferlay had been there. I gather that that's one popular lad. What the Nan's become of him, anyway?"

Presently the radio carried a speech by Jovain. It was short and conciliatory, urging people to go unafraid about their daily business, promising a detailed program later that would serve the needs and aspirations of the entire Domain. "The bedbug letter," Terai muttered.

"What?" asked Wairoa.

"Never mind. An archeologically ancient joke. We're descending."

At the airport the two got a carriage to the riverside dock where *Hivao* lay and went aboard. There Terai stopped to gaze around him.

The scene was a colorful and peaceful skin stretched across events. Shore leaves had been canceled and every crewman was back. However, they had made the most of their stay, not only in excursions but in cultivating friendships. Being exotic helped vastly. The skipper saw no immediate reason why they should not have visitors. Flutes and drums resounded, feet danced, girls laughed and chattered and embraced and sometimes slipped below with a nautical companion. Men were guests too, mostly sailors and navvies, come to drink and talk and gamble. Terai noticed one, afar at the taffrail, who did not resemble a Breizhad—tall, gaunt, sandy-haired, horse-faced; he played a stringed instrument and sang for a group of listeners, when he wasn't upending a jug.

Several meters beyond lay the ship from the Northwest Union, a catamaran that bore an aircraft pod similar to *Hivao*'s. Her crew had avoided the Maurai, not even being sociable when in the same taverns, doubtless under orders. To Terai, that meant they weren't civilians as alleged, but Navy. Those on watch today stared forward at the festivities here, surely more than a little envious.

The afternoon was warm and bright. Water clucked against hulls. A steam dredge chuffed and dumped a load into its barge, maintaining basin and channel. Tarry odors lifted from the wharf. Above the warehouses, Terai saw the twin towers on the cathedral, remembered their antiquity, and for a moment felt dwindled to a dayfly.

He kicked the notion from him. "We've got work to do," he said.

"What?" inquired Wairoa.

"M-m-m . . . for the time being, I suppose, we wait to see how things go. I daresay Mikli and company will soon get here. Whether or not they had anything to do with what's happened, they can't be certain either what'll come of it. Better stay close to base, eh?"

"He should not find out you are in the Domain."

"Oh, no. Agreed. Until he arrives, though, I suppose I can move about pretty freely, if I don't give my right name."

"What have you in mind?"

"We've already seen the local higher-ups. I don't think they're involved in any plots, do you? But yon ship's been seven months in this port. Ordinary people are bound to have had plenty of contact with the Norrmen, and scraps of information are bound to have slipped out. Not that townsfolk would recognize it for what it signifies. But we—" Terai chuckled. "Yes, we have a great excuse for pub-crawling."

5

A few kilometers north of Dulua, for it took no more to be deep in the forest, Vanna Uangovna had her communion shrine. Individual seers and seeresses differed in the settings where they could most readily and fully know Gaea: a hilltop, a cave, a riverbank, a grove. . . . Vanna wanted more than untouched nature, she wanted a place to which humanity was integral, on which she herself could work as air and sunlight and unseen tiny life did. So had she commanded years before, and so had it been done for the proróchina.

One dawn she went there, neither alone nor leading a class as often aforetime, but with a single attendant. The air was still cold and damp, tendrils of mist a smoke over the ground, but already full of pine and earth fragrances. Radiance from the right stole among surrounding evergreens, lost itself in their needles and shadows, then suddenly glowed on a high branch or gleamed off a dew-wet spiderweb. Birdcalls had begun trilling and pealing, mosquitoes whined as they sheered off from repellent, a squirrel halted its comet-pace up a bole and chittered, otherwise the woods were hushed. Nearly hidden by duff, the trail was soft and whispery underfoot.

Having left cultivation behind, the two walked in fitting silence among the trees for a while before Vanna said low: "You are troubled, child."

Jiyan Robbs swallowed hard. She was of pure Merican blood, or a throwback to it, her blond head looming above her ucheny's, her fullness straining a linsey-woolsey frock; but she was not quite sixteen, and a sluga. Her hands, coarsened and reddened by the housecleaning tasks to which her steward had most recently assigned her, writhed together.

Vanna dropped back a pace, to walk alongside and lay a hand of her own, feather-light, on the girl's arm. "Tell me, dear," she murmured. "Let me do whatever I can toward easing your mind. Afterward let Gaea give you peace."

"I—I am afraid—" Jiyan could not go on.

"Fear must be a servant, never a master, not to be overworked, ultimately to be retired from service as no longer needed." *Yet you must not ignore the fact that reality can be brutal.* "What are you afraid of? Mistreatment? A word from me should put a quick stop to that."

"Oh, no, reverend lady. But I—I'm afraid I can't leave home after all." Jiyan knuckled her eyes. "I'm so sorry."

"What?" Vanna kept her tone serene. "The major hasn't said anything against it, has he?" The Robbs family were slugai of the Kharsovs, born to serve that house. They were not bound to a patch of soil, though, but had been towndwellers for generations, many of them in skilled jobs or positions of trust, modestly well-to-do.

Admittedly Bors Kharsov, major in the Blue Star Polk that owned half the property hereabouts, was not happy about letting Jiyan go. He had complained that it was fine for her to be a disciple in her free time—yes, yes, we are One in Gaea, sluga and Soldat alike—but sending her off for advanced study was something else again. Whether or not she showed promise, the example would make others of her class restive. . . . When Vanna insisted, he had not ventured to oppose the Librarian on a matter of that kind.

"No, but—his younger son, Olgh, you know—oh, reverend lady—"

The story stumbled out piece by piece. That Olgh had seduced her was nothing unusual. That he talked of making her his acknowledged concubine, respected in his household, after he got married, was not too surprising either; he was the same impulsive age. The problem was that Jiyan was desperately in love with him. She didn't think she could bear the thought of going away for years. But—but—the gift was in her; already, under Vanna's tutelage, she was coming to see what full Oneness could mean.

"Oh, my poor darling." Vanna stopped. "Here's a log, let's sit down, let me hold you while you cry. Weeping is natural, you know." *I know.*

Afterward she led the girl through exercises and mantras, until calm returned like an incoming tide. She made no attempt to force a decision. That must come of itself. Vanna hoped it would be for departure. Here, Jiyan would never have the freedom to pursue truth undisturbed. Not only would that be her loss, mankind as a whole would have lost a potentially inspiring ucheny.

The morning was well along when they continued on their way and reached the shrine. It was an arbor in a small meadow, edged by flowerbeds. In winter Vanna sought it on snowshoes, warmly clad, and her perceptions and meditations grew frosty, turning out toward the universe through which Gaea danced. Summer was the season for contemplating life, and yourself as an organelle amidst the energy and wonder of it.

Vanna lifted her arms. The birds came to her, robin, goldfinch, bluebird, flew around her head as a halo of wings and song, settled on wrists and fingers; she thrilled to the gentle clench of their feet. A doe and fawn trotted past, but were shy of Jiyan and did not come to be scratched behind the ears. It had taken Vanna a decade to win such friendship—as valuable, as Insight-giving a time as she had ever spent. Nowadays a bear who denned in this vicinity would gladly share with her the blueberries in a nearby slough.

Oneness, Oneness, love, peace. . . . It made hard the task of explaining to disciples that pain and death were aspects of the same ever-evolving unity, that even as she stood amidst her animals the white cells in her bloodstream waged war against predatory bacteria, and that this too they must understand and wholly accept before they could hope to know Gaea.

The birds fluttered off. They had their own living to do. Vanna and Jiyan went into the arbor. It contained no more than a dais of swirl-grained oak and a glacier-scarred boulder on which was chiseled a mandala. The humans took lotus position before the stone.

"I suggest you choose a leaf today," said Vanna, nodding toward the wild grapevines that twined over the lattice and passed the light through in golden flecks. "A single, particular leaf. Make it central in the cosmos, as everything is." Her voice fell into a hypnotic softness. "Observe its stem, veins, infinite shadings of color, the stirring at each least breeze. Think of its life cycle, ancestry, cellular architecture down to the quantum, its identity with you. . . ."

For her part, Vanna closed her eyes and sought to sense, to be, every odor of the thousandfold subtleties pervading the air.

Clouds piled up, moved forward on a loud wind, covered heaven. Rain came. It did not interrupt meditation but enhanced it. The humans removed their clothes and went out to be laved by the sky. Jiyan had learned how not to feel cold in this weather.

When the storm had passed and they were dry, they dressed again. Now speech was appropriate. Vanna found objects, twigs and stones and the like, wherewith to illustrate elementary principles of physics. That was a subject which gave her pupil difficulty. "You shall have to learn the basics of it, if you wish to approach true Oneness," the Librarian said, as she had done before. "Gaeanity is not mindless mysticism, whatever the majority of those who call themselves Gaeans may think. Or perhaps I should put it this way, that its mysticism springs from the mystery at the heart of reality. We *do not ever* observe the world in detachment. That is not possible. The wave functions not only set a limit to the accuracy, the certainty of our knowledge; they make us a part of what we are studying, and of all else. Probability cannot become equal to unity before an experiment is performed. We create reality as much as it creates us." She saw a glow of eagerness on the girl's face, smiled, and cautioned: "Yes, it sounds wonderful, and it is. It's boundlessly wonderful. The universe is a miracle. But I've been giving you words of grand sound and scant meaning. The right language for the Ultimate is mathematics."

She could almost hear the mind before her: *Might that kind of understanding not be worth more than . . . than Him?* To head off an anguished *No!* she took Jiyan's hand. "I talk too much," she said. "The afternoon's gotten old, you've had nothing to eat since breakfast, and you're healthily growing. Come, we'll go home."

An old scar twinged. Vanna too had surrendered a love, once and forever. Marriage ought not to be incompatible with enlightenment, but it often was. The wholly enlightened future would be different, but so would marriage itself be. Not that she'd live to see that. She would long since have returned her being to the Life Force.

They walked back at a brisk pace, in silence except for breath and footfalls.

Cleared land opened and Dulua lay red-roofed before them, along the huge argency of the lake. Vanna hugged her disciple goodbye and made her way alone to the Library. Various prosaic duties remained before she could seek her cottage, cook a simple meal, and settle down with a book—nothing weighty this evening, just a light historical romance, unless Chen Yao's latest novel had arrived from the publisher. He was fantastically funny.

When she entered the building, an acolyte met her in its foyer. "Reverend lady," he said, after he had bowed and received her gesture of blessing, "a message has come for you, a coded radiogram from the High Sanctuary in Chai Ka-Go. I put the transcription on your desk and have stood guard outside."

What? Vanna willed her pulse back to normal. "Thank you, Raiho." She could not make herself proceed in philosophical slowness. Adepts did not communicate thus unless something portentous was afoot, and this communication originated in the nearest thing to a central headquarters that Gaeandom possessed. Having closed the office door behind her, she sought her stool and hunched anxiously over the papers.

A number at the top indicated the cipher matrix used. She could decode in her head as fast as she could from a book. Dipping brush in ink, she began to write. After a minute she was amused to notice that she was doing calligraphy.

Humor froze and fell out of her as the burden of the message began to appear. At the end she sat motionless, while the sun set and night flowed upward in the room.

"—to those of principal grade throughout the Five Nations, enjoining them to absolute secrecy. Until permitted, you should give to no one the least sign that you possess the following information. Within the hour, you should perform the Exercise of Discretion. . . .

"—you know about a mad quest by an unknown faction, seeking fissionables. . . .

"—authorities ordered monitoring, seismological and radiological, terrestrial and atmospheric. . . . No public mention of this effort has been made, but of course the Minister of War in Yuan stands in a confidential relationship to Prorók Chepa and habitually seeks his counsel. . . .

"—above Chukri. A slight but measurable increase in the background radiation count was observed and aircraft were dispatched to collect samples. . . . Unequivocally products of uranium fission—

"—source unidentified. There were no unambiguous ground tremors on which to triangulate. Either it was an air burst or it took place very far west of us. Both could be true, of course. . . .

"—Northwest Union is not the sole possible culprit. It was never made public, but Yuanese military intelligence has ascertained that a Beneghali attempt to construct a fusion generator was approaching success when the Maurai learned of it and mounted a commando operation which destroyed the plant. Elements within the Federation itself may conceivably be planning revolt. The Domain of Skyholm seems implausible, but certainly the potential capability exists, as it does in Espayn, Free Merica, Meyco, and perhaps some of the marginally technological societies. The explosion or explosions did occur in a high latitude, but there are plenty of uninhabited lands and untrafficked waters to which anybody could send a testing expedition. An accusation like this is much too grave, too apt to bring a violent reaction, for us to make blindly. . . .

"—Soldati governments are keeping the knowledge to themselves for the nonce, informing no foreign powers. . . .

"—you have been told because you are among the Custodians of Humanity. Yours is the task of guidance away from a new Death Time and, very likely, Gaea's casting off of our whole species. On the practical side, you are in a network that covers much of the globe. Keep alert. If you believe you have any smallest clue, report it in cipher. . . .

"—whoever is responsible for this must be found out and annihilated. You are the defensive cells of Gaea. Through you, now, acts the Life Force."

—Vanna sat long in the dusk, alone with this newest truth. Finally she folded the papers and tucked them into her bosom, to carry home and burn. They felt harsh against her skin. Abruptly she put elbows on desk, buried face in hands, and wept.

XII

The door at the top of the front stairs opened and afternoon sunlight struck dazzlingly downward into the Pey-d'Or. A dozen drinkers looked up from their tables, as did Sesi from her stance, and saw a pair of bulky shadows athwart that brilliance. The door closed again behind them and boots thumped. Wariness fell on the men together with the returned gloom, for these newcomers were strangers, and armed.

They stopped at the bottom of the stairs and peered around. At this hour, nearly all patrons were sailors from ships in port. Among their burly, shabby-brightly-clad forms, four were conspicuous as outlanders. One was Plik, who sprawled against the board, legs across the floor. Opposite him, in conversation until now, sat a short, sallow man with short, grizzled hair and beard, long nose, ready smile but wintry eyes, dressed in a high-collared tunic and buckskin trousers. Two benches away, a Maurai had been plying the barmaid with jokes and propositions; she giggled and encouraged him when she wasn't taking orders. Off by himself in a corner was another Maurai, to judge by his blouse, sarong, and sandals; but he was a bizarre sort, short-bodied, long-legged, hair in black and brown stripes, features disharmonic, skin covered by dark splotches of which one made a domino mask. He alone did not stare at the arrivals.

Dressed alike in green, they had insignia of military rank on their sleeves and the emblem of a globe on their shoulders. Their heads bore sklerite helmets, and at their belts were not just combat knives and truncheons, but a pistol apiece.

Sesi moved toward them through an uneasy silence, smiling and swinging her hips a little more than usual. "Greeting, sirs," she said in her accented Francey. "What is your pleasure?"

When the sergeant replied, his own intonation was Eskuara: "We are here on business of the Domain. Attention, everybody!"

A half-drunken deckhand bristled and jeered, "The Domain? Hai, what the devil's going on? I never saw uniforms like yours before, and I've been around, I have."

The corporal took the word, sounding as if his home state was Marnaube: "We belong to a new force, the Terran Guard. The Captain has ordered it."

"A couple of weeks after taking office?" muttered Plik. "Oh, no, hardly. This must be the preorganized outfit that occupied those key points on the ground—and Skyholm—during the glorious revolution. Eh, my friend?" he asked his tablemate.

Mikli Karst leaned close and answered low, "Yes, obviously, but don't say it aloud." He grinned. "You perceive and understand a great deal for a souse, but you're not used to government from the center and I'd hate to see you get in trouble."

Plik scowled and swigged.

"At ease," the sergeant called. "We're going around town making an announcement. Too important for the radio or newspapers alone. Pay heed."

He took a document from a pocket, unfolded it, cleared his throat, and read aloud:

"Talence Jovain Aurillac, Captain of Ileduciel, to the people of the Domain, for its welfare and safety.

"You are aware that an imminent danger has lately compelled the posting of troops aboard the aerostat. This danger still exists. While it does, visits on other than essential business must be suspended. Normal functions and services will be maintained, and the authorities and inhabitants of every state shall continue their normal routines unless otherwise directed.

"Perils and uncertainties confront us on every side—conflicting ambitions and mutinous discontent at home, hostile nations growing in strength abroad, the entire configuration of the world changing at storm speed, politically, socially, economically, technologically, even religiously. Although I am vowed to preserve the integrity of the Domain, that is not possible by freezing ourselves into a new Isolation Era. We must be ready to institute whatever changes are healthful. Some will be radical. Most obviously and immediately, the Domain cannot continue as loosely organized as it has hitherto been. We must have a stronger central authority, prepared to act as swiftly and decisively as needful. To this end, I have established the Terran Guard, a security corps taking precedence over any state militia or police, coequal with the regular armed services but with distinct responsibilities and under the direct command of the Captain.

"People of the Domain, you too can help your country in its hour of peril. Investigation of enemy plans and actions against us is proceeding apace, and you shall have a full account immediately after your government does. Meanwhile, at present certain crucial individuals are missing.

"The most urgently wanted is my kinsman Talence Iern Ferlay, a Senior in his Clan and lieutenant colonel in the Air Force. You have probably seen or heard reports of his violent behavior in Skyholm and his seeming escape from it, aided by persons unknown. One is reluctant to speak ill of a popular figure, and at present he is only under summons as a material witness. However, it has become increasingly clear that he knew much more than he pretended. If he is alive, his testimony will be of the utmost significance in our pursuit of the factions that would undermine us, and withholding it is treasonous. If he is dead, that will at least be a clue for your guardians.

"By this warrant, I demand the help of all who may have knowledge pointing to his whereabouts. I remind them that their first allegiance is to Ileduciel and its Captain. For information leading authorized agents to Talence Iern Ferlay or his body, a reward of five thousand golden aers is offered."

The sergeant read on: "—automatic amnesty . . . preferment . . . physical description as follows—" while Plik shaped a silent whistle, Mikli stroked his beard and smiled, the sailors and Sesi grew wide-eyed, and Wairoa sat observing.

At the end, the sergeant barked, "Is that clear? Any questions?" None came. He snapped a salute and clicked his heels. The corporal imitated him. "In duty to the Captain!" he exclaimed, ritually although it was a ritual new in the Domain. The two men wheeled smartly about and departed.

Again silence prevailed, until the half-drunk seaman slapped palm down on board, a gunshot noise, and bawled, "Zhesu up the mizzenmast! Are they after the Stormrider? Just because he stands against that mother-diddling Gaeanity?"

A nearby man tautened. "Watch your language, mate," he said. "I'm a Gaean, and proud to be."

"Why?" asked a third. "No insult meant, I'm not looking for a fight, but what is it in Gaeanity, anyhow?"

"Truth, that's what's in it," replied the second. "Oh, aye, the fine points are too much for me, and belike I'll never feel Oneness myself, but I know it's real. And so do a holdful of people brighter than you or me, mate."

"It's the coming thing," opined a fourth man. "It's getting harder and harder to deal with Gaeans unless you're a Gaean yourself, or respectful of the creed, anyhow; and a lot of those deals are fat, very fat." He rubbed his chin. "Ye-e-es, I could use five thousand aers. And I've seen Iern myself, strutting around in this same tavern, not long ago."

"Hold on!" shouted the first. "Whoever turns the Stormrider in to his enemies will answer to me." He lifted a knotty fist. "I'm from the Etang. My wife and kids would've been dead, save for him. And by every devil underneath your arse, Iern should've been Captain, too. *He* wouldn't take the kind of shit we're in for. Because mark my words, we're in for plenty."

"Then where's he gone?" demanded the second. "Why'd he run away? What's he got to hide?"

Plik, who had sat inhaling and sipping the mustiness of his wine, murmured to Mikli, "What he has to hide is his hide, I think." The pun came across in the Angley he used.

The Northwesterner nodded. "Your esteemed Captain is being, shall we say, decisive," he replied, low-voiced. "But then, I gather that Iern's action forced his hand."

Plik regarded him closely through the aromatic dimness. The two of them had struck up an acquaintance bordering on friendship. Mikli enjoyed the songs, Plik the accounts of the Northwest Union, each the sardonicism of the other. "I wonder what else you've gathered," the Angleyman said. "What is your real business in Uropa? Your vagueness about it has approached the poetic."

Mikli made his eyebrows repeatedly rise and fall. "Have I been vaguer than the Maurai over there? Nobody brags about commercial and quasi-diplomatic negotiations in progress. That fun gets too expensive."

"But you seem less upset than you might be about what's happened, in spite of Jovain and his followers being frankly cool toward your nation."

"They're cooler toward the Maurai." Mikli started a cigarette and used it for a baton in between puffs. "Interesting paradox. You'd think Gaeans would favor the Maurai, wouldn't you? Ecologically minded society, conservative but tolerant, whereas we Norries tend to be infatuated with machinery and to look on Earth less as a house than a warehouse. But in practice, the Maurai claim a stewardship over the planet that the Gaeans want for themselves, and the Maurai attitude is too rationalistic and pragmatic as well. Also, of course, making the Domain a world power entails sapping the Federation hegemony, something we in the Union would be delighted to help along. On this account, perhaps we'll write yet another chapter in the tortuous history of alliances."

"I wouldn't lay money on that."

"Oh, not now. Jovain isn't about to break off relations with either party soon, or anybody else, assuming he could do it. The authority of the Captain has its limits, which can't be greatly expanded overnight, and besides, he'll naturally want to keep his options open. Expect simply a shift of emphasis, while he consolidates his position —starting with disposal, one way or another, of that cumbersome Talence Iern Ferlay. Pending our airman's apprehension, his reputation is a convenient target. Have you heard the news about his wife?"

Plik nodded, tossed off his drink, and signaled for more. "You needn't repeat the obvious to me," he said, "especially since I disagree with your implied prediction."

"Oh? Why?"

"Granted, I am a souse, but a well-read souse, and a bit of a poet to boot. They say that only mathematics can make sense of the physical world. Well, only poetry and music can make sense of the human world, because humans are the least rational of the animals and how else shall we symbolize their madness?" Plik shook his head. "No, my chum whom I am about to cadge a refill from, no, you lay out a neat scheme for Captain Jovain, but I guarantee you it won't come to pass. It's neat, you see, logical, self-interested, therefore not human."

"Indeed? It was formulated by a human, wasn't it? What fatal flaw do you detect?"

"It's a matter of the soul of the people—for every people has a soul, and if not strictly immortal, it's damnably hard to kill." Plik spread his hands. "I can't explain, unless indirectly through a song." Sesi arrived. He threw an arm around her buttocks and rubbed his cheek across her belly. "A fresh charge, Vineleaf, provided this gentleman pays."

"I will," Mikli said, "if you'll promise me that song."

"I can't," Plik answered. "Such things come if they choose. When you try to force them, they send idiot changelings instead. But I think that this one has chosen to come. Give me another day or two."

"Fair enough." Mikli laid a coin on the table. "And another calvados for me, dear doxy."

A buzz sounded. He was alert instantly as a cat. "No, hold mine." From a pouch at his belt he took a miniaturized radio transceiver, laid it to his ear, listened for a moment, and brought the input disc before his lips for a brief reply in Unglish.

Rising, he said, "I'm sorry, I must go. Drink my share of the money in good cheer, Plik, if not exactly good health."

"You've been waiting for that message these past few days," said the Angleyman.

Mikli smiled, his smile that was peculiarly fetching despite the bad teeth. "No epochal deduction. Yes, we've had a party in Alleman country, searching out trade possibilities, and they've just called in that they'll arrive here shortly. I have to make arrangements. You make your song—and the barmaid, for that matter."

He left. A few minutes later, Wairoa the lonely did likewise. Emerging on the street, he sauntered idly back and forth a while, until he had the information he needed to send him in a particular direction. Given his distinctive appearance, he was a most implausible spy, provided he kept out of normal earshot and did not seem unduly interested in his surroundings.

Thus he saw a weary, dusty, sweaty group ride into town, a light wagon with a covered load in their midst, a large blond woman at their head. He saw Mikli lead a band of men from the Northwestern ship to meet them and escort them back, politely but absolutely fending off curious passersby. He saw the wagon unhitched and a cargo boom lift it onto the deck. Although at a distance, he saw exultation upon Mikli, who capered about and repeatedly kissed the woman's hands; it was not her that the little gray man welcomed, but the freight she had brought.

That night, like a drift of mist, Wairoa slipped aboard. The gangplank was drawn in. Besides the regular watch, a detail stood sentry around the cart. None of them noticed the soft thunk of a rubber-sheathed grapnel he cast from the water where he swam, nor his climbing the rope and creeping over the planks—but then, he took hours, and when he poised motionless, his dappled nudity melted into moonlight and shadow. He did not come nearer the wagon than a hatch coaming he used for concealment. It was not necessary. The sole instrument he carried was a hand-held ultrasonic beam generator; it was small and simple because he, alone on the ship and in the world, could hear and analyze the echoes of its probing.

As cautiously as he proceeded, he did not regain the wharf until the stream had begun to shiver with a wan eastern gray. Thereupon he hastened to the inn where Terai had quarters.

2

Night came again, bringing wind and wrack. The moon, well past the half, had risen when Plik left the building that stood over the Pey-d'Or.

Almost sober, he walked as fast as the murk between far-spaced street lamps allowed, for cold blew about his threadbare coat. Nevertheless the moon, as it seemingly flew in scud, caught a smile on his mouth, and he hummed a tune against the whine of air, scrit and rattle of paper trash; when a tomcat commenced a serenade to some puss behind some pair of shutters, Plik laughed aloud. "Good luck, my friend," he called. "Try going down the chimney."

His way to the decrepit house where he rented a room for himself and another for his books led across the square beside the Cathedral of Corentin. Only the moon shone on it, fitfully, for at this hour it was empty save for him and a dust devil. The church lowered above like a shadow cast on the sky by a twin-peaked mountain. He passed the southwest corner. His footfalls rang hollow on stone.

"Plik! Stop."

He obeyed the voice, turned, and moved in his awkward fashion toward the one who had so quietly hailed him. Iern stepped out of the darkness between wall and tower. Plik broke into a run, reached and embraced him. Iern gave back the hug till the Angleyman groaned, "Please. My ribs may be poor things, but they are mine own."

"I'm sorry." Iern let go and withdrew a pace. "I'm just—glad—too weak a word—glad to see you. Been waiting for hours. Wondered if you'd ever come. Since when has the tavern stayed open this late?"

"It didn't. But Sesi was in a mood for me. She usually gets that way when I'm doing a poem. Psychic pheromones?" Plik's tone sharpened. "Happens you are the subject, old chap. How've you fared?"

He squinted through the shifty light. The Clansman wore a pysan's blouse and baggy trousers. A slouch hat cast obscurity over his countenance, but it could be seen that he was shaven, scrubbed, and well nourished, more than could be said for the balladmaker.

"In haste," Iern related. "You may have guessed I left Skyholm by parachute when Jovain took over." He nodded a trifle smugly as he glimpsed awe. "I knew who I could trust hereabouts, and made my way from place to place, generally at night. Early on, I took the added precaution of swapping my clothes for this outfit." His high spirits faded like a moonbeam sundered by a cloud. "I dared not linger anywhere. Outsiders are always noticed in the countryside, and the news of them spreads faster than you might suppose. I'd endanger any household where I stayed, and probably be tracked down in short order. Obviously I can't go to my mother and her husband; they'll be watched. Kemper seemed my best bet. Much easier to disappear in a city, right? I entered after dark and took my stance here, expecting you'd pass by."

"Me?"

"You're my hope now, Plik. You know every back alley and thieves' den Kemper has got, and who in them would be willing to help, for a price or for love." Iern doubled his fists and hung his head. "I know it's asking much. We've been drinking companions but scarcely blood brothers. This isn't even your country. But where else can I turn? The respectable folk who might agree are too conspicuous, and have no experience at this sort of thing anyway. That's why I decided against trying Beynac and its environs. I don't think you'd run a great risk yourself. All I want is for you to introduce me to someone who'll hide me until—till—I can see what I ought to do next. I've been counting on it."

Plik stood silent a while. The wind ruffled his thin hair. He began to shiver a little. Then, slowly: "I don't believe I'd better."

The pilot stared at him, mute.

"Not that I wouldn't," Plik went on. "I'm with you more than you can understand, Talence Iern Ferlay. Your cause goes beyond you, beyond the Domain. There's a transcendence about it that I can't prove but do feel, through and through my marrow. Who am I to deny the gods what they are groping after, whatever that is?"

The other man's eyes widened further. "You're a weird one."

"True. Always have been. Else I'd never make a line of poetry. It'd all be mere verse. I freely admit most of it is." Plik's grin, crooked as the moon, straightened out into somberness. "The trouble is, I don't know anybody we can rely on." He described the announcement of the reward. "Five thousand aers is a fortune in that class of society—in fact, it's a way out of that class; and additional help is promised too. If a given person kept faith, somebody else would be bound to find out and turn you in."

Iern looked away, down a street that was a tunnel of darkness. "Jovain wants me worse than I realized," he said, word by word. "Why? I'm not leading the opposition to him. None exists yet, except in certain hearts." He paused. "Yes. When I'm dead, soon my wife — Yes, provided she doesn't learn he had me murdered. He tried it himself, about three years ago."

Again Plik stood dumb, shivering more violently, until Iern perforce looked back at him. Pain twisted the homely face. "I'm sorry," the singer mumbled. "I thought you knew."

"What?"

"About her. Well, the mails only go weekly between our Breizheg farms, and few have radios. It's common knowledge here. Clansfolk newly returned from Skyholm have talked, and now the very newspapers—" Plik laid hands on Iern's shoulders. "Talence Faylis Ferlay is openly living with Captain Jovain. She stood by his side at the inaugural. She lent her name to a call for unity under his leadership. Yesterday she announced she'll start a divorce process against you. She spoke of cruelty, infidelity, and desertion."

He dropped his clasp and waited. Iern did not stir. His expression was unreadable below the hatbrim. The wind piped. Cloud shadows fled across pavement and made the carven stones above appear to move.

Finally Iern whispered, "I was afraid of that. Her brother— But I kept telling myself I was being unjust, Faylis herself would never . . . conspire, betray—" A shudder went through him. He cleared his throat, spat, raised a boot and slammed it down so it boomed. "The bitch!" he roared. "The treacherous little bitch!"

"Sh, sh, keep quiet, a police squad might hear."

Iern spun on his heel and blundered back into the murk where wall met tower. He struck his fist on the hardness, kept it pressed there, jammed his brow to it, squeezed his eyes shut.

Plik, waiting in the open, could not see that. He did hear strangled words—"I loved her once. She loved me"—and afterward the harsh, gut-deep sobbing of a man who has had no practice with tears.

It didn't take long. Iern came forth, gait machine-firm, back straight and head borne high. The hat still masked him. His tone was flat and remote: "Your pardon. It was a shock. Probably I can steal a boat and singlehand her to Angleylann or Eria. Can you suggest any good possibilities there?"

Plik hugged himself and made his teeth stop chattering. "No, I'm afraid not. In the more prosperous nations, word about you would soon get back here, if the hunt is out as seriously as I think, and agents would come regardless of whatever sanctuary you'd been promised. You could go to earth in some wretched half-barbarian village, but do you have the skills to support yourself under those conditions? Nobody there can afford to feed an idler. And how would you keep in touch with your partisans on this side?"

"Why should I? What's the use?"

"You will because you must," Plik said gravely. "I tell you, you smell of fate as the air before a thunderstorm smells of lightning." He pondered. "I've no idea what your destiny is. Maybe fate itself doesn't yet know. Maybe you won't save but will destroy the soul of your people. I only know that when something alien to a spirit enters it—and Jovain is bringing alienness with him—then demons break free."

"Arh, you and your flights of fancy!" barked Iern. "No sense in standing about freezing. I'd better find me that boat and be away before dawn."

It blazed in Plik. He grabbed clumsily at the pysan blouse. "No, wait, wait! A refuge that could also become a base of operations—" He dragged on the coarse fabric. His feet jittered beneath him. "Come on! We can talk while we go. I have the waterfront in mind anyway."

Iern's manner remained metallic, but he fell into stride. The two left the square and started down a street beyond. It was narrow, lampless, hemmed in by walls; they must move carefully. "What is your notion?"

"You know about the ships from the Maurai Federation and the Northwest Union, don't you?" Plik replied. "They've lain in port for months, while personnel of theirs scuttled hither and yon about the Domain. Everybody's irritatingly secretive, but I'm convinced that whatever their different objectives may be, both crews are from their respective governments." His laugh clanked. "Maybe they're assigned to spy on each other."

Emotion tinged Iern's voice: "By Charles, yes! Why didn't I remember? The Maurai—"

"M-m-m, I wouldn't. I've tried to cultivate those sailors, and they've been cordial, invited me to parties aboard ship—and never let slip a flinking word that meant anything. I realize you favor closer relations with the Federation, but that doesn't give you such a claim on their gratitude that they'd likely take the substantial risk of compromising their mission by hiding you. I repeat, they're a quite unknown quantity. Besides, I doubt they could hide you. You couldn't be tucked away indefinitely below decks, I suppose, because visitors like me get guided tours all over the ship, and they plan on a lengthy stay. A white man in their midst would stand out like a hay-fevered nose."

"Well . . . who besides them? The Norrmen?"

"Yes. I've gotten to know their chief somewhat, an amusing scoundrel by the name of Mikli Karst. My strong impression is he'd take you aboard, if only for love of mischief—though I daresay, too, he'd think of options that a popular member of the Aerogens, in exile, might open for his country. Remember, the Northwest Union is the underdog vis-à-vis the Maurai, and determined to change that condition. This requires taking chances.

"Furthermore, he gave me to understand yesterday, when he stopped in for a drink, that he expects to leave betimes. Evidently he's accomplished something important; he did fairly well at hiding his excitement, but I saw it aquiver in him, oh, yes, I saw. In fact, he was making arrangements—notifying the harbormaster, et cetera—arrangements for a cruise of a day or two, starting this morning, as an exercise for his men before they begin the long voyage home. Which gives you that much time already, out of sight of your enemies. For the short while left that the ship lies docked again, why, it shouldn't be hard to keep you hidden. I imagine you could actually appear on deck at intervals, if you're dressed like a Norrman. Those fellows come and go so much that a casual glance would lump you in among them."

"You're persuasive," Iern said, "but I see a large non sequitur or two."

"Why should they not collect the reward for you, eh? Well, Mikli won't, I warrant. The money is nothing to him; he has other sharks to fry. At worst, he'll refuse and send you off—because he *is* a secret agent of some kind, who'll not want to attract unnecessary attention to himself. If he does take you in, I assure you none of his crew will speak of it. I've found them as close-mouthed in their way as the Maurai."

Still Iern hesitated. "You talk fast," he said, "but your trade is words. Are you certain you're a judge of people? And I—I'm a flyer and castlekeeper. Nothing more, really. What do *I* know about people, or politics, or, or anything? Where do you get this fantasy, Plik, that I could possibly lead more than a squadron of aircraft?"

The street opened on the docks. Beyond shadowy hulls and raking, rocking masts, the water glimmered beneath the hasty moon. Watchmen's lanterns were like stars in their loneliness. The wind was quieting down but growing colder yet.

Iern looked west, toward the two great ships that had traveled halfway around the planet. He squared his shoulders. "We'll try it," he said. "Lead on."

They met scant delay in gaining admission onto *Mount Hood.* Her commander, if not her captain, had left orders to inform him of any unusual happening, no matter the hour. After a brief colloquy, the guards at the rail extended a gangplank, and quite soon after that, Iern and Plik were having brandy-charged coffee in Mikli Karst's cabin.

The atmosphere was warm in there, thick and acrid from the host's cigarettes and the poet's clay pipe. Iern resisted an urge to fan the smoke off with his hand. It curled blue through the glow of two lamps. Outside came a strum of wind in rigging, slap of waves against strakes, creak of hawsers. The deck swayed slightly, to and fro. The men sat on a leather-covered bench that curled around a table. A filing cabinet and typewriter were secured nearby. Additional were a bed with a beaverskin blanket, a bureau, and a door to a private bath. Otherwise bookshelves, enclosed against motion, occupied bulkhead space. The volumes were in a variety of languages, and several were ancient—not from the century before the Judgment, for most such were long decayed, but from two or three hundred years earlier, when paper and bindings were durable. No pictures were displayed, though Plik had said Mikli was married and a father. The single personal item to be seen, held fast on its shelf by guying threads, was a statuette of a cat-headed woman in a pleated skirt. Mikli had remarked that he had recovered it, years ago, from what seemed to be the ruins of a museum in the Nile swamps.

Talk had gone on until dawn was turning the portholes gray.

"We're agreed," said the small man. "I'll get you to my country, and it will grant you asylum. Naturally, I cannot guarantee the conditions, but they'll be loose."

"How can you be sure?" asked Iern, and coughed.

"Why, that quaint institution we are pleased to call the government of the Northwest Union has no power to keep anyone out whom a Lodge would make welcome, and I know that Wolf will be happy to receive you. Discreetly, no doubt; secretly if possible. You'll have to bide your time before you contact any underground movements in the Domain. But at best they'll need time themselves to organize . . . if they actually decide to. Never fear, Colonel Ferlay, we'll meanwhile keep tedium from your doorstep."

Plik blew a smoke ring and watched it dissolve in the haze. "Human schemes," he said. "Ah, well."

Mikli raised a finger. His gaze pierced Iern's. "Now please understand," he said. "As of this moment, you are free to go ashore and forget us. However, once you have accepted our protection, we'll have to think about our own security too: which means you'll have to obey orders. Are you prepared to do so?"

"Of course," Iern told him. "I understand entirely, and accept your protection and thank you for it."

"Splendid!" Enthusiasm rose in Mikli. "Then I can tell you that you'll be in the western hemisphere quicker than you guessed." His look sought Plik. "This is not matter for drunken babble, or even for verse."

The Angleyman smiled. "I do babble in my cups like the proverbial brook," he said, "though I hope less monotonously. But have you ever heard me spill anything I shouldn't? Most of being a poet is knowing what to omit."

The Norrman smiled back. "I wish we could talk further, you and I. We're equally addicted to circumlocutions."

He turned to the Clansman. "We're not going out today exclusively to refresh our seamanship," he said. "You may have noticed an aircraft pod aboard. We're not supposed to fly over the Domain, but once we're below the horizon, who cares? Not that we planned to mention the pod will be empty, when this ship returns here." He felt after a fresh cigarette. "The case is that we have urgent reason to send something home. Never mind what."

"Home?" snapped Iern. "How?"

Mikli put a lighter to his cigarette and inhaled. "Ah, you would be aware of the problem, wouldn't you? That the Maurai restrict what types of aircraft we may have. Nothing that could get from here to the Union in a single flight except perhaps, barely, the eastern wilderness fringe. Humiliating, no? Well, we'll refuel along the way."

Iern visualized the globe. "That must be in Mong country."

Mikli gave him a sharp glance. "Eh? Why do you say that?"

High-keyed as he was, Iern's mind raced. "I don't imagine you would leave a stationful of valuable fuel by itself in the wilds. Too big a temptation for local savages, to capture it, fill their lamps, and plunder the metal. Besides, you'd have trouble keeping its existence secret from the Maurai for long. So you have a hushed little arrangement with somebody. In Krasnaya, I think. It's reasonably well located for the purpose, and not poor and primitive like Chukri or bustling and officious like Yuan."

"You'd better cultivate some hushedness yourself, Ferlay," snapped Mikli, before he donned amiability and suggested, "Concentrate your interest on the pilot. She's a charming young lady who's completed her task in Uropa. Alas, I do not recommend you make your attentions physical. She's also a cougar."

He reapproached earnestness: "You cause me to modify the plan. I wasn't going to ride along. But in light of this remarkable development—your imaginable potential—well, I'll come too. I'd like to be a witness and have a voice when you meet our leaders."

Iern gave him a hard stare. "Besides," the Stormrider said, "you've more or less finished your work here, at least for the present. Otherwise you'd never consider leaving. And the coup in Skyholm means that you, like the Maurai, had better do nothing more about the Domain until you can get a line on how things are likely to go."

Mikli cackled laughter. "Marvelous! Congratulations! You're absolutely right. It's as plain as a corpse at an orgy, but you are right."

He rose. "Well," he proposed, "what say I have Ronica Birken called, she's the pilot, and a special breakfast prepared, and we get acquainted over it?" He looked at the third man. "Um-m, Plik, I hate to be inhospitable, but perhaps it would be better all around if you don't hear certain things."

The Angleyman smiled and unfolded his lanky length. "Oh, yes," he said. "Anyhow, I'm dog-weary, and after getting some sleep I have a song to finish."

Iern glanced uneasily upward from his seat. "Is that the one you mentioned, about me?" he asked.

Plik nodded. "Yes, but have no fears. It's much less about you than about the myth of you."

"What myth?"

"Ah, hardly more than a fresh-begotten cell in the womb. It'll grow, and when it's born— But only poets recognize myths for what they are, and who really listens to poets?"

Plik stooped. His arms went around Iern, his lips close to the Clansman's ear. "Farewell, Prince," he breathed. "We may never see each other again, but when you've become a god, or a hero or a demon, I'll still remember you were a damned good drinking companion."

"What the chaos do you mean?" Iern returned the embrace. "Oh, never mind. You're crazy, but you did save me and I do thank you, more'n I can ever tell. Goodbye."

Plik straightened and left the cabin. Mikli followed him to the door and signaled the watch, who let the visitor go down the gangplank.

The sun was not quite up, but whiteness lifted above eastward roofs, few stars remained to see, and the moon and Skyholm stood pallid in a haze that had come to rest after the breeze dropped. As yet, the docks were virtually deserted. Dew glittered on their tarred planks and bollards. A couple of early seagulls slanted above a sleet-colored river. Plik's breath smoked. He shambled fast. His fingers plucked invisible strings while he sang, low, what had come out of him thus far.

"They have cast the Prince from his throne on high
And proclaimed a strange new day.
They have named it with freedom's ancient name
In Caesar's ancient way.
They enjoin our souls that we seek fresh goals,
Since loosed from tyranny,
And abjure the Prince and his wicked works,
For theirs is mastery."

His voice loudened, and suddenly the tune was a set of trumpet calls.

"But hear a dusty bugle rave,
The snarling of the drums,
A whisper from a sunken grave
Where the bones are astir: 'He comes! He comes! He comes!'
And see his flag of moonlit clouds advance
Across a waste where cold winds roam.
The ghosts of old go riding through the dark to meet him.
So shall the Prince come home!"

3

Helpless, Terai stood on his ship and watched the North-westerner leave her moorings, pass him by, and glide on downstream. The sun had barely cleared eastward roofs; its rays made vivid the green-and-white flag that mocked him with a wave of farewell. No sail was on the catamaran. Mikli Karst wasn't waiting for the tide, but was expending fuel in his auxiliary to get away.

What to do, what to do? For the hundredth or thousandth time, Terai beat thoughts against an immovable rock of fact. His mind felt bruised and bleeding.

That slut and her gang—or those bold patriots, no matter which words when the truth they clothed was deadly—they had brought a load of fissionables aboard. Wairoa had reported no doubt of it. Nor was there any doubt that the stuff was bound for the Union . . . though where, in that vast wild realm, remained a question.

Terai had considered pursuit, but, irony, *Mount Hood* was swifter if less capacious than his monohull. He had considered a radio call to N'Zealann, asking the Navy to intercept, but that task would be next to impossible, as wide as the seas and as few as the suitable aircraft were. Besides, he expected the ship would return here in a day or two. Her captain had said she would, and several of her personnel had stayed behind. If she did not, it would excite comment, the last thing Karst must want. (But he had probably completed his political undertakings in the Domain for the present, whatever they had been. They seemed to involve a relationship with Talence Jovain Aurillac, whose regime would need a while to consolidate its power before it could be useful to anybody else. If in the meantime it proved unviable, then the Norrmen had better not be caught in close touch with it. Therefore Karst himself should be going home before long.)

Given this much, Terai's conclusion was that the enemy would fly their ghastly treasure back, launching their plane when beyond sight. They'd need to refuel, but must have made provision beforehand. Where and what—a ship at sea, an island, someplace on their continent—was unforeseeable without knowledge of their destination; and they might well take the precaution of following a circuitous route.

The aircraft aboard *Hivao* was superior in aces and spades to anything they could have: a jet, not a propeller job, speedy, armed, with at least a fourth again the range, and as crippled in this situation as Terai himself. He'd considered using it for surveillance, but of course Karst wouldn't launch his vulnerable machine then; he'd radio an excuse for keeping to sea and wait till the Maurai tanks ran dry. It wouldn't take too long, even given refills from the mother vessel, since the kilometers added up in a hurry during such an operation. The Domain lords wouldn't sell more fuel because they didn't allow foreign overflights, and their claims included the Bay of Bisky. (Doubtless Karst counted on taking off unnoticed.)

Terai had seriously thought of sailing out, getting aloft, and trying to sink *Mount Hood* from above. Telescopes in Skyholm—his glance sought its disc, but sun-glare still hid it—might well pick that up, leading to criminal charges and diplomatic difficulties; could be worthwhile, though, if it worked. It would not, he decided. His jet being a fighter, not a bomber, he doubted he could send a full-sized ship to the bottom, especially if the Domain dispatched warplanes to interfere. And if he did, the casings of the plutonium wouldn't last in salt water, and he'd have released whole kilos of poison into the sea, he, a man of Oceania. For what good, anyhow? The devils in Noramerica must already have such a hoard that the loss would make no critical difference, and the secret of their intentions would die with *this* crew of them.

The catamaran decreased in sight. Terai thumped the rail, hurting his flesh in hopes that that would soften his agony.

"I think I'll go get drunk," he rasped.

The first mate, who had been standing beside him, nodded. "I plan the same when my watch ends, sir. If you want, I can give you the name and address of a fine little piece. She's clean and not too expensive."

"No, thanks." Terai turned convulsively away and lumbered to the gangplank. *Sex for hire—how corrupt are we getting in these damned idle months?* He winced. *Besides, I doubt I could do anything in that line at the moment.* A billow of longing: *Except with you, Elena.*

As he debarked, he didn't notice who had come onto the wharf. Fingers plucked at his elbow. He forced his head around and looked into the mask of Wairoa. "I've word, skipper," said the man who claimed nine mothers.

"Aii?" Terai blinked. A leap went through his breast. "Hope, do you mean? Come *on!*"

He hustled his associate back aboard and into his cabin. It was more homelike, and more secure, than the suite he kept at an inn so that he might have space for entertaining business guests. Tatami mats gave back the light that poured in, together with pungent coolness, through opened ports. The bulkheads were covered in burlap and pictures from his house. Books lined a big desk, mostly reference works, a couple of biographies and the like; Terai was not much for fiction or poetry. Between the desk and his bunk he had rigged a workbench, where in free hours he often turned wire, stones, and shells into jewelry, when he didn't borrow *Hivao*'s metalworking shop.

He virtually thrust Wairoa into a chair and stretched an arm—muscles moved like pythons—toward a liquor rack. "What'll you have?" he asked. "Tanaroa! A chance for us after all?"

"Plain soda water, if you please."

"Well, um, well, yes, we've a way to go till noon, but—" Terai cracked a bottle for his visitor and poured a stiff whiskey for himself. His mass could absorb it without his feeling more than summery. He plumped himself down at the desk and got busy stuffing his pipe. "Speak, man. Don't keep me on the hook like this."

"I promise no deliverance, you realize," Wairoa said in his most pedantic style. "What I have is some new information, which has led me to an idea."

Terai curbed his impatience and invoked his brain. It wasn't the world's best, he acknowledged, but it was well stocked and reliable. "Carry on."

"Since learning that *Mount Hood* was going out today, I've maintained close watch on her," Wairoa said. Terai wondered when, where, and how the fellow ever slept. "Late last night, two men came aboard. One stayed. The other left just before sunrise. Judging from portraits in periodicals and verbal descriptions, that one who remained was the Talence Iern Ferlay who is being sought by the new Captain."

Terai sucked in a breath. *It was a thick, windy night, and Wairoa must have been at a distance, but he has owl's eyes.* "What in Nan's name could that mean?"

"Please let me finish giving you the data, then I'll offer my interpretation. Ferlay's companion was an alcoholic Angley balladmonger you may recall from a low-life tavern near the cathedral—Peyt Rensoon, nicknamed Plik. The colloquy between him and the men awake aboard the ship made plain that he persuaded them to rouse Mikli Karst, whereupon he and Ferlay disappeared into Karst's cabin for hours. The watch was too close by for me to slip on deck. When at last he emerged and made his way home, Rensoon was exuberant, bawling forth a song that I interpreted as a recent composition of his own and rebellious in sentiment. I didn't track him far, thinking I'd better keep *Mount Hood* in view. Nothing significant occurred, however. Ferlay must be aboard her yet, outbound."

"Gr-r-rum-m." Having gotten his pipe going, Terai drew comfort from it while he pondered. "What do you make of this? You've had longer to think about it than I have."

"I've gathered that Ferlay was an habitué of Rensoon's favorite tavern whenever he was in Kemper, therefore doubtless a friend of Rensoon's. He must have made contact and requested help in finding a refuge. Now Rensoon, in turn, had grown friendly with Karst. You didn't see that, of course, but I did. The idea would be natural, would it not, that the Norrman could very well convey the fugitive to his homeland. The Union would have nothing to lose and possibly something to gain. Such an escapade would appeal to Karst; and he's presumably dispatching his fissionables anyway."

Terai rolled smoke across his tongue and cradled the warm little bowl in his hands. "Well, all right, they give a refugee a ride. Likeliest on their plane. What of it?"

"Rensoon was in that cabin a long while," Wairoa said. "He may well have picked up clues to their destination."

"*Ho!*" Terai leaped out of his chair.

"If we got an intimation of the flight plan—mainly, where they propose to refuel—we could follow and overtake them."

"Yes, yes!" Terai bellowed. "Lesu Haristi!"

He paced the narrow confines, back and forth, back and forth, the pipe raging between his teeth. "Yes, if we could time it so we caught them over uninhabited land, we could force them down. That's the real gain, Wairoa. You did a tremendous thing when you discovered that they are, definitely, Norrmen who've been collecting that vile stuff over the years. But we've no proof beyond your word. Our superiors will believe; who else? You know how cynical people have gotten in the Islands. They wouldn't support another war on somebody's naked word, and a full-dress war is what it'll take to eliminate this monstrosity, especially if we don't know what it really is or a damn thing more than that it *is.*" He snatched his glass and poured fire down his throat. "If we capture them, though, we have the physical evidence. And we have them, to interrogate. By the Triad, I've never used torture in my life, but with these hands I'll do whatever is necessary to get the truth out, and lose no sleep afterward. I have a wife and children; I hope for grandchildren."

Unaccustomed to speaking at length, he jerked to a halt, settled back into his chair, and regarded the multiple man.

"Torture should not be required, certainly not where Rensoon is concerned," Wairoa said. "He'll have scant motive to stay silent, if we promise a reward and point out that we have no reason to harm his chum Ferlay. I anticipate the main problem as being the paucity of his information. Karst will scarcely have divulged anything on purpose. I'll need to hunt for data accidentally let slip, of which

Rensoon may well have no conscious recollection. A long-drawn business, I'm afraid, preceded by the lengthy process—bribe or threat or appeal—of getting his cooperation."

Terai glowered at the coals in his pipe. "And at the end we may draw blank. I understand. But we must try, of course. Where is he?"

"Asleep in his rooming house, I'm sure. I've just come back from reconnoitering it. We can't kidnap him out of there. He wouldn't take kindly to being shaken awake, no matter what we offered, and a card game downstairs bids fair to continue all day."

"M-m, yes, we hardly want the police on our necks. But meanwhile that cargo of misery and death will be winging off—"

"My thought is this," Wairoa said. "Let us spend the next several hours getting our ship cleared for her own 'exercise.' Short notice, but you can claim the Norrmen inspired you and today happens to be convenient for it. I'll keep Rensoon's house under observation. When he finally emerges, I'll let you know. You can handle the matter in a way I can't. Seek him out, be genial, stand him a drink, invite him aboard *Hivao* for an impromptu celebration. Once we have him here, we'll lock him away and put out to sea. When it's feasible, we'll launch our jet—you and I and he, prisoner—and take off in a westerly direction. I'll interrogate as we fly. If we get a lead on where the enemy plane is bound, we'll adjust our course accordingly. If not, we'll get Rensoon back to Kemper and pay him an amount of drinking money for the trouble we've caused him.

"There is my proposal. Do you see flaws?"

"No," Terai said after a while. "Nothing important that we're likely to lose. And maybe a world to gain. Or at least to save."

XIII

The airplane was rather small, except for capacious fuel tanks, and its present load took up most of what space there was in the fuselage. Ronica Birken at the controls, Talence Iern Ferlay beside her, Mikli Karst behind, had scarcely more room for movement than their seats offered. That was tolerable, because they should be breaking their flight in about twelve hours. The craft was a twin-engined propeller-driven monoplane with the additional capacity for vertical takeoff and landing that operation from shipboard required.

Well designed within the limitations the Maurai impose, Iern thought. *No wonder the Northwesterners chafe. I certainly would.*

He glanced at the big young woman. *The pilot's well designed too. And she did a neat job of getting us off, in those heavy seas.*

They ran beneath him now, gray and green, shaking their white manes, but the night wind that raised them had died down and fifteen hundred meters of altitude made a vast circle of them, intricately and shiftingly patterned. Only a few clouds, sunlit from aft, broke the blue above. Skyholm had dropped under the eastern horizon.

Iern's pulse beat high. He should have been tired after his sleepless night; excitement had forbidden his getting a nap while *Mount Hood* bore him off. He wasn't, nor did he feel dread or grief anymore. An underground part of him reproved the rest for being lighthearted, even joyful, when the Domain and everybody he held dear lay under a weight of trouble. He paid small attention. He was free, off to do battle but first to explore the world!

Faylis' betrayal had stopped hurting. *At least things have come out in the open. I don't suppose I'll want revenge on her* when *I return. Already she seems like a dream dreamed long ago.*

And meanwhile— He was growing acutely aware of Ronica. He hadn't had a woman for worse than two weeks, Faylis reluctant and he too busy to seek elsewhere (which would doubtless have been wrong anyway when the land mourned good old Captain Toma) and afterward on the run. This Norrie wench was, indeed, magnificently engineered and obviously full of life. If he wasn't being wishful, he also felt a—perhaps not exactly sultriness—a banked fire in her, ready to blaze up at a touch.

"I'd be interested to fly this craft myself," he ventured.

She gave him a straightforward look. Her eyes were ocean-colored in the strong features, her hair fell past her shoulders in thick amber waves, contained only by a beaded headband. Her bosom stretched a shirt unbuttoned halfway down it; trousers hugged full hips and long legs. A huge sheath knife added an arousing suggestion of wildness. "Why, sure." Her voice came husky through the engine-throb that filled the cabin and made it tremble. "I was sort of counting on you to spell me, in fact, since learning you're a Stormrider. Maybe you can teach me a few tricks." Her Angley was more accented and less fluent than Mikli's, but it sufficed.

Iern grinned. "Gladly, mamzell. What sort of tricks have you in mind?"

Mikli's ashtray breath reached him as a laugh at his back. The Norrman laughed often, though the sound was more like a fox-yelp than a peal. "If you're thinking of flying a mattress, which you probably are, dismiss the idea," he advised. "Insistence can be hazardous to life and limb. I know."

Ronica flushed under her tan but did not appear offended. "I don't muck around with married men," she said matter-of-factly.

"Oh, you can't call me married—" Iern began.

She did show a trace of anger. "Mikli is. His wife's a sweet person who's been kind to me, but she has the misfortune to love him. You watch out yourself, Ferlay. He'll proposition anything on two legs, and I'm not sure about some of the quadrupeds."

And he her superior! Iern braced himself for unpleasantness.

Mikli only laughed again. "We make a fine team, Ronica and I," he said. "She does bait splendidly, doesn't she? And gives as good as she gets. It passes the time. I miss her when we aren't working together, and for her part, she's been known to enjoy jokes of mine, proving that she has her human share of low-mindedness."

"Enough of this frogfart," snapped the woman. She turned her attention forward. "Yes, you can try your hand later, Ferlay, but she's running nicely on automatic and I'd sooner leave it that way as long as can be."

"I understand," Iern said. "A light plane is vulnerable to weather;

that's when it wants a pilot. Do you think we'll get some?"

"Oh, weather we've always got," she pointed out with a renewed smile. "As for the bad kind, who knows?" A cloud drifted across her mood. She sighed. "Once people did. We could ourselves. A station in orbit—"

Mikli cleared his throat. Ronica chopped her words off. Mikli took over: "Missy Birken isn't my subordinate—not in my corps at all. Lucky for me. How would you like to try keeping her under military discipline? But occasionally she takes off from her regular work and does something entirely different, and a few times this has brought us into cooperation."

"What is your work?" Iern inquired of her.

She hesitated, shook her head, and replied, "Better change the subject."

Iern thought of the crates behind him. He had been emphatically informed that their contents were no affair of his. Books, maybe? But what could be secret about a book? Dangerous drugs? He couldn't imagine the woman trafficking in that, and besides, if he remembered aright, the Northwest Union had no tariffs or restrictions on trade, foreign or domestic. Valuable metals? Every ancient site in western Uropa had lain stripped for centuries, and while he'd heard mention of her having gone east, he didn't think anything salvageable remained there either. The tribes had brought nothing of that nature to exchange for civilized wares for generations.

What *had* the outlanders been doing in the Domain? Plik's impression that it was government rather than commercial business seemed vaguely reinforced by Iern's recent experiences, but might be mistaken. Moreover, from what the Clansman knew about the Union—exceedingly little, he realized—he wondered if you could make a distinction between public and private agencies there.

His exuberance shrank. He was going to be very much alone for a while, in a strange land among folk whose purposes were unknown. "May I ask some questions?" he said. "You don't have to answer any that you, um, shouldn't."

"Sure, go ahead." Ronica smiled at him once more, reached over, and patted his hand. Hers was warm and hard. Her sleeves were rolled up; sunlight struck gold from the tiny hairs on her arm. He found it an effort to concentrate on collecting information. "I gather you've been through a rough spell. Why not put you at ease? Remember, though, I want your story in return!"

"With pleasure . . . well, not complete pleasure, under the circumstances, but— Oh, for a start, was my guess right about a stop in Krasnaya?"

"Yes," Mikli responded. "Let's hope the opposition doesn't make the same guess."

"Opposition?"

"The Maurai, who else?" Ronica snarled. "We'll ride a flamer if they catch us."

"They won't try, actually," Mikli said. "What reason do they know to? Doubtless they'll notice that you and I have not come back to Kemper on the ship, and conclude that I've finished my dirty work and you are flying me home. But whatever my villainy was, it must be finished; whatever report I intend to make, I must have alternative channels of communication for it. Besides, we'll be in Seattle before the ship returns to port. Chasing us would be an expensive exercise in pointlessness. No, I was simply hoping that any investigation they do make doesn't lead them to our cozy arrangement in Krasnaya."

Iern felt his throat and shoulder muscles tighten. An electric tingle passed through him. "The way you talk," he breathed, "it's proof— you and they, secret agents, foreign agents, in the Domain—"

"No comment," Mikli said lightly and kindled a cigarette.

Ronica wrinkled her nose at the smell and made a production of cranking down a window several centimeters. The chill air that came in was somehow calming to Iern, as was her speech: "Well, this much comment. We were busy, aye, but not to your harm. The Maurai are our enemies, not your beautiful country and nice people."

"What *were* you doing?" he dared to challenge.

"Nothing against you! And Mikli—well—"

"She's been told no more than she needed to know, which was minimal," the Norrman said. "Standard precaution in intelligence work. Yes, most of my assignment was to gather intelligence, especially about Maurai activities in Uropa. Also, I hoped to give a few of your leaders second thoughts about closer interaction with the Federation. I'll be happy to explain to you, at length, why that's a bad idea for the Domain as well as distressing to the Union."

"Did the coup take you by surprise?" Iern demanded.

"Oh, my, yes. I'm frankly underjoyed. Captain Jovain can be expected to cultivate Gaeanity, which is opposed to everything we stand for in the Northwest. And he speaks of the Domain's taking an active role around the world: beginning in eastern Uropa, guiding civilization as it revives there. A Gaean-dominated continent— Well, maybe you can do something about that, my friend."

Ronica gave Iern a regard first startled, then thoughtful.

"And yet," the Clansman protested, "you are making for Krasnaya, a Gaean country."

"That's different. Haven't you heard? The Mong Wars are over," Mikli replied with mild sarcasm. "Relations between their states and the Northwest Union are correct, if not precisely ecstatic. True, Yuan, the largest and strongest, does still throw its weight around to a degree. But Krasnaya no longer gets involved in any shenanigans. It's peaceful to the point of timidity."

"What have you in mind?"

"A certain polk—regiment, you might say—in Krasnaya maintains an airfield in a fairly isolated location. Its commander is willing to sell supplies to Northwestern flyers who happen by. We do have treaties allowing us a limited number of flights per year over Mong territory. The Maurai know that, of course, but I think we've kept knowledge of this particular field, I mean its cooperativeness, from them. Our pilots don't use it often, bonus payments keep its officers discreet, and why or how should the enlisted personnel notify foreigners? Generally the place serves us as a refueling station for exploratory flights to the wild country east and south."

Exploratory in search of what? wondered Iern.

Ronica asked his next question for him: "I've not been through there myself. Not my stamping grounds. A chance to see Uropa was irresistible, but otherwise— What'll we do, Mikli? How guard our cargo from snoopers? Camp by the plane?"

"No, it would be an insult to refuse hospitality. But the seals on these crates will be unbroken when we leave in the morning," her associate said. "The commander does not wish to lose his little sideline, nor have the details of it passed on to higher echelons."

"Good! I'll really be wanting to stretch myself, come nightfall." Ronica moved her elbows in circles, an exercise with incidental effects pleasing to Iern. He felt relieved by what he had heard, a sense of being among comrades.

Her glance at him buttressed it. "You must be plumb worn raggedy," she said. "Why don't we have lunch, and afterward you try for a piece of sleep? When you wake, I'd like to hear about you."

He nodded. His head was, in truth, beginning to feel both scooped-out and heavy.

"I put sandwiches and a bottle of wine in that red bag on top of our luggage, next to you, Mikli," she went on. "First, though, I got to piss." She unbuckled her safety belt. "Hand me the pot, will you?

Hell, when we don't even have any aisle space— It makes no big difference, and the contortionist act needed by a girl will probably be fascinating, but I'll think the better of you, Iern Ferlay, if you'll just stare out the window for a few minutes."

2

The hour was past noon when Terai got aloft. He opened the pod, boarded his jet together with Wairoa and Plik, and stood it on its airy tails just as soon as *Hivao* had cleared the river mouth. To an indignant call from the coast guard station, he replied, "I am sorry, I know this is illegal and I apologize, but an emergency has arisen. It is my own action and responsibility, no one else's. Please note I have not overflown any land and am bound west overseas. If you wish to make a formal complaint, please contact the Federation ambassador." As yet, there was insufficient traffic between the two nations to warrant consulates.

He pressurized the cabin and climbed steeply. Nothing in Uropa could overhaul this machine except, maybe, a Weather Corps vehicle of the first class, and to the best of his knowledge, all such were too distant from here, and unarmed as well. He turned for a glance, through a rear panel, at the dwindling, sinking moon of Skyholm. If they yonder wanted to fire-blast him, they'd better hurry. He did not expect they would, when his infraction was minor and they had everything else to think about.

The cabin had places for half a dozen, twice as many as were here. Terai had seen no reason to bring more. If he found his quarry under suitable conditions, he could force it down by himself, and either he or Wairoa could use the guns to cover the other if that one had to go out on the ground and secure their prisoners. If he failed to make the capture, extra men would have wasted their time, possibly risked their lives, for nothing; and much remained for them to learn and accomplish in the Domain, he hoped. According to doctrine, he, the chief of the expedition, should have dispatched a subordinate rather than himself. But their mission was not of a nature to make him indispensable. His second in command could perfectly well take charge, whereas Terai and Wairoa had become a uniquely qualified team in the field.

Moreover—the huge body tautened—that was probably Mikli Karst ahead. Terai had a score to pay off.

Sitting alongside a resentful Plik, Wairoa strove to mollify him: "Yes, we did lure you on board in order to kidnap you like this. We regret it far more deeply than we regret violating Domain airspace, but after we have explained, you may agree we had no choice. We will do you no injury, and we will return you as soon as possible and pay you a generous compensation."

The Angleyman leaned back, let knobbly fists fall open, and regarded his seatmate for a while. "How will you return me?" he inquired. "I doubt the authorities will let you land, after what's happened."

"We can call our ship to stand out to sea and take us aboard. Or if that isn't practical for some reason, we can get you passage of a different sort, through Espayn, for example. It would take longer, but I repeat, you shall be well paid for your time."

Plik stared around him, at the sleek cabin, gun posts, windows full of sky but equipped with steel shutters. His gaze went back to the abnormal form beside him, and thence to Terai. Both Maurai had donned white uniforms that stood forth against his own shirt and trousers (faded, patched, darned) like snow against fallen leaves. "This must be a large matter," he said slowly.

Wairoa's tone became stern. "It is."

Terai looked around again. "Y'know, Plik," he drawled, "it should be an adventure for you. See a bit of the world, hey?"

The singer coughed out a laugh of sorts. "Shrewd! . . . Well, we can talk, at least." He rubbed bloodshot eyes. "First, what about a drink, followed by breakfast?"

Wairoa nodded, unbuckled, and went aft to a cabinet. He brought back a flask of whiskey at which Plik snatched, before he returned to start heating food and making coffee on a hotplate. Terai leveled the jet off at ten kilometers and put it on autopilot. It hissed along at close to the speed of sound.

He moved to seat himself across the aisle from Plik, lean over toward the passenger, and rumble, "We haven't much time. We need your help fast, or it's no good, none of it. Can we start talking at once?"

"Aaah!" Plik's Adam's apple, which had bobbed an impressive number of times, came to rest as he lowered the flask. "Yes, I feel better already. But you owe me an explanation, you realize. Suppose you begin."

Terai brought forth pipe and tobacco pouch. He kept his look upon them while they occupied his hands and he said awkwardly: "We know you guided Talence Iern Ferlay aboard the Northwestern ship, and take for granted he's being flown to what he thinks is refuge. Understand, we're sure he's quite innocent in this ugly business. We mean him no harm, and in fact we can offer him asylum ourselves—honest asylum. What made us seize you was the hope you can give us clues to exactly where he's headed, so we can overhaul him and the rest before it's too late."

"Too late for what?"

"I wish I didn't have to say this. That plane is delivering the stuff for a new War of Judgment."

Plik almost dropped the bottle. Terai moved his head up and down, up and down. "Yes," he said, "nuclear explosives."

He described the evidence in harsh words. "Iern Ferlay must simply have happened along," he finished. "I daresay Mikli took him back because he might be a useful pawn. Besides, Mikli lives for troublemaking—stirring up the anthill, he called it once when we talked. Do you know, the rest of his gang may be sincere, but I believe Mikli Karst is mad. That he wants to put the torch to the world so he can see it burn."

"Nuclear explosives," Plik whispered. "My feeling was truer than I knew."

"What?"

"Archetypes," said Plik wildly. "The demons are stirring against the gods. But who are the demons and who the gods?"

He took a hefty swig before he twisted around to peer at Wairoa. "Who are *you?*" he called.

Wairoa did not look up from his work. "I have given you my name," he said.

"What are you, then? The same question, of course." Plik became owlish. "I . . . do not . . . wish to give gratuitous insult. But you are a strange one, I have wondered about you before, and now I need to know somewhat." He looked at Terai. "I can't agree to help you, whatever my help may be, until I understand what myth we are in—can I?"

Well, if he's a lunatic too, I think he's harmless, and best we humor him. Terai explained the genetic mosaic.

Plik's face stiffened. "Thanks," he said in no friendly voice. "That gives me a better idea of why the Gaeans regard you Maurai as the ultimate enemy."

"Hunh?" replied Terai, astonished. "Are you a Gaean?"

"No, no. I am a Christian; a Nicene Christian—laughably archaic, no? Yet God has always allowed much strangeness to go about in the world, and reveals Himself in ways that are often terrible. I referred to your so coldly making free with life."

Wairoa brought a tray whereon stood a plate of ham, eggs, and buttered toast, a glass of tomato juice, and a mug of coffee. "You have not asked me whether I object to existence," he clipped.

Plik looked long at him, while Wairoa arranged the tray in its rack and after he had sat down again. "I think you may be the loneliest human creature on Earth," the Angleyman murmured finally, "but you control yourself like a steel spring."

Wairoa started the least bit, and almost spoke.

"Your special senses and abilities—" Plik went on. "Yes, it is something to be the great Watchman. And at the end of the world, you can let that coiled spring fly free."

Terai lost patience. "What in Nan's name are you blithering about?" he exclaimed. "See here, you, the power to smash several cities is escaping westward. We need your cooperation to stop that, and by Tanaroa, we'll have it. You are not going to slip into a drunken stupor till we've gotten your information out of you!"

At once he regretted his bullying note. The relief was enormous when Plik nodded vigorously and said, "Oh, you shall have it, whatever it is and whatever it may be worth. I've read my history books. Should I want Vineleaf screaming among ruins, the skin burned off her and her eyeballs melted? Only let me feed first." He gave hearty attention to his tray.

The dread that lay in the bones of every Maurai crawled out of Terai's and into his flesh. "How can you say something like that," he mumbled, "and then sit and eat like that?"

Plik engulfed a forkful of ham. His answer was quasi-cheerful: "Why, I am a poet of sorts, and horror is the proper business of poets."

After a conventional interrogation, the interplay between him and Wairoa became an event which Terai could only watch in awe and incomprehension, with chest aching from held breath and strained muscles, while the aircraft speared westward. Later Wairoa said it had been unique in his own experience. He had never before worked with anyone like Plik, nor did he imagine he ever would again.

The two of them felt their way forward through nuance after nuance. There was hypnosis, to bring out buried memories, but there also came to be a kind of mutual trance, wherein a silence might have as much meaning as a sentence, and the words gave little to listening

Terai. Subliminal whispers and shifts of expression (and posture, odor, what else?) must likewise have passed back and forth, as Plik lay on a pad in the aisle and Wairoa hunkered above him.

—" *'Krasnaya,' he guessed?*"

"*Mikli's face, his body— That guess was right.*"

—"*Mikli was amused?*"

"*Yes, to me he felt somehow, creepily amused by all this.—*"

In the end, after the better part of an hour, Plik rose, shuddered, got back in his seat and groped for his bottle. Wairoa settled down cross-legged in the aisle for a time before he too stood up, sought Terai, and said, expressionless:

"They intend to refuel in Krasnaya. It is reasonably close to being on a direct route to the northern tier of the Union, where secret activities can be most readily carried out; and they have no reason to suppose we have reason to pursue them. Besides, Mikli was making snap decisions, including the decision to go along himself. It's his way. I've gained a number of clues to his character which may prove useful. But they aren't immediately relevant. As for his precise destination, I have considered the airfields in Krasnaya and narrowed down the possibilities to a fairly small territorial range. Give me a map."

Terai did not pause to marvel at the encyclopedic mind which had so incidentally revealed itself. He just obeyed. Wairoa pointed to an area not far north of the greatest of the Great Lakes. "Air traffic is slight over that region; it's mostly wilderness. Make for it, use radar when you have approached, and the chances appear good that we can detect them and intercept them well ahead of whatever goal they have."

"Lesu Haristi—" Terai breathed.

"If you have no further need of me, I would like to rest awhile," Wairoa said. He withdrew to the rear of the passenger section, settled down, and did not sleep but . . . meditated?

3

While the Captain's office was not large, it was, above every place else in Skyholm, tradition-hallowed. No photograph of those who formerly occupied it had ever been replaced on the bulkheads, though time had turned the oldest nearly faceless. Beneath that of

Charles Talence and directly above the desk hung, framed, the original copy of the Declaration of Tours, signed by him and the entire Ancestral crew—a seed from which the Domain would grow. (*"We pledge ourselves to more than a rebuilding of what the material world has lost. It is to the causes of peace, order, justice, and ultimate reunion that we dedicate our lives and this instrumentality whose warders we have become. . . .* ") The desk itself was a gift from High Midi when that realm joined; glass protected the ivory inlays on its top, but five centuries of use had left their scuffs and scars on oak panels. A modern console—radiophone, video screen, computer terminal, printer, et cetera, et cetera—was the wellspring and channel of information, but on a shelf beside it stood books that had risen with the Thirty. None but scholars could now read that French Bible, the novels by Jane Austen and Castelo Branco, comedies of Holberg, poems of Villon and Goethe, but they were the last such relics that had not crumbled away. The wool carpet covering the deck in subdued colors was no antique, but it did express the gratitude of Devon in Angleylann after Skyholm had blasted a pirate fleet a generation ago. Hundreds of years earlier, a Captain had caused to be engraved above the outer door the words *We Serve.*

Seated in a chair that threatened to buckle under his weight, Mattas Olvera was like a boot kicked through a museum case. He grunted, snorted, belched, scratched his armpits and bulging belly. Fleas hopped in his whiskers and greasy robe. His cigar filled the room with stench. Behind the desk, Jovain must keep insisting to himself that this new arrival was his ucheny, come to advise him on matters of doctrine, and that perhaps the Captaincy had indeed shriveled to a museum exhibit and the time was overpast to give it fresh life.

"I'm no politician," Mattas gobbled. "The fine details of wheedling and diddling aren't for me, except where it comes to getting at a juicy young wench, haw-aw-aw! But I do understand you can't press forward too fast, oh, yes." He wagged a finger. The nail was black-rimmed. "However, boy, there's such a thing as moving too slowly, also. Right now most people will go along with you, because they don't know any clear reason not to. They've families to worry about, positions, possessions, their own sweet necks; they hope if they obey, they'll be let continue living as usual. That includes the opposition. Don't give it a chance to harden."

"I know." Jovain suppressed his irritation.

"What are you doing, then?"

"The hunt is out for Iern Ferlay, and Faylis is helping break down his reputation among the populace, reveal him for the puffball he is."

Her condition was that I guarantee his safety and freedom. Well, yes, but I can't control events like a puppeteer, can I? "I'm in daily conference with Seniors and other leaders who incline toward me for their different reasons—Gaeanity, pacifism, social progress"—Jovain sketched a smile—"or, for that matter, restoration of social virtue."

"Not incompatible, those. I never claimed to be a good example." Mattas spread his arms wide. "Gaea is in every aspect of what we are. Go ahead, denounce the latter-day decadence, call for the purity of old. If it turns 'em toward Gaea, it's right."

"You know about my Terran Guard," Jovain continued. "It's just a nucleus, of course. But as it grows, it will give us every reason to proceed with the disarming of the Aerogens and the various states. More efficient, more controllable, therefore less provocative to foreign countries." *And obedient not to any homeland lord, but directly to the Captain.* "The Espaynians are ready to cooperate."

The day before, Yago Dyas Garsaya had sat in that very chair opposite the desk and discussed that very subject.

"Yes, Your Dignity, my government is prepared for a certain amount of humiliation," he said. "Was that not the plan? You justify your actions by a threat from my country. We apologize for not having had better curbs on our extremists. We can swallow that much pride for the sake of the larger purpose." His palms made a gesture that looked negligent but, Jovain knew, was studied. "After all, every informed person is aware that our regime is not yet totally settled into every part of its territory; and as for the Domain public, the admission makes us more human, less sinister. Both governments pledge to work together for a lasting peace. Reduction of armaments is an early step."

"Can the Zheneral actually afford that?" asked Jovain. He had been over this ground before, but there was so much to keep in mind, and everything so damnably fluid—

"Oh, yes, if it is genuinely mutual," said the Zheneral's envoy. "What real menace do you and we face except each other?"

"Well, eastern Uropa is in ferment," Jovain must say.

"Allied, we can keep those tribes polite, with minimal force. The Maurai have shown us how." The Espaynian paused to choose words. "*They* are a long way off, Your Dignity, like the Northwest Union, to name our two most important rivals. We need not worry seriously about either in the near future."

"I am not so sure," Jovain answered, remembering a fragmentary report he had gotten this morning. Two aircraft headed west, one of them launched in sly defiance of the sovereignty now inherent in him, and one blatantly— He should summon Mikli Karst, by the code that the outland agent had given him, and require a statement. But a thousand pieces of business were clamoring at him, and he didn't even have a proper staff organized.

"Maybe," the delegate conceded. "Doesn't that make solidarity of our two countries the more urgent?" He smiled. "A paradox, that in order to strengthen ourselves against the misguided, we begin by cutting back our armed forces, no? But so the situation is."

True: because the military of both lands have hitherto been regionally based, their first loyalty to a Clan or a neighborhood or some such archaism. Hope stirred in Jovain. How could a world that included Faylis not be full of it? "Right," he said fervently. "Lowered barriers between us, increased trade, an open road for the missionaries."

"This will take time, you realize," he reminded Mattas. "We have to overcome inherited distrust, vested interests—well, you know."

"I know about gnats and their concerns," the ucheny snapped. "The which are not mine. I'm here to ask how soon you'll start letting in the Truth."

"The Domain has never restricted freedom of religion," Jovain said, roweled afresh. "Or philosophy."

"You know what I mean, son."

Jovain stroked his beard. The silkiness was soothing. "I do," he said. "Haven't we talked about it through the past two or three years? Financial help for the teachers and seers, out of the Captain's treasury; eventually, a requirement that all children be exposed to the teaching, as part of their education—" In haste: "Oh, I'm not betraying you. Those are still my goals. But I begin to see how long-drawn and complicated it'll be—"

Mattas could be strict when he wished. "And I've told you, mold while the clay is soft," he retorted. "The reactionaries are off balance. They don't know what to expect, and they'll rejoice if you give them, forthwith, things like strengthened peace and a call for moral renewal. Let the package include a little aid for *us*—not much at first, nor especially marked for what it is— Do you follow me?"

Jovain returned home late. He always did. When would the day come for him and Faylis to be their own people? As was, every moment they had alone must be stolen from something else. Well, he kept assuring her, well, he was barely in office, he must consolidate his position and set the work of their common dream in train.

Hitherto she had taken it calmly. He was getting an impression that she was more interested in the idea of love than she was in making love. Unlike Irmali—but between him and Irmali there had mostly been a courteous coolness, for longer years than he cared to number.

He found Faylis in their apartment. It was as meager as any; equality aloft was another tradition. She had servants, though, and could occupy herself with the book research that she enjoyed and that was, in fact, valuable to him.

He found her weeping.

He knelt before her chair, embraced the slight form, begged her to tell him what was wrong and thereafter crooned at her. Finally she could lay a hand across the paper on her lap. "M-m-my father," she wrung out. "A letter from my father. He disowns me. Because of what I've done . . . with you— *O-o-o-oh!*" she screamed, and hugged herself to him. "O-o-oh, oh, oh."

He let her cry, wishing she would finish, while his mind raced: *That means worse than the family Mayn; it could mean the whole Clan Ashcroft against me, except Lorens, after the old man gets through corresponding back and forth. As if I didn't already have Irmali's Lundgards on my neck— This will jerk every traditionalist knee in the Domain. Never mind whether Castle-keeper So-and-So keeps half a dozen concubines, his Captain is supposed to be perfect, never sullying the anim of Charles, right?*

Iern would have been better schooled in hypocrisy than I am.

The rowdy power of Mattas stood forth in Jovain. He lifted his head above his shoulder, where the head of his woman lay, and told himself: *Okay. As Mikli Karst is fond of putting it, okay. This had to be met sooner or later. I shall overcome. I will overcome.*

XIV

Flying west lengthened a day, but the sun had swung low when the Maurai overtook their quarry.

Refreshed by sleep, Iern was telling Ronica about himself. He had intended to concentrate on the glamorous aspects, but despite her wide-eyed fascination she kept asking questions that struck deep. Nevertheless he was having a marvelous time.

A part of that came from the wonder unrolling beneath him. He had not imagined such an immensity of forest, like a dark-green ocean, broken only by a frequent gleam of lakes or a silver thread of river—and now he flew parallel to the greatest lake of all, an inland sea. It shone on the left as if it too were silver which the long yellow sun-rays had turned molten.

The aircraft droned and shivered. He fancied that it strained forward, in the manner of a horse when it scents the stable near the end of a ride. Mikli had consulted a map a short while ago and estimated that an hour's travel remained. Iern would welcome release from this cramped, noisy, vibrating room; and yet while Ronica gave him her full heed, he felt no hurry about it.

"—flitted down to Pireff," he said. "That's the chief port in Ellas. Its master is friendly to the Domain, which sends a fair bit of trade his way. Our plan was to hire a boat and spend a couple of months knocking about the islands—"

The airplane rocked. An angry whine sawed through fuselage and windows. Smoke trailed. The intruder craft swept about in an arc of kilometers, ahead of this one, tilting back and forth, well-nigh speaking the taunt: "Take a good look."

Iern did. It was a sizable twin-engined jet, gray-painted, so that light off metal did not dazzle him and he could make out gun turrets and rocket launcher. It bore no insignia, but he had read everything he could find about the world's flying machines and knew those rakish lines.

"Charles!" he yelled. "That's a Maurai fighter!"

Sweat sprang forth on his skin, icy and gamy. His pulse almost drowned out Ronica's blast of profanity. Behind him, Mikli's voice came faint: "They've tracked us. How and why? Tune in the radio, girl, for hell's sake! Standard band."

Ronica nodded and obeyed. Her lip was curled back from her teeth.

Basso out of the receiver: "—calling you. Come in and be quick about it." Iern identified a N'Zealann accent in the Francey. The speaker shifted to a different language, of which he caught just a few words—Unglish, he supposed. A thrumming calm took him over. He had small idea of what this encounter meant, and none of what course it would take, but he was a Stormrider.

Mikli leaned past him and ripped out a reply. The jet climbed from sight. Its spokesman answered in his turn. Unable to follow the dialogue, Iern glanced back at the Norrman and saw apprehensiveness flicker across his furrowed countenance.

Silence fell, save for the engines. Ronica switched off the transmitter and explained starkly to the Clansman: "They demand we surrender. There's a broad stretch of beach not far ahead, for landing. If we don't, they'll force us down."

"What . . . is this . . . about?" he asked.

"Wrong place to discuss that." She continued in Angley as she inquired, "Any thoughts, Mikli?"

"Well, we could honor their request," her associate replied.

She missed his derision. "No!" she flared. "I'd pull the sky down first. If they took us prisoner, they'd find out about Orion—from *us.*"

A secret, and enormous, Iern guessed. Aloud: "I've never heard that the Maurai torture people."

"They would if necessary, after they'd seen our cargo," Mikli answered. "But I doubt they would need to. They have consummate doctors and psychologists. Drugs or . . . whatever means they used to get the information that put them on our trail. . . . Oh, yes, they'd wring our knowledge from us, to the last drop."

Ronica turned steely. She peered before her, laid fingers around chin, and murmured, "We could land as they say, then make a break for the woods."

"And starve to death?" Iern protested, before he remembered this wasn't his battle, maybe.

"Oh, I'd get us to civilization, and in fine shape," she said mechanically. "I'm a professional at that sort of thing." Her look sought him.

"You sit tight. They've no cause to hurt you, I think."

"You forget what Lohannaso told us," Mikli reminded. "We are not to get out until commanded. He can make a vertical landing the same as us, his guns covering us every centimeter of the way. If we run, he'll open fire. I know him; we've sparred before. He hates inflicting death or injury, but when he reckons he must, he doesn't waste time agonizing over the decision."

Ronica nodded. "And anyhow," she said slowly, "they'd clap hands on the plutonium."

The what? It was like a thundercrack in Iern's head. *No, I misheard, surely I misheard.*

Ronica nodded again. "Okay, we've got a single choice," she went on. Her tone was quite level. "I'll crash us in the lake. They won't recover a thing."

"Wait a minute!" exclaimed Iern and Mikli together.

Her gaze went back to the passenger. "I'm sorry, Ferlay," she said low. "You could've parachuted first if I'd watched my tongue. But you've heard what only dead men are supposed to know, outside of Orion."

He tensed himself to seize her. Her knife leaped from the sheath and pointed at his throat. He knew expert handling when he saw it, and pulled back. Her left hand operated the stick and brought the airplane banking around.

"They'll blast us if we act suspiciously," Mikli warned.

Ronica grinned like a skull. "Let them. We'll crash and burn among the trees. If they have any sense, they won't come near the wreck. The crates and those brittle old warheads will be broken, the plutonium scattered everywhere around. Not nice."

Mikli spoke in Unglish. Ronica shook her head and told Iern: "He's not anxious to die, but there isn't a thing he can do about it. No weapon on him, our firearms stashed out of reach, and if you behave the least bit funny, Mikli, dear, I'll put us into a dive on the spot. Notice how low I've brought us; it'd be impossible to pull out. . . . Iern, I really am sorry. I couldn't do this to you if I weren't here myself. I think you'd have loved to see Orion rise. I would have."

"She's crazy, a fanatic," Mikli babbled.

"No," Ronica said. "I gave my oath, that's all."

The lake filled more and more of the world-circle. The Maurai jet screamed past. Ronica uttered a brief laugh. "They're wondering what the devil *they* can do," she observed. Her wariness toward the men never slackened.

Low above conifers, the sun filled the cabin with a haze of luminance. *Sun!* It exploded in Iern. The duel that he and Jovain had fought, over a dreamland a million years ago and a million light-years remote— He didn't pause to think further.

"Hold, hold," he said, while the knife poised under his jugular. "We may have a chance yet. To keep your secret and save our lives. Barely possible. I am a Stormrider."

Something akin to dawn shone in the woman's face. A whisper in Iern declared that she was in truth no fanatic, she savored life more than most. But her blade remained unwavering. "Say on," she ordered. "Fast."

"We'll need parachutes," tumbled from him. "While we put them on— Mikli, talk to the Maurai. Deceive them. I gather that's your specialty. Afterward, Ronica, let me have the controls." They were dual. He had already taken them, and found the airplane a nimble little beast. "I'm more skilled than you. I'll climb well aloft, and collide with their jet. Both will go down, but we'll be warned, we can bail out."

She stared. "They won't let you steer close."

Energy crackled in Mikli's voice: "I believe they might, once I've blarneyed them. Okay, Ronica, I'm about to scramble after the parachutes, and I'd like to get a pistol while I'm at it, but I don't want to put a bullet through your brain. Do you trust me that far? I too look forward to Orion rising, and the glorious chaos that will follow." Iern heard him unbuckle and crawl back across the freight.

Plutonium, the Clansman thought. *What sort of monsters are these I'm with? But dead I can do nothing, learn nothing, and I won't stay alive unless I save them.*

Mikli handed him a parachute pack. He went through the irksome exercise of securing it to himself in the space available. Meanwhile Ronica returned the plane to an obedient course. "Put on your own gear," Mikli said to her; and to Iern: "Don't get playful, my friend. I did retrieve a pistol, but it's cocked for you, not the lady."

Having seen a possibility of making his goal, he's willing to walk a tightrope, Iern decided. *It probably gives him pleasure.* For his part, he felt altogether alive. This was like daring a hurricane again.

Mikli stretched forward and switched on the transmitter. Unglish barked to and fro. Wilderness passed beneath. Finally he signed off and reported:

"I told them what's plausible, that we considered crashing ourselves before we'd yield to them. Next I said we'd changed our minds, but want assurance we won't be massacred. Lohannaso claimed he has no such intention, which is doubtless correct, but I insisted we come down simultaneously, rather than he second. That way, I said, we can bargain when we're on the ground, instead of sitting helpless under his guns. I'm sure he expects we'll attempt a dash in among the trees. He also, obviously, means to catch us or shoot us. And at worst, he'll have our plutonium—that wasn't mentioned, but of course he will—and he'll have Ferlay, too, who may well be able to tell him something. He does know you are in our midst, Ferlay; I'd be very interested to hear how he learned it. . . . Well, that's what I've negotiated. Satisfactory?" A flint snicked, a plume of harshness streamed.

"I hope so," Iern said. "May I fly us now, Ronica?"

"Go ahead," she answered. The knife was once more in her hand.

He grabbed altitude. That should not alarm the opposition. They'd assume he was looking for the beach where he was supposed to go. The jet buzzed him, impatiently, and climbed higher.

Soon he did spy the destination, a white crescent shadowed by the pines that gloomed behind. He moved toward it. When above, he went nose up and started backing earthward. After a short while the Maurai craft entered his view, a hundred meters off, matching his descent. He felt how his light vessel shuddered in the turbulence of yonder exhaust.

An inner trembling went through him. He was about to attack brave men who had done him no harm and would have made him welcome, in order to save a pair of devils who— *And to save me. And maybe afterward, somehow, Ronica can explain, can justify—I always have wondered about the rightness of the Power War.*

Go!

He kicked the pedals and shoved the stick. Vision and equilibrium spun dizzily, propellers howled, metal rang. He saw how the Maurai veered; but he was the Stormrider, and his aircraft was a limb of himself.

They struck. The force slammed back through him.

"Out!" he roared, slipped his safety belt, and lunged for the door on his side. Ronica went the opposite way. Mikli followed.

Iern twisted through whistling air, he pulled his ripcord, the chute blossomed white and smote him with deceleration. Then he was free, shrouds in hand, steering for earth. Not far away he saw Ronica and Mikli, likewise liberated.

His gaze pounced on the planes. The Northwestern fell in ruin, along a stone's trajectory, ablaze. It struck water; waves fountained, steam roiled; it was gone. Fleetingly, Iern thought of its cargo. The lake must have softened the impact, kept the containers from breaking open. Eventually they would disintegrate and release the poison. *Let there first be time for a salvage expedition.*

The jet was still in flight, staggering. Iern had tried for a frontal collision, to wreck the controls, but instead had taken out the starboard engine and, it seemed, slewed around to crumple the portside wing. The Maurai pilot was good. His machine could not land without smashing, but somehow he forced a direction upon its descent and used what was left him to slow down. He brought it to the lake, a kilometer out. Spray flew, golden in the evening light. The fuselage bobbed for several minutes before it sank. Meanwhile the people within emerged and started swimming. Only one of the three bothered with a flotation cushion.

The knowledge that he had not killed them made Iern sob for joy.

He, Ronica, and Mikli rolled over on the sand, sprang to their feet, shucked their parachutes. The woman had kept her knife, the Norrman his automatic pistol. He gestured at a tangle of bleached driftwood. "Get behind that," he said. "They're bound our way, those kanakas. I suppose they figure they can't survive by themselves in an environment this unlike their South Seas. They may be armed. But we'll have the drop on them."

"Take it easy," Ronica answered. "They won't get here fast." She swung toward Iern. "Oh, great work!" she cried, radiant. "By God, you didn't lie, you are a flaming hell of a flyer!" She seized him to her and kissed him for a thunderful time.

The sun dropped under the pines. Heaven turned greenish. Cold shadows engulfed the beach. *Lap-lap* said wavelets that came in aglimmer from the edge of the world.

As the swimmers drew nigh, recognition lanced through Iern. "Anim of Charles! Plik!" He leaped up and started to cross the log behind which he had been lying.

Ronica grabbed his leg. "Down, you gruntbrain," she rapped. "A well-oiled gun can fire even if it's gotten wet."

Mikli discharged his, a warning shot. The noise went flat and loud across quietness. Startled birds left the boughs where they had settled. Some fluttered high enough that their wings caught sunlight. "Attention!" he shouted in Angley through the tangled dead roots before him. "If you fellows want to come ashore alive, you'll wade in with hands raised and any weapons discarded."

"How'll we get food without guns, or fix it without knives?" bellowed the basso Iern had heard over the radio.

"Oh, fout, you didn't expect to bag anything with those toys, did you?" Ronica called back, almost merrily. "I have a knife, and that's plenty. If I didn't, I could improvise. Behave yourselves, boys, and I'll nursemaid you to safety."

Motion in the water indicated reluctant obedience. The three reached the shallows and walked toward the beach. Drenched garments, clinging to them, revealed no questionable bulges underneath.

Mikli rose. "Very well," he said, and holstered his pistol. "Please remember I'm quick on the draw, Terai."

The huge gray-haired man nodded. Ronica vaulted the driftwood and advanced to meet him and the freakish figure at his side. "Better shed your clothes and let 'em dry," she advised. "Wrap yourselves in parachute cloth. I can't do much about a case of pneumonia, and your race— Oh!" She stopped in her tracks. Her right hand went to her opened mouth, her left clenched into a fist.

Iern scarcely noticed. He was speeding toward Plik. The singer's teeth chattered; he shook and hugged his skinny frame. Iern took him by the shoulders. "What have you done, you bastard?" the Clansman raged.

"N-n-not what . . . what I expected." Misery regarded him. "The aim was to f-f-force the Norrmen down, take them . . . prisoner, con-confiscate their shipment—but you'd have gone free, they'd have brought you to refuge—if those maniacs you're with hadn't— Iern, they were carrying *fissionables.* Judgment stuff! What could I do but cooperate with the Maurai?"

"I discovered that myself. All right, I understand, Plik." Iern released his grip and patted the other on the back. "Not your fault or mine, what's happened. Let's make the best of it together."

"You wouldn't have a drink about you, would you?"

Iern could not help laughing. "No, I'm afraid the nearest obtainable alcohol is a long way off."

"And Sesi still farther." Plik slouched on up the beach.

Approaching Ronica, Iern caught words passing between her and the tawny-skinned giant. "—Then it *is* you," she breathed. "I wasn't sure, I was just a kid and that was twenty years ago, but I could never forget—"

"But do you remember I was your father's friend?" the response rumbled, most gently. "Not his enemy, though bad luck put us on opposite sides in the war. His friend. I came to see your mother because I felt she deserved to hear whatever I could tell her about him, and maybe I could help her."

"We'll have to talk more, later." Ronica turned her back on him and walked off, stiffly. Silent tears gleamed on her cheeks, amidst deepening shadows.

The Maurai men stripped. Iern tried not to stare at the grotesque one. Mikli did not try. Ronica knelt by a parachute. Her blade flashed as if in anger. She cut pieces to serve as towels and togas. "You do the same, Plik," Iern counseled.

"If the lady will look elsewhere," the Angleyman replied.

A grin of sorts passed across her. "Don't be shy," she said. "I know that what cold water does to a man is temporary."

"I never supposed you were inhibited," Iern remarked.

"You've never seen me sober," Plik answered dourly. Ronica heeded his wish and soon he too was sheeted. His shivering began to abate.

Mikli hopped onto a log. "Hark, everybody!" he called. "Gather 'round. We've got to settle things between us."

"Who appointed you boss?" Ronica demanded.

"Chairman," he corrected her. "That's more my métier than yours, no?" The rest of them came to stand before him: the Maurai on the right, Plik and Iern on the left, Ronica alone in the middle. "As a matter of fact," Mikli continued, "you—this girl here, gentlemen—she'll be in charge because she knows how to stay alive in wilderness. You've no way of compelling her, when she has to be free in order to operate. Therefore obey her, if ever you want to see your own womenfolk again.

"Introductions first." He named those present, except for the domino-visaged man, who stated, "Wairoa Haakonu," and no more.

"Now, then," Mikli said sharply. "Why were you pursuing us? Breaking Domain law in the process, I'll bet, and certainly violating Krasnayan airspace. What's your excuse?"

Terai bristled. "You know bloody well," he growled. "Plutonium."

Mikli raised his brows. "What? What are you talking about?"

"You had kilos of plutonium aboard your plane. Federation intelligence has been working for years to nail whoever's been collecting that hell-garbage. We learned you had. Wellantoa has a report from us, of course, but no proof. All that our bare word can do is make them busier in your country than they have been; and you were already the prime suspects. We need physical evidence before we can properly crack down. Did you imagine I'd let you fly off with it, you swine?"

"This is ridiculous. What put such a fantasy into your head? I credited you with common sense, Terai."

"Wairoa slipped aboard your ship after the freight arrived. He had a detector."

"Really? Infallible? See here, I'll explain the situation. We did bring some material from an ancient bomb crater, by request, for scientific study at home. It did have a slight residual radioactivity. If you'd been less excitable, I could show you, but now it's at the bottom of the lake."

Appalled, Iern saw how such possibilities would have the political force to stay the hand of the Federation. "You lie!" he gasped. "Or why did you bespeak plutonium to me when the danger came?"

"That settles it." Terai lifted a fist like a sledgehammer. "One extra word of denial, Karst, and I'll break your back across my knee, if I don't smash your skull and spatter your foul brains." He glared around. "*Nuclear weapons.* After the war, I'll recommend we encase your whole gang in the same concrete we sink them in."

"No!" Anguish rang through Ronica's voice. She lifted her arms. "Not weapons. I swear it."

Compassion softened Terai's tone. "That sounds genuine," he said. "But what are you building, then? Secret powerplants? Doesn't make sense."

They call it Orion, Iern thought. He could not bring himself to reveal that. It would hurt her further, and serve no clear purpose. *Though why should I care?*

"I can't tell you." She drew a shaken breath. "I can only give you my oath it isn't a nuclear weapon. If it were, and I'd found out, I'd have denounced it to the world myself. I swear this, Lohannaso, by my father's memory, my mother's decency, the honor of my Lodge and my people."

I believe she's sincere, Iern thought. *Not that I know her, not really, not yet. But I cannot imagine her as a dissembler.*

What is she, then? A half-barbarian, no doubt; she mentioned living in Laska. Could she have been hoodwinked in her ignorance? That doesn't seem likely. Her talk and behavior show a first-class brain.

Plik's expression, like Terai's, reproached her. "You did gather plutonium in the East," the Angleyman said.

Her nod was jerky. "Yes. For a good end, I repeat. Folk are scared witless by nuclear energy. They have been for centuries. They refuse to think about it, to understand how it can serve, not destroy."

"It is the dragon of the Apocalypse," Plik said. He looked from face to face, and into the forest murk beyond. "Have we, precisely we, come together like this by chance?" He quaked and wrapped his cloth tighter about himself.

That interchange triggered something in Iern. Abruptly the wildwood woman was uttering sense, the civilized man gibberish. Reading accounts of it, Iern had in fact wondered if the Maurai were right in waging their Power War. Why must the unbound atom necessarily be a menace? Surviving chronicles declared that before the Judgment, Old France got perhaps half its energy from that source; and Old France was the lost country in which human beings had been happy and prosperous. They had reached for the stars. . . .

Decision crystallized. *Until I know more, I won't commit to either side. But there does appear to be a fair chance that Ronica is . . . not unjustified.* The realization that he need not shun her went through him in great warm billows.

Laughter of a loon shrilled across the water. Treetops were losing the light that had been theirs.

Mikli cleared his throat. "I'll confess what I suppose you've already deduced," he said. "I overreached myself. My mission was not to acquire fissionables. I simply failed to resist the temptation, and invited Ronica along to see what she could do on the side."

So she's done it before, on this continent, Iern thought. His lust after her grew tempered by . . . fear? No, not really that. . . .

"What was your mission?" Terai inquired.

"What was yours?" Mikli countered.

"Gathering intelligence, especially on any calamities you might be brewing in Uropa."

Ronica had recovered her self-possession. "Hold on," she said in a voice of command. "Stuff the politics. It'll soon be dark. Nobody has a flashlight, hey? Well, we can start a fire with your cigarette lighter, Mikli."

The Norrman felt in his pockets. "I seem to have lost it, probably while whirling head over heels out of the airplane."

"Damn."

"Yes, I call that downright petty of the gods."

"Okay," Ronica said, "we'd better make ready for tonight while we can see what we're doing."

"What will that be?" Iern asked.

Mikli jumped down from the log and gave Ronica an exaggerated bow. "You have the podium, my lady," he said.

She took it, in a catlike upward step, and stood poised against woods and dusking sky. "The three basic survival requirements are water, shelter, and fire, in that order," she declared, "and fire we can do without in a pinch. We'll have to till tomorrow, when I can make a fire drill. But this is late summer in a cold climate. We must have shelter."

"Um, what about food?" Terai wondered.

"That's not urgent. You should be able to manage on air for a month. Actually, though, I'll have something for us to eat before noon."

"Shouldn't we begin work on that shelter?" urged Iern.

She surprised them by replying: "We can put it together in a half hour or less. Let's take a little time first to get straight with each other.

"We're two pairs of rivals and a pair of neutrals, in a country foreign to us all. Except for a few savages, this region is practically uninhabited. If we struck inland, we might find a civilized village, but the odds are against it, when we have no maps. We could blunder around for weeks, and fall is coming on, winter close behind. I propose we follow the lakeshore, more or less southwest. That'll bring us to a fair-sized town—Dulua, if I remember the name right. The distance is, oh, three hundred kilometers, I'd guess. We'll have to keep moving. But we can certainly get there."

"And when we do, what next?" Terai challenged.

Ronica shrugged. "Depends on the locals, no? But Krasnayans are generally pleasant. Or so I've always heard."

"Yes, yes," said Mikli.

Terai glanced at Iern. "Good for you that we're not in Yuan," he said.

"Why?" asked the Clansman.

"You didn't know? Well, what information Wairoa and I gathered is sketchy, but does give strong reason to think the Yuanese supplied most of the equipment for Talence Jovain Aurillac's private army. It was smuggled in through Espayn, which suggests his dire words about that country are a smoke screen, hm?"

Iern stood dumbfounded.

"I told you, take the politics and stick it!" Ronica snapped from above. "Uh-huh, I understand the problem. We Norries don't want you Maurai to go home with whatever additional data you've picked up about Ori—about our project. Like the confirmation that we are the fissionables gatherers, or whatever clues there may be in my identity and Iern's presence. You don't want us to go home full of secrets you haven't learned, plus a warning about what your high command has heard from you. Well, we've got to hang together on the trail. Else we may not live to backstab each other in Dulua. Give me your pledge—cooperation, yes, comradeship—or by God, I'll strike off alone and leave you here to die!"

Iern suppressed a protest; Plik wet his lips; Mikli seemed thoughtful; Terai glowered; Wairoa waited impassive. After a moment, they mumbled agreement.

"Good." Ronica sprang down, smiling. She touched Iern's hand. "I wouldn't really have abandoned you two guys," she whispered. "You're innocent. But I figured we needed some dramatics along about then." She raised her voice. "Okay, let's make that shelter. Follow me."

Plik nudged Iern. "Innocent?" he murmured hoarsely. "Perhaps, in a sense. But not harmless. You're a mightier threat to the world —the old world we've known—than any of these, my friend."

"Do you truly mean that?" the Clansman asked. "How?"

"Upheaval. The forces are gathering for it, and you are at their center. Merciful Christ, but I want a drink!"

Ronica soon found what she sought: a long bough that had fallen and weathered into a pole; a pine with a branch low above the ground, and no dead trees nearby which might topple in a storm, on a site sufficiently elevated that rainwater runoff would not course through; surrounding deadwood and other forest debris, ferns, shrubs, lesser trees which included some broadleafs.

"We could do better if we had more time," she said. Light was failing fast; only the sheen of the lake, visible between trunks and sweet-smelling shoots, relieved gloom. Chill deepened minute by minute. An owl hooted. "A thatch hut, for instance. Or at least a fire in front of our entrance, rocks piled behind to make a reflector. We will do better after tonight, I promise. This is kind of an emergency, and I'll settle for not freezing."

Meanwhile she propped an end of the pole in the fork and started collecting thinner pieces to lean against it on either side. Under her direction, the men did likewise; thereafter they wove sticks and saplings between; foraged for material—branches, moss, fronds, punk, anything—to pile on top until it lay five or six centimeters thick; added a second layer of wands to keep this covering from blowing away. "Check the duff underneath for stones and twigs," Ronica said. "It'll be your mattress. Later we may sleep in luxury on juniper boughs. We do need blanketing. You three drowned rats use the parachutes; the rest of us have dry clothes. But come on, get leaves and stuff to put over you."

They crawled into the shelter and composed themselves, close together, just as night was giving birth to stars. Animal heat made it warm, and weary bodies found the bed amply soft. However, Iern was a while about falling asleep. He had contrived to lie beside Ronica, and became overly aware of her.

2

The trek began, and soon he was astounded. He was having a perfectly glorious time.

Half of it was in bleak, sluicing rain. Afterward mosquitoes came in clouds, and their whine was an irritant almost equal to their bite. Ticks drilled into flesh; extracting them was an art that required care, lest the head stay behind and produce an ulcer. Advised by their guide, men gave a wide berth to the bears they sometimes came upon, and feared rattlesnakes much more, and learned to keep an eye out for poison ivy. There were also brush, windfalls, quagmires, streams, ponds to contest their way and often force them to detour beyond sight of the inland sea. Farther on, they encountered hills along it, and the hollows between were apt to be worse going than the slopes. (A few times they saw mounds of a different sort on the banks above the water, with shards of brick and glass visible through the overgrowth, and shunned them. Those had been villages, centuries ago, and that was too sad a knowledge.) In camp the chores were many for unskilled, uncallused hands to toil at, from the first collecting of firewood to the last stowage of supplies away from thievish animals. The march went on but the forest still reached ahead and around, endless, tenantless, pitiless.

Only when riding a storm or a woman had Iern enjoyed himself so hugely.

He had the wit not to exult aloud, as others did not complain aloud. Much of his pleasure was due to nothing save luck. He was young, in excellent physical condition, naturally dextrous, and possessed of adequate footwear. Poor, raddled Plik must lurch along in shoes that rubbed him raw. Mikli's elegant boots held out, but he admitted that they pinched, and that his wiry frame had fewer reserves of strength than he had thought. Terai commanded plenty, and the versatile hands of a sailor or a smith, but these brooding green intricacies made him feel trapped and wore at his nerves. Wairoa seemed totally adaptable—yet who could tell, when he himself did not?

Iern, though, learned from Ronica.

He learned that rain was a bath, not a scourge, and the way to stay comfortable in it was to strip down to almost nothing, for the chill factor in wet garments was what could kill. (Her body was dazzling, her nudity or seminudity casual—not provocative, as an amicable but cranium-rocking clop across the chops taught him early on.) The juice of wild mint or plantain repelled insects, and the immune system was presently dismissing effects of those that got through. Noises changed from annoyance to fascination; the forest was a treasury of sounds, as it was of odors, tastes, textures, sights—here a muskrat burrow, hidden until Ronica pointed out the traces, there the prints of a fox, meaningless until she read to him the long story they told —never before had he been this aware.

Travel became simpler after she taught him the ways of it. For instance, you parted brush with your shins and then, in the same flow of motion, your forearms, and glided on through. She did not force the pace, anyway. "What's the hurry? You guys should improve as we go. Meanwhile, if we pushed somebody to the point of collapse, that really would keep us too late in these boonies. Let's shoot for an average of, oh, twenty klicks a day."

On four occasions she decreed a layover, two nights on the same spot while they rested and did various jobs such as laundry; they might be soapless, she said, but that was no excuse for being rancid. The first time, she treated Plik's feet, making pads of moss and cloth for the sores while remarking what a variety of alternative materials existed—birdskin, bast. . . . "You're not going anywhere till we've got you properly shod, fellow. Yasu Krist! Didn't your pappy ever tell you a hole in the sock means a hole in the foot?"

"Yesterday you mentioned you could make a boat out of—birchbark, was it?" he said. "Why don't you, and save us this walking?"

"It'd take a while, and we'd be weatherbound a lot, or paddling against winds that'd wear us out worse than any swamp. Also, we'd have to come ashore for most of our necessities. No, for us shank's mare is faster."

Ronica rose from her crouch above Plik's ankles. "I'll get some rawhide for moccasins." She sighed. "I hate killing a deer when we'll have to leave most of the carcass behind. But I've got to, and Brother Crow or Sister Worm will benefit, so the waste isn't too bad."

First she stood in the smoke of the fire she had kindled, using a drill she had made, twigs, tinder, and careful breath. (The drill was wood and parachute cord. She had remarked that sinew could have substituted for the latter, or gut, or various vegetable fibers. Lacking a steel knife, she could have chipped a serviceable blade out of stone.) Iern wondered why she fumigated herself. "Animals fear human scent," she explained. "After all, we've been predators for a million years or more, the paleoanthropologists tell me." (Her vocabulary was another surprise to him.) "They haven't the instincts to understand smoke-smell, unless an actual forest or prairie is burning."

At his request, she demonstrated how she would track her prey—by faint marks in soil and grass, pellets of dung, leaves nibbled in characteristic patterns—and stalk it—in slow, high-arching steps, freezing dead still whenever its constantly shifting attention drifted near her. "At home in Laska, it's fun getting close enough to touch them." Clearly, she would fail if anybody else went along. She vanished in among pines.

Mikli having declined to release his pistol, she would make the kill with her knife. Her sole additional piece of equipment was her rabbit stick, which she carried everywhere "on principle." It was a straight piece of dense wood, about a meter long and as thick as she could comfortably grasp, usually tucked beneath an arm. With it she knocked down anything from a dry branch for fuel to small game spied on the way.

"Once in Laska," she had related, "I met a grizzly, and plain to see, he was in a bad mood. I brandished my stick. It'd be no use in a fight against him, of course, but it made him stop before he charged. 'Why, you nasty little tramp, you,' he thought—which gave me time to reach a tree, bigger'n he could uproot and higher'n he could grab. Eventually he got bored and wandered off."

She returned in the evening, blood-splashed, a skin slung on her back full of meat and selected parts, whatever she expected they could use. As twilight fell and her group settled around the campfire, she needed a while to become cheerful; she sat cross-legged, staring into the flames. Iern asked why. "Today I felt a life run out between my fingers," she said low. Again he must wonder what she really was.

Less personal killing didn't bother her. She whittled out bits of wood which, set in a figure-four shape and baited, upholding a boulder, frequently provided a squirrel or the like for breakfast. She caught fish on wooden spears or bone hooks, or in stone weirs if the party happened to overnight by a stream. Sometimes her hurled stick felled a bird; jay turned out to be delicious. One misty dawn she stripped, camouflaged her head in grass, and swam slowly, silently, off into the lake, until she could slip beneath a flock of ducks and seize two by the legs.

By then, her fellows were generally not spitting meat over a bed of coals. She had taught them how to cook with water in hollow stumps or pits, using heated rocks, or bake in ovens of stone and turf. It conserved vitamins better, she said. For the same reason she tried to make the men eat all organs of an animal; and she boasted of her maggot stew, but in that case she encountered a marked lack of interest.

She didn't press the point, if only because there was no dearth of vegetable food either: berries of numerous kinds, clovers, grass seeds, select parts of cattails, sedges, thistles, dandelions, nettles. Some things required special treatment, such as boiling; some must be avoided, such as purple grass seeds that might carry ergot; some were not available at this time of year, such as the pollen cones of pines, or would require too much processing, such as acorns. However, Ronica proved her claim that the wilderness was a cornucopia for those who knew how to seek and take—"always with care and love," she said in one of her earnest moments.

The moccasins she made for Plik and Mikli were a hasty job, she admitted, but they should serve for the rest of the trip, and they did.

As a rule she was gone throughout most of the day, foraging, while the men hiked. In the later afternoon she reappeared, bearing provender, and guided them to a campground. They had acquired regular duties, whatever they did best or least badly. Plik and Mikli scavenged firewood and cooking stones; Terai dug a hole if that was wanted, or did other heavy labor; Iern and Wairoa, Ronica's aptest pupils, helped her in more skilled tasks, mainly constructing and equipping a shelter.

As they learned and toughened, the travelers began to have leisure: a lunch break, an hour or two around the fire at night before going to sleep—or inside in rainy weather, warmed and dancingly illuminated by another fire safely beyond the entrance, reflecting off a rock wall at its back and roofed if necessary. By tacit consent, talk steered clear of the divisions between them. Ronica might reminisce about the vast variousness of Laska, Iern about Uropa, Terai about the South Seas and the Asian countries he also knew; Mikli might throw in a cynical, funny story; Plik might sing; on a memorable evening, Wairoa told of what he had found in Africa.

The moon dwindled and waxed anew.

3

They were not far from the edge of cultivation. Another four or five days should see them in Dulua.

The night was unseasonably mild, and faring had been easy. Iern could not sleep, he could merely drowse. When he sensed that Ronica was leaving the shelter, he came altogether awake. Lately she and he had been exchanging long glances. He awaited her back soon, from a simple errand of nature, but she did not come. Finally, impulsively, he got up too, picked his way among slumbering forms, and stepped outside.

The moon was full, as it had last been when he fell like Lucifer, how long and long ago. Low above the great lake, it cast a glade which ripples broke into countless tiny golden wires upon obsidian, each with its own life. Elsewhere, stars gleamed. Light made hoar the grass that sloped back toward the trees; it filled them with silver and shadow, while the cone of the thatch hut became a finger pointing at the galaxy. Silence dwelt under heaven. A breeze ghosted moist, subtly pine-tinged.

Iern had left his wrapping of parachute silk behind. Like the others, he hung his clothes up to air before he retired. Coolness caressed his skin, dew his feet. Somehow he knew where to seek, a rivulet that glimmered and faintly chimed on its way across a hillside into the lake. Ronica sat there, on turf that summer had turned thick and sallow. Her knees drawn up and arms laid around them, she gazed out over the water. Moon-glow frosted the hair spilling down her breasts.

She lifted her face toward him. "Hi," she said tonelessly.

"May I join you?" he requested.

"Sure." She hesitated. "I may be in want of company. Or maybe not. Let's see." She patted the ground beside her.

He lowered himself. Through the centimeters between them, he thought he could feel the radiant heat of her blood . . . drumtide of her heart—? . . . She turned her eyes back outward.

A time passed. Now and then her mouth or brow twitched slightly, as if in pain. Finally he could not but murmur: "What's troubling you, Ronica?"

She made no reply. He waited before he said, "All right, I'll keep quiet."

"Thanks for that, Iern," she answered. "You're good people."

Still she looked eastward, to where moon and constellations were ascending. The sky wheeled majestic around the Pole Star. He remembered Orion. . . . No, not yet. Orion was for winter, when the year must die and a new year come to birth.

Suddenly she leaned over, caught his hand, and cried from deep within: "Oh, God, Iern, what am I going to do? We're almost there."

She is surprise upon surprise, he thought. Hope flared, but he kept himself moveless, save for returning the pressure of her fingers, and his own voice muted. "What do you mean, Ronica? What's wrong?"

Her free hand made a fist and beat the earth. "We—trailmates—Terai's such a decent man, and Wairoa—oh, I don't know, he's a mystery, except that he may be the bravest human being I've ever met—

"Not too much worry about you or Plik," she blurted. "I think we can do pretty well by you in the Northwest Union, and not badly by him. But those Maurai, they're enemy, it can't be helped, they are, and we cannot let them carry back the news they've gotten. We cannot. It would end any last uncertainty in Wellantoa, you see, and give clues, and our venture is so desperate at best. Mikli talked to me about—his pistol or my knife while they sleep—but no, no, no, wasn't that deer bad enough? I said I'd kill him if he tried. They've been our trailmates— What am I going to do?"

She cast herself against him. He held her close. She did not weep, but she shuddered.

Until she raised her countenance, and smiled beneath the moon, however shakily, and said, "Okay, no decision yet. I will *not* allow murder, but— Anyway, meanwhile. I need, no, I want— Never mind. Don't think I, I haven't noticed the looks you've been giving me. And you're an almighty attractive man, and I've grown almighty horny. M-m-m-m?"

She was a storm, a delirium, a lioness. In between times, they were both astonished to find what merriment and peace were theirs to share.

XV

They were near the end of the wilderness when Ronica noticed things that brought her to a halt. It was early in the day, but she had already bagged a fat woodchuck and hoped she would soon get enough else that she could rejoin Iern. Let the others trudge onward, she thought; she and he could take their time and, later, catch up.

"Oh-oh," she breathed, plus a brimstone curse. The traces she had come upon required scrutiny. Those broken branches, slashes through brush, heavy tramplings over ground were from last year. Since, the forest had been healing. Maybe nothing less than a Survivor's eye would have seen the scars. *I damn near wish I hadn't.*

She curbed her emotions. Iern was a splendid lover, but that could wait. In fact—she grinned abashedly—her supply of Afterward capsules, which she had slipped into a pocket before leaving Kemper on a just-in-case basis, was getting low. What most of her wanted was simply his company, and even that wish had less to do with his glamour as a Stormrider and (Plik's phrase) exiled prince than it did with his own self.

Better postpone the fun and games. Something big has happened hereabouts, and we could blunder blind into a hell-kettle of consequences. She went on all fours. Nose close to soil, she used a twig to tease away leaves and needles that had fallen over the tracks she wanted to read. They were well-nigh obliterated; the fact that any indication of them whatsoever remained gave her ideas which made her uneasy.

Sunlight filtered through greenness, or struck between openings to bake aromas out of earth and duff and speckle them with gold. Insects buzzed; crows made rusty noises from afar; a wild dog barked. She paid only the peripheral heed of caution. Lay cheek to ground and study those hints of shadow that make visible the remnants of a print....

By now the men were competent to pick a resting place in her absence. They had pitched camp on a bluff above the lake. Though the trees were more than a hundred meters back from it, the sun had gone behind them when Ronica arrived. Their crowns stood black against a yellowing western sky. Beyond the shade they cast, the water seemed doubly bright. Bats and swifts darted through silence. The turf underfoot kept warmth that the air was losing, and springiness and a hay scent of the summer that was waning.

Iern sped to meet her. "Hai, where've you been?" he shouted. "I imagined the most awful things—" He embraced and kissed her. His whiskers were thin and soft, and always would be till he found a razor and got rid of them, but the rest of him was man, plenty of man. She responded as vigorously as weariness allowed. Their relationship was no secret.

At length he stepped back and said, glancing at the marmot in her rawhide carrier: "Plain to see, you were busy. That isn't much you've brought."

"It'll have to do," she replied. "If my dead reckoning isn't way off, we should reach Dulua tomorrow, where they'll feed us. If we decide against that route, I'll scrounge us a proper meal."

The rest, similarly puzzled, had congregated around, hulking Terai, pinto Wairoa, gaunt Plik, Mikli the carrion cat. It was the latter who asked sharply, "What do you mean? What have you found?"

"Spoor," she reported. "A good-sized bunch of men were busy in these woods last year. They brought in a heavy load of equipment and supplies, mostly on horseback. I found a site where they spent a while, operating out of it on foot, before moving on. The alignments of tent-peg holes, latrines, and what-have-you told me they were soldiers." She paused. "Not local soldiers. Their clumsiness proves that. I've never been in these parts before, but I do better—hell, you guys have learned to; and I understand most Krasnayans have some woodcraft, considering how many of them are loggers or trappers. Any guides they furnished must've been run squanch-footed, trying to herd those cheechakos."

She fished in her pocket. "I poked around and came on trash the party had left. Remnants of cardboard containers for field rations, that sort of stuff. The labels are still legible in spots, but I don't read their alphabet. Mikli?"

He took the moldered scraps from her and squinted at them. "Yuanese," he said. "Imperial Army of Yuan, yes, clear identification."

Ronica saw Iern whiten beneath the weathering of this trip. *Yuan!*

she remembered. *The Maurai claim they have evidence that Yuan grubstaked his enemy. He must feel trapped.* She wanted to take him in her arms and console him.

Mikli addressed her: "Last year, did you say? No war was going on. What was?"

Terai stiffened. Immediately he tried to relax, but Mikli had seen. "Do you know?" the Norrman demanded.

Terai hunched his bull shoulders. "Why should I answer that?" he replied, like distant cannonade.

We're close to civilization again, to our olden hates— Ronica clutched Iern's hand.

"Let's pool our data," Mikli was saying, his tone gone mild. "We've assumed we'll be hospitably received and can arrange our passages home. But Mong societies have a xenophobia built into their foundations, and we'd better not walk into a crisis without some idea of what's safe for us to do and what isn't."

Terai glared. "All right! I recommend this, you filthy uranium hunter—that you don't say a word about what you've been engaged in, or you'll likely get torn to shreds. Not that that would bother me, but I'd be sorry about Ronica." He glanced at her more kindly. "You've been duped, lass. I think I understand how and why. Someday you will too, I hope."

"Ah, so." Mikli stood for a space in thought.

"Terai," Ronica pleaded, "I swore we aren't making Doom weapons or, or anything evil. You Maurai are just fanatical about atomic energy. Won't *you* ever try to understand?"

Mikli laughed. "Well," he said, "we may feel friendlier after we've had a bite to eat. Let's get that animal cooked, shall we? I noticed a currant patch too, not far from here. And the light will soon fail." He sauntered off toward the shelter.

Wairoa surprised by breaking his habitual silence: "Ronica, we are not fanatics, we are students of history. I know atomic powerplants could be safe—much cleaner and less harmful than the coal you burn so lavishly in the Northwest Union. Why, the isotopes released from the coal spread more radioactivity by orders of magnitude, not to speak of what the fumes and fly ash do to living things, or the mines to a land. But the atom would allow a high-energy industry to come back, worldwide, and that is what the planet cannot bear."

"Are you sure?" Plik asked softly. "Demonic, yes, destructive of the old order; but likewise were fire, stone tools, the first farms, the first ships, metal, writing, printing, on and on. Man has always raised demons, and I think that once again—"

Several meters off, Mikli whirled about. His pistol jumped from the holster. "Hold!" he called. "Not a move, or I fire!"

Ronica felt no shock. She never did, at the moment of danger. She was aware of how Iern recoiled and reflexively, uselessly went into a fighter's crouch; Terai trumpeted fury; Wairoa grew motionless; Plik cast himself belly down. Her mind focused on the little man with the gun, and the evening became as clear and sharp as a splinter of glass.

"My apologies," Mikli said. He peeled his teeth in a grin. "I really must insist we talk. Please remember I'm rated expert with this type of weapon."

"What the chaos do you want?" Iern rasped.

"Nothing you personally need fear, I believe," Mikli assured him. "For openers, I would like to think aloud, if I may." His free hand stroked his beard as he murmured:

"Like the Imperial Yuanese Army, Terai, you've left more clues lying about than you realized. You suspected us of seeking fissionables in Uropa. This implies that, earlier, your service had discovered that somebody was gleaning them wherever possible. It would be natural for Maurai to assume the Northwest Union was involved, and thereafter to alert the Mong, requesting their assistance. Your Federation hasn't the resources to investigate everywhere by itself. But I'd guess that your primary assignment in Uropa, Terai, was to find out if collection was being attempted there, and, if it was, to enlist Skyholm in tracking it down and suppressing it. . . . In any event, I don't think you'd have suggested that Krasnayans are ready to kill anyone accused of looking for fissionables, unless they've heard about this activity. No public announcement, no; as much discretion as possible; however, inevitably, quite a few civilians will have gotten wind of what all the official excitement was about. Especially after Yuanese military detachments entered this country. Krasnaya hasn't the capability of rummaging its own hinterlands. Doubtless the Tieñ Dziang offered, ah, assistance to his good friend the Supreme Gospodin. I don't suppose the search turned up anything. At last the Yuanese went home. But they left their scat for Ronica to find, eh? And thereby hangs a tale that *my* service will find very interesting."

It couldn't have happened like this before the Doom War, flashed through Ronica. *Then everybody was under everybody else's surveillance. But spies today, or even observers, they're widely scattered, they lack the equipment and the sophistication— Do I really want that ancient world revived?*

Mikli's voice crackled: "Is my analysis right?"

Terai kept silence, but Wairoa, perhaps less used to the malevolent games that governments play, let out: "Yes, you are! Now do you see why you'd better not brag in Dulua?"

Terai laid a warning clasp on his countryman's arm. Mikli smiled anew, askew, and said, "Oh, indeed. Nor should you, tomorrow or ever. . . . Ronica, stand aside. I had to give you your way earlier, but from here I can make the rest of the distance alone. Behave yourself, and you can come along."

Terai roared and plunged forward. Mikli took aim.

Execution! Ronica knew. *He'll shoot the Maurai, and anybody else who might be inconvenient—*

The rabbit stick flew from her hand. Strangely, what was in her mind at that instant was Terai's talk once while he and she were at work together, about his children when they were small and his desire for grandchildren.

The pistol banged. It missed Terai, who was charging crouched and zigzag. The stick hit straight and hard across Mikli's right arm. He yelled. The pistol dropped. He staggered, dazed by pain. Ronica reached him barely ahead of Terai.

Rage made a lion mask of the big man's face. He must intend killing. Ronica snatched up her stick and rammed it into his midriff. Hard muscles were a corselet, but Terai also lurched, went to his knees, and gagged.

Ronica took the firearm, ran to the bluff edge, and cast the thing as far as she could into the lake.

When she returned, her victims were on their feet. Wairoa assisted Terai, Iern and Plik hovered uneasily in the rear. She slid her knife forth, resheathed it, and looked them over. "Okay," she said, "there'll be no more of this foolishness, and we'll let bygones be bygones. How about starting a fire? I'm hungry."

"You were magnificent," Iern told her after dark; and he proceeded to be.

During the night, a nudge and whisper aroused her. Their softness was sufficient, for she had been sleeping warily. "Come outside," Mikli hissed. "We must talk. For the sake of Orion."

They left the shelter and sought a point some distance off, under a giant spruce. Tinged by a waning moon, its branches roofed them beneath fragrance, and a measure of warmth stole from the forest at its back. They were nearly invisible to each other in its shadow. Beyond, turf stretched rime-pale until the bluff toppled into the lake, which mirrored stars in its darkness.

"Listen," said Mikli's disembodied voice. "Listen well. This day you were idiotic to the point of betrayal—"

"Shall we take that matter before a Lodge court?" she retorted.

He chuckled. "I don't belong to any Lodge, remember? I only serve, in my fashion. Well, you wanted us to forgive and forget. I can't forget—my arm still hurts abominably—but I do see what motivated you, and I've grown resigned to the fact that the human species has a capacity for idealism which costs it megadeaths per century. So let us two dismiss the past and simply resolve that Orion shall rise."

Those words never failed to make her spine tingle. *And this bastard knows it,* she thought. *Just the same—* An ancient saying crossed her mind. *He may be a son of a bitch, but he's* our *son of a bitch . . . I suppose.*

. . . "Okay," she said. "I couldn't allow cold-blooded murder. But I agree we have a problem. How do we keep the Maurai from spilling their news? It could bring their outfit onto the real scent, couldn't it? Before Orion is ready."

"I admit I was too impulsive," he replied. "A fault of mine. I should not have invited you along to Yurrup, either. What you could do was irrelevant to my mission, and ended up compromising it." He clicked his tongue. "Done is done, and we may yet reap some benefit from the situation. In fact, we already have a better idea than before of how closely the Maurai are on our track. We need to inform our associates and get started on countermeasures."

"What do you think we should do?"

"This. To the degree that chance permits. And I always have been rather good at rolling with the dice.

"During the trip I established, in conversation, that neither Terai nor Wairoa knows any Mong language. A considerable advantage for us, hm? The difficulty I mentioned to you, earlier, was that the Krasnayans would innocently help everybody in our group go home." Sardonicism: "Except for Iern, of course. We know whom he'll accompany. . . . Now we've deduced that the Krasnayan authorities have gotten reason to be twice leery of foreigners who come from the woods. Such an attitude can be used."

Ronica poised herself.

"Here's the plan I've worked out," Mikli thrust at her. "I'll see to it that we all get detained—not mobbed or shot or anything like that, but detained on suspicion. Except you. I'll have to improvise the scenario as we go along. Basically, you get away from the rest of us at some appropriate point. You make your way to Yuan. You're expert at sneaking, and the border isn't far south. There you contact a certain person. You'll have to go through the usual bureaucratic quadrille first, but I'll give you key names to cite, and the phrase 'Code Nineteen.' Do you follow that? 'Code Nineteen.' When finally you're brought to an official who knows what it means, you'll explain that the entire project is in danger—"

"What project?"

"You have no need to know, my dear. An elementary principle of secret-keeping. 'Code Nineteen' will serve. And the word that Yuan had better dispatch an armed force in a hurry, to take charge of the prisoners. After that, leave matters to me. I'll get the lot of us, including your precious Maurai and your priceless Clansman, bundled off to our country."

"I . . . don't have more than a few words . . . of Mong."

"No problem. Plenty of Soldati know Unglish. They wouldn't like their serfs having a language they can't eavesdrop on. The dialects aren't too different from those in the Union. You'll manage.

"Is this operation permissible under your principles?"

She ignored the sarcasm. Her pulse accelerated. "Yes," she said. "The way you've put it. Tell me more."

2

Vanna Uangovna was at meditation in her bower when the strangers appeared. Wind blew sharp, whipped a gray heaven, brawled in trees and tossed their limbs about, rippled the grass of the meadow. It was turning sere, that grass; her flowers were gone; the vineleaves decking the arbor were red and crackly, while a pair of birches showed gold against somber evergreens. In girlhood, Vanna would have shivered in the cold, as thin as her robe was. Today, a Gaean adept, she had chosen to make this weather the mandala she would contemplate, the Aspect that would take her into itself and so open the way to Oneness.

Again Earth spun toward Northern winter. Heat radiated out and out, until it belonged to that energy which pervaded the cosmos and whispered of the mystery at the beginning of all things. No mathematical physicist had yet developed a wave function for the primordial event, and there were those who maintained that none ever would, that paradox was the very core of reality. . . . But she was not separate from the farthest star or the earliest instant. The dear, familiar water she drank and that coursed in her bloodstream, most of the molecules in her quite ordinary body, these held hydrogen atoms which had formed during the first second or two of convulsion. They would endure while the universe did, save for those that escaped to space and became the stuff of new stars forging new iron. . . . If she was so intimate a part of the galaxies, how ultimately integral she must be with Gaea, the living Earth!

Let this austere day strip self from her—an expression of the Life Force that had had its role in evolution but could now best die out, like the seasonal rut of ancestral animals becoming transfigured into the love between man and woman. Let her, for the short while she was able, perceive, however dimly, the Organism, and seek an Insight into how she, this portion of Her, should function in the service of the Purpose. The wind blew, the wind blew. . . .

Meditation was not trance. As she merged her being with the world, she opened her senses more and more widely to it. Thus she heard the strangers afar, though they did not walk clumsily. She might have let them go by unhailed—no one from the vicinity would disturb her without urgent cause—but a while later they were close enough that her heightened perceptions captured their talk, and she realized from the cadence that they must be outlanders.

Prospectors for bomb stuff. Detonations in the West, such as ushered in Death Time. Memory stabbed through her inner peace, which drained from the wound. Suddenly alone in her head, she stepped out and stood where the wind could stream unhindered across her.

That raw vigor brought calm, determination. *They may be harmless. In any case, what reason would they have to attack me?* Early in her discipleship she had learned how not to be afraid of death or pain; fearlessness about her own person became as natural to her as breathing. However, she rejoiced in her usefulness—proróchina, ucheny, Librarian, human being—and did not wish it to end before Gaea was through with her.

Following a deer trail, the newcomers emerged in the meadow. They saw her and stopped. For a minute, looks went back and forth.

They were incredibly diverse, and weatherbeaten, unbarbered, ragged. The biggest of them could only be Maurai. To judge by what was left of their clothes, the tall blond woman and the short gray man were Northwesterners. The young fellow and the scarecrow figure were puzzling, and as for the sixth member of the party—no, he was not deformed, but he was alien.

The gray man smiled, advanced, and bowed. "Greeting, my lady," he said. His Yazik was fluent but the accent did, indeed, identify the Union. "Please don't be alarmed. We're travelers in distress, searching for aid. Are we near Dulua?"

"Yes," Vanna answered, less calmly than she had expected to. "I'll take you there if you like."

"Many thanks. You are most kind, my lady. Permit me to introduce us. We are a mixed bag." He pointed about. "My name is Mikli Karst. Ronica Birken and I hail from the Territories, as I imagine you've guessed. Terai Lohannaso and Wairoa Haakonu are from the Federation. Talence Iern Ferlay and, ah, Plik are more exotic, from the Domain of Skyholm in Yevropea. We regret that I alone among us speak your language."

The Domain!

Vanna realized she was gaping like a child. She mustered graciousness. "Thank you, sir. I hight Vanna Uangovna Kim." In Unglish: "I bid you welcome." She said the same in Maurai and Angley.

The young man was the most startled. "I didn't expect I could talk to anybody here!" he exclaimed.

Vanna must proceed slowly: "I am the Librarian. As such, I have to be able to read the principal languages of the world, and I have seen much fascinating material from your country, sir."

"But you speak it, too. Without even a strong accent."

Vanna smiled. She liked him. "I have recordings, and practice reading aloud. How else could I appreciate your poetry?"

Talence, she recalled. *A sort of royalty in the Domain. What events have brought him to Merica, in the company of these?* "I am eager to hear your story," she said.

"Well, that may pose a few problems, honored Vanna," Mikli warned. "What we are free to tell is limited." He addressed the blond woman in Unglish: "I think this is the strategic moment for you to take off, my dear."

Starkness laid hold of Ronica. She nodded, once, and said, "Aye." She flung herself against Iern and they exchanged a fierce kiss. She vanished into the woods.

Dismay shocked through the Librarian. "What is this?"

"Be at ease," Mikli replied patronizingly. "We aren't under arrest, are we? It isn't compulsory to proceed to Dulua, is it? But the rest of us plan to, and will be glad if you come along. By all means, take us straight to the appropriate security officers."

Fissionables gatherers, then? But it doesn't make sense, not really. Vanna called upon the wind for coolness. She observed the remaining strangers, each by each, and used her gift for reading people.

Mikli stood smug. Terai was curbing belligerence, Wairoa freezing his features into immobility, but it seemed they were both surprised by Ronica's disappearance—as was Plik, who looked around in a vague fashion. Iern appeared to have been forewarned (predictable, when he and the woman were obviously close) but not to be nursing any particular scheme, only to be trying for stoicism. No, these were no united conspirators.

Well, what are they?

"You will have explanations to make," Vanna cautioned.

"I realize that," Mikli said. "Shall we go make them?"

Almost automatically, she started for the homeward path. They trailed her, save for Mikli, who walked alongside. She didn't want that; she distrusted his glibness.

Therefore she said in Angley: "Do we have this language in common? Then let us use it."

"Tanaroa, yes!" exploded from Terai. "What I could tell you about that treacherous little skulk—"

"Easy, easy," Mikli interrupted. "Your word against mine, an exercise in futility until our Krasnayan hosts have carried out a proper investigation." Menace: "If you accuse me, I'll accuse you right back, and we may find ourselves mutually dead."

Vanna moistened her lips, which had gone dry. "Can you tell me anything?" she asked. "Perhaps I can advise you, if you are innocent of wrongdoing. I am an influential person in Dulua."

Clearly, Mikli had not anticipated her, but assumed he would be the sole spokesman. She must needs admire how he improvised. "The story is less than pleasant, my lady. It involves official secrets, too. I imagine you will be interpreter at the hearing, and so find out the different things we shall have to say. Meanwhile, I thank you for your generous offer, but believe we had all better give careful thought to our testimony before we make any admissions.

"For example, Terai and Wairoa," he said over his shoulder, "you Maurai have intelligence agents throughout the Five Nations. I know who a number of them are. If I named them, the Soldati would have to take steps, and your service would be vastly inconvenienced. I won't, I will observe professional courtesy—as long as you do. Shouldn't we let the governments concerned settle the matter quietly between them?" To Vanna: "I hope I haven't shocked you, my lady."

"Oh, no," she said in a dull voice. *Of course the Maurai have planted spies among us. They want to be sure we don't get adventurous, or Gaeanity get out of hand.*

"And you, Iern, Plik, it would not be in your interest to reveal everything you *think* you know," Mikli continued. "If you hope for support from the Lodges, and eventual repatriation— But, honored Vanna, Iern has a great deal to tell which is no secret, about his life in the Domain and the coup there that you have probably heard about. And Plik will entertain us with a song or two, I'm sure, if you promise him a drink. Come, let's be friends."

In their different ways, they yielded. The Maurai whispered together and went mute. Iern shied off from describing how he had gotten here, but was candid—in a swimmingly romantic fashion—about his experiences before. Vanna bore with his anti-Gaeanism; he knew no better, he was capable of learning, and in truth he did appear to have suffered injustice. Gaeanity did not by itself make anybody wise or moral. Like a religion (in the strict sense of that word), to most of its followers it was just a set of myths, phrases, and rites. Generations, perhaps centuries must pass before it had become more than this to all mankind. *The Life Force is millennial.*

That odd man, Plik, presently offered a song, which he entitled "Statecraft," but it was wild and weird and Vanna didn't like it.

"—Now the chief of those who have seized the throne
Lays his peace upon the land.
There shall be no more war against his will,
And false beliefs are banned.
If the Prince is gone, he who led us on
Down endless roads of night,
We must surely welcome the sane young sun
And thank our lords for light.
"Like blades our fathers drew from sheath,
As winds and wolves give tongue,
The lightnings flare above a heath
Where the thunders cry forth what witches long have sung,
And on the hills a darkling host takes arms
And once again the balefires burn.
The Law of old, cast out, has raised an outlaw warfare.
So shall the Prince return!"

Bors Liuvich Kharsov, major in the Blue Star and magistrate of Dulua Prefecture, leaned back. His Merican-style chair creaked. He looked across his desk at those who sat on the bench before him, twirled his mustache, fiddled with the ornate collar of his tunic, and said unhappily, "Your stories don't match, and none of them rings true."

"Sir," Mikli Karst replied, "I have explained as much as my duty allows. To repeat, we were bringing Talence Iern Ferlay to political asylum when these Maurai overtook and assaulted us. The conflict brought both planes down, and we must perforce join in a march to civilization."

"Yes, yes. But why did your female companion abscond?"

Dustmotes bobbed in the sunlight slanting through a begrimed windowpane. Air in the office was stale. Four armed guards stood against the wall. "She is a woodsrunner. Claustrophobiac. She feared detention."

"That doesn't make sense, you know." Bors glowered at Iern Ferlay and Plik. "What have you to add?"

Vanna Uangovna translated the question. The Clansman's answer was more clipped than she rendered it: "No comment, sir."

"And what of you from the Maurai Federation?" Bors persisted, using Unglish as he had been doing.

"Karst lies," Terai Lohannaso snarled. "Excuse me, sir, I can't say more than I have. He's the outlaw, in a violation so gross I'm certain your authorities will agree we had a right of hot pursuit. But I cannot give you details. Not to anybody except the principal diplomatic representative of the Federation."

"I will send after her," Bors promised, "but you must be patient. We don't have your advanced radio communications in Krasnaya. We're a poor country, and electronic parts are expensive, relay towers prohibitive, telephone networks unthinkable. I'll dispatch a courier tomorrow. You can send a letter by him, which I shall want to read first. At this season, though, the Gospodin has gone into retreat, as is his custom. Court has shut down, officials and envoys are taking a holiday. I have heard that the Maurai legate likes to fish our wild lakes. It may take a week or more to find her, and then she must get here."

"I can wait," the big man said, grimly satisfied. How curious, Vanna thought, that Mikli Karst and—yes—Iern looked satisfied too. The Norrman had probably anticipated delay; it was plain that he was well acquainted with the laws and customs of Krasnaya. How and why?

Bors addressed him: "The nearest Union consulate is in Jinya, no great distance. Or you may write to your embassy in Minyatonka if you prefer."

"No point in that, sir," Karst answered. "What would either of them know to exonerate me? May I, instead, give you addresses in the Union and the Domain to which you yourself can write? The responses will show that my companion and I were on a legitimate assignment."

"That will take a considerable time."

Karst smiled and imitated Lohannaso's voice: "I can wait."

Bors stiffened in his chair. "Meanwhile," he said to the group, "you must admit your accounts have been inadequate. No offense intended if none is called for, but you could be smugglers, bandits, or . . . or uranium hunters. . . . I have no choice but to detain you, pending further investigation."

"I quite understand, sir," Karst purred. "Indeed, no offense."

"You shall have comfortable quarters—"

A thought had been querning in Vanna. It burst forth. "Honored Major," she said, "I would claim privilege."

He was surprised. "What is your desire, reverend lady?"

"House the gentlemen from the Federation and . . . honored Karst . . . where you see fit. Separately, I suggest, but properly, of course. However, let me be responsible for the other two gentlemen. The Library has guest rooms, you know. You can post guards if you wish, though I don't imagine they will cause any trouble."

Bors raised his brows and twiddled his mustache. He and she had collided ere now; but they had also cooperated. "May I ask your reason, reverend lady?"

"Why," she said in perfect honesty, "we've never before had visitors from Yevropea. I've a million questions to ask them, a million aspects of Gaea to learn."

3

The garden was large and beautiful, but in ways unheard of by Iern. Here was neither the many-flowered lushness of Bourgoyn nor the formal beds and topiaries favored in Brezh. The space enclosed by the Library on one side and walls on the remaining three was intricately but sparely laid out. Those walls were of stone and timber interspersed, each piece chosen and placed to create a harmonious whole. Opposite the great building, a portal crowned by an arc of wood held a gate whose wrought iron formed a Yang-and-Yin symbol. Graveled paths wound among banks of moss, clover, or herbs. Here and there were trees which had been bent as they grew, into curious but pleasing shapes. Goldfish and water lilies graced pools of varying size and form. Several plots consisted only of ground cover or bare earth, daily raked, surrounding a boulder, a stele, or an abstract sculpture. Then abruptly you would come on a patch of weeds, unselected, untended save to contain them in their place, a reminder of the primeval, and somehow this too belonged.

Bathed, groomed, nourished, freshly clad, Iern paced beside Vanna. Though they had talked till far into the night, and bells and gongs calling to rites had wakened him at dawn, he felt well rested. The morning was young, after a breakfast as light but tasty as dinner had been yesterday; Vanna had rushed through her duties in order to meet him. Plik was sleeping off the wine she had told a scandalized servitor to keep bringing him on demand, while pity was clear to see upon her.

Gravel scrunched underfoot. Walls gave lee from a wind that soughed in the tallest trees. This day was cold but sunny, with scraps of cloud hurrying by overhead.

For the most part, conversation had hitherto dwelt on him and his world. Given all that there was to tell, he had not found it hard to steer clear of those events about which Ronica had asked for his silence. Now Vanna agreed his turn had come to inquire of her. Besides, she said, smiling in her shy manner, what he asked her and how would tell her yet more about him. They had reached a point where they could touch on personal matters.

"Mine has been a quiet life," she related. "To you it may seem tedious, but I have found it measurelessly rich."

His glance admired her. She was small and slight, but a loose gray robe did not hide litheness or delicately female curves. Her head was large, its brown eyes oblique, nose snub, chin rounded, lips that made him think of flower petals. The ivory skin showed faint lines and the black hair, clasped at the neck and falling halfway down her back, held streaks of white. Her voice was almost too soft, but that was because she spoke of herself. Enthusiasm would make her vibrant.

"I was born into the Aldan Polk, whose range lies northward. My father taught school. I grew up among foresters, lumberjacks, hunters, trappers, fishers, artisans. Living thus, the Aldans keep few slugai and do not regard any task as menial. This was doubtless healthy for me; otherwise my studiousness might have kept me entirely among books. As was, they joined with the nature around to make me feel a Gaean vocation early in my life."

"Pardon me," Iern interrupted. "Let's make sure I understand you. Polk? Slugai?"

"M-m, that requires a discussion of history."

"I don't mind. On the contrary. Please talk away."

"I suppose 'polk' can be most nearly rendered as 'regiment,' though that is no longer exactly what the concept implies. See, when our ancestors came to Merica, driven by terrible need, they must fight their way. Besides, a military type of organization was essential to everything they must do in an unknown land. That included fighting each other. They did not come over in a single wave, after all, nor from a single place. If nothing else, a stock of medicine or motor fuel could become the occasion of a battle. Only slowly did the Five Nations coalesce, and wars between them continued frequent until modern times.

"So the regiment became the basis of every Mong society. A Soldat is born into his or hers, and often marries within it; when not, the wife enrolls in the husband's. It has its unique emblems, honors, customs, traditions. It sends representatives to its national government, yet if it finds reason to change allegiance, that is no disgrace, for the regiment is what commands ultimate loyalty.

"Of course, over the centuries its nature has evolved. Today, though everyone still receives military training and stays in the reserves, the actual soldiers are a minority. Most of us are . . . almost anything else." Vanna smiled. "For example, a Librarian."

Iern thought back over what little he knew. "And the slugai, then, are the nonmembers?" he guessed. "Descendants of the old population. Regimental property."

"No, not that, not slaves." Her tone was a little defensive and again she spoke at length, but faster than before.

"This also began in the Migrations. Agriculture across the plains had broken down during Death Time. Grass took over; and the Soldati were accustomed to a mobile life. What more natural than that they became stockbreeders, nomadic herders? Yet they still required the productions of sedentary people, everything from flour and fruit to machinery and chemicals. So was it not also natural for a polk to protect those surviving Mericans who lived in its range, and in exchange receive their labor?

"Yes, a sluga is born to the service of a particular Soldat family, with no legal provision for release. But he or she has rights, guarantees against abuse; they include the right of appeal directly to the colonel. The Soldat family is responsible for the well-being of its slugai, and to fail in this is a criminal offense. Very few are bound to the soil anymore, and those who are generally prefer it thus. Remember, they cannot be evicted. Most are free to choose their lifework. As a rule, the only requirement is that they keep their masters informed of developments and pay a modest tax on earnings. When any of them wish to change residence, permission is seldom withheld; the master reassigns them to relatives of his. Quite commonly, a Soldat family will see that a promising sluga child gets an appropriate education and a start on a career. Feelings between Soldat and sluga usually range from tolerant to deeply affectionate. Legal intermarriage is impossible, but unofficial marriages are not rare, and the acknowledged children of such unions become Soldati."

Iern recalled how Plik had expressed skepticism yesterday evening, after Vanna had been tending to represent her country as altogether peaceful and benevolent. She had later tried to get information about the collection of fissionables. Obviously she knew it was going on, and it seemed as if she knew yet more, something dreadful which she must not reveal. Iern claimed ignorance; Ronica, Ronica. . . . "Whoever is busy need not be an absolute monster," Plik had drawled. "How pure is Krasnaya? How pure would it be if it were a world power? Not a jot, I assure you. Incompatible." He took a gulp of wine. "No rudeness intended, my lady. You are sincere. It's just that you believe mankind has a potential for becoming orderly and moral, and going on from there to transcend itself, whereas I consider this to be the newest version of the Pelagian heresy." He was apt to use obscure words when in his cups.

Now Iern thought: *Nearly all people I've ever met or heard about have accepted the conditions they live under because they must, and made the best they could of their lives. It doesn't follow that they think those are the best lives possible. Who would be so uncouth as to shock this gentle academician with accounts of sordidness and brutality? What would be the point in it?*

She appeared to sense his reservation, for she touched his hand, moth-lightly, and her tone grew twofold serious: "Please don't think we are barbarians, or that our forefathers were. They were perforce rough, but they seldom ravaged wantonly. And knowledge, such knowledge as is in books, was sacred to them. With a book, a Soldat could carry a piece of civilization in his saddlebag. The attitude has persisted."

She fell silent. They walked on through the bleakly bright day for a minute or two, until a laugh trilled from her. "Oktai, how I do talk!" she said. "I forget I am not on a platform lecturing to my acolytes."

"I was not bored," Iern assured her. "But if you've finished that digression, won't you tell me more about yourself?"

"Shall we rest for a bit?" She gestured at a bench, a granite slab, which faced a seven-meter circle defined by rocks whose erosions and concretions made each one unique, an object for contemplation until you appreciated its special beauty. White sand covered the ground. Placed upon it, in a pattern so subtle that it almost appeared random, were a number of sea shells, from gaudy conch to minute and spiraled cone. Just off center loomed a man-high mass of coral.

Vann settled herself and gazed at its rosiness. *She can't be tired,* Iern realized. *She must want to . . . do what? Draw strength from this? Calm?* He wondered if she had ever seen an ocean.

Joining her, he found the seat faintly warmed by the sun. *Does she take that into her awareness too?* Irreverence: *Revelation through the buttocks.* And: *Why not? To her, as nearly as I can discover, every part of a living thing has its dignity. Its mystery.*

"You said," he prompted, "when you were a child, you decided you wanted to be a priestess."

Her look remained fixed on the coral, but she smiled afresh. "No, no. 'Priestess' is a totally misleading word—as misleading, I admit, as the churchlike practices, rites, costumes, organization that Gaeanity has developed over the centuries. Those are merely aids, comforts. Gaeanity is not a religion, it is a philosophy and way of life, in conflict with no faith that I know of. There is nothing ecclesiastical. True, there is intercommunication, and in grave matters it is best for someone like me to accept the guidance of the Great Center, and persuade my disciples to do likewise. But we are never compelled. To stifle individual judgment would be to stifle that expression of the Life Force which it is."

A hint of pain flitted across her countenance. *What is she remembering? A recent crisis?* That question reminded Iern of too much. "You're digressing again," he made haste to tease.

Her smile was wider this time. "Well, I warned you!"

She sighed. "I have little autobiography to give, my friend. A polk can always use another ucheny—teacher, ceremonialist, scholar. If perchance I developed into a proróchina as well—adept, seeress; you have no exact Angley word—that would bring honor which my polk would inscribe on its banners. Therefore it underwrote my education, which in the course of ten years took me as far as Chai Ka-Go in Yuan."

She broke off, and was quiet for a time before she said low: "At last I returned to Krasnaya, but went into retreat for a year more—on the rim of the ancient iron-mining pit at I-ping, that unhealed wound in the earth. It helped me understand how and why the Life Force begets pain, destruction, grief: another unfolding and discovery of itself. . . . Eventually I came here, to Dulua, by request. As an ucheny, I made extensive use of the Library, and so succeeded the former Librarian when he went into his Last Seclusion. That is my main work, though I also teach and counsel and—am fortunate in having the love of small children.

"But this approaches boastfulness, Iern. Enough."

Her voice, which had dropped to a croon, fell silent, and she stared at the coral as if hypnotized. He thought she must be more open than modesty made her pretend. Not that he wished to pry or seduce—already he liked her too well—but he hoped to know her better, and perhaps even bridge the gap of belief that sundered them.

Therefore he ventured, "No. You haven't told me the real things, have you?"

She stirred. An eddy tossed a lock of hair across her brow.

"I'm an outsider, of course," he said. "If I intrude on your privacy, tell me and I'll get out."

"No," she answered. " 'Privacy' is a weaker concept among us than I gather it is among your people—and weaker in your turn than among the Northwesterners, who often seemed obsessed by it. Here we simply try to observe the common decencies."

Again she sighed. "But what is to tell, Iern? I daresay you wonder why I have not married. I planned to, in Chai Ka-Go. But first I went to the House of Revelation, not as pilgrim or supplicant but as disciple, and . . . experienced that which has since made a proróchina of me. He was a disciple too, but, but the Insight and the Power come more strongly to certain women than they do to any man, and he could not face being married to such a one. . . . Don't feel sorry for me. I told you before, my life is immeasurably rich, in Gaea and in the love of living creatures I know."

The Power, he wondered. *I've heard claims that the primary adepts can read minds, walk on air, foresee the future, raise the dead. Superstition only? I know a little something of what training and concentration can do. I'd never have been a Stormrider or been able to parachute from Skyholm if old Sergeant Galvain had not drilled us Cadets without pity.*

How I hated him, then. But surely Vanna does not force her disciples like that. I think she must lead them, open doors for them.

"Psychic power," he said aloud, scarcely noticing that he did. "If nothing else, total discipline and dedication. Yes, that must be awesome. It inspires fanatics, but I can see how it might frighten an ordinary man who'd have to live with it."

Vanna turned her head to give him a hurt look. "What? Iern, I am no fanatic, am I? Have I denied you the right to your opinions and the expression of them—or anybody else?"

"No, not you," he said quickly. "And I suppose few of your fellow seers would. You're too busy seeking enlightenment. You're saints of a kind." *Unlike we of the Aerogens, who bear that name among some pysans.* "But those you've taught, who haven't gotten as far as you—well, maybe they feel less secure. Maybe they think they have to make belief in the Life Force compulsory, or it might die out."

"Iern," she said in the gentlest of tones, "that was your bitterness speaking, not you. I sympathize. You've suffered hurt and loss; you're seeing your entire civilization begin to go under, and, yes, in its day it did serve humankind magnificently. I don't say that what you've been through is justifiable in human terms. The Life Force is also the Heautontimoroumenos, the Self-Tortured. I can merely say the events happened, and hope you will come to accept."

Resentment flared. "Accept the inevitable? But I don't agree that it is."

She kept her mildness, her air of explaining and consoling. "Gaeanity, which is another word for sanity, is spreading across the world. And why not? What's so terrible about peace, love, reunion of the human body and mind and spirit within the Oneness of all life, all Being?"

He borrowed ideas from the commentators he had read at home: "Is this the universe in action, or is it because Mong governments give the movement fat subsidies? And ruling classes abroad often do favor it. Their people are getting restless, and Gaeanity encourages submission; never mind liberty or traditional rights, just retreat into your head. Or it can be useful in marshaling force against a rival . . . as I found out."

She was quiet, while the clouds and their shadows flew, before she said, more kindly still, "Iern, you are a moth—no, a hawk, battering yourself bloody against a glass pane. If only you could slide it aside, you would know that what lies beyond is no image, but the veritable future, and your freedom." She took his hand. "Let's change the subject. We've treasures to give each other."

He swallowed. "Thank you. Let's."

Inwardly: *The Mong nations are waning. They've lost the will to prevail. But the old warrior spirit lives on; it has become missionary.* He regarded the woman beside him. Her gaze in return offered care, compassion, and not a millimeter of ground surrendered. *She is a daughter of the Soldati.*

4

By the fourth day, Terai was barely able to maintain control, and Wairoa was showing signs of strain.

It was not that their confinement was onerous. They shared a vacated sluga cottage, simply but adequately furnished. The food and drink brought them were good, the crisp vegetables and lightly fried meat not unlike Awaiian cuisine, the herb tea and beer full-bodied. The armed watchmen at the single door were alert but genial, eager to talk in Unglish. Daily, under doubled guard, the internees were allowed out for an hour or two of exercise, which could well happen to be a game of handball played with soldiers off duty. For their private amusement, they were lent cards, chess and go sets, and any available books they wanted. Meanwhile they had assurance that the Maurai legate would soon arrive and negotiate their release.

"The trouble is that Mikli swine," Terai had growled early on.

Wairoa nodded his striped head. "He was tense in the office, but basically confident. I could smell it. Unfortunately, he does not subvocalize, and his body language is peculiar to himself. I got no clue to his thoughts."

"He has a plan." Terai rumbled a laugh. "He didn't send Ronica away to spite her lover! She'd have torn his ear off for suggesting it. But what is her errand, then?"

"To report to a Northwestern agent and get help?"

"What sort of help? A message, possibly, via the Yuanese connections we think the Norrmen may have. But a raid—ridiculous."

Wairoa leaned elbows on a windowsill and considered the rainy, windy night. "The objective could be to silence us," he proposed.

"He's already done that, for the time being," Terai pointed out. He rose from his chair and prowled the clay floor. It was cold beneath his bare feet.

Wairoa's glance trailed him. "I don't actually understand why, or how. I admit I tend to be naive about human affairs in general, and about the Mong in particular. But why don't we reveal it's the Norrmen who are gathering fissionables? We could tell where to go, to dredge the evidence from the lake."

"Didn't you hear? He threatened retaliation. He'd compromise *our* intelligence in the Five Nations by blabbing what he knows, and he may well know plenty. The Union's been interacting with the Mong for centuries, they must have a network of agents who'd make it part of their jobs to keep track of ours, and Mikli personally must have operated here before, as familiar as he is with local situations. Stalemate." Terai smiled sourly. "As for Iern, he's reliable. He won't breathe a word that could get his dear Ronica in trouble. Plik will oblige his request."

"Are you certain Mikli isn't bluffing?"

"No, but I can't take the risk while alternatives are open. Besides, in any case, I can't predict how the Mong would react to the information—or the Domain, once word reached there, which it surely would —or our own Federation, for that matter. We could find a global, bloody mess on our hands. Most dangerous, I suspect, is the Union. What would *it* do, after its secret was out beyond any question? Those plotters must have contingency plans. And . . . Ronica vows they've built no nuclear weapons, and I think she's honest and she may be correct, but can we be sure? At best, we could all stumble into a war we don't want, and need not fight if this business is handled properly."

Terai took pipe and tobacco off a table. The pipe was a corncob, given him because he had lost his in the crash. He missed that old briar and hoped he would soon get home to his collection. *And Elena, the kids, the house, our friends, the land and the sea—how far away they feel tonight.*

"Yes," he said, "that quandary keeps my mouth shut at least as much as does any threat to our corps mates. I've no doubt Mikli counts on my reasoning this way. But damnation, it is the right way! Far better to inform only our government, and let it study things and decide what to do."

"How will you convey the information?"

"I'll tell the legate when she arrives, if I can get a private conference for us in a secure place. If not, I'll make her understand that she absolutely must get us released and brought to—Inspectorate headquarters in Vittohrya, I suppose. She can surely manage that. We're not under such black suspicion that a local magistrate, or the Gospodin himself, will care to provoke the Maurai Federation on our account."

"Mikli must realize what your intentions are," Wairoa said.

Terai tamped the tobacco harder than was needful. "Aye, he must. And still the son of a teredo was cheerful. . . . If worst comes to worst, we will tell the Mong."

—At midafternoon of the fourth day, the troopers from Yuan entered Dulua. At their head, beside the commander, rode Ronica Birken.

A drizzle chilled the air, blurred roofs and walls, slicked pavement. The crowd that had gathered to stare might have been dissolved by that weather, for chatter had died to a mumble while the horses and stocky, gray-green-clad, Asian-faced soldiers who encircled Terai and Wairoa blocked off view of any watchers, anybody known to them.

Save Mikli. Arms akimbo, feet braced wide, he looked up into their faces and grinned his triumph. "Those cords will come off your wrists and those gags off your mouths after we're well out of town, if you've been well behaved," he told them in Maurai. "However," and he wagged a forefinger, "each of you will at every moment be in charge of four riflemen whose orders are to kill if you utter a single word. Or try to write one. Or look as though you might. They're picked men, and they've been told you're uranium smugglers such as they've been hunting for. You could have miniature radio transceivers planted in your bodies, and warn your complotters if you get a chance to speak. It's general knowledge that the Maurai have that sort of gadget, but by and large, Mong don't know their limitations.

"So, not a word—to repeat what I warned when we called you out of your house—not a word, or you die. Which wouldn't trouble me in the least. It's Ronica you have to thank for your lives, once again. She insisted. And, I grant you, this is less gauche, it will cause less comment . . . and I look forward to talking with you later, under easier conditions."

He threw back his head and cackled laughter. "Forgive me if I gloat. It *was* a dicey thing, far too many factors that could have made the bones roll wrong. Now cooperate and we'll treat you reasonably well. In due course you can be repatriated. Relax and enjoy."

He sauntered off. The Yuanese soldiers made way for him before closing their ring afresh about the two men on whom their looks dwelt in utter hatred.

—Public displays of affection were bad manners here. Iern and Ronica held hands and looked into each other's eyes. Her hair was damp, aglitter with droplets; her breasts rose and fell. Plik watched wistfully and glugged from a bottle he had had the foresight to snatch when summoned.

"Zhesu, how wonderful!" Iern breathed.

"Just you wait till we're by ourselves, lad," she muttered in reply. "I'll show you what wonderful is."

"I was terrified for you."

"And I for you," answered the throaty voice. "How've you been?"

"Fine, except for the worry. The local, m-m, adept took me in, and I learned Gaeans can be very decent people. We had fascinating conversations, and she showed me a little of her, her influence over animals, children— But what happened to you?"

"I did my job, more or less as I'd told you Mikli had instructed me. Got across the border, found a Yuanese military base—or constabulary, or whatever you'd call it; no real distinction—Well, I made enough ruckus that finally they put me through on a radiophone to a high-level officer in Chai Ka-Go, and he found somebody who knew what my code phrase meant, and after that I got action. Hoo-hah, did I get action! All they asked was Mikli's name, where he was, and did he want out. Messages started going back and forth, and meanwhile this troop was marshaled, and at dawn today, we *rode.* You've noticed how lathered the mounts and remounts are, haven't you? Poor beasts, I hope they don't catch cold, standing around untended like this. Anyhow, when we reached town, the noyon required the local colonel to take us to Mikli, and from then on, it was Mikli in charge —except that I talked him out of having Terai and Wairoa shot out of hand."

"How'd you do that? Plain to see, he wants them dead."

"I told him they'd become friends of mine; also, there is such a thing as the honor of the Lodge, and I'd complain to Wolf; also, in the near future I'd catch him alone and secure him and beat the living shit out of him. He saw my point."

"What's next?"

"I don't know exactly, though I'm certain we'll get home, to the Union. How I look forward to showing you around my country."

And how I hope I will learn that you are not monsters there, went through him.

—When Orluk Zhanovich Boktan was based in Dulua, commanding his bootless search for clues to the death-stuff runners, and during subsequent, shorter missions to this area, he and Vanna Uangovna had gotten on cordial terms. Their unlikeness made their encounters stimulating, while at the same time he respected her intellect and Power and she found him to be a kindly man at heart.

Thus she stood in the thin rain and listened while he told Bors Kharsov: "No, sir, I'm sorry, I can't say more. Besides, I don't know more. My orders were to get Karst's release and bring the rest of them back to base, dead or alive, according to his directions and my judgment. The two men we have tied up seem to be first-chop suspects in the uranium smuggling, and that isn't a business that can wait."

"Maurai—dealers in the horror—I can't believe it," Vanna stammered.

"Could be a ring of them, operating on their own," Orluk said. He had clearly been thinking hard as he rode hither. "The Federation's as mixed a herd as the Five Nations, and spreads over all Oceania. Or could be an international criminal syndicate, members from everywhere. Or . . . could be the Maurai high command is sorry its forerunners junked what explosive they could find, these days when new factions are on the way up."

"Nevertheless—" Vanna subsided, shivered, and stared at the armed strangers everywhere around.

"The Norrmen seem to have a spoon in this kettle," Bors said, his tone mistrustful.

Orluk nodded. "I know. But are they necessarily our enemies any longer? If they got a clue to something, and warned our upper echelons because we're in a position to act fast—well— Truth is, in the last several years, off and on, I've noticed Norrmen going in and out of important Yuanese offices—" He snapped his lips shut. His was not to say more than he must.

"What shall I tell the Maurai legate when she arrives?" Bors wondered.

"Don't ruffle her feathers unduly," Orluk counseled. "Explain that her countrymen, if they really are her countrymen, were extradited on criminal charges, you had no choice but to obey, and she can apply to diplomatic channels for information." In his hand he held a gauntlet. He slapped it against his thigh, a whipcrack noise. "Let's be away!"

Bors rustled the papers he had received, to show that he had in fact had no choice. "You cannot stay for refreshment, honored sir?" he asked as politeness required.

"No, sir, my humble thanks, but I regret it is impossible." They exchanged bows, followed by salutes. Bors departed.

Orluk turned to go. Vanna plucked his sleeve. Fear knocked in her breast. "What do you really think?" she asked him.

"Wai?" He blinked in surprise.

"About this. What is behind it? I sense—utter wrongness—*evil*—" She must force the last word out. It was not one which a true Gaean would use save in the cruelest extremity.

Orluk's leathery countenance registered unease. "How, reverend lady?"

"I don't know. This is so sudden. And yet it isn't, either. Dreadful forces loose, unnatural alliances, everywhere lies and secrets, lies and secrets. . . . Orluk, a wind blows from tomorrow and it smells of war. Not a few battles and a treaty, but a war, violence and worse than violence, to bring down the world. What can you tell me? What can we do?"

Were they drops of mist on his brow and in his beard, or sweat? She saw him force himself into starkness. "Reverend lady," he said, "I know scarcely a thing beyond what I've already told. Something very bad is going on, but it's still hidden in the dark." He squared shoulders which had slumped a little. "Come what may, come the demons out of hell, I hope I'll do my duty, whatever it turns out to be.

"I must go."

"A minute more," she craved, from a tide that—in this hour when serenity was torn to rags and scattered on the wind from the future —bore her toward Oneness. "I have a brother who's a soldier. And are we not all reservists, all Soldati? If something happens to rouse those bone-deep fears we bear, ancestral memories of Death Time, and we must fight, you know how shaken the troops will be. A proróchina in their midst could make every difference to their morale. Call on me."

"Reverend lady!" He was overwhelmed.

She smiled, for now that she had spoken, calm was rising in her, the calm of absolute resolution. "There will be many such volunteers," she said. "The fight will be for Gaea . . . and for humankind, lest Gaea be forced to cast us off. I approach you because we are acquainted. Krasnaya cannot field any large army, and it will doubtless be under Yuanese joint command; you can expedite my recruitment; I would like to ride to battle with a friend."

He gave her a bow of Third Humility; his Tien Dziang only rated Second. She gave him her blessing. He bustled off and barked orders.

Once more at peace, Vanna sought Iern. (Afterward she would

withdraw to her home and let Oneness possess her and she possess It.) She wanted to bid him farewell. They would never meet again. He had gusted into her life like a breeze off the sea she had not seen except in pictures and poems; for a tiny bit, she had daydreamed; but of course that was impossible. The marvels he had described, the revelation of his spirit in their few days together, were as much as she could have hoped for, and enough.

He had his love. Maybe she would have the kindness to stand aside while Vanna and Iern said their decorous goodbyes.

5

Mist rolled white across the earth, but heaven was clear and the sun a dazzlement low in the east. Breath was still sharp as it went in the nostrils, visible as it went out, but sweet odors of horse had begun to rise. A hush lay yet over the company, but hoofbeats, creak of leather, jingle of metal, surrounded it with sound. Then from afar, dwindled but unutterably clear, came the ringing of a bell.

It clanged in no cadence of Franceterr, and a drum which must be huge boomed slowly beneath its tones. That call completed Iern's sense of unreality—or was it he that was the phantom? Kilometers distant, he made out the temple, multiple-roofed, rising to an onion-domed tower, awakening the village beneath to devotions and labor, and every shape was grotesque. The landscape might likewise have been on another planet. Curiously laid-out fields reached from yonder horizon to this road; no fence, hedgerow, wall, or boundary stone identified any plot of ground as anybody's own; trees stood only where they could serve as windbreaks or give shade to a worker while he rested. The feeling Iern got was that this countryside was tended in total care by the people who belonged to it.

On the right side of the road, a line of poplars went parallel, as they often did on both sides at home. Here they had untrimmed poles woven between them to make a cattle-proof barrier. Beyond reached grass. Near the edge of vision, a herd and a pair of horsemen seemed to float on the mist.

Yesterday he had felt nothing strange, in the excitement of liberation and departure; and then when he and Ronica had slipped out of camp to a haystack they'd marked— ("Who cares about the wet?" she laughed. "It'll steam right off, I promise you.") This morning, his body weary and nerves aquiver from released tension, he knew how lost he was.

In search of assurance, he glanced behind him at the soldiers. They should be solid. But their forms, faces below the crested helmets, dress, banners were foreign; their very style of riding was, the rhythm in which lances swayed and flashed. Their outfitting sloppy and their formation well-nigh nonexistent by his standards, they nonetheless conveyed a sense of coiled-snake readiness. Yawns were giving place to talk, in ordinary human fashion, but when somebody cracked a joke in their high-pitched language, they did not laugh like Uropans.

He brought his attention back to the commander, on whose right he traveled. A compact man, Orluk Boktan bore himself so erect that he appeared taller than he was. A countenance craggy apart from the flat nose held slant gray eyes, gray mustaches and forked beard, a scar puckering the left cheek. He was bareheaded, his shaven pate stubbly, his collar open, and he puffed on an atrocious cigar. His voice was harsh but his manner affable—if Iern read it aright, which was not certain—as he responded to questions.

Ronica, on his left, conducted the conversation, translating between Unglish and Angley. Plik and Mikli rode close behind. Terai and Wairoa were at the tail of the column, not to be seen from here. *Poor fellows,* Iern thought. However, Ronica had explained the necessity of keeping them silent. Whatever cause she served, she herself must not be endangered! *How splendidly she rears in her saddle against this enormous sky. Am I falling in love?*

"Yes," Orluk was saying through the woman, "I am from Yo-Ming in the West, and know the mountains of the Border well. The Bison Polk has a range at their feet, and there my older wife dwells, and our children and grandchildren. I visit when I can."

"How do you come to live this far east?"

Orluk grinned. "Thanks to your folk! I had the luck to be in several of our last clashes with them. It got me quick promotion and the notice of my superiors. The Bison Polk has a good many members in the Chai Ka-Go area, who moved that way as the city grew. When their old noyon died, I was invited to take his post. Not easy, shifting from hills to plains, leading troops drawn from ranches and towns instead of hunters, trappers, timbermen— Well, I was needed on that same account, because these parts keep woodlands too, where the Bisons may someday have to fight. A proper Soldat doesn't refuse duty. But I wanted my youngsters raised in the country of their fathers."

"Have you been here long?"

"Fifteen years. It's not bad. I've a fine home in Chai Ka-Go, which is a place where you can have fun; a nice little wife there, children by her, grandchildren in a few more years, I hope. I can brag that I've done well in my command. Who was dispatched to scour the Krasnayan woods for bombrunners? The Bisons!"

Reminded, Orluk lost his geniality, scowled, and puffed savagely on his cigar. "We found nothing, though," he said, "till your group — When I think about my women, children, grandchildren— Ha, if you want their story squeezed out of those two dogs, ask me. Start by putting pliers to their balls, I would."

"That isn't so Gaean, is it?" gibed Mikli.

"I'm not a Gaean," Orluk said. "I give the Principles and adepts their due respect. They may be right. But meditation and theory aren't for me, and what honor do they have from lip service? My homage is to the old gods—Oktai, Erlik, Lenin—and the ancestors." He brooded. "Not that I think a true Gaean would be tenderhearted in this matter. What *are* they scheduled for, those two?"

"That's out of my department," Mikli said.

"Is it?" Orluk threw him a backward look. "I wonder. You know a hellful more than you've told."

"Indeed I do," replied Mikli blandly. "For example, the ways by which my team identified what that pair were up to and how Ronica and I tracked them down. Details of that kind would point at too much else my service prefers not to make public. I do not question your trustworthiness, Noyon, but you have no need to know. As a military man, you understand."

"Yes, I do. But things weren't this tangled and strange when I was young—"

Actually, Iern did not hear what the men talked about until later. Ronica had stopped translating when Orluk gave her an irritated glare. She continued to ride alongside the commander and listen to the Unglish. The sense of isolation grew colder within Iern. He dropped behind to join Plik, while Mikli rode forward.

The Angleyman was sober, for lack of supplies, and subdued. He regarded his companion for a while before he said, "You're troubled, my friend. Not worried or frightened, nothing so superficial, but troubled. Aren't you?"

Iern stared ahead of him. The sight of Ronica against the Mong landscape stabbed with realization of how alien she, too, was. "I suppose you could call it that," he mumbled.

"Do you know why? Presumably you're bound for safety in the Union, and in charming company."

That last phrase brought back recollection of Vanna yesterday. She hadn't seemed to mind when he violated her society's customs, took both her hands in his, and kissed them. How delicate they were, exquisitely formed. "Blessing be upon you, Talence Iern Ferlay," she had murmured. "May you win happiness, as you well deserve." *She's mistaken there,* had gone through him, in an arrow flight of his past misdeeds. She chanted a few lines in her language and explained: "Those were not a prayer for you. We do not pray to Gaea. They were a wish, with what force is mine behind it, that your share of Her life become whole." Her ritual solemnity broke. "I, I will remember you, often and often. Fare gladly."

To Plik, Iern blurted, "I'm flying blind, that's why, blind and the instruments gone dead."

"It is indeed disturbing to find oneself in a foreign myth."

"What? No, listen, I admit our stay in Dulua has made me doubt a great many things I took for granted. I wasn't so narrow-minded I didn't believe Gaeans can be good people individually. I knew some in Uropa who were—are. But they did seem to be on the side of the enemy—in a fundamental way, against everything the Domain lives by—and wrong, wrong! Now Vanna—those patient explanations of hers, and her own self—" Iern looked near the sun through eyes almost shut. His lashes made rainbow colors. She had made him aware of countless small miracles like that, and gotten him to think about them and feel them.

"Yes, she has the ultimate Gaean personality, doesn't she?" Plik mused. "Or an aspect of it . . . as St. Francis of Assisi and St. John of the Cross have two aspects of the ultimate Christian personality. . . . Why do I use that mincing word 'personality'? I mean 'soul.' 'Emotional' is another cowardly word. I will say 'spiritual.' The real meaning of a faith is spiritual, beyond comprehension except by the spirit. She explained hers to you, in part, by being what she is."

"Could she possibly be right?"

"Is a poem right or wrong? Hers is a powerful myth, yes."

Silence fell between them. Mist thinned off the ground, revealing lands on the left harvested or under preparation for winter wheat, silvery-green prairie on the right. Blue-clad slugai were emerging from their row houses of rammed earth. Birds passed overhead. The air had warmed further and carried odors of soil and vegetation as well as horse and man. The manifold noises of the cavalry troop had settled into a steadiness of syncopated beats.

"And these Yuanese," broke from Iern. "Can they be fundamentally different from the Krasnayans? Oh, I admit how little I've seen of either. But less and less can I believe they'd conspire with Jovain, away off in Uropa, and arm him for his coup, as we've heard they probably did."

"Why have you changed your mind?" Plik asked.

"Well, naturally, a Gaean regime in the Domain would please them, and some of their officials may have given him a little secret encouragement and help. Otherwise . . . they act far more interested in the Northwest Union. And well they might. Same continent. They don't give me any impression of being imperialists, directly or indirectly. Gaeanity at its heart is not militant. I've learned that much. Its nature is to persuade, not compel."

"You *have* learned," Plik said. "Not that you have logical proof. Our species is gifted where it comes to interpreting doctrine so as to justify whatever one wants to do. You're here because some Gaeans are adventurous and warlike, aren't you? And what's happening in the world goes beyond logic, beyond all rational explanation."

Iern gave him a sharp look. "Are you getting weird again?"

"The universe is weird. I'm not sure whether 'reality' is a word that can have a meaningful definition."

Plik leaned close. "Here me," he said, and never had Iern seen him more grave. "I am an alcoholic wastrel, but I'm also a minor poet, and therefore from time to time I deal in things that cannot be spoken straight out.

"What I feel upon us is a gigantic conflict of . . . mystiques—a conflict so deep-going that human beings and whole civilizations are turning themselves willy-nilly into archetypes and reenacting immemorially ancient myths—for only myth and music can even hint at such truths. . . . The Apollonian Domain and Arthurian Maurai are up against Orphic Gaeanity and the Faustian Northwest. Or if you'd rather, the Norrmen are demons readying to overthrow the gods of sky, sea, and earth—though chthonic gods have always had their own dark side—and the war that is coming will bring an end to the world."

Ronica— "No!" Iern shouted. "You're crazy!"

He wanted to gallop his horse till wind, speed, exertion drove the horror out of him. *Why horror? Those were only words, that Plik likes to play with. He's only eccentric, not a madman, not a prophet.* Orluk would scarcely allow him to leave the troop. He trotted ahead, drew next to Ronica, and poured talk at her, any talk that came to his tongue.

She answered merrily. His nightmare faded. It left him altogether when she brought her mouth close to his ear and proposed, in a straightforward sentence, what they should do while the company took its midday rest.

They reached the military base toward evening. The outlines of a blockhouse, hulking athwart heaven, recalled centuries of history that Uropa had not shared; but lesser buildings were reassuringly prosaic, functional. Familiar as well were a little airfield, a few planes parked on it, and a whiff of synfuel scent.

One craft was Northwestern, a large version of the one that lay on the lake bottom with its deadly cargo. Iern made out an insigne painted on the tail, a running wolf from whose neck hung a broken chain. As the column approached, half a dozen men stepped forth to meet its leader. Among them were two unmistakable countrymen of Ronica's; others waited by the plane.

A Yuanese officer saluted, said some words, and handed a sheet of paper to Orluk. The noyon read it, frowned, and sat pondering. Mikli spoke to him, got a curt response, and rode over to where Iern, Ronica, and Plik were waiting.

"Orders flown in from Chai Ka-Go today," he informed them. To judge by his manner, this was not unexpected. "He's to let us go home immediately, taking Terai and Wairoa along."

The Clansman's pulse bounced. On a night flight, he wouldn't see as much as he had hoped. *But she'll be beside me, and when we arrive—*

"Our esteemed commander doesn't approve of such haste," Plik observed shrewdly. "He suspects a hustle, and wonders if his superiors were wise in endorsing it."

Mikli leered. "They weren't," he said in Francey. "The imperative for our side has been that at all costs, we must not let anybody else interrogate the Maurai. No doubt our spokesmen's argument was plausible—that, being those who got on the trail of the conspirators, we know most and are best able to interrogate in depth, and no time should be wasted. But doubtless it was certain additional considerations that made certain key Yuanese individuals agree the argument was indisputable. Come, let's pay our devoirs and be gone."

Courtesies went to and fro. Armed Norrmen took charge of the prisoners. Hand in hand, Iern and Ronica were the last to embark. They paused at the cabin door and looked back. Sunset light scattered unreal gold across a land that again, itself, seemed unreal. Still on his horse, Orluk loomed out of a long shadow, peering after the departing foreigners.

XVI

His first month in the Northwest Union became for Iern more than an idyl. It turned into a voyage of discovery.

The inaugural surprise was his reception, or rather the lack of any. There were no passport requirements, no customs, no money changers, no officials. The plane landed on an airstrip near a village simply because agents of the Maurai Inspectorate might be present at a city port. Terai, Wairoa, and a couple of their guards stayed aboard simply because the sight of men under detention would have caused gossip. Everybody else made straight for a nearby hostel.

When Iern expressed amazement, Ronica snorted. "What'd any country in its right mind want with that kind of garbage?" she said. "We hold that busybody types should also earn an honest living."

After a few hours' sleep, the party met for a gargantuan breakfast, served by a staff that presented no reckoning. "This place belongs to the Wolf Lodge, and we're on Lodge business," Ronica explained. "Otherwise we'd pay. If we were nonmembers, we'd pay double."

"You and I shall have to call on the local Lodgemaster before we go on," Mikli told the Clansman. "Be discreet."

That was in a home down the street. Iern had seen occasional photographs and read occasional travelers' descriptions from the Union; not many were available in Uropa. He was somewhat prepared for architectural styles which were, moreover, less exotic than the Mong's. The office within the house was plainly furnished except for pictures, relics of local history, and a carven plaque above the desk—the wolf with the broken chain and the motto *Run Free.* The Lodgemaster, who in the present case was a robust middle-aged woman, heard out Mikli's brief account, asked some eager questions through him, but soon, at his urging, shook the newcomer's hand, wished him a pleasant stay, and bade him goodbye.

Iern had expected that here he would receive formal asylum, or else be referred to someone who had the power to grant it. "But this was just a courtesy call!" he exclaimed when back outside.

"Why, of course," Mikli said. "It pays to observe the proprieties when they don't cost too much effort. At that, Dorda was rather miffed when I told her this was a concern of the Mother Lodge, acting for the whole, and we could only give her a short time and some noncommittal chitchat. Provincial chapters complain chronically about how snotty the leadership is."

"Whom shall we report to?"

"Nobody, unless you count a small number of people whose help we'll need. You aren't going to be held incommunicado, exactly, but it wouldn't do to attract attention to you."

"Isn't this illegal?"

Mikli yipped mirth. "You have considerable to learn, duckie. As a matter of fact, the appropriate officers of the Wolf Lodge will have to okay such things as the internment of Terai and Wairoa. Otherwise, if they found us out, they might hold us guilty of unjustifiable invasion of personal liberty. We'd have to let our prisoners go, and face a hefty damage suit for sullying the honor of the Lodge, as well as whatever claims the two Maurai wanted to bring against us."

"But the government—" Iern gave up.

Two automobiles waited at the airstrip. They were large, their aluminum and woodwork brightly painted. Iern could see that they used steam engines, automatically fired by powdered coal; he smelled it, too, in the reek of exhaust. He could not tell whether the tires were of synthetic elastomer, as in the Domain, or natural rubber obtained through trade.

Their warders joined the captives in one. Mikli, Plik, Iern, and Ronica took its mate. "Let me drive," the woman said ardently. "Yasu Krist, I don't think I've held a steering wheel for an ever-loving year!"

She spoke Unglish, but Iern understood. At odd moments along the way, she had led him in practicing it, and Vanna had shown him books in it. The written language was sufficiently near Angley that he knew he could quickly learn to read, if not to write very reliably. Speech would take a while longer. As yet, he could only follow Ronica, because he was used to her voice, and only in fragments. However, it had become clear to him—as Mikli had remarked on an evening at the campfire—that the two speeches transformed into each other according to fairly regular rules. Once he had mastered those, fluency would become just a matter of exercise and of acquiring vocabulary.

The dialects of Ingliss prevalent in various parts of Oceania were something else again. As for Maurai, while its grammatical structure was basically Hinja-Uropan, scarcely half its words were related to Angley or Francey, and their line of descent had seen countless mutations.

Ronica engaged the motor. The car took off like a rocket. Though the road was smoothly graveled, Iern thought a hundred and fifty kilometers an hour a trifle excessive if you weren't airborne, especially when she roared in an arc around indignant drivers of horse carriages and oxcarts. The second chauffeur probably agreed, for his vehicle was soon lost to sight behind a cloud of dust.

Otherwise the scene was peaceful. Sunlight and cloud shadows flowed across alternations of evergreen forest and cleared farmland. Afar in heaven he saw a mighty snowpeak, Mount Rainier. Cloven air hooted. A partly opened window let in a breath of coolness, hay, smoke, damp, autumnal odors advancing as summer retreated.

Eeriness tingled through him. "Those farms," he said at last. "Utterly strange to me—almost every detail about them—but even so, they . . . they remind me of my grandfather Mael's, where I was born. And I can't think how."

"Freeholds," Ronica answered, referring to earlier reminiscences of his. "Most of these, the same families have had for generations, beholden to nobody. Hirelings and tenants, too, have generally been around for lifetime after lifetime. They belong here the same as their landmasters."

"It's neither that ideal nor that solid an existence. It never was," Mikli scoffed from the back seat. "Like most of our institutions, Iern, this kind of husbandry originated out of need for defense during the Mong Wars. It's obsolete now. More and more farmers are selling out to agribusinesses . . . because their sons and daughters have moved to town. Three or four years ago, the Grand Council passed a resolution deploring this decay of the yeomanry, the backbone of the Union, and calling for remedies. Heh-eh! One virtue the Northwestern government does have. By its rudimentary character, it makes obvious the fatuity of all government: something which the heavy-handedness of most tends to disguise."

"Oh, I don't know," Ronica said. "I think we've got a damn fine system, or did till the Maurai horned in. We will again, by God." She lifted her head, and Iern remembered that secret battle cry, *Orion shall rise.*

Between them, as much in argument as in exposition, she and Mikli sketched the unwritten constitution of the Northwest Union.

Membership in a Lodge was voluntary and revocable for cause.

These days, a substantial part of the population belonged to none, and even members carried on most everyday activities independently of them. Regardless, they remained fundamental to the society—or societies, in this huge and diverse realm.

What actual government the Union had was principally local, elected, and highly participatory through public meetings which often got highly vocal. It provided little more than police and courts. Other services—roads, schools, libraries, hospitals, fire protection, waste disposal, and on and on, frequently including police—were furnished by private enterprise or by a Lodge on a fee basis. (Twice, en route to Seattle, the car stopped at a turnpike and Mikli paid toll.) Competition kept the price low, since law provided for no exclusive franchises.

Above municipalities were the Territories, fifty-two regions widely different in size and character, all of them organic outgrowths of land, ethnos, and history. Their own governments ranged from parliamentary to aristocratic, and met periodically to deal with matters of regional concern. (To this extent, Territories resembled states of the Domain or tribes of the Federation.) However, they usually had such meager executive authority that they were dependent on the goodwill of a community to carry out, in its area, any measures they enacted.

A vague analogue of a federal parliament, the Grand Council of the Union met annually for a short time around summer solstice, unless emergency required an extraordinary gathering. The location was on an island in the straits, from which the major cities thereabouts were accessible but not so readily that their fleshpots would tempt legislators to hold long sessions.

This legislature was bicameral. The House of Delegates was the larger, comprising representatives of the Territories. Each Territory could have from one to three, according to how much it contributed to the national treasury, a matter which it decided for itself, as it did the manner of choosing its representatives. The House of the Lodges had one member from each, including Injun, Eskimo, and Aleut tribes that had opted for an equal status. (Some, with entire control over their home Territories, saw no reason to.) Presiding over both was the Chief, elected by the Delegates with the advice and consent of the Lodges.

The Delegates passed legislation; the Lodges could veto. Nothing that was passed applied to any Territory whose own laws contravened it. However, unreasonable or unduly selfish denial was apt to bring reprisals, such as a general boycott. The Grand Council concerned itself mainly with the common interest in broad matters—public health, protection of environment, inter-Territorial cooperation in general—and this to a very limited degree. It did not even directly issue money. The Territories did; the Union dollar simply registered what they, at current rates of exchange, saw fit to pay into the common fund. (Currencies were variously based, but always on something tangible, usually silver, copper, or real estate. They had better be; paper money was in use, but nowhere was it legal tender.)

The Council maintained modest clerical and research facilities at the otherwise sleepy fishing village where it customarily assembled. More extensive resources were available via radiophone, printout, or a boat to one of the cities.

The offices of the Chief were permanently in Vittohrya. They handled defense and foreign relations. As for defense, it relied on the Territorial volunteer militias, though a cadre of professionals existed. The Chief appointed and removed diplomats, while the treasury supported a small organization of career experts and underlings. Any international agreement, no matter how trivial, required the approval of both Houses. This had not originally been cumbersome, for in its glory days, between the decline of the Mong and the coming of the Maurai, the Northwest Union had had scant reason to care what foreigners wanted.

These years were more humble. If they would continue speaking for their peoples at all, Chief, Grand Council, and Territorial authorities must cooperate with the occupying Inspectorate in its searches and seizures. "I see the bear trap they're in, and sympathize, sort of," Ronica said. "Our native toadies and opportunists don't exactly help their prestige, either. The more power they think they need to claim over us, the less compliance they get, so they call for more laws, more snoops, and folk get their backs up higher and find new ways to evade."

"It isn't that simple," Mikli maintained. "Quite a few among us *want* a stronger government. They say if we'd had one, we wouldn't have lost the war; and now we need one to . . . ah . . . 'bring us into the modern world' is a popular phrase among intellectuals."

"Oh, sure," Ronica sneered. "There've always been a lot of infantiles who want somebody else to make their mistakes for them, and the intellectuals have always been glad to oblige." She glanced at Iern. "In the past ten or a dozen years, Lodge membership has been increasing from a postwar low. Ordinary people are deciding, the way they did when the Mong were on the rampage, they've nowhere else to turn."

"When fever has burned off fat," Plik murmured at her back, "we begin to see the real flesh again, and the skeleton beneath."

2

As he neared Seattle, Iern saw how villages grew closer together, roads were paved, and automotive traffic waxed. A military convoy in the Domain would have had fewer motor vehicles per kilometer than civilians were driving here. While trucks predominated, buses, motorcycles, and even private passenger cars were common; the metropolitan area must contain thousands. And this was in spite of numerous railroads, where steam locomotives pulled interminable trains. Lines appeared, strung on wooden poles, which he learned transmitted electric power, or telegraphic and, in some cases, telephone communications. Daylight or no, colored fluorescent signs blinked outside many shops. After dark, nearly all illumination would be by carbon-filament electric incandescents, and no few families would tune in radios they owned for an evening's entertainment.

"How can you do it?" Iern marveled.

"By good luck," Mikli replied. "After the Doom War there was abundant metal lying around. A single sky-piercer, as a tall building was called, yielded I know not what tonnage of steel and copper; abandoned automobiles became a major resource; et cetera. Besides, nature has blessed the Northwest with abundant hydroelectric potential, and we import coal from enormous fields farther east. So we've no lack of energy or chemical feedstocks. We get aluminum from clay, magnesium from seawater, synthetics from coal and wood products— Well, you can find the details in an engineering library."

"It's more than luck," Plik declared. "You had to be the kind of people who do such things."

"Aye," said Ronica proudly. "Free people, everybody minding his own business, including the business he makes his living by."

She maneuvered through a crowded intersection. "Shoulda been a traffic-control signal there," she said when she had gotten past, after an exchange of curses in which a muleteer came off second best. "We have them downtown. But they do require materials, mainly electrical, which're in heavy demand for other things. We hear talk about replacing power lines with underground ceramic tubes of salt solution, then we could reclaim that much metal, but the labor required would be unbelievable."

Bitterness ripped from her: "What we could do if the Maurai'd let us! Energy, resources, boundless, a universe full! But no, that would upset their precious little hegemony, wouldn't it?"

Mikli reached out to lay a hand on her shoulder. "Easy," he warned.

—Seattle was big. Though a census had never been held in the Union, population was estimated as high as fifty thousand. The city was also, to Iern's mind, ugly. Its streets were admittedly clean; horses, oxen, and the like wore plastic diapers in town, as they did in the Domain. Otherwise, here was none of the venerability of an industrial section in his country, nor any piously preserved ruins such as towered over Chai Ka-Go. Most construction was brick and concrete, boxlike, smoke-begrimed. Traffic brawled, factories belched soot and stench, marts were garish: a chaos wherein houses left over from an earlier era seemed pathetically lost.

Ronica gave a defensive answer to a remark of Iern's: "This is a working town. We don't need parks, when it's just a short ferry ride to an island or bus ride to the nearest woods. The air isn't usually this bad; rain washes it for us. And you'll see a nice district or two."

All the same, he was disturbed, at a deeper level than the esthetic. *Why?* he wondered. *Could Plik be right about this being Demon Land? No, that's absurd. But why, then, am I uneasy?* He wasn't accustomed to looking into himself.

Ronica kept her promise. Crowded with ships, the waterfront was a rousing sight. When she turned north, its docks and warehouses soon gave way to homes surrounded by lawns and gardens. Fresh breezes blew off the Sound, which sparkled around winging sailboats and islands intensely green save where fall colors had begun to blaze. Mountains limned the sky.

The car went up a driveway and stopped under a carriage porch. The building was impressive, long, high, massively and darkly timbered. Above the main doorway stood the sign of the Wolf. "The Seattle chapter house," Mikli said. "The Mother Lodge is south on Mount Hood, where it was founded, but this is the largest chapter and here we'll spend the night."

—Dinner was ceremonious, presided over by a white-bearded Lodgemaster in a blue robe, who kept a hat on his head and, when they rose to go, took a staff which a postulant waiter handed him. Two other Lodgemasters were present, one female, and several more persons whose counsel was obviously wanted. The seafood offered was delicious, the regional wine surprisingly good. Despite the formal atmosphere, in a dining room where portraits on the wainscot looked from across centuries, and despite the need for translation, talk went vigorously. Iern found himself telling at length about his nation, background, experiences, hopes.

Afterward the party repaired to a chamber whose somber sumptuousness was both relieved and deepened by the relics on display. Ronica showed them to the Uropans: banners and weapons from battlefields where Norrmen rolled back Mong; a sliderule belonging to the chief of the first engineering team that restored a hydroelectric dam, while sickness ravaged them and resentful savages raided them; the log of a ship that had dared Arctic fogs and storms and ice for three years, to rechart those waters—remembrances of Wolves who had served their people well and brought honor to their Lodge. Iern was especially moved by a set of logarithmic and trigonometric tables. They had been hand-copied in an isolated community, not long after the War of Judgment, from a printed book that was rotting away.

Meanwhile servitors laid out drinking and smoking materials, and disappeared. Curtains shut away a night that had turned rainy. The group found armchairs and settled down for serious discussion.

Ronica tried to keep the foreigners abreast of it, but was handicapped by the fact that she kept putting in her own oar. A couple of times she got into stiff arguments. It was Mikli who, after hours had passed, summed the decision up:

"We cannot risk our secret getting out. Not that you'd willingly betray us, I know. However, your presence could give the enemy clues, as active as they're likely to become after Terai's report from Uropa.

"So, Iern, you shall have the asylum you asked for, in a safe place. I'm afraid we can't let you establish contact with your homeland, even clandestine, for some while to come. But what could you expect to accomplish immediately? Wait a year or two and see how the cat jumps over there. Meanwhile, I think you'll enjoy learning more about us." He snickered. "Considering who your teacher will be, eh?"

Ronica didn't blush. "I sure am ready for a furlough," she said.

"What about me?" asked Plik. "When can I return?"

"Sorry. You'll have to wait too," Mikli said. "We'll make your stay as pleasant as we can." He cleared his throat. "I imagine your friends will prefer to be by themselves at first. We'll provide you comfort and amusement, Plik, and Iern will revisit you in due course."

"I see," the Angleyman answered slowly. "Well, this is better brandy than I can afford at home, and as for Vineleaf—" Breath hissed in between his teeth. Tossing off his glassful, he refilled, his hand not quite steady. "You won't mind if I keep helping myself, will you?"

"And what of Terai and Wairoa?" Iern demanded. "Where are they?"

The Northwesterners heard the names. Their faces hardened, like molten metal setting. "We consider them prisoners of war," Mikli said. "We won't maltreat them."

War. Iern and Plik exchanged a look. Rain hammered on windowpanes.

"I expect they can go back after Orion has risen," Ronica made haste to add.

"Hold!" Mikli exclaimed.

She gave him a whetted glance. "I'll not spill anything," she told him in the same Angley she had been using, "but neither will I lie to Iern, by words or by silence."

The Clansman braced himself where he sat. "I would have liked to bid Terai and Wairoa goodbye," he said.

"They'll be okay, I swear, if they don't get reckless," Ronica promised. "And you might very well see them again before you're free to go home, all of you—when the world is free."

3

Vangcouve Island, across the Strait of Wandy Fuca, hardly seemed a place of exile.

Under assumed names, Iern and Ronica spent their first three days in Vittohrya. Given clothes in local style, Iern attracted no attention from the city's cosmopolitan dwellers, in spite of clean-shavenness and comparatively short hair, while Ronica drew no more than she did everywhere there were men. When in public he kept a bandage on his throat and she explained that her husband was recovering from laryngeal surgery and could not speak. His condition did not prevent him from dining well; the Wolf Lodge had provided ample money.

Vittohrya was very nearly the opposite of Seattle. A cultural and, to a lesser degree, political rather than a commercial center, it preserved (or had in the course of centuries regained) the legendary graciousness it had possessed before the Doom War. What ancient buildings survived had been lovingly restored; most new architecture was in harmony with them; parks and gardens were everywhere. Ronica showed Iern about, historic sites, viewpoints, museums, the university she had attended. Each evening they enjoyed a presentation—concert, ballet, Injun dance—before going back to their hotel and enjoying each other.

And yet, he came to see, "very nearly opposite" was superficial, misleading. Folk might tend to be more cultivated and less bustling here, but the same demon of energy and will dwelt in them. He saw it in breakneck boat races, swimming, ball games; in the tense curve of a bridge or a statue; in Venturers' Hall, where reports arrived daily of prospects for profit around the globe; in crowded, noisy, smoky taverns, as beer went down by the liter and distilled spirits followed close behind; in walls that bore scars of street fighting during the Power War and later riots; in the free-swinging gait of man and woman alike.

In the glowers and curt responses given what few uniformed Maurai he noticed.

"I feel sorry for them," he admitted once when he and Ronica were by themselves. "That must be some of the loneliest duty on Earth."

"I s'pose," she answered. "Inspectorate personnel are spread almighty thin. Of course, I'll bet you silver to skunk cabbage that a lot of so-called Maurai sailors, business people, scholars, and tourists are undercover agents."

"What sort of treatment do they usually get?"

"Depends. Some among us still won't speak to one, unless you count spitting on the street as he walks by. Some are cold and correct. Most, nowadays, are willing to meet an individual halfway and give him whatever he deserves. And some fawn on them."

"Surely genuine friendships happen, even affairs and marriages."

"Oh, sure. Bound to. Speaking of which—" She reached for him.

—They moved to a housekeeping cabin the Wolf Lodge owned and spent the rest of the month there. It stood by itself in a lovely place on the west coast. Land dropped steeply to the sea, forest dreamed, mountains reared behind. They had ample supplies, books, radio, phonograph and music library, boat, fishing tackle. When they wished to explore elsewhere, they took bicycles over several kilometers of trail to a dirt road where a bus stopped. Ordinarily their quest was into natural splendors, for the great island was lightly populated, but sometimes they found themselves in a fisher village and its cheerful pub.

By then Iern could talk, less and less haltingly each time. Ronica made him learn Unglish by insisting they use nothing else for at least half of every day. Among others he stayed mute, until toward the end she decided they could safely call him sufficiently recovered to speak a few cordial words in a voice which had not yet gotten back a natural intonation. She continued to carry on the actual conversations for both of them, shifting easily from truthful reminiscence to shameless prevarication.

These were a hardy, hearty folk. From low little houses, built strong against gales, they set forth in low little boats to reap the ocean. Among the headstones in the graveyards stood memorials to those who never came back; centuries had eroded away many names but no courage. The lucky men returned to their wives, who had been working at least as hard, and their children, who also had tasks but always attended school. They returned to a church, for most of them believed in Yasu; perhaps a general store, and certainly a tavern, though it be but a single room in the landlord's home; bus, bicycle, or pony cart bringing them to larger communities where they found shops and a chapter house of whatever Lodge was theirs, though it be but a weathered cabin.

"I like your people," Iern told Ronica, in their cottage. "The more I see of them, the better I like them—"

She smiled. Lamplight glowed amber across her hair and skin; shadows shifted, bringing out by turns the strong molding of her body, the deep cleft of her bosom. She was making dinner, and the air in the room was warm, aromatic, faintly resin-smoky. Windows were full of night, but the world came through them as a sound of surf, soughing in trees, call of an owl. "You like just about anybody," she said. "You're that kind of guy."

"—but the less I understand them," he went on, from the chair where he sat admiring the view. She being infinitely the better cook, he washed dishes after meals. It was as reasonable a division of labor as her skillful splitting of firewood with a flint-headed ax on which she chipped a fresh edge as required, his carrying the sticks inside.

"How so?" She continued busy. The stone slab topping the brick stove was hot, water boiled in a vessel of heat-resistant glass set over an opening above the fire, a synthetic-lined aluminum wok had received its oil and was ready for stir-frying.

He fumbled after words. "I don't have the right terms, I can't ask the right questions. But, oh, what seems completely contradictory—on the one hand, this outspoken individualism, the freehold farmer or the small businessman or the skipper who owns his own boat, those the ideal—"

"My mother and stepfather have told me that people didn't make such a fuss about it before the war. They took it for granted. Since, we've gotten the Maurai to react against."

"Well, but on the other hand, the Lodges, and members centering their lives on them— Or am I wrong about that?"

"It'll take a slew of explaining," she said. "I'm not sure how well I can explain, seeing as how I grew up with it. You, looking in from the outside, might actually make a few things clearer to me. Let's talk it over as soon as dinner's on the table."

He felt a sheerly intellectual thrill. By now he knew full well that she was not in any degree a barbarian. He did not know what she really was.

The Northwest Union was never founded as such; it grew. The name dated from the Assembly of Vittohrya, which formalized relationships already in existence, but another hundred years would pass before the last Territory joined.

In the dark and poorly chronicled era following the Doom War, their cities destroyed or dying on the vine, climate turned cold and stormy, nature itself fallen sick, their only outside contacts the Mong invaders, somehow those Northwesterners who survived rallied themselves to prevail. Out of the need to stand together, shoulder to shoulder and back to back, the Lodges evolved.

These people had always been both self-reliant and gregarious. They had had their churches, clubs, civic organizations, volunteer service groups, and the like. The oldest of the Lodges—Elk, Moose, Lion, Mason—traced their origins to the time before the catastrophe. They were nuclei and examples; but likewise were the remaining nonwhite aborigines, some of whom had kept a vestige of tribalism and now revived it in new forms. (This was almost the sole analogy to early Maurai history.)

The typical Lodge began as a male outfit for mutual help. Much of that was of a military or constabulary character. In region after region, a Lodge became a militia, recruiting, training, procuring and storing matériel, building and garrisoning strong points, and fighting when called upon. Add to this its civilian functions. It organized medical and fire-protection teams, provided for the aged and disabled and bereaved, salvaged what it could of books and other relics, set up schools for the children, exerted social pressure toward civilized behavior. Rituals, costumes, initiations, ranks, mystique gave its members strength to endure; such things were both recreation and re-creation. Membership was always voluntary, because for a long time the ghosts of the old United States and Canada haunted the minds of men; but once a Lodge had arisen, few individuals wished to stay outside its shelter.

Gradually, fitfully, Lodges spread beyond their original homes.. Members who moved elsewhere founded chapters, which stayed in touch and worked out a hierarchy for decision-making. The fraternities had always kept certain secrets, and their warlike functions had reinforced this trait. Eventually their top officers came to wield considerable power. It was not unlimited, for a disgruntled member could try to stir up a vote against it, or appeal to civil authority, or just resign. However, when it called upon the resources, economic and human, of a society whose chapters reached from the Bering Sea to Cape Mendocino, and which had investments in everything from farms to intercontinental trading companies, that power became intense.

Apart from some aboriginal tribes which had taken the name, a Lodge was not identified with a Territory. Geographically, Lodges interpenetrated. In early centuries, members of the same one might occasionally find themselves on opposite sides of a firing line. (The period rarely saw a clean-cut situation of Mericans versus Mong. Rather, there were intermittent clashes between different quarrelsome and usually short-lived little polities. When Norrman fought Norrman or Mong fought Mong, he was apt to seek allies among the aliens. Complexities and treacheries were numberless. Then during spells of peace, powerful families made advantageous marriages across borders, trade in goods and ideas grew brisk, a brilliant center of art and learning might develop and attract as many foreign as domestic admirers.)

Fraternity did, though, tend to mitigate strife and draw kindred together. The upshot was that the Norrmen stood off the Mong, drove them back from the eastern mountains, and in the course of doing so forged a new, eventually unified civilization.

In that civilization, most things a man did were of his personal choice. He shared in the bulk of public business through his Lodge. Not much was left for the state to do, and he preferred matters be that way.

He; or she. Since before the Doom, Northwesterners had borne a tradition of equal political rights for the sexes. Few communities of theirs ever lost it, and those regained it afterward. A ballot might be meaningless in the age of the folk-wanderings, but the labor and marksmanship of a wife meant everything, and she was entitled to her voice in township council. From the beginning, Lodges recognized their "ladies' auxiliaries" as essential to survival. As times grew less desperate, childbearing grew less urgent, while simultaneously activities in which women could fully participate became more important. Piecemeal, Lodges admitted them to first-class membership. ("They were already telling their husbands how to vote, anyway," Ronica laughed.)

Nowadays, when members of two different Lodges married—which happened more often than not—or a member married an outsider—which was becoming fairly common—it was usual for one to adopt the affiliation of the other. Usual, but not compulsory. A person might not wish to sever old ties, or go through a second postulancy.

The ordinary member paid dues, performed service-type duties, took part in rituals and celebrations. He or she might stand for office, or might become a salaried employee. The rewards of membership were, first and foremost, solidarity, a sense of heritage, an ideal of mutual helpfulness; schooling, insurance, medical care, housing when away from home; recreational and research facilities; the inner glow that came from free-will service; color, pageantry, fun.

And sometimes more.

The Wolf Lodge originated around Mount Hood, an area which the Mong never reached and where defense against native troublemakers was comparatively easy. Thus it was less concerned with war than with restoring order and productivity, while preserving as much material of the lost civilization as possible. It took its fair share in the general defense, but supplied a disproportionate number of officers, especially technical and staff officers. Later it provided many teachers, engineers, physicians, and similarly well-trained people, demand for whose work caused chapters to spread like dandelion seeds. Prestige allowed it to be more selective than most about whom it admitted, and more demanding of them after they were initiated.

To this day, its dues were the highest at every grade of membership, its interior pomp and public display almost the least, of any Lodge; yet none had members more influential, in technology, science, commerce, art, scholarship, the military, civic and national affairs.

It had its rites, of course, beginning with those customary at the start and end of a regular meeting. The most solemn was Return, when on Midwinter Eve a chapter met to remember its dead. Midsummer Day saw the pleasant ceremony of Honors. Revelry was in order following an initiation or an elevation in rank, as well as a wedding, christening, or golden anniversary. Funerals were stately, courts of dispute stern. The Wolves took part in communal festivities, though not very conspicuously, and maintained their philanthropies, schools, cultural and scientific activities, militia—in short, the usual—plus their equally usual collective enterprises, their shares in private businesses, and their representation in the Grand Council.

On the whole, though, the Wolf Lodge, even more than most, expected its members to create their own livelihoods and lives. It gave help rather than support. It required effort as well as dues, and not too many questions asked. Democratic enough at the day-to-day chapter-house level, it was oligarchic and close-mouthed higher up. Members who did not like this continuation of what had been an obvious wartime necessity, twenty years ago, were free to complain, call for investigation or impeachment, or resign. Few had done so, and fewer yet had paid any attention to them. Among the Wolves, the ancient bonds of the pack remained as strong as the bonds between Captain and Aerogens had once been under Skyholm.

Hence this was the Lodge that had conceived of Orion, and still dominated the endeavor to make Orion rise.

4

Beneath a westering sun, waves flamed green, gunmetal, mercury. They rolled mightily landward, reared, and crashed in foam-fountains on cliffs. The wind that whistled over them deepened its noise to a roar when it entered the forest above. It thrust and flowed and swirled, it flung coldness, salt sting of spindrift, smells of kelp and distance. Gulls wheeled and mewed; black brant took wing as a sea otter swam close; farther out, from time to time one of a pod of migratory whales broached and then dived; a ship slipped under the horizon but her sails remained in sight like a memory.

Evergreen boughs tossed dark against a sky where clouds flew in streaks. The wind tore scraps of yellow, red, bronze off broadleaf trees and sent them whirling away to their fates. A strip of turf along the cliff edge where Iern and Ronica sat was thick, harshly fragrant, tawny with autumn.

They had been for a tramp through the woods and had stopped on their way back to rest and watch the whales go by. After several minutes he glanced sideways at her. She had drawn up her knees and clasped hands across them. Her gaze had wandered from the waters and gone northwestward—toward home or toward heaven? It was a somehow blind stare. Her lips drooped.

He touched her sleeve. The wool of the mackinaw was rough beneath his fingers. "You look sad," he offered.

She turned her face to his. Her hair was coiled in braids, but a lock had escaped from her watch cap and fluttered on her brow. He had never seen a more endearing sight. "Oh, do I?" she asked as if coming slowly awake.

"You've been like that all day. You've tried hard to conceal it and be jolly, but I've come to know you a little, Ronica."

She sighed. Her smile was pensive. "Well, okay, why not be frank? I'm sorry this will soon end."

Dismay smote him. "No, it can't! Mustn't!"

"Been a wonderful month, right? None better in my life. But I can't go on parasitizing forever. I've work to do, kinfolk—the Lodgemaster and I agreed beforehand I'd get a month's vacation with you. That was fine by me." The green eyes were focused unwaveringly upon him. "I didn't know, then, how hard it would be to say goodbye."

For an instant he was dizzy, and blood in his ears shouted the wind out of them. "For how long?" he croaked.

Pain crossed the strong-boned countenance. "No telling. I'll try to get leave and rejoin you before . . . Orion rises . . . but—depends on how things go, how badly I'm needed. Don't be afraid, Iern. You saved Wolf's bacon in the air above Krasnaya, and the Lodge won't forget. We dare not risk the Maurai finding out about you, because you know too much, like the location I'll be heading for, and there is no way in the world you could keep it from their drugs and doctors. But you'll have a decent place to wait in, and afterward I dare hope we'll help you return to your own."

"How long?"

"A year, two years—I can't tell. I'm only a junior engineer, and I've been absent for such a stretch—"

"Am I supposed to wait—" Abrupt rage exploded in Iern. He cracked fist into palm. "No, God damn it!" he yelled in Unglish. "I'll not stand for that! I love you too much!"

She gasped. "Oh, Iern, oh, Iern." And they were in each other's arms.

—Laughing, while tears glistened on her cheekbones, she raised herself to an elbow and said unsteadily, "Okay, flyboy, you win. I kept telling myself it was just an infatuation. You were foreign to me, exciting on that account, but also a great lay, a human being I could like and respect, and I'd been alone ever since— Well, anyhow, I was wrong. This turned into more than a party. I want to go on with you for always."

"And I you." He rolled over to nuzzle her in the hollow where throat met collarbones. She was smooth and warm and smelled of summers gone and summers to come. "It won't be easy, Ronica. Besides the different nationalities—entire cultures—I am—" He must force it out, even though it was to her and his face was hidden against her. "I've begun to see how childish I've been, my whole life. I won't improve overnight."

"Aw, now." She rumpled his hair. "How about we get our pants back on before we freeze our buns off?"

They did, sat up, held hands, exchanged smiles and kissing motions. Wind, whales, chill, declining sun went unnoticed. "You'll come along to Laska," she said happily. "I can wangle that. As a matter of fact, there's no safer place to hide you."

"I, uh, I don't want to scandalize your family. Marriage. . . . I don't know what the legalities are. Under Aerogens law, Faylis can't have her divorce till a year and a day after she's filed suit, assuming it's uncontested. But what does Union law have to say about a marriage performed in a different country, that no longer is a marriage?"

"Union law doesn't have a mucking thing to say. Did you think we'd let the government meddle in something so important? Don't you worry your pretty little head. My folks will understand, and we'll straighten out any formalities at leisure."

They embraced. When she drew back, she had turned serious.

"Let's give this some further thought, darling," she advised. "Where we're bound for—if we both are—is no nice retreat where you can have plenty of amusements while you rusticate. It's in the outback. You will not be permitted to leave or have any outside communication until the work is done, and I've told you that could be a couple of years yet. I'll be busier than a one-armed octopus, and often bone-tired when I get home; they're really pushing hard. I may get sent off again looking for fissionables, which takes skills you haven't got. Laska does have grand scenery, hunting, fishing, and so forth, but it has a lot of rotten weather too, and winter is moving in. Expect to be housebound most of the time."

"Well," he said, "I believe I could—"

"Iern," she interrupted bluntly, "you've called yourself childish, and maybe you are in a few ways, but for the most part you're a man, and an energetic, restless man at that. Can you stand being a . . . a sort of he-concubine?"

Can I? he wondered in sudden shock. "Must I?" he heard himself ask through a tightening throat.

Her expression grew stark. "Yes. And—oh, God—" She hammered at the grass. "The more I look at it, the more it seems that the situation could poison what we've got between us. Maybe we, we would do better to separate . . . for however long it takes."

"No!" Wrath flared in him. "Why should they keep me a prisoner? Haven't I earned their trust?"

"Orion means too much, darling. Too much to me myself." She wrenched the statement forth. "And you did, when you were a Clan Senior, you did show a particular friendship for the Maurai."

I can yell at her and wreck this joy we've just won, said a new voice in Iern's head. *Or I can answer carefully, while thinking harder than ever before in my life.*

The effort to choose each word and keep his tone level made him shiver. "Ronica, listen. I favored closer relationships with the Maurai, true. That was because they seemed to have the future in them, science, high technology. But here I've learned that the Union does also, perhaps more. And are the two incompatible, anyway? Does the liberation of the Union mean the destruction of the Maurai?"

"Oh, no," she whispered. "I told you Orion is not a weapon. At least, not a thing to kill people by the millions. If the mission goes as it should, nobody will die."

"So you can work on it in good conscience?"

"Yes."

An uneasy recollection of Plik crossed Iern's mind. He threw it out. Purpose thrilled upward within him. It was like riding the hurricane or leaping from Skyholm again. He sensed that his decision had been secretly coalescing in him for weeks. Now all at once it had set him free.

"Why can't I join you?" he challenged.

"What?" she cried.

His voice resonated in his skull. "Enlist me in your cause. From clues you've let drop, I have a vague guess as to what Orion may be. If I'm right, magnificent! I'll want to help. If I'm wrong, I'll still do my best for you. I'm offering you my commitment, you see. And I have a technical education, and I am a first-class pilot. I might actually make a useful suggestion or two. Ronica, take me."

"Iern, Iern, Iern!" She toppled into his arms. "Iern, together we'll see Orion rise."

Wind shrilled, waves marched, the North Pole circled toward winter.

XVII

Another wind whooped off the Sound, whirled through city streets, dashed rain against houses. The water streamed back down, gurgled along gutters, shimmered on pavement wherever a lamp broke the early darkness. Traffic still thronged and boomed: pedestrians in hooded coats, bicyclists and motorcyclists in ponchos, bubble shapes of private cars, lumbering bulk of buses, now and then a horseman or an animal-drawn cart. Hoot, clang, rattle resounded from railway station and yards, docksides, factories working overtime. Lights beckoned from taverns, restaurants, gambling halls, theaters, bawdyhouses. Derelicts huddled in doorways or slunk from alley to alley, clutching to them whatever warmth might lie in a jug of cheap booze or a marijuana cigarette if they had any.

An Inspectorate patrol passed through downtown Seattle. Silence spread around it like ice freezing outward, until the men's boots racketed unnaturally loud. They were armed, not simply with the knives and truncheons that had been standard, but with pistols and rifles. They moved in close formation and their visages were dour. You got the impression that they would almost have welcomed a reason to open fire, these easygoing Maurai who since the war had tried so hard to make friends.

The house of Elwin Halmer saw nothing of this. It was among the old mansions which remained as enclaves in the industrial sections that had grown up around them and devoured their neighbors. The living room was warm and softly lit, pastel-papered, full of heirlooms. Flames crackled in a fireplace designed for efficiency but built of rough stones. Above the bone candlesticks on its mantel hung the emblem of the Wolf, burned into a piece of walrus hide.

"Check . . . and, I do believe, mate," said Plik.

His host and warden studied the board. "Damn! You're right. Well, it was a good game." His tone begrudged the words.

Plik unfolded himself and left the table, glass in hand, to get a refill of whiskey at a sideboard. The Norrman shook his head. "How do you do it?" he wondered. "You've been drinking at a rate that threatens to bankrupt the Lodge, and still you beat me three games out of four."

"Perhaps you should drink too," Plik suggested. By now his Unglish was adequate. "If the Lodge is kind enough to provide for my material wants, presumably you can take a share. Don't feel you would be embezzling. I'm supposed to be kept as happy as detention allows, but I do miss drinking companions."

Elwin scowled. "You know I can't do that. I've got to lose weight." His fat would not have been unusual among Maurai his age, but here, as in Uropa, it was abnormal.

Plik grinned. Liquor clucked from a bottle. "I do know. I've been devising a song for you, my friend."

"What do you mean?"

"Why, I've told you that at home I'm a balladeer of sorts. If you will let me sing a capella—

" 'The doctor said, "Diet." I nodded my head
And wondered just what it was I would be fed.
I looked at my ration. The ration was small.
I reached for my glass. There was no alcohol.'
"No alcohol! No alcohol! A very small ration and no alcohol!
No alcohol! No alcohol! A very small ration and no alcohol!"

"Easy for you," Elwin grumbled.

Plik returned to his chair. "But listen.

" 'Oh, sweetheart, dear sweetheart, I'm full of despair.
I feel I am living on water and air.
The ration allowed is exceedingly small,
And the worst thing of all, there is no alcohol.'
"No alcohol! No alcohol! A very small ration and no alcohol!
No alcohol! No alcohol! A very small ration and no alcohol!"

"(The next really needs a female voice.)

" 'Oh, lover, dear lover, pray do not feel blue.
I've got the most marvelous treatment for you.
Let's hop into bed and you'll have such a ball
You'll forget your small ration and no alcohol.'
"No alco—"

"Hold on!" Elwin exclaimed. He doubled a fist. "Are you making fun of me, you miserable sot?"

Plik reached for a pipe and tobacco jar given him. "Why, no, not really. At least, no more than I'm wont to make fun of myself."

"A whole mucking month I've put up with you and your guards—"

The Angleyman's thin, drink-flushed cheeks grew redder. "As a service to your bloody Lodge, which may promote you for it, to the next higher order—Fleascratcher First Class or whatever the title is. Do you think *I've* enjoyed being cooped up and only allowed out on what amounts to a leash?"

"Yah, to the nearest cathouse, mainly. They picked my place to hold you not just because of its location but because—you know it, you bastard—my wife's less than a year in her grave, and I don't get around—"

"If you think I'd purposely— That's an insult, sir."

They glared across the table in tension that had been gathering for weeks as if beneath a thunderhead. A lightning rod appeared and discharged it: one of the two knifemen who made sure Plik stayed in the house or, accompanying him on occasional excursions, made sure he stayed discreet. "Somebody to see you," he reported.

Iern followed. He had shed his rain gear, but the wet sheened on his face and he seemed to exude cold dampness. Behind him, impassive, trod his own attendant. "Good evening," he said in Unglish.

"Welcome, welcome, welcome!" Plik sprang from his chair and half ran, half staggered to hug his friend. "None but Vineleaf could be a happier sight," he burbled after he had stepped back. "How have you been, old chap?"

"Occupied," Iern said reminiscently. "You?"

"Hm, they've given me comfortable quarters and made every reasonable effort to provide distraction—local tours, theater, books, you can imagine—but time has inevitably become a stream of glue. . . . Well, never mind the self-pity, especially if you bring release. Do you?"

Iern hesitated. "In a way."

They had been talking Angley. Elwin Halmer made an uneasy noise. "It's all right," Iern told him in Unglish. "Ask my guard. Ah, I'm sorry." He performed introductions. "I've come to discuss my plans with your guest."

"Why this late?" Plik inquired.

"The obvious reason, not to draw attention. Maurai are starting to beswarm Seattle—every town in the Union they can reach, I imagine —and more are expected."

Plik scrutinized Iern. "You have joined the Northwest cause, I see."

"Um-m, well, in a way. I'm not free to explain till, till you've made a decision for yourself."

They sat down. Elwin mustered the hospitality to offer drink. Thereafter the Uropans ignored everybody else.

"—I'm going with Ronica, north. You can doubtless guess the destination a little closer than that, but I promised to say nothing, and in fact I'll be told nothing further before we're safely on our way. Would you like to come along? Be warned, it's a commitment you make for the next year or two. If you refuse, they'll keep you confined for the duration anyway. But you'll have those distractions you mentioned, which will be in short supply where we're bound."

"Do you know, you're sounding like her?"

"I am? Well. . . . I asked, and she got her superiors in the Lodge to agree, so you're invited. I felt you deserve the choice. You might feel less lonely. On the whole, though, it's probably not an invitation you'd be wise to accept."

Plik blazed back: "Wise? What's weak little whimpering wisdom, when there's a chance to witness the wreck of the gods? Of course I accept!"

Iern stared. Shadows chased across the gaunt face before him. Eyeballs caught firelight and flickered. "I don't understand."

"You, the exiled Prince, don't?" The words tumbled from Plik. He gestured wildly. "Well-a-day, he seldom does, he knows not who he is, before he comes to his kingdom or his death. You're in the myth now, you know, completely in the myth. You've identified yourself with Orion, and here he is the sleeping hero who shall wake to set free his people—or else the Giant in Chains, who shall burst his bonds and storm forth to take vengeance. The dead are leaving their graves. In this rainy land I have seen the old Merican spirit rising huge from where it lay centuries buried, and the foundations of the world are atremble—"

"You're drunk, Plik, drunk again."

"What else? Come, join me, let's drink while we can."

2

Fog hung thick and white, turning nearby trees into blurs of dimness, obliterating all that lay beyond. The dank air made Terai wheeze and think morbidly of tombs. Silence pressed inward. From time to time a horn lowed, not as if in warning but as if it mourned for ships long sunken.

Though the cabin was warm enough and well lit, a sense of the outside chill pervaded it. Terai thought that that was because it was a prison, the windows hastily but stoutly barred, the door to the outside reinforced and nailed shut. He and Wairoa had this half to themselves, but through a functioning door he heard their guards in the adjacent room. A poker game was in progress. He was tempted to go in and join it—anything to break the unending sameness—but he had no money. Besides, no matter what the game, he doubted he'd be well received. Monotony had turned the Norrmen resentful of their captives. He and Wairoa might have cultivated better relationships, but had instead armored themselves in sullen pride, and it was probably too late now for camaraderie.

He prowled from wall to knotty-pine wall. The pipe between his jaws had made a haze of its own, blue and biting. His tongue felt like scorched leather. But what was a man to do?

Wairoa sat reading a book. The Wolf chieftains had been generous about providing those. Also available were a radio, phonograph, record library. The Lodge maintained Shaw Island as a resort for members. Neighboring cabins stood vacant at the present season; perhaps a few occupants had been persuaded to move elsewhere for the rest of their holidays. It would have helped if Terai had been allowed to use the hobby shop, do things with his hands, but the keepers had their strict orders to be wary of him. He and Wairoa could walk and exercise outdoors when they chose, but always under heavy guard.

"Mong to Norrmen," he muttered. "I wish we could have stayed with the Mong. They treated us mast-high better."

Wairoa continued reading, but made reply. He could divide his attention like that. Once he had broken his reticence and described the peculiar neural connections between his cerebral hemispheres, but most of what he related had gone over Terai's head. "I suspect we would have had our throats cut, after polite apologies," he said. "Our presence was potentially most inconvenient for various influential persons."

"I know, I know. How often have we been over this ground before? I don't see how you can stay so calm, Wairoa, I truly don't."

"Deprivation drives you crazy. I have no family to miss. I do have an ever-changing reality to perceive on this patch of soil, the waters around, the sky above. Don't you remember what Ronica Birken pointed out— Hold." Wairoa lowered his book and raised a hand.

For a minute silence prevailed in Terai's hearing, then he caught the noise too, remote but approaching, the stutter of an outboard motor. Surprised remarks, delighted oaths, chairs scraping back across planks showed that the guards had also heard. *Who in Nan's name might that be? No random boatsman, I'll wager, if he burns fuel like that.* The heart slugged in Terai's breast.

The motor stopped and different sounds drifted from the wharf. Several newcomers walked up the trail to the cabin, guided by men whose forms were almost as unfamiliar in the eddying fog. They were led off, presumably to shelter—except for one, who stepped closer to this building and vanished from sight around its corner.

Soon he came in to the Maurai. And he was Mikli Karst.

—"How cordial do you expect us to be, for Haristi's sake, when you tried to murder us?"

From the chair he had taken, Mikli smirked at the man looming over him. "That was professional, not personal," he said. "In your place, I'd take a sporting attitude."

"And keeping us locked away like animals, that's damn near worse," Terai growled.

Wairoa sat quiet in a corner, watching from the mask around his eyes, surely perceiving with every enigmatic sense that was his. Fog in a window behind him was as revealing as his countenance. No sound reached Terai from the next room. The guards had withdrawn to it and were poised alert behind the door, doubtless hoping that this dismal service of theirs was near an end.

Mikli waved his cigarette. "Oh, I'd say you've been pretty pampered animals," he laughed. "We had no choices, you know, except to kill you or hold you incommunicado."

Yes, we've too much to tell, Terai thought wearily, for the hundredth or thousandth time. *Where to find the plutonium and its carrier, absolute proof of Northwestern guilt, a casus belli that should satisfy the most rabbity pacifist. Just as critical, the information that the Wolf Lodge is in this business to the tips of its hairy ears. Our corps can't learn a worthwhile thing from the Union government, because that gaggle of powerless clowns doesn't* know *a thing. But a lead to Wolf—and to Kenai in Laska, from words that got dropped along the trail—yes, that's the exact kind of clue the Federation needs, to track the monster down.*

"After all, your people have been aware for a while that fissionables are being collected," Mikli went on. "They alerted the Mong governments—"

"How do you know it was us who did?" Terai demanded. The answer might point toward something that would be useful, if ever he got loose. "They could have found out for themselves, couldn't they?"

"Unlikely. They weren't geared to notice. Consider how blandly ignorant the Domain has been. The Maurai doubtless saw no reason hitherto to notify Skyholm, because they had no indications of any such antics in Uropa until lately."

Mikli trickled smoke from his nostrils. His lazy voice continued: "Now, of course, the Federation authorities have had your report to alarm them further, as well as one or more actual nuclear explosions."

"What?" Terai bellowed, and Wairoa stirred in his corner.

Mikli nodded. "Yes. It happened about the same time as Jovain's coup and all the interesting action that followed, so there was no chance to notify you. I didn't hear about it myself till I'd returned home. But, yes, Mong observers picked up clear traces of atmospheric detonations in a high latitude and west of them. They notified the Maurai, who confirmed it. Communications have been super-tiptop hush-hush. Mustn't poke the anthill unnecessarily, at least not before the party responsible is identified beyond doubt. Otherwise the devil alone knows what would come of the global hysteria that'd follow.

"Meanwhile, the Federation is rushing additional personnel to its Inspectorate in the Union. Its fleets are converging from around the planet on Awaii—closest major base to us, and we are the most obvious suspects."

"You are guilty," Terai said in a flat voice. The effort not to seize the creature before him and kill shuddered through his body.

"Well, you and I know that, but where's the clinching proof?" Mikli retorted smugly. "What shall the Inspectorate search for, and where? Whom shall the Navy attack? A new war against the Northwest Union would be essentially a war against innocent bystanders, who'd fight but not have had the least part in . . . Orion. It would drag on as long as the last one did, or longer, because you're not mobilized for it as you were then, and—in the absence of anything except allegations—it would be unpopular at home."

Terai swallowed. He felt sick. Everything he had heard was correct: not true, if "true" meant "honest," but correct. He remembered learned professors in Wellantoa who described the Power War as militarism gotten out of hand—oh, yes, nuclear generators could never be permitted, but the abandonment of that project could have been negotiated. He remembered commentators and preachers who denounced the continued Maurai presence in the Northwest as cultural imperialism, a boot stamping down on the very diversity that the Federation claimed to treasure. He remembered demonstrations by the youthful and their graybeard imitators, many of them affecting bits of Northwestern garb, in favor of peace and freedom, which they seemed to think they had invented; some had jeered at him when he happened to be in uniform. (And he remembered youth in cities of the Union, aping Maurai fashions.) More to the immediate point, he remembered talking with mature and sober tribal leaders, from end to end of Oceania, who wondered if the cost of patrolling the world was not falling too heavily on their folk. . . .

But no matter that. The fact was that while the Maurai chased shadows, and maybe even put an army back on the mainland, the Wolves and whatever allies were theirs would keep busy; and it seemed they had begun testing their instrumentality of damnation.

Wairoa's words crackled dry through Terai's despair: "A question, Karst. How do you know the Mong detected a blast and informed the Maurai, if this has otherwise been kept secret?"

Taken aback, Mikli said, "Intelligence operations," in a tone less cocky than usual.

"Furthermore," Wairoa pursued, "why were we sent from Yuan in your custody? Why should the Yuanese trust Norrmen with something so major as interrogating us?"

Recovering his balance, Mikli grinned. "Well, yes, we have succeeded in getting cooperation there."

"From certain Yuanese officers only. Else the whole world would know of an alliance, or at least a partnership, between the former enemies."

Mikli stubbed out his cigarette and reached for a fresh one. "You're smarter than I supposed, Wairoa Haakonu."

"Infiltration," the hybrid said. "Not by your nugatory government, but by Wolf and whatever other Lodges are in the plot. You have had twenty years. The polks are no longer nomadic war bands where everybody knows everybody else; they have members widely scattered, who move wherever circumstances may take them individually. You could introduce agents who could pass for Mong and work their way up—Injuns, Asian-descended Norries, or some of the actual Mong who still live here and there in your eastern Territories. Or white men, for that matter; the Mong are a heterogeneous lot. You could bribe, you could blackmail, you could convince sincere people that helping you was in the best interest of their countries. You wouldn't try for the top echelons; that would be too risky, especially given the regimental hierarchy and merit system. But you could have your agents in place at nexuses through which information and command pass—your sleepers, your whole network to call upon at need. The Mong are naive to a pitiful degree. You and your kind are not.

"Ye-e-es, I daresay also that when their legitimate officers imagined they were dealing with your government, its representatives were Wolves, who passed on to Vittohrya what they saw fit, and no more. Congratulations on a bad job well done."

The sheer purposefulness of it—twenty years!—broke over Terai like surf.

Plain to see, Mikli did not like to be on the receiving end of talk. He rose. "Well," he snapped, "you may get a chance to ask further, when you've rejoined your friends of our little forest excursion."

Terai hunched his shoulders against whatever blow would land next. "What do you mean?"

"Why," Mikli taunted, "Iern Ferlay has enrolled under our banner, and Plik is inevitably tagging along. My home is in Laska, where we're going to need better security arrangements, so I'll come too. Why not keep the old gang together? We shouldn't hold you here any longer anyway, what with the Inspectorate dashing about like so many waterbugs. We'll take you with us. Pack up. We leave in an hour, while this helpful fog lasts."

He turned and went into the next room. The door slammed behind him. For a while both Maurai were mute and motionless. Then Wairoa said slowly, in the language of their home: "That is an evil man. Not simply an opponent. He radiates evil. Can't you smell it?"

"No," said Terai. "But I believe it."

He stared into the cold formlessness outside before he finished, "I'll get word back. I will, or die."

3

Clouds drove low across Dordoyn. Their grayness veiled the heights and turned somber the hues of autumn on the steeps beneath. Wind wailed, a sound as cold as the air itself. Damp odors blew about, in between spatters of rain. Roads had become rivers of mire, squelching to weary hoofbeats.

More than ever, Castle Beynac seemed to belong here. The modern additions looked dream-unreal against those stark old walls and towers. Riding from Port Bordeu, Ashcroft Lorens Mayn had come to yearn for warmth, firelight, ease, and he was no weakling. He had chosen to fare in this manner with his retainers so that the pysans could see their new castlekeeper and feel assured that he meant them well. They had given him flinty stares and returned none of his genial gestures. Now he wondered how much comfort awaited him at journey's end.

A reception committee stood outside the gate, wrapped and hooded. They had mustered an honor guard, too, which was encouraging—militiamen in uniforms and crested helmets, daggers at belts, pikes, crossbows, and rifles at shoulders. Lorens urged his horse to a final canter up the approach, drew rein, and lifted an arm in salutation. From visits in earlier days, he recognized faces. The first officer, Iern Ferlay's fellow Clansman Hald Tireur, waited in the forefront, his back and time-plowed countenance held stiff. The secretary, a young groundling named Ans Debyron, waited nearby, a parchment in his hands, no friendliness in his face either . . . or in any of those confronting the newcomers.

At Lorens' back, a score of mounts snorted, stamped, and came to a halt. He counted the men before him: twice the number of his, two dozen among them armed. Wishing to avoid provocation, he had confined weapons in his party to knives, a few pistols, and four lances that were mainly for display of pennons.

"Greeting, Clansmen and goodfolk," he said. "Peace and welfare be yours." Wind seized the formality and scattered it like the dead leaves that tumbled past.

"Greeting," responded Hald. "May I ask your name and errand?"

Dumbfounded, Lorens could merely exclaim, "You know me!"

"These witnesses require your name and errand, sir."

Some point of Dordoynais law or custom? This is not gentle Bourgoyn, where Faylis and I played as children amidst the vineyards. "I am . . . Ashcroft Lorens Mayn, colonel in the Terran Guard, lately made castlekeeper of Beynac and environs. I have come to assume my duties." Impulse: "You knew that! I called ahead, after you received written notification—"

"We have received no notification of your appointment according to ancient usage. Therefore we have received no notification at all."

Lorens struck fist on saddlebow, mastered himself, and said with a mildness that cost him much: "Hald, you know these are extraordinary times. This is an area vital to the security of the Domain," *these wild and rugged hills, shelter for bandits or rebels.* "Its proper superintendence could not wait on conventional procedures" *when not a single qualified Talence will accept the post under Jovain.* "The Captain used his emergency power to appoint me. I am the brother of the missing castlekeeper's wife. My intention is to care for the interests of his family, and especially of the people, your people, Hald. As soon as someone of the blood can be regularized, I'll step down in his favor."

"When will that be, and how many garrisons will you first have set in our midst?" Hald also must struggle for restraint. His followers stirred and glared. Guardsmen's knuckles whitened above the grips of their weapons. The officer turned to Ans Debyron. "Read the declaration of refusal," he said thickly. "You drew it up."

The secretary bowed, stepped forward, and unrolled his parchment. Red and white chased each other across his smooth cheeks. His voice sometimes wavered or cracked. But the words fell forth like stones:

"Imploring the mercy of Deu, invoking the anims of the Ancestors, we, the men of Py Beynac, assembled on this date of—"

Lorens heard a mumbled curse or two behind him. He sat half listening, feeling less shock than might have been expected, and more tiredness.

"—old rights confirmed by the Treaty of Périgueux, whereby Dordoyn became a state of the Domain—" *But that was centuries ago. The time is long overpast for Franceterr to be once more a true nation, oneness within Oneness. How dare they set their will against it?*

"—call upon all sons of Py Beynac and their brothers throughout Dordoyn—" *They dare.*

"—do not recognize the authority, under any circumstances whatsoever, to name a person as castlekeeper who is not legitimately a Ferlay—" *Faylis has cast Iern from her, now they cast her from them.*

"—maintain loyalty to the Domain and its established institutions, which include Ileduciel and the Aerogens, while such loyalty be mutual; but violation of law, usage, and rights is treason. We call for a meeting of the Clan Seniors and the heads of the several states, to inquire—" *They aren't actually rebelling, yet. Skyholm can blast into smoke any army they may field. But what of guerrillas? What of refusal to deal? Skyholm cannot scorch the land itself. That would be an offense against Gaea second only to unleashing the atom; and without supplies from the ground, Skyholm will soon fall from heaven.*

"—wherefore, Ashcroft Lorens Mayn, we ask that you go from us peacefully, but we require that you go."

He heard out the signatures and titles. Ans withdrew, breathing hard. Lorens formed a smile of sorts. "You make things very clear," he said through the wind. "You are sadly misled, but of course I don't want trouble and I will return home. Are we offered hospitality for the night?"

"No," said Talence Hald Tireur.

Lorens turned in the saddle to gesture caution at his indignant party and informed Iern's Clansman, "We'll find an inn. Don't punish the landlord for receiving us. Let's keep relations as smooth as may be."

Hald responded with a brief nod. Lorens brought his horse around for the downward ride. It began to rain in earnest.

4

In the Captain's lofty office, Jovain peered across his desk and said, "This is a grave matter. Perhaps a capital matter."

The lean, white-haired woman sat unmoved. "Then please get to the point, sir," she replied. "I told you when you summoned me back here, it was a damned inconvenient moment."

"You did not explain why, Colonel."

"Wasn't it obvious?" Vosmaer Tess Rayman asked. He must needs admire how skillfully she modulated her tones. The note of scorn was never quite identifiable as such. "My command is as restive as any. The boys know nothing except that your announced intention is to cut down on the military in general and storm control in particular. When, how much, in what ways? Uncertainty is worse than the ax itself. They bitch, they get into trouble off base, they start thinking more about home and kin—the old securities of the regions they came from—than about their service." He opened his mouth; she hushed him by lifting a finger. "I don't so much mean pilots and staff recruited from the Aerogens. They're more conspicuous and more articulate, but the Air Force is just a fraction of their lives. I'm thinking of career personnel, mostly groundling-born, few of them flyers—mechanics, traffic controllers, computermen, electronicians, quartermasters, cooks, the whole underpinning of our organization. Their morale is pretty badly shaken."

"Already? Nothing has happened yet." Jovain frowned. "Nor have I heard about this problem."

"You wouldn't have . . . yet. Sir. A person has to be close to such things—in the beginning—to see. After they explode, anybody can tell, but then it's too late. We of the officers' corps have been trying to find ways we might head off trouble and recommendations we can make to the Captain."

Distracted despite himself (*Do I encounter anything but distractions, I who meant to bring a benign revolution?*), Jovain tugged his beard and said, "Consider reminding them that the armed forces and auxiliaries exist to serve the Domain, not the other way around. If a reduction in size and role is called for, be assured that this will be a phase-out, not a chop-off, and nobody will lose what he or she has earned a right to."

"Apart from the meaning of their lives—a meaning they'll have to seek elsewhere," Tess retorted. "Your Dignity"—he realized that she reverted to the principal honorific as a method of emphasis—"please bear in mind that a large part of what's held the peoples and states of the Domain together has been the things they *do* together."

Jovain gathered resolution. "I am not unaware of that, Colonel. I submit that it is time for us to abandon obsolete institutions and practices and seek new goals. But meanwhile, as for unity—"

He straightened till he felt his back muscles stretch. "Let me be frank," he said. "I believe you deserve no less. There can be honest differences of opinion as to what's best for the Domain. I respect them. In fact, I'm eager to take them into account, and disappointed at the lack of response to my overtures. But what we must have is unity. Dissent, properly expressed, is one matter. Conspiracy, or outright insurrection, is another."

"Indeed it is," she said dryly.

That stung. "Colonel Tess," he snapped, "I am giving you the privilege of discussing with me, personally, a very serious question that has been raised about your actions." He drew breath. "A warrant of inquiry is out for Talence Iern Ferlay. It has been widely publicized. If he is willfully failing to appear, that makes him a fugitive from the law. If he has not appeared because somehow he came to grief, then whoever withholds pertinent information commits a felony." He attempted a smile. "I myself wish him well. We've had our disagreements, true, but I'm genuinely anxious about him."

"Indeed you are, sir."

Is she being impassive or is she being sarcastic? Ignore that. Attack. "Colonel, either he parachuted from here or he fell to his death. There is no third possibility. Our teams ransacked Skyholm and every departing aircraft, as you well remember. Investigators ascertained that a man answering closely enough to his description bluffed his way past a sentry out onto an inspection platform, did not return, and had a parachute. It's well known that you and he were rather close. Investigators found another guard who, earlier, noticed a certain person carrying off the equipment for such a dive. Depth-recall technique brought out a description which could belong to your son Dany.

"The inference is obvious," Jovain finished. "Have you any comment?"

"Yes, sir." Her manner remained cool. "This is nothing but hearsay, from a span of time when the whole aerostat was in turmoil and nobody could possibly be a reliable witness to anything—least of all those outsiders you imported."

"Then you deny complicity?"

"Sir, by the code of the Aerogens, *you* have no right to ask such questions." Tess reared her head more high than before, amidst the relics filling this room.

"Where is Vosmaer Dany Rayman?"

Tess grinned. "How should I know? I gave him a well-earned furlough, and he's a healthy young bachelor."

"You force me to issue a warrant of inquiry for him too."

"The Captain of Skyholm has that prerogative."

"I can bring charges against you, Colonel."

"The Captain of Skyholm may request my superior officers or the Seniors of my Clan to bring charges." Tess gave him a moment to consider her precise phrasing. "I suggest you refrain, sir. I've explained that those so-called statements are worthless. A court-martial, let alone a Clan court, would throw them out like garbage."

The Clans and the officers stand by their brethren. Acid washed up into Jovain's gullet and burned. "I can arrest you on my own authority, remember."

"And hold me for a limited time before I must be tried. Sir, again I don't recommend it. My associates and I are too busy already, trying to knit an unraveling fabric back together."

Against what contingency?

Jovain swallowed the acid. "Very well, Colonel," he said. "Since you refuse cooperation"—humor flickered—"or else deny that cooperation is possible, you may return to your . . . duties. You will inform the Terran Guard as soon as you have word of your son Dany. Please be advised, I do not regard the officer corps as an independent entity, and will take measures to make it more candid and responsible than hitherto. Good day, madame."

She rose, saluted, and left.

Quietness succeeded her, the whisperings and quiverings of Skyholm amidst thin stratospheric winds, the eternal silence of the infinities beyond. A stench of his sweat insulted Jovain. Exhaustion rolled over him. He put elbows on desk, buried face in hands. *Faylis, Faylis!*

But no, first he had work to do, always more work. Vosmaer Tess Rayman might be an extreme case, but she was also an early warning. Disaffection in the armed forces—no direct menace to Skyholm, which could smite any unit of theirs with lightning; but as an element of unrest throughout the land— He needed to confer with persons he could trust, those who supported him and his cause. He rang for his aide. This day was going to turn into a long night.

5

At sunset, the women left Carnac. It was a clear and frosty evening, wherein a streak of red above the western horizon soon smoldered out, leaving a greenish sky that rapidly darkened. Eastward the color was purple-black, and Ileduciel glimmered low above a line of forest whose silhouette was turning skeletal. When the town was behind them and they were out on the highway, the feet of the women rang on frozen dirt, crackled over thin ice patches, rustled through fallen leaves.

They numbered about a hundred, ordinary Breizheg housewives, maidens, grandmothers suddenly become strange in their cloaks and cowls. They carried no lanterns, for the road was familiar to them and the moon would have risen when they went home; but each bore a candle and a means of lighting it. They walked in no particular order, and had no ban on talk, but somehow they made a procession, and what muffled speech passed among them was like a dirge.

"—blasphemy . . . bad luck . . . saint-forsaken . . . murderers . . . revenge, so the poor ghosts may have peace—"

Rosenn kept reminding herself that what had happened the day before was only a riot, and what was to happen this night would only be a gesture. The Gaeans wanted to establish a center in Carnac for the benefit of visitors who shared their beliefs—and, admittedly, in the hope of making converts. Captain Jovain was frank about his intentions; he would "encourage cultural exchange" and "guarantee freedom of expression for all faiths and philosophies." No community might forbid construction of a Gaean center on real estate bought and paid for. The rumor flew that the Captain's treasury was assisting such purchases, which was within his discretion but did not sit well with sailors and farmers who had also heard rumors that there was to be no more storm control. A deeper root of trouble, Rosenn thought, was the conservatism of these pysans. Jovain had not understood that. Carnac, why, Carnac was not far from cosmopolitan Kemper, and a seaport itself. . . . He claimed his world-view embraced eons, but he had no real conception of ancientness. He could not admit that a people may have a right to preserve their own nature, a right to be intolerant.

And thus, last week a group armed with knives, fish spears, scythes, and clubs had told the imported workers who were breaking ground to cease and desist. The mayor of Carnac rejected protests directly from Ileduciel, and cited guarantees of autonomy in the treaty of union. The Terran Guard sent a detachment to protect the workers; a mob gathered; stones were thrown, shots fired; three young men of the town lay dead. Work stopped again, and careful, conciliatory phrases went between mayor, Mestromor, and the lords aloft.

A regrettable incident, such as history had known beyond numbering—no more, and here was nothing except a traditional reaction, futile save insofar as it bled off some of the grief and rage. Striding through the chill twilight, Rosenn found she could no longer believe that.

Why am I here? she wondered, almost frantically. *I am a woman of the Aerogens, the wife of its greatest man while he lived; I have an excellent education, I have traveled from end to end of the Domain, I know better than to partake in a primitive rite of resentment, especially when it's certain that Jovain has me under surveillance.*

She glanced downward at Catan. Side by side, the mother and the foster mother of Talence Iern Ferlay led the procession to the standing stones. *Obligation to my hostess? But why did I seek her at all? She and I have seldom met. We have no ties, except for our separate memories and for the son of his that she rendered unto me, a son who may well have died.*

The anguish ripping through Rosenn told her suddenly what her reasons had been, and were. She reached to grip the other woman's hand. Catan gave back the pressure, and a long look, but in the deepening dusk Rosenn could not know if she smiled. Maybe, silently, she wept.

Skyholm faded away. Stars twinkled forth.

When the women reached the stones, there was enough light that they could see what they did, from crowding constellations and the icy Via Lactea. On one side of the road, fields reached ghost-gray into darkness. Lamp-glow from a distant farmhouse felt as remote as the stars. On the opposite side, forest made a wall, where bare branches stood against heaven like the spears of warriors. Between it and the road were the megaliths.

The rows of them marched beyond sight. Hoarfrost glimmered on their rough shapes; otherwise shadows lurked thick around and underneath. *Shadows of time,* Rosenn thought, *shades of the unknown folk who raised them in ages before history.* Against all reason, she felt the power in them, a remorseless patience, a communion with the inhuman stars. *How did they get back their sacredness? Was it that in the chaos after the Judgment, when everything else slipped from man's grasp, they abided?*

Snicks and flickers ran through silence, as the women lighted their candles. Each flame brought forth a face within a cowl; none was the face that daylight, husband, or children saw. *Shadows, shadows, only a cheekbone, an eyeball, a gleam of teeth.* Hands shielded fire as every woman sought her stone, then the goblin glows stood clear and tiny, illuminating the way toward night.

Catann led Rosenn to a stance in front of the lines. At their backs were the remnants of a cromlech, below their feet were sere grass and frost; the planet spun toward Northern winter and soon Orion would rise. "I should not," Rosenn whispered half wildly, "I don't know anything about this, I don't belong here—"

"Oh, but you do," Catan murmured. "We belong together, leading them, we, his mothers, he the true Captain who'll bring back rightness. Just hold your candle up, a beacon for him to steer by, and wait."

She lifted her own above her head and lifted her voice. Rosenn knew hardly any Brezhoneg, but Catan had told her in Francey what the chant would mean.

"*In the holy name of Deu, by Zhesu-Crett and every saint on earth and on high and in the Afterworld, we are gathered to call desolation over evildoers. May the sorrow they have wrought and the wrath they have raised turn upon them, upon them whose names we now name—*"

Foremost was Talence Jovain Aurillac.

XVIII

The *Graym Trader* departed Seattle early on a clear morning. Pujay Sound sparkled gray-green and whitecapped, already well trafficked. Islands and mainland lay vivid with fall, snowpeaks reared afar. Gulls and clouds cruised before a wind that blew cold out of the northwest.

The ship was nothing fast, nothing special such as might have aroused Maurai curiosity. She was a small coastwise freighter of a type common in these parts. Amidships, above the deckhouse, a girder tower upbore a four-bladed rotor, tailed and swivel-mounted so that it could always point itself into the wind. Through a virtually frictionless magnetic transmission it drove twin screws and supplied a modest amount of electricity. A tiny diesel was a standby, grudgingly used; synfuel was expensive.

Coal was too, not so much directly as in the amount of steel required for a steam engine sufficient to drive a vessel of any size. Few stacks were sullying the air—a welcome change from shore, Iern thought. An alcohol-burning turbine would have needed less metal and been clean to boot, but even the Northwesterners were no longer producing that stuff on a large scale; too much land had been ruined in centuries past by consumption of vegetable matter that should have been returned to the soil.

Standing with Ronica at the rail, he saw mostly sails, some rigs of ancient type and some aerodynamically sophisticated. A majority of the larger modern craft flew the Cross and Stars.

In the long run, Northwestern civilization is doomed, he thought. *While atomic power is forbidden, it can only maintain its kind of high-energy economy by importing coal. Someday, either the Mong will cut off the supply or the fields will give out. Then there are two choices: a technically advanced, somewhat progressive, but diffuse and carefully managed society like the Maurai's; or an aristocratic, labor-intensive, basically static society like the Domain.*

Unless Orion— And everything is in upheaval.

Ronica brightened his mood by stretching her arms wide and laughing for happiness. The shadows of the rotors pulsated across her; they made her hair shine twice bright when the sunbeams touched it. "We're on our way," she exulted. "Yasu almighty, I'm bound for home, and I've got *you* along!"

He laid an arm around her shoulders and hugged. A deckhand nearby winked at him. "Now can you tell me what we're going to do?" he asked.

She sobered. "Not yet, darling. That is, I could, but it'd be kind to wait till Terai and Wairoa can listen in."

"Eh?"

"Bad enough that they'll be in lonely confinement for the next year or two, knowing their people at home are mourning them for dead. Let them at least learn we aren't monsters."

"Where are they?"

"Under guard below decks. Brought aboard during the night. We can't risk giving them any freedom in these crowded waters. Terai, for instance, might bull his way to the side, jump overboard, and swim to yonder Maurai ship. Just the commotion of an attempt might draw too much notice. Once we're in the Strait, nobody else close, we can loosen up."

—Nevertheless, when they appeared a few hours later, the captives were hobbled, and the two who accompanied them bore sidearms. The skipper and his six-man crew had been chosen carefully; most of the time they plied a regular trade, but occasionally they were called on to do things about which they were to ask no questions and tell no tales.

Ronica, Iern, and Plik waited in the saloon, where a leather-upholstered couch curved around three sides of a table. Sunlight danced in through glass ports. The deck rolled a little and quivered faintly underfoot. Plik's pipe sent aroma eddying through the air.

Ronica sprang from her seat and seized Terai's hands in hers. "Welcome," she said. Her sincerity was unmistakable. "How good to see you again." To Wairoa, in haste: "And you." She had confessed to Iern that she couldn't help feeling the hybrid was both pitiable and uncanny.

Terai returned her a sour smile. "I'd have preferred it be under different conditions."

"Yes, you've had an utter bitch of a time, haven't you, poor dear? And I'm afraid the end is not yet. But I do hope that what I'm going to tell you will make you feel better about it." Ronica gestured at the guards. "Okay, you can go."

"Uh, wait, Miz Birken, Captain Karst ordered us not to let these guys out of our sight," protested one.

Ronica snorted. "I countermand the order. If Captain Karst doesn't like it, he can squabble with me when he's slept off last night's drunk. Wait beyond the door if that'll make you happier." She shooed them through and closed it behind them.

"I suppose we could've used Angley in their presence," she explained, "but I'm not damn-all fluent in the lingo, especially technical terms."

"If you will not reveal the secret to your own men, why to us?" Wairoa asked.

"Well, you're safe," Ronica answered bluntly. "You aren't going anywhere till Orion has risen. I want you to understand we mean business. That should keep your horns pulled in. I'd hate for you to get killed trying some or other heroic idiocy." She smiled. "We are trail buddies, remember. Come, let's have a drink in fellowship."

She poured for everybody from a carafe, and remained standing while she lifted her glass and proposed solemnly, "Here's to the day when we can meet again, and every one of us free because the world is."

Iern sipped. The wine was pungent in his mouth, but the headiness he felt came from her tone, her stance, herself a young goddess of victory. Plik emptied his glass in two swallows and reached for a refill. Wairoa hesitated, shrugged, and drank. Terai kept motionless.

Ronica noticed. "I understand," she told the big man. "Maybe you'll be willing to join in my toast after you've heard."

She sat down, but only physically. Enthusiasm radiated from her. Iern, on her right, imagined he could feel it, a flame. Plik was beside him, the Maurai at the end opposite her.

"What is Orion?" she began. The words cataracted forth. "Not what you feared, not a bomb or any such hellish thing. Orion is a spaceship. A fleet of them."

To Iern, the revelation was not totally unforeseen. Nonetheless it went through him like a lightning bolt. Terai grunted, as if hit in the belly; Wairoa did not stir; Plik looked bemused.

"A ship that can go to the planets," Ronica said in glory. "They had the beginnings before the Doom War, you know. They orbited Earth and got as far as the moon, and even beyond for a little. Afterward people lost the dream. They were too busy surviving, and resources were too lean. The old spacecraft were chemical-powered.

They burned fuel at a horrendous rate. We could never go back in force if we depended on their sort. Besides, nobody could hide the effort. You Maurai would've stopped it at the beginning. And maybe you'd've been right, not just maintaining your cozy little supremacy, but right. Where *would* the energy come from, on this poor exhausted world of ours?"

Her fingers tightened along the stem of her glass. "From the atom," she said.

Terai shuddered and waited for more. Wairoa widened his strange eyes. Plik gasped. A song shouted within Iern.

"The idea goes way back," he heard. "To that interplanetary age which died aborning. A man named Freeman Dyson had it and did some theoretical work on it. What a wonderful name for him—'Freeman.' And he gave it the name 'Orion,' too.

"Nothing more happened, mainly for political reasons, I've heard. Then civilization went under. The idea lay forgotten for hundreds of years. You've never heard of it, have you? Nobody did. Not till folk in the Northwest Union got interested in nuclear power and started going through old material in detail. The Orion papers were there, with references to a huge literature on spacecraft in general. Actually, they weren't papers anymore, they were mostly on microfiche and so forth, but distributed widely enough that what did not last in one place where the archeologists had dug usually did in another.

"Well, I've heard that some individuals were excited about Orion. But the first order of business then was to get atomic energy plants designed and built. You recall how our searchers located fissionable material the Maurai had missed in their earlier sweep, and expected they could find more. Realizing the Federation would hate this, they kept as discreet as possible, and publicizing Orion would've been unnecessarily splashy."

Ronica sighed. Bitterness entered her voice. "The Norrmen did not expect the Federation would react in the fanatic way it did. The Power War . . . is history. Since, we've been saddled with the Inspectorate, and all your limitations on what we may do."

She tossed off her wine and poured more. "Already during the last couple of war years, when it was pretty clear we'd lose, Orion came up as a thought. That was among members of the Wolf Lodge. Ours has always been heavy on scientific, technical, and managerial types, you know. Orion's been basically a Wolf undertaking, though of course we've brought in useful and trustworthy people from elsewhere."

Terai nodded stiffly. "Yes, I see," he mumbled. "A widespread, wealthy, influential . . . but private . . . organization, whose members generally feel close-knit but don't demand an accounting from their top leadership—yes."

"How does this spacecraft work?" asked Wairoa in impersonal wise.

Her exuberance returned to Ronica. "Offhand, the idea looks insane," she said. "But it isn't. You throw out a series of small atomic bombs and detonate them behind a thick plate at the rear of the ship. The explosions accelerate her. I can't go into too much detail because I'm not in the drive department. My work's been on control systems. However—" She laughed aloud, as she had done earlier on deck, a peal of joy. "Listen. I didn't learn this myself till very lately, when Iern and I came back to Seattle. (Sorry, sweetheart. That day I left you in the chapter house—)." She squeezed her lover's hand. "They made a test shot two or three months ago, unmanned, telemetered, the vehicle recovered at sea. The results were perfectly splendid. Twenty years of work and sacrifice, and by God, we sent her beyond the sky and brought her home again!"

"It *is* insane," Terai groaned. "Bombs. Radioactive trash. How many will die of cancer because of that one shot? How many children will be born deformed?"

"No number you could measure," Ronica retorted. She flushed. "Okay, some contamination. A firing pit contains most of it, but, yes, a detectable amount of radioisotopes does get into the atmosphere. It increases the background in the immediate neighborhood about as much as you would if you moved that neighborhood to the top of Mount Denali. Everywhere else gets less, and the stuff decays fast.

"How many die of cancer each year, Terai Lohannaso, because you force us to burn coal? I've seen figures on that. Several thousand."

"We don't force you to burn coal," he said. "We wish you'd stop."

"And turn ourselves into another satellite of yours, same as our Southwestern kinfolk? All right, tell me this. How many people every year, around the world, live in ignorance and squalor, and die of starvation or sickness, because you damned smugmugs won't allow the world a productive technology?"

"Tanaroa, woman! We're doing what we can, and we'd do better if we didn't have to mount guard on the likes of you, but the fact is that Earth, the biosphere, can't afford—"

Wairoa raised a palm. "I suggest we spare the rhetoric," he said coolly. "Everybody here has heard it before." Through the silence that fell, his question thrust: "How have you maintained secrecy for two whole decades?"

"Organization," Ronica said. Plainly, she was glad to be relieved of the fight that had been building. "Mikli tells me we could never have gotten away with it in ancient days, but no intelligence corps now has the equipment or the expertise they did back then. And the actual Orion site is under the Leutian Mountains of Laska. They're not just isolated; enough of them are volcanic to mask stuff like heat emission."

Terai winced. "I came so close, once—"

"You must have conducted numerous tests," Wairoa persisted.

"Well, yes, of course. Nearly all of them underground—developing the bombs, for instance." Ronica grinned. "The locals expect to hear an occasional loud noise and maybe feel a tremor."

Wairoa nodded. The sunlight sickled across his tiger-striped hair. "Indeed. Vented radioactivity would be too slight to notice, when no one knew any reason to monitor a background count that varies naturally. But your test launch, that is another story, no?" It was chilling how still he sat. "The Wolf chieftains are aware that the Maurai have learned that somebody is collecting fissionables. They must realize that a global alert for fallout is a logical consequence of this knowledge. How could they hope to escape detection of their shot?"

"They didn't," Ronica said. "Well, the planners prepared for the worst case. Given the spotty detection network, how can you pinpoint the source? You can suspect Norrmen are responsible, and you can get kind of nasty about it, but how are you going to identify and catch a person who really has information?

"Go ahead and search," she defied his corps. "It'll be a long hunt, because you've not got what it takes to comb our country from end to end in a hurry. Meanwhile, seeing as how this test was successful, I doubt we'll have many more. We should, but you don't leave us the option and maybe on that account we'll lose a few ships, a few lives." It rang forth: "So all right, even if my life is among them. Before you can find us, Orion shall rise."

A wintry tingle went through Iern. *Bon Deu, I didn't imagine what I was committing myself to!*

Where Terai stared like a sick man, Wairoa pursued: "What is the military purpose of this? It must be military."

Ronica nodded. She had gone as stern as he. "Because of you, yes, that's the first objective. To win for us Norries the freedom to be ourselves again.

"Iern, Skyholm inspired the idea. All by itself, it controls Franceterr, because nothing can strike at it and it can strike at anything. What of higher ground yet?

"We're building ten Orion spacecraft, twice what we estimate we'll need. Allow for misfortune. What we do put into Earth orbit—their crews can follow the movements of single vessels down below. Their carrying capacity will be enormous; with the system we've developed, a kilo of uranium or plutonium will boost something like seventy-five tonnes. How'd you like a weight—shaped, pinpoint-guided—dropped on you at meteorite speed? We figure one such object, a few tonnes' mass, hitting the ocean, would sink every ship for ten kilometers around. And lasers—we'll deploy solar-collector mirrors, to power Skyholm-type lasers, but bigger. Precision lightning bolts, my friend!

"And there will not be a single God damned thing you can do about it."

Silence. Ronica sat back. After a time she raised her glass to her lips and, having drunk, said very softly: "Not that we want revenge or any such nonsense. We assume the Maurai have the wit to know when they're beaten. After Orion is aloft and we've performed a demonstration or two on uninhabited targets, we take it for granted you'll agree to live and let live. Then we can get on with the work we really want to do."

Silence. Terai and Wairoa looked at each other. Iern felt dizzy. Plik startled the company by speaking for the first time.

"Oh, yes," he said around pipe and wineglass. His tone was almost calm. "Your proper business. To raise the Old Serpent and bring about the end of the world."

Ronica gave him a hard glance. "No," she said. "If anything, to save the world."

"Not as men have known it," Plik replied. "Including you, my dear; 'man' embraces 'woman.' No, the gods are doomed—everybody's gods—and what new ones will come striding through their ashes, we shall not live to understand."

Throughout the furious talk that followed, he would say no more. He simply drank himself to sleep.

2

Ships to the northwest radioed warnings of a storm. The captain of the *Graym Trader* decided to steer around, following the coastline though with ample sea room, rather than make a direct run from the mouth of Wandy Fuca to Cook Inlet.

On the fourth morning of the voyage, Iern came out on deck from the stateroom he and Ronica shared. She was napping after a post-breakfast romp; he lacked her feline ability to sleep almost at will, and went up for some fresh air.

It had turned bitterly cold, that air, blowing from a murkiness in the west. It stung his face, flung salt on his lips, whined and hooted in the framework of the tower, where the vanes spun as if lashed frantic. Wrack blew like smoke under a leaden sky. The sea was leaden-hued also, save for foam on the thick waves and spume off their crests. The ship rolled and shuddered to their anger. Mountains thrust above the eastern horizon, their brutal outlines gone dim.

Crewmen on watch stayed inside. Iern was astonished to see Terai at the starboard rail. The prisoners were no longer subjected to the indignity of restraints—what could they do, where could they flee?—except for being locked into their stateroom at night and having their guards occupy the adjacent cabin. However, they held aloof, appearing only at mealtimes and for exercise topside, seldom speaking to anybody. Iern couldn't blame them.

Moved by the loneliness of that big form, the Clansmen went to join Terai. "Good day," he ventured in Unglish.

The Maurai grunted and continued staring landward.

"Isn't this weather hard on you?" Iern asked. They both wore watch caps, pea jackets, and canvas trousers issued them, but Terai's body strained his garments, and his feet, which could fit into no shoes aboard, perforce had a pair of thin shoreside slippers.

He appeared to thaw a trifle. "Not now," he said. "Yesterday a sailor found me a set of long woolen underwear. It's too tight and it itches, but it keeps me warm."

"They're not such bad fellows, the Norrmen, are they?"

"N-no, not as individuals." Terai hesitated. "As a matter of fact, I've just begged half a kilo of butter from the cook." He took a hand briefly out of a coat pocket to show the cube in its waxed-paper wrapping. "The extra calories will help me survive those unheated quarters."

"Oh? I never heard—" Iern broke off. Maybe the idea was true, maybe it was superstition, or maybe the Oceanian race had a metabolism unlike his. Whatever he said might give offense, as edgy as the captive must be.

"Most people mean well," Terai added. "I haven't met many I'd call evil. The causes they can serve, though, that's where the evil is."

"Well, obviously you, in your position, you can't approve of Orion. And yet, well, you've learned it isn't diabolical, like a nuclear weapon, or a direct threat to your country." Iern essayed a smile. "The Northwesterners will never be imperialists. They're too—ornery, is that their word? Trying to make a conquering army out of them would be like herding cats."

Terai gave him a glare. "Don't you know what poison those bloody ships of theirs will spew across the world?"

"You heard Ronica's data. The contamination will be negligible compared to—"

Terai's words trampled Iern's down: "Do you imagine they'll stop with a single set of launchings? And supposing they get their way, they'll loot the planet and rape the biosphere same as their ancestors did. And they'll build nuclear powerplants—breeder reactors, fusion generators—and others will have to do likewise, out of fear if nothing else, and soon there'll be bombs again—" The Maurai swallowed an uneven breath. "Son," he declared, "I'm not a historian or a philosopher, but I've seen considerable of this globe and the people on it, and I can tell you one absolute certainty. Whenever a capability exists, it will be *used.*"

"No," Iern argued, "you're the ignorant one. Ronica's told me about the safeguards they mean to establish after the, the liberation."

"Whereupon they'll overthrow your enemies for you at home and you'll live happily forevermore," Terai fleered. "That's what's bought you, isn't it? That, and your lady love's delectable carcass. Well, she's not the first who whored for a gang of conspirators. Listen, and I'll give you a few surprises about what your precious Norrmen have been at in your Domain—"

Fury exploded through Iern. "Shut your filthy mouth!" he shouted. "Before I kill you!"

Terai took his great hands forth and waited grimly. A ghost of reason whispered to Iern beneath the thunderclaps, *Don't try, you can't, and besides, his words don't mean anything, they're merely a cry of pain.* He turned his back and stalked away, around and around the deck until calm should return. Terai stood in place for a while, regarding him, then went below.

Faylis screamed and fled down the sky, but she was the moon and the wolf that will devour the moon was at her heels. Blood of battle reddened the snow that had lain on the ground through years of unending winter. Ravens tore at corpses. The tree in which Iern crouched helpless had frozen to death; its branches reached stark across a heaven where the sun was guttering out. Now the dolmens gave up their dead, now from the North a black ship fared, while out of the sea rose a snake, writhing till the waters boiled, spewing venom in a fog. Skyholm was falling, each moment more near, more enormous, the noise of its coming shook all Earth so that the slain men trembled on the snow, and behind Skyholm the stars fell, trailing fire, and each of them wailed—

"What the hell?" Ronica exclaimed. "Darling, wake, something's happening."

She shook him. He had the upper bunk. He groped his way to awareness of her, a shadow in the murk of the tiny room but a real, solid, sane hand and a breath of woman-smell. A fresh cry, a tattoo of hasty feet, yanked him alert. He swung from under his blankets and dropped to the deck. It was chill beneath his soles.

"Let's see." Ronica opened the door a crack and peered out. Light from the corridor spilled yellow across her mane and bare skin. "Nobody. The trouble's topside." She glided forth. He followed.

Another door sagged half-splintered. Wairoa stood in the cabin behind. The adjoining door swung to and fro as the ship rolled, but neither of the guards was there. Mikli emerged from his quarters, bristle-haired, attired in a nightgown. Wairoa saw him and stepped back inside. Plik was in too boozy a sleep to be aroused.

A howl rolled down the companionway, together with a frigid blast. A voice followed: "Ma-an overboard!"

Ronica bounded up the ladder. When Iern emerged too, he found added lights being turned on. Their glimmer picked out drops of a rain that was half sleet, flying on the wind. The cold struck fangs in him. Amidships, the guards stood in their pajamas at the port rail, gripping pistols, squinting down. The night lookout slumped nearby on his knees, face a mask of blood that dripped onto the planks. A fourth sailor and the captain approached; they had flung on jackets and trousers. A fifth was evidently at a searchlight which probed from the deckhouse roof, while the steersman in the bridge had reversed the screws. The ship lurched toward a stop.

"What the fuck is this?" Ronica demanded through the keening of the air.

"The big Maurai," said a guard. "He's overboard."

"You, you, you." The captain pointed. "Take the lifeboat. Orik, you stand by to throw a lifering if we see him in the water."

"What went on?" Iern asked through a sudden sickness.

Mikli plucked at his arm. "That's what we'll have to find out," the intelligence officer said. "Meanwhile, none of us is much use. Go below again. We don't need a case or two of pneumonia added to our problems."

Chon Till, captain of the *Graym Trader*, could almost have been a native of southeastern Merica. In him, the African strain that had for the most part diffused throughout the general Northwestern population manifested itself anew: brown skin, kinky hair, broad nose and lips. He was no impoverished barbarian, though, but very much a man of the Wolf Lodge. He had actually donned a uniform tunic, blue with ivory buttons, for his inquiry.

He glowered around the saloon. Outside its stuffy warmth, wind yowled, sea whooshed and rumbled, hail tapped on glass. Inside, an electric lamp shone dull from the overhead. Seated around the table with him were Mikli, Iern, Ronica, and, opposite him for a direct confrontation, Wairoa.

"I've interviewed the witnesses among the crew," he snapped, and ticked points off on his fingers. "The men on guard duty heard a loud noise that roused them. They were prompt to respond, but apparently Lohannaso had broken his door open in a single rush and started running. The guards glimpsed him headed up the companionway. One pursued, the other quite properly stayed to keep Haakonu under control—until he heard the 'Man overboard,' at which point he also went on deck. The lookout saw Lohannaso burst into the open, dashed to intercept him, and has a broken nose for his trouble. He's too dazed to be sure what came next. Maybe the Maurai slipped and fell over the side, maybe he jumped. I want to know which."

"How do you propose to interrogate a dead man?" Mikli scoffed.

Till raised his brows. "Are you sure he's dead?"

"We've been searching for more than an hour. He's a strong swimmer, but—how long would you guess a man can survive in this water before the cold kills him, Ronica?"

The woman shrugged, though sorrow dwelt on her face. "Half an hour, maybe, give or take some," she replied. "In his case, I'd take; he's not a white man, nor used to subarctic temperatures."

"He could have stayed afloat long enough," Till said. "We'd soon have gotten to him, especially if he hollered. The question in my mind is whether he struck his head on a strake or something like that and immediately went under, or whether it was deliberate suicide, or —or whatever else." He fixed his gaze on Wairoa. "What have you to tell, Haakonu?"

The response might have come from a machine: "The noise of the lock breaking woke me. I saw him go through. He was enormously strong; it would have been easy for him. By the time I was out of my bunk, men were dashing around so busily that I deemed it best to stay where I was."

"But you were his friend!" ripped from Iern. "You must know what he wanted, what made him do it." *Poor Terai. His stories about his home, that he told by our campfires in the woods, made me hope to visit him there someday. I should write to his widow—when they let me, after Orion has risen. . . .*

"I do not read minds," Wairoa said. "Like everybody else, I saw him brooding. He may have decided he would rather die."

"No," Ronica declared. "Never. He had too much life in him."

"Besides," the captain said, "the witnesses told me he was fully clad. If he intended suicide, why should he take that trouble beforehand?"

Mikli scratched in his beard. "You never know about suicides," he observed. "They do the most peculiar things. I knew a physician who contracted an inoperable cancer. Perhaps he could have been saved if we were allowed to manufacture radioisotopes. As was, he gave himself a lethal injection. First he sterilized the needle."

"And Terai did belong to an alien culture," Iern said, however it hurt. "A situation like this might drive a Maurai over the brink. Is that possible, Wairoa?"

"Oh, yes," said the man with the mask.

Ronica slammed a fist on the table. "No, God damn it," she insisted. "I've been exposed to plenty of Maurai in my time, and I know a real he-man when I meet one, too, and in Terai's case it is *not* possible. What are you holding back, Wairoa?"

The reply was whispery: "He did not confide in me. If you are thinking of drugs or torture as means to find out whether I lie, please be advised that my peculiar constitution will make it a waste of your effort."

Ronica grimaced. "Krist, what sort of swine do you suppose we are?"

An idea came to excite Iern. "I have a suggestion," he said. "You remember I made an unlikely sort of escape myself. Terai may have hoped to do similarly. If he could—well, disable the lookout, throw heavy things to put anybody else out of action for a few minutes, lower the lifeboat—"

"And row from us?" Till derided. "Let's imagine he raised the mast and sail before we got organized. A mighty big imagining, if you ask me. He'd still have only a fraction of our hull speed."

"But it's a dark and wild night," Iern argued. "He was a physical prodigy. He just might have carried it off, and eluded you for the hour or two he'd need. How far are we from land?"

"About five nautical miles. That's to a chain of islands. Beyond is the Inside Passage, and the mainland beyond it. Everything wilderness, scarcely an inhabitant anywhere, for at least a thousand kilometers in any direction."

"The boat carries stores and equipment. Sir, I realize it'd be a gamble against astronomical odds, but I can picture Terai deciding that cast of the dice against his life was worth it, if conceivably he could get to his people and tell them what they need to know to stop Orion. He wouldn't have told you, Wairoa. Why involve you, when you could scarcely help him? Better to leave you in reserve against his likely failure."

The Maurai nodded. "Your hypothesis sounds plausible," he said in a level voice.

Mikli gave him a look that warned: *Don't think you'll get any chance to act as his backup.*

The captain tugged his chin. "Well," he murmured, "it does appear to fit what facts we have. Yes, a brave man might have tried it. We'll never be sure, of course."

He glanced around. "Any further comments? If not, no point in keeping station here. The corpse won't rise for days, and we've no idea where it'll be carried first. You may as well turn in. I'll start us on our way again."

—The bunks were narrow, but Iern and Ronica spent the rest of the night in hers, holding each other, only holding each other close. They both wept a little.

3

Surf raged among skerries below ramparts of cliff. A boat or a man could not live through it. Terai was nearly blind in the windy, sleety, foamy dark, but he heard the waters roar and felt them recoil. He turned left at random and swam parallel to the unseen coast. Maybe he'd find an accessible shore before he drowned.

The pain of exhaustion, the gnawing of cold had faded into numbness—how long ago? He remembered vaguely that he had estimated three hours for the passage. They might as well have been three centuries. He was a thing that swam.

But then, and then—He came into a quietness aflow beneath the wind. His cracked lips tasted less salt. Scarcely more aware than a homing salmon, he started landward, and where a stream emptied into the sea he felt stones under his feet.

He reeled ashore and lay for a while upon blessed hardness.

The wind savaged him. He forced into himself the will to move, sat up, crawled out of his garment. Once in a half-forgotten dream, Ronica had warned that the chill factor in wet clothes could be deadly.

Yet the stuff had saved him. Had freed him. In the minute when a friendly sailor offered a—what did they call it?—a "union suit," he had thought what to do, how he might escape and be taken for dead yet remain alive.

"Wool's the best survival fabric there is," Ronica had said by the campfire. "Nothing holds heat better, whether or not it's wet. Raw wool, the natural grease in it, is preferable, but the ordinary cloth is good too. A shame we haven't got any here."

Terai had it on shipboard. He and Wairoa latched their cabin door and spent an hour rubbing the underwear with butter. When he sundered that door he was fully clad, but merely to hide the fabric beneath, lest someone guess his intention. Overboard, he shed the outer garments—he had loaded his pockets to sink them—and swam off in what amounted to a diver's wet suit.

At that, he'd barely survived. He would still die if he didn't seek cover.

He climbed centimeter by centimeter to his feet and staggered toward the glooms that soughed before him. Probably his best bet was to heap a lot of pine duff, leaves, humus, and so on over himself and wait for dawn. Later in the trip he could do better.

Later . . . better. . . . He was doubtless on an island. His single possession was a piece of smeared underwear. He was almost certainly the sole human being around. It was an unknown but huge distance, over mountains and through primeval forests, to civilization and the Maurai Inspectorate.

He went in among the trees. They broke the wind and he began to shiver slightly less. He began to think.

First thing in the morning, he should find some suitable rocks and chip out an edged tool, a knife or handax. Then he should construct a shelter, and traps for small animals, and a weir for fish—and, oh, yes, meanwhile live off grubs, roots, tubers, pine nuts, remnant berries, whatever he could get. Presently he should have accumulated bones for awls and daggers, sharp stones for scrapers, gut and sinew for making such things as a fire drill. He'd have to see about clothing; the wool wouldn't last unless it had protection from brush and ground. Maybe he could kill and skin a large beast. Likelier, for the time being, he must settle for plaiting grass, or something of the kind. Improve the tool kit, smoke meat, collect trail rations in general, develop a way—paddling on a log?—to get his stuff across the narrows to the mainland. . . .

He dared not dawdle. Winter was fast closing in. He might well perish. But (for a moment of pride, he raised his weary head) he thought his chances were fair. He was strong, and had skillful hands, and had learned a great deal from Ronica Birken.

XIX

Beneath the mountains in Laska there was coming to birth a terrible beauty.

Eygar Dreng, director, did not look like a sorcerer. He was a short, stocky man, half Eskimo, his features heavy and rather flat under a shock of grizzled black hair. A wound suffered in the Power War made him limp and use a cane. He dressed carelessly. His manner was affable unless incompetence had angered him, then he could outswear a longshoreman. He was cozily married, with four children whose ages ranged from twenty-five to thirteen; the oldest was wedded too and had overjoyed him with a grandchild. When time allowed, he would attend a party or a hard-fought poker game, and he was active in the Kenai chapter of the Wolf Lodge.

His background was scarcely more spectacular. A native of the area, he had moved south to study mechanical engineering and, later, work on aircraft development. During the war he served in the volunteer army, attaining the rank of major before he was invalided out. While the last battles were fought, he was among the first to dream of Orion and scheme for it. The site was picked at his suggestion, and he was a leader throughout the initial, most cruelly difficult years of preparation. Nevertheless he found moments in which to "generate notions"—his phrase—that engineers drawing up the basic designs found useful. When work on the actual hardware could commence, fifteen years ago, he was a natural choice for boss. Here he had been ever since, coordinating efforts that began with experimental parts, crude, small, scarcely worthy of being called toys, and that failed heartbreakingly at every level of advance, as men and women strove to create a thing which had never existed before.

And yet— "The man is a wizard," Plik said to Iern after they had met him. "A Faust. But with what devil has he made his pact?"

The dedication, the sheer will that drove Orion was in its way more awesome than the achievement. Eygar Dreng never went far from here; likewise his family, and the several hundred workers under him and their families, including spouses and children who had no direct role in Orion and very little knowledge of it. An occasional specialist visited from outside, consultant on a knotty problem, but only when the security officers had convinced themselves absolutely of his trustworthiness. Secrecy was, however, not the ultimate reason why this community sealed itself off year by year by year. That would have been impossible, especially for Northwesterners, were these not selected for desire as well as abilities. The vision was what held them. Whether or not they knew it, they were preparing the way for their god who had been prophesied unto them.

"Freedom first, yes," Eygar Dreng told the Uropans. "We've got to have that before we can go on, and when we do, a lot of us will happily retire. But not all; and new ones will pour in. Freedom first, not foremost!"

"What afterward?" Iern asked, though Ronica had spoken of it to him earlier.

Thereby she had kindled in him some of the flame that blazed in Eygar: "Space! The planets and the stars!

"Sure, we can't launch many of these nuke ships from Earth. Too much fallout. Besides, we'd soon run out of explosive. But we won't have to, either. Given the payload capacity they've got, in a few trips we can put the apparatus in Earth orbit and on the moon for a bridgehead, a permanent human presence yonder. From then on, it'll grow of itself. Can't help doing so, among all those opportunities. The resources are unlimited. The ancients proved that. We've got perfectly feasible plans of theirs in the files, waiting. The lunar regolith alone contains nearly every raw material we need. The asteroids contain more, and in more concentrated form. A single asteroid, nudged or solar-sailed into Earth orbit, or maybe mined on the spot by robots that catapult the stuff back—a single nickel-iron asteroid a klick or two in diameter would supply world industry for at least a century. Not just ferrous metals, either, but everything critical for alloys and electronics. And not just the Union, but world industry, including what the retrograded peoples need to lift them back to a decent life.

"And energy." He paced his office like a polar bear in a cage. Its narrowness and bleakness strengthened the image. Folk in these caverns had not taken time for making them luxurious. "As much energy as we can ever use, clean, free, inexhaustible. Only build enough solar collectors, big enough, in space. No limit. No night or weather or dust or birdshit to interfere, ever. Though I'd rather revive another ancient idea, myself. Instead of hanging them in the sky, build Criswell stations on the moon, out of lunar materials. Either way, beam the power down here as microwaves and turn it into electricity. Shucks, in due course we Norries could make the Maurai happy and dismantle the nuclear powerplants we'll have built on Earth. We won't need them any longer.

"Given that kind of energy, we can make all the fuel anybody wants, and not from coal or biomass, but hydrogen straight out of seawater. That includes fuel for chemical spacecraft boosters—unless we decide on laser launches and strictly aerodynamic reentries. No more nuclear blasts in the atmosphere.

"Actually, with that prospect before us, unlimited power, we can afford to burn up a certain amount of present-day fuel in launches at the beginning. Ten Orion shots to liberate us; ten or twenty more to orbit the really heavy stuff needed for an early start on space development; and that's all. From then on, the Orion system will only operate out yonder, where it belongs. Where *man* belongs. Of course, it'll soon be obsolete. Fusion-powered craft are already on some drawing boards."

"You'll transfigure the world," Plik murmured.

"Maybe less than you think, son." Eygar's words, which had tumbled and crackled, took on a calmer tone. The fanaticism faded out of his narrow black eyes. "Aside from civilizing it. Manufacturing should follow mining out into space. We won't need to take our raw materials from the hide of mother Earth, nor rub pollution into the wounds. Come back in a hundred years or so, and you may find us living in a pastoral paradise."

Plik shook his head. "Only angels are fit for paradise."

Eygar scowled. "What're men fit for, then?" He dismissed his irritation. "Work, at least. Okay, come have a look at ours."

More than a hundred meters deep, below their camouflaged covers, ten shafts in a mountain were the wombs of Orion. Between them, and elsewhere under the range, ran a web of corridors, rooms, vaults, rails, pipes, cables, machines at their business like trolls.

Simply building the physical plant had been a superherculean task. Some natural caves and extinct fumaroles were a nucleus, but mostly the means had been dynamite, a limited amount of power equipment, and human muscle—through day and night, sunshine, rain, fog, snow, frost, thaw for worse than four years. The cost had been gigantic too, and continued so: the cost of concrete, metal, apparatus, labor, fuel for the generators whose electricity powered everything from fluorescents and ventilators to furnaces and groundwater pumps.

(Construction workers were hired in the South, none for longer than a year except those few who knew the truth. They heard that they were building an industrial site to exploit Northern natural resources, for a consortium of entrepreneurs. Local inhabitants heard the same. They didn't complain too loudly about being excluded. They had work aplenty of their own, and reckoned it bad manners to pry when people didn't care to talk. . . . At last Eygar took a small part of the uranium-235 that had been collected and faked a volcanic eruption. The consortium announced that the shock had ruined everything. It could not afford to rebuild. Luckily, the disaster smote in a pause between excavation and furbishing; few personnel were there and casualties were nil. Then the Wolf Lodge, members of which had been leaders of the project, kindly offered to purchase the site for a wildlife refuge and scientific base it had been contemplating. . . . The Maurai were only marginally aware of all this, and not interested. Their Inspectorate was still new and overextended in the South, Laska was remote and inclement, they had no reason to suspect trickery.)

Not much showed aboveground: cabins, sheds, primitive roads, a laboratory, what an ecological research station would reasonably maintain. None of it was on the mountain of the spacecraft. Nor was much else visible except peaks and the forests below them; Tyonek, on Cook Inlet, lay eighty wild kilometers to the east.

Staff, their families, and their community facilities were housed underground. It was not as claustrophobic a situation as Iern had imagined. Living quarters were small but adequate, more comfortable and healthful than those wherein most of humanity huddled; interior decoration had become a folk art; places existed for meetings, games, sports, hobbies, celebrations; the school and the public library were excellent; if dining was perforce in mess halls, the food and the kitchen help were superior; individuals found themselves in countless permutations of mutual-interest groups. They could and did go topside almost anytime off duty that they wished, into a land where they could hike, climb, ski, hunt, fish, boat, picnic, frolic, or simply enjoy its magnificence. Sometimes parties of them took cruises by bus or yacht, which might include a fling among the fleshpots of Sitka.

Indeed, the isolation was not and could not be total. A fair number of persons, such as Ronica, had frequent occasion to go elsewhere. Then there were those, integral to the organization, who never had reason to come here—her mother and stepfather, for example. Living in Kenai, they were agents for one of the Wolf Lodge's commercial enterprises. It was a genuine job, but it was also cover for their service as a liaison, arranging the unobtrusive shipment of needed goods to the establishment across the firth.

On the whole, for nearly all concerned, and counting in the sense of vital achievement, rewards outweighed sacrifices.

Not that they dwelt in perfection. Everybody hated censorship of mail to the outside, and most longed for a glimpse of the South, a change of scene and neighbors, knowing they would not leave this cranny of the world until Orion rose or they died. They quarreled, connived, divorced, fell sick, knew loss and grief and frustration. A few committed crimes, punished by a tribunal of the directorate that governed here. Three who had developed psychoses were humanely but permanently confined.

Adolescent rebellion was less than might have been expected. The majority of those growing up in this place had only dim memories of anything else, or none. It was taken for granted that as they came of working age they would serve the undertaking, in whatever capacities they were able, until it was finished. A minority cherished no such wish, and resented the fact that they must remain after they reached adulthood. Their parents had contracted to live under what amounted to a dictatorship; they themselves had not, and weren't Norrmen supposed to be freemen? Could they not be trusted to keep their mouths shut?

The answer was no, they could not; yes, this was a gross violation of their liberty; once the nation was free, they would receive generous compensation, or they could file damage suits for larger sums if they saw fit. Thus far, none had attempted escape, though it would be possible if carefully planned. After all, they were the children of intelligent couples, who had raised them in an atmosphere of patience, hard work, and exalted hope. How would they feel if, somehow, they betrayed Orion, or simply if they let Orion rise without them?

The entire arrangement was metastable at best. Sooner or later, some random event must tear secrecy asunder, unless the great purpose was attained first. But then, the enterprise itself was marginal, a desperate, wildly daring venture. By that very fact, it caught at the spirit. Orion was a huge thing for which to live. These people had it, and it had them.

The spacecraft were at different stages of construction. In one case, it was demolition. Engineers were taking apart the unmanned test vehicle that had flown this summer, to study piece by piece. They planned to rebuild her, but along modified lines. She had been designed for flotation, to be recovered at sea where no outsiders were watching and returned here in sections. The rest were intended for ground landings.

Just two more preliminary flights were scheduled. Iern had the technical background to know how dismaying that paucity was, but the staff had scant choice. Every shot was a clue to the nature and location of what was under way, and the Maurai hounds were chasing down every other possible trace, too. On that account, the search for fissionables was now suspended, a decision whose rightness the narrow escape of Mikli's group underscored. Nevertheless, given time, it was sheerly inevitable that the enemy would find this stronghold. Eygar did not propose to grant the time.

The second excursion would be manned, to check out controls and landing gear. Eygar hoped to launch it in a few months, as soon as certain alterations were completed which the first experiment had indicated were desirable. The third flight, also manned, would carry lasers, solar collectors, and solid projectiles for testing; it should be ready in a year or so. Assuming no out-and-out fiasco or disaster, its results would be the basis for equipping the whole fleet. Orion ought to rise in full strength less than two years hence.

"That's cutting it almighty thin, I know," Eygar said. "We'll launch sequentially, over a period of a week, unless the Maurai are right on our necks by then. That should give a chance to correct some mistakes, as experience shows us what they are. My guess is we'll lose a couple of vehicles, and a couple more will prove useless because of malfunctions. Give me five that work, though—" he held a palm upward, fingers crooked like talons—"give me a hand of ships, and we'll set ourselves free."

Electric chills went along Iern's spine as he beheld *Orion Two.*

The corridor through which he had come debouched on a platform ten meters up the ascent tube. Ladders, catwalks, and wheeled scaffolding wove webs through cold, echoing dimness. A pit at the bottom, where fans and scrubbers would receive the really bad toxins from the initial explosion, was like a lake of night. Workers who moved about on the frames, in and out of the hull, were dwarfed; he felt eerily that they did not service the spacecraft, they served her.

Plik crossed himself.

Poised at the center, the ship gleamed with a sinister loveliness. Below her spearhead bow, ports and an airlock were visible. Farther down, she flared gracefully out to a larger diameter which occupied most of her twenty-seven-meter length; therein were equipment and life-support housing, followed by a radiation shield, the cargo space (which would hold weapons in the next war, and again afterward if the peace needed patrolling), another radiation shield, the propulsive machinery, and still another radiation shield—this last to protect metal, plastics, and electronics, not crew. About at her midriff, short wings swept backward. From his angle, Iern spied hatches above and below them, whence three-point landing gear would emerge. He also made out the scaly pattern of heat-buffering tiles, though their ceramic shimmered as burnished a blue-white as the bare metal. At the very stern, three thick plates were successively wider, to a maximum of some fourteen meters. They varied in shape as well as size, and their interconnections were intricate.

"We've changed the original design every which way, of course," Eygar said. Ardor throbbed beneath his dry phrases. "But it was hardly more than a sheaf of calculations and sketches. Old Dyson never got his chance. I wonder what the world'd be like today if he had. . . .

"His would've been bigger, and assembled in orbit. We need a vehicle that can go from Earth and come back again, and maneuver freely in both air and space, and put down on any reasonable runway or even any reasonably level patch of dirt. She has to be independent of ground control, too, since we can't set up worldwide stations like the ancients. She'll carry her own computers, and employ crew at several control boards. Building an integrated system that one man could fly would've added years to the project. What she lacks in elegance, she'll make up in brute power. If she misses on a pass, she'll have the reserves to try again.

"What we had to go on was the old astronautical literature, such of it as survived; ditto the stuff on nuclear engineering, especially explosive devices; our own civilization's experience with things like aircraft; and the raw belief that it *can* be done."

He pointed downward. "Not much finesse, no. We'll do better in the next generation of Orions. Here, essentially, on command, the machinery dispatches a bomb down a chute. Valves open in front of it and close behind—sturdy valves! The bomb detonates automatically behind the after plate, unless the pilot sends an override signal. The design derives from ancient tactical warheads. There are several varieties, with yields from fifty tonnes to five kilotonnes; the pilot chooses the mix and sequence. He can have a lesser push still by unleashing a minimum size and sending a 'muffle' signal along with it, though that wastes the full available energy. You can't see them from here—they look like shallow rib segments—but he's also got solid-fuel chemical rockets to help him maneuver in space, plus gyroscopes inside.

"That first explosion gets the ship moving!" he exulted. "And then it's bang again, and bang and bang and bang. Little contamination from the atmospheric bursts; none from bursts in space. The delta vee is limited only by the number and size of bombs she carries. She can prowl above Earth any way the pilot wants, or carry a small ocean freighter's worth of cargo to the moon or an expedition to Mars—and return."

"Hold on," Iern said. "Space is a high-grade vacuum. How do you couple the energy to the ship, there?"

"Good for you," Eygar laughed. "The bottom plate consists mainly of synthetic material that absorbs the energy, shrinks, and rebounds, giving the ship a healthy whack. It's a compressible lattice of doped fluorosilicone chains and assorted carbon rings, forming a cellular structure. The same stuff supplements the hydraulics in the upper plates, which time-attenuate the impact. You don't get a jerky ride; it's fairly smooth. In spite of the Maurai, we've learned a bit more basic science than the ancestors knew."

Because of the Maurai, we know far more biology, and perhaps things about the psyche, passed through Iern. *Is their attitude altogether unreasonable?* He cast the thought from him. Ronica's cause was his.

"When your ship has completed her mission," Plik asked, "how does she fall?"

Eygar gave him a hard look before explaining: "If she isn't in Earth orbit already, she assumes it, and fires a retroblast or two to reduce speed. She could theoretically back down through the atmosphere on nuclear, but our control systems aren't up to that, and besides, it'd make unnecessary contamination. So the descent will be aerodynamic. You see the wings and heat shielding. Those pods under the wings contain turbojets, which have ample fuel. So she won't come down deadstick. With the lift we've got, we can afford the extra mass. In fact, if it weren't for the need of concealment, she could fly high before releasing the first bomb. But as long as we had to hide the construction work anyway, we did it in these shafts, and installed the pit apparatus to swallow the initial radioactivity—and, of course, to make it harder for the enemy to identify just where the ship is rising from.

"Oh, she won't fly like a hawk, no, nor an eagle, I suppose—but a dragon, a dragon."

2

Wairoa sat hunkered in his cell, contemplating the subtleties of air currents. A shutter slid aside and a guard looked through the window in the otherwise solid door. "Hello, there," he said.

Wairoa brought his attention back from hypersensitivity, rose, waited. "The chief would like to see you," the guard explained. "Uh, if you want."

The Maurai quirked a smile. "By 'chief' you mean Mikli Karst, head of your intelligence and security group," he replied in the same Unglish. "I doubt the director would be that sardonic."

The guard frowned. "Damn it, cut that out, will you? We try to be nice to you and— Oh, never mind. Will you come?"

Wairoa nodded and slipped on the undergarments, tunic, trousers, and sandals issued him. He had been naked, observing with his entire skin. The door opened and he stepped forth. Two armed men stood nervously aside. They were career soldiers, normally keeping watch against intruders aboveground, occasionally doubling as constabulary below, unused to the role of jailers. The captive was a spooky sort, too, they thought.

"This way." One before, one behind, they conducted him through coldly lighted tunnels. Ventilators whirred and gusted breezes which smelled a little of oil and chemicals. Beyond the detention section, folk went to and fro on their work. They cast startled glances at Wairoa. The official bulletin about the new arrivals had been terse. The sight of him turned voices off.

At the end of the walk was an anteroom where an officer was handling documents while a secretary typed letters. The former wore a sidearm. "Go in," she told Wairoa. "You fellows wait here."

Past a door was a second chamber, not very spacious either, its rock similarly covered with soft, blue-gray material. The portal to a vault occupied most of the rear wall. A bookcase filled the left side. Across the right wall, above a large glass-topped desk, a pair of mammoth tusks curved mightily. On the desktop were a telephone, an intercom, an onyx penholder in the form of a yoni, a crystal ashtray, and several reference volumes between bookends made of human jawbones—no pictures anywhere, though Mikli Karst had a wife and children. The air was blue and a-reek with cigarette smoke.

"Greeting," the Norrman said cordially from behind the desk. He waved at a chair opposite. "Sit down. Would you like coffee, tea, something stronger?"

Wairoa shook his head, lowered himself, crossed his arms, and leaned back.

"You needn't sulk." Mikli's tone continued cheerful. "You've been pretty well treated for a prisoner of war—which you are, you know—haven't you? A comfortable cell, your privacy respected, decent food and drink, plenty of books, exercise periods, a promise of medical care if you should need it. And human interaction, if you'd accepted the overtures of your guards. They were curious and wanted to be friendly. It's not their fault that you rebuffed them."

"And you are about to offer me more," Wairoa said.

"Shrewd, shrewd. Can you tell me why?"

"You too are curious. Not being stupid, you do not expect me to let out any secrets, but you may acquire a few usable insights from conversations with me. If nothing else, they will be diverting."

Mikli reached for a cigarette. "You might credit me with common humanity. You'll be here for many months. I've arranged matters so that keeping you in close confinement any longer would be a pointless cruelty."

Wairoa's voice remained calm. "About that last motivation, you lie."

Mikli narrowed his eyes. "I don't recommend insulting me."

"You cannot be insulted."

Mikli cackled a laugh. "Good for you! Instead, I'm amusable."

He ignited the cigarette, inhaled, blew a smoke ring, and said: "This is my proposal. You'll be free to move about the residential-recreational sections. The critical areas are restricted, as you must have guessed; the sentries admit nobody without a pass. From time to time you may go topside if you like, under guard. Below ground, you may call on anybody you wish and talk freely, though you can also guess what kinds of questions will go unanswered. Nobody will accompany you on such excursions. We've better uses for personnel than to have them clumping after you.

"The restrictions are these. You must spend the nights in your cell, locked up. By day you must report in person, every four hours, to the officer on duty in the anteroom here. And you must wear this gadget."

From a drawer he drew a padded ring, hinged at one point and equipped with a locking mechanism where it stood open. "It fits around your neck," he said. "It's loose and comfortable, you can wash beneath it, but you see that it won't slip over your head. Inside are wires, transistors, and a small but adequate battery. If any suspicion about you arises, the officer will press a button to trigger a radio signal which, in turn, will activate a transmitter in the collar. That will enable us to pinpoint your location. Would you like to examine it?"

Wairoa accepted the device, turned it over once, and handed it back. "Obviously any tampering will also switch on the transmitter," he said. "The frequency must be suitable for alarm circuits in this complex to pick up and carry, else the walls would screen so weak a signal. Above ground, it should be detectable by a sensitive instrument for a significant distance, independently of line-of-sight. Therefore I would judge the frequency to be in the range—"

"Who cares?"

"I am interested in the configuration that generates such a waveband, given its physical dimensions. Ingenious."

"I have no doubt you can redesign it in your mind. Myself, I just gave the specs to one of our electronic witches, and she delivered the goods two days later. Do you accept my terms?"

"Yes."

Mikli rose. "Then let me do the honors. Please bend over the desk. M-m-m . . . don't try anything violent. I'm tougher and faster than you may think. Besides, where would you go?"

"By resisting, I could deprive you of the sexual satisfaction," Wairoa replied, "but it would not be worth the trouble."

Mikli stiffened. After several seconds he said, harshly: "All right, come on." Wairoa got up and complied. Mikli locked the collar around his neck. Both sat back down.

Mikli had recovered equilibrium. "Apropos your remark," he said, "I can introduce you to a woman who'd find you interesting. She's no beauty, but then, neither are you. Or if you prefer a young man, I can oblige also."

"No."

"As you like. You could have said, 'Thank you.' "

"Why?"

"Look, my time is reasonably valuable. I can't waste it on your surliness."

"I am simply a precisionist," Wairoa said. "Let us by all means talk whenever you wish. You are an interesting creature."

"And you. How human are you, anyway?"

Wairoa made a slight shrug. "What is human?"

Mikli nodded and ground out the stub of his cigarette. "You and I have quite a few likenesses," he observed thoughtfully. "We both feel . . . detached . . . and at the same time, as if we had been born into a war going on forever . . . no? I'm not sure but what there is such a thing as ancestral memory. Certain nightmares— Do the races of man remember the wrongs they have done each other?"

"Curious to hear you employ the word 'wrong,'" Wairoa remarked.

Mikli blinked, shook himself, and took out a fresh cigarette. "Well, even on a strictly scientific basis, it's ridiculous to suppose the races have identical psyches. When everything else is unique, stature, proportions, color, tolerance of environmental factors, how could brains and nerves not be? Look at the temperaments of different breeds of dog—"

The intercom buzzed. Mikli flipped a switch. "Excuse me, sir," came a woman's voice. "I need a file from the vault. Okay?"

"Okay." Mikli shut off the instrument. "Let's get acquainted before we get metaphysical," he proposed. "Would you care to tell me something about your past life?"

"Let me think about that for a minute," Wairoa said.

The outside officer entered and sought the massive, iron-reinforced oaken door of the vault. "Kindly look away while she dials the combination," Mikli ordered. Wairoa swiveled his chair around and sat silent until the door swung open. Then he turned back, which gave him a sidewise glimpse of a chamber walled with filing cabinets and the officer sliding out a drawer.

"No, I believe you have the sequence reversed," he said. "My observation has been that people know each other somewhat before they exchange autobiographies. Why don't we begin by talking shop today? What were our respective teams doing in Yurrup?"

Mikli puffed hard. "You'd tip your hand to me?"

"No, of course not. However, a few details about what is obvious anyhow could be worth trading. For example, your primary mission was concerned with the coup d'état in Skyholm, wasn't it?"

The officer caught her breath. Mikli frowned. "If you mean, were we a party to it, the answer is no," he replied.

"We, our team, learned you had been in Espayn and later traveled about meeting with various high-ranking Clansmen—and you were not the first Northwestern agents in that area. In fact, it was word about earlier ones that decided my command on sending investigators."

The officer took out the folder she wanted, closed drawer and vault, departed. Meanwhile Mikli said: "Such things could scarcely be kept hidden. However, use your common sense. Naturally, my corps wanted to know what was going on in the Domain, especially since you Maurai were expanding your presence there. What were *you* up to?" He bent lips into a smile. "An old saw goes, 'Ever pointless are point-blank questions.' We had the unglamorous job of collecting the usual countless bits of a jigsaw puzzle which might or might not form a coherent picture. Oh, yes, we'd have been glad to see a regime come in that favored us and was hostile to you. But what did happen? A Gaean takeover, an ideology in the saddle that's four-square opposed to us. Would we have promoted it? Come, now, man, come, now."

"You maintain trade and cultural relations with the Mong."

"Mutual expediency. If they find out about Orion, prematurely, we'll have a two-front war on our hands, you from the sea, they from over the mountains. As is, they, like you, suspect us of being the uranium gleaners, and relations have grown strained."

"Somebody gave Jovain the help he needed."

"The evidence points to Yuan. Didn't you fellows get clues?"

Wairoa nodded. "We can expect the new Domain government to start freezing us out," he said. "It will use its sizable resources in aid of converting the eastern Uropans to Gaeanity, which will bring their growing strength under its leadership. An intercontinental alliance—could that be the long-range hope of the Yuanese leaders? Could the imperial Soldat spirit be stirring again?"

"You worry," Mikli said. "But Maurai policy has always been to uproot trouble at the earliest stage, before it's had a chance to grow—eh? What do you propose to do about Yurrup?"

"I am not in Her Majesty's Cabinet or the Admiralty."

"No matter," Mikli said with the ghost of a sneer. "When Orion has risen, we'll protect you, too, against aggression. You see, then it'll be in our interest to preserve the status quo, while we proceed to shower the benefits of space upon all mankind."

Wairoa regarded him. "You do not believe that. You never did."

"Oh, no." Mikli laughed. "Let Eygar Dreng and his think-alikes enjoy their fantasies. It stimulates their engineering genius, which you must agree is impressive. At the same time, it's a textbook case of wish triumphing over logic."

"What do you predict, assuming Orion succeeds and the Northwest Union becomes the dominant power on Earth?"

"Well, out of curiosity I've quietly commissioned technical studies, by people who have no emotional ax to grind where space is concerned. And I've done my own thinking."

Mikli made a throwaway gesture. "Visualize," he said. "We can't garrison the globe, and would not if we could. So we'll need Orion, and an enlarged support structure, to maintain the upper hand, the threat in heaven. Little or nothing to spare for peaceful endeavors until a separate fleet has been built, and that will take a long while —especially when investment capital won't be forthcoming very fast for such an expensive and unproven venture. Even if it were, Dreng is ludicrously optimistic about the possible pace of development. He closes his eyes to any economic or social hurdles. Meanwhile, every society, ours included, will be changing. Orion alone, and its check on the old Maurai balance wheel, guarantees that—but the changes are totally unpredictable." He grinned like a shark. "Except for this: we will never, never see Earth turned into a residential garden supplied by industrial parks throughout the Solar System. It is in the nature of man that he fouls his own nest."

After a silence, when the ventilator alone had utterance, Wairoa stirred in his chair and asked softly, "If you bear so little faith in your cause, why do you serve it so well?"

"It's the liveliest game in town," Mikli said, "and it should lead to some glorious fireworks. Why do you serve yours?"

"Because I think you are right about what will happen if your side prevails."

"Why do you care?"

"It is in *my* nature to be a watchman." The Maurai was mute for another space; then, mâtter-of-factly: "We were born to kill each other, you and I. On that account, we can be more open with each other than with anybody else in the world."

3

"—Once again the vintners have wrought their humble miracle,
To give us in communion a year that long has passed
On an autumn stormwind's blast.
Here there is remembrance of vineyards flaming scarlet,
As vivid as your spirit, which must also go at last
To wherever it is cast,
And oh, how fast!
Then taste that summer once again which dreams within the cup

Of sun-gold wings upon a hawk at hover
No higher in the sky than our hearts went winging up,
And dance your way through music to discover,
Wine-renewed, that I remain your lover."

Plik ended his song with a ripple of chords and put the guitar aside. His left hand reached for a glass, his right arm went around the waist of the young woman who sat beside him. He smiled down into her countenance, then lightly kissed her.

Applause spattered about the mess hall. After dinner it became a tavern which had acquired a name, the Boot Heel. (Nobody knew how, but everybody knew why: Northwestern engineers had an immemorial saying, "The instructions are printed on the heel.") The bar was a shelf under a selection of bottles and a beer keg; you helped yourself, tossing money into a jar on the honor system. Ornate lamps took over from fluorescent panels, for a festive look and romantically shadowed corners. Pine scent blown into the air joined the ventilators to keep down stenches of burning oil, tobacco, marijuana, hashish. Only a handful of drinkers were still on the benches at this late hour. The one day off that workers got was staggered through the week, and many did not take it, nor vacations either; Orion possessed them.

"Who was that song for?" asked the young woman. Earlier, when the room was filled, Plik had given his numbers various dedications, generally ribald.

"Why, you, my dear. Who else?" he purred around a sip of volcanic local whiskey.

Lisba Yamamura contracted her brows as she helped herself to sherry. "Um-m-m, in that case you called me 'Vineleaf,' and pretended we'd been acquainted a fairish time."

"Poetic license," said Plik.

She gave him a sidelong glance. "Or licentiousness? I think it was a piece you wrote for some other woman, back in Yurrup, and translated into Unglish while you were washing dishes." He had gotten daytime employment in the kitchen, where they were always shorthanded. Most evenings he sang for drinks and tips and did rather well, since entertainment was hard to come by.

Plik cocked his head at her. She was on the stocky side but her face piquant, with its hint of Asia, and she was lively and bright, a technical reference librarian. "No, not really," he maintained. "That is, I admit the original composing was done there, and uses certain literary conventions, but never until now have I found a lady worthy of the sentiment."

"Well—" She smiled and snuggled. "I'll be conventional too and pretend I believe that. You're kind of a charming rascal." His lips wandered across the fragrance of her blue-black hair. "And a foreigner. That's exciting. We're so isolated here."

"You aren't working tomorrow, are you?"

"No, I don't have to."

"The same for me. We could keep busy nevertheless."

"Eager, aren't you?"

"I've been lonely."

"Your friends—"

"Oh, my co-workers and the chaps in the bachelor section are kind, interested, but, let's be frank, alien to me, as well as being male. Iern and Ronica invite me to their room for a drink and chat, but not often. Nearly all their time necessarily goes to their own work, or to each other. Wairoa, since his release . . . Wairoa observes."

"Captain Karst? I heard—"

Plik grimaced. "Why should he care about me? He has bigger mice to whom he can play cat."

Lisba drew a little away from him. "What do you mean? The Maurai?"

He hiccoughed and drank afresh. "No, they're the hounds on his track. He'll double back to their kennels if he can and gnaw their pups to death. The mice are ordinary people, helpless and hapless, millionfold. And, to extend the metaphor, if the world burns, he'll crouch before it and purr."

She disengaged entirely. "I don't like your implication," she said.

"I beg your pardon." His speech had turned overprecise. "Perhaps I misspoke myself. Too much to drink. Maybe we should abandon these glasses half-empty and—"

"No, wait, mister." She sat stiff and glared at him. The rest present could not hear their low voices, and grew chattersome themselves, determined to ignore what went on. Privacy was another thing valued in the Union, scarce in the Orion complex. "I want to know just what you did intend by that crack. Mikli Karst is kind of a hero around here, you realize, considering what he's done for the project. If he's evil, then the bunch of us are; and I deny that."

"Oh, so do I, so do I," Plik hastened to say. "We needn't discuss his individual morals. *You* honestly believe you're doing what is best for the world. That's enough."

"No, it isn't." Her nostrils flared. Though the light was too dim for certainty, it seemed she had gone white. "You're claiming I—my colleagues and I—we're such blind fools we'd serve a cause that could bring on a new Doom. You're showing the same hysteria as is built into the Maurai and— Well, I thought better of you. I truly did."

He bridled. "The reality is," he said, "every Orion ship will be able to take out several cities. Who shall control the masters—forever? And what about fissionables brought from space, fusion reactors built on Earth, biotechnics such as created poor Wairoa? You're loosing a demon, you and yours are, the demon of power."

"Power doesn't have to be misused."

Plik shook his head, drank, slumped. "Your claim is almost a meaningless noise, my dear. At best, irrelevant. We don't use power, ever. It uses us, feeds on us, and long after its first purpose is behind it. It exists for its own sake, it is its own God. You believe Orion will set you free. And maybe it will, for a time. But afterward, afterward—"

Lisba rose. "Goodnight," she snapped.

He caught her wrist. "Oh, wait, please! I meant no offense. Let's say the spirit wasn't talking but the spirits were."

She pulled away. "And let's say I got tired of listening to them. Goodnight, I told you." She walked out.

Plik stared after her, brought his gaze back to the company that remained, encountered a wryly sympathetic smile, and declared aloud, "She can entertain no doubts of her rightness. None of you can. You dare not. I had better keep it in mind." He lifted his glass.

4

Fog was the most terrible enemy. This was not a cold country, even when winter strode nigh, and the islands sheltered it from the worst of the wind. Rains were seldom violent either, though scarcely a day saw none. A few times snow had fallen, but thinly, melting almost before it reached earth. Terai could keep going through such weathers until sundown forced him to make shelter.

But then clouds descended, full of chill drizzle. They drowned the world, made him grope through gray formlessness, robbed him of the early and late hours of a daylight that grew daily more brief. Blind beyond a few meters or less, he could not plan his route across whatever heights and depths lay ahead. He must stumble forward at random, yet stay close enough to the water that he could hear its waves lap on rocks, lest he stray irretrievably from their guidance;

and the clouds muffled noises, distorted them, blurred any sense of the direction from which they came. More nightmarish still was the dankness, which seeped through garments and into flesh and marrow as no gale was able, made him cough and shudder and wonder if the South Seas had ever been aught but a dream.

He could not camp and wait for it to clear. That would cost him too much of his dwindling time. On his best days, he estimated that he won thirty kilometers of distance, and those victories were rare. Oftenest, terrain slowed him. Necessity kept forcing a halt—to prepare for night, to sleep, to wring what he needed out of the wilderness and work it into a form he could use, with inexperienced hands and tools of the Old Stone Age. Fog or no, he must make what headway he might.

This coast was a strip beneath mountains, interrupted again and again by their roots, over which he clambered, or by fjords around which he detoured, or by rivers he swam or forded. Yet he had no other path. Striking east in search of easier ground, he would soon have been lost, when the heavens were nearly always hidden; before long, a high-altitude blizzard would have claimed him, if an avalanche, a tumble, or a grizzly bear did not first. Here he at least had the straits for a compass, the wooded lower slopes to sustain him—deer were plentiful at this season—and the chance that he might come upon a settlement or see a fisher boat and get help.

He had passed many marching hours in devising the story he would tell, if and when he met human beings. It had better be a good story, as wild as his appearance was. Gaunt, weathered, scarred, unshorn, unwashed, clad in his rank woolens and in untanned skins lashed together with sinew, that he changed not when they grew putrid but when they grew stiff—rabbit stick in his grasp, crude pouch full of stones for cutting and throwing at his waist, whatever food he had in an equally primitive woven-withe carrier on his back—he would shock the poorest of the savages who roamed this outback.

He was not a savage, though. He was a man of the Maurai, who had a mission to fulfill and a home to return to. Every day he made himself remember that and believe it.

Terai Lohannaso slogged onward through the weeping cloud.

5

Fire crackled cheerily behind mica panes in the door of a ceramic stove. Warmth gusted from vents. A low whirr sounded in the chimney, where a fan captured some of the energy in the flue gases; much of what remained went into a heat exchanger and thence back to the house. Lamplight glowed on wallpaper, curtains, pictures, furniture, carpet, and reflected off window glass as if to deny the night beyond. Lingering odors of dinner, fresh scents of coffee and brandy drifted about the living room.

"But are you sure Iern's presence won't be a giveaway?" Tom Jamis asked. "He's bound to meet people on his visits—Kenai is an overgrown village, and what'd really make gossip buzz would be that your fiancé did not get introduced around—but somebody on a trip south could happen to mention him when the wrong ears overheard."

Ronica smiled at her stepfather. He was a large man, balding, his beard gray, not unlike Launy Birken in looks and heart. "Yes, that's one matter to brief you two about," she told him and her mother. "Not to worry as long as we're careful. Mikli Karst himself okayed the arrangement, the cover. Iern is a Free Merican—from Corado—whom I met on a trip about which I'm not supposed to talk. We do have a few foreigners co-opted into Orion, remember; but officially he's a visiting scientist, in the ecological study area on a fellowship. His name is Erno sunna Fernan, which ought to let possible slips of the tongue go unnoticed. His accent will pass for a dialect of Unglish used near the Meycan border, under Spanyol influence." She inhaled and drank pungency from her snifter glass and sent a wallop of strong coffee after it. "We won't be here much anyway, you realize. But damn if I wouldn't see my folks and show them my man!"

Iern reached between their chairs to take her hand and give it a squeeze. Adoration torrented back and forth. Momentarily her universe left its moorings and soared. After three months and more, he could still do that to her. *I'll have to get awful old and feeble before he can't; and likelier we'll chase around in our wheelchairs, cackling lustfully and shocking our grandchildren.*

"You're a dear," said her mother. "In your hoyden fashion." Anneth might be prematurely white-haired, but that was almost the sole concession she had made to time. "And I like you, Iern. Probably I'm going to grow very fond of you."

"I would be honored, madame," answered the Clansman, unwontedly shy.

"That is, I hope Tom and I will get the chance to," Anneth said. "We hardly will before Orion has risen. And later—your business in Yurrup— Well, let's not borrow trouble. The interest rate is exorbitant. How are you enjoying things across the Inlet, now that you're settling down?"

Glory replied: "Oh, wonderful. Fascinating. Even the conferences, reports, all the drudgery that takes up most of the time—it's getting us into *space.*"

Ronica understood. She had herself been in the simulators, in the course of her work on control systems.

It was natural for Iern to train as a pilot. His past career made him the most qualified airman ever to enlist in the undertaking. Already, gaining a feel for the vessels he might someday fly, already he had made practical suggestions for improvement, for combing out what bugs the research and development effort was discovering. And then too, his role was as closely intertwined with hers as they themselves were when alone and in the frequent mood. He was there, in her nearness, during the day—

Except in the simulators. Then he leaves me, and doesn't come back to me right away after he climbs out; his look, his soul, they're elsewhere. I can't blame you, Iern, darling. I only envy you—though you're never more lovable than when you're full of stars— And it's just a computer-generated shadow show, images on a screen, well-faked instrument readings, roughly faked sensations, to give us an idea of what we must build and do. The ancients were free to keep a huge ground-control apparatus and a tracking network that spanned the planet. We are not. Instead, we must create ships in which the crews can fly free—in which you can, Iern, Iern. And I by your side?

—They would stay overnight at the house. Before going to bed, they donned parkas and went forth, hand in hand, for the uncommon sight of an entirely clear sky. Here, on the outskirts of town, the dark and the stars were theirs. Cold caressed their cheeks and made breath stream snowpeak-white. Frost underfoot crackled through the silence. The Milky Way shone aloft, and again in an ebon mirror of water. Brilliances crowded around it. And mightily over the eastern range came striding that winter constellation called Orion.

XX

Their number is so small, they with whom I can speak freely. Here were two of them. Jovain looked across the Captain's desk and felt how alone he was. He could share his mind with these men, but never his heart. For that, there was nobody.

"What do you think?" he asked Bergdorff Pir Verine.

The magnate shifted in his seat. He was on the short side, but a well-known sportsman who had had a distinguished record as an officer in the Italyan campaign. At home he was a decisive administrator of his family holdings in the Lake Zheneve region, and of a brokerage he had founded. Yet now he hesitated. "I need more information, sir," he said.

Mattas Olvera uttered a thunderous obscenity. "What more?" he demanded. "Truthtellers are being persecuted across the Channel. It's a clear violation of treaty—under the eye and lasers of Skyholm. If we hold still for this, who'll be next in line at our rear ends? The eastern barbarians?"

"Wait, wait." Jovain lifted a palm. Silence fell, deepened by the eternal soft breathings of the aerostat. In the Gaean manner, he brought himself to awareness of his surroundings, ancestral possessions and creations, glacial hardness of the glass top under his hand. Thence he drew strength to curb his Gaean mentor: "I've already heard the rhetoric, Mattas. What I want today is advice."

The ucheny turned red, made a gobbling noise, sank back into his chair and smoldered.

"I'm tired of hearing the Allemans called barbarians," Pir Verine added. "Some are, but those who live near me have won back to civilization. They have a growing literate class, trade, law, ambitions. Which, to be sure, will eventually make them rivals of the Domain, as their confederacy expands and modernizes." He gave Mattas an irenic nod. "To that extent, you are right. We owe it to our grandchildren to look ahead and provide."

"The question is, what and how?" Jovain said. "We cannot dawdle, either, or we risk the Domain falling apart beneath us. Soon, *soon* I shall have to call in my official counselors, discuss matters with them, and issue my orders. First I need to know what direction to take. I summoned you, Pir, because I believe you can give me a sound, independent opinion." *Or the closest approximation to one that I will ever see,* he thought. Unease passed through him. *Is even that much true? Pir Verine has gambled for high stakes in the past, but always after calculation and precaution. He found it expedient to support my coup—and was prepared to disavow me had it failed. He could find it expedient to betray me in my turn.*

The other Clansman ran a palm over his bald pate. "Well, then," he said, "if I may be frank, I see no reason why we should take this business in Angleylann very seriously in itself."

"What?" exploded from Mattas. He swung to his feet and stamped back and forth. When he passed before the desk, Jovain caught odors of unwashed skin and robe. "Ignore, if you will, that a gang of narrow-minded reactionaries forbid the people they rule to hear the Truth. You've claimed you're sympathetic to Gaeanity, you, but—Argh!" He barely refrained from spitting on the carpet. Instead, he pointed at it. "Do you remember what that signifies? That we rid Devon of pirates plundering its coasts, though it's never belonged to the Domain and Skyholm owes it nothing. Nor has that been the single favor we've done it over the centuries. And what gratitude do those chingaros return us? Flat-out violation of treaty, that's what!"

"Let's consider this in perspective," Pir replied mildly. "The pirates, and their ilk throughout the past, were robbing goods we wanted in trade, ruining markets of ours—and would doubtless have gotten cocky enough to raid our shores too. Skyholm was no more altruistic than governments usually are." He lifted a forefinger. "True, the Concord of Guernsey guarantees free entry into the countries of southern Angleylann, to persons of the Domain on legitimate business. However, Devon is a hierocratic state. Its Bishop decided, not quite wrongly, that Gaeanity will undermine its church and faith. Therefore, he says, the business of our missionaries is not legitimate. Well, is this worth fighting a war over? Why not concentrate on making converts closer to home, ucheny?"

"Who spoke about war?" Jovain said. "Economic sanctions—"

"Oh, no," Pir answered, his voice grown softer still. "No, not that, sir, my friend. Your promise to the neo-isolationists, that you'll restrict foreign trade, has many of us adequately unhappy. We'll be striving to get that program put on the shelf. But at worst, trade with, say, the Maurai has not reached a large volume. Trade across the Channel is a different matter. An embargo would do grave damage to me and everybody like me." His gaze sought Jovain's and held fast. "The Captain cannot wish to hurt his supporters, can he?"

How cold the air feels. Imagination only, but I shiver.

"I wasn't talking about a war, either," Mattas grumbled. "Firm diplomacy, an ultimatum if need be, mobilization on our side, those should turn the trick."

Pir smiled. "Ah, yes. And out of the crisis, we should get further commercial concessions. Please recall what I said. The business is nothing to take very seriously in itself. That does not mean we can't make a fulcrum of it."

They gave him sharp looks. "As a single important instance," he explained, "think of our military professionals. They don't like the idea of rapprochement with the old enemy, Espayn. Far less do they like the idea of their own reduction, their eventual replacement by men whom Skyholm recruits directly. Yes, up in my Alps I too have heard complaints that approach the mutinous. Mobilization will give the cadre something to do, something which you control, Captain."

"I . . . was . . . thinking . . . along those lines," Jovain admitted.

—Hours later, he stood by himself. His back was bent, his hands clasped behind it. He stared at the time-browned paper whereon was the Declaration of Tours, scarcely seeing, while the words throbbed below his mind. "*—the causes of peace, order, justice, and ultimate reunion—*"

I, having lived through war, am a man of peace. But if I threaten war, and am defied, I shall have to wage it. Why? How did all this happen? What has gone wrong?

He squared his shoulders. Pain and death were among the workings of the Life Force, which he served. Let him never forget.

The clock said that Uropa had rolled from the short day of this season into the long night. He should seek home, to his apartment, to Faylis. Maybe he could draw strength from her. Likelier, she would want it from him, comfort, consolation, hope. Well, at least she had stopped complaining about the irregular hours he kept.

2

Terai saw the village at a distance, by the glow of its windows through dusk, and forgot weariness as he hastened his stride. He had known it was there, a fisher community at the head of a fjord; the Injuns whom he encountered earlier had told him. They also gave him shelter, food, clothes, but after a single night he declined further hospitality. The news he bore could not wait.

Besides, he fled from a sense of guilt. The Northwest Union was their country too.

He must serve his own, and mankind as a whole, and the living planet.

Meadows reached dim around him. The graveled road whispered beneath his moccasins. As yet, chill had not turned to cold, but it would before long, for the sky was clear and the Injuns had remarked that this day which was ending was the first of winter. Stars blinked forth in a purple that rapidly deepened to black. Somewhere a dog howled.

The road bent down toward a gleam of water, and heights cut off most of what light remained. Terai could just make out the radio antenna above one building, which he supposed was the hall of whatever Lodge had a chapter here. Its leanness and guy wires made a mast of it, on a ship bound among the stars to an unknown port. Orion stood huge behind.

Terai groped through rutted streets to that goal. He met nobody. Folk were indoors, mostly at table. He glimpsed them there, husband, wife, children, perhaps a parent or two dwelling under the same roof or a friend come to visit. The scenes were infinitely comfortable and cheerful, and infinitely remote from him.

The house he sought was the largest in town, as suited a meeting place, but of the same timber and shakes as the rest. Its door was unlocked. Terai decided he had better use the knocker regardless, for luminance at the rear showed someone was present, doubtless a caretaker who got an apartment in exchange for part-time services. The wood banged hollowly.

After a while the door swung aside. A middle-aged man confronted Terai. The candle that he held in a stick showed him gnarled but powerfully muscled from a lifetime's toil. He peered at the big newcomer in the ill-fitting garments. "Who are you and what d'you want?" he asked at last. Suspicion of strangers was not normal in these backwoods.

But I am Maurai, Terai thought. *He can see that.*

Aloud: "Good evening, sir. I'm sorry to disturb you, but I have an urgent call to make, to Vittohrya."

"Um," said the caretaker sourly. "Let's hear your name and errand."

"Look, I was shipwrecked, made my way overland till yesterday, when I came on a tribe who took me in and directed me here. I only want to call my company to explain what happened. They'll arrange transportation for me."

"What office would be open this late, and on a holiday? I wonder—" The enmity became naked. The man's free hand dropped to a sheath knife at his belt. "Let's just go see Ola Noren, you and me. He's the mayor, and he's more in touch with outside than the rest of us."

Perhaps Terai should have agreed. The chances were that his story would be accepted. But he had come too near disaster too many times on his trek; "chance" was to him almost a dirty word. Unobtrusively, he assumed a judo posture, muscles relaxed, senses alert, organism ready. "I'll be glad to pay my respects to your mayor after I've made my call," he said. "Now, if you please, I'll do that."

"I don't please!" The knife flashed forth. "We've had our bellies full of your sort snooping around, aye, even here. Whatever you're after, be damned to you. Come along."

There was a flurry of action, an impact, a thud. Terai scooped the knife off the porch, looked at the man who gasped on the boards, and murmured, "I'm sorry. I didn't want this and I mean you no harm. But you'll follow my orders, understand?"

The caretaker crawled erect, retrieved his taper, relit it, and shambled ahead, across a dark lobby and down a dark corridor. Another candle glimmered. Behind it came a woman, stout, her fingers made grotesque by arthritis and her teeth obviously false, a sight all but unknown in Oceania. "Bob?" she called. "Bob, dear, what's the matter— Oh!" She halted, agape, aghast.

"Don't be afraid, mizza," said Terai patiently. "Your husband is okay. He was a little unreasonable about letting me send a message, and I'll have to keep him for a hostage till my mates arrive, but that should be pretty soon. If you go out, please tell your neighbors not to make trouble. Afterward I'll try to arrange a compensation payment for you good folk."

"You . . . do like he wants, Mara," the caretaker mumbled.

She departed, trembling, trying not to sob. Terai set him in a chair, closed the door of the radio room, and leaned above the transmitter. "You may be a castaway," the Norrman said, "but you're no common sailor."

"Navy," Terai answered. "I hoped not to provoke a hostile reaction, but it seems I got one anyhow."

"Well, why *are* you Maurai pouring men into our country? We hear from the Straits towns—"

Terai hushed him and completed his connection. The rating on night duty in Vittohrya called her officer. Terai would have preferred reporting to someone superior, but a courier would take a while to bring such a person, and by then this village would be in turmoil. He trusted the agitation would remain under control—a jeering mob outside the hall, indignant spokesmen coming in—but that was another risk he dared not take. "Listen carefully, Ensign," he said in his own language, "and pass my message on to Captain Kurawa. Nobody else, not a word, do you hear me?"

When he was through, the reply stammered, "Yes, sir, yes, sir. We can get a VTOL craft there inside an hour, with a squad aboard, to fetch you. Will that do?"

"I think so. It will have to."

"Do you need, want, something special, sir?"

"Well—" Terai indulged in a smile. "You might send a bottle of rum along. And after you've dispatched that runner to Captain Kurawa, maybe you can set a business in motion for me."

"Anything we can do, sir! Tanaroa, what this means—"

"Nothing large. A message to N'Zealann, concerning arrangements for me to talk with my wife at home."

3

The chamber wherein Arnec IV, Mestromor of western Brezh, had assembled his guests was high in his palace, overlooking much of Kemper. Standing at a window, you saw roofs whitened by a recent snowfall, the two streams flint-gray, hulls and masts along the waterfront, cathedral spires in silhouette against an overcast that veiled the heights beyond. Where streets were narrow, night was seeping upward. Lanterns glowed there, ruby, sapphire, emerald, amber, but as subdued this year as the holidays they lit. Cold breathed from the panes.

Nor did lamps and hearthfire seem to lift gloom inside entirely. Perhaps wainscots, carpet, heavy old furniture were too dark, ancestral faces too forbidding in their frames. Or perhaps the shadow was in the people themselves. They numbered a score, mostly men, mostly middle-aged, divided between Aerogens and prominent groundlings. All were richly clad for this occasion, but all the hues were somber, aside from a short red mantle that Vosmaer Tess Rayman kept about her shoulders. Wine and hors d'oeuvres stood on a sideboard, but everyone partook only slightly, absentmindedly. They circulated as small, interchanging groups and spoke low.

At length Arnec raised his voice, in accented Francey: "My ladies, my sirs, please be seated." When they had found places around the central table, he stood at its head and lifted his hands for silence. He was no impressive figure, being short, stooped, white and sparse of hair, with spectacles always about to slide off his nose. A scholar whose work on the post-Judgment evolution of the Celtic languages was considered definitive, he had seldom taken a more active role in politics than was required by the position he had inherited. On that very account, his invitations drew heed when his messengers delivered them person to person—especially since they pointed out that agents of the Terran Guard were paying no particular attention to what went on around his professorish self.

"You know in a general way why we are here." He might have been lecturing at a Consvatoire. "It will be for you to clarify that purpose, in the next several days, and decide what shall be done. I am not a man of action. At most, I can see when action may be indicated. However, I suggest we begin by an informal exchange of ideas, at once. Thereafter we can go downstairs without too many unspoken thoughts gnawing at us, and enjoy the first supper of those festivities that are our announced reason for coming together." He settled into his chair.

Silence prevailed for a space. It was not that these individuals did not know each other. Members of leadership classes normally do. Rather, it was as if nobody wished to speak out, lest that make every restraint crumble.

Talence Hald Tireur, who had traveled the farthest, broke through: "The question is simple. How much more outrage are we going to tolerate from that usurper?"

"Hold, hold," said Dykenskyt Zhan Hannes in some alarm. "I

realize you at Beynac have a special grievance—"

"Not only us. Ask anywhere in Dordoyn. We could not have turned Jovain's appointed lackey away if we didn't have the whole country behind us."

"But outright rebellion—"

"I am not talking about that, sir. I am talking about a convention of the Clan Seniors, to vote Jovain out of office."

Lundgard Simo Ayson thumped the table. "Will the swine allow a convention to meet? Will he obey if it does? He has Skyholm."

Vosmaer Tess Rayman gave him a look partly cynical, partly compassionate. After all, he was a cousin of Jovain's cast-off wife, Irmali. "He does not necessarily have the military," she said. "In fact, isn't that what this meeting is about?"

Arnec's colleague, Sozen III, Mestrogoat of eastern Brezh, shook his troubled head. "Not so, Colonel," he replied. "The problem goes deeper. I listen to my commoners. Bad enough that Ileduciel means to support a cause away off in Angleylann that they see as pagan, subversive of rightness. They can suffer it as a move in a political game they have never wanted or pretended to understand. But an impeachment—the saints falling out among each other—that would shake them to the heart. They would ask why Ar-Goat should stay in the Domain."

"Unless they had an acceptable successor, someone who ought to have been Captain after Toma," said Kroneberg Stef Lanier excitedly; and he was the brother of Rosenn, who was the foster mother of Talence Iern Ferlay. "Wherever he is— Or if he's dead, as seems too likely, well, then, won't your pysans agree to punishing his murderers and installing a righteous new Captain?"

"Who should that person be?" Dykenskyt Zhan Hannes gave Talence Hald Tireur a dour glance. "We're seeing what amounts to mutiny, if not outright secession . . . thus far." In haste: "Mind you, I agree we should not allow the mobilization to occur. We need a united front to get that order countermanded. But neither can we let regionalism get out of hand."

A portly groundling, who was a well-traveled merchant prince, rumbled: "I'm naturally concerned about a disruption of trade, but believe me, I'm more concerned about the possible disruption of the Domain. *Can* the military cadre refuse to assemble their units and meet 'if negotiations fail,' as I understand the order says? If they do, isn't that the true rebellion?"

"Maybe things won't go so far," suggested the Grand Mayor of

Elsass. Her tone was more wistful than hopeful. "Maybe our best course at present is simply to temporize, do nothing."

Vosmaer Tess Rayman cleared her throat. "No, I'm afraid not," she answered. "You see, matters are already in train. We're already being used, as a menace to Devon. If we acquiesce— Well, but let's think a minute. Who are 'we'? Of course, I can't speak for every soldier, sailor, and flyer, but I know that they are not a few who'd rally around for a curbing of the Captaincy. We are the professionals, the skeleton and minimal muscle of the services. We depend on our reservists for the real flesh, when they're called up in an emergency. Now, they're not many either; the Domain hasn't faced a serious threat for centuries. And they have their homeland ties and loyalties, the same as most of the cadre do. And they're not stupid."

She looked around the table. "It seems plain to me," she said, "Jovain is less interested in protecting a handful of Gaean preachers —less interested in 'the sanctity of treaties,' however many words he issues about how our commerce and safety depend on it—less in any of that, than in providing a diversion. Bring the services, the men and women trained in fighting, together. If he can send them off on a foreign adventure, fine. If not, at least they'll be assembled, vulnerable to Skyholm—not scattered among their folk, potential nuclei of guerrilla bands. Meanwhile, his Terran Guard and political agents will tighten his hold on civilians everywhere."

"How long can he maintain such an obviously unstable situation?" Arnec inquired.

Tess shrugged. "Until he can think of the next thing to do, sir. I'd say he's as off balance as we are. I'd also say we should find a balance ourselves, soon. Take a firm stance. We'll have legal and historical precedents, the ancient rights of the states and their peoples."

"He has popular support of his own, especially in the South," Sozen warned. "Remember, he claims to be restoring and protecting traditional ways. Those are not so much the traditional ways of Brezh or of most of our lands—but—" He hesitated before speaking it: "Civil war? Not overnight, not for years, but eventually?"

"Impossible," growled Lundgard Simo Ayson. "That's part of our problem. He controls Skyholm."

Talence Elsabet Ormun spoke softly. She was a young woman, from a minor family in the Captain's Clan, invited on her kinsman Bram Gunhouse's recommendation because she was a technician in the aerostat. "He . . . he need not control it always," she said.

4

Snow had fallen heavily a few days before and was imminent again. Thus moisture in the air made the earth a gift of warmth. Vanna Uangovna could walk in the Library garden wearing simply a robe and boots.

She was alone. The twelve days of Solstice were not over, and most folk were celebrating—at home, among friends, in regimental ceremonies—quietly, noisily, desperately, however their moods were after the news that had come.

Vanna's was . . . elegiac, she supposed. She did not share the common belief in astrology and cycles; Gaea's embracing dance with planets and stars was subtler than that, and ultimately stronger. Yet she could not help feeling it appropriate that this interval, when debts were paid, ushered in the Year of the Rattlesnake. Destruction, decay, millennial winter sleep, and renewal—but what was the life like, that flowed through time toward the hour of its birth? Would it remember her schoolchildren?

The sky hung almost black, as if just above her head. With no leaves astir against them, the patterns of stone and timber in the garden walls had become a stiff calligraphy in an unknown language. Attendants had cleared the paths—gravel mumbled underfoot—but otherwise there was little here save naked trees, rocks, steles, sculptures, fishponds emptied and frozen over. An occasional evergreen bonsai should have been an affirmation of endurance, but today, for her, it could not.

She came to a slab bench facing a circle of stones and a coral mass. Seashells thrust their tips above snow; the next fall would quite bury them. For a moment she stood irresolute, then smiled the least bit at herself and sat down on the side Iern had once used.

She had brought a clipboard and writing equipment. When they were ready, she first contemplated the coral, let her thoughts sink far down into tides and depths, before she put brush to paper. Though she wrote in Unglish, she took pains to make each letter beautiful.

Vanna Uangovna Kim of the Ardan Polk, in Dulua of the Krasnayan Gospodinate, to Talence Iern Ferlay of the Domain of Skyholm, wherever he be, upon the last day of that year when we met:

Greeting and well-wishing.

It is not sure that this letter will reach you. I will send it while traders still ply between Mong lands and the Northwest Union, accepting incidental mail for a small fee. You may recall my asking where I could write to you, if occasion arose, and your lady Ronica Birken giving me an address, a trading post somewhere in the Yukon. She said that certain persons who stop there will know where to carry such a message.

Doubtless it will be inspected along the way. Well, I have nothing secret to tell you.

Indeed, my reason for writing is equally unsure. I cannot think that you will be granted any opportunity to reply, even if you desire to. Where are you, what are you doing, how do you fare? I have often wished to know since we said goodbye, but told myself that it would be foolish to attempt communication. So now, when an answer seems impossible—why?

To this I can only say that it is not impossible. You would have to be a Gaean, an adept at that, feeling the wholeness of the universe, to understand fully what I mean. However, think of how you recall, reach out to, those you care about who are absent or dead. Coming as you do from an old society, think of the communion you have with your forebears. While you cannot respond, I can speak, and that is more than you perhaps realize.

After you and your companions left, we returned to the everyday here in Dulua. Oh, yes, the strangeness of the episode kept us bemused, but less and less as the weeks passed. I was exceptional, trying to regain serenity and never wholeheartedly succeeding. I could not forget the ominousness of your coming and going, nor how your decency shone against it. Pity me not, for I had my work and my world. May you too have been inwardly calm and glad.

But today— Censors, please note that I tell nothing which will not long have been general knowledge by the time this can arrive. Note as well, please, the words of a famous Norrman writer, "A fight is public, a love or a hate is private." Though Iern and I be opposed, if we are, we keep the right to remain friends.

Iern: Yesterday the word came. "Intelligence agents have discovered actions in the Northwest Union which pose an unequivocal, immediate, and enormous danger. Governments of the Five Nations are in emergency conference at the highest levels. Diplomatic representations will be made, but it is expected that an ultimatum must be given. The nature of the threat cannot be divulged at present, for that might close the option of a peaceful settlement. Meanwhile, the Five Nations shall demonstrate their determination to avert the worst while praying for the best."

Words to that effect, although, inevitably, much longer-winded. I cannot recollect them exactly, nor do they matter. What does matter is that the Soldati are being mobilized for joint operations.

I am not the sole person who can guess what this is about. Rumor of the uranium gleaners has flown widely around. I assume, myself, that it is the Maurai who have found something specific and terrifying, for traders do bring tales of how they are steeply increasing their presence in the Union. It would be logical for them to inform our leaders. They and we and all humankind have a common interest, a common peril.

Yes, *all* humankind, including those elements in the Northwest who are guilty. They must imagine themselves liberators. I do not, cannot believe that you are among them, Iern. I cannot believe that the vast majority of Norrfolk are. They may once have been misguided about "peaceful" atomic power, but can they stand by while madmen light the torch for a new Death Time?

And this is the little I know today, this and my personal decision. I would wait to learn more, except that trade and mail could be cut off at any hour, so that I must write now.

As for myself, if you are interested, I will be getting in touch with Orluk Zhanovich Boktan, the noyon who took you down to his country and released you to the Northwest. My Aldan Polk and the Blue Star are both small and no longer very militarily oriented. They will doubtless come under the same Yuanese command as his Bison. He and I are friends, after a fashion, and have worked together in the past, after a fashion. He will welcome my presence as what you would, misleadingly, call a chaplain. Unless the crisis abates, I shall probably leave in another week or two. After that, it will certainly be impossible to write to you, for however long the conflict lasts.

What news comes in from your country is not good either, unrest, outbursts of violence, tensions abroad, and then I think how those who love you must wonder and grieve. In this language I could say, "May life continue well with them as with you," but of course that is meaningless in Gaean terms. Gaea is in upheaval again. To the extent that we are reasoning and dutiful beings, we must open ourselves to Her Who is us, and *be,* as organelles of Her. That is all. It is everything.

[The brush slipped and made a blot.] But Iern, Iern, I do not wish to preach! I have only been trying to explain. Maybe someday we will meet and explain better, we two.

Please convey my regards to Ronica Birken and your friends.

The brush hovered. She started to write "Yours affectionately" but changed it to "Yours in memory." Light was failing; she must hunch over the clipboard and squint. The first tiny snowflakes drifted down.

5

From behind his desk, Jovain returned his visitor's salute. "Be seated," he said.

"Thank you, Your Dignity." Talence Elsabet Ormun took the edge of a chair. Her hands clenched together on her lap. She was nervous, Jovain saw—nervous but determined.

He regarded her more closely. The technical staff of Skyholm had never intruded much upon his attention, what with everything else that did. They were simply there, like the machinery. When this electronician requested an appointment, declaring that she bore a message from a number of colleagues, the realization had jarred him that he should not have taken them for granted.

Her appearance was reassuringly undramatic, neat, skinny, homely except for lustrous dark eyes. Often she gulped, and her voice was strained. He proffered her a smile. "At ease," he said. "If we can't be comrades in the stratosphere, where can we be?"

"The Captain is . . . most gracious," she replied.

"What can I do for you, mamzell?"

"Listen. Just listen, we beg you."

Warmth rose within him. *She needs something very badly, she and the others she mentioned. They will allow me to be kind to them.* "Say on. The Captain is the premier servant of the people."

"That's not the original idea of him—" She broke off, as if frightened by her impulse. "I pray pardon. Irrelevant."

The warmth chilled a little. "Well, what do you have to say?"

She straightened, returned him stare for stare, and drew breath before it rushed from her:

"My corps has been discussing things. Not in a body, but individually. A number of us are distressed at what has been happening lately. And what threatens to happen. We have kinfolk, ancestral homes that we see on furlough, allegiances older than our work here. I intend no disrespect, but the, the manner of Your Dignity's election was, was irregular. Some question it. Some ask what became of Iern Ferlay. They express doubt of, of his alleged suspiciousness. Sir, please understand that I, the persons for whom I speak, we are not denouncing or anything like that. For the good of Skyholm and the Domain, we wish to give you a warning."

Jovain stiffened until his back twinged. *No, such a reaction is not wise, not truly Gaean.* The interior voice was almost inaudible. "Proceed," he snapped.

"There is unhappiness with Your Dignity's policies, and anger, and —and disobedience. And now the trouble with Devon, that many people think is unjustified. More and more cadre officers announce they won't answer a call to arms for that issue, but will stay home and lead the pysans and townsfolk in keeping their ancient rights. Sir, this is terrible!"

"It is." Jovain mustered his own will. "It cannot be allowed. It shall not be."

"What does the Captain propose to do, if we come to the brink?"

"Let us hope we do not. That common sense, if nothing else, will prevail. Skyholm does hold the final power."

Her hands quivered. "Sir, that is why I am here. To warn you this isn't true. A substantial part of the staff, aloft and aground, have decided they—we cannot let Skyholm fire on its people. Or on a foreign country that has done us no real harm. We cannot, we will not."

It was like a hammerblow. Jovain sagged back. "Your oath," he whispered. "Your tradition of service."

Her diffidence vanished. "We read the oath as a pledge to keep Skyholm for the benefit of the Domain. *That* is the tradition of our corps. We are not about to change."

"What do you want?"

"Nothing but reconciliation, sir. If the Captain would consult more widely, and heed more opinions, everybody could agree on a settlement. We, my group, we aren't politicians. We don't presume to set terms. We simply implore you to make peace before too late."

Jovain braced himself afresh. "And if I try and fail, what then?"

"Sir, you must not fail. I repeat, we will not operate Skyholm against any part of the Domain or any innocent foreigners."

" 'We'! Who are the lot of you? Name them."

The dark, primly covered head shook. "No, sir. That might invite reprisals. Can't you see that we are trying to prevent an open breach?"

"You speak for—" Rage flared. It tasted metallic. "You bitch, you're the one who started this sedition!" Jovain screamed. "You!"

She rose. "Perhaps I should go," she said quietly. "Anytime the Captain desires to talk further, he can find me in my quarters or at my station."

Jovain sat alone and shuddered. After minutes, he became able to send for Mattas. When the ucheny entered the office, Jovain groaned, "Help me. Ease me."

An hour of yogic exercise, chant, meditation brought calm. It was not the deep inner peace of Gaea, it was like the flatness of a sea while the air gathers itself for a storm. "We'll forestall them," Jovain said. "Whom shall I contact first? Counselors—Terran Guard—loyalists—not sufficient. Necessary, but not sufficient. The Espaynians, Dyas Garsaya for a liaison—" He stared at the photograph of Charles Talence, which centuries had rendered nearly faceless. "And the Maurai?" he murmured. "Yes, maybe in due course the Maurai. Whatever I decide, 'due course' had better be soon."

Mattas dragged on his beard. "I don't like that last," he said. "But if you must, I suppose you must. We can't let slip what we've won. It means too much to Earth."

Abruptly Jovain recalled that, aside from a brief ceremonial visit to Tournev, he had not since he became Captain set foot on ground. The lands that he ruled had become a clouded map far below, less real to him than yonder picture. He could at least take the picture off the bulkhead, handle it, cast it on the deck and grind it underfoot if he chose. The world had shrunk to this globe in heaven, most often to this single cell within it. Would he ever be free to leave Skyholm?

XXI

"—The government of the Northwest Union declared itself powerless to act. Her Majesty's representatives pointed out steps which it could take to help: forbidding any further work on the infamous Orion project, requiring the surrender of the facilities, proclaiming those persons outlaw who do not promptly obey, and calling upon all citizens to cooperate in the abolition of that worldwide menace. When the Chief and Grand Council refused this minimum, Her Majesty's government perforce considered it a rejection of the ultimatum. The grace period has expired, and a state of war exists between the Maurai Federation and the Northwest Union."

The order of the day echoed in Terai's head next morning, as the armada stood out to sea. He had known that matters must come to this, known it from the moment he stumbled into an office in Vittohrya and saw who awaited him—not only Kurawa of the Intelligence Corps, but the director of the Inspectorate and the supreme commander of occupation forces, there in the middle of the night.

But then a month followed that was like a fever dream after the wilderness. Medical examinations, treatment of injuries, rest and diet, yes, except that the rest and the diet were snatched on the run. Interrogation, flight to the great base on Oahu, truly intensive questioning, interviews with officers of every rank and specialty, a number of them flown in from N'Zealann, sessions under drugs for total recall, conferences, and several drunken parties to make it bearable. Meanwhile the diplomats wrangled and the harbors filled with warships, as Oceania marshaled her strength. Sometimes a piece of news from elsewhere drifted past . . . the Mong nations were likewise preparing to fight, the Free Merican states agreed on a boycott of their Northern cousins and talked of alliance against them, the Captain of Skyholm issued a proclamation of deepest concern and support, Beneghal set grudges aside and offered assistance. . . . None of it quite registered on Terai.

What did burn its way into him was what he witnessed in the streets whenever he left base. Awaii had been in the Federation for hundreds of years. More races had mingled their blood here than in N'Zealann itself. Yet the public announcement of Orion's existence—a desperate attempt at generating pressure on a Union that was flatly not interested in meaningful negotiations—had in this ancient Merican possession touched off madness. Not in everybody, or even a majority, no. But in appallingly many, above all the young. They swaggered about in imitations of Northwestern costume. They scrawled *To the stars!* on walls and pavements. They danced in torchlit parades, they kindled bonfires on mountaintops, and chanted. They shouted down campus speakers who tried to explain what a monstrosity Orion was, or they just declined to come listen. In a few areas they rioted. And it was not as if they understood the arguments on either side. The news had exploded over them too swiftly, too recently, for education. It was that *their* tribe of old was daring this thing. *Let the Norrmen go! Let the Wolf run free!*

For Terai, the flareups only reinforced his conviction that war was inevitable. That odd man Plik (how did he fare? How did Wairoa?) had been right, in his way. A hurricane of the soul was rising; reason, wisdom, consciousness itself were no more than spume blown on the wind.

Nevertheless, when the loudspeakers carried Admiral Kepaloa's iron voice across decks where sailors waited row upon row, when he uttered the unrecallable word, Terai would have wept if he had been alone.

This day he stood at the taffrail of the flagship *Rongelap* and watched the mountains of Awaii drop under the horizon. They were blue-gray at their distance, between a turquoise heaven and a sea which ran sapphire, cobalt, indigo, laced with foam more white than the clouds towering aft or gulls skimming above the wake. Sails and sails bedecked those waves, banners flew brave from a hundred hulls, out over the edge of the world. Behind him the dreadnaught swept grandly bow-ward in teak and bronze and myriad crew, six masts upbore her own multitudinous wings, the breeze sang in lines and thrummed in spars and eddied back down through odors of pitch and salt. The power and pride of Oceania bore north on crusade, and Terai knew he should have rejoiced.

To him came young Lieutenant Roberiti Lokoloku, also of Intelligence, who had become a friend during the debriefing, and stopped by his side, and after a little said shyly: "You don't look very glad, Captain Lohannaso."

"Are you?" Terai retorted. "We're off to kill people, you know."

The black Papuan countenance flinched. "Yes, true . . . and some of them are known to you personally, hu? But what we are doing is right."

Terai continued to stand arms folded, eyes aimed at the receding land, while he nodded. "Aye. If I didn't think that, I wouldn't be aboard."

"Er . . . I must admit I, I don't entirely understand why you are. I mean, after everything you've done, they must have offered you a long leave, and afterward an assignment at home."

"They did. I volunteered for the expedition. No, I insisted."

"Why? If I'm not being nosy."

Terai unbent his arms and clasped the rail. The motion set muscles astir under tattoos and T-shirt; he had almost regained full weight. "I'm not certain myself. But I had to—to see this thing through? Or carry out one last duty before—before what?" He snorted. "Enough. I don't believe in fate."

"What do you believe in?" Roberiti dared ask.

"Grandchildren." Terai gusted a laugh. "I've enjoyed life. I want them to be able to."

"—no further disorders in Seattle, but the policy continues in force, that no Maurai, military or civilian, may go outdoors unaccompanied. In Portanjels, an explosion damaged a Navy freighter. There were no casualties. It is theorized that saboteurs planted a bomb on a piece of driftwood and launched it on the tide. The hinterlands remained quiet after last week's savage firefight on Mount Rainier. However, aerial scouts, taking advantage of a rare break in the weather, report signs of preparation for major guerrilla attacks. Intelligence has confirmed that a massive exodus did take place, apparently northward, by ship, boat, motorcar, and aircraft. The scale of this movement seems larger than had been supposed. The cause is obscure. It may be panic, although the high command has repeatedly assured Northwesterners, including members of the notorious Wolf Lodge, that they will be safe in their persons and property as long as they keep the peace.

"In Wellantoa, Prime Minister Lonu Samito addressed Parliament. His broadcast speech declared that the situation is well in hand and the nation's most urgent need is public calm. He decried hysteria at any mention of nuclear explosives, pointing out that whatever supply the enemy has accumulated must be small, and apparently committed to the Orion project. As for it, Sir Lonu said, the lunacy of the whole idea proves that the Wolf gang is too irrational to pose a serious danger."

"Which is why we're sending the Grand Fleet against them," Terai muttered.

The officers in the wardroom paid no attention. They were listening to the radio news or playing cards. All at once he wanted out of this stuffy air and bland voice. He took his pea jacket off the rack and sought the companionway.

It was not unduly cold on deck, but raining again. The water fell straight, so thick that its silver-gray drowned vision within a few hundred meters. It sluiced chill across his skin, drummed dully on the ship, gurgled off through the scuppers. Windless, *Rongelap* throbbed ahead under power, sails folded, but waves still ran high from half a gale in the night and the hull rolled to their booming pace.

Companion vessels that he could see were dim. Nearest was an aircraft carrier. The flat silhouette was unmistakable; that class necessarily ran always on engines. Her twin hulls were about as long as the battleship's one, a hundred and twenty-five meters. Twenty VTOL planes rested on the forward half of her catamaran deck beneath the bridge, like bullets stood on end.

No—nineteen. The twentieth broke through the ceiling and swung, aglisten, into an approach path. It must have gone to take a noon sight on the sun, as a check on inertial navigation systems. The sound of its jets came faintly to Terai.

He wondered afresh how anyone could endure the high North. Rain—rain at home was quick, joyful, alive with light, and left a rainbow for a mark of its blessing. Here it was a ceaseless presence. When it did not fall, which it seemed to do more hours than not, it brooded in cloud and mist; even the monstrous winter darknesses rarely saw heaven. Could the North have driven its dwellers insane? Could they be embarked on their Orion hellishness not as a wild strategic gamble—that being merely what they told themselves it was—but because they were starved for stars?

Dolphin-graceful *(O Hiti, our romps together!)*, the airplane descended.

A flaw came out of nowhere. Ship and flyer lurched. The pilot missed the deck. A wing struck and crumpled. The plane cartwheeled. The time felt like days before it struck water, but then it sank instantly.

Sirens wailed. Men scuttled about. *Rongelap* drew to a halt of her own, and lifeboats dropped from davits. Useless. The armada had taken its first loss, and what killed the man was the North he had come to tame. Terai bruised his fist, hammering on the rail.

That night, a heavy fog arose. Despite radar, a frigate and a fuel tanker collided. Both ships were disabled, and several more crewfolk perished.

"—*In a radio communiqué, Fleet Admiral Alano Kepaloa denied reports of extremely high casualties. 'We have had a setback, not a disaster,' he maintained. 'Nor can it properly be said that we were taken by surprise. Our hope was to force Cook Inlet, disembark our marines at Tyonek town, and send them inland to find and seize the Orion site. Aerial reconnaissance showed only a single warship in the firth, an obsolete steam-driven ironclad which the Union was allowed to keep after the last conflict. It has been secretly and illegally refurbished, with missile launchers as well as gun turrets, but should be no match for us.*

" '*Nevertheless, we did not commit ourselves to an all-out assault, but dispatched a squadron to probe. This proved wise, when concealed batteries opened fire from both shores. Admittedly that was unexpected, especially in its intensity. The Wolves had prepared themselves with remarkable thoroughness as well as cover. But they had a decade or more to do it. They sank three light vessels and inflicted severe damage on others, including a dreadnaught. However, the squadron disengaged in good order.*

" '*An alternative plan will shortly be executed.*' "

It was.

Afterward Terai and chosen fellow officers sat at a conference table aboard *Rongelap,* heard the tale of the slaughter, and debated how the Navy could have brought such a catastrophe on itself.

Terai needed no report. They had not let him join the invasion, for his knowledge and abilities were too valuable to risk. But when the survivors began to straggle back, bearing their wounded and what few of their many dead they were able to, he had taken a boat to the receiving station ashore. In between getting accounts out of dazed minds and pain-twisted lips, he had assisted in a hospital tent, where surgeons did what they could for the remnants of men. The blood, the mutilation, the stench, the cries, probably most of all the attempts at cheerfulness, would be with him while he lived.

Beyond the tobacco reek of the cabin, ports showed water fitfully agleam as clouds drove across the moon, and the heights of the Laska Peninsula. Wind whistled drearily. Waves smacked on the hull, making it rock and creak. Terai cradled his pipe in his hands for whatever warmth the bowl might give, though this room was hot enough to bring out sweat.

Silence fell upon the dozen men and women. Terai let it ripen before he said, "Figures can wait. We took a beating; the rest is details. And I know what brought this on."

The haggard faces turned his way. "You did not state that earlier," Kepaloa reproved.

"No, sir, because I'd had no chance to think about it. And the admiral will remember that since returning here I've been occupied in grilling such prisoners as the marines brought along and comparing their stories. By the way, hanging on to those Norries was heroic. The men who did so should be recommended for the Te Kooti Cross."

"Well, then?"

Terai squinted through the blue haze. His eyes smarted, his head felt full of sand, weariness dragged at every bone in him. "Our scheme was sensible in itself," he said. "Rather than lose more to the artillery, let's land farther south, where there's practically no habitation, and slog up through the mountains to the objective. The trouble was, the enemy saw as well as we did that that was sensible, and took measures, just as he'd done to defend the Inlet."

"But what measures?" cried the flagship's captain. "Lesu Haristi, yonder country's empty because it can't support a population! Aircraft surveys showed nothing. But still the marines walked into an ambush and were wiped out. *How?*"

Terai clamped teeth about his pipestem. "That mass flight from the southern tier of the Union, by every available conveyance—and the Norries have a great many conveyances, sir, with small commercial fuel depots everywhere. It wasn't panic, as we supposed. It was a rush to these parts, through the Inside Passage or by air or over the upland highways. Men by the thousands, munitions by the tonne, bound north to resist the attempt that it was predictable we'd make."

"No, wait, please," said a woman in his corps. "That's impossible. No entire nation could be organized for such a mass action without us learning about it beforehand. Certainly not the Norries!"

He sighed. "True. But you see, organization wasn't necessary. The conspirators simply stockpiled matériel: portable rocket launchers, machine guns, and the like, including plenty of ammunition for the small arms that almost every Northwestern household keeps."

He rested elbows on table and gestured with his pipe. "You can't understand what's happened unless you understand the Norrie character," he said. "Which isn't easy, as foreign to ours as it is. I'll try to explain.

"They're individualists, but they're also cooperators. Their basic social unit, above the family, is the Lodge—even nonmembers tend to follow that lead—and precisely because it is a voluntary organization, a Lodge need not be democratic. So a few persons can command large resources and give no accounting to anybody else for an indefinite period.

"Next consider the spirit of the people." *Plik called it Faustian, whatever that means.* "They had no chance to assemble militia against us, as they did before the Power War. Events moved too fast; scarcely any of them knew about Orion. But they are giving us a hard time all the same. The news of a space force a-building has not left them thunderstruck. Instead, it's charged them with lightning. They *want* the atom set afire again, for the power it'll bestow on them to do things, and Nan take the consequences!

"A very cunning man made this the basis of his contingency plans." *Surely it was Mikli Karst, guiding genius of the genii.*

"When the crisis came," Terai proceeded, "word went out to the Lodgemasters. They were to inform their members, discreetly, and ask for volunteers to defend Orion. They could tell those volunteers where to pick up munitions, food supplies, reserve fuel, everything that had year by year been stashed away for them.

"The ragtag army flocked off. Cadre officers met it and posted it around the peninsula. Probably it outnumbered our marines. We weren't expecting significant resistance. Besides, the Maurai never have been good at land warfare; we are the Sea People. Most Norrmen are used to inland wilderness, and to firearms, machinery of every kind—they're a nation of mechanics. That made up for their lack of soldierly training.

"The upshot was, they destroyed the flower of our Marine Corps."

Terai leaned back. His eyelids drooped. That much talk had exhausted his remaining strength.

"Well," said a man presently, roughly, "I suppose we must believe you, fantastic though it sounds. You do have information from prisoners, and past experience with these folk. The question is, what action shall we now take?"

Kepaloa swept his glance around the gathering, checkreined his own pain, and said: "At the moment, we can do little. I see no point in capturing the Inlet, at high cost, when we no longer have the troops to send on to Orion. Furthermore, a concentration of ships would be vulnerable to a nuclear weapon, and we must reckon with the possibility that the enemy possesses some." It was a measure of his self-discipline that he could say that in a level voice. "I will deploy the fleet accordingly and attempt a blockade. Meanwhile, our army in the South can try to keep the irregulars from being supplied overland. Maybe after a while they'll grow hungry."

"But what if they get their damned spaceships up in the meantime?" asked another man.

Terai rocked back and forth, trying to stay awake. "My impression from what I heard while among them is that they can't do it soon," he told the group. "Not for a year or more, at earliest."

Kepaloa nodded. "That seems probable. Well, whenever we have reasonable weather—not often!—we can try bombing the general area, though I suppose the Orion installations are well reinforced."

"Sir," Terai said, "I could lead a small party ashore and try to sniff out precisely where the target is."

"I will take that under advisement," the admiral replied, "but I doubt the possible gains would justify the risk. Haven't we had sufficient losses?"

"Sir," proposed a major of the marines, "given replacements, we can punch through that rabble. The South doesn't matter. Once we've scotched Orion, we can reduce the South in detail, same as we did in the Power War. Why not send our army up here?"

"I imagine they are considering that in Wellantoa," said the admiral. "But I mean to recommend against it. If we evacuated the South, there would be nothing to prevent a huge flow of men and supplies overland to Laska. We don't want a bloodbath—not on either side.

"You heard Captain Lohannaso. Except for one or two possible test shots, Orion cannot rise for at least a year. That should give us ample time. Frankly, I felt from the beginning that the Cabinet was paying too much attention to public funk, when it ordered immediate full-scale action. That phrase 'atomic energy' made so many knees jerk. Now let us hope we shall be permitted to proceed rationally, and not cut the enemy down but strangle him."

For the first time in recent memory, Kepaloa smiled. "And such a long period may not even be required," he finished. "My information is that we can expect help quite soon."

"Today the Five Nations issued a joint declaration of war against the Northwest Union. Crack troops, already stationed near the Rocky Mountains, are moving toward the passes, which appear to be only lightly defended. In Chai Ka-Go, the Tien Dziang himself predicted that the allies will occupy the Orion site well before summer solstice."

2

More and more as the months passed, Faylis kept to her apartment. Despite the loneliness, she felt almost glad that Jovain must work the long hours he did. Were he free to entertain, as a Captain normally was, she would have had to be the hostess and do him credit. She had come to dread meeting people and avoided it whenever possible. Her servants took care of things, and the shuttle brought books from the Consvatoire library.

It wasn't that anyone was openly rude to her. If she received cold looks from many of the aerostat staff, especially women, she also received the phrases that would be hers by right when her divorce was complete and she was truly the Captain's wife. Members of the Terran Guard showed her a sincere respect. Various of its officers attempted cordiality.

She did not know how to respond. Those were soldiers, creatures of another species. Most no longer had home ties, which reminded her, wrenchingly, of her own estrangement. Their conversation bored her, when it did not turn to military matters or politics and repel her; they knew nothing of scholarship or esthetics and cared less.

As for Mattas Olvera, he was a stinking vulgarian who could not keep his moist paws to himself. She had finally summoned the courage to tell him she wanted no further instruction in Gaean principles.

With her brother, Lorens, she could be somewhat at ease, but he was usually traveling about the Domain as Jovain's spokesman and troubleshooter, and would land here wrung out by the stresses.

Skyholm itself had turned eldritch. At first she had hated the crowding. Now, since Jovain had dismissed the Cadets and suspended Clan-right visits for the duration of the emergency (whose nature she never could quite understand, because it always seemed to change), nobody was left except the staff, their spouses, Jovain's few confidants, and a hundred Guardsmen who rotated monthly. The occasional persons who flew up on business were unknown to her, commonly foreigners, and stayed less than a week. She sensed how huge and high aloft the aerostat was, when she passed through its present echoing hollowness, and must fight to remember that the dreads this raised in her were senseless. Or were they? Their very irrationality made them horrible. She had frequent nightmares.

There was a small compensation, in that the Garden was never overrun. Many times she savored its beauty and calm without encountering anyone else. Otherwise she felt best in the apartment, reading, listening to music, dabbling out a watercolor or a fragment of writing for Jovain's dutiful praise.

He was kind and attentive, held her close and murmured to her when she cried, unfolded his wonderful mind in their conversations over wine, yet listened in his turn. Those talks—about art, literature, history, languages, astronomy, everything—should have been recorded, she thought. They were surely as brilliant as any had been in a Pinckard Era salon. That he and she seldom made love did not trouble her. Poor dear, he came home exhausted, and she was safe from the shock of recollecting two or three days later that she had not taken her pill, something which the messiness of it all did tend to make her forget. But if only he were not gone so much!

Faylis realized she was withdrawing from the world. It was no great loss. Someday Jovain would bring his opponents to heel, and he and she could go live in a grand place among cultivated friends. Meanwhile, perhaps she drank a wee bit more than she ought, but it kept the melancholy down, and she was growing well informed on a wide range of subjects.

Thus his action came as a whipcrack surprise.

He had not sent word he would be delayed, and did arrive before the cook finished dinner. Faylis laid aside a Coimbran novel. (It was fascinating in its subtleties, and new, too, barely ten years in print. She thought she might try translating it into Francey.) "Good evening, dear," she began. His grimness struck at her. "Oh. What's wrong?"

"I want a drink," he said, went to the liquor shelf, and poured himself a hefty apéritif.

Though the Captain's quarters were comparatively spacious, suddenly they appeared too small for him. The walls pressed inward, as if the pictures sought to take him prisoner. They were not his or hers. She had had no chance thus far to exchange Toma Sark's possessions for new ones. At least, she had not made the chance, finding it easier to learn to ignore those family portraits and banal landscapes. Jovain stood surrounded. He drank fast and refilled his glass.

"I hope . . . nothing terrible has happened," Faylis essayed.

"No, no." He shook his head. A laugh clanked from him. "Not today. But tomorrow will be busy."

The cook gave him a quizzical glance. He had imported her from the Valdor estate, remarking that she was skilled, loyal, and limited in her command of any tongue besides Eskuara. Faylis felt sorry for her, as lonesome as she must be here, but it was a relief not to be able to carry on any real conversation with her. Jovain smiled and addressed her. She brightened. *How charming he can be,* Faylis thought. *Why do they harass him? He only wants the good of the Domain. Of the whole planet.*

The cook set the table. Savory odors filled the room. Because Jovain was brooding, Faylis returned to her book until the woman had left. A maid would appear in the morning, while Faylis still slept, to clean house and lay out her breakfast.

Seated for dinner, she asked, "Now can you tell me, dear?"

Wine clucked from the bottle in his hand, into crystal goblets. "I suppose I must," he answered. "No, I'm sorry, that was a wrong way to put it. I've had to prepare in secret. But I'm ready at last."

Fear breathed through her. "For what?"

"I thought about telling you before," he sighed, "but—well—you've been unhappy enough, without lying awake nights wondering if I would ruinously overreach myself. Which could have happened, yes. But the alternative is powerlessness, the Captain reduced to a figurehead, control in the hands of the reactionaries." He clenched a fist on the tablecloth. That whiteness brought out how sallow his skin had become, how bulged and blue the veins. "We *can't* let the Enric Restoration be undone, when the world stands in mortal danger."

"No, certainly not," she said, and tried to admire his resoluteness. He was like the hero of an old romance or epic. Except that, well, he didn't blaze with will and vigor. He was a tired man stumbling along from day to day, ever more openly defied by Aerogens and groundlings both, hagridden by doubts of his own wisdom, even his own righteousness.

"Eat," he urged. Faylis put food on her plate, despite having no appetite. Her throat felt constricted and her pulse stuttered.

"Let me explain." His tone gained energy. "Several weeks ago, an element within the Skyholm staff decided they would not man their posts, they would not do their duty, in case of war or insurrection. Nor would they identify themselves, beyond a speaker. Oh, I have a close idea of who most are. But probably I have not guessed the name of every traitor, nor can I foresee how the rest will behave if matters come to a head."

Faylis heard knife and fork clatter from her grasp.

Jovain nodded. "You understand," he said. "Well, I agreed with the speaker that nobody on either side would mention this. Public reaction would be unpredictable too. Meanwhile, you recall, I eased my demands on Devon, and the Bishop for his part was eager to compromise. Gaean missionaries remain banned, but Gaean centers are allowed for the use of believers."

"Yes. I . . . I was overjoyed."

"I remember." Jovain winced. "It hurt me to deceive you with a half-truth. For I repeat, I cannot and must not let the Captaincy weaken. Suppose, for example, the Northwesterners throw the allies back—the Norrmen and their atomic power—what then?"

He took generous portions. "I went quietly to work," he told her. "Your brother was among my invaluable agents. The Espaynians proved cooperative. So did the Maurai. Their ambassador sent an immediate call to Wellantoa, and soon the Federation flew in the team I asked for. Tonight a full replacement staff is waiting down in Tournev. Tomorrow an airship will bring a contingent of them here, and I will tell the present staff to depart on it, and those who are now on ground duty to relinquish their posts and go home."

Dizziness swept over Faylis. "No, you can't—can't—"

Jovain grinned. "Indeed I can. I have my Guardsmen. There's nothing secret about the construction or operation of Skyholm. Any group of competent technicians can learn the tasks in a few days. And these will serve no factions in the Domain. They will answer to none but the Captain."

"The ground . . . replacement parts, food, airfields—"

"We will command the Loi Valley—if necessary, through the Guard—and it has sufficient industries to maintain us. No rebel would dare attack it." Jovain cut a piece of meat and chewed lustily. "Can you see what a burden off me this is, what a liberation?"

Faylis covered her face. "Oh, no, oh, no. Skyholm against its own country!"

"Not in the least." He reached across the table to pat her head. "Here, don't cry, darling. Skyholm will render the same services as always, defense, communications, weather, safety monitoring, power supply, everything. We'll merely put certain insubordinates in their place and reassert the ancient rights of the Captaincy. Wounds will be free to heal. In another year or two, the Domain will be more united, more happy, than ever before."

She raised her glance. Tears blurred the view of him and tasted bitter on her mouth. "I, thought, that, at first," she hiccoughed. "But it's just gotten worse and worse. And now, *foreigners* in charge of Skyholm— How do you know they'll get along with each other? How do you know they won't turn on you?"

Jovain regarded her for a while before he said slowly: "I admit we've a difficult transition ahead of us. And you have been isolated, a virtual prisoner. Do you wish to return to ground? The townhouse in Tournev, perhaps? I'll miss you, but I shan't be offended."

"No, never! I want to be with you!"

He came around to her chairside and comforted her until the storm of weeping passed. Then they picked at food gone cold and found little to say. When that had been endured, Jovain rose.

"No coffee for me," he said. "I must be early awake. A cognac, music, a sedate book, and bed."

Faylis stood too. "I'm going for a walk," she replied. "I won't be long." She would seek peace for herself in the Garden.

Jovain embraced her gently and brushed lips across hers. His beard made the caress silky, but he smelled of stale sweat.

She hurried down corridors and companionways, to escape their emptiness as soon as possible. Bare surfaces and bright lighting made them the more desolate. Dust and shadows might have held ghosts from the past, the safe past, but these reaches swarmed with the future, whose phantoms had no faces. Stairs clattered underfoot, ventilators whispered, Skyholm quivered.

To reach the catwalk she had so often betrodden, rough vines, damp moss, greenery and its odors, was like returning home to her father's forgiveness. Her pace, breath, heart slowed. Chill ebbed out of her. Muscles eased, one by one, and she grew aware that they had been hurting from tension but that this also was being soothed away.

A bridge, another companionway, a rivulet, a walk among metal abstractions, birds and butterflies. Her course was for the bower which was especially hers and Jovain's, where she could look down upon Gaea under the moon and become whole again.

She emerged at a small openness. A fountain leaped and sang; rows of bonsai lined the path leading by the Winter Lord. A woman stood in contemplation of the statue. Faylis thought she recognized that lean little shape, though the back was turned. *Talence Elsabet*

Ormun. Iern's Clanswoman, arctically correct toward me. No, please, I don't want to meet her, not this night of all nights—

Memory flashed. A booth was tucked in among the bushes, marked "Service." She had never had the curiosity to look inside, but there it was on her left, a refuge till Elsabet should take her presence elsewhere. Faylis scurried across turf, parted branches, opened the door, slipped through, and shut herself in. Once more she was breathing hard and her heart pounded.

The booth was barely of a size for her. Fluorescents made its plastic walls sheen in dull verdancy. A ladder led steeply down a hatch. Warmth, moisture, and pungency drifted upward. Machinery—pumps?—throbbed.

She might find a less uncomfortable place to wait on the lower level. At least it should be interesting to see what kept this bit of Gaea alive in the sky. Faylis gripped a handrail and descended.

At first she could not make out the murky tangle of pipes, vats, switchboards, instruments, structural members. A forced draft blew heavily into her eyes, bearing chemical whiffs that stung them. She ventured a short distance along the passage before her, glanced aloft, and spied the roots. The entire ceiling was a mat of roots.

Some were long, thick, gnarled like arthritic hands; but they ended in tendrils that the wind made stir, that reached down and brushed her. Most were short, thin, corpse-white, and they wriggled and wriggled and wriggled. She was back in a nightmare, which went on beyond sight.

A tiny voice wailed that here was only aeroponic cultivation, only to be expected. Her screams overrode it. The slowness wherewith she turned and ran—fingers caught at her ankles and tangled themselves in hair. They sought to hold her in this grave, forever.

—She stumbled into the apartment. Jovain put aside his book and forgot his music. He hurried to go meet her. "Darling, darling, what's wrong?"

"I want to leave," said death-dry mouth and throat. "I must. Tomorrow. No later. Please, please, no later."

3

Excursions above were scarce and brief. That was not due to fear of Maurai bombers. They came over when the weather was reasonably clear, which was a rare event in winter, and for the most part confined their attentions to areas where man had visibly been at work. This let them shatter buildings and crater roads, but the damage was confined to short radii. One crew missed its way and, by sheer accident, dropped its load near a launch tube. Steel and concrete stood firm. The camouflage layer of dirt was churned about but not blown from its retaining lattice.

What kept folk below was their enterprise. Eygar Dreng and their own desire drove them like slaves. They took no more holidays, and generally a person did little away from the job except eat hastily and sleep.

Yet some relaxation was required, especially for those who had the most intellectually demanding tasks, lest brains collapse into porridge. On such an evening, Plik called on Iern and Ronica. He had stopped singing in the Boot Heel, because now it had almost no trade.

He had brought along a bottle. Iern snatched at it. "Hoy, you're looking woebegone," Plik said. To the woman: "And you are no angel of hilarity, my dear. Why?"

"The news," Iern snapped. He dashed whiskey into glasses. "Or the lack of it. Did you know, before the Judgment there were global news organizations? You could follow what was going on halfway around the planet from you. We get what trickles in, random items in radio messages or a post bloody near as random."

Plik squeezed his shoulder and said sympathetically, "Yes, tales of spreading chaos in the Domain. It must be hard to bear."

"And the Mong on the march!"

"Eh? But we heard that days ago. And surely you also heard what Dreng claims. Given the difficult terrain and long supply lines easy to cut, he expects our men can delay them enough."

Iern plucked three folded sheets of paper off the bureau and flung them on the table. "Read this. It came today, in a military courier's pouch. I don't know by what route it reached him."

Plik folded his lankness onto one of the four straight-backed chairs the room boasted. Otherwise it held hardly more than a double bed, the small board, and storage for clothes. As a childless couple, its tenants rated nothing larger. Ronica had softened it with a reindeer hide on the floor, pictures and a map of Laska on the walls, a fine hardwood gun rack, a knot of bright cloth streamers to flutter in the whirr from the ventilator. Her old cat Pussifer curled asleep on the coverlet.

Plik read, reread, laid the letter down, and reached for his drink. "A touching remembrance of a sweet if somewhat enigmatic little lady," he said.

"Don't you understand?" Iern rasped. "She's joined that army. She might be killed or, or anything."

Ronica, who had stayed seated, kept her face toward her man. "You really do care a lot, don't you?" she murmured. "You've been trying not to let on, but you're no good at it."

"Don't you care?" Iern replied. "I mean, you've no cause for jealousy. Vanna and I got to be friends in Dulua. When you were gone and I needed a friend. That's all."

Ronica chuckled. "I could wish for her sake you were lying, stud, but I believe you. Well, think. She ought to be reasonably safe for the time being, anyhow. She won't be in front-line combat, will she? Not that I'd predict much of that at the outset. We've precious few strongholds in the East, and they must be grossly undermanned where they aren't deserted, what with reinforcements rushed to the West and to Orion. Probably the worst hazards the Mong will meet are blizzards and slides."

"But later the Norrmen must fight them," Plik said.

"Yes," Iern muttered.

"Can amateur, underequipped, ill-supplied war bands really stave them off for as long as necessary?" Plik wondered. "And what if the Maurai bring up overwhelming strength of their own? I hear rumors of countries such as Beneghal offering them troops, not to speak of the unmobilized manpower scattered across their islands."

Iern tossed off the lower half of his drink. Slightly eased by its fieriness, he sat down too, poured himself a fresh shot, and looked across the table at Ronica. She smiled and reached to stroke his hand, as if signaling that come defeat and the quenching of the dream, they would still have each other and that was what most mattered. Light from the fluorescents lost its bleakness in her amber mane, in the highlights and curve-cast shadows of a blue robe she wore.

"Nobody knows," he answered the Angleyman. "The equinox is our ally, but I think that come summer weather it will be touch and go on the battlefield. If those men can buy us a year, and if *Orion Two* tests out satisfactorily—at least to the extent that no major modifications prove necessary—then we can quite possibly do it, complete the rest and launch them in time. If not, then not. That's why Dreng is pushing construction. We've nothing to lose by advancing our schedule. If it turns out we've committed to a faulty design, well, we'll get no chance to alter it anyway."

"Do you mean that everything depends on the next mission?"

"Yes. First, it will show whether the basic systems are good; but in view of the successful unmanned flight, they probably are. Second, most important, it will gather data we must have and don't yet —data that, ordinarily, a research and development effort would accumulate through a series of trial shots. For instance, how the weapons should be installed—because time forces us to cancel the third flight, which would have provided us the parameters for that. In addition, the crew will handle those matters originally planned for *Two,* gaining experience in free fall, testing maneuverability, atmospherics—"

Plik raised his palms. "May I be excused?" he laughed. "You waste your technicalities on my pig-ignorance."

For her part, Ronica turned grave. "This means Iern, like the other pilots, damn near lives in a simulator," she said. "I'll bet he could fly the real thing in his sleep by now. Meanwhile we engineers and computer programmers and life-support specialists and who-all else tinker away like demented beavers, and, Yasu, do we get a tongue-lashing when he finds out we've made the rig still worse!"

Iern grew able to smile, in pride. "It's frightening to spin out of control, even if it's only pretense," he said, "but you beavers have become marvelous at gnawing. We're practically ready."

Plik started. "Do you mean the ship will fly soon?"

"Very soon. As I told you, we're not installing any actual military equipment, only the experimental apparatus that should give us an idea of how to install it in the rest that are under construction. Work on *Two* herself has dwindled down to whatever afterthoughts the scientists are having. What may delay us is weather. Not a storm; *Orion* should be able to thunder her way through any wind. But we want the region thoroughly socked in. It wouldn't do for the Maurai to identify the precise site. That could make their bombing effective."

"Pilot, copilot, three engineers, a computerman, their standbys, plus the data-collection team, eh? Do you expect you'll be among them?"

Iern sighed like a boy in love. "I can hope."

A knock on the door interrupted. For privacy's sake, the panels were too thick to pass a called invitation. Ronica padded the short distance and opened up. Light from room and hall spilled across Wairoa.

He waited for no word, but stepped directly through, closed and latched the door behind him, and halted motionless. They saw him clad in the coveralls usual here, though his feet were bare. The masked, disharmonic face looked the more strange above drab cloth and judas collar. Beneath an arm he carried a large book.

"Well!" Ronica said. "Howdy. Been quite a spell. Sit yourself and tipple."

Plik glowered. His companions had never before heard such hostility from him: "What harm do you intend?"

"Hold, fellow," said Iern, shocked. "Never mind politics. Wairoa's our trail-friend."

"He's the friend of Mikli Karst," the Angleyman rasped. "Haven't you noticed? They're together every time Karst is in these caves."

"Well, m-m, Mikli did give us a rude incident—"

Plik grinned acidly. "That could be taken as all in the day's dirty work. But he's evil, fundamentally evil. Can't you sense it?"

"Stop," Ronica ordered. "This is my home, and Iern's. Have a seat, Wairoa, and if Plik won't give you anything out of his bottle, we have one in a drawer." She took a fresh glass off the bureau and waved the Maurai toward the table.

He did not step forward immediately. "I have something to show you, Iern," he said low. "But if the authorities learn about what we know, we could be dead. Maybe Ronica and Plik should go elsewhere."

The woman stared at him, strode to her man, and stood by his side. "No, thanks," she answered.

Plik stroked his chin. "Conceivably I've misjudged you, Wairoa," he said. "I'm curious. I'm also careful of my neck, therefore discreet. Please let me listen."

Wairoa nodded, advanced, and took the fourth chair. Iern poured for him, but he ignored it. Ronica lowered herself and poised catlike. Iern shivered the least bit, while sweat broke out on his skin. Plik sat back and drank.

"I must be quick," Wairoa said. Nevertheless, his tone remained level, the Angley softly accented. "Yes, I have cultivated Mikli Karst. It was easier to do than he would like to know. He has a jackdaw mind for facts, and of course he hoped for data useful against my side. But mainly, he is a very lonely man. Solipsists are."

Plik registered surprise at the phrase.

"I have found his company interesting," Wairoa continued. "It has lightened captivity and idleness for me. However, my principal motive has been ulterior. I meant to spy."

"What?" Iern exclaimed. "How? What for? You could never get any information out to your people."

Wairoa caught his gaze. "I could get it to you," he replied.

After a silence: "I had my strong suspicions from the beginning, an idea of precisely what to look for. Her Majesty's Naval Intelligence has collected clues over the years, and especially during the last mission to Uropa. I believe Terai sought to tell you, but you rebuffed him, being by then dedicated to Ronica's cause."

"Terai," Plik whispered. "Do you suppose *he* brought the Maurai down on Orion?"

Nobody responded. It was a question which had been asked many a time since the ultimatum was delivered. Wairoa proceeded, relentless: "While here, I convinced myself totally, but that was by means you would even more refuse to accept, Iern—body language, overtones, subvocalizations, a logic which is less inductive or deductive than intuitive. What I needed was tangible evidence."

He laid the book on the table with a *smack* at which Iern and Plik started, Ronica flared her nostrils. The cat woke, yawned, stretched, jumped to the floor and thence to her mistress' lap. Ronica patted her absentmindedly. She purred. The sound made a curious obbligato to Wairoa's voice.

"Early on, I learned the lock combination of his office vault. He had me turn my back, but hyperacute hearing can follow swiveling dial and clicking tumblers. I confirmed my result by dropping numbers casually into remarks to his subordinates over the days, and paying close heed to their expressions. Meanwhile I obtained Mikli's permission to borrow books. Since I must report regularly to the officer on duty in the anteroom, it was natural that I go in and browse when he was not there. After the first few such visits, nobody kept me under surveillance. He never leaves important material lying loose, nor did I seem in any position to spy or sabotage. Rather, he wanted me to share his collection. I took care to give him commentary that he found amusing, upon the more outrageous parts of it."

"And at last you saw your chance to ransack the vault, when the officer went to the can or something," Ronica said hoarsely. "What've you found?"

Wairoa's tiger-striped head wove to and fro. "My procedure was different. In these hermetic surroundings, security is lax because everyone assumes it can safely be. I entered the vault for several brief periods, reconnoitering, until I had identified what I sought. Tonight I lifted it." He gestured at the book. They observed the title: *Pain: Concepts and Techniques Around the World.* "This is my portfolio."

Iern half reached for the volume. "What did you take, in Zhesu's name?" he asked.

"Correspondence, memoranda, excerpts from reports—proof," Wairoa said, like a hammer striking iron. "It was never Yuan that supported Jovain and made his coup possible. Certain high Yuanese officers were involved, yes. They provided a conduit for messages and matériel. When the emergency of our capture by the Krasnayans occurred, they arranged for our transfer to Northwestern agents. But essentially, Iern, your secret enemy has been . . . the Wolf Lodge, the builders of Orion."

The blood fled Ronica's countenance. "No, you're crazy!" she yelled. "What earthly use to us—a Gaean regime, just when our trade with the Domain was getting well started—no!"

Wairoa maintained his erosive steadiness: "Mikli gave me the same argument. I lulled him by not disputing further. But the facts are otherwise.

"The Yuanese in the cabal merely provided assistance and a front. They were ignorant of Orion, of course, but took for granted that certain Lodges in the Northwest Union were plotting to throw off the Maurai yoke. From their viewpoint, they were helping promulgate Gaeanity in Uropa, gaining Norrman allies on the far side of the rival Mong realm Bolshareka, and making a personal profit. Oh, yes, Mikli and his gang meshed them in a spider's web, piece by piece. They became exceedingly vulnerable to blackmail. And some were Norries from the first, infiltrators passing for Mong and working their ways into key positions.

"The impetus against Skyholm always came from *here.*"

"But why, why?" Iern stammered.

"It would be to the benefit of the entire Union to abort an incipient close relationship between Domain and Federation," Wairoa said.

"Why grant the Maurai a foothold in Uropa, profitable commerce, technological exchanges? Rather, get these for oneself, for the Northwesterners—as well as unhindered, unquestioned access to eastern Uropa, where fissionables are. Moreover, trouble in the Domain would distract the attention of the Maurai while Orion neared completion."

"But Gaeans are gut-set against our whole ph-ph-philosophy." Tears stood in Ronica's eyes. "No such arrangement could last."

"Mikli and his associates were only interested in the short term. Once Orion was up, it would make little difference who reigned in any country." Wairoa opened the book. It had concealed a sheaf of papers. "Consistency has no relevance to politics, nor do loyalty or morality. Jovain must be horrified by the news of your undertaking, and ready to support my nation against you. The Federation in turn will accept whatever help it can get in this war. Ultimately, though, it would be glad to assist a more congenial party into power in Skyholm.

"I think you are entitled to know who your enemies are, Iern."

"Let me see that!" The Clansman grabbed at the file. Ronica's chair tumbled and her cat sprang off, indignant, as she hastened to look over his shoulder.

Plik leaned close to Wairoa. "Why did you do this?" he whispered. "What did you hope to accomplish?"

"Perhaps nothing," the Maurai conceded. "But I must needs try."

"Oh, you did enough. You played your role." Plik hoisted his glass. What he had drunk did not account for the unsteadiness of his hand. "You opened the gates of the hell through which he must pass."

"Must?" Wairoa asked.

Plik did not reply. Wairoa sipped sparingly and observed the readers.

At last Iern shoved the papers aside, raised his head, and pushed from his throat: "You appear to be right. What next?"

Wairoa collected his evidence, tucked it away again, and stood up. "For my part," he said, "I shall report as usual, prior to my curfew. I had better take the opportunity to return these documents, under guise of looking for another book to borrow. You know where to find me if you wish. Goodnight."

He went out. Iern twisted around in his seat, toward Ronica. She stooped and received his face in her bosom. "Oh, darling, darling," he mumbled.

She ruffled his hair. "It's bad, beloved, and I'm ashamed," she told him. "But things like this happen. We'll make it right, I swear we will. Hang in there." A chant: "First the stars, your flight beyond the sky, a way outward for our children and their children, forever—"

Plik departed, mute. He left the bottle. They might need it worse than he would.

XXII

In the morning, Iern went to the nearest telephone, called his team chief, and reported himself and Ronica sick. It was not really a lie. After the night they had had, they would be of less than no use on the job.

They dressed warmly and set out for the surface. "Looks like this clear spell is going to last a while," the guard at the head of the ramp warned. "The kanakas might come over."

"I heard they'd pretty well given that up," Ronica said. "Waste of good bombs."

"Yah, but you never know about those bastards. If they just fly a reconnaissance, the pilot might still take a fancy to a little machine-gun practice on a couple of Norries."

"No. *They* aren't monsters!" Iern snapped. His vehemence took the guard aback.

Besides camouflage, a stand of spruce concealed this door. Sunlight struck between towering clouds to glow on murky-green boughs and ruddy trunks. The air was cold in their shadows but held a faint sweetness that was theirs too. Beyond, the mountainside swept away toward neighbor peaks and steep-sided valleys. The snow on the ground was old, surviving in streaks and patches, wan of hue. Boulders and crags jutted above it and what winter-gray turf lay exposed. A flock of Dall sheep wandered in the distance, led by a splendidly crowned buck. Breezes whittered.

Here two persons might find peace.

Iern set out on an upward-slanting course. Ronica took note of landmarks before she joined him. Weather was not ordinarily severe in this country, thanks to the warm Kamchatka Current, but it was treacherous; rain, snow, or fog could close down the horizon without warning.

They strode for a while in silence, until she asked, "Do you want to talk about it now?"

Sleeplessness hoarsened Iern. "Didn't we thresh things out till close to dawn?"

Her head shook within the hood of her parka. "Not really. We talked the obvious to death. And you—" she squeezed his arm—"you told me a worldful about Skyholm and the Domain and your life, trying to explain to me what it has meant to you. Trying to explain to yourself as well, I think."

"I said I would continue in Orion."

"Well, you haven't much choice, have you? I want you to continue willingly. As is, if you quit, it wouldn't stop anything, with the ship all set to go. Nor would it let you out of here. You'd just make people wonder what ailed you, and that might lead them to Wairoa. We agreed his poor little attempt at sabotage doesn't deserve the punishment Mikli would doubtless lay on him."

"Mikli!" Iern spat.

"That's what I'm hoping to set you free of today, dearest," Ronica said. "It's no good, you feeling like a prisoner. That would poison everything—yes, between you and me also."

"I intend to kill Mikli Karst."

Ronica's smile was a grim one. "An excellent idea in principle. In practice, not smart. You couldn't get away with it here, and they'd probably put you to death, because, damn it, he *is* invaluable. I happen to know that the shore batteries that stopped the Maurai at Cook Inlet, and the stockpiling of war stuff and the scheme for irregulars to come north that saved our bacon on this peninsula—those were his ideas, and in large part his doing. The secret could never have been preserved this long without him, his tireless tightrope dance. I suspect he's got more surprises up his sleeve."

"What he did to my country—"

"I agreed before, that's inexcusable. The end did not justify the means. Mikli is a sadist, and this must have been an irresistible prospect, playing Satan on a continental scale; so he persuaded the Wolf leadership it was desirable. I suppose from a strategic viewpoint it was. For one thing, it entailed suborning a lot of high-ranking Yuanese, and I imagine those fellows are frantically busy on our behalf, trying to blunt the Mong attack. But I agree, the Domain didn't have to be made a sacrificial goat. It was doing us no harm, and Jovain's gratitude has evaporated overnight, hey?"

Stones scrunched underfoot. A raven flapped past, blackness momentarily blotting out the sun, and croaked, startlingly loud.

"But you know something, sweetheart?" Ronica said. "I realize this isn't a logical argument. Just the same, if you'd become the Captain of Skyholm as was your right, I'd never have met you. I can't help my selfishness, I'm glad."

He stopped. She did. They gazed at each other. He seized her to him. Her cheek was cool against his. "And I, and I," he avowed.

She stepped back a pace, took both his hands in hers, and said: "Okay, if we can revenge you later on Mikli, fine. But he isn't worth a lot of trouble. What we should make our goal is giving the Domain a legitimate government, that'll restore order and justice and hope. It can be done. It will be, Iern. Every report tells how shaky Jovain's rule is. It may well collapse of itself. If not—after Orion has risen, a word from on high is all that will be needed. And that word can be yours, Iern, you who helped us in our dark days. We Norries are no angels, but we do honor our debts."

"Yes—yes—we discussed that last night—"

"It deserves repeating today, when the booze is out of our heads. And I've thought of something else. I warn you, darling, this could be a shock."

Iern flashed a grin. "Your shocks are generally high-voltage. I'm prepared."

She became earnest. Her voice dropped, her eyes held as steady as if she were sighting over a rifle. "About that next Captain in Skyholm. We've been taking for granted he would be you. But do you really want it anymore?"

"What?" broke from him.

"Think. You were rambling on last night about a heap of things. Including mention of how you'd always wished to travel around the world, and being Captain would nail you in place. But it was a duty, maybe, and a big challenge, certainly. Since then, however—wouldn't you rather lead the way into space?"

He stood wonderstruck.

"The Domain must be full of Talences who'd make suitable Captains," she pursued. "You'd fulfill your obligation if you saw one of them in Skyholm. We haven't got too goddamn many genius pilots. And Orion isn't just for the Northwest Union. It's all humanity's last chance to get out into the universe."

He was still for a minute or two before he said, nearly under his breath, "You were right. You have rocked me back."

She kissed him.

He knuckled his eyes. "You read me truly," he sighed. "But, well, could be I've seen a little more of politics in action than you have, in spite of your haring around with Karst. I can't be as idealistic as you about this undertaking here."

"After your experience," she replied low, "I wouldn't expect you to be. Nor do I suppose we humans, any bunch of us, are more than glorified apes. Sure, we'll fuck up in space same as we've done on Earth. The point is, we'll *be* there, beyond the death of the sun."

"And learn, and do, and dare—" Iern laughed aloud. "What a pair of orators we're becoming!"

Again they stood silent in the wind.

"Very well, Ronica, most beloved," he said. "I am with Orion . . . and my heart is. It'll be a dreadful thing if we lose that: not the war, but Orion. Partly because I think we belong out there, partly because—you're right—it's what I most want to do in the world, except for loving you—and mainly because I do love you, and this is where your own heart is."

She came back to him.

"But I have swallowed as much as I can," he warned. "I will not condone any further monstrosities."

"Nor I," she promised through unexpected tears.

2

After the days-long turmoil of assembly and the two days and nights of horrible crampedness aboard a troop train, it was incomprehensibly marvelous to be out in the open again. Kal-Gar, railhead and frontier settlement in southwestern Chukri, was no shrine of grace or delight, and the ruins left from before Death Time made it melancholy in a way that the relics looming above big, hectic Chai Ka-Go did not. Winds blew bitter across whitened plains, dry snow whirled, clouds went in tatters or joined to hang low as the ceiling of a tomb. Yet Vanna Uangovna felt she had been set free.

In part, this was true. Back east, and still more on the train, they had incessant need of her—the young, scared soldiers, abruptly plucked from home and dispatched to a war they did not understand. Thrown together into a strange camp, then jammed together in the stinking, rattling gloom of freight cars, they engendered ghastly rumors. Ucheny and proróchina, she moved among them, spoke to them jointly and individually, led them in chant and meditation, made them remember that it was Gaea for Whom they fought. Fear bared its teeth at her, shrank, and scuttled off to chitter from dark corners. But she could not radiate serenity like that without draining her own wellsprings.

There was again uproar at Kal-Gar, as men and horses burst forth. There was more life to it than had been at the loading. For two days the troops got leave, by turns, to seek what wineshops, gambling dens, and joyhouses the outpost boasted; and Vanna could walk the prairie alone, breathing clean air, and return to her bunk and sleep. Meanwhile Orluk Zhanovich and his fellows in the leadership organized for departure.

The Western majority of his Bison Polk had come north through Bolshareka to join his command. Units from all the Five Nations assembled likewise, putting themselves mutually under a Yuanese Grand Noyon. These were the elite cadres and their drafts, that could be mobilized fast and efficiently. Their assignment was to invade the Northwest Union through several Rocky Mountain passes. They would seize positions bestriding both valleys of the Fraser River, and thus interdict enemy passage north or south. Concurrently, the rest of the regiments would gather their strength and bring it up. And then the Soldati would follow the routes of their ancestors, back to the Yukon Flats, before they swung down again to seize and bind Orion.

Few of them knew that that was the objective. The Maurai announcement had not reached many pastoral homes, and even a townsman might be excused bewilderment about the idea of a spaceship. The commonest impression was that the Norries had been hatching the same kind of evil egg as a generation ago, and this time the Maurai needed help in a new Power War. After that had been won, soldiers growled, the whole devil-ridden country should be occupied and domesticated.

The Mong army uncoiled itself into half a dozen serpents and struck west.

Vanna had never seen mountains before. Words and pictures had brought to her no ghost of their beauty.

On the fourth day she rode with Orluk and the staff, about a third of the way back from the van. She would rather have been off by herself. Surrounded by men and their racket, she could not truly seek Oneness in the awe everywhere about, as she had been able to do earlier on the march. However, yesterday skirmishing had taken place between forerunner patrols and Norries who came down from the heights. Today spotter aircraft had reported enemy activity originating at a small fort some twenty kilometers ahead.

Orluk heard the latest bulletin, replaced his miniradio in its bag, and nodded, stonily satisfied. "We'll see action before this day is done," he said. "They're deploying field artillery, including a pair of fair-sized rocket launchers, while their foot are digging in."

"Oh, no," Vanna whispered.

An officer laughed. "Did you expect them to strew roses?" he gibed.

"Major, one does not address the reverend lady in that style," Orluk rapped.

The man stiffened in his saddle. "I'm sorry, sir."

"You will apologize to her, not me. She's done more to hold this outfit together than any of you."

"Reverend lady, I was thoughtless. I abase myself."

"No, please," Vanna said. "It doesn't matter in the least. I . . . I should not have spoken as I do. We *must* go on."

Orluk said, unwontedly awkward: "As a matter of fact, reverend lady, it should not be much of a fight. They seem to be the usual unprofessional Norrie militia, scarcely at more than battalion strength. I expect they'll tease us with shells and sniping as we come in range. But two can play at that game, and we can call in a few fighter-bombers as well, if they get too troublesome. We may or may not find it worthwhile to root out their sharpshooters or reduce the fort."

"Sir," another officer said, "may I suggest we don't delay for that? We've been lucky so far. A snowstorm could do us more harm, cause more delay, than some holdouts at our backs."

They had indeed been fortunate, Vanna reflected. Clear, stingingly crisp weather the whole way. No need for shovels or snowplows, because the Norrmen themselves had reopened the road after the last blizzard. On the other hand, though they were plainsmen, she didn't think her dear, hardy boys would suffer unduly from anything the highlands could throw at them, or be unable to carry on. And the vernal equinox was only a few days off, the beginning of spring. . . .

"Yes, probably," Orluk said. He laughed aloud. "How long since I was campaigning in mountains! How good to be back!"

And how I understand him—now flowed upward in Vanna on a wave of affection.

Almost, she could ignore the column that trotted, trudged, and rode on groaning wheels, through this defile and heavenward. Or else she could take them as another flowering of the Life Force, comely in their fashion. Leather creaked beneath her, muscles surged between her knees, a sweet smell of horse sweat softened the chill of the air, reins in a hand and mane rough under a palm when she stroked the beast confirmed her own aliveness. Filling the road, helmets nodded above uniforms, as rifles did across the shoulders of infantrymen; the lances of riders swayed like wheat before the wind, while pennons and banners made bright splashes. (O flags inscribed with honors! Her name was on one of them.) Wagons and field guns rumbled behind mules. The occasional armored car was almost jewellike in its polished workmanship, at its distance among these distances. A sound rolled through the division, the reverberation of its advance, that she imagined would recall the sound of an incoming surf to those who had seen the ocean.

On the right, a river brawled merrily in reply. Gray-green, it dashed brilliant sprays off rocks, swirled, eddied, surged. Beyond it, and to the left, the mountains reared, incredible in their steepness, their grandeur. Precipices, talus slopes, outthrusts stood blue-gray above snow that remained utterly white, save where sunlight sprang off it in diamonds or shadows lay blue as the sky overhead. She could not see either summit from here, but crowns gleamed before and behind, too splendid for arrogance.

The sun had advanced far enough toward noon that it shone down into the gorge, on into her bloodstream. An eagle hovered up yonder.

Iern told me of the Alps in Yevropea.

How can it be wrong to rise high? Karakan Afremovek himself cited ancient records, how the spacefarers of those days saw the planet suddenly as our home in the cosmos, alive, infinitely precious.

Flat, booming sounds echoed down between the rock walls from afar. "They're enfilading our advance company," Orluk said. He might have been discussing a deal in cattle. "It's supposed to retreat and draw them on, while we advance in close order. Hoot the bugles."

Word went back. Trumpets awoke to wildness. Echoes cried answer. A kind of muted roar went along the ranks, in which the shouts of sergeants were nearly drowned.

"Now whatever happens, reverend lady," Orluk told Vanna, "you stay by Lieutenant Bayan here." To the young man: "Lieutenant, don't forget, you are responsible for the proróchina's safety. Don't forget, either, she's worth as much to us as any single corps we've got."

"Oh, no," Vanna protested. "Please—" Pain jagged through her. *Us? Our aim? Destruction of those spaceships. Yes, true, we cannot let the heedless Norrmen lay hand on all Earth. But could we ourselves not, later—we, and you of Skyholm, Iern—?*

"Look there!"

The cry brought Vanna's gaze aloft. Something flew. It gleamed silver against azure, a maned head and a long tail, heart-stoppingly lovely.

Orluk shaded his eyes and peered. "A rocket of theirs," he said. "Well, we know they don't have but a few, and that bugger's poorly aimed. We may not take any casualties at all from it."

Rocket, Vanna thought. *What would Orion have been like, rising?*

The sky exploded.

She crept back to herself and to her feet. Naked, she rose. The blast had stripped the garments from her, as it dashed her against the road. Asphalt clung to the smashed bones of her left arm, from which its moltenness had eaten off the flesh.

First she must set the agony aside. It seemed that nothing existed but agony, that the fire would burn her forever. From somewhere infinitely deep she raised a mandala. It had the form of Earth, small, cool, blue, amidst the stars of space. The mantra that sounded around it was *Living, dancing, forever love. Living, dancing, forever love. . . .*

As she returned to herself, she saw smoke blow off sprawled black unshapes. Vapors roiled above the river, though it had ceased boiling.

Other things were crimson, swollen, cooked but not yet dead. They staggered or crawled about, making noises.

Vanna heard them only dimly. She thought her eardrums must be broken. Her right eye was missing, too; she fumbled a finger into the socket, then withdrew her touch from the jelly beneath and the char and protruding bone beneath that. Her left eye saw through a blur, but clearly enough, what the rest of her was like.

No matter. She shambled off, searching through the dust and ash that drifted under a cloud like a mountain-high fungus. A dark spatter on the ground, as if of wings—the eagle, hurled from heaven?—no, likelier a man's head split open, and his burned brains. Forms mewled at her feet. She went on downward. Farther from ground zero might be some who could understand her.

She found them after a while. One had no face. He sat cradling in his arms a comrade who had little skin, but who could see and croak, "It's her, I think, the Good Lady, I think."

Vanna sat down with them. Because of her left hip joint, she could not assume lotus position, and because of having just a single hand, she could not properly bless them. However—

"Peace, and we return ourselves to Gaea. Peace, and we return ourselves to Gaea, to That Which we are, to Her Who is us. It is done in beauty, it is done in beauty—" She strangled on her words and died.

3

The auditorium was packed, seats and aisles, stares and stares and stares. Ventilation could not carry away body heat or body smells; air grew stifling and loud with breath. Afoot near the entrance, Iern and Ronica looked down across what seemed almost a single shadowed mass, to the stage. There light glared.

Eygar Dreng stood at a microphone. His wide shoulders were hunched, and the words dragged out of him. At his back, two banners were spread across the wall: the green (for forests alive) and white (for purity of mountains) of the Northwest Union; the wolf and his broken chain of this Lodge.

"—no more information has reached me as of now. I repeat, yesterday the Mong invasion was halted by the annihilation of every force they had in our eastern Rockies. Tactical nuclear weapons accomplished this. The troops were the pick of the regiments, and it seems unlikely that more can be fielded for a long time. Reports are coming in of consternation throughout their homelands."

No triumph was in his tone: "Our news monitors are also receiving accounts of horror and fury around the . . . civilized world. In Vittohrya, the Chief denied any foreknowledge or complicity by our government, pledged full cooperation with the Maurai, and called on every Norrman to help find and kill the guilty parties. It seems, though, that no mobs are storming Wolf halls or attacking members. Instead, I've heard an account or two of celebration in the streets. In Wellantoa, the Queen and Prime Minister issued a joint statement— Oh, shit, you know what they said as well as I do, and the same for everybody else."

He straightened. "Yes, those were Wolf units posted in the East, at exactly those points where the Mong could be expected to enter. I didn't know that myself until today, but it would not have been hard to arrange. Nor did I know that any of the nuclear fuel for Orion had been diverted to weapons. And supposing this was a necessary backup for us, I don't know why a party under flag of truce did not arrange a demonstration for the Mong, instead of slaughtering them by the tens of thousands. Well, true, they did pose a first-order threat, and I am not a military man.

"I'm going to turn this platform over to Captain Mikli Karst of Naval Intelligence, chief of our security operations. He has said he'll tell us more."

Eygar stumped off the stage. Mikli sprang onto it.

He was in dress uniform, medals aglisten, himself vibrant with victory. He seized the microphone as if it were a weapon and brought his wolf-gray head close to it. His free hand gestured—waved, pointed, chopped, cut—while his voice rang:

"Okay, ladies and gentlemen, comrades in Orion, I'll explain why. Afterward you can tear me to pieces if you choose, because I, *I* have been the prime mover behind it all. Not alone, of course, but the instigator, the arranger, the encourager when the going got tough, the man finally responsible . . . and damned proud to be!"

The audience moaned. It sounded orgasmic.

"Almost from the start," Mikli hammered at them, "I saw we might well find ourselves in a desperate situation. In fact, that was a great deal likelier than not. Orion always was a gamble, by brave men and women willing to risk everything for freedom. Did you, my comrades, and did our country and our cause not deserve what insurance we could devise against catastrophe?

"What is so awful about atomic energy? It's cleaner and safer than coal or synfuel; it's equal to the long-range requirements of a high industrial civilization, which solar energy is not; it's our key to the stars. Your parents knew this, and tried to bring it back for peaceful use. The Maurai crushed them, because it would have upset their own cushy dominance. You know the truth yourselves. That's why you've been building Orion, to free your countrymen and the human race.

"Then I ask you, what is so bad about a limited use of nuclear weapons? Is a man less dead with a spear or a bullet through him? Does it hurt less to get hit by shrapnel or a flamethrower? What have we got, what have we had through the centuries but a taboo? It was the ancestors of the Maurai who gave us that word, you know: taboo, a senseless prohibition."

Mikli let his statement sink in before he proceeded in quieter wise.

"No, we are not about to throw multimegatonne weapons around the globe and bring on a new Doom. We would not do that, and besides, we haven't the means. What we have done, what we propose to do, is simply defend ourselves.

"The Mong, like the Maurai, were unprovoked aggressors. In the Power War, free men and women fought to defend their homes and liberties. They failed, not for want of courage, but because their hands were tied—by taboo. And at least that was a one-front war. This time, as always, we had not the manpower to hold our eastern frontiers against the Mong while the Maurai were at our throats in the West—not unless we gave our few defenders what they needed to make their devotion tell.

"Director Dreng asked, reasonably enough, why our action was not to fire a single such weapon where the enemy would see and be warned. He is understandably shocked. Events and his many responsibilities have given him no chance to think about this question. I hope you will do so now, Eygar Dreng. Put that fine mind of yours back to work. And you likewise, my companions in Orion.

"I give away no secret in reminding you that our supply of such weapons is limited. Most of what fissionables we could scrounge over the years is tied up here, waiting to raise Orion. Given a warning, the Mong would doubtless have withdrawn . . . and been free to try a different strategy. Meanwhile the Maurai and, yes, our own government would have had warning too. They would have reacted. Instead of an overwhelming feat of arms, which does indeed seem to have united all our peoples behind the Wolf Lodge, we would have had indecisiveness—counterattack—quite possibly, Norrman against Norrman, while the tyrants gloated in Wellantoa.

"As is, we have terminated the eastern threat for as long as we shall need. Like our forebears of old, we have rolled back the Mong midnight from our homeland. Now we are free to deal, once and forever, with the Maurai."

Cheers began to sound.

Mikli signaled. "Let me bring before you a man who can say more about war in a dozen words than I can in a thousand—Colonel Arren Rogg, cadre commandant of the heroes who held the Laska Peninsula for us, and still hold it!"

A big person lumbered onstage. He pointed to his empty right sleeve. "I left this flipper in a valley south of here, where we bushwhacked the enemy," he said without dramatics. "Not much for me to lose, when so many fine young men left their lives in the same place. Those Maurai marines fought well, I've got to admit. They did not die cheap. A lot of graves are out there this morning, along with the fellows still alive, still on guard. I wish we'd had nukes then. I think the dead and the living and their kinfolk wish it too. If we need to meet another attack like the last, and us without reinforcement, we'd better have nukes.

"Thank you." He limped back down.

A roar followed him.

Mikli shouted into it: "Are we really sorry, friends? Sure, it was regrettable, but which would you rather be, a killer or a slave? And I have battlefront reports, news to share with you. Identifications are in for most of the Mong regiments that were wiped out. If you've read your history, or listened to your parents and grandparents when you were a kid, you'll remember them. They killed plenty of Norrfolk in their day, they, the pride of the Mong. And now their core is gone. Hear the list: Whirlwind, Faithful Shepherd, Dragon, Sons of Oktai, Bison—"

Ronica snatched after Iern's hand. He stood absolutely motionless.

"—St. Ivan's—those the main ones, but lesser allies as well—gone, gone, gone!"

The crowd was on its feet, stamping till the concrete reverberated, waving fists on high, screaming.

Mikli's amplified voice interwove: "—power—let the niggers learn from what happened to the gooks—yes, I say to you, we shall overcome—we have the might; the warning *has* been given—the future is ours—*Orion shall rise!*"

Iern wrenched free of Ronica and made his way out the door. She gasped, looked after him, started to follow, then pulled her lips together, folded her arms, listened and watched.

4

The builders of the site had provided a common room for religious and meditational services, with three nichelike chapels, Yasuan, Jewish, Buddhist. Nothing was large, because congregations never would be; pagans held their ceremonies outdoors or at home. Then somehow a tiny chamber elsewhere, little more than a volcanic bubble smoothed out, came into the hands of a few Old Christians, who made it theirs. It could hold perhaps twenty worshipers, though it seldom did.

Plik found himself quite alone when he entered. The vault was silent, cold, full of shadows; it had only a single fluorescent plate in the ceiling, thirty centimeters square, while light from the corridor outside must seep in past a grille of withes. Wooden too were the chairs. Cushions for kneeling lay upon them, together with prayer books, for the damp stone floor would have rotted leather and paper. The walls, plastered, bore frescoes of lily patterns, dim and hard to make out. Opposite the entrance, a communion rail ran before an altar that was a block of native basalt. On either side stood empty candleholders. The vessels upon a homespun altar cloth were bone. The crucifix above was carved from driftwood, crudely, yet with a sense of how the contours strained in the sea-bleached material.

A holy water font at the entrance was equally rough, a soapstone dish on an oaken pedestal. Plik signed himself. He went in, genuflected, found a candle, dropped an offering in a box, planted the taper and lit it with a piston lighter—a Maurai import. In the murk around, the flame burned star-small.

Plik knelt on the bare floor before the rail, put his hands together and bowed his head above them. Thinly clad and thinly fleshed, he shivered.

After a time he rose. He unslung the guitar that had been across his back, strummed a few notes, and sang to its accompaniment, very low, while he confronted the crucifix:

"Lord beyond eternity,
Fountainhead of mystery,
Why have You now set us free?

"You, Who unto death were given,
By Yourself, that we be shriven,
See, Your world will soon lie riven.

"After Easter, need we dread
Fire and ice when we are dead?
Hell indwells in us instead.

"From our hearts we raise a tower
Wherein sullen monsters glower.
Save us from our hard-won power!

"You Who raged within the sun
When no life had yet begun,
Will You let it be undone?

"We have wrought such ghastly wonders,
Lightnings at our beck, and thunders—
Help, before this poor earth sunders.

"Lord beyond eternity,
Fountainhead of mystery,
Why have You now set us free?"

The last chords rang away into stillness. He stood for a while longer. All at once he seemed to buckle. He dropped the guitar on the floor as he returned to his knees and hid his face.

"Redeemer," he begged, "forgive me, I am overwrought, forgive so bad a verse."

XXIII

Except for basic maintenance and security, the Orion establishment was shut down this morning, everyone gathered in the auditorium to hear the word. Hurrying through empty, susurrant, whitely lighted corridors, Iern thought of catacombs—when he thought of anything except nightmare and tactics.

Wairoa had not been in the audience. He would surely have been if he were able. He would have stayed prudently in the rear and thus been visible to the Clansman. Therefore he was in the confinement section, doubtless by order of Mikli or a cautious subordinate.

A single guard was on duty in the office, amidst a stench of cigarette smoke. He looked nervously up from his desk and snatched for the submachine gun on its top as Iern entered. Seeing who it was, he brought his hand back. His voice was high and uneven: "What's the news, sir? Did we really hit the Mong yesterday like the radio said?"

Iern made himself halt and nod. "Yes. Nuclear warheads on rockets. Destroyed them." *Were you there, little Vanna? Are you yet? I believe I hope you died. Living, you would grieve too much for the dead and the unborn.* "What do you think of that?"

The sergeant shook his head. "I don't know what to think, sir. I'm, well, kind of stunned. Are we going to have a new Doom War?"

"Captain Karst promises us a glorious victory."

The sergeant gave Iern a closer regard. "You don't look too happy yourself, sir. Pale and shaky."

"Letdown, I suppose. They could have stopped Orion from rising." *Now for the part that had better sound convincing.* "The reason I'm here is that I need the release of the Maurai prisoner."

"Sir?"

Iern was faintly amazed at his own readiness. In the past, he had been glib only during a seduction. "You probably know he and I are acquainted; were before we arrived. I have hopes the shock of this news will make him more cooperative. Whether as a source of information, or a go-between, or both, he might prove valuable in getting his people off our backs."

The Norrman was dubious. "I don't know, sir. My orders—"

"No time for niggling," Iern snapped. "Captain Karst himself told me I could try. You've routinely let him go every day, haven't you? Today he's been in protective custody, else he might have been lynched. That danger's past. I'll sign him out." Iern gestured at the inner door.

His guess was evidently right, that the detention order had been casual and verbal. Save for armed guards at critical points—who had never needed to do more than turn an occasional drunk aside—this home of the Minotaur had had no reason for wariness *(yet)*. Moreover, Iern bore the enormous prestige of an astronaut. "Yes, sir," the sergeant said, took keys from a drawer, and rose.

There were only a few cells in the block, most vacant. Offenders gaped, a psychotic bleated as Iern was led down the passage to Wairoa's place. The hybrid was reading. He laid down his book when the door opened, got to his feet, and stood impassive. "We . . . I want to talk with you," Iern said, no longer smoothly, while he wondered how much knowledge the brain behind those strange eyes already had of him.

Wairoa came forth. The blue coverall issued him was ill fitted to his proportions, but somehow he made it an imperial uniform. In the office, Iern scrawled an acknowledgment. A part of him speculated how he would explain his action to Mikli. If everything went well, Mikli wouldn't learn of it until far, far too late. If not—no matter.

Thoughts like these were nothing but eddies. His will was the stream, flowing on toward its cataract. Last night, after the newscast, both he and Ronica had been very quiet. They spoke little about the event, and only clichés ("Awful. . . . Violation of trust. . . . Maybe necessary. . . . War knows no honor. . . . Wait for more information; this is all so vague and confused. . . .") uttered in flat voices, and they seldom looked straight at each other. He went to bed early and was surprised to find himself soon drowsing off. Numb, he supposed. He awoke happily, until he remembered. Then, after a gasp, he set about preparing for the day—washing, dressing, eating if not tasting breakfast in a hushed mess hall—like a machine. Within him, the stream rose and gathered force.

He didn't know when Ronica had sought sleep or if she ever found it. When the alarm roused him, she lay awake at his side. Her eyes were dark-rimmed and she had even less to say than he did. They went together to the announced assembly, but not holding hands as usual.

—"We need a private location," Iern said when he and Wairoa were in the corridor. "I think the library will serve best."

He meant the public library, not any of the technical collections. Ordinarily it was busy, reading being a favorite pastime here. Today the long room was deserted, as if nobody would ever again care what the philosophers and poets had to offer. The men chose a table at the far end, took opposite sides, and began to talk. Presently Iern noticed how low their voices were. He yelped a laugh.

"What is funny?" Wairoa asked.

"I . . . I imagined . . . Vanna Uangovna's ghost . . . telling us please to be quiet." Iern swallowed. *I will* not *cry. We haven't time for that.* He finished his account of the proceedings.

Wairoa appeared unsurprised. "Once," he remarked, "in an old book—pre-Downfall—I saw mention of a still older epitaph on a tombstone. It read, 'I expected this, but not so soon.' "

"I did not," Iern said raggedly. "I truly did not. Nor, this morning, did I expect the sort of reaction Karst evoked. The glee, in those people I'd come to like, that was the most horrifying experience of my life."

"You do not agree the weapons were required to save Orion?"

"Can anybody sane agree that *anything* is worth that price? I thought . . . nuclear power need not be misused. I was wrong. You Maurai are right. Given the potentiality, the weapons are inevitable. And they'll provoke the building of more and worse, until we bring a new Judgment on ourselves. The only survival course is total prohibition."

"Which entails the conquest of the Northwest Union and the suppression of Orion," Wairoa said in a calm tone.

Iern nodded violently. "Yes! These . . . Wolves . . . have proved they're unfit to hold power over Earth."

"No people are fit, my friend. No individual is. The best that can be said for my nation is that we have merely aspired to maintain a balance advantageous to us, not to gain an empire. And nevertheless we have done our share of terrible deeds."

"Damn your niceties! Listen. If we hurry, we, you and I, today, we can stop Orion."

Wairoa's pupils dilated, then narrowed in the mask of his face. "How?"

It flamed from Iern: "By taking the spaceship up!"

Wairoa grew felinely attentive.

The words rushed out of Iern on the torrent of his will. "*Orion Two* is the prototype. The tests and studies made in her are going to be absolutely essential to the completion of the rest. She's ready. Crews and backups are too. I suspect the actual selections have been made, though not yet announced. The launch is just waiting for thick weather, so the Maurai can't see where the ship rises from. They'll be caught unawares, and won't get a radar fix on her, either, before she's out of range, at her acceleration. The crew will conduct their experiments and maneuvers, voice-radioing down whatever isn't automatically telemetered, to make sure the data are received here whatever happens to the craft. According to plan, she'll land on an airfield north of the mountains—which one will depend on conditions—and be trucked back. But if this doesn't work out, it shouldn't make a large difference, provided the mission itself was successful.

"We can abort it."

Wairoa pounced: "You intend to fly her yourself."

"Yes. Immediately. While that obscene rally is going on and the air outside is clear. Your Maurai *will* see the ascent, and surely triangulate on it. Knowledge of the site ought to make their bombing more effective. Probably that alone can't do serious damage, as armored as these installations are, but it should do some. More important, loss of *Orion Two* will set the project back months. Dreng's gang can't ready a new prototype any faster. That should give the Maurai time to muster ample force—even against the few nuclears I daresay are stored somewhere in this neighborhood. If Dreng is wise, he'll surrender at once. Whichever way that goes, I hope afterward they burn Mikli Karst alive, but I'm afraid they're too humane. He wouldn't be!"

"How do you propose to accomplish this? All entries are well guarded."

"Yes, but I've become a big figure, you know. We have two key points ahead of us. First is the portal control, near the top of the launch shaft. Obviously the way has to be clear before the ship can rise. We'll have to take that by force, but we can bring guns from my apartment, we can exploit surprise, and nobody else will be around to give help or sound an alarm. I'll show you how to operate the mechanism. Next I'll proceed to the entry near the bottom. The guards ought to let me in when I explain I want to look the pilot console over with a view to recommending certain adjustments on the basis of my simulator experience. You open the gate, I raise the ship—I can't otherwise, because of a safety interlock—we do that—" Iern's hands lifted, fingers talon-crooked—"and Orion is dead!"

Wairoa was silent for half a minute before he murmured, "You and I will also be dead, what?"

"If you're lucky," Iern replied, "you can slip off in the confusion, fight past an exit sentry, and escape into the mountains. You've told me about that collar you wear, but you should have a chance to get out of range before they overhaul you, and later make contact with your fleet. True, the odds are against it, but it's not impossible."

"And you?"

"The single thing I have left to care about," said Iern out of his forsakenness, "is taking that ship away from the Norrmen."

2

He entered his home, and there was Ronica.

Dismay rammed through him. He halted in midstride. She set down the cat she had been hugging to her bosom, rose from the bed on which she had been reclining, and moved toward him. The features were drawn taut over the strong bones of her face; tear tracks glistened. "Iern, dearest, are you ill?" The husky voice laid a whiplash across him. "You look awful." She noticed Wairoa at his back. "Oh, hullo," she said absently, and reached her man and took him in her arms.

I know what I must do, he realized. *It makes me glad I haven't long to live.*

Her warmth strained against him. Her hair smelled of summer. He brought an ankle behind hers and pushed. They fell to the floor together. She swung hands downward in time to soften the impact. His weight was on her loins and thighs. His right forearm came across her throat to pin her head down. Stupefaction stared at him. "Shut the door, Wairoa," he called, "and come help me."

"What the living fuck?" she gasped. "Has this business driven you crazy?"

She began to struggle. How often had he felt that supple solidity astir beneath him? His left arm fended hers off. He might not have held her long by himself. Wairoa arrived and took possession of her wrists. He at her hands, Iern at her feet, they used sheer mass to keep her captive. Her hair spilled amber over the carpet. Above, the rainbow streamers she had hung before the ventilator grille fluttered forlornly. From the bed, her cat watched round-eyed.

Ronica snarled. "Darling," Iern begged, "listen to me. Please listen. I love you. We mean you no harm. We have to do this, and hate it, but it's for your sake as much as ours."

She drew a deep breath. Her lips bent into a stark smile. "When a man says he wants to do something to me for my own good, I run," she flung at him. "But you have me staked, you bastards. Say on."

His intent rushed from him.

"We can't allow you to carry a warning," he finished. "We'll bind and gag you. That will prove your loyalty; you couldn't help what happened." Abjectly: "I'm more sorry than you will ever know. I didn't expect to find you here. I love you . . . more than *I* will ever know, I think."

She had quieted while he talked, save for the quiverings of tension. Now the green stare burned. "Then why in Satan's name are you doing this?" she exclaimed.

"Do you remember . . . topside . . . I told you I, I would not condone any new . . . abomination?" he stammered. "Well, it happened, and I will not. I c-c-cannot."

"Why can't you? Why don't you just go on strike, instead of ruining everything for the rest of us?"

"Because the rest of you—no, not you, Ronica, never you, but . . . the murderers, who'd be overlords of the world . . . they, the consequences of their, their egoism—would ruin everything for everyone. For my people in the Domain, and Wairoa's, and, and yours too—the children I hope someday you'll have—" Abruptly, the river of Iern's resolution flowed fast and grew Polar-cold. "In the end," he said, "I am a Talence of Skyholm. I don't rejoice at that, but it is so. A master who does not serve is no master.

"Time is short. We have to secure you and be off. Please don't resist. Please don't hate my memory forever."

"I see," she answered slowly. "It's what I thought." Her tone sharpened: "You realize you plan a suicide mission, don't you? That ship isn't meant for singlehanding. They simplified—speeded up—the design process by omitting an escape module. You can launch her, but unless there's at least an engineer on the after controls, you can't execute more than the simplest maneuvers. You can't bring her down without crashing, if you don't burn up in the atmosphere first."

Iern nodded. "Of course. I'll switch off the telemetry and head straight out." He shaped a smile himself, and it was honest. "She's stocked for eight man-weeks. Given the accelerations she can make, I ought to see some splendid sights. I'll think of you."

Her laughter rocked him back. Wairoa showed disconcertion. "Indeed you will, lover," she cried. "I'll be right on deck."

He could only stare.

"Let me loose, huh?" she said. "This pose is ridiculous. I couldn't dash out the door and holler. Nobody to hear me, anyway."

Iern and Wairoa exchanged a glance, released her, and stood up as she did.

She surged to Iern and gave him a fierce kiss. "You flinking idiot," she said into his ear, before she gulped back a sob. "Did you imagine I'd let you go and leave me behind? You don't know me very well yet, do you?"

"But—but your Lodge—"

She stepped back, caught his gaze, held it as strainingly as she held his hands. "Sure," she said. "It hurts like fire. But what hurt worse was that our captains lied to me, to all of us—gave their word of honor we were not helping let the Doom loose out of its hell—*used* us, as though we were their subjects and not the Free Folk! If the Northwest Union doesn't stand for liberty, straight down the line, what is it but another God damned empire?"

She shuddered. "And today, when they learned for certain—they did not kill Mikli. He invited them to, even, but he knew them better than I did. I saw them howl hosannahs as he ranted—howl like curs for a Glorious Leader. Our calm, educated, sensible, kindly team boss, he was prancing for joy, he was yelling for more and more of that mind-buggery. Eygar Dreng, I'll give him credit, Eygar stood aside and looked grim, but not Rainier Abron, oh, no, not him nor the huge most of 'em."

Ronica snapped after air. "I left. I came home to do some howling of my own, over the corpse of everything I'd believed in. I hoped you'd be here already. But instead—" Iern saw the countenance of a Fury. "Oh, now I know how much I love you! You've got your engineer. We'll do our justice together. And afterward we'll land somewhere—a Mong field, maybe—and start winning Skyholm back!"

"But—but—no, the hazard, I won't allow—" For an instant, he wondered if this was a ruse. *No. She can't betray, it isn't in her.* Wairoa gave him a slight nod. *His weird perceptions tell him she's true. And she may be the help we must have to take the ship.* "Yes," he sighed.

Ronica sank cross-legged to the floor, closed her eyes, spent a minute bringing nerves and muscles and brain back toward oneness. The men stood almost as quiet, not daring to disturb.

She sprang to her feet. Her breath was even, her motions flowed. "Okay," she said crisply, "let's hash out a few details. Two rifles in yonder rack." While neither she nor Iern killed for amusement, they had maintained their marksmanship. "Each can knock a man over. Better take extra ammo clips, in case things turn sour. And, oh, yes—" She whirled toward the bureau, snatched notepad and pencil, scribbled as she stood. "This is to ask Cluff and Sonaya Browen to adopt Pussifer," she explained. "They're cat people, they'll give her a good home."

3

In a high-level corridor, a ladder fixed to the wall went up through a three-meter shaft. This gave on a horizontal passage, short but zigzagged, which in turn led to another ladder and shaft. Having completed the second climb, Iern emerged at the end of a thirty-meter hallway. Halfway down that length, a massive ironwood door stood open. Shutters covered loopholes in it. The near side was steel-plated, the farther side heavily lined with spongy, sound-absorbent material. Similarly padded was the rest of the tunnel. At the midpoint of that section, a control board was set flush in rock and concrete. The mouth of the tunnel stood open on a dimly lighted emptiness: the ascent tube. A narrow balcony with a safety rail projected out.

Two guards sat at a table by the door, near the entrance to a lavatory. They were playing a card game but clearly had scant interest in it. Their casual garb identified them only by the brassards they wore, and the sidearms. Close at hand, a rack held two automatic rifles.

They rose warily when Iern appeared. He walked nearer, they recognized him, a little relaxation came upon them. One was a middle-aged man, grizzled and burly. One was a woman, red-haired, young but with laughter lines around mouth and eyes. She wore a dress rather than coveralls or blouse and slacks, because she was about six months pregnant.

"Hi, Iern," she called. He had made the acquaintance of both, as

he had of many in his outgoing fashion. "What can we do for you?"
"I've something to show you, Jori," the Clansman replied. He stopped where he was, a distance off, and nodded at the man. "You too, Dalt."
"Is the meeting over?" the latter demanded. "What's happened?"
Jori's scrap of good humor blew from her. She reached out as if pleading. "The story isn't true, is it?" she asked unevenly. "About the . . . those weapons. I couldn't believe it."
"I'm afraid it is true," Iern told her. She whitened.
Dalt peered at him. "No wonder you're in such a plain-to-see spinout," the Norrman said. "Well, I'll be damned if I'm sorry, and you shouldn't be either, Jori."
"What will happen next?" the woman choked, and caught at her filled belly.
Dalt shrugged. "The kanakas will get their ass out of our waters in an almighty hurry, if they've got any sense. Uh, Iern, *is* the assembly over? What exactly did the speakers say? And why've you come way up here?"
The flyer stayed where he had been when hailed, five meters off by the opposite wall. "It developed that you may have emergency duty to perform," he said. "I thought I'd better show you in person, since I might be involved also." Deliberately, he had dropped his voice.
"Eh?" Dalt said. "Can't hear you. Speak louder or come closer, will you?"
"Emergency duty!" Iern shouted. *The signal.* He moved slowly toward them.
He had their full attention. Ronica had swung out of the shaft and was well down the hall before they noticed. They knew her too, and suspected no evil. In a moment they would see that her left arm was behind her back. Iern retreated.
Ronica whipped her rifle around, out in front. "Stop!" she yelled. "Not a move! Raise your hands!"
Dalt snatched for his pistol. Ronica's firearm barked. The bullet whined nastily by his ear. She bared teeth at him while she loped close. "Not a move, I told you," she said. "You know I'm a crack shot."
Wairoa followed. He bore the second of her guns. Around his shoulder hung strips cut from a bedsheet. Jori screamed. Both guards lifted their hands.
Wairoa joined Ronica. From the side, Iern said fast: "We won't hurt you if you behave. We'll hog-tie you. On the safe side of the

door, naturally. But I warn you, we're desperate. We mean to hijack *Orion Two.* That should prove what sort of people you're dealing with. Behave!"

"Oh, no, no," Jori moaned.

Dalt roared, half moved to charge, looked into the muzzle of Ronica's rifle, and let his foot slam back down on the floor. His gullet worked. "The kanaka, yes," he said. It sounded like vomiting. "And the foreigner. But you, a Wolf woman. Couldn't you just have turned whore?" He spat.

"No words," Iern ordered. He was about to instruct them in the position they must assume for binding, when Jori spun on her heel and ran for the control panel.

"Hold, you fool!" Ronica shrieked, and fired a fresh warning. Jori never wavered. Iern bounded in pursuit. She had a head start and it was incredible she could run so fast, she'd reach the alarm switch before—

A third smack resounded. Jori's skull burst open. Blood and brains spurted. Her body lurched forward, fell, rolled over and over, arms and legs flopping. It ended below the panel. More blood ran out. The trail and the pool of it were luridly red.

Iern's knees failed him. He sank onto them and fought for breath. Darkness went in rags before his vision and a roaring through his head.

He grew aware that Ronica knelt beside him, held him close, cradled him to her. "Are you all right, darling?" she cried low. "You weren't hurt, were you?"

He clawed his way toward full consciousness. "Did you shoot her?" *If she did—what then?*

"No," Wairoa answered. He stood above Dalt, whom he had made lie prone, like a dark-visaged figure of Death, masked and tiger-hooded. His voice was loud enough to carry but quite level. "I did. Her purpose was obvious, and she would have achieved it. A merely crippling shot was too unlikely to strike right, as charged with adrenaline as her system was."

"I . . . could not . . . have done that," Ronica said. Tears flowed quietly from the green eyes.

"A woman and an unborn kid," Dalt raged at her. "Are you satisfied, traitress?"

It's still alive in her, I suppose, passed through Iern. *How long will it take to die? Could it possibly be saved? No, I forbid myself that idea.*

"She would have thwarted our purpose," Wairoa declared in his calmness. "Orion would have risen at the behest of the nuclear weaponmasters."

Dalt retched.

"I didn't say what you did was outright wrong," replied Ronica. "I doubt if I'm proud of the fact that I was unable to." She rose, and helped Iern do likewise. "C'mon, dear. Time's a-wasting."

We do what we must, what we must, what we must. The chant in his head joined the task of binding and gagging Dalt and dragging the prisoner well away from the door. Together, they loosed the Clansman from thralldom. Later, when he had time, he could mourn. Wairoa mounted guard. Ronica tugged the body aside, laid it out, covered the remnant of its face with a towel from the lavatory, and used another towel to wipe up the worst of the spill.

Meanwhile Iern finished his chore. Returning to Wairoa, he said, hearing how mechanically the words marched, "We can't delay. Let me demonstrate the setup."

"Can the shots have been heard?" the Maurai asked.

"Hardly." *How blessed are these technicalities.* "We're near the top of a hundred-plus-meter shaft designed for sound absorption. So is this area, and the staggered passages to it are meant for sound baffles as well as precautions against debris or radioactivity if something goes badly amiss. However, we can't tell when that meeting will adjourn. Mikli was enjoying himself, and perhaps planting the seeds of a political career, but he does have other things to take care of."

Iern led Wairoa to the balcony. A chill breeze muttered from the depths of the tube. A rustle of ventilators and throb of pumps were barely discernible. Darkness reached downward and downward, lights firefly-feeble at intervals that seemed enormous, until it came to a white cascade of radiance. There poised the ship. At that remove she was small, exquisite, a piece of jewelry beside the spiderweb of her access frame. In the upward direction, sight ended after twenty meters, blocked off by metal dimly aglimmer.

Iern pointed that way. "The portal," he said. "It's not a simple door, it's an elaborate machine. It has to be extremely massive and totally integrated with the rest of the structure, if it's to survive the forces Orion unbinds. A conventional bomb, direct hit, would hardly make it shake.

"The panel here controls a set of motors that move the complex. First an outer valve tilts back. That's the one onto which the camouflage is secured. Then the inner valve retracts, and the way is clear for the ship. The initial blast flings her out, while the fallout pit at the bottom—the equipment and solvent tanks built into its walls—capture the bulk of the material given off."

"A remarkable achievement," Wairoa commented.

"Yes. It involves an ablative layer that dissipates most of the fireball energy—but you've doubtless studied the subject; you study everything, don't you? . . . The ship passes this point on momentum. She's held to a precise path by high magnetic fields, high, generated by superconducting coils behind the shaft lining. The opening of the portal activates them automatically.

"The gate can't close ahead of the second blast, in atmosphere. It comes too soon—but at an altitude from which it won't damage works built like these, especially since it'll be weaker. Well, we needn't consider that. Your job is ended when you have opened the portal and I have raised the ship."

"It has never been clear to me why there is a separate arrangement for the gate," Wairoa said. "Why don't they operate it from the Mission Control centrum?"

"A number of reasons, including the general principle of decentralization and defensibility. And economy—less electronics required, simpler construction. This whole undertaking has been a wild gamble using a bare handful of resources—a handful that had to be replenished again and again by the most ticklish means—and why are we chattering?" Iern snapped.

He started back inside. "Doctrine is as follows," he said. "After the portal has opened, an observer on the balcony takes a last-minute look at conditions, chiefly the treacherous weather. Then the entire team leaves the site. They close that heavy door behind them. You can guess what the detonation of an atomic bomb in a confined space, plus a hull rising faster than sound, will do to the air. Besides the concussions, it'll still be hot enough after helping accelerate the ship—still be hot enough when it gets here to cook your lungs. The engineers think the controls have the ruggedness to escape damage, after modifications following the first shot, but that remains to be seen. Anyhow, the door, together with the noise-absorbing stuff, protects the team. Just the same, they're supposed to scramble down to the hall below."

"I observe the door can also act as a barrier to enemies."

"Yes, an extra precaution, against saboteurs or commandos or whatever—like us. Your case is going to be rather special."

Iern reached the panel and quickly explained the array of meters, switches, and buttons. Wairoa was as swift to understand.

"When the gate opens, an alarm sounds," Iern said. "That's automatic; we can do nothing about it. The purpose is to make sure everyone seeks the safe place assigned him. The mission plan allows twenty minutes, but the interlocks disconnect at once and the ship can lift at any time. I'll try to make the interval short, so you can dodge out before the Norries arrive."

Wairoa nodded. "I must hold this post for us until you are away," he agreed steadily. "Can you send me an advance notification?" He pointed to a loudspeaker.

"Not directly, I fear," Iern told him. "Communications to and from the ship do go through Mission Control, which is shut down at the moment."

"And wouldn't likely cooperate anyway," said Ronica from her scrubwoman's posture.

"The pilot is supposed to activate a three-minute advance signal," Iern said. "That will shut off the gate alarm, which sounds like a—a trumpet, I've been told. The ship's is a high, sustained note. I'll be sure to send that, of course. Three minutes should give you time to slip out the door—you had better have it closed and barred in advance, against possible assault—slip out and try for escape."

Ronica got up, checked her coverall and shoes for telltale stains, and put all firearms at the gun rack. She and Iern could not carry weapons through the longer, more direct passage to the crew entrance without being challenged. Iern finished his lecture. Ronica came back to the men. She took Wairoa's right hand in both of hers. Compassion dwelt in her visage and tone. "Luck fly with you, trail-friend."

He gave her one of his rare smiles. "Do not fret about me," he replied. "I know what the odds are, and feel no fears. Rather, it will be good to stand as what I am, a watchman. Blessings be yours."

"Goodbye," Iern said. He could not utter more to the hybrid, nor shake his hand.

Wairoa folded his arms. His gaze followed the others until they were gone. Thereafter he checked on Dalt, secured the door, refreshed his knowledge of the control board, paused for a while at Jori's body, and went out onto the balcony.

In thirty minutes, Iern had decided arbitrarily, he was to open the portal. It was about the time his companions would need to reach their goal and prepare for launch, assuming they encountered no trouble. Wairoa did not require a view of the clock on the panel; he always knew its reading. He leaned over the guard rail to contemplate darkness and the light flashing in great banners off the ship far below.

4

Every entry to the ascent tube had a defensive door and sound-absorptive lining fifteen meters from the end of the corridor that led to it. However, on lower levels where workers constantly went to and fro, the approach was straight. Admission into the main shaft was past a valve as ponderous as the one at its mouth. When closed, this would block off most of the air shocks from Orion. At boarding level, the distance was considerable from the last cross passage. No possibility existed of coming upon the guards by surprise.

Walking toward them, Iern was not afraid. He had even set aside his grief over Jori. There was too much else to do. Never had he been at a higher pitch of aliveness, though the note that keened through him was winter-cold. His mind seemed to observe each last detail that heightened senses brought in—scuffed gray tiles underfoot; smudges on dull-green walls; off-white ceiling and pure-white fluorescent plates; whirr, breeze, chemical whiffs from ventilator grilles; the sharp smell and salt of his dried sweat; Ronica glimpsed beside him, head aloft, and her rangy gait—Ronica, who was surely torn and tormented beyond anything he had felt, but they could not now pause to deal with that, either—

As above, the guards sat at a table by the outer door, which was fully swung back. Today, when work had been suspended, the valve beyond was shut, a great oblong sheen of steel. These sentries were both men, both known to Iern and Ronica. Alfri Levayn, the younger, slim, dark, bespectacled, wore a gaudy shirt but read a book that was probably weighty. Torel Hos, balding and kettle-bellied in a dun coverall, puffed a cigar. He was the one who called, "Hey, what's the word?"

"True about the nukes," Ronica told them.

"Um." Torel took the cigar stub from his mouth and looked gloomily at the lit end. "Well, the Mong did invade us."

As the newcomers reached the table, he gave them a scrutiny that became careful. "You two seem mighty shook up," he said. "And you've been sweating like mules. How come?"

"The news was a shock, and the auditorium was packed beyond what the air conditioning can handle," Ronica replied.

Alfri laid his book down. The title showed: *A Short History of the East*

Roman Empire. "I knew such weapons must have been built," he said dispassionately. "Only a few, of course, because no more could be spared from Orion. But it was not conceivable to me that there were none. What astonishes me is that the Maurai and the Mong ever assumed otherwise, that they failed completely to allow for it."

"I suppose they did allow for it as best they were able, but figured they must take the risk or see us win for certain," Torel guessed. To Iern and Ronica: "How'd the assembly go? Is it over yet? I haven't seen or heard anybody except you guys."

"We left before it ended," Iern said. "The audience seemed enthusiastic. But it had developed into an oratory session. Ronica doesn't care for that, and as for me, I have no business in your Northwestern politics, do I? It struck us that this is an ideal opportunity to check out some details about the ship."

"What?" Torel said. "I thought everybody had the day off, except poor slobs like us."

"Correct. Which means no horde of workers to push through and engineers to argue with."

Alfri's eyes narrowed behind the spectacles. "Wait a little," he objected. "They'd be working on the rest of the fleet. *Orion Two* is finished."

"Yes, yes. But don't you realize cut-and-try modifications are being made all the time, searching for improvement? The simulator has convinced me we could do better with the piloting-power interface. Too late to modify this ship, but Ronica and I will examine her again with these new ideas in mind, to see what we can propose for later models."

"We'll be testing various controls," the woman added. "Strictly dry-run, of course. Don't worry when the 'Systems Active' sign goes on." She gestured toward an inset glass panel.

"M-m, this is irregular," Alfri demurred.

"Oh, balls, you know us," she said. "We have our passes on us, if you must see them."

"Our orders— Uh, Miz Birken, I'm not questioning your competence or anything like that, but we were informed that operations are postponed till tomorrow, and the rule is that no one ever goes in except in regular line of duty or on a special pass."

"Yeh, yeh," Torel agreed. "You understand, don't you, folks? No offense. If something should go wrong, Alfri and me'd be in the manure, and you too."

Iern had hoped to avoid this, but known he might well encounter it. Ordinarily Norrfolk abided by the spirit rather than the letter of any policy, and the spirit tended to be whatever a given individual felt it ought to be. But in the present crisis, and with the outcome of twenty years under the lash of a dream dependent on yonder solitary vessel—

He and Ronica had discussed the problem on their way down. They could make no real plan, but they could think what the likeliest of the contingencies were, and arrange signals.

"*I'll refer them to our chief!*" he said fast and harshly, in Francey. She returned a tiny nod.

"What's that?" Torel inquired.

Iern shrugged. "I was swearing in my native language. Not at you, you have your duty, but at the stupid situation. Rainier Abron personally approved our suggestion. In the excitement, he didn't write anything down. Try calling him at his office or his quarters, will you?"

"Sure," Torel said. "I am sorry about this, Astronaut Ferlay." He settled himself before a telephone on the table.

"No use anybody getting mad," Ronica said. Smiling, she hunkered on her heels.

"Er, here, wouldn't you like this chair?" asked Alfri, and rose in haste.

"No, thanks. I'm comfortable. Do sit. While we wait, Iern and I can describe the meeting to you, if you want."

Alfri resumed his seat. "Probably no need as far as I am concerned," he said moodily. "I can guess. In fact, I volunteered for this assignment today, when I could have gone."

"Hm-m. And you'd been taking for granted we had killer nukes and would use them if hard pressed. What are you, precognitive?"

"No. In my leisure, a student of history. My people tend to be. They've endured so much of it."

"Your people?"

"Yesterday evening Rabbi Kemmer went about lamenting. He called for atonement, he recited Kaddish for the slain Mong. Others of us, like me, remembered Joshua; and the Captivity; the Maccabees; and the destruction of the Temple; the Khazars; and the Holocaust; Ben-Gurion; and— It went on, Miz Birken, it went on in my mind. This is in the nature of things. The trick is to survive. In spirit still more than body."

"Then you're glad we have the weapons?"

"Of course not. The point is that we do, and Orion is saved." Alfri winced. "As for whether or not we should have built and used them

—I'm weak and selfish enough to thank God that that wasn't my decision to make."

Torel put the telephone in its cradle. "I can't raise Dr. Abron either place," he said. "Probably the, uh, rally hasn't let out. Do you want to wait, or what?"

Iern glanced at a clock on the wall. In . . . seventeen minutes Wairoa should open the portal. "We may as well wait," he replied.

Alfri beamed. "Wonderful," he said. "At a time like this, it'll be especially nice to have such good company."

—"Oh, yes, the Domain is really something," Ronica declared. "I do recommend you visit it yourselves if you ever can. Not just monuments and quaint folkways, either. Some mighty jolly places. That dancing song, Iern, how's it go?" Her voice lilted Francey to a melody she probably improvised: "*The alarm will be startling. If we're ready, close to them, I think we can overcome. Try for a grip from behind and get their pistols.*"

The Clansman forced a smile. "You know I can't carry a tune in a wheelbarrow," he said. "But if you'll endure my croaking—*You take the younger man, I the older. Be sure that neither can reach a rifle.*"

Unspoken was the likely fate of Wairoa.

Alfri winced. "You're right, sir," he agreed. "You can't."

"The dance is easy to learn, and fun." Rising, Ronica took his hand. "C'mon, I'll show you."

"Some fellows have all the luck," Torel grumbled.

"Oh, I'll teach you next," she promised. "Meanwhile stand aside and watch. Over there is a good vantage point." She indicated the opposite side of the corridor.

"We're not supposed to leave—"

"Pooh! Scat." She leaned above the table and pulled lightly on what was left of his hair. With a sheepish grin, he got up and ambled off as directed. Iern accompanied him. Ronica guided Alfri to the middle of the floor.

"Have a care, sir," he called to Iern. "I'm falling in love with your lady."

Torel gave the flyer a sidewise look. "You're pretty glum, yourself," he remarked. "And tense."

"It's hard not to be," Iern said. "I'm glad Ronica can snatch a little enjoyment out of this mess."

One minute . . . . I used to think she had no acting talent. Will she tease me if I mention it, tell me to beware? . . .

Ronica executed a few kicks. "La, la, la, la," she warbled. "Like that. Do you see? Now we start back to back."

"Shucks, I'd rather be seeing you," Alfri laughed.

She fluttered her lashes. "The second measure is more interesting. Okay, dosey-do." She slipped behind him. "La, la, la."

Time!

"La, la, la, kick," she sang. "Oops, you got my ankle there. No harm done. Let's take it over."

Well, exact synchrony wasn't possible. Was it? Or has something gone awry?

"La, la—"

The horn sounded.

It was a deep, brazen roar, blasting out of a loudspeaker—out of loudspeakers placed everywhere—ringing, echoing, snarling down the corridors under the mountain, a warning, a call to battle, Orion shall rise!

Torel lurched, planted his legs wide, and stood dumbfounded. He would only remain so for a second. Iern cast himself at the blocky form. He might have delivered a deadly blow, but had decided he couldn't. Torel was a decent man, a husband and father. Iern attacked him at his back. His right arm threw a lock on both of his opponent's. His left hand darted to unsnap the holster.

Torel bellowed. Bull-strong, he wrenched loose and went for the sidearm himself. Iern got him again, but in a grip that immobilized the pilot too. They stamped and swayed about. The trumpet clamored around them.

Ronica's voice cut through the noise. "Hold! Not a move. You're covered."

She had used the instant of Alfri's paralysis to release and snatch his weapon and skip beyond his clutch, back toward the table where the rifles were. He stood as if she had clubbed him. "Stop that, Torel," she yelled. "I don't want to hurt you."

The older man sagged. Slowly, he raised his hands. Iern took the pistol and went to join Ronica.

"Yes, this is a hijack," she said. "Please don't make us shoot you. We'd try not to kill, but we might not succeed."

"Ronica," Alfri gasped. "No, no, not you, no."

"Yes. Go ahead, run off and tell. But be sure to remind 'em that anybody who comes after us will die. We'd rather take time to prepare properly for liftoff, but if the door cracks, we'll assume there's a party headed in equipped to stop us, like by shooting a rocket into the drive assembly, and we'll launch on the spot. They'll get the blast right in their faces, and the radiation will spew out here. You savvy?"

"I do," Torel groaned, "yeh, I do, you—" The rest was anguished obscenity.

"Go!" Iern interrupted, and fired a shot for emphasis. The men turned and ran. Twice Alfri cast glances back over his shoulder.

Iern yanked the telephone cord free. Ronica took both rifles. They sped to the inner door. He pulled the switch to Open 5; the valve would close itself after five minutes. It retracted with torturer slowness.

"I hope," Ronica said, almost too faintly to hear through the alarm, "I hope . . . nobody . . . thinks to cut off power to this section. The door couldn't shut, the catch pit couldn't work, the contamination would be horrible."

"They should have thought of that before they fired on the Mong," Iern answered.

The steel mass had withdrawn to a point where he could slip past. Ronica followed.

Tail-heavy as she was, the ship required no support. Scaffolding for workers was gone. What replaced it was the access frame, its semicircular lattice movable on wheels and adjustable by motors to make any part of the hull reachable. Recollection jarred Iern: once the crew was aboard, that structure was supposed to be dismantled and removed before liftoff. What damage would its flying fragments wreak, white-hot or molten or vaporized, neutron-blasted into filthy new isotopes? Plik's Angley drawled within him: *Too bloody bad.*

He and Ronica stepped onto a platform. He thumbed a switch on a post and the gangway slid forward along its runners.

The spearhead nose of the ship loomed before him. Light was everywhere, a candent blaze, cold as the air that eddied over his sweat-drenched garments. He could see nothing beyond. In this muffling place the alarm sounded remote, like a trumpeter blowing defiance on the rampart of the world.

The boarding platform stopped a few centimeters short of the crew entry lock. That was closed, but a key hung on the post. Iern brought it against the center of the circular valve and twisted its head. Magnetic fields intermeshed; a servomotor started; outer and inner valves swung aside. An identical device was within.

Iern put a hand on Ronica's hip, wondering if he would ever embrace it again as it deserved to be embraced, and urged her to the airlock chamber. She hefted the firearms she carried, seemed ready to throw them away, then kept them. *Respect for the craftsmanship,* he thought. He gave her the pistol he had carried. "All right," he said, "but do secure them."

She nodded. "I'll take the first engineer's station."

"Not necessary when we're just bound straight up. I'd rather have you beside me."

She passed her lips over his and crawled through. He came after. Crouched in the narrow space, he reached across to the control switch on the frame and set it for retraction. The valves he made fast behind him.

The pilots' cabin was forward of the space he entered, which held seats for passengers—scientists, engineers, *whose day I am certainly spoiling,* he thought. He climbed the rungs provided for vertical position and weightlessness, into the compartment and the left-hand seat. Lying on his back, knees above head, he buckled himself to thick-padded resilience. The smell of the leather brought memories alive, Grandfather Mael's easy chair, where he sat while he told a little boy stories of elves who lived in the dolmens and came forth at dusk to dance by the light of Ileduciel. . . . Through the window before him Iern looked onward and onward, the length of a monstrous tunnel, but in the glare around him he could not be sure whether he saw any sky at the end.

Enough. He brought attention and fingers to the many-studded intricacy of the pilot board. *Click,* a bulb glowed green, a needle moved on a dial, *click,* a fan whirred and a breeze touched his cheeks, *click,* a computer display sprang onto a screen, *click—*

Has this delay doomed you, Wairoa? I'm sorry, it's not rational of me, I don't wish it, but somehow that would atone for the killing—the double killing—and put an end to sorrow.

Well, more likely than not we're doomed too, my love and I. No spacesuits aboard; those are individually made, and the flyers hadn't been named before we did it ourselves. Untried ship; the robot craft was different in many ways. No ground control to help; no real crew; no emergency ejection system; no landing field for which I've practiced on the simulator, unless we want an executioner waiting for us to debark— Ronica, Ronica! Iern beat his fist on the chair arm. Designed to cushion acceleration, it yielded maddeningly. After a short while, he swallowed hard and got back to work.

Having taken care of various duties aft, she slipped in and established herself. "Keep watch for intruders," he said.

"I'm not a total butterbrain," she snapped.

Stricken, he stopped his preparations again to turn his head her way. "Forgive me," he blurted. "I didn't mean that."

"Of course you didn't, and I shouldn't've reacted. I'm on edge too." She laughed. "Damn the safety factors! We can't strain across the gap between us for a kiss, can we?"

"I'm amazed at you. If I'm in turmoil, you must be in agony."

"Well, I was, sort of, until . . . I decided. But now we're doing what's right, or what's least wrong, anyway. And laying our own lives on the line. And Iern, Iern, we're going out! Into space!"

He couldn't help it. She kindled something of that joy in him, regardless of everything. He *would* not dwell on the fact that his purpose was to keep Orion from truly rising, ever.

5

"—avenge the wrongs we have suffered—"

The horn roared.

Mikli's harangue broke. For seconds he poised like a cat. A surge passed over the crowd, with a sound as of breaking waves and screaming gulls.

Mikli's lips peeled back from his teeth. "Oh, oh," he muttered. "School's out." He addressed the microphone again. His voice boomed into the clamor: "That's the launch alarm. Take it easy. We've got trouble. Probably nothing we can't handle, we Norrmen, if we keep our wits about us. Stay put." He lifted his arms and the half-panicky confusion died away. "All security personnel present, leave immediately and report to your regular duty stations. Equip yourselves and stand by for orders. The rest of you remain seated until your guardspeople are out. After that, make an orderly exit and go to your quarters."

Dreng had mounted the stage. Terror writhed over the heavy countenance, not for his own safety. "Talk to 'em, Eygar," Mikli said. "Keep 'em from stampeding. I'll rescue your precious ship." Into the microphone: "Be of stout heart, Norrfolk. I'm on my way!"

He hurried off, along the aisle and through the door. Some cheered him. The sound was lost in the trumpet call.

When out of sight, he ceased his fast but confident walk and pelted down the hall, up a stair, down the hall above to his office. The subordinate manning it stood pistol in hand. She snapped the barrel aloft in salute. He waved merrily. "Any information?" he asked as he passed by.

"No, sir. Not yet." Boots pounded in the corridor, men shouted, echoes flew, the horn raged.

Mikli laughed. "That makes this all the more fun, eh?" he said from the inner office.

At his desk, he snatched the telephone and began calling. "Level One, okay, guards haven't noticed anything except the alarm," he announced while he punched for the second entry. "Level Two, same. . . . Level Three—hello, hello—a dead line, seems. And that's the crew port. . . . Level Four, okay, no disturbance. . . . Level Five —Hello, hello, hello—it rings, but nobody answers—and *that* is Gate Control." He grinned. "Uh-huh. We've got us a case of the galloping piracies."

The duty officer's instrument shrilled. She listened for a few seconds. "Yes, I'll switch you over," she said. Her tone trembled: "Sir, it's a man from the Level Three post."

Mikli listened. "A-a-a-ah," he breathed. "Very well, Hos, you and Levayn report to your command center, draw new weapons, and wait for orders with the rest of your team. No time now to worry about whether you were negligent. Move!" He put the phone down. "Shaira, dear," he called to the outer office, "check the whereabouts of Wairoa Haakonu."

"Why, he should be confined, sir, shouldn't he? But—" A throttled shriek. "He isn't! He's at Gate Control!"

Mikli nodded. "Figures." He consulted his watch. "Ferlay and the Birken slut must be snugging themselves into the ship at this moment," he said, as if to himself. "Normal countdown would be an hour. They can easily shave off most of that—or all of it, if we try to force an entry and they see nothing to lose by blasting off at once. But they'll prefer going through at least the basic checkouts and warmups. Twenty minutes, perhaps." He raised his voice anew. "Shaira, call security HQ and have a squad equipped with a couple of rocket guns proceed to Level Five, pronto. If the door is shut, which it doubtless is, they're to blow it down, and get in and shunt that valve back in place before the ship rises. On the double!"

Once more he lifted his phone, and punched a special number. "Battleship *Sea Serpent,* Commander Scarp on the bridge, speaking," he heard.

"Captain Karst," Mikli snapped. "Listen well. Code Volcano. D'you read me?"

"Yes, sir. Absolute priority."

"Get up steam and man battle stations. Warn personnel not to look west. It's possible there'll be several flashes in that direction which could blind them—yes, they'd better not be exposed without full clothing, gloves, and face masks."

"What?" The appalled man mastered himself. "Have civilians been alerted?"

"Yes, ever since this pig got out of its poke, the alarm has included a radio 'cast, and a receiver is always open in Kenai. They'll be in bed with the blankets pulled over them. I thought everybody knew that," Mikli said impatiently. "If our spacecraft does go up, you put out to sea. Your primary mission will be to destroy the Maurai aircraft carriers, so they can't lay precision bombing on us after they've taken a sight. You will do that at all costs. If thereafter you can inflict further damage, why, that's fine; but try to disengage and return here while you still have some missiles in reserve against whatever they may try next. Do you understand? Repeat."

When the navy man had obeyed, his own words shaken, Mikli said, "Have fun," lowered the phone, and left his chair. For a moment his vision lingered on the mammoth tusks. "I hope you did in your day, old chap," he murmured, "and that I can leave as impressive a memento behind me." He stroked the smooth onyx of his penholder, turned, and walked out.

"Where are you going, sir?" his subordinate inquired.

Mikli chuckled amidst the trumpeting. "Why, to Level Five. You didn't imagine I'd miss such an entertainment, did you, love?" He patted her head, laughed at her annoyance, and hastened off.

An officer stopped him, wanting permission to lead a breakthrough at Level Three. Mikli lost several minutes; the request must be refused so emphatically that the attempt would not be made regardless. Finally an elevator bore him to the corridor just below his objective.

There the racket of the horn was loud enough to shiver his jaws. A dozen armed men stood at the ladder. One bore a launch tube across his shoulders, two more each carried four of the small solid-fuel rockets with explosive warheads which the device projected, the rest were conventionally outfitted. The entire squad was in disarray; men looked grim or slouched in despair; they reeked of fear; the pain that showed upon them was not only in their eardrums.

Mikli dashed to meet them. "What in hell's shitpits is the matter with you?" he yelled. "And I ordered two rocketeers."

The squad leader saluted. "Sir," he answered against the noise, "the second man is dead, along with four others. There's a rifleman defending, and he's murderous. Whoever raises his head out of the shaft gets a slug straight through it. No time to deploy the weapon." He gulped. "And, uh, sir, you know this's a suicide task, don't you? The armor on that door 'ull throw chunks back—cut the rocketeer to pieces."

Mikli glared from face to face. "A man should be proud to die that Orion may rise," he stated.

"*Orion Two* will rise any minute," whimpered another. "Without the door, whoever's up there won't live to tell about it. Even down here—"

Mikli put arms akimbo. For a few seconds, only the trumpet had voice. "And you call yourselves Norrmen," he said.

Suddenly: "Okay. Load that tube and give it to me."

"Sir?" They goggled at him.

"*I'll* open the door for you. Be prepared to follow. You—" he pointed to the most woebegone of the group—"I'll have your side-arm. You run on home to your mother and see if she can't supply the cojones she overlooked when you were on the assembly line."

The man flinched. "Sir, this is crazy," the leader protested. "We can't afford to lose you! I'll try it again myself."

Mikli shook his head. "No. I've got a notion, but I won't waste time explaining, and you haven't the craziness to execute it properly anyway." His laughter shrilled. "Also, I'm not about to miss a chance like this for making havoc!"

They shuffled their feet and looked away. "Jump," he ordered, as quietly as possible under the racket. They regarded him and made haste to obey.

Pistol at waist, loaded launch tube on his back, Mikli put foot to rung. "When you hear this thing go off, follow," he directed. Monkey-agile, he swarmed aloft.

A haze of horn-sound filled the zigzag passage. At its end the dead men lay sprawled in a heap. Their eyes stared, their mouths gaped, blood and brains and excrement besmeared them. Mikli made a slight moue and picked his way over them to the next ladder.

When his brow was almost at the verge, he stopped. Clinging one-handed, he unbuckled his dress belt and passed it around the rung at his midriff, refastening it to make a loop against which he could freely lean. He unshipped the rocket launcher and raised it, with some effort, until its front half rested on the floor above. His left hand took hold of the stock, which should have been at his shoulder, and tilted the barrel upward.

Bullets whanged. Wairoa had seen. The tube jerked to the impacts. Mikli grinned wider than before. His right hand reached for the firing switch.

It was a madman's plan, therefore it had not occurred to the guards. He could aim only by blind estimate, and the barrel wouldn't hold steady. The odds were immense that the rocket would not strike near the vulnerable point where the bolt met its housing, but merely dent the steel somewhere else. Mikli relied on his luck. Speaking to the gathered Wolves, he had called it destiny.

The alarm cut off. Silence crashed down.

For a short while, he could not know that it had, as stunned as his ears were. Then he heard the signal that came after, high and icy, a sound like a winter wind.

In three minutes, *Orion Two* would rise.

Mikli fired. Smoke and flame whirled above him. Fumes scorched his breathing. The *whoom* of the missile ended in a doomsday crash. Knife-edged shards of it flew glittering and wailing, caromed from the walls, hailed past him where he pressed himself tight to his side of the shaft. He scarcely felt the lacerations. They didn't matter. Nothing mattered but stopping the ship.

He sprang upward. No bullet greeted him. Soot-stained and battered, the door sagged ajar. "Ya-a-ah!" he screamed in his victory, and plunged toward it.

Wairoa stood fast while the trumpet cried its summons. Eye to loophole, weapons ready, he waited. When the guardsmen appeared, he picked them off. He paid no heed to the one who lay bound on the floor. Afterward, though, his gaze strayed to the dead woman. He stooped, briefly laid a hand on her belly, straightened, and resumed his vigil, a gaunt night figure amidst whiteness and machinery.

The rocket launcher poked over the verge. He fired several times, but that was no fleshly target.

The horn ceased blowing. Orion whistled.

Wairoa eased. His watch was ended.

Almost.

The blast sent him staggering backward. He dropped his rifle. Dazed, he went to his knees. Blood dripped from his nose. He crawled back erect. Mikli Karst had slipped through the crack that had opened. His pistol was drawn.

Orion whistled.

Mikli shot. Wairoa stumbled, caught at a wall, leaned panting against it. From the hole in his guts, crimson spurted and flooded. Mikli made for the control board.

Wairoa gathered himself and scuttled to intercept. "No!" Mikli howled. "You can't!" He shot again, nearly point-blank. Wairoa did not seem to feel. He reached his enemy and grappled.

Embraced, they reeled by the panel, on outward. Mikli could not bring his gun to bear, against the grip on that arm. Wairoa twisted, bones snapped, the pistol clattered to the floor. Mikli's free hand gouged. Wairoa ignored. He was using his own right arm to steer his opponent, keep them both moving.

"No!" Mikli shrieked. "No!"

Wairoa smiled. "Yes," he said.

They lurched onto the balcony. Mikli sank teeth into Wairoa's throat. Wairoa levered him over the guard rail. Mikli did not let go. They fell together, a hundred and more meters down the shaft toward the pit.

—Below, the squad leader exhorted his men. A few who were brave rallied to him. They climbed the ladders and burst into the control section. That was just in time for them to perish in the fire and thunder of the ascent.

XXIV

This time the angry magnates had not met in Kemper under false pretenses. They made known their purpose, and gathered in Dordoyn, at Castle Beynac, whose warders gave Captain Jovain his first open defiance. There were many more of them than had been at the previous conference. Their entourages filled every spare room in the keep, every possible place nearby, and not even the innkeepers would take money for lodging.

Sessions began early each day and ran until well after sundown. The matter dealt with was as grave as any in the history of the Domain, or more so. Everybody demanded to be heard, repeatedly and at length. Disagreements and doubts ranged from basic principles to the pettiest procedural details. Personal enmities flared. Intrigues, covert threats, crass bargaining went on in the darker corners of the castle and the clock. Yet slowly, inefficiently, humanly, the meeting bumbled toward a consensus.

At last Vosmaer Tess Rayman could stand before it and offer a summary. She had been elected chairman at the beginning, rather to her own and the collective surprise. The feeling had seemed to be that as a service officer whose career had made her intimate with Skyholm and respected among Aerogens and groundlings alike, she might be the least controversial person present. She soon disabused the rest of that notion, but nobody seriously ventured to challenge her style of riding herd on the assembly. Most were somewhat grateful for it.

The auditorium had been added to the fortress a pair of centuries ago, a long and narrow-windowed chamber. Beneath each sill was a statue of an Ancestor, in the abstract style of that era. A turret above was actually a camera obscura, whose electronics filled a screen girdling the room above the windows with a view of the outside as seen from a height. This evening it showed dusk setting in over trees that were still leafless, valley muddied by rain, river wanly agleam. A few stars had blinked into sight and Skyholm hung low in the north like a moon across which tiny lights glittered. The coldness of the scene pierced an air grown hot, stuffy, and tobacco-laden.

From the podium, Tess looked over the scores who sat before her. The colors and cuts of regional garb bespoke what a mixed lot they were—Clan Seniors and managers, merchant princes, regional lords and ladies who ranged from the shy and scholarly Mestromor to the elegant Grand Mayor of Elsass, from the severely black-clad President of Bourgoyn to the shaggy mountaineer who was Chief of Jura — She cleared her throat.

"I would like at this point to sketch what we appear to have agreed upon," she said. "Not that any individual here will endorse every part of it. However, my impression is that we've reached a point where compromises bringing us to unity have become possible.

"Jovain's replacement of Skyholm personnel cannot and must not be tolerated. It does worse than giving him—him and his pack of mercenaries, Espaynians, Maurai 'advisers'—total control over the most powerful instrumentality in Uropa, perhaps in the world. He can blast us to ash. We have no check whatsoever upon him, except outright rebellion and ruinous guerrilla warfare. It may well be that nothing stays his hand but the knowledge that that would destroy the Domain . . . and, let's give them credit, probably the Espaynians and Maurai in the Skyholm crew wouldn't obey such an order without extreme provocation from our side.

"They are doubtless honorable, by their own lights. I myself will concede that Jovain may be. The point is that *he* and *they* decide what shall happen, not *us*, not the peoples and the ancient usages of the Domain." She pointed at the image of the aerostat. "Once that saved civilization in Franceterr. Later it guarded and nurtured. Now he has turned it into the means of absolute power.

"And that is what's worst. Skyholm rightfully belongs not to him but to the Domain—to our forebears and to children yet unborn, as well as us. It's the heart of everything that we are. You may or may not personally believe that the anims of the Ancestors live on up yonder, but you know full well that their heritage does. Our purpose is to claim that heritage back."

She paused. A rustling went through the audience. She made her voice dry.

"What do we propose to do about it? Well, first, obviously, we petition for a convention of Seniors. They can't meet in Skyholm as always before, but that may not be legally required. They should vote Jovain's impeachment and removal.

"Meanwhile, in earnest of our resolve, we should announce that henceforward our allegiance is withheld. Our states shall pay no dues to the center, recognize none of its officials, and heed none of its decrees; and we call on other states, corps, Ligues, companies, organizations of every sort to do likewise.

"Several among you have argued in these past days that such action will tear at the very fabric of our society. This is true. Nevertheless—"

A young man darted through the main door and along the aisle. "News, news!" he howled. Tears coursed down his face, which was stretched out of shape. "The radio—"

Tess lifted a hand to stay the unease in the group. "What the devil?" she demanded. "Unseemly, if it isn't an emergency."

"It is," Ans Debyron said through his weeping. He reached the podium and sprang up beside her. "Hear me, my sirs and ladies. The Mong armies attacking the Northwest Union have been wiped out—by nuclear weapons. Deu deliver us!" He sank to his knees and sobbed.

Tess held her place while horror made chaos below her. At last her gaze sought the image of Skyholm, ice-white above deepening darkness. "And what will you do now?" she whispered.

2

Terai Lohannaso was in his cabin, writing a letter to his wife, when *Orion Two* blasted free. Blue-white radiance flashed through the port, bright as a dozen suns.

His chair crashed back. The cabin abruptly seemed nighted, except for the banners of dazzlement that flew across his vision. He groped his way out. Another burst came down the ladder that led to the deck. It was less fierce than the first, and even then he gauged that the angle was much more steep.

By the time he was topside and the afterimages had cleared from his eyes, there had been a third flash, but it showed star-tiny and was the last seen. Crewfolk boiled about in near panic or squatted stunned. Those who had happened to look straight at the initial explosion were recovering their sight, but more slowly than he.

Terai plowed the mob from his path, reached the rail, and stared around.

The morning had grown calm again, save for a flock of terrified cormorants whose wings beat black against a sky that held only a few clouds. The sea sparkled greenly; a slight, cold breeze sent wavelets smacking against the hull and made it roll a bit. *Rongelap* lay anchored off the little Barren Islands, to keep watch on Cook Inlet. To starboard the mountains of the Kenai Peninsula reared over the horizon, and forward the peaks of the Leutian Range, distance-hazed but brilliant in their snows. Besides the dreadnaught, half a dozen lesser ships were in view—no more, since the fleet had dispersed in squadrons well away from each other.

Afar to the north, beyond the heights Terai could see, a thread of vapor reached heavenward, slowly twisting apart and dissipating, the track of the comet.

"Now hear this!" bawled the loudspeaker from the bridge. "Now hear this! We have no cause for fear. All personnel to battle stations —smartly, look alive!—like seamen of the Queen!"

That rallied the Maurai. They trotted to their posts, resolution in their gaits and countenances. Terai felt proud of them.

"Will Captain Lohannaso report to the admiral's office?" the voice called. He was already bound in that direction.

The muted thunders reached him after a number of minutes which confirmed that their source was in the neighborhood belonging to Orion.

Palu Halaweo, skipper of the flagship, gave Terai an expression of dismay. "Do you mean their spacecraft are ready?" he asked.

The intelligence officer kindled his pipe and took a puff that tingled soothingly over tongue and palate. "No, sir," he replied. "That was a single launch. A prototype vehicle, I'm certain, intended for tests and data collection. No matter how much information the Norries have from astronautical archives, it's just not possible that they could design and build something so ambitious on a basis of pure theory. I've told you before, my investigations have established they'll need months yet to finish the work; and at that, the reliability will be questionable."

"But why did they send this one off in sight of Tanaroa and everybody?" Admiral Kepaloa demanded. "I would have waited for a fog, at least."

"That's a puzzler, sir," Terai admitted. "I suspect something went rather drastically wrong—for which, three cheers, hm? Did we get a triangulation on the site?"

"I'm waiting to hear—" A rating appeared with a sheet of paper in her hand. Kepaloa laughed. "Speak of Nan and you'll feel his teeth in your butt! I do believe this is the report."

"Yes, sir, three accounts, almost simultaneous," the sailor announced.

Two were from aircraft which had been on patrol off their carriers; the third was from Kodiak Island, which the surviving marines had occupied. In addition, aboard this vessel, young Roberiti Lokoloku had coolly hastened to a binnacle and taken a compass bearing on the trail while it was still clearly defined. Terai drew the lines on a map and examined their point of convergence. "Ye-e-es," he murmured, "this identifies the area a great deal more precisely than before. May I suggest that the admiral let me compose a message for radio to Wellantoa? The geology department at the University will either have details about those mountains or know where to get them. That will give us clues to where the other launch facilities *can* be, and we'll proceed to bomb them to flinders."

"Aye!" exclaimed Halaweo. "They must be well hardened, but how many tonnes of high explosive can they stand? We'll bring it in by the convoy load if we must."

Kepaloa scowled. "Why are they inviting it? Damnably queer—"

An intuition thrilled along Terai's nerves. "Sir," he said, while his fist smote the table, "I suggest also that we keep receivers open to every plausible channel. It could well be that we'll get a communication . . . from space."

The rating reappeared. "Sir," she declared anxiously, "we have a report from a scout plane. The ironclad that was lying near Omer village is southbound at full speed. She's sent up small, fast flyers of her own—spotters for her guns, we think."

"Hm. Well, well." Kepaloa considered the chart. "About three hours till she heaves in sight of us. A desperation maneuver? We'll prepare a suitable welcome for her, eh, gentlemen?" He saw how Terai stiffened, heard the breath go in between his teeth. "Aii, what's the matter, Lohannaso?"

"*Hello, Earth. Hello, Earth. Spacecraft* Orion *calling Earth and mankind.*

"*Talence Iern Ferlay of the Domain of Skyholm speaking. With me is Ronica Birken of the Northwest Union. We are in orbit around the world. It's unbelievably beautiful. . . .*"

"Ronica Birken speaking. I am of the Northwest Union. I helped take this ship away from the Wolf Lodge in hopes she'd carry off the guilt my folk must otherwise forever bear. Treachery, mass murder, hazarding a new Doom, and the vision of an empire— I dare not imagine that you will follow along, once you have understood. Listen down there! You've been lied to, used, treated like interchangeable pieces of machinery. You who were the Free Folk, what you've gotten is a government, and it's handling you the way governments always do their subjects. . . ."

"Talence Iern Ferlay again. I don't agree with everything my lady has said, but we're united in this, that we will not condone what has happened and it shall be avenged." The Unglish changed to Francey. *"To my mother and her family, my foster mother and hers, all my kin, all my comrades, a word of love and comfort. We don't know what we are going to do next or whether we can make a safe landing somewhere, sometime. But if we die, don't grieve. We won back our honor and we are out in the middle of a miracle. . . ."*

Terai did not hear the broadcast as it came in. He was in his cabin again, finishing his letter home. "Farewell, best beloved," he wrote, signed his name, put the paper in an envelope and sealed it. He had a fair idea of what would presently happen. Seeking back to the admiral's office, he found the tape of the message. As it played for him, the gray hair stirred on his head. "Tanaroa!" he whispered. "How I envy you, Iern, boy. Luck be with you."

Early that afternoon, *Sea Serpent* rounded the southernmost cape of the Kenai Peninsula and headed for the Gulf of Laska. She was a huge and ugly vessel, low in the water, her upper works harshly angular: bridge, deckhouse, gun turrets, missile platforms, lifeboat nacelles. Armor gleamed in sunlight that a rising mistiness had turned pale. Three stacks fumed forth stench and murk.

High above, several Maurai jets circled helpless. They had chased away the enemy planes, but when they attacked the ship, their missiles could not seriously damage her, and murderous antiaircraft fire brought down half their number. Bombers had come, to drop their loads from a safe altitude; and laser beams detonated the bombs in midair.

Terai heard the reports with rage—rage at the smugness and stupidity of the Federation's Ministry of Defense, at the public apathy and intellectual mendacity which had mired down every effort that anybody did make toward restoring the strength and alertness that had won the Power War. Oh, yes, he remembered, they knew in Wellantoa that *Sea Serpent* existed, old and obsolete. The Norries were allowed to keep her as a mother ship for their coast guard in these waters. But her actual owner was the Wolf Lodge, which contracted her out.

No one had thought to tell Terai, or any of his service, to check on her while they were in Laska. She had simply, quietly gone off to some isolated workplace where she was transformed into this monster. Armor, armament—electronic weapons, copied from Skyholm, such as the Royal Navy itself did not possess . . . defending Orion directly, they would have revealed what exact location it was that they guarded, but this was a mobile stage for them—

And there the thing came.

Under power, sails folded, *Rongelap* and her squadron moved to engage. The time had been too short for reinforcements to arrive. And now the time had shrunken to nothing.

A rifle bellowed, the shell flew invisibly fast, seeking range. A fountain erupted white near the ironclad.

She returned no shot. Instead, it flashed at her forward launch pad. The rocket streaked aloft, a silver spear trailed by firelit smoke. The sound of its passage boomed across kilometers.

On the bridge, Kepaloa brought his binoculars down as the projectile crossed the sky and dropped from sight. "I am afraid your guess was correct, Captain Lohannaso," he said roughly.

"It was logic, of a brutal sort," Terai answered. "And not a Nan-devoured thing we can do about it, except—"

Incandescence flared on the southeastern horizon. A dreadful grumbling noise followed, and vapor made a new snowpeak on the sea.

Halaweo snatched a microphone. "Now hear this!" he intoned. "That was a nuclear warhead, as you have been notified might be the case. Stand fast to your posts. They can't throw one at us, this close, without destroying themselves. As for those rays you have also heard about, they seem to be for air protection only. In any case, a beam that can touch off a warhead will not have the energy to do much against a hull. No ship could carry the generating capacity for that. You face no danger you have not faced before, and you have a vital job to do.

"Prepare for action. We're going after those kea birds!"

Engines woke to full speed. The Maurai craft surged forward. Their guns raked before them. Blast and shrapnel went furious over the ironclad.

She had courageous men aboard. Regardless of casualties, they launched a second rocket, a third, a fourth. The skies blazed.

Radio reports were coming in. The Wolf spotter planes had done their work before they must flee. No target vessel that they identified was fast enough to get out of the nuclear kill radius. Each explosion claimed an aircraft carrier and her attendants. Elsewhere, horror immobilized Maurai crews, or whipped them close to mutiny. "*We're beaten, we can't fight this, it's the Downfall*—"

Terai was not sure why heart remained in the sailors here. Well, he and others had been frank with them before exhorting them, and a fiend confronted is less terrible than one unseen.

"I love you, Elena," he had started his letter. He didn't know if she would ever receive it. Maybe only the fishes would.

Morale must be drawn close to breaking. Terai saw it snap in Halaweo. "Merciful Haristi, we're ruined like the Mong," the captain groaned.

"No!" Terai seized him by the shoulder, hard enough to bring a gasp of pain. "Not if we can sink that ship. She has to be their last atomic resource. They can't have had much for combat use, if they wanted Orion to rise. They don't even have missiles with the range and accuracy to shoot from inside the firth. On!"

Hostile turrets swiveled. Guns bawled. *Rongelap*'s mainmast splintered and fell. Flames licked over its length. Wounded crewmen screamed. Their comrades kept stations, returning the shots.

The ironclad heeled about and throbbed toward the mouth of Cook Inlet, where the shore batteries waited. Some distance off, a Maurai frigate was burning and sinking.

"We'll have to let her go," Kepaloa said. "She can knock us to pieces."

"No, sir, no," Terai urged. "Don't you see? She must have more nukes aboard, probably all they have left. She *is* their nuclear weapon. And she'll smash the next force we can bring to bear—unless we send her to the bottom this day."

Kepaloa gave him a long regard before replying, "I think you have just assumed command, Lohannaso. Very well, we pursue till the end."

A chemical burst rocked the dreadnaught again. Slivers of metal and wood hailed into human flesh. Fire blossomed and crackled on the port side. Men lay moveless, like broken dolls, or dragged their crippled bodies off in search of help.

But other men served the guns of *Rongelap* and her companions. *Sea Serpent* lurched in the water, listed, slowed to a crawl. Her after turrets were wreckage. Her stacks were blown away; the black gang must be choking. What conventional shots she could get off made geysers in the sea. And still the Maurai closed in.

"Ho-o-o!" Terai shouted. "You didn't think we'd have the manhood, did you?"

Hulled and aflame, *Rongelap* was nonetheless the faster vessel. She drew alongside. Her riflemen interdicted the opposing deck. Terai bounded down off the bridge. On his way, he snatched a fire ax from its rack and swung its crimson-painted starkness over his head as if it were a lightning bolt. "Grapple, board, and scuttle!" he called. "For the sake of your children!"

No fear was in him, nor any anger. He moved like a storm or a tide. Within him was the cool memory of swimming with his dolphin friend through the waters of home.

Nobody ever knew, afterward, whose was the vengeful hand that armed and set off a remaining nuclear warhead. A fireball whirled upward. Momentarily, waves boiled. Birds fell from the air, seared. The crash echoed through far valleys and loosed avalanches down the sides of mountains. A wind howled into being and bore the fallout poisons eastward across the Gulf.

Later there was a great stillness, and the sea lay empty.

3

After the weight and violence of acceleration, free fall was like a dream, half-wakeful by an open window in a morning of early springtime.

Earth gleamed in blue-and-white purity, greening Northern lowlands, sculptured heights, quicksilvery rivers and lakes, weather aflow. Then a new sunset went red-gold down the curve of the planet, as the spaceship ended another ninety-minute circuit and swung around over the night side. She found no darkness. The stars crowded it out of heaven. Alone in the unlighted control cabin, Iern let his spirit soar amidst radiance.

Ronica winged back to him. She had been on inspection. He embraced the fragrance and litheness of her. The Milky Way brought her face frostily forth in the shadows. They floated hand in hand.

"All okay," she told him. "We've got us a better machine than the designers themselves knew. . . . Have you had any response to our broadcast?"

"No, not yet. But it will require special relaying arrangements, and they are . . . preoccupied . . . down there—and to be honest, I would rather not hear for a while what has been happening."

"I understand," she sighed. "I'm close to collapse too. Reaction. But here is healing for us."

He nodded. "Healing for the human race, maybe. Ronica, we cannot let this be lost. I thought we had to keep Orion from rising, but now, when we've seen— Somehow, it must."

She kissed him. "Yes."

"On that account," he said, "I think we should wait to return. I mean longer than the time for rehearsals, familiarization. A week or more, till the situation has stabilized someplace, if it ever can. Till we know where we can land without having the craft taken away and forever grounded."

"My same idea, darling. We've ample rations."

Eagerness lightened the exhaustion in his voice. "And ample power. The computer capabilities aren't great, but we don't need much finesse, given the drive energy available. We don't have to remain in Earth orbit." Suddenly, in the teeth of everything, he laughed. "How would you like a leisurely trip around the moon?"

 4

"I did what I did for love of her," Jovain mumbled. "Oh, also because I wanted to remake the Domain in my own image, and get revenge on Iern—but chiefly it was for her. Now I have none of them."

Mattas Olvera laid a hand on the Captain's shoulder with an unwonted gentleness that matched his voice: "You were serving Gaea."

"I was serving myself." Jovain made a chopping gesture at the prism window. "And She denies me likewise."

The ucheny had found him in the Garden, at the bower of the roses. He had gone there to look down upon the ground, where Faylis was. Golden-white under an afternoon sun, against the deep-hued sky, cloud deck hid both land and sea from him. Reports were that a devastating gale raged beneath, such as the Stormriders had formerly gone out to do combat with.

"You speak wrongly," Mattas admonished. "She no more can withdraw from you than you from Her. Life is One. Only when organelles grow diseased—" He veered from that. "And you haven't actually lost your, m-m, wife, have you? My impression has been that she wearied of this environment but is waiting for you in Tournev."

"How long must she wait? How long can she? Will she? We had drifted well apart already." In a rush of bitter-tasting wrath, Jovain shook his fist at the immensity around and above him. "And I can imagine how her romantic little heart is aflutter at the word—Golden Boy Iern alive, circling the planet like a god set free, and hallelujah ringing from end to end of the Domain! While I stand here abandoned, disowned, a prisoner in my stronghold—"

Mattas' tone sharpened. "Self-pity doesn't become you. Be a man again. You were."

Jovain smote fist in palm. "I, I'm sorry. The catastrophe in Merique, climaxing all those mad revelations, and my own realm falling apart—" He held his eyes turned outward while he reached a degree of steadiness. "I'm astounded at how composed you've stayed. I should have thought you, a Gaean adept, would be in torment. Victory is in sight for that horde of ruthless technolaters."

Mattas' words harshened further. "I don't agree."

"Why not?"

"Gaea will prevail. That's what I came about. Rewi Seraio asked me where you were. He urgently wants a meeting of the leadership. I guessed you might be here, and in need of some psychic help before you saw him."

"What?" Jovain straightened. A tingle ran down his spine. "Thank you, but we'd better not delay. I'm in control of myself." *The prospect of action, any action, after this impotence, is like blood given a wounded soldier.*

The men walked rapidly among blossoms and leaves. They tried not to see how much was faded, withered, or dead. Persons detailed from the new staff to tend the Garden lacked the time, experience, and devotion of the former keepers. The very air had lost its sweetness.

The higher levels were empty, a maze of echoing corridors and deserted rooms, save for the occasional technician or Terran Guardsman. The latter saluted crisply. Few of the civilians did, because few were Francey. Skyholm today was crewed largely by Espaynians and Maurai. Jovain often wondered how many of them were even civilians. The heads of their contingents, Yago Dyas Garsaya and Rewi Seraio, avowedly were not, but officers in the intelligence corps of the Zheneral's Army and the Queen's Navy.

He had wanted a band obedient to none and nothing other than himself. Instead— Well, he did keep the upper hand militarily, but he was not certain what measure of real control that gave him.

Reaching his office, he sent for the foreigners and settled himself under the portrait of Charles and the Declaration of Tours. The glass desktop felt cold beneath his hands. Mattas took a chair that stridulated under his bulk. "We want revenge," he growled, red-faced. "Or cautery, if you like, burning the cancer out of Gaea before it spreads."

"What can we do?" Jovain responded dully. "Once the Domain could have dispatched help to the Mong, but what is left us?"

As if on signal, Ashcroft Lorens Mayn entered, erect in his green uniform, his features haggard and yet twistingly akin to his sister's. He came to attention. "Sir, I'm afraid there is more bad news," he said. "A couple of hours ago, before the storm got so intense we lost most radio signals, a pair of messages came in. High Midi has renounced allegiance. So have the Seniors of Clan Kroneberg, unanimously."

"They too?" Jovain sighed. "Scarcely a surprise. Sit down, Lorens. Have you heard anything lately from Faylis? I haven't."

"No, nor I," the young man said with compassion. "But I had no time to visit her when I was last in Tournev. You remember my concern then was that masked attack on several Guardsmen."

"No clues to the thugs so far? We might do best to impose a curfew. If we can't control that one city and its hinterland, we're finished. Skyholm itself is."

Yago Dyas Garsaya came in, found a chair, lit a cheroot, and smoked it in nervous whiffs. "I have had some information passed to me by my home office, from the Mong countries," he said. "The Gaean network, you know, as well as what few agents we have there."

Jovain's pulse quickened. "What do you hear? Are they planning a new attack?"

The Espaynian shook his head. "Apparently not. The Soldati seem utterly demoralized."

Mattas' beard bristled. "And they claim to be a warrior race!" he snorted. "The Norrmen must have spent their stock of hell-weapons, or nearly so. The ashes of the slain cry on every wind for vengeance."

Yago shook his head. "Those regiments that were ready to go, and died, were the ones where some of that spirit survived from of old—and evidently a more crucial example to the rest than anyone understood," he explained. "After all, Gaeanity does not make for a warlike ethos. And it does heighten the shock of something like . . . like that which was done. Whole polks in the Five Nations are refusing to join the colors. Those that say they will are being gutted by desertions."

Mattas sagged. "The birthplace of the Insight."

"Besides, it appears the governments have abundant trouble at home. Reports are starting to come in of slugai running off, or meeting to organize and demand equality. Many have been seen armed, in public."

"That society must be further decayed than it knew itself," Jovain said slowly. "The minute the grip of the aristocrats slackened—and, yes, the fact that kinsmen, fellow Mericans, had broken the pride of the Mong— What do you think will come of it?"

Yago shook his head sadly. "Who knows?" he responded. "Unrest on a continental scale; possible disintegration; at the very least, the end of the old order. I think the Northwest Union need no longer worry about its eastern front."

"Until we—" Mattas stopped as Rewi Seraio entered.

The Maurai was a brown-skinned man in late middle age whose portliness and professorial manner did not make him appear the less formidable. Before he was seated, he was talking, in flat, rapid Angley sentences: "Captain, gentlemen, I asked you to join me because my country has suffered a disaster of its own and may soon, as a consequence, be in a crisis without precedent. Naturally, this strikes at those of Her Majesty's subjects who are here, and thus at Skyholm."

Foreknowledge clamped a hand on Jovain's heart. "A nuclear strike against you," breathed out of him.

Rewi nodded. "Yesterday."

Mattas made a noise as if he were being strangled. Lorens did not stir, but now he did not look young at all.

"I only received a report on it lately," Rewi continued. "Matters have been so chaotic that it's taken this long to get anything like a coherent account together. That sensation about the spaceship started the confusion, and may have precipitated it."

"How? What happened?" Jovain asked faintly.

"You have heard the broadcast Ferlay and Birken made, or a replay, haven't you? They declared they had taken the prototype vessel in order to deny it to the Northwestern slaughterers. This was admirable, of course, but quite likely it was what forced the Norrmen to their next action.

"They dispatched a battleship armed with nuclear-headed rockets. It took out our aircraft carriers, which was doubtless its primary assignment, and in the course of doing so destroyed or crippled nearby ships to a total of a fourth or more of our Grand Fleet. A final explosion demolished it, but among other things cost us our flagship and commanding admiral."

Jovain sat motionless. He did not know what else to do. Yago punished his lungs with smoke. Lorens crossed himself. Mattas belched a Douroais obscenity.

After a silence, Rewi's impersonal voice resumed:

"One wonders how far to trust a leadership that has inflicted such egregious miscalculations and negligences on Her Majesty. However, I think the assessment is correct, that the enemy vessel was not only his last carrier for such weapons, but went down with his last stock of them. You may recall that the Ferlay-Birken message included descriptions of the Orion spacecraft, with key technical details. Thus we know how much fissionable material is tied up in them, and we can estimate an upper limit for what amount could have been scavenged. Surely all that the enemy could spare for warheads has now been expended. He will scarcely sacrifice spacecraft to get more. Not only does he lack reliable means of delivery, it would negate the whole purpose of his effort."

"Nobody can predict what a madman will do," Jovain said. "Whoever ordered that battleship out must have been insane, no?"

Rewi gave him a grim smile. "Insanity is a relative matter, sir. I can imagine demoniacal hatred behind the move, but in spite of the price, it's paid off handsomely."

"Indeed?"

"Consider. Bombing has become out of the question until we can build more carriers or else invade Laska in force and construct air bases there. Either would take the better part of a year, at least, even if we accept the foreign help we've been offered. Similarly for a massive landing on the peninsula. Meanwhile those people are free to carry on their work. They've lost their prototype, but I should think they'll need less time to produce a second one, especially since the first has proved out remarkably. It ought not to take very much longer than that to ready their entire space escadrille.

"Meanwhile, too, the blockade is ended. Worse than the losses sustained is the collapse of morale. The report sent me says that it's no use telling the crews that the nukes are all spent. An obsession about the atom is built into them, into our entire culture. Nothing now prevents the southern Territories from pouring reinforcements and supplies north, by sea as well as by land. We can't control those parts, aside from enclaves—not when a whole people has the taste of victory in its mouth.

"And what of reaction at home and abroad? This is not a popular war, you know. The report mentioned riots or demonstrations in a number of Maurai communities. Terror and, yes, a certain rebellious admiration for the sheer audacity of the foe. I suspect Ferlay and Birken have fired millions of imaginations; and *our* sworn objective is to dismantle those spacecraft. I wouldn't be surprised if Beneghal backs out of the negotiations about an alliance with us. I'll wager a year's pay that the Free Mericans in the Southwest do."

Rewi's look pierced them, one after the next, ending at Jovain. "In short," he said, "the odds at present are even or worse that the Norrmen will succeed in their undertaking, and a handful of irresponsible adventurers will come to dominate this planet. They may then encounter the kind of difficulties that you have, Captain, but our civilizations as we have known them will go under."

"Unless," Mattas said.

"Yes," Rewi replied. "We discussed this, you and I."

Comprehension crashed through Jovain. "Wait!" He heard his voice as a thin shriek. "Skyholm?"

"Yes, Your Dignity," the Maurai told him. "The aerostat is dirigible. We can take it over the Pole and station it above the enemy within a week. We don't need precise targeting information, when we have unlimited solar power. We can maintain laser fire for as long as need be—flame down his troops, burn out his support in the region, keep his mechanics and their works below ground, drill down into his caverns, until he surrenders."

"Almighty Deu," shivered from Lorens. He crossed himself again.

"Nothing could touch us," cried Yago, "nothing!"

"No, wait, wait," Jovain stammered. "Here at home . . . the Domain would be prey to my own enemies—"

"Is it not, as things are?" Rewi retorted.

"Iern could freely land in Franceterr. They'd swarm to him."

"What danger is a single unarmed spacecraft? You would return as a hero, sir, a conqueror, invincible. And . . . I think I can safely promise that the Maurai Federation will be beside the man who saved its world."

"Who saved Gaea," Mattas urged. "Saved Her from a second Judgment. Exacted justice for atrocities, not only committed against human beings but against Her own self."

Skyholm, rang in Jovain. *The most powerful single fortress and engine in existence. Its Captain the shaper of the next thousand years and more—if he shows the decisiveness that becomes a man—*

Glory mounted in him. He sprang to his feet. "I will!" Beneath the tumult he was aware of the sun-arrows he would be sending to kill and burn, kill and burn, he, a revengeful god.

5

Once more the Boot Heel roared.

Addressing a regathered assembly that day, Eygar Dreng had ended with a shout: "—We can win, and before God, we shall! If we've lost heavily, the enemy has lost more. He won't be back soon. Tomorrow we get busy again, and we're going to work like trolls. This night, though, we'll hold a celebration and a wake, a celebration of our victory and a wake for those brave men and women whose lives bought it for us. Drink your thanks to the memories of Mikli Karst, Bryun Scarp, everybody who died so the Wolf may run free. In their spirit, Orion shall rise!"

He was in the mess hall himself that evening, seated on a table as if it were a throne. His brawny hand gripped a glass of whiskey, his short legs kicked, and his voice rumbled through the racket. The chamber could hold only a fraction of the folk, especially counting militiamen off duty. Most spilled out into the halls, to pass their own bottles around, bellow forth song, stamp forth dances, embrace, often drop a few tears, then hoot defiance or laughter. Air was hot, smoke-blue, rank, but it could have been a winter wind that whipped them to life.

Tides of them struggled in and out the doorway, across the floor, around the bar. A scarecrow figure appeared in their midst. He had been able to move fast along the corridors, but here the crowd trapped him. Snarls lifted, curses resounded, fists threatened, while quietness spread in waves from the center as people turned to stare.

"—traitor, spy, tear 'm apart, string 'm up—"

"Belay that!" Eygar boomed. "Let him be." The growling and milling about were slow to die away. "Are you the Free Folk, or a rabble o' Mong city-serfs? What's happened can't be Plik's fault. Let him be, I say!"

The crowd moved from the Angleyman, pushing and shoving each other, until there was as much space as possible around him. Eygar beckoned. "Come on over, fellow," he called.

When the singer had done so, the director proffered the flask at his side. "Have a swig," he invited.

Plik tilted it at length. "Aaah!" he sighed. "God bless you, sir. I needed that enough to risk my bones in this place. You're most kind."

"I've enjoyed what I've heard of your stuff. And I don't imagine you bear any responsibility for what your, uh, your friends did."

Plik returned a steady look. "No, sir. However, they remain my friends."

"You've a right to your sympathies."

"Oh, but I have none, except for the innocents whom these vast causes have killed, mangled, bereaved, and for those whom they will."

"Well, do your job and watch your tongue," Eygar advised. "A lot of the boys are pretty touchy, after what we've suffered, and I can't spare you a bodyguard. Okay, proceed to the bar if you want."

Plik could not get away immediately through the human press. Thus he heard an officer who stood next to the chief say in anxious wise: "About the stolen spacecraft, sir. I do think we should discuss the hazard it poses."

"Okay, I'll finish what I was telling you, and then we'll get down to serious drinking," Eygar replied. "Tomorrow we can go over the details if you insist. Basically, I don't agree it is a danger. Ferlay broadcast that his intentions are peaceful, if not favoring us any longer. I believe him. And in fact, I hear from a couple of radar tracking posts that he's taken off for outer space."

"He'll return, sir. And *Orion Two* will still have atomic bombs in her drive racks."

"He can't drop them on us. Not unless the entire system is redesigned and rebuilt first, and who's going to do that for him? The Maurai? No; dead against their whole ethic. Besides, Ferlay and Birken left because the use of nukes in war disgusted them beyond endurance." Eygar bit his lip. "I can't say as how I blame them too much."

"Nevertheless—"

"Oh, I'm not relying on psychology alone. Ferlay *could* land in Federation territory without cracking up, maybe. The Maurai *could* be so desperate they'd convert his bombs into warheads and fly a special mission over us. Remember, though, those aren't high-yield units; they'd vaporize the ship if they were. If the total kilotonnage were put into a single weapon, and struck fairly close, it could take out one of our launch tubes, no more. They're reasonably well dispersed, remember, and damn well hardened. If the fissionable stuff were divided among a sufficient number, then each of them would have to strike precisely. The Maurai don't have information that exact . . . nor bombsights that good. Nobody's fought a real air war since the Doom. Today's technology for it is primitive.

"I credit them and Ferlay with the common sense to recognize all this."

"The ship herself is a potential weapon, sir," the officer argued.

"You mean her blast," Eygar said. "Yeh, theoretically Ferlay could stand her on her blast and torch out our sites, one after the other. It'd be a feat of piloting beyond belief, no matter what a crackerjack he is, especially when he has no copilot and just a single engineer. But it is a far-fetched theory. Well, simply to put minds like yours at ease, Jayko, I'm having the militia bring some rockets to this area."

"Nuclear?"

Eygar gestured forcibly. "No! I'm informed that we've shot our wad of those filthy things, and don't mind admitting I'm glad. These are small solid-fuel jobs with chemical warheads. They can get up to about ten klicks' altitude. The spaceship would have to hover closer than that if she was to inflict any real damage, and a single missile forward of the plates would bring her down."

His fist hit the table. Bottle and tumblers rattled. He took a hefty swallow of liquor. "Repeat, I don't expect any such attempt," he said. "Ferlay must know better. Besides, I suspect he loves that ship as much as I do. Maybe more, since he's had her out yonder, the lucky bastard. We are prepared against contingencies, Jayko. Therefore, God damn it, let me concentrate on this booze."

Plik edged his way out of earshot in the hubbub. Though he continued to draw hostile stares, nobody abused him further.

An arm linked with his. Glancing down, he spied Lisba Yamamura of the library staff. "Hi," she said, almost timidly.

"Why . . . hello." He was surprised. They had chance-met occasionally since their quarrel of several months ago, but a degree of coolness had prevailed between them. "How are you?"

"I'm not quite sure lately. You?"

Plik shrugged a little, smiled a little.

"If you're thirsty, which I bet you are, be warned you'll need half an hour at least to belly up to the bar," she told him. "Care for some of mine to tide you over?"

"Thank you." He accepted her glass and took a modest sip. "But how do I deserve it?"

She gave him a long look. "You must be very lonely these days," she said.

"Hm, well—"

"Nobody wants to hear your songs, do they? Have you composed any new ones? These events ought to've inspired you, whether or not you'd be wise to make it public."

From the hall came a sound of deep young voices. The melody spread and strengthened, bringing in man after man.

"Let a long-imprisoned thunder
Shake the mountains and the skies
While the stars behold a wonder
As we make Orion rise.
    Death to tyranny!
    Now the Wolf runs free!
    Defy the gods on high, for they shall die.
    And we're faring,
    And we're faring,
    And we're faring forth to liberty! Liberty! Liberty!"

Plik shook his head. His lips had gone pale. "No," he said. "I wouldn't try to compete with that."

"What?" Lisba asked. "Stirring tune, yes, but I don't think the words are anything special."

"They're doggerel," Plik replied, while the rest of the song overrode all else. "However, don't you see? I'm a poet of sorts, or claim to be. I invoke demons and afterward do my best to report what I saw. But this is the tongue of the demons themselves."

He disengaged his arm from hers. "I'm sorry," he said. "I've doubtless offended you again."

"No . . . not really. I sought you out because I did remember what you are and— Oh, I won't betray my Lodge or Orion, nothing like that, but it seems as if you might understand what's happening and help me understand—" Lisba took his hands and leaned close. "I've got a room in the bachelor women's section." She spoke fast. "A cubbyhole, but private, and there's a jug of wine. Come along. Please."

6

The storm ramped over western Uropa until about sunset. Faylis kept indoors (what else could a delicate woman do?) and heard wind scream, thunder roll, rain gallop on the roof and rush in the streets, gusts of hail like drum tattoos. When lightning flared, the cataracts down windowpanes gave it an evil flicker, as if something burned outside. The Aurillac mansion in Tournev was cold; sabotage had disabled the city power station that received from Skyholm. She could huddle near a tile stove, by the glow of lamps, but beyond lay sarcophagean darknesses. What few aged servants slippered around did not come to her unless she rang, talk to her unless she talked first, or give her other than rudimentary replies. She had no appetite and noticed only vaguely that her cook had been careless.

The wine cellar and liquor cabinet offered wares more attractive. Toward evening, as the weather diminished, she felt sufficiently eased, warmed, to carry a book to bed, a collection of favorite verses. They caused her to weep for all the sadness and terror walking the world, those poor people killed so awfully on the far side of it, poor Jovain, whose lifework was crumbling when he had scarcely begun it, her poor father, who must miss her terribly, poor Faylis, whose husband traipsed around the sky with a barbarian hussy and proclaimed his faithlessness to the whole human race. . . . Nevertheless, she had the largeness of spirit that might forgive him if he returned to her. . . . She slept ill, plagued by dreams.

She woke from one, panting and sweat-bedewed, before dawn. The windows were not dark, for light poured through brighter than any full moon, to cast whiteness and shadow across the rug. The air was cool, so quiet that she heard the old house creak as its joints settled. Her night candle guttered low.

She could not get back to sleep, nor lie alone for hours until the maid brought her chocolate. *I will look outdoors,* she decided. *Yes, why not take a walk?* Hesitation. *Those terrorists.* But they had done no worse to date than drub some soldiers and demolish some machinery. No man of the Domain would attack a woman out of political resentment. Nobody had done worse, really, than shun her and be distant, albeit correct, when conversation was unavoidable. *Outdoors. A glimpse of nature. The peace that is in Gaea.* She dressed quickly, in a plain gown and hooded cloak that would hide her identity from casual observers, lighted her way downstairs, unbolted the main entrance, and stepped through.

Stairs, pavement below, walls and roofs opposite, sheened beneath the enormous disc of Skyholm. Far-apart gas lamps were dimmed well-nigh to invisibility by that unreal brilliance, and she could find no stars above, merely a few snowy scraps of cloud. The street was deserted, save for a cat slinking by; it gave her a glance out of eyes turned opal. She went down to the sidewalk and started off. Her footfalls rattled in the silence. Her breath formed cloudlets of its own.

I think, yes, I will go as far as Riverside. She quickened her pace. The motion pumped the lingering nightmares out of her and raised a slight exhilaration. *My life is not ended. Hardship, injustice, lack of discernment in everybody, those have wounded me, but I will recover, I will achieve Oneness, and the right man may come courting.*

If not—

She emerged on an esplanade. Trees, balustrade, time-blurred statues reached hoar. Beyond them the Loi flowed ashimmer, and beyond it open ground, where farms and orchards nestled, rose toward the crest which the Consvatoire occupied. At this remove its spires were ivory miniatures, but beneath them dwelt the beauty, wisdom, and calm of centuries. The east was rosily brightening. A carillon began to ring from Scholars' Tower, the same welcome to the sun that had sounded for half a millennium. She could not tell whether she heard the distant music in her head or in her soul. *Yes,* she thought, *my true abiding place may well be there.*

She lifted her gaze toward Skyholm. For a few minutes yet it would reign alone, luminous and numinous. More lights than usual glittered across its face. And did not something move along the edges?

What? No, no, no!

The chimes stopped. Faylis stood screaming, and a hidden part of her wondered if she would ever stop screaming, as Skyholm slowly drifted north, then faster and faster until it had dwindled out of her sight and heaven was left inhuman.

XXV

Orion Two rounded the moon and Earth rose before her. The sun now at their backs, Iern and Ronica saw their planet as a white-marbled sapphire amulet, only a little worn away by night. Its radiance dazzled stars out of vision, though elsewhere the galaxy made a frosted highway through their brilliance.

The ashen craterscape fell away aft and beneath. Daylit harshness became shadow and mystery. Where eventide dusk was clear, men at home beheld the old moon in the new moon's arms.

Ronica and Iern floated behind the pilot window. Tears glimmered in her eyes. "Each time that sight is lovelier," she breathed.

He nodded, himself struck dumb by it.

"Here I see what before I only understood," she said into the hush that filled the ship. "The Gaeans are right about the wholeness of life, the aliveness of Earth. How alone it is, and how infinitely precious. We *can't* let Earth be killed. There is nothing else."

He found an awkward voice: "Well, someday, habitats in space, maybe even worlds beyond the Solar System."

"I hope for that, of course. But this will always be our mother."

Catan, Rosenn, he thought in a stab of pain. *How do you fare?*

"Not that the moon isn't marvelous, in its gaunt fashion," Ronica went on. "I want to come back, and make a landing . . . in the Sea of Tranquillity, I think, to pay my respects to whatever is left from the *Eagle.*"

"Would you really consider that worth another crossing?"

"Why, this one's been magnificent—"

"For me, yes, when I could take a rare moment of leisure."

"And me. Chores, cramped quarters, smelly air, indifferent rations, sanitation woes, all the drawbacks of weightlessness—wonderful anyhow. Besides, we've gotten things fairly well licked into shape, haven't we? And the hang of working in orbit. The return leg ought to be a lot easier."

"Right. We'll probably need a small course correction or two, but otherwise I expect three holidays for us. Except for deciding what we'll do when we arrive, where we'll go."

"Have you had any further thoughts on that?"

"I'm afraid not. A place which won't treat us as criminals, and won't confiscate this vessel. Meyco? Okkaido?"

"Too vulnerable to Maurai pressure, as I told you before. How about my suggestion of a backward region, well inland?"

"I considered that," Iern said reluctantly, "but the more I come to know these controls, the more certain I am we can't land without adequate ground facilities. A full crew might conceivably set down on an Asian steppe or an African savannah, though *I* wouldn't care to risk it and I'm a moderately reckless sort. We can't by any manner of means. A single pilot won't have sufficient data input, nor could I by myself direct you, fast and accurately enough, how to operate the engines—which are badly undermanned too. When we hit atmosphere, I'll mainly have to make snap guesses about most of the parameters, including the most important ones; and as an aircraft, rather than a spacecraft, this thing is a pretty good brick. We'll be doing well—better than well—to make a safe landing on the best, and best-monitored, airfield in the world."

Ronica sighed. "Uh-huh. Say, don't look so down in the mouth, or I'll spin myself around and make you seem like smiling. At worst, we turn ourselves in to the Maurai. They should treat us fine, seeing what we've done for them, and from what I've heard, Oceania is not a bad place to live. Maybe eventually we can talk them into reconstructing Orion for themselves. Or—who knows?—maybe when we reach Earth, establish proper radio contact, and get some news, we'll learn of a country that'll welcome us on our terms."

"Maybe. More likely, bioscience will have developed a giant moth that can fly between planets." Iern jerked. His fingernails whitened on the seatback to which he held himself moored.

Ronica reached for him. "Hey, sweetheart! Trouble?"

He wrenched the words out, while he stared before him and did not really see Earth. "Yes. Earlier I was too exhausted, or else too busy, or else too caught up in this experience . . . for the fact to sink in . . . that we can very easily crash, or burn on our way down . . . and you be killed."

"Aw-w." She rumpled his hair. "Come off that Francey chivalry, will you? I knew what I was doing, and never for a wingbeat wanted anything else. No, of course I'm not anxious for us to die, not before we're too old and decrepit to screw, but this way, if it happens, we'll go out fast—crack!—and together. And we've had better lives by several light-years, both of us, than most of the human race ever imagined. Don't you dare feel sorry for me."

"Well—" He kissed her. They lost their holds and drifted off, embraced. "You're the greatest wonder the universe has, Ronica, you."

By Earthlight, as it flooded the darkened cabin, he saw her eyelids droop, nostrils flare, lips grow fuller. "In that case," she proposed from down in her throat, "let's go to the cargo section, where there's more room. I've figured a way around the problems in making love in free fall."

2

For eight hundred years, Skyholm had simply maintained station against stratospheric winds, save for the briefest of test cruises after a major engine replacement; and none of those had occurred in living memory. Its voyage across the ice-crown of the planet became an epic of daring, ingenuity, and will.

Jovain encountered little of that himself, except as tales told him by men who trembled and whose words dragged in weariness. He knew that inexperienced Aimay Roverto Awilar had lost footing in an unexpected gust, while on a team changing a blown-out skin panel, and gotten his parachute lines fatally ensnarled; that inexperienced Katarina Papetoai, returning from a reconnaissance, had missed her landing on the flange, been caught in turbulence, and blasted into unconsciousness and a lethal tailspin when her small jetplane passed under the hot-air vent; that others had promptly volunteered; that engineers, electronicians, work gangs frantically made repairs on systems stressed beyond design limits, as pilots contended with forces that were huge upon a thing of this size, navigators peered and hunched over inadequate charts and muttered profanely to themselves, preachers preached but a few determinedly lighthearted amateur entertainers did more to keep morale high— He heard of these things, and for his part issued commendations and honors, but nothing was entirely real; he was lost in the passage itself.

The continent, the Channel, Angleylann amazingly verdant, Scotalann still bleak, a sea wild and murky when it was not wild and green, rocks heaving gray-blue around fjords and then the inland glacier that seemed to have no end until storms drowned the sight, unseasonable stars and shuddery auroras after dark, and always, always, the purpose before him, the thing he must do: while Skyholm lumbered on toward his destiny.

The time came at last when it halted.

"General checkout," he ordered. "Combat teams to their stations, three-watch schedule." He felt no exultation. He was inexorable but tired, and Laska had cloaked itself against him. Nothing but clouds showed beneath Skyholm, from rim to rim of the world. The navigators could tell him no more than that he was approximately above his goal, plus or minus fifty kilometers. The sun stood wan in blue-black heaven.

No importance. The roiling whiteness below must break for a spell and he could get a fix on the target area. Meanwhile, always, he poised invulnerable and omnipotent. The subarctic day at this time of year was equal to any on the planet, and it would lengthen beyond aught the Domain summer knew, until he had power to maintain bombardment almost the whole twenty-four hours. He did not expect he need be here nearly that long. Well before solstice, he could have laid the region waste in the course of a methodical raking that must eventually find and annihilate all of Orion. The enemy ought to surrender much sooner than that.

He sought the central control compartment. Mattas accompanied him. Rewi Seraio was already present, to represent his government, on whose side Skyholm had gone to war. The three of them stood at the center of a circular chamber ringed in by instrumented panels where technicians sat alert. Screens presented images of the world, downward, sideward, spaceward. A hum and a faint ozone smell pervaded the atmosphere. The deck vibrated very slightly underfoot.

"You may proceed when ready." Jovain's words felt enormous in his skull.

Bolts flared, more lurid than lightning, as the outraged air rushed back and discharged.

A boss technician removed his earphones and swiveled his chair around. "Operation satisfactory, sir," he reported, "and radar ionoscopy shows adequate power delivered to the ground."

"Good," said Jovain. "Stand by." He departed from the uncanny squiggles on the oscilloscope screen, to the familiarity of his office, and wished Mattas and Rewi did not follow him. *Why did they come to that room? Curiosity? A need somehow to participate? An exorcism of fear? Why did I?*

Arrived, he ordered a radio call to ground and an intercom patch-in for himself when the Orion chief was on the line. Thereafter he stared across his desk, the desk from High Midi, at the others. "Well," he said. His skin prickled and felt cold. He noticed wet patches under the sleeves of his uniform. *Faylis,* he thought, but she was infinitely remote.

The resolve abided that had launched him on this enterprise. *It's for her, mankind, Gaea, my fame (no, I'm not supposed to think about that), sanity, righteousness. In this terrible hour, we must ourselves be terrible.* "Well," he repeated.

"Would you like me to deliver the ultimatum?" Rewi offered.

"No," Jovain said. "Thank you, but—no, I am the Captain. Of course, if you should want to add something—"

"I told you earlier, sir, that could give a false impression of indecisiveness and prolong matters," the Maurai answered imperturbably. "I trust you'll not falter."

"It won't be easy," Mattas said. His beard waggled as he talked. A scrap of bacon was caught in the grizzled shag. "You may have to conduct massive destruction. Remember always, it's surgery. Gaea will heal."

And we'll go back to our customary lives? Jovain thought. *No, Gaea never raises the dead. She brings forth new lives. How sinister did the mammals seem to the dinosaurs?*

The intercom buzzed. He stabbed its accept button. A woman's voice spoke accented Angley: "Your Dignity, please hear Eygar Dreng, director of Orion for the Wolf Lodge of the Northwest Union. Dr. Dreng, you address the Captain of Skyholm, Talence Jovain Aurillac."

Mattas and Rewi showed the same tenseness that Jovain felt in his belly. His chest muscles hurt. *Not Gaean, not Gaean. Relax, like a tiger.*

A hoarse masculine tone: "Hello, Skyholm, hello."

"Greeting, sir," Jovain said, and waited for the interpreter.

"This is Dreng," he heard in Angley about as good as the underling's. "Proceed, if you please."

Jovain recovered from his surprise. After all, the master of Orion could not be an ignoramus. A substantial literature on aerodynamics and related sciences existed in the Domain, and since the Enric Restoration, copies had gone abroad. Dreng had doubtless wanted to read the originals; if he had an ear for languages, he could have acquired a conversational knowledge with slight extra effort, for Angley and Unglish were close kin; maybe he had kept in practice by periodic talks with that woman, secretary or research librarian or whatever she was—Jovain snapped off his speculation. His business was too deadly serious.

"I am the Captain," he said. "Do you, eh, do you understand what the situation is? We were broadcasting announcements of our intentions, appeals to your reason, on every usual band while we approached. But we got no answer."

"You did not rate an answer, as long as we could hope your balloon would puncture and go down in the drink."

Anger flared cleansing through Jovain. "Well, it did not!"

"So?"

Jovain wrestled for self-possession. "Hear this. The aerostat is positioned above you. Its accumulators are fully charged and indefinitely rechargeable. Any aircraft or missiles you may send against us —not that I believe you have any with the capability—will be blasted out of existence. Our lasers will ruin your project, your entire goal in this senseless war. I beg you, surrender before it is too late. Your own government has disowned you. I have a representative of the Maurai at my elbow, ready to help negotiate reasonable terms."

"Sure," Eygar Dreng said contemptuously. "The trouble is, your idea of 'reasonable' and ours have nothing to do with each other. Look, we here have considered this, the bunch of us, since your first message came in. We're agreed, we'll take our chances. We'll keep the same channel open for communication, and you might do well not to sizzle our transmitter out. Don't you realize you're laying your entire civilization on the line?"

Mattas pulled his hips from his chair arms as he rose. The seat clattered to the deck behind him. "How much harm will you make us wreak on Gaea?" he bawled.

"Fuck you," Eygar Dreng said. *Click.* The intercom went dead.

"Punish them," Mattas said thick-tongued, while his fists punched about, "punish them, punish them."

3

An unseen sun loosed wrath upon the land.

Clouds and rain could not stop such bolts. They seared their way through; water turned to live steam, so that vapor trailed after every flash; thunder banged; electric sparks and streamers rushed eerie blue; the wind was troubled in its course, it eddied about and whined.

Where a beam smote, trees exploded and their fragments burst aflame. Herbage vanished at the center, became charred in broad rings about such a patch of baked earth. Rocks glowed red. The beasts and men that took direct hits were lucky, for they perished too fast to know it. Those on the fringes were cooked alive, or took a superheated breath and felt their lungs shrivel. At larger distances, any that chanced to be looking in the direction of a ray were blinded —and the rays went everywhere.

Some were winks, that did their havoc and then, recreated, struck nearby. Some lasted for a minute or more. They did not hold steady, for there was no sense in drilling at a target the gunners could not see. Instead, they walked around on the mountains, down into the valleys, up across snows that gave way in avalanches. As the hours passed, square kilometers of wilderness turned into blackened, smoking, steaming, flood-riven desolation, save in random spots where things that had been animals might still writhe and scream.

Toward evening the rain ended and the sky began to open. Men who had been elsewhere, who had glimpsed the fury from behind shielding ranges, and by cowering had saved their sight, now saw a foreign moon above them in dusky heaven. So huge was it that it seemed to be falling down upon them, and that was when many lost their last wits, cast their weapons away, and ran haphazardly, howling. Its sunset-ruddy light made the stormclouds around it glow, as if with inner fires that would soon break forth.

Pickets on the heights, who had taken shelter during the onslaught, used the luminance to observe that which had been done. They put portable transceivers to their lips, and radio waves swept to and fro through a dusk grown hideously quiet. The men huddled into their parkas against deepening cold. The invader moon faded as the sun dropped farther below the horizon, but they saw how the circle of it blotted out stars, and knew they would see it again, coldly ashine, ready to kill the rest of them.

Eygar Dreng sat in his office, as alone as ever a man could be. It was a homely, cluttered room, mostly full of overloaded bookshelves and file cabinets, communications and computer equipment, a few such souvenirs as a kayak paddle from the racing championship he had held in his youth. Upon his battered old desk were two pictures, one of his family, one out of ancient archives, a Voyager view of Saturn. The ventilators whispered.

He held a radiophone to his ear. Colonel Rogg's voice, relayed from the field, sounded faint and thin, as if a ghost spoke: "No, sir, we have no hope whatsoever. I thought we might, but the enemy has demonstrated his capabilities—and he was, in effect, shooting blind. Tomorrow looks like clearing weather. A technology like his must include optics that can pick out individuals on the ground. Sir, I am responsible for my men. Today I've seen too many of them—well, we've a hospital tent here at base, you know, and the rescue and medic teams have been absolutely heroic, but— No, sir, tomorrow we withdraw."

"You realize that leaves Orion open to ground attack, as soon as the Maurai can muster more troops," Eygar said. His own voice dragged, as did every muscle and bone in his body. "No replacements for you, when the aerostat interdicts every approach."

"They wouldn't come anyway, would they, to certain death—and for what? Sir, we're licked. Our duty is to salvage what we can."

"You suppose the Yurrupans will let you evacuate."

"That's for you to arrange, sir. You have a line to them, don't you? I . . . I assume they wouldn't hunt us just for fun. Whatever happens, we're leaving. Surely you'll help save lives."

"I'll do my best."

"I'm sorry, sir," the colonel said. "Myself, I'd be glad to die leading a charge against them. But they're up in the sky."

"I understand," Eygar told him gently. "Commence what preparations you're able. I'll be in touch again before . . . before sunrise."

After a few technical details, he set the phone down and punched his intercom. "Get me Skyholm, Nona," he instructed dully.

The answer sounded appalled: "Not to surrender? Already?"

"No, not yet, I guess. But I do have to parley." Eygar sat back and waited. Once he smiled at the image of his wife, children, son-in-law, grandchild; once he touched the Saturn picture.

The phone rang. He fitted himself to it. Preliminaries babbled. Then:

"Captain Jovain speaking. Dr. Dreng? I trust you want to talk reason. Believe me, we have not enjoyed doing what you forced us to do."

"I wonder— No, pardon me. This has been a shock."

An oddly sympathetic tone: "I know. Please say what you wish."

"I suppose you learned, from your Maurai allies, approximately where our militiamen are, and selected an occupied area for a demonstration, as closely as you were able given the weather."

"Yes, we did. I warn you, my meteorologists tell me that tomorrow it will clear."

"Uh-huh. Okay, Captain, the militia have had enough. If you permit, they'll leave in the morning."

"Splendid! I *am* happy. Naturally, in common humanity, we will permit. But let me give you another warning. We will monitor, and consider any evidence of bad faith to be an intolerable provocation."

"Oh, sure, sure." Discussion turned to routes and schedules. The Norrmen would meet at Tyonek, and Maurai ships would be on hand to transport them away, probably to Seattle. The march and embarkation would take several days.

"Meanwhile—" Joy belled through Jovain's words. "About your installation. I suggest you bring your personnel to the same pickup point, for the same conveyance home. The Maurai will require guides and the like, of course, on their way to the site."

Eygar grinned lopsidedly. "Oh, no, Captain," he said. "That was not on the agenda. We stay."

"What?" Jovain yelped. He recovered equilibrium. "Your position is hopeless. I repeat, Skyholm will fight until you surrender or are destroyed. You are already outlaws, yes, in the proclamation of your own government. Do the decent thing, give up, spare lives, and amnesty should be possible for most of your group."

" 'Outlaw' bears a rather special meaning in this country," Eygar said. In the recital of a tradition there was strength. "We don't hold with locking human beings in cages or turning them over to professional killers. An outlaw is a person who's forfeited his right to redress for anything anyone may do to him. It's about as effective a deterrent to crime as I know of, and less expensive than the rest. But declaring a man outlaw is the gravest business we can undertake, a lengthy process with every safeguard our forefathers could devise, much too important to trust to a government. Besides, at present the Northwest Union has no government. We don't count those miserable puppets of the Maurai."

"Don't preach anarchism to me!" Jovain rasped. "The world has seen, in the Rocky Mountains and the Gulf of Laska, the world has seen what that leads to. The time is ripe for ending it."

"Ah, so." Eygar laid hand around jaw. "In other words, you'll not be content with dismantling Orion."

"Certainly not, after the lessons of the past several decades. The Northwest Union will be made into a civilized nation. The criminals who built and used forbidden weapons will be brought to justice.

. . . Ah, I myself take for granted you were not a party to that, Dr. Dreng. Conduct yourself properly and I think a later investigation will clear you. I see no reason to penalize individuals who were simply misguided."

"Have you discussed these policies with the Maurai Federation?"

"Only en passant. But I think their general intent is obvious. They do not propose to have a war every twenty years! And my government intends to participate in the peace conference."

"You've got the power to insist on that."

"Yes." Triumph: "Therefore, shall we arrange an armistice?"

"No," said Eygar Dreng. "Orion hasn't quit yet."

"You're insane!" yelled the voice at his ear.

"Stubborn, yes. Insane, no. We're well provisioned, heavily armored, and you don't know exactly where to aim your shots at us. You'll need weeks or months to reduce us, or the Maurai to ferry soldiers north. Meanwhile, anything could happen. I've read a fair amount of military history, Captain. Now and then it's paid off for a garrison to hold out till the bitter end. But I hope you'll allow our militia to go. That you won't try using them to blackmail us."

"Oh, yes, oh, yes. World opinion—" Jovain breathed heavily. "Do you imagine I'll retreat? If I keep station till the Maurai troops come, my Domain will have disintegrated beyond retrieval. If I probe randomly for your launch sites, I will inflict dreadful harm on Gaea. Do you see me caught between those two horns?"

Eygar said nothing.

"I will do whatever is necessary to crush your misbegotten society," Jovain said. "And I have a third possibility open to me. Where I am, I command an enormous area, land inhabited by your people, waters plied by their ships. Furthermore, Skyholm is movable; it came to you, didn't it? I can punish your whole nation until it rises and marches against you itself. Not its nature but its artifacts, cities, villages, farms, roads, mines, everything men have built, with surgical precision.

"Across the Inlet from you is another peninsula, settled, prosperous-looking. Dreng, I tell you most solemnly, if you have not yielded by tomorrow noon when the cloud cover will be gone, by tomorrow night that will all lie a desert. Which will be the merest beginning."

Eygar shook his head as if clubbed. "And you condemn us for using a few nukes," he said.

"Enough!" Jovain shrilled. "I'll hear no more. You shall *not* desecrate Gaea—" For a space, his breathing shuddered, until he could finish flatly: "You are overwrought, Dr. Dreng. Let's adjourn this. Think it over. Ask your personnel how they feel. Then—well, before noon I shall expect to hear from you. Do you follow me? Very well, goodnight."

Click.

Eygar Dreng sat long by himself, staring into emptiness.

"I suppose I should go," Plik said. "Even for me, it's grown late."

Lisba held him close. Her look flew around the cubicle that was hers, walls where a few pictures hung garish, cot, chair, dresser, clothes rack, tiny desk doubling as a washstand. The caverns mumbled around her.

"No, please, don't," she begged. "You can have the bed. I'll throw my sleeping bag on the floor for a mattress."

He stroked her hair. "I would never allow that," he said, "a lifelong gynolater like me. What on—what inside Earth prompted you? I admit this evening has been not only consoling but delightful, like its predecessors, for me at any rate. Nevertheless, your offer is the most undeserved honor that has yet come my way."

She clung. "You're company. Those ghastly rumors, that thing in the sky, a general assembly after breakfast tomorrow— Do *you* want to lie awake alone?"

He flinched. "No. But you . . . you could easily invite someone who's more handsome, less alcoholic, and not wistful about a barmaid afar in Uropa. Why me?"

"You, you sing songs, merry or crazy but songs, and you make a weird kind of sense out of everything—"

"My dear," he sighed, "I am no prophet. Nothing is pledged us. Ofttimes the exiled Prince has returned too late, or merely to die. And at best, I tell you naught for your comfort. I feel the whole world dying, to be reborn in a shape altogether strange—and birth hurts worse than death, remember."

"I still want you here."

"Well, well," he said unsteadily. "If otherwise useless old Plik can share a little warmth. . . . Whatever happens, Sesi—Lisba, yonder gloriously rumpled cot shall be yours tonight. But let us try if we cannot both sleep there, together." He held her in his left arm while his right reached for the bottle.

XXVI

"Oh, no, no," Ronica moaned. "They can't. You mustn't."

Eygar Dreng's voice crawled out of the receiver: "We must. At least, we will. The vote was overwhelming to fight on. Maybe Jovain is bluffing. It's not been the way of the Domain to make war on noncombatants, has it? Or if he isn't—well, we hope the Free Folk will stand fast against him till we can raise Orion. We've warned them on the Kenai Peninsula to evacuate their homes, in case."

"But if they lose everything they have— Oh, I suppose the Maurai will send ships for them, but they'll be destitute and— You can't spend their hopes like, like money . . . for your own ends. You're being a government!"

Bitterness lashed back: "Don't you tell me what to do. We wouldn't be in this fix if you hadn't betrayed us."

Ronica shrank into her seat and covered her face. From his pilot's chair beside her, Iern heard breath raw in her mouth.

He gazed outward. The spacecraft was positioned to give a forward view of the planet she orbited at a height of some hundred and fifty kilometers. Beneath a sun close to noontide, Earth filled well-nigh half his vision. Directly before him, a cloud deck was falling from sight as he moved. Rifts in its whiteness revealed sea turquoisely aglimmer and land brown, ruddy, freshly green. Even as he watched, the gaps widened. Northward, skies were clear. He could see across forests and meadows of the Yukon basin and a silver vein which was the river, on to snowpeaks athwart an azure deepening to starful blackness.

Over the clouds hung a sphere of duller hue. At this remove it showed as a disc, about half the size of a full moon. Here and there, metal flung back light in fierce little sparks.

"Calling Skyholm, calling Skyholm," Iern croaked into his own transmitter. "Jovain, come in, answer me. You can't do this thing. For the honor of the Aerogens—by the anims of the Ancestors—"

Surely they heard him in the rover globe. He was using a band to which a main receiver was always tuned. The Maurai high command, in response to his earlier call, had agreed to link him to its worldwide radio relay network while he circled. Its agents were listening in, of course, but so should the Captain have been, while Ronica called her old chief. But Jovain did not reply, he did not reply.

Orion Two swung north, on a near-polar track that would also take her above N'Zealann and, as Earth rotated, Franceterr. Soon the aerostat hunched above the rim, a shrunken, malignant lunar crescent. It dropped beneath. The ship hurried on toward night.

Ronica wept. Tears escaped from her fingers and bobbed about in microgravity. Rays of the lowering sun splintered into diamond shards against them. Iern's own, unshed, thickened in his throat.

"That is no bluff," he said heavily. "I don't know Jovain well, but I do understand him—the whole Clan spirit—enough to realize how totally he is committed. One does not make a threat without meaning it. And then, I think, the personal element. He scorned to speak to me as part of his revenge. When I see him release his laser beams, that will be another part of it."

"Merciful Yasu," she, an unbeliever, implored.

"The Wolves should surrender, and pick up their lives as best they can. What future has a corpse? But they seem to be fanatics, no saner than their enemies."

She lifted her head. "Don't say that!" she exploded at him. "They are of the Free Folk!" She slumped. "I belonged to them once."

He gripped her shoulder. "You still do, darling. Dreng was . . . unjust . . . as hurt as he's been." Sickly: "We did what we thought was right, in a swamp of lies and treacheries. It would have sucked everything down regardless."

She stiffened and shivered beneath his hand. "But, yes, they are my people, they are," she grieved. "And all that was theirs will go down in wreck, and they will go into slavery."

Exaggerated, he thought. *Subjection, not slavery; and the Maurai will be gentle masters.*

Masters nonetheless.

Plik.

Now why should I remember Plik, out beyond his heaven?

That night in Seattle. "In this rainy land I have seen the old Merican spirit rising huge from where it lay centuries buried, and the foundations of the world are atremble—" Yes, that is why my beloved mourns, the true reason, for the soul that her people will lose.

Her people who yearned for the stars.

It cracked through his head: *What soul remains to Skyholm?* The darkness into which he was entering flooded him; he hung alone in it and could not breathe.

Ronica caught at his arm. He saw her countenance close to his, anguish thrust away by love and concern, and heard, "Darling, Iern, what's wrong? Are you okay?"

"I—yes—" He struggled for self-command. "Yes, I just had a, a rather frightful idea."

She braced herself. "What?"

He looked from her, gathering resolve. Never would he have a task more cruel than the speaking of his mind, here in this quietly hurtling heaven-farer. The Arctic Ocean sheened vast, wrinkled, white-swirled. Icebergs and a northern cloudbank flung light back over the waves; the blueness within them was like swords unsheathed.

Finally he said, his eyes aimed past her, his tone level: "We may be able to save them. Your kin and even, perhaps, Orion. For your sake."

Air whistled in between her teeth.

"Of course, we may well fail," he added. "And whichever way that goes, if we make the attempt we will probably die."

2

"Your Dignity," said the voice of Ashcroft Lorens Mayn, "the hour is past noon, your ultimatum has expired, and the weather is currently favorable. We can commence bombardment anytime."

"Prepare," Jovain replied, "but hold fire until I reach the central control compartment."

He switched off the intercom and sagged at his desk. *Why?* he wondered. *My presence isn't necessary. I could stay where I am, issue my orders, and not witness what happens.*

I must, he knew. *I need the torture. I believed I kept silence before Iern to make him writhe, but no, it was because I dared not respond.*

Silence closed in on him, save for the endless susurrations of his stronghold. He imagined words in them, which he was glad he couldn't quite hear. He rose in haste. His calves slammed against the chair bottom. *No more dithering!* he instructed himself. *Do what you have decided and go on to your destiny.*

For a minute, though, he lingered in his office. His glance searched among the relics, passed over the Declaration, reached the portrait of Charles, and saw how after all the centuries it had no face. He turned and walked out with long strides.

Through the hollownesses and among the ribs he passed, to the chamber of controls, instruments, and images. The foreign technicians poised at their panels. The atmosphere seemed charged and cold. Faylis' brother was absent, overseeing his Guardsmen, but Mattas, Rewi, and Yago were present, for reasons Jovain suspected were obscure to themselves. Maurai and Espaynian gave him the salute due from their rank to his. Mattas brooded over a screen. It showed a milky edge of cloud and, below, ranges, valleys, shoreline, channel, a smudge that was Kenai.

"Start by flaming the town," the ucheny said. "Next give them a respite, a chance to agree we are in earnest, before we hit the villages and farmsteads."

Irrational anger stirred in Jovain. *Who is the Captain? Who gives orders here?* Terror: *Nobody?*

He suppressed it, but could not refrain from: "Suppose they hold out after that second stage, what should the third be?"

Mattas lowered at him. "Before we go elsewhere, we burn the entire hinterland, as we did that valley across the Inlet yesterday. Give them an object lesson right next door."

"Gaea—"

"We *are* Gaea."

Jovain ran tongue across lips. They were dry, cracked. "Very well," he said to the boss technician. "Bring your units to bear, and fire when ready."

Brilliance hunted the sun out of sight. The Wolf Lodge hall burst asunder and collapsed in a pyre. House after house kindled along streets where wooden blocks turned to coals and asphalt bubbled. Smoke off the docks blew thick, swart, pungent as its blazing tar. Boats lay aflame at their moorages. Water steamed around them. The roar of conflagration rolled back from mountainsides.

The attack ceased. Inhabitants beheld, afar, their dwellings a pillar of blackness above a crimson tarantella. Some of them sobbed, some cursed, most stood mute in the wet grass while their children keened, a few tried to keep alive patients carried from the hospital.

There was silence in heaven about the space of half an hour. Then the bolts struck again, again, again, from end to end of that land.

In the computation cabin, Iern leaned back from his terminal and flexed stiffened fingers. Ronica, at hers, had finished before him. "Done," he said. She nodded and pressed the final keys. Numbers and graphic displays flashed onto screens. Printout clacked.

Iern studied the results and turned toward her. "Everything checks," he said. "We do it on our second pass from now. First, of course, I have to modify our orbit, but not immediately."

She smiled the least bit. "Good," she answered. "We'll have that much time for our own."

He unbuckled to seek her. She met him midway. They floated together between machines, hands joined. She had not braided her hair today but simply tucked it down the back of her coverall. The motion pulled it loose and it streamed from her headband, awave in the ventilator breeze like a field of ripening wheat. Her eyes were sea-green, her skin earth-tawny, and she smelled of sunlight.

"Oh, Deu, this is wrong," he said. "That you should go."

"We've been over the same ground before," she replied. "If I go, it'll be along with you, and who says it has to happen, anyway? A pilot of your caliber—"

"But under those conditions? And . . . and my own feelings about it. I'm not certain but what I'll fail at the reentry itself—"

Once more tears broke from her to make tiny planets, but they were few and they were for him. "I do see, my most beloved. Come."

She led him to the cargo space, and there she comforted him, only held him, comforted him, gave him of her strength.

3

Mountains reared blue, gray, agleam with snows and glaciers; haze blurred their mightiness, but they were bones of the planet, they would endure. Below them, dark-green forest yielded, westward, to openness and lighter hues of growth, until the peninsula met the firth. Beyond that troubled glimmer uprose further heights. A rainstorm was approaching from the south. Its murk loomed over the sun, so that dimness had fallen upon the earth. Wind whistled chill in its vanguard, soughed through trees, strewed flame off burning Kenai and tattered the smoke of farmsteads. It fanned the blaze which gnawed at a stretch of woods, but the quenching rain followed on its heels.

In such a half-light, Skyholm stood pale and gigantic. Tricked by the weather, it no longer sent its bolts probing slowly and carefully, but sought to wreak every harm it was able. No buildings were left to ravage. The energy stabbed in arcs outward from the townsite. Perhaps the gunners were not searching for humans, perhaps their vision was mist-blurred. Surely, though, they cared little where anyone might be underneath them. Their intent was to bring down, speedily and forever, that nation which had rekindled the torch of the Judgment.

The Kenai folk fled east on galloping horses, in wildly jouncing wagons, or running their hearts out afoot. Many a one who rode carried an infant thrust upward by a mother. None could find shelter before the lasers overtook.

Light flared on high.

Those who cast a glance thither saw a wink and a wink, star-small but sun-bright. Afterimages wavered before them. Brilliance echoed from cloudbanks.

"What in Nan's deepest hell?" exclaimed Rewi.

"An electronic spasm of some kind, that flash," suggested the head technician.

"In every screen?" Jovain scoffed. *The wakened anger of Gaea,* flitted through him. *No! That is us.*

The glare returned. Overloaded systems blanked out.

As images wavered back onto them, the meteor appeared. Its fieriness waxed. Mattas screamed, flopped, groveled.

"Hold fast!" Jovain shouted.

An instant afterward, he knew what this was. *Faylis, Faylis.* The noise struck him. It turned his skull into a bell, which roared as hot as the meteor. The deck pitched underfoot. He toppled and rolled. He struck against something that did not yield, but gouged and hammered. Stunned, barely aware, he felt how everything fell, down and down forever.

The immensity swelled before Iern. It grew until it was like the whole Earth he had been orbiting. No, the moon, for it did not live.

Nor did it have heights, plains, rilles, craters, mysteries. Behind its spiderweb ribs, it was only a horrible facelessness. Yet that was Skyholm, Skyholm.

He did not truly ken it, save in a remote sanctuary for those who mourn. The all of him was too engaged. *Orion* did not merely, blindly follow a trajectory. Too much had been unknown for such aiming. The aerodynamic controls were under his hands and he must use them, by guess, instinct, will; he himself must be the hurricane.

Push the stick, twist the wheel, flip the toggle, punch the button. Needles jittered across dials, computer displays snaked and trembled. Did he need another bomb to correct his path? No. The stratosphere shrieked. The hull shook and groaned. Heat went over him, a tidal wave. And still his target widened in sight.

It filled his vision and his being. There was naught else. *Now.*

Strange how slight the shock was, when *Orion* speared through the heart of Skyholm.

Nonetheless it threw the ship out of control. Iern's blood surged to the spin. He saw Earth below him, awhirl. It sprang toward hugeness, as his prey had done before it died. Snowpeaks reached upward; or he might find his peace beneath yonder sea. The thickening air smashed at him. Its incandescence began to lay a hood across his eyes. His fingers flew, sending their word to motors, wings, and Ronica, where she crouched at the power board. But he could not regain command and he did not care, he, slayer of his heritage.

Thunder crashed.

It rolled from horizon to horizon, zenith to nadir and back again. Mountains took it up, cliff to crag. Birds staggered in flight. A fireball crossed the sky and vanished behind the Arctic Pole.

In its wake, Skyholm fell. Rags of fabric peeled off, tore loose, fluttered away on the thin winds high above. Sunlight rippled along them. The skeleton tumbled, over and over. When it reached the lower distances, it broke apart. Pieces flew in a hundred different shapes, a grotesque hail. Where they struck water, geysers fountained; where they struck soil, impact quivered through its mass; where they struck rock, it rang.

Stillness descended, until the rain arrived.

Ronica's voice on the intercom fought its way across tumult: "We did it, huh, Iern? Goodbye. I love you. Thank you for loving me."

If we—our children—I wish— No, I will not *surrender her!*

Within the Stormrider lifted a resolve to do what he had believed was impossible. He never knew how it happened. He did not really come back to himself until he had made *Orion* rebound off dense layers, in leaps that took her halfway around the world, had climbed on a fresh nuclear blast, regained orbit, and circled at rest.

In the hush that followed, he could weep.

XXVII

"Where we are, it's like seeing Earth reborn," said the man from space. "Utterly beautiful, peaceful, as if it would bear fruit that was never sown. . . ."

"We're at sunrise again," said the woman. "Wings of light over tall clouds; they make me remember an eagle that flew by a waterfall once in an upland wilderness. . . ."

Radio relays afloat and ashore bore their words across the globe.

"Hear us," Iern pleaded. "We've had time to think, these past days while we soared around and around our planet, everybody's planet. I suppose you have likewise. What reports we've caught tell of battle at a halt, and now of a truce called, while Maurai and Norrmen together brought help to Kenai and the homebound soldiers. That much compassion and common sense give hope for more. But you've not watched from beyond, as my lady and I have. You've not been out where Earth *is* one, alone among the stars. Listen to us who are there."

"Oh, we don't expect we'll convert anybody," Ronica joined in. "What we want to do is call for thought, and for the courage to make a new beginning.

"You've got to, you know. It's either that or go under. The old order of things is no more, it lies dead where brother slew brother.

"Maurai Federation, Northwest Union: after those losses you've taken, do you want to fight on? Can you, even? Aren't your societies already too hurt? If you let the war bleed you till the end, one or the other may prevail, but scarred, crippled, and nothing akin to what it was.

"Soldati of the Mong: your reign is finished. Will you die in your tracks, or lead the way toward freedom?

"Franceterr: you may build another Skyholm, but the Domain is forever in shards. Meanwhile you're open to your enemies—and,

Espayn, the barbarians threaten you as much. What will you do about that? World: will you stand by while Uropan civilization perishes, or will you join to save and share in that legacy?

"Men, women, of every nation, every race and condition: how much longer are you going to let yourselves be used? When are you going to tell your leaders, 'Enough!' and claim the right to live your own lives?"

The ship flew on, above an ocean that had come abrim with day.

"We have no power, we two," Iern said, "nor do we want any. It's power of humans over fellow humans that's brought us all to this evil pass. Nor do we imagine we can talk you into some grandiose reconstruction. Things don't work that way, and it's probably well that they don't. What we think we can do, from our perspective, is make some proposals. We're sure they have occurred to many of you before. But we've heard no mention of them, and suspect nobody in authority has ventured to broach any such ideas, for fear they'll be cast back and damage that same authority.

"Ronica and I have nothing to lose, and millions who are listening.

"The Maurai Federation denies wanting to impose its will on humankind. However, that is precisely what it has done, for lifetime after lifetime. Be honest, you in Oceania. Why would you stamp down the Northwesterners, if it were not that their scientists, engineers, and entrepreneurs would inevitably undermine your scheme, your sway?

"The Lodges of the Union also deny having imperial ambitions. They also should be more honest with themselves. They've never once admitted that others may have a right to self-preservation, to raise barriers against them, to resist their doing anything whatsoever that they damn well please. What have you been grasping after on behalf of your realm, Wolf, except the power to kick the rest of mankind out of your way?

"Will the two of you fight to the death—the immediate death of the loser, the slow death of the winner? Or will you come to terms and for better or worse both change, in unforeseeable directions, into something else?

"We say from outside your world: end the strife and get back to work. Let Orion rise, but not as a weapon—no, as a tool, which you build and use in partnership.

"Yes, it will release radiation, but the time is overpast to become reasonable about that. The contamination will be slight, bearable, and temporary, until we have a permanent human foothold in space.

Soon afterward, Earth should stop being an impoverished planet. How far we'll then go, how much we'll achieve, is for our descendants to reckon up, a billion years hence.

"Meanwhile, let the industries grow, fusion generators included, but under proper safeguards. Let Maurai and Northwesterners join together to help their sister civilizations, the Mong, Uropa, and their old allies. Help the barbarians and savages as well, and offer them a hand, be patient—but, I would say, not let them suppose they're your equals until they are civilized. There is no more virtue in backwardness than there is in domination."

Ronica took the word: "Well, this goes pretty far. We can't lay out a program for attaining paradise. Nobody can. Prophets who became kings have always brought disaster. We do ask you to think, think hard, and make peace and *wage* it.

"You'll need precautions, of course, so the Maurai won't be tempted to seize the space fleet for purposes of demolition, or the Norrmen for purposes of supremacy. But I believe the strongest shield the peace and the undertaking can have is that they are what the people want. Make it known, folk. Be ready to overthrow whoever would give you any less.

"Orion shall rise, for all of us."

Iern forgot to switch off the transmitter before he whispered, "How else may I win my own forgiveness?"

2

The *Terra Australis* departed Laska for N'Zealann early in the summer. She was a monohulled neobarque, white as her sails, upper works ashine with brass and glass. The Triad stood at her prow, the Cross and Stars flew from her staff, and a pennon on the foremast head proclaimed her the royal yacht. Ordinarily it was at her maintruck, but for this voyage that place of honor belonged to the flag of the Northwest Union.

The second day was bright and not unduly cold. Clouds stood in the north like snow mountains; otherwise the sun trekked alone through blue clarity. The ship heeled to a wind that strummed in her rigging and skirled across white-maned waves. They were green on their backs, amethystine under their crests; the sound of them was an ongoing low torrent. Foam blew off and carried salt to lips.

Three left the deckhouse and sought lee at the starboard rail. Nobody else was about, unless you counted the wahine in the wheelhouse. This vessel required fewer sailors than servants.

Plik drained his goblet and refilled it from the wine bottle he had carried out of the guest saloon. "Stand with me here upon the deck," he said, mildly drunk, "for it may be the last quiet talk that we shall ever have."

"Our first, anyhow, in the hooraw since Iern and I landed," Ronica replied. She had not drawn her parka hood forward, and brushed at a stray lock of hair which the wind tried to make into a banner.

"It costs, being charismatic figures, and when you do it on a global scale—" Plik shrugged. "Thus far the officers aboard have been courteous. They know how badly you two need a rest, and haven't pressed their company on you. The feeling cannot persist. I'm glad I'm an obscure ne'er-do-well, tolerated on your account." He held his cup high, admired the ruby glow within, and drank.

"Why did you ask to travel along?" wondered Iern.

"I couldn't resist the opportunity. However, I only plan on a brief stay before catching passage back to my tavern and my Vineleaf. You two are in a different case. Gods are less free than mortals."

"Aw, c'mon!" laughed Ronica. "Okay, we did grab the popular imagination, we do have some symbolic importance, and this tour of ours may help nail down the peace. But the sensation won't last. While it does, we figure we'll make damn sure of a place for ourselves in the space exploration program."

Iern drank of his own wine and looked out beyond the horizon, as he often did. He had lost the haggardness that had been upon him, but certain lines in his face would never go away. He could once more be blithe, but his ghosts would never leave him. "You see," he tried to explain, "we have no countries, either of us."

"You can have any you want," Plik said.

"Not really."

"I think I know what you mean. Whatever glories they heap on you, they will not be your motherlands. The gods of those went down in fire, and strangers inherit the temples."

"Yes. Besides—well—"

"Besides, nowhere can you be merely yourselves. You are those from whose loins the new race, the new world, will spring."

"Whoa, now," Ronica protested.

"Oh, not in hour-to-hour existence," Plik said. "That's as full as always of grubbiness, conflict, connivance, short-sightedness, greed, stupidity, laziness, cruelty, waste, every charming usual human quality at play. But . . . you have mana, you two, and it will not let you go, no, not even after you are dead. I hope for your sakes you can resist the appeal, and the urge, to set the time a little more nearly right. My hopefulness, though, is very small."

He pondered before he finished: "Unless—by blazing the trails beyond Earth, you can beget and nourish an entire myth unfelt in the past, that will live on in the lives of your children's children's children. . . . Come back in a thousand years, part the weeds on my grave, give my bones a shake, and tell me."

"Hm." Pain dwelt in Iern's grin. "How? We'll scarcely be in shape ourselves to do that."

"Wrong," Plik answered. "For better or worse, your two spirits will walk crowned through the whole cycle to come—and, it may well be, the ages that follow."

"We're only us!" the woman cried as if struck.

"Is anyone ever only human?"

"I don't know," Iern said awkwardly. "I just know that at journey's end Ronica and I will someday slip off to Terai's house, and tell them there about him, our trail-friend. Not to forget, not to forget." He held out his glass. "Pour, will you, Plik?" Raising it filled: "Here, while we can, here's to Terai . . . Wairoa . . . Vanna Uangovna . . . yes, Mikli, Jovain, everybody— We remember. Do you hear? We remember."

His free hand sought Ronica's. Rims clinked threefold. Wind quickened. A whale surfaced. The ship bore onward, in quest of the Southern Cross.